CRAFT AND VISION

CRAFT AND VISION

THE BEST FICTION FROM
The Sewanee Review

EDITED BY ANDREW LYTLE

DELACORTE PRESS / NEW YORK
A SEYMOUR LAWRENCE BOOK

ACKNOWLEDGMENTS

All selections are reprinted in the form in which they originally appeared in *The Sewanee Review.*

"Sled" is reprinted with the permission of the author, Thomas E. Adams.

"The Marquis and the Crocodile" (Copyright © 1965 by Harry Brewster) is reprinted with the permission of Charles Scribner's Sons from *Into Deeper Waters,* by Harry Brewster.

"The Unattached Smile" is reprinted with the permission of the author, Harry Crews.

"A Courtship" (Copyright 1948 by Random House, Inc.). Reprinted from *Collected Stories of William Faulkner* by permission of the publisher.

"Cloud Nine" is reprinted with the permission of the author, Caroline Gordon.

"The Fugitives" is reprinted with the permission of the author, Madison Jones.

"The Wheel" is reprinted with the permission of the author, Smith Kirkpatrick.

"A Matter of Family" (Copyright © 1962 by Claude F. Koch) is reprinted with the permission of the author and of Chilton Book Company. This story is part of *The Kite in the Sea,* by Claude F. Koch (Chilton Book Company, 1964).

"Something Just for Me" is reprinted with the permission of the author, George Lanning.

"The Guide" is reprinted with the permission of the author, Andrew Lytle.

"Lula Borrow" (Copyright © 1956 by University of Missouri Press) is reprinted with the permission of Mrs. Thomas Mabry and of the University of Missouri Press. This story also appears in *The White Hound,* a collection of short stories by Thomas Mabry and Ward Dorrance (University of Missouri Press, 1959).

"The Lame Shall Enter First" is reprinted with the permission of Farrar, Straus & Giroux, Inc., from *Everything That Rises Must Converge,* by Flannery O'Connor (Copyright © 1962, 1965 by the Estate of Mary Flannery O'Connor).

"By the Waters" is reprinted with the permission of the author, Charles Rose.

"Jujitsu" is reprinted with the permission of the author, Eleanor Ross Taylor.

The Death of a Kinsman (Copyright 1949 by Peter Taylor) is reprinted with the permission of the author, Peter Taylor.

"Statement of Ashby Wyndham" (Copyright 1943 by Robert Penn Warren). Reprinted from *The Sewanee Review* by permission of Random House, Inc. This story is part of *At Heaven's Gate,* by Robert Penn Warren (Random House, Inc.).

"Moon Lake" (Copyright 1949 by Eudora Welty). Reprinted from her volume *The Golden Apples* by permission of Harcourt Brace Jovanovich, Inc.

CONTENTS

ANDREW LYTLE, *Foreword* vii

THOMAS E. ADAMS, *Sled* 1

HARRY BREWSTER, *The Marquis and the Crocodile* 9

HARRY CREWS, *The Unattached Smile* 53

WILLIAM FAULKNER, *A Courtship* 62

CAROLINE GORDON, *Cloud Nine* 78

MADISON JONES, *The Fugitives* 111

SMITH KIRKPATRICK, *The Wheel* 128

CLAUDE F. KOCH, *A Matter of Family* 141

GEORGE LANNING, *Something Just for Me* 179

ANDREW LYTLE, *The Guide* 202

THOMAS MABRY, *Lula Borrow* 224

FLANNERY O'CONNOR, *The Lame Shall Enter First* 273

CHARLES ROSE, *By the Waters* 310

ELEANOR ROSS TAYLOR, *Jujitsu* 327

PETER TAYLOR, *The Death of a Kinsman* 332

ROBERT PENN WARREN, *Statement of Ashby Wyndham* 366

EUDORA WELTY, *Moon Lake* 415

BIOGRAPHICAL NOTES 453

FOREWORD

THE SEWANEE REVIEW is now in its seventy-ninth year of continuous publishing. Its interests and policy have always been literary. In the earliest days it did print some scholarly articles, but more often than not the scholarship even then sustained the literary event. I feel I can say that during the last four editorships sound scholarship underlay critical reading and judgment, but the *Review*'s interest did not seek the professional article with extensive footnotes. There were journals already for such. We have always looked for young and gifted talents. I have been particularly conscious of this need, especially in fiction, which seems to me to languish. Recruiting, of course, does not and cannot depend upon the young. Excellence must be courted, but an excellence which will sustain the magazine's tradition, a word not much in use these days. Nevertheless, without being too rigid, the editor should seek like minds and belief without dogmatic standards or the obvious opinion of prejudice. Eclecticism will not maintain a tradition. The editors must have come out of a culture which still maintains a common understanding about values, or else must assume such values. *The Sewanee Review* has been fortunate in this. What the future holds the future knows. At any rate there will always be the common editorial affliction, how to distinguish opinion from judgment.

The list of contributors includes minds and reputations long familiar to the world of letters. The names below, picked at random out of various issues, show the catholicity of taste and skill, as poets, as fiction writers, and as those who judge these arts. In the most real sense the magazine is John Peale Bishop, Cleanth Brooks, Robert Penn Warren, William Meredith, Arthur Mizener, Marshall McLuhan, Reinhold Niebuhr, Jacques Maritain, Katherine Anne Porter, St.-John Perse, Denis Devlin, Marianne Moore, Randall Jarrell, Robert B. Heilman, Robert Lowell, Donald Davidson, Wallace Stevens, John Crowe Ransom, Horace Gregory, T. S. Eliot, Eric Bentley, Francis Fergusson, F. O. Matthiessen, Jean Stafford, E. E. Cummings, Mark Schorer, Wallace Fowlie, Mark Van Doren, Peter Taylor, Delmore Schwartz, R. P. Blackmur, Wyndham Lewis, Hannah Arendt, Howard Nemerov, Ezra Pound, John Berryman, Joseph Frank, Theodore Roethke, Robert Wooster Stallman, Adrienne Koch, D. S. Savage, F. R. Leavis, Austin Warren, René Wellek, Alan S. Downer, Thomas Merton, Albert Camus, William Empson, Flannery O'Connor, H. H. Watts, John Edward Hardy, Eliseo Vivas, Malcolm Cowley, Yvor Winters, Herbert Read, Vivienne Koch, Robert Fitzgerald, Theodore Weiss, Caroline Gordon, C. M. Bowra, Richard Eberhart, Philip Wheelwright, Reed Whittemore, L. C. Knights, Russell Kirk, Stephen Spender, Madison Jones, John Frederick Nims, James L. Dickey, Thomas Mabry, Walter J. Ong, Arnold J. Toynbee, Charles T. Harrison, Arthur Gregor, Denis Donoghue, Daniel G. Hoffman, William Arrowsmith, Samuel H. Monk, Merrill Moore, Geoffrey Tillotson, Lionel Trilling, Glauco Cambon, Mario Praz, Walker Percy, George Garrett, Ted Hughes, John Hollander, Wayne C. Booth, Hollis Summers, Frank Lissauer, James Wright, Maynard Mack, Brewster Ghiselin, Sister Mary Gilbert, Emilio Cecchi, Sergio Baldi, Nicola Chiaromonte, Elio Chinol, Nemi D'Agostino, Agostino Lombardo, Giorgio Melchiori, Eugenio Montale, Alberto Moravia, Cesare Pavese, Larry Rubin, Elio Vittorini, Edward Dahlberg, John Hall Wheelock, Louis O. Coxe, Makoto Ueda, Harry Crews, Boris Pasternak, Sister M. Bernetta Quinn, Kathleen Raine, Ashley Brown, John Hawkes, Louis Rubin, John Logan, Allen Tate, Andrew Lytle, Henri Michaux, Kenneth Burke, Richard Wilbur, Frank Kermode, Bonamy Dobrée, Conrad Aiken, Richard Chase, Frederick Morgan, William J. Smith, Richard M. Weaver, F. Cudworth Flint, Howard Baker, Edward McCrady, Walter Sullivan, J. A. Bryant, Jr., Carolyn Kizer, Robert Hollander, Monroe K. Spears, Harry Brewster, Radcliffe Squires, John Palmer.

A special issue in 1966, edited by Mr. Allen Tate, was devoted to Mr. T. S. Eliot. Its table of contents shows the following: I. A.

Richards, Sir Herbert Read, Stephen Spender, Bonamy Dobrée, Ezra Pound, Frank Morley, C. Day Lewis, E. Martin Browne, Helen Gardner, Robert Speaight, Conrad Aiken, Leonard Unger, Frank Kermode, Robert Richman, G. Wilson Knight, Mario Praz, Austin Warren, Wallace Fowlie, Cleanth Brooks, Janet Adam Smith, Robert Giroux, Francis Noel Lees, H. S. Davies, B. Rajan, Neville Braybrooke.

These names represent a new era, its most distinctive era, for *The Sewanee Review*. It began in 1944 with Mr. Allen Tate's editorship and persisted through that of Mr. John Palmer (now editor of *The Yale Review*), Mr. Monroe Spears, who held the post for nine years, and now myself. Mr. Tate's wide acquaintance in the world of letters, both at home and abroad, his judgment of what is good, and his ability to solicit the authors set the tone and quality which his successors have followed. Previous to this, during a short interim before Mr. Tate took over, I held the office of managing editor. There was no secretary, no business manager, no proof reader—no one but the managing editor, who had to do everything. Nor did the magazine pay contributors; the editor of necessity went begging, but beggars who make a habit of it lose friends. Fortunately Mr. Tate was able to persuade the Vice-Chancellor of The University of the South, Dr. Alexander Guerry, to alter the situation. Mr. Tate became the first editor independent of the English department, and the budget was increased so that the staff could be enlarged and the magazine could pay contributors. This was a real triumph, because in the early forties we were still suffering from the depression. The fees for contributors were not much, but they made a beginning. Craftsmen are loath to give away their wares, and quite rightly so, for nearly everywhere—and certainly in this country—what is free is held in contempt. The common and mass audiences still measure the good of a thing by the money it brings, not by what it is. These audiences do hold a vague and uncomfortable sense that another good is involved, but not being readers they are incapable of reaching a definition.

When we decided to bring out an anthology of selections from *The Sewanee Review,* and choose from all the arts, it at once became clear that to do so would make the physical proportions of the book beyond publishing reason. Even if this could have been managed, the selection still would have been unfair and unrepresentative. You have only to glance at the list of contributors to understand this. So we decided on fiction. We have used one short play and parts of three novels. The rest we offer are long and short pieces of fiction. I hope the reader will find this collection varied in its effects, but only as experience is varied. The stories are written out of a conscious use of the craft. As widely different as are the subjects and styles, this fiction represents the oldest tradition in the world, the perpetual understanding of the human predicament and the sense that it can only be imparted formally.

And since the soul is the form of the body, form inheres in the imagination, and without the imagination the word could never be made flesh. The fiction writer, therefore, only seems to be inspired by the objective world. It is the imagination which selects what it wants from the discrete phenomena the eye takes in—not the other way around. The term creative writing is a bad term. Only God creates. The artist imitates, but he imitates not the surface of things but the inward and complete nature of man, caught and surrounded as he is in nature and society. Because fiction, unlike verse, is discursive, the author's risk is often excessive. But once his subject is found and recognized, the craft may be consciously used, so long as he remembers it is a tool. In the end the sudden discovery of form and subject conjoined is a mystery. It is instantaneous; and nobody, including the author, takes in quite how the two fuse and thus allow the drama to unfold.

The stories offered here were written out of this formal sense of craftsmanship. At present, sensation seems to be the prevailing subject, and its form as uncertain as appetite. The *Sewanee* authors differ absolutely from this kind of appeal, which is most brutally offered in the films from the underground. It is no secret that behind the lenses of the camera stands Peeping Tom. Not only in the underground has he achieved freedom from secrecy; above ground he is viewed with some sympathy. One wonders if the loss of his secrecy will not also lose him his chief characteristic. All of us, being human, have curiosity about Tom's interests; but to equate this with a more complex knowledge is a dangerous thing. It makes what is private public, thus erasing the distinctions between these two separate parts of being and behavior. My complaint is not so much the obscenities; it is the conscious effort on the part of the producers, actors, and writers, to eliminate categories and bring forth a succession of unrelated scenes, distorted or salacious, as meaning. This is formlessness for its own sake and the opposite of the traditional understanding of craftsmanship. Lacking form, the subject is dissolved into sensation or monotony —finally only monotony, because the bestial, the infantile, the erotic, removed from all other events or knowledge, turns the means into the end. This is Satanism. The tool, whether it be a hammer or a mind, cannot be the thing it makes or transmits, with all due respect to Mr. McLuhan. Binet's lathe in *Madame Bovary* turns out napkin rings. Even though the rings are without utility, for he does not use, sell, nor give them away, nevertheless the ring is an object apart from the machine and the man turning. This monotony is the death of an art. The same accusation can be brought against fiction, where too often in serious fiction the authors seem impelled to introduce erotic scenes which do not add to the complication. I mentioned the movies because the subversion of the arts shows itself most clearly in the visual image which pictures make. Words are more difficult. Their connotations imply too long a history.

We offer the reader a variety of actions, but actions which have a common view. Knowledge is always superior to sensation. Nor will sensation and appetite in themselves serve as a substitute for the work of art. In the *Sewanee Review* collection we hope to present actions which reveal a lasting kind of entertainment.

ANDREW LYTLE

CRAFT AND VISION

SLED

BY THOMAS E. ADAMS

ALL the adventure of the night and snow lay before him: if only he could get out of the house.

"You can't go out," his mother said, "until you learn how to act like a gentleman. Now apologize to your sister."

He stared across the table at his sister.

"Go on," his mother said.

His sister was watching her plate. He could detect the trace of a smile at the corners of her mouth.

"I won't! She's laughing at me!" He saw the smile grow more pronounced. "Besides, she *is* a liar!"

His sister did not even bother to look up, and he felt from looking at her that he had said exactly what she had wanted him to say. He grew irritated at his stupidity.

"That settles it," his mother said calmly, without turning from the stove. "No outs for you."

He stared at his hands, his mind in a panic. He could feel the smile on his sister's face. His hand fumbled with the fork on his plate. "No," he said meekly, prodding a piece of meat with the fork. "I'll apologize."

His sister looked up at him innocently.

"Well?" said his mother. "Go on."

He took a deep breath. "I'm . . ." He met his sister's gaze. "I'm sorry!" But it came out too loudly, he knew.

"He is not," his sister said.

He clenched his teeth and pinched his legs with his fingers. "I am too," he said. It sounded good, he knew; and it was half over. He had control now, and he relaxed a bit and even said further: "I'm sorry I called you a liar."

"That's better," his mother said. "You two should love each other. Not always be fighting."

He paused strategically for a long moment.

"Can I go out now?"

"Yes," his mother said.

He rose from the table, glaring at his sister with a broad grin, calling her a liar with his eyes.

His hand plucked his jacket from the couch and swirled it around his back. The buttons refused to fit through the holes, so he let them go in despair. He sat down just long enough to pull on his shiny black rubbers. Finally he put on his gloves. Then with four proud strides he arrived at the door and reached for the knob.

"Put your hat on," his mother said without looking at him.

His face, toward the door, screwed and tightened with disgust. "Aw Ma."

"Put it on."

"Aw Ma, it's not that cold out."

"Put it on."

"Honest Ma, it's not that cold out."

"Are you going to put your hat on, or are you going to stay and help with the dishes?"

He sighed. "All right," he said. "I'll put it on."

The door to the kitchen closed on his back and he was alone in the cold gloom of the shed. Pale light streamed through the frosted window and fell against the wall where the sled stood. The dark cold room was silent, and he was free. He moved into the shaft of light and stopped when from the kitchen he heard the muffled murmur of his mother's voice, as if she were far away. He listened. The murmuring hushed and he was alone again.

The sled. It was leaning against the wall, its varnished wood glistening in the moonlight. He moved closer to it and he saw his shadow block the light, and he heard the cold cracking of the loose linoleum beneath his feet.

He picked it up. He felt the smooth wood slippery in his gloved hands. The thin steel runners shone blue in the light, as he moved one finger along the polished surface to erase any dust. He shifted the sled in his hands and stood getting the feel of its weight the way he had seen his brother hold a rifle. He gripped the sled tightly, aware of the strength in his arms; and he felt proud to be strong and alone and far away with the sled in the dark cold silent room.

The sled was small and light. But strong. And when he ran with it, he ran very quickly, quicker than anyone, because it was very light and small and not bulky like other sleds. And when he ran with it, he carried it as if it were a part of him, as if he carried nothing in his arms. He set the rear end on the floor and let the sled lean against him, his hands on the steering bar. He pushed down on the bar and the thin runners curved gracefully because they were made of shiny blue flexible steel; and with them he could turn sharply in the snow, sharper than anyone. It was the best sled. It was his.

He felt a slight chill in the cold room, and in the moonlight he saw his breath in vapor rising like cigarette smoke before his eyes. His body shivered with excitement as he moved hurriedly but noiselessly to the door. He flung it open; and the snow blue and sparkling, and the shadows deep and mysterious, and the air silent and cold: all awaited him.

"Joey!" From the kitchen came his mother's voice. He turned toward the kitchen door and refused to answer.

"Joseph!"

"What!" His tone was arrogant, and a chill of fear rushed through his mind.

There was a long awful silence.

"Don't you forget to be home by seven o'clock." She hadn't noticed, and his fear was gone.

"All right!" he answered, ashamed of his fear. He stepped across the threshold and closed the door. Then he removed the hat and dropped it in the snow beside the porch.

He plodded down the alley, thrilling in the cold white silence —the snow was thick. The gate creaked as he pushed it open, holding and guiding the sled through the portal. The street was white, and shiny were the icy tracks of automobiles in the lamplight above, while between him and the light the black branches of trees ticked softly in the slight wind. In the gutters stood enormous heaps of snow, pale and dark in the shadows, stretching away from him like a string of mountains. He moved out of the shadows, between two piles of snow, and into the center of the street, where he stood for a moment gazing down the white road that gradually grew darker until it melted into the gloom at the far end.

Then he started to trot slowly down the street. Slowly, slowly gaining speed without losing balance. Faster he went now, watching the snow glide beneath his shiny black rubbers. Faster and faster, but stiffly, don't slip. Don't fall, don't fall: now! And his body plunged downward, and the sled whacked in the quiet and the white close to his eyes was flying beneath him as he felt the thrill of gliding alone along a shadowy street, with only the ski-sound of the sled in the packed snow. Then before his eyes the moving snow gradually slowed. And stopped. And he heard only the low sound of the wind and his breath.

Up again and start the trot. He moved to the beating sound of his feet along the ground. His breath came heavily and quickly, and matched the rhythm of his pumping legs, straining to carry the weight of his body without the balance of his arms. He reached a wild dangerous breakneck speed, and his leg muscles swelled and ached from the tension, and the fear of falling too early filled his mind; and down he let his body go. The white road rushed to meet him; he was off again, guiding the sled obliquely across the street toward a huge pile of snow near a driveway.

Squinting his eyes into the biting wind, he calculated when he would turn to avoid crashing. The pile, framed against the darkness of the sky, glistened white and shiny. It loomed larger and larger before him. He steered the sled sharply, bending the bar; and the snow flew as the sled churned sideways, and he heard suddenly a cold metallic snap. He and the sled went tumbling over in the hard wet snow. He rolled with it and the steering bar jarred his forehead. Then the dark sky and snow stopped turning, and all he felt was the cold air stinging the bump on his forehead.

The runner had snapped; the sled was broken. He stared at the shiny smooth runner and touched the jagged edge with his fingers. He sat in the middle of the driveway, the sled cradled in his lap, running his fingers up and down the thin runner until he came to the jagged edge where it had broken.

With his fingers he took the two broken edges and fitted them back into place. They stuck together with only a thin crooked line to indicate the split. But it was like putting a broken cup together. He stared at it, and wished it would be all right and felt like crying.

He got up and walked slowly back down the street to his house.

He sat down between the back bumper of a parked car and a pile of snow. Cradling the sled across his legs, he put the two edges together again and stared at them. He felt a thickness in his throat, and he swallowed hard to remove it, but it did not go away.

He leaned back, resting his head against the snowpile. Through his wet eyelids he saw the lamplight shimmering brightly against the sky. He closed his eyes and saw again the shiny graceful curve of the runner. But it was broken now. He had bent it too far; too far. With his hand he rubbed his neck, then his eyes, then his neck again. And he felt the snow coming wet through his pants. As he shifted to a new position, he heard the creaking of a gate. He turned toward the sound.

His sister was walking away from his house. He watched her move slowly across the street and into the grocery store. Through the plate-glass window he saw her talking with the storekeeper. He stared down at the runner. With his gloves off, he ran his fingers along the cold smooth surface and felt the thin breakline. He got up, brushed the snow off the seat of his pants, and walked to the gate to wait for his sister.

He saw her take a package from the man and come out of the store. She walked carefully on the smooth white, her figure dark in its own shadow as she passed beneath the streetlight, the package in her arm. When she reached the curb on his side, he rested his arms on the nose of the sled and exhaled a deep breath nervously. He pretended to be staring in the opposite direction.

When he heard her feet crunching softly in the snow, he turned. "Hi," he said.

"Hi," she said, and she paused for a moment. "Good sledding?"

"Uhuh," he said. "Just right. Snow's packed nice and hard. Hardly any slush at all." He paused. "I'm just resting a bit now."

She nodded. "I just went for some milk."

His fingers moved slowly down the runner and touched the joined edges.

"Well . . ." she said, about to leave.

His fingers trembled slightly, and he felt his heart begin to beat rapidly. "Do you want to take a flop?" In the still night air he heard with surprise the calm sound of his voice.

Her face came suddenly alive. "Can I? I mean, will you let me? Really?"

"Sure," he said. "Go ahead," and he handed her the sled very carefully. She gave him the package.

He put the bag under his arm and watched her move out of the shadows of the trees and into the light. She started to trot slowly, awkwardly, bearing the sled. She passed directly beneath the light and then she slipped and slowed to regain her balance. The sled looked large and heavy in her arms and, seeing her awkwardness, he realized she would be hurt badly in the fall. She was moving away again, out of the reach of the streetlight, and into the gray haze farther down the road.

He moved to the curb, holding the bag tightly under his arm, hearing his heart pounding in his ears. He wanted to stop her, and he opened his mouth as if to call to her; but no sound came. It was too late: her dark figure was already starting the fall, putting the sled beneath her. Whack! And her head dipped with the front end jutting the ground, and the back of the sled and her legs rose like a seesaw and down they came with another muffled sound. The street was quiet, except for a low whimper that filled his ears.

He saw her figure rise slowly and move toward him. He walked out to meet her beneath the light. She held the sled loosely in one hand, the broken runner dangling, reflecting light as she moved.

She sobbed and looking up he saw bright tears falling down her cheeks, and a thin line of blood trickling down her chin. In the corner of her mouth near the red swelling on her lip, a little bubble of spit shone with the blood in the light.

He felt that he should say something but he did not speak.

"I'm . . . I'm sorry," she said and the bubble broke. "I'm sorry I . . . your sled." She looked down at the sled. "It'll never be the same."

"It'll be all right," he said. He felt that he ought to do something but he did not move. "I can get it soldered. Don't worry about it." But he saw from her expression that she thought he was only trying to make her feel better.

"No," she said, shaking her head emphatically. "No it won't! It'll always have that weak spot now." She began to cry very hard. "I'm sorry."

He made an awkward gesture of forgiveness with his hand. "Don't cry," he said.

She kept crying.

"It wasn't your fault," he said.

"Yes it was," she said. "Oh, yes it was."

"No!" he said. "No, it wasn't!" But she didn't seem to hear him, and he felt his words were useless. He sighed wearily with defeat, not knowing what to say next. He saw her glance up at him as if to see whether he were still watching her, then she quickly lowered her gaze and said with despair and anguish: "Oh . . . girls are so stupid!"

There was no sound. She was no longer crying. She was looking at the ground: waiting. His ears heard nothing; they felt only the cold silent air.

"No they aren't," he said halfheartedly. And he heard her breathing again. He felt he had been forced to say that. In her shining eyes he saw an expression he did not understand. He wished she would go in the house. But seeing the tears on her cheeks and the blood on her chin, he immediately regretted the thought.

She wiped her chin with her sleeve, and he winced, feeling rough cloth on an open cut. "Don't do that," his hand moved to his back pocket, "use my handkerchief."

She waited.

The pocket was empty. "I haven't got one," he said.

Staring directly at him, she patted gingerly the swollen part of her lip with the tips of her fingers.

He moved closer to her. "Let me see," he said. With his hands he grasped her head and tilted it so that the light fell directly on the cut.

"It's not too bad," she said calmly. And as she said it she looked straight into his eyes, and he felt she was perfectly at ease; while standing that close to her, he felt clumsy and out of place.

In his hands her head was small and fragile, and her hair was soft and warm; he felt the rapid pulsing of the vein in her temple; his ears grew hot with shame.

"Maybe I better go inside and wash it off?" she asked.

With his finger he wiped the blood from her chin. "Yes," he said, feeling relieved. "You go inside and wash it off." He took the sled and gave her the package.

He stared at the ground as they walked to the gate in silence. When they reached the curb he became aware that she was watching him.

"You've got a nasty bump on your forehead," she said.

"Yes," he said. "I fell."

"Let me put some snow on it," she said, reaching to the ground.

He caught her wrist and held it gently. "No," he said.

He saw her about to object. "It's all right. You go inside and take care of your lip." He said it softly but with his grip and his eyes he told her more firmly.

"All right," she said after a moment, and he released his hold. "But don't forget to put your hat on."

He stared at her.

"I mean, *before* you go back in the house."

They both smiled.

"Thanks for reminding me," he said, and he dropped the sled in the snow and hurried to hold the gate open for her.

She hesitated, then smiled proudly as he beckoned her into the alley.

He watched her walk away from him down the dark alley in the gray snow. Her small figure swayed awkwardly as she stepped carefully in the deep snow, so as not to get her feet too wet. Her head was bowed and her shoulders hunched and he humbly felt her weakness. And he felt her cold. And he felt the snow running cold down her boots around her ankles. And though she wasn't crying now, he could still hear her low sobbing, and he saw her shining eyes and the tears falling, saw her trying to stop them and them falling even faster. And he wished he had never gone sledding. He wished that he had never even come out of the house tonight.

The back door closed. He turned and moved about nervously kicking at the ground. At the edge of the curb he dug his hands deep into the cold wet snow. He came up with a handful and absently began shaping and smoothing it. He stopped abruptly and dropped it at his feet.

He did not hear it fall. He was looking up at the dark sky but he did not see it. He put his cold hands in his back pockets but he did not feel them. He was wishing that he were some time a long time away from now and somewhere a long way away from here.

In the corner of his eye something suddenly dimmed. Across the street in the grocery store the light was out: it was seven o'clock.

THE MARQUIS AND THE CROCODILE

BY HARRY BREWSTER

THAT ghastly sight! The horror of it all, when I opened the door and looked in! It still sticks to the lining of my thoughts and clings to the seams of my dreams however much I try to shake it off in the gust of daily activities, and when in desperation I proceed to rub it away from the surface of consciousness, yes, it condescends to fade like a smear of chalk from the blackboard leaving however a thin, persistent dust of particles. No sooner I relax than the dispersed members of the image re-assemble, taking shape and unity again, creeping back to the very forefront of my mind, and then I feel as if my whole being were shaken by the grip of that horrid thing. And yet there is an element of absurdity, of the grotesque in it all, maybe something even pathetic. You might find it funny once I have told you my story, but to me, perhaps owing to my female frailty, it remains horrid. My uncle Andrew thought and still thinks me silly, quite silly.

A marquis as a husband and an old villa in a beautiful Ionian island! My uncle had offered them to me on a silver platter as it were. He had warned me though, I must in due fairness admit, and had said:

"Rosalind dear, I think you will like him in the end, but mind you he's a bit of a crank and you might be discouraged at first. However a marquis and a fine old villa are not to be sniffed at." As a matter of fact when the time came, it was not *at first* that I shrank back but *at the end*. It was the end.

"For instance his looks," my uncle Andrew went on. "The marquis is middle-aged, portly with a round pink face and a moustache; he's bald moreover. But then looks are not that important in a man. You'll soon discover that he's kind-hearted, good-tempered and well provided with a sense of humour. He can tell amusing

9

stories, not only at dinner parties. He is a great lover of animals as you yourself are and can prove interesting on the subject. He loves entertaining, delights in Scottish reels and is generally liked. Though not intellectual, he's an excellent linguist and he's well travelled. In fact he's a gentleman."

"Apart from his looks what other snags are there?" I interrupted.

"Well . . . let me see. He's a bigot I'm afraid, not only devout but a bigot. He's eccentric and conventional, the two things go together very often you know."

"In what way exactly is he an eccentric?" I pressed. "He's not a sadist is he, or a masochist?"

"No, he's not. But first of all let me tell you the conditions on which you would be admitted as a candidate, since they reflect some of his most characteristic traits. You see he has been wishing for an heir and looking for a wife for over twenty years now. I've tried to help him, but there are five conditions on which he insists and which don't make the task easier. First of all she has to have a pedigree, a good one; secondly she has to be English, Scottish or Irish; thirdly she must be extremely fond of animals; fourthly she must be Greek-Orthodox by religion or willing to convert to it immediately; and fifthly she must be attractive. You see, it's the combination in one person of all five requisites that's so hard. Mark you, money is not one of the conditions, and this is a significant as well as an interesting point, don't you think so? I introduced several girls to him, all very nice, mainly from the Embassy in Athens when I was First Secretary there—you know the sort of girl. Of course they were all willing, but not one of them passed the test. In spite of my trouble and care he turned them down one after the other. They all fell short of the required standard. Poor things, they did their best, but he proved merciless. However he has not lost hope; he keeps coming every year to the British Isles on his quest. It has become an ingrained habit. First he puts up at his club in London and then he visits various parts of the United Kingdom and Ireland as the guest of a peer or a country squire, searching and even finding and wooing, but up to now without success despite his title, his money, his villa, his island and all the moral qualities I can vouch for. So I have thought of you Rosalind. You have a pedigree, you are British, you are attractive, you like animals don't you, and I feel sure you wouldn't mind becoming a Greek-Orthodox."

"But you are not serious are you? The suggestion is preposterous. Why on earth should I marry an unattractive elderly gentleman for money? Do you want me to sell myself?"

"Rosalind dear, don't misunderstand me. There's no question of your selling yourself; I'm not asking you to consider a marriage in which there would be no mutual liking. Of course if he accepts you and you accept him it will be a reasonable bargain, but then all marriage contracts come about as the result of a bargain, an agreement to exchange, a willingness to give and take, even the most romantic ones. If the offer is made to you, well, why not consider carefully all pros and cons and then accept or turn down accordingly? You are free. There would be no harm in your accompanying me to Sepheria, seeing the estate and being introduced to him and his Swedish mother from whom all the money comes. You love old houses, don't you, you are a bit old-fashioned yourself and you are interested in architecture. My friend's house would please you I think. Of course you wouldn't have to commit yourself. As you know we also had a country house in the island of Sepheria years ago and I used to spend my holidays there. My parents, your grandparents, were in the habit of going there for the summers and autumns. I remember walking over very often to Acratas, the estate of our Greek friends, and playing with the present marquis when we were boys. Years later, after our house had been sold, I went back to Sepheria quite often from Athens when I was stationed there. So I know the island thoroughly."

After all these years I find it hard to recall the exact nature of my reaction. Doubtless I was shocked by my uncle's absurd plan to get me married off to his friend the marquis. Andrew was a bit of a rogue with a baroque sense of humour which had contributed to his expulsion from the Foreign Service. He was young for his age and great fun. I liked him and I think he liked me even though he probably regarded me as a hopelessly silly girl on whom one could play a trick. There was always a streak of cruelty in him which, however, I deliberately ignored. I adored Greece, I was attracted by the idea of visiting an island I had never seen before, I liked old houses and was intrigued by my uncle's account of his friend. So l went.

On our journey to Sepheria I asked uncle Andrew to tell me more about the island. He described it as follows. Being already at that time interested in writing I took down his own words in my diary to which I am now having recourse in recording this chapter of my life after so many years. I have jealously kept my uncle's description because I have always regarded it as a characteristic expression of his mind which delights in mixing nature with sex. Even his sketches, of which I have collected a few, disclose a response to scenery which goes beyond the limits of ordinary propriety.

"Sepheria is situated in the Ionian sea and is one of that group of isles off the mainland of Greece which escaped the blight of Turkish rule, having been saved by the hand of its patron saint who raised it and said: *Stop*. The Turks saw the hand and heard the voice from across the sea and stopped. Like its sister islands it was governed for centuries by Venice who planted olive trees, and then for half a century by Britain who introduced ginger-beer and cricket and finally handed it over to independent Greece in 1864.

"The inhabitants speak Greek and belong to the Greek Orthodox Church. There is a local landed gentry of mixed Greek and Venetian descent who had their titles bestowed upon them by Venice. They do not mind using them abroad, but in classless Greece, like the Phanariots, they cautiously forget about such appendages for fear of the ridicule. Most of them are impoverished, but some still own attractive country houses and large olive plantations.

"Sepheria is a great cluster of limestone crags, basking in the sun shamelessly naked and surrounded with prudish hills which are decently clad in luxuriant woods of olive and cypress. These creatures of vegetation keep scrambling up the bare limbs and rugged crests in a praiseworthy attempt to bring decency to the mountain-tops; but the attempt remains a desperate one. The mountain-tops prefer the nude. Down the valley they are more successful where it is easy to rush and mingle with orange and lemon. They become quite outrageous in the creeks and coves, in those folds and hollows where they bustle and romp down to the beach. There even they are apt to forget all manner of decency, for they keep fingering the sand and rocks, and ogling the sea, lifting their skirts in provocative curtsies. The sea is a gentle, patient sea which lets itself be touched and played about with, seldom reacting with more than a ripple. Once in a while, however, perhaps when the teasing goes too far, it allows itself to be lashed into fury by all the winds of Aeolus."

Andrew and I were met by the marquis at the port of Sepheria. Orestes was his name and his looks were much as Andrew had described them, but what struck me most at the time was his jovial good nature which put one immediately at ease. Everything seemed a joke. We laughed about the weather, the seasickness I had endured, the people around us, the news of the day—he had a knack of communicating laughter over things trivial and important alike. He had a white mouse crawling up his trouser leg, a guinea-pig in his waistcoat and a hamster in a side pocket of his check suit. He attended to them and us with equal care and cordiality. From the quay he led us to his car and the chauffeur drove us away over hills and valleys to Acratas, the family seat.

I was expecting a villa situated, like most of them there, on the slopes of a hill with a view to the sea and the mainland beyond. But no sooner had we started climbing than down we went again and up, weaving our way ribbon-like into the interior of the island through olive groves, clusters of cypress and woods of pine and oak. Soon the walled-in gardens gave way to a much wilder scenery of ravines, crags and boulders where the olive as big as oak still grew but had ceased to look planted by man. At length the countryside widened out and we drove through farmland cultivated with greater care.

Swinging suddenly to the right through a gate and up an alley, we entered a wild entangled park of pine, ilex, cypress, eucalyptus, poplar and oak interspersed with a variety of exotic trees I failed to identify. Then, through a great doorway in a long brick wall overhung with creepers, we drove onto a gravelled garden-front where we got out. What struck me at first was the atmosphere of neglect which in the light of that evening hung over the place like a sleepy mist, an atmosphere of deliberate, sophisticated neglect, rather than one of abandon and dilapidation. I have seen many fine country houses in England and on the continent, but none which gripped me from the start with such feelings. They were pleasant feelings, yes, but . . . it was precisely this *but* which I found hard to explain there and then, for indeed I was enchanted, though I had no time to examine the details of the place.

The outside garden did not face the house straightaway, for between the two there was a brick entrance with stables and great store-rooms to the right and left. They formed part of the walled enclosure of the inner garden right in front of the house. In the dusk I was unable to single out the architectural features of the façade, but at a glance I could see that the building, over which bowed huge pines and poplars, presented a rambling appearance probably due to additions. Along the façade there was an arcade, or loggia, which seemed of mediaeval origin, standing on a lower level than the garden, somewhat like a basement. A bridge of steps led to the veranda above, which stretched along the whole length of the main floor.

Orestes and Andrew had been engrossed in a pleasant exchange of news, while I had kept silent, walking a few steps apart, to take in as much of my surroundings as the fading light would permit. Now the two separated and our host came up to me, took me by the arm and led me up the stairs. Andrew followed. The butler opened the door with a bow. There was an inner glass door with coloured panes and traces of Art Nouveau. We went in and the old marchioness greeted us. She was very old, bent, wrinkled, her hair bright mauve. Her eyes were sharp, penetrating, and contrasted with those of her son, mild and bovine. She was not lacking in friendliness however and said she wanted me to feel at home.

It was hard to feel so immediately, for I suddenly found myself in an enchanted world where delightful things of the past had merged and crystallized with less pleasant things of the present. I felt as if I had already entered the crystal. Was it comfortable to be there, to remain there, transparent, hard, fixed? But I was tired and now that night had fallen, and the oil lamps and candles were lit, my mind began to falter. The shafts of light pointed like glowing fingers towards shadows which extended too far and deep for me to follow. Family portraits kept looking down at me with eyes critical and cold, not like the kindly ones of the portraits at home. These had eyes which felt like blades probing my softness, my silliness, and striking through. I was getting dizzy I thought. Teasingly uncle Andrew had always said that my mind was feeble. Yes, I knew he said so only teasingly, but . . . well, I was tired. I pleaded fatigue and urged to be forgiven, to be allowed to go to bed without the formalities of dinner. They were kind, understanding, and led the way to my room. Having closed and locked the door I undressed. It was hot; so I lay naked on the sheets of the four-poster bed. My eyes wandered from the wooden crucifix overhead to the terra-cotta pine cone in a corner across the room, which, stuck on a pillar of shining plaster, stood up, as Andrew would have said, like a phallic symbol newly dug out from prehistory. A great Venetian mirror tilted towards me and nodded with glimmering iridescent stains. I blew out the candle and sighed with relief at the sight of the open window at the far end of the room. Outside the stars shone bright between the branches of oak and poplar and through the rifts in the heaving mass I stretched and stretched and breathed the immensity of space.

On awaking the next morning I found the sun shining through the openings. Everything was spotted with splashes of light and for a while I could hardly understand where I was. I lay agreeably in a daze.

I was brought back to the present by early morning tea and a slice of lemon which a peasant girl carried in on a tray, I got up, washed and dressed. By then all traces of the daze had vanished.

In the morning, on an empty stomach, one is apt to view things with rational, merciless self-criticism. Suddenly I was aware of the whole absurdity of my circumstances; I felt ridiculous, vulnerable, and intensely annoyed with Andrew for having got me into this grotesque situation. What on earth was I doing here, silly fool. I slammed the door of my bedroom and angrily went down. I was received by half a dozen yelping Irish terriers and the butler who led me into the dining-room where I was served a continental breakfast with excellent coffee and milk. The coffee was not Turkish, but of the bitter *espresso* type. Hot toast, butter, and honey with a flavour of mountain herbs began to soothe my temper. Then the door opened and Orestes came in wearing his check tweed suit. He explained that he had got up early, as was his habit because of the farm. But his mother stayed in bed until noon, and Andrew was still asleep. How had I slept the night? Was the bed all right? While these conventional but friendly enquiries were being made I had leisure enough to examine him from head to foot. He was not exactly prepossessing to look at; uncle Andrew's negative description had been if anything an understatement. He was so funny-looking however, with his puffed pink cheeks, little moustache and tufted ears, that soon I felt my irritation dissolve. The white mouse kept running up and down his trouser-legs, while the tawny guinea-pig pushed its head in and out of one of his pockets.

"Isn't it sweet?" commented Orestes. "But you must see them all, my animals, you know; has Andrew told you about them? They live upstairs, as well as in other parts of the house, and in the garden; Mama won't have them on the first floor. The birds and rodents are upstairs, the tortoises in the garden."

While I was observing him talking away in his cheerful manner I suddenly became aware that though he was chatting without concern, as if his mind were all with his animals, he was nevertheless keeping a watchful eye upon my person and face, and I then realized that I myself was under close scrutiny. This made me feel uncomfortable. I got up and said: "Yes, do show me the house and the animals."

So he led the way from room to room. They were strung out the whole length of the house with, alongside, a connecting corridor. The floor was made of simple unpolished planks of wood, but covered with oriental rugs, some of them very fine if I remember rightly. The rooms varied in size and gave onto the back-garden overgrown with a wild tangle of plants, many of which seemed to me of an exotic species, and bordered, beyond a wall, by pines and ilexes. The drawing-room was long and big, with a glass door and steps leading to the back-garden. The furniture consisted of a few eighteenth-century Venetian pieces and simple English Regency chairs. An old-fashioned grand piano stood in a corner by one of the three windows. A full-sized portrait of a glamorous lady was hung over a Second Empire sofa. Great-aunt Irene had been to the Czar's court where the picture had been painted, commented Orestes. There were other family portraits and a prettily framed Madonna which could have been fourteenth- or early fifteenth-century Italian. Sienese? And yet there was a Byzantine touch about it. Where did it come from? Orestes did not know.

The dining-room was almost as big, with only male family portraits on the walls, ancestors in military or naval uniform. The early Victorian dresser and oblong table covered with English silver, the chairs of the same period, the flowery plates fixed to the walls, the wooden mantelpiece and painted ceiling, all gave the room a rather fanciful nineteenth-century atmosphere in keeping with the wild verdure of the garden. The adjoining sitting-room was small, panelled and intimate, with armchairs, a desk, engraved note paper, pen and ink and faded photographs framed in tortoise shell or silver. The *arms room*, as Orestes called it, where grand-papa had arranged his collection of weapons, was even smaller, but the display was gorgeous: Syrian and Spanish daggers, Persian and Turkish scimitars with ivory hilts studded in emerald, Arabian long-barrelled rifles, Italian eighteenth-century blunderbusses, elegant French rapiers, Moroccan sabres, African bows and arrows, spears from America, boomerangs from Australia, and many strange weapons whose provenance and exact method of use were unknown to Orestes himself. They covered the furniture and festooned the walls, on one of which there hung the only painting in the room, a portrait of their ancestor Capodistria, the first prime-minister of Greece, who was assassinated at Nauplia in 1831 and from whom Orestes descended on his grandmother's side. But there were scores of old prints on the walls fitted between the weapons and also an elaborate well-framed family-tree.

From this room we passed to the library, which was situated in the mediaeval part of the house. It was long, low and dark and the panelling showed through where the books did not cover the walls, while oak beams ribbed the ceiling in black. There was a desk in a corner by the window; near it stood a globe, faded and yellow, on three legs, and round the chimney-piece, which looked as though it had not been used for many years, were grouped a sofa and arm-chairs covered in heavy dark leather. An atmosphere of gloom and desertion pervaded the room, I thought, and yet I felt a presence, the presence of someone searching for something, a lost manu-script, a letter or a document. They say I'm psychic. But I've never seen a ghost. Evidently the most I can do is to feel one.

Perhaps what fascinated me most was a small terrace which crowned a low truncated tower or buttress and to which one had access from the sitting-room. Overgrown with creepers and vines, it looked onto the back-garden. There was a low table that had been a millstone. The seats consisted of sections of Roman columns, varying in height and diameter, and of a few blocks of stone with inscriptions in Greek. There were also some comfortable bamboo chairs. The view was enclosed within the wall of trees round the house; the atmosphere of intimacy it created with pomegranates, vines, oleanders, and Japanese medlars drew me into a world more personal than that of the house itself.

Orestes explained to me that the floor above contained his own rooms at one end, the guest rooms including my own occupying the centre, his mother's suite and other rooms towards the far end to the south. But first he took me to the ground-floor, half underground. It was the oldest part of the house, the original building of a monastery, with its dark vaulted chambers and loggia. Here were the servants' quarters. First we visited the spacious kitchen, fitted with great ovens in the wall for baking bread, open fireplaces with cauldrons hanging from the chimneys, old-fashioned stoves, and four huge spits worked by elaborate machinery. Strung along the walls were rows of brass pots and pans which glistened in the light of the white vaults. There were endless pantries, store-rooms with casks of wine and olive oil, and winding passages leading down steps into cellars, dark closets and dungeons. We did not go far down; I felt ill at ease there and I wanted to see the farm.

Outside the house appeared to me, as it had already the night before, a large rambling building with pleasant but not outstanding architectural features. The ramshackle effect however was deceptive, for on closer examination I realized that the core and oldest part consisted of the main block and of the two lower wings stretching forward at right angles, parallel to each other, the whole forming a structural unity. The lower wings contained the stables for the horses, which we visited later, and other store-rooms, so I was told. Now he proceeded to an outlying brick shed at the far corner of the house, almost detached, which stretched away amongst the trees. Here were the wine and oil presses. Orestes, who evidently took active interest in his farm, went out of his way to explain to me the whole mechanical process of pressing the olives and collecting the oil. The machinery was new and well kept, recently imported, he informed me, from Italy. He also showed me the generator which supplied power to the household and whole farm, though for aesthetic reasons he insisted on retaining in the actual house the old method of oil lamplighting. He also pointed out the pumps for the water supply system. Then he led me back to the main cluster of buildings and took me into the chapel, where I admired the richly carved iconostasis and questioned him on the family tombs and inscriptions. Thence we went to the stables where we spent a good half hour examining the horses and watching them being groomed and fed. His farm-hands were pleasant and gay, and I noticed that they talked to Orestes without a trace of that obsequiousness which one so often comes across on similar estates in other parts of western Europe. They addressed him in the usual Greek second person singular and treated him as one of their own. The cows were in the fields, the pigs, poultry and geese were in separate buildings a mile away where the peasants also lived, so I was told. It was evidently too far to go there that morning. Orestes being anxious to show me his own animals; so we went straight up to his rooms.

These were like a zoo, an unusual one however, for I had never before seen a set of rooms with delicate Venetian furniture and upholstery crowded with birds of the most varied species, local and rare, as well as cats, mice, guinea-pigs, hamsters, lemurs, lizards, chameleons and many other creatures. Several of them, of course, were shut in cages, especially the parrots, canaries, budgerigars and the like, but other birds flew about the room apparently free and unconcerned. The pigeons snuggled and cooed on his pillow and flew in and out of the window as if the room were a dovecot. The rodents in the room next door were also free, quite undisturbed by the Siamese cats which showed an exemplary lack of interest. Orestes explained that he had trained his animals to live happily together. Needless to say, the mess over furniture and bed from the droppings of this vast and varied animal life surpassed description, and yet an impressive staff was employed to keep the rooms from turning into Augean Stables. I pulled myself together and showed the greatest interest in every little creature. My words and questions seemed to work wonders; he purred like a large spoilt pussy-cat, especially when I caught and fondled a pigeon which had been cooing and defecating on his pillow. He would have kept me there till lunch time, but I was determined to get out. So I said I wanted to see the garden, which indeed I did.

After having led me into a closet for a quick look at his collection of stuffed birds he reluctantly took me downstairs and out into the fresh air, where a very different smell came from the roses and lemon trees. The walled-in garden in front of the house was a mass of orange and lemon with roses creeping up the walls, geraniums in pots, and beds of dahlia and carnation bordered with box bushes. Water was plentiful and the system of irrigation by means of open stone ducts remarkably efficient. Beyond the well-tended inner garden the park stretched, all around, overgrown and as if deliberately neglected. We passed by a lawn, very green and lush and likewise watered by carefully laid-out ducts, which was crawling with tortoises. I had never seen so many in my life. Orestes jumped in their midst, picked up a large one and held it out to me. It was indeed a magnificent beast and he beamed as I tickled its head, which kept ducking in and out. "I like prehistoric animals, I mean those which are still linked with a distant past," I lamely remarked.

We continued along a path under the walls of the house till we came to a sheltered spot facing south, where a pond had been curiously dug out against the wall and carefully fenced round with wire-netting.

"Here's the pool I used to keep . . ."

Orestes did not finish his sentence. He hesitated.

"You kept what?" I said.

"Er . . . ducks."

"But why then did you have it closed in with wire-netting?"

"Oh, to prevent them from getting all over the place."

"And why did you get rid of them?"

"They were a nuisance, so I had them removed."

"But I thought you liked animals."

"Not ducks."

I was about to persist: "And why don't you like ducks?" But he looked so distressed that I dropped the argument. There was a strange, pained expression on his face, as if something preyed upon his mind.

We walked on beyond the walls of the house and came to a place which held me spellbound. I had already noticed it out of the corner of my eye on our arrival the evening before. It lay not far from the main entrance, about a hundred yards to the right, and consisted of a clearing in the wood overlooking a lower level of tangled vegetation with an opening away to the west. Distant olive-clad hills, bespeckled with clumps of cypress and lit up by the dazzling sun of noon, drew my gaze out, over the fields to the horizon. The opening of brilliant light contrasted with the dark shadows of the wood and illuminated the ground where we stood, which was strewn with drums of columns, capitals and carefully hewn blocks of stone suggesting an ancient site. Under a huge weeping willow there was a swing which looked as if it had not been used for years. The ropes were frayed and rotten, but having caught hold of them I could not help sitting on the little worm-eaten plank. Orestes did not stop me. I pushed with my right foot and gently swung to and fro. A mild creaking descended from the frame above along the ropes down to the tingle in my hands, like the muffled squeal of a child.

"Does anybody use this swing?" I enquired.

"Apart from the occasional visitor like yourself willing to take the risk, I was the last to enjoy it as a little boy. We lack children here. . . ."

He pronounced the last words wistfully and I turned my eyes away to the distant landscape through the opening.

"Don't you feel . . . somewhat closed in here?" I remarked.

"What do you mean?"

"If you look at those hills over there . . . "

"Well, what about them?"

"I mean . . . from a house up there you would have a fine distant view over the sea, wouldn't you?"

"I see. Yes, there are villas with fine distant views. They are turned outwards. The view from this house is turned in. It's a world within, a life within."

"Yes, it's very beautiful here. But I like to look out, to live. . . ."

"I think that here you'd grow to appreciate a different kind of beauty; you'd grow to understand and love the quality of a self-sufficient world turned upon itself, the quiet rhythm of security and peace which family life needs so badly nowadays."

"Do you really think I would?"

He had come quite close now and sat down on a broken column, while I kept swaying, but more gently, under the weeping willow. When at length I stopped he took my hands in his and I could not help looking into his eyes. They were not so cow-like as they had seemed to me the night before, no, they were large and deep, almost attractive I thought. And who had said he was bald? He didn't seem to me bald now, his brow was fine, Shakespearian, yes Shakespearian. There was hair, all right, further back, dark brown and curly, doubtless a bit grey but still fairly dark, and his moustache was not a tooth-brush one at all. And who had said he was fat? Andrew? No, Orestes was heavily built, of course, but not *fat*. I was sure now it was all muscle, he led such a healthy life, didn't he, the life of a country squire interested in farming. No, his complexion was not pink as Andrew had described it, but of a healthy out-door ruddiness. Poor Orestes, so lonely in life. I was beginning to feel quite sentimental, surely not sloppy, but sympathetic, moved . . . the spot was so poetic, so full of nostalgia and conducive to sentiment, genuine sentiment. The hot wind that had been rustling the leaves overhead dropped as if by magic and suddenly a stillness settled more soundless than silence. The swing stopped creaking, I thought, and for a split-second even the cicadas held themselves back from their midday dizziness as if time were in suspense. Was this the *Panic-hour* I had read about? How I wished it was. Perhaps it was. He came closer, closer still, and I could hear him breathe, the only sound that came to my ears after the first second of stillness. His mouth seemed to me very near and rather pleasant, a full, well-shaped mouth which made one forget the nose. I was feeling mellow, receptive, yielding. "Would you . . . er . . . I . . . I love . . ." he started to say, but suddenly the hamster popped its head out of his breast-pocket and I burst into a fit of nervous giggles. I could only see the nose now and I giggled and giggled. And then . . . then the swing ropes snapped.

"Well, how are you liking it here? Do you see yourself as the *châtelaine*? I do."

When my uncle made such remarks I never quite knew whether he was facetious or in earnest. After the siesta hour I had gone to his room, knocked on the door and walked in. He was stretched out on a deck-chair by the window reading a book.

"Listen Andrew, you've got to tell me more about this man you've entangled me with. I can't make head nor tail of him. So please start from the beginning. After all, you've known him since childhood, haven't you?"

"Yes I have. But a detailed life history would hardly explain more than a few significant facts. You've had a glimpse of his most eccentric side, the twist which love for animals has given him. For a Greek that's unusual, to say the least. No doubt there are reasons for it, his English grandmother for one. Then his upbringing. There were certain psychological circumstances, but I'm not an analyst. This much I can say however. When a small boy Orestes was apparently starved of all that natural human affection a child needs within its family circle. I know this both from hearsay and from his having once mentioned it to me. Being a few years younger I was far too small at that time to notice anything myself, but I have since gathered that his parents were particularly harsh towards him; they doted on his sister, the only other child, who later died. He had a nanny, of course, who happened to be even harsher. So all his natural affection went to his pets, dogs, cats, and any other animals he could get. Evidently this annoyed his parents, who insisted on having such objects of weakness and self-indulgence removed from the premises. So Orestes had to hide his pets, in a desperate effort to save them from probable death. These circumstances developed in him a protective, possessive spirit directed towards, if not limited to, animals, which in the end became the sort of passion you've seen. His father was as upset as one who discovers that his only son is homosexual. This Orestes was not, at least I think so, and although there were no signs of depravity in his attachment to animals his father was nonetheless disgusted.

"The old-fashioned gentleman used to go off on distant, prolonged journeys to the tropics and once he came back from Uganda with a baby crocodile, which, as a grim joke and in a mood of bitter irony, he donated to his son. Little did he realize the kind of revenge he was laying himself open to. I still recall the tiny creature, scarcely bigger than a lizard, when it arrived and was presented to Orestes in a box lined with cotton-wool, fragile, delicate, helpless. Orestes took to it immediately and lavished on it all the care it needed for survival. The problem was not during the hibernating months, when it lay motionless without needing food, but when it came to life again in the spring. Then it had to be encouraged to eat and was liable to fall dangerously ill if exposed to any sudden drop in temperature. However, thanks to Orestes, it survived and gradually grew. I remember going often as a boy to Acratas for the day from our house and playing with Orestes and the crocodile. My friend gave it the name of Pylades. Years went by; they became inseparable. The beast developed into a centre, an institution, a being worth living for. Already before the war it had achieved considerable length and girth; visitors from all over Europe and America were admitted to its stately presence, though only twice a week and at a fixed hour of the day; they stood in awe before it as the major sight of the villa. Then there came the long interruption of the war and when I saw Orestes and Pylades again in 1946, the latter had become huge. It measured at least ten or eleven feet in length and its girth round the middle was formidable. I remember I used to tease Orestes at that time by insinuating that he had been feeding his pet on the bodies of German and Italian soldiers killed by the partisans.

"Orestes was now master of the estate, his father having died. Pylades had become the hub of life on the farm and in the household, except of course during the winter months. The entire staff of servants were detailed, under minute instructions, to the care of the beast, whose well-being took precedence over everything. Even the peasants of the farm had to lend a hand from time to time. The task of keeping such a creature properly fed with suitable food was not easy. It thrived on raw meat, if possible live flesh, and poor Orestes had qualms of conscience in having to decide whether any of his beloved animals had to be sacrificed and tossed wriggling and writhing to the jaws of the monster. But his love for the creature he had reared from the cradle, as it were, and brought up alive and healthy through the most difficult years of its existence in a climate unsuited to its constitution prevailed over everything in the end. Of course he suffered, poor man, being so kindly and gentle by nature, from the inconsistency of this course dictated by love and at the same time in opposition to all his principles of love. But, Rosalind, when prompted by love is there anything we aren't prepared to do?"

"There's something wrong somewhere. Your mind is twisted, Andrew."

"Well, no matter. The monster grew and dominated Acratas. The old marchioness protested—in her heart she loathed it—but she had to keep quiet now, she who had been domineering and ruthless in her son's upbringing. He was inflexible. The crocodile came first.

"Did you notice, Rosalind, a sort of pond in the garden with wire-netting round it? Well, when the first days of spring came and the danger of a frost was over, Orestes would lead four stalwart peasants with a stretcher down to the dungeons of the ex-monastery, to a dark vault connected with the central heating system. Still hibernating and lethargic, his eyes stiff and glazed, Pylades lay there wrapped in straw, but ready to wake up. With some difficulty they would place him on the stretcher—he weighed over four hundred pounds—and would then strap him down for safety's sake, though there was little danger at this early stage of the year. Then they would carry him up and place him in the pond where, except at meal times, he would lie for hours on end motionless, like a log of wood. I recall how Orestes, whenever he took visitors round, would use a stick to prod Pylades and bring out some signs of life. He knew the most sensitive spots. The beast would then hiss furiously like a steam-engine or the dragon in Siegfried. The visitors would stand there struck with wonder. In actual fact the poor crocodile was hissing out of sheer boredom or pain perhaps and, no doubt, as a sign of protest at the indignity of the treatment. But if not thus stimulated Pylades insisted on looking perfectly innocuous as well as uninterested, which was deceptive and even dangerous, as I learnt from personal experience. It was part of his hunting technique to lie motionless, unless prodded, looking like a log of wood, but with a purpose, for if you observed him closely you could see that he was watching you out of the corner of his tiny eye. So exasperatingly wooden did he persist in looking that I once stuck my hand through the mesh of the wire-netting in order to draw his attention. Suddenly he snapped round like lightning. Luckily my reflexes were quick and I managed to withdraw my hand in the nick of time. But believe me it was touch and go that my whole hand wasn't bitten off.

"Orestes not only doted on the beast but developed a unique relationship with him and knew every intimate aspect of his life. For instance his sex life . . . It was fabulous, so I gathered from the accounts my friend gave me of his habits. Poor creature, he felt the lack of a mate. Orestes went out of his way to find him a female companion, but failed. So he ended by becoming like an ordinary sex-starved tomcat, only a hundred times bigger and more lecherous. It was a real problem which only Orestes knew how to cope with.

"Now Rosalind, lest the picture of my friend remain incomplete, I must not omit to mention another important centre of attraction in his life which luckily did not clash with his commitments to Pylades. This was the Church. I've already hinted at it. Neither of his parents had been pious, in fact religion had not entered their lives. In understandable reaction Orestes turned to the Church with a vengeance. He became a regular church-goer and has lived, ever since his father's death, on the closest terms with the local parish priest. Distinguished members of the Greek Orthodox clergy come to see him regularly. I think he would have been in the Church himself long ago if he did not consider, rightly or wrongly, his position as a country squire incompatible with the responsibilities of a priest or a bishop, a dignity he would no doubt reach if he took holy orders. And besides I think he would find it too hard having to give up his six months' freedom and comfortable wanderings in Britain and Sweden. But there's no question his not being devout, even a bigot, I fear.

"Of course one can't help feeling a little sorry for his old mother, who had no use for the crocodile and even less for the priests and who has spent her days at Acratas retired in her rooms in helpless rage. I've noticed that she now stays with her brother at his country house in Sweden for periods which tend to get longer. But Orestes finds it hard to oust her even after the terrible event I shall now tell you about. He hates her and yet is attached to her.

"Early in the month of April three years ago, when I was still at the Embassy in Athens and just before that absurd scandal which led to my resignation . . ."

"Dismissal, you mean."

"Nonsense, resignation; I received a telegram from Orestes. It said: *Distressed please come Pylades dead.* For various reasons I could only catch the boat to Sepheria two days later. The next day I came across an obituary in one of the Athenian daily papers which gave the mere facts. Apparently he had died of pneumonia, aged forty-one. When at last I got to Acratas I found the household in mourning and Orestes in a state of mental prostration. The old marchioness had left for Sweden the day before. It took a little while and some humouring to get Orestes in a communicative mood, but in the end he told me the whole story. He had been spending the months of that winter skiing in Sweden as he was in the habit of doing every year, while his mother, who at her age needed a Mediterranean climate during the cold season, had remained at Acratas.

He had left the usual instructions for Pylades to be carried out from his straw couch in the underground vault and placed in his pool as soon as the warm spring of Greece had started. He had also asked his mother to supervise the delicate transition period from rigid hibernation to the less lethargic stages before Pylades reached full wakefulness in the water and mud of his sun-conditioned pond. The tricky problem of diet could not be left to the household staff, for Pylades had first to be fed on milk with a spoon like an infant needing encouragement and every reaction or lack of reaction had to be watched. Then little by little more substantial food would be provided, viz. boiled chicken and lamb at first, and finally the real thing, live creatures, duck, rabbit, goats, stray dogs and cats. Evidently he needed blood if he was to prosper."

"How disgusting."

"Well Pylades was not a crocodile for nothing; let me get on with my account. The old lady had been entrusted with this delicate task; she had done it before. Orestes left with his mind at rest, or more or less at rest for I think he never quite trusted his mother. The truth of the matter was she hated Pylades, though she had been wary not to disclose her feelings beyond a display of indifference which Orestes chose to interpret as whimsical affectation. When he received a telegram from the major-domo announcing Pylades' sudden death, Orestes hurried home by air and after a few enquiries came to the conclusion that his mother had actually killed him. Wilful neglect on her part amounted to that, he maintained. Besides, there might have been poison in the food. So he publicly accused her of murder. There had been a terrible row before my arrival, so I gathered, and the old lady had left in a huff. Orestes was heart-broken. I tried to comfort him. Little by little he recovered his balance and I was glad to see that in due course he resumed his normal rhythm of life and his periodical voyages to the British Isles in quest of a wife."

"And this is the man you want me to marry?"

"Now Rosalind, don't let his past history upset you. It shows you of course that Orestes is an unusual man, but I do know he's kind-hearted and extremely faithful by nature. He would make an attentive husband, believe me. Pylades is no more and Orestes is ready for a wife. He's satisfied, he tells me, with your pedigree and other qualifications. Are you satisfied with his?"

I did not answer but remained pensive and silent.

That evening there was a dinner party at Acratas, apparently in my honour. The bishop of Sepheria had been invited and a few other prelates. After dinner we were strolling in the drawing-room admiring the bibelots while coffee was being served when the old lady approached me and tugging me by the sleeve drew me away into a distant corner of the room. She had been drinking at table a little more heavily than the others; her wrinkled cheeks were flushed and she seemed more animated than usual.

"What a son, what a son!" she muttered wringing her hands. "He should have been a priest! I hate priests. He keeps neglecting the estate, don't you see, everything is falling to pieces, he won't let me run the place, he takes no interest in the management of things, how can he, those animals, everything is going to the dogs, look, look!" and with a swoop of her withered arm from out her tasseled silk shawl she waved at everything around, butler, coffee-cups and tray, the windows and beyond. "All these priests! He should have been a priest himself, don't you think so?" she added with a grimace. "I'm clearing out of here. Sweden for me. And all these animals of his!" she repeated. "Do you like animals, Rosalind? I loathe them. Priests and animals. And that crocodile, oh that crocodile!" Her voice went strident, but she had cautiously turned her back to her son and the guests as she stood there facing me. Her lips trembled.

"I thought the crocodile was dead long ago," I ventured to remark.

"Dead? Did you say dead? Dead indeed! Can a crocodile ever die in this house?"

Her voice had risen to a hoarse pitch, and in the flickering light of the candles so dear to Orestes her eyes glowed with the fierceness of desperation. She kept them fixed upon me while her bent frame shrank out of the room into the darkness.

I returned to the party and sipped a glass of brandy.

Orestes seemed in the best of spirits, cracking jokes with Andrew and the bishop, though I felt that all the while he had been keeping me and his mother under close observation. He now edged towards me and under pretext of wanting to show me an icon led me to the opposite side of the room. He lifted a double candlestick with his left hand and, while pointing out various features of the icon, casually remarked:

"I saw my mother talking to you a little while ago, before she slipped off to bed, so as not to disturb her guests; she's so considerate. Poor Mummy, she's a bit tired these days, overwrought you know. In a heat wave like this she feels it and a change back to Sweden becomes essential for her. As a matter of fact the climate there suits her far better naturally, and now in her old age the time she spends here every year is reduced to a few weeks. Incidentally what was she telling you? Did she say the house was falling to pieces and that I took no interest in the place?"

"Well, yes, I believe she did."

"She always does. Poor thing she has a screw loose by now." And Orestes lifted a forefinger to his right temple in a rather unflattering gesture. "Don't mistake me however, I'm very fond of her, very devoted, but you know old age, it's inevitable, sooner or later we all have to face it, unless we die on the way. As a matter of fact everything is all right here, don't you think so? You had a good dinner didn't you, *dolmades* and *kalamari?* And the service was adequate, wasn't it? Spiro, the old butler, is magnificent, the bishop told me. And the farm, well, you had a glimpse of it yourself this morning. All is well, don't you think so? Poor old Mummy."

He did not propose. After that incident by the swing when he had been about to, I expected it every day during the fortnight we spent there. However he did not and I was immensely relieved, for I was not sure of myself and feared another fit of giggles. Evidently I was not quite so old-fashioned as I had thought. Andrew however knew better; he knew that it was but a question of a few more days.

When we got home and before a week had gone by, a large envelope was delivered to me with a Greek postmark. It contained, on beautiful note-paper with *Acratas* embossed at the top of the sheet, a formal proposal of marriage couched in flowery but tender language. Although I had been expecting it I needed another ten days to consider the offer and make up my mind.

Did I love him? One well may ask and indeed that was the very question I at once put myself. Good heavens no, I was not in love with Orestes. I was at a loss when I found that the answer turned out to be so, if by *love* romantic love was to be understood. Then my reaction was to be honest, honest to myself, honest to him, and to reply no thank you. On further consideration, however, the idea of getting married to him was not without attraction, not without a certain wisdom perhaps, in fact an offer not to be turned down out of hand simply because I was not *in love*. Nowadays we invariably expect to find an ideal love sooner or later, but do we ever? Look at my own friends, I kept saying to myself, look at my sisters and the girls I have known from my early childhood, and what has happened to them. They have all married men they thought they were in love with, and now, a couple of years later, are either separated or divorced, one married again, another not, a third living with a man who cannot or will not marry her, their families disrupted, their children without a real home, and they still hope to come across real love. Was I to follow in their footsteps? Why not act instead as our great-grandmothers used to do on the advice or under pressure of their parents? They seldom married for love and yet their marriages were hardly less successful than those of today; on the contrary the records suggest they were reasonably happy and their family life united and harmonious. And if they had love affairs, as no doubt they had, these did not break up the unity to which they belonged. We insist, I thought, on being too honest nowadays, too idealistic, that's the whole trouble. Why should I not marry Orestes even if I was not yet in love with him? Admittedly he was neither young, nor handsome, nor outstandingly intelligent, but then look at myself. Young? Yes. Pretty? Only just. Brains? Well, to be frank, not particularly bright. Money? None. And what's a pedigree worth nowadays? Nothing, except to a crank or a morbid snob who usually wants money as well. Then, if you came to think of it, Orestes was not a *mauvais parti*. He had plenty of money, a sense of humour, a lovely house, a kind-hearted, faithful nature, so Andrew had assured me. No doubt he would prove a good husband, a good father. Surely I would grow to love him in due course. There was that crocodile story which had left a feeling in me like a peculiar taste in the mouth. But it was a thing of the past, silly nonsense we could all forget about. Change in religion? Well, I would remain a Christian after all and I never had anything against the Greek Orthodox Church. My father was in favour of the match, Andrew, the architect as it were, almost insisted, and my sisters, who had at first made fun of me about it, were equally anxious I should accept as they saw themselves, so I guessed, coming out to Acratas for long holidays at my expense.

After ten days I answered the letter and said yes.

I consented to be received immediately into the Greek Orthodox Church and two months later the wedding took place in London. It was a formal wedding with all the conventional trappings
and for our honeymoon we went to the Riviera. Then the turn
came to go to Acratas. I was thrilled.

Acratas! What a memory, that rambling old house amongst the
pines and ilexes, the forlorn garden and the drums of columns half
sunk into the herbs and thistles! Acratas! Wrapped in that light of
Greece which there breaks into fragments as if by magic and darts
through the rustling leaves like shooting-stars! The vision recalls
me with a cry.

Love! Yes, I think I was in love with Acratas long before there
was any chance of my loving Orestes, so much so that that feeling
of apprehension, of evil, which had touched me like an invisible
hand on my first visit was soon lulled to sleep. Can one be in love
with a place, with a house? Where have I heard these words which
cling to my mind:

"Think of a beautiful villa with a garden of unsurpassed dignity in a malarious, desolate country. It is ague and almost death to
linger there, and yet almost impossible to tear oneself away."

Acratas was not in a malarious, desolate country and yet the
ague was there, the touch of death, and I lingered, I lingered too
long perhaps.

Our arrival on a mid-September day was charming. The impassive major-domo received us with a smile. I had never seen him
smile during my first visit. Spiro, the butler, was effusive with welcome, while Katina, my own personal maid (a peasant girl whom
Orestes had had specially trained) made me feel instantly at home
and at ease. My mother-in-law was not there. After having attended
the wedding she had decided to remain in Sweden indefinitely. So
everything was tactfully arranged for me to take over my new
home. On the surface it was easy, but I foresaw difficulties which
would need delicacy as well as perseverance. It is difficult for a
woman from outside to step in as mistress of a house where old tra-
ditions, acknowledged habits, and well-established rules have hardened into architectural features of life. But the first gesture I
made to establish myself and refresh the air, where so many beauti-

ful objects cried out to breathe, was to rush into the garden. I picked flowers and arranged them in vases here and there in the principal rooms which, perhaps for several generations, had not seen such colour and gaiety.

Orestes and I spent our first three weeks of married life at Acratas peacefully and harmoniously. We proceeded to sound each other gently, to explore each other without treading too harshly on the tender edges of our respective susceptibilities. I had to make allowances for his animals, he for my mania to move furniture about, my insistence on making full use of the flowerpots and vases and my habit of pinning to the walls specimens of abstract art. I found him amenable, patient, anxious to please and full of understanding, but stubborn on certain points. I already liked him more than when I had first met him, but there was something in him which escaped my understanding, something he kept to himself which he could not, or would not, share with me and which made him look absent sometimes, as if his mind had wandered to an object far more attractive than myself. However I was determined not to be worried by any incongruity at this stage of our marriage and so those first days at Acratas went by almost as happily as one could have wished.

From the moment of my arrival it had become my aim and task to get on with the servants. I practiced my Greek by talking to them more than was necessary for the household. Katina, my maid, was simple, gay and inquisitive. Fresh from the village she had no inhibitions or former loyalties to contend with. Ignorance and simplicity did not detract from her inborn dignity, and treating me as an equal came naturally to her. She was collecting her *proika*, or dowry, and once this could be achieved, her marriage would be secured as well as her freedom from us. Servitude to a husband would be of a different order. Heleni, the cook, much older, better looking, more fussy, attached to the house like a cat, was a widow. She hated interference, regarded me at first as an intruder, but her sense of humour was so boisterous that I quickly found the key to her heart.

I have already referred to Spiro, the butler, with whom I felt at ease from the moment I set foot in the house. His jovial talkative manner, without a trace of deference, at once conquered my heart.

He called us both by our Christian names and barged into the drawing-room conversation as often as he liked even when guests were there, as if he were a member of the family. At the same time there was not an ounce of rudeness about him, of suppressed resentment or class-consciousness. It would have been impossible to find someone like Spiro in any other country but Greece. A pity only that he was getting on, and suffering from asthma.

I need not mention the lesser members of the domestic staff. There were many of them, mainly on a part-time basis, for the innumerable chores connected with the kitchen, the laundry, Orestes' animals, and the disheartening task of keeping the house clean. They lived in the farm buildings or their own villages with their families and came and went every day according to a plan. But apart from the gardener and the regular servants there was one man who lived on the premises about whom I should say a few words. I have called him the major-domo and I took an immediate dislike to him. He was half foreign and very un-Greek I thought. Strictly speaking he was a sort of general steward for the whole estate. His ubiquitous presence kept casting a shadow on every facet of life at Acratas and he acted, I thought, more in the nature of a spy than in that of a helpful co-ordinating hand. His long vertical shape, lean angular features cut by a sardonic smile which I had at first failed to recognize as a smile, his habit of suddenly appearing behind my back, round a corner, or silently through a door, upsetting what I was about to do with a polite but firm remark that I should not do it because it had never been done before, would drive me to suppressed fits of rage. His presence, which tapered away into absence and back into presence without those edges of human substance one is accustomed to, was like the presence of an evil angel exuding some of that malefic influence I had sensed on my first arrival at Acratas. He may not have been the source of it; this I felt lay elsewhere, but surely he was connected with it. After three weeks in the house my awareness of such influence had shrunk and might have been swept away by the healthier breezes of Acratas had it not been for the major-domo constantly crossing my path. I would have to have it out with Orestes. I knew it. When I first ventured to mention the question to him, pointing out the uselessness of this man's services, at any rate in the house, where I could now take over the duties of household management myself,

Orestes seemed embarrassed as well as surprised. He said he could hardly dispense with him, the major-domo being such a skillful taxidermist. But I knew there was no room at Acratas for us both. I would have to bide my time and carefully choose the moment for my attack.

One morning, after about three weeks, Orestes told me that urgent business called him to Athens for five or six days. I suggested that for the period of his absence the domestic staff, including the major-domo, should be given a badly needed holiday and go home to their respective villages. I assured him that I could manage by myself in the house and that with the assistance of the gardener who occupied a room at the far end of a wing, I would be able to cope with the feeding of the animals. After much cajoling on my part and hesitation on his, Orestes agreed. Before leaving he handed me a bunch of keys and said:

"Here are the household keys, darling. I forgot to give them to you before simply because the need for your having them had not yet arisen. But as you are going to be alone in the house for a few days, you'd better take charge of them now. It's only the house-door that really matters, since most of the inside doors are always unlocked. However there are a few rooms, as you may have noticed, which are kept locked because they are not being used at present, for example my mother's suite, but you have the keys on the bunch in any case. There's one room nevertheless, at the far end of the top corridor, of which I alone have the key. As all the locks in this house are old and somewhat primitive, one of those keys on the bunch might fit into it at a pinch. But please don't try and open the door. It's a private study where I keep personal papers and mementoes of a purely sentimental interest and I don't like anybody else to go in. Will you promise me? The window is the far corner one up there, do you see?"

We were in the back-garden by the pool; I was digging with a trowel and sowing some seeds in a flower-bed. Orestes pointed to the window above.

There and then I was more vexed than amused by the restriction, but as I did not wish to start any disagreement at this stage I laughed and promised to be good and obedient. After he had left, however, I did think it funny to find myself in a sort of Arabian Nights tale with keys and permission to open any door I liked except one.

When the servants had also gone I was immensely relieved. At last I was alone at Acratas except for the gardener, who stayed quiet and unobtrusive at the far end of the south wing. My elation at being alone in a large eerie house wrapped in the shadows of the past, both far-off and recent, may seem surprising, but I have always loved old houses. I felt that I would never come to grips with this one and discover the ways and means by which I would make it alive again as well as my own, unless I was for a while left alone to my own devices, without being watched, without comments, advice and looks from others. I wanted to be alone and free to put my ears to the walls and floors and try and learn their secret. For every house with an atmosphere is anxious to speak to you, but you must catch its words and the meaning of its language. If there was something nasty at Acratas to discover, muffled under the veils and layers of so many pleasant features, now was the time to find my bearings and tackle things good and bad.

My first impulse was to rush to the kitchen. I have always loved drawing-rooms and kitchens more, I should say, than dining-rooms and bedrooms, though the exact precedence has often changed in the course of my life. I used to despise bathrooms; now they come foremost on my menu of domestic dalliance.

The kitchen at Acratas was magnificent but had remained aloof. For whereas in the drawing-room I was already mistress of the situation and had succeeded in imposing upon prejudices a few abstract paintings, whenever I ventured to make my presence felt in the kitchen Heleni would persistently keep me at arm's length with the poker, as it were. Now, with Heleni and the poker well out of the way, I put the kettle on the charcoal fire for a cup of tea and set about revelling in the shapes and objects of this realm over which I was determined to rule. With pencil, notebook, and tape-measure in hand I paced about or sat on a table making plans for the future. I would introduce the efficient and the new while conserving the ribs and hollows of the solid old architecture. Heleni would be made to learn new dishes and cultivate cleanliness; with tact and perseverance I would achieve it. She would yield to my moulding in the end.

After the kitchen and an exploration of the other basement rooms, vaulted and dark, I turned back without proceeding lower into the dungeons. I had more pressing things to do that day and I climbed briskly to the second floor which, compared with the first,

I hardly knew. There, sure enough, was my bedroom, *our* bedroom I should say, for I had insisted that I could not sleep with the doves and that Orestes would have to choose between them and me. After some cajoling he came to share the bed in my room. His habits were still those of an inveterate bachelor; he too would require some moulding, I thought, to become a normal husband. But it remained my room with my drawings, books, gramophone and records, my pot of basil and my red hibiscus in flower outside the window; and his room with his doves and birds and rodents remained his.

I went to see whether all was well with the birds, then returned along the corridor past my room. First came the two guest-rooms, then my mother-in-law's suite, which I had only partially visited when I first came and remembered but imperfectly. So I proposed to examine it now, but having pressed the handle of her bedroom door I found it locked. I remembered then the bunch of keys, unhooked it from my belt, and with a proprietary feeling fumbled about till I found the right key. The large well-proportioned room was much as I had seen it when my mother-in-law was occupying it, only the windows were now carefully closed and a thin layer of dust covered the Louis XV furniture and the pink bed-cover of lace. I crossed the room and opened the door into the boudoir, which was new to me. It was a small exquisitely furnished room with full-length looking-glasses framed in gilt and hanging on light blue wallpaper of a flowery design which harmonized with the Louis XV dressing-table, though perhaps not quite with the Empire sofa. There were two doors in the opposite wall, one leading to the bathroom tiled with Art Nouveau patterns. Even the bidet and W. C. were embellished with blue and pink convolutions in the same style. There was a smell of stale toothpaste and talcum powder merging into Eau de Cologne. The other door from the boudoir led to her sitting-room, fairly large with two windows and yellow silk curtains; there was an old-fashioned piano in the corner of the room, a sofa and a couple of arm-chairs in chintz, and here and there three or four paraffin lamps with blue opaline shades.

My inspection did not last long, for although I was almost over-anxious to tarry and let my mind sink into details that fascinated me, something—I knew not what—was urging me on. I stayed there long enough, however, to notice that the atmosphere was stuffy, meticulous, but neither lacking in taste nor unpleasant; nor was there anything sinister as one might have been led to think from a first encounter with the old lady.

Retracing my steps I passed through her bedroom again, locked the door, and continued my exploration along the passage. This end had only been indicated to me by Orestes and dismissed with a wave of his hand as a totally uninteresting part of the house. I could still hear the canaries singing and the pigeons cooing from Orestes' room away at the opposite end, but as I walked on, such sounds springing from sun and light yielded to a creaking of boards under my feet. The corridor now was much darker for there were no windows as there had been before, giving onto the front garden. I noticed another couple of doors to my right which I unlocked in turn and found that they opened into large low rooms, one almost empty, the other crammed with furniture in disuse, partly in need of repair. They looked as if they had served as nurseries once upon a time and I pictured to myself how I would arrange them should they again be required as such. Here, however, I sensed an atmosphere I did not like, an atmosphere I could not define but which no nursery should ever possess. It felt like a layer of neglect which had accumulated as the result of some unhappy event or experience, sticking as it were to the walls, ceiling, and floors, and even to the furniture. No doubt it could be scraped off and cleaned out; fresh paint would do the rest; I would see to that. Oddly enough, after having opened a shutter to let some light in, as I walked up and down examining the rooms, I thought I heard, above the jingle of the keys, a noise of footsteps close behind me. I thought I recognized them as the major-domo's and turned round in anger at being again followed by this man. I knew he had a key to the house—but no, not a soul was to be seen, even though I searched and called out. Irritated with my faulty imagination and surprised at the sound of my voice, I closed the shutter and withdrew to the corridor once more. I found myself walking again towards the darker end.

The corridor seemed endless now, the light was getting fainter and fainter, the chirping of birds had faded away, silence was complete except for the creaking of the boards under my feet. There came a stretch of blank wall, everything seemed lengthened, including my own thoughts, but I felt there must be a door further on, over there, at the far end, yes, it must be the door Orestes had forbidden me; well then, why go further? But something was drawing me on, could it have been curiosity, the curiosity aroused by a forbidden thing, no, not only curiosity, at any rate, for it was something both unpleasant and irresistible, as if an invisible hand had grasped my sleeve, was pulling me on, in a trance as it were, I felt like in a dream, for I had often had a dream of that kind had I not, surely it was a familiar one, that of an endless corridor in which I keep finding myself walking on and on towards an end which will finally come, a malignant end, yes, but luckily I wake up before I get there don't I? Now it seemed to me as if this dream were materializing, as if it had been projected into the present, or was I being projected into the past? As I walked on I felt my grasp on reality weaken. I knew that the house was big, but surely not that long. I should have reached the end ages ago. Perhaps I was living at a different tempo, could it be possible? At last the end came and I found myself facing the wall. But was it the end? I turned sharply to the right before I knew what I was doing. *There* was the door I had been expecting, the forbidden door. I examined it closely and passed my hand over it in the semidarkness. Unlike the doors of the other rooms it was heavily carved, a double door which felt solid. The joints closed tight and there were two projecting knobs of brass which shone provocatively as if they expected to be grasped and pushed. I did push, but the door was firmly locked. Instinctively my hand went to the bunch of keys and fumbled there for a while until I felt ashamed and pulled myself together, but not entirely, for without meaning to, I put my left ear close against the wooden surface as if something was to be heard from within. There was nothing but complete silence, so I peered into the key-hole thinking I might see through. But the hole was dark, the door solid, unyielding, impenetrable, that is, from my side impenetrable, evidently not from the other, for I became aware of the presence of something exuding through it like a miasma. I began to feel faint with nausea and as if I was about to drop, when a sharp ring from the house-door bell shook me back to the reality of the outside world. Who could it be at this time of the day? Not the major-domo, who had a key. Almost relieved I hurried down and found the postman at the door with a telegram. After handing it to me he rode off on his motor-cycle waving his hand.

The message was from Orestes saying he would be back a day or two later than planned owing to unforeseen additional business and asking me not to worry.

The evening sun was shining on the lemon leaves in the garden. The gardener came with milk, eggs, and vegetables from the farm and took them to the kitchen before retiring. I went out for a stroll with the dogs and everything proved so welcoming and cheerful that the weird experience I had just gone through was at once swept clean from my mind as if the light of day had dispelled the heavy shadows of a dream.

When I got back I buried myself amongst pots and pans in the kitchen, prepared my supper, and after having had it on the flagstones of the front garden I went up to my room. The trees were bowing outside in the evening breeze, and as I combed my hair over the window-sill I thought I heard my hibiscus sigh, a sigh that rose to fill my heart and drown the croaking of frogs from the crocodile pond of Acratas. I turned and hugged my pot of basil; it smelt good. I switched the gramophone on and after hesitating between the Moonlight Sonata and jazz I chose the latter. I felt I needed it that night. Then I lay down on my pink sheets and let myself sink away. The night proved exquisitely peaceful, my sleep deep and restful, and at the sun's first touch upon my brow I rose relaxed and full of energy.

The morning I spent in the back-garden. I loved it, for unlike the front-garden it was untidy, neglected, ready to yield, waiting for a mind and hand to transform it into the garden I felt it was destined to become. I had the mind and hand, or so I thought, the will and strength to shape it as I wanted. I had sketched it on a sheet of paper, I kept planning it in my mind and now I was checking with my notebook and tape-measure. Plan, yes, of course there would be design, a clear pattern with gravelled paths, box hedges and walls, but not too much plan; there was enough of that in the front-garden with its cones and cubes of green. Mine would be less formal with flowering bushes and herbs, rows of rosemary, sage and basil, delicious herbs of all kinds and flowers, beds of flowers, oleander, myrtle, more pomegranates, more hibiscus, more geraniums, and mimosa of course, daffodils, crocuses, sun-flowers, hollyhocks, roses, masses of flowers including asphodels from the shore of Elysium or from round the corner up the stony hill-side, they would be brought to new life in my garden. I felt as happy as Johnny Crow. There was all the water I wanted—not enough sun, did I say? Perhaps. But I would make the sun. I would not cut the trees down, no, but I would prune them, taper them back; one needed a wall of trees, for protection I suppose, in any case there it was and had always been; I had not come to uproot but to mould; it would be a retreating wall of trees to let the air and sun in, and the sun would play and work with the water.

The area of the back-garden was so large that I realized there would be room enough for the dream of my life, a kitchen-garden of my own planning. I like gardens, I love kitchens, but I adore kitchen-gardens. I sat down on a large stone and gazed. I would lay it out over there to the left, to the south-west, beyond the crocodile pond. It would be bordered on two sides by the whole of the south garden-wall and the far end of the west wall which faced the back of the house; to the east it would have the house and crocodile pool, to the north the garden itself. Once the tangle of weeds and shrubs had been cleared it would have pears, apples, and roses growing against the walls, and beds, well watered by a system of ducts, laid out for the cucumbers, marrows and melons. Of course there would be tomatoes, beans and peas, and above all row beyond row of the architectural artichoke. Along the drier edges and in the further corners sage, mint and oregano would cluster.

I got up excited, my imagination was running wild. What would I do with the crocodile pond? There it was in front of me, shapeless and muddy, and round it an unsightly wire-netting. A fountain? A swimming pool? Yes, I would combine the two and have both in one. The quarry was not far off. Stone was easily available. Away with the beastly mud, cart-loads of it would be removed. And in the place of mud I could already see spouts of marble, and falls and steps of water running over stone, flat soft stone for the bare feet and naked body. I fancied myself rolling into the deep pool from a flight of sparkling foam and dripping moss. There would be large amphorae on the edge, with overhanging geraniums and pomegranates. My kitchen-garden on one side, my garden on the other!

Flushed with excitement I sat down again by the crocodile pond, mapping out every detail, my pencil dashing lines across the

pad, my imagination digging, building, planting, as if I was about
to create "a miracle of rare device, a sunny pleasure dome with
caves of ice." Who would pay? I thought I heard a muffled mutter
bubble up from the mud of the crocodile pool asking the question.
Orestes of course. No, that was not the point, I said to myself. It
was a question of measure and taste; my imagination had carried
me too far, for I now realized that within the precincts of Acratas,
which were designed for meditation, anything even slightly over-
done, would seem ostentatious and verging on vulgarity. I would
have to be more cautious with my plans. Why not leave things as
they were? Suddenly I felt very weary; my right hand fell from the
pad and hung limp at my side as if a heavy claw was holding it
down. Why not leave things looking back with dreamy eyes? It was
all so beautiful, why change anything? But surely—I struggled—
surely a whole world lay between passivity and inappropriate action. My kitchen-garden, my beloved kitchen-garden, would surely
be in harmony, wouldn't it? My hand felt heavy and slothful, but
my heart still clung to the dream. Those walls over there, they
would do nicely as a prop and protection for fruit trees, vines and
roses, but not for every creeper. Most of the ivy would have to be
cut down of course. What was that dark patch on the wall near the
far corner, a stain or a shadow? It was hard to tell; it had an uncanny shape, rather nasty in outline I thought, like that of a beast,
a horrid thing that had once sprawled over a large area leaving a
legacy one did not want. Well, I would anyhow have the whole
garden wall white-washed with lime, bright clean lime. It burns.

The weather was sultry. I was infinitely weary, my mind heavy,
but not sleepy. It occurred to me that whenever I came close to the
mud-pond I would invariably feel weary. Now indeed I was overcome with a kind of paralyzing apathy, as if my energy was being
sapped, my plans and buoyancy overwhelmed, by the obtruding
sluggishness of a presence I could not rationally grasp, but which
seemed bent on contesting every inch of my way, every ounce of
my will to act and mould, bent on crushing my determination to
make Acratas my own. What was it that kept holding my hand
back, softening my mind into acquiescence? As I sat there, on the
edge of the pond, I felt as if something or somebody was watching
me. Uneasily I looked round and up to the windows of the house.
Those of the drawing-room were open and so were those of my

bedroom above and of the room with the birds. All the other windows were closed. Indeed, except for those rooms, the whole upper floor looked as shut and unperturbed as a face of a Buddha with a smile. The smile lay in the stone moulding which framed the seventeenth-century windows. The rest was blank and silent. There was nobody of course, and yet I thought eyes could watch through closed window-panes. Nonsense, I kept repeating to myself. I knew perfectly well there was no one there and I leant back against a yielding pole of the rickety wire-netting. It would be a stone pillar soon without wire-netting, I thought, stretching myself into the future.

But my mind was being pulled into the past, a past I knew not but could sense, yes I could almost see it, the crocodile in the pond like a log of wood! It lay as still as the air, the colour of mud, but rigid like the silence of Acratas. And suddenly a live rabbit flew over the netting and dropped with a splash into the water. Like lightning the crocodile snapped; a squeal was followed by crunch, crunch, and then again another live thing squealing for its life came down with a splash, a pink piglet this time, and the crocodile snapped and crunched, blood running from its jaws. When it had had its fill it waddled out of the water, leaving a rippled wake that closed into smoothness again, and after slithering up the bank lay basking in the mud and sun, its jaws wide open and motionless to let the birds come and pick the teeth still pink with blood.

Where were the birds that pecked at Pylades' teeth? The birds were no more and silence was like death, the silence of Acratas. But where were the pigeons that cooed and nestled on Orestes' pillow, the pigeons that picked Pylades' teeth? Tell me, o tell me, do pigeons pick crocodiles' teeth? The pigeons of Orestes' pillow—I could hear them again in the distance and I shuddered. Their cooing was as gentle as the whisper of death. And a torpor descended upon me, spreading around like the breath of a fever-stricken marsh. With a gasp I tore myself away from the image, from the touch and feeling of it in my flesh, in my bones, in the fibres of my brain. I broke out of the mire and ran for my life to the north, the far north of the garden, and collapsed at the foot of my hibiscus which, red and silky, quivered in the draught I had stirred. The air was lighter and I breathed more freely.

I bit my lips with anger at letting myself be overcome by fancies which had no place in the reality of the moment. The present was mine, the present of Acratas, and above all the future. If unwholesome shadows were still sticking to the walls and earth like overgrown ivy and weeds, was I not there to scrape them out and let the bare stone of Acratas speak for itself? I toyed with my penknife which felt like a hatchet and paced the garden with fresh determination.

An emptiness in my stomach brought me back to the time of the day. It was past noon, so I was glad to be able to hurry down to the kitchen for a drink and a bite. Nothing is so efficacious as food, I have found, in restoring the mind and steadying the nerves. By the time I had come up to the drawing-room and settled myself on the steps to the garden with a book and a cup of Turkish coffee, I felt ready to conquer the world. If there had been some hitches that morning, well, they were part of the campaign, part of the obstacles without which there could be no conquest.

Were the obstacles in Acratas or in me or in us both? I sat there musing on this question, but then swept it away as immaterial. Whatever and wherever they were, the obstacles formed part of my battlefield. I would carry the day in the end. But now I felt sleepy. It was an extremely hot and sultry afternoon early in October, so I went up to my room for a welcome siesta.

When I woke up a couple of hours later it was time to take the dogs out and I fetched them from the gardener. Through the wood and up the hill we went, following the tracks of the goats, over the crest that overhung Acratas and amongst the great olive trees, on by the cypress grove and down the little valley to the stream and mill, and up again through the fields of asphodel in bloom to the dens of jackals where the dogs rushed about in excitement. But soon we turned back, for it was breathlessly hot and the air heavy with dark clouds gathering on the horizon, where flashes of lightning seemed to herald an approaching storm. When we got back I left the dogs at the lodge with the gardener and turned to that eminence of flat ground I cherished by the swing, which I had had mended a few days before. As I sat down on the broken drum of a column I felt the ground covered with pine-needles slip like silk under my sandal-clad feet. Unlike the mud pond and its immediate neighbourhood, unlike certain parts of the house itself which I liked so much but which had not yet yielded, this spot, with its stones and scattered pieces of columns, with its distant view through the opening in the trees, had always filled me with a pleasure free from any shade of oppression. Here I now tarried to rest and to watch the storm sink into the valley from the towering crags of Mount Kratanos. It crept over the hills and along the dells, stretching out from the mountain towards Acratas, licking the earth with vapoury tongues, black and sticky, and lighting up the neighbourhood with flashes as yet silent but ominous.

Where I was sitting the air was still untouched. Silent and damp it hung in suspense, waiting as it were to be drained of its moisture and lashed free into lightness. Already a few yards away I could see minute whirlwinds of dust touch the thirsty ground with kisses that sucked, lifted, and blew about particles of straw and seed. Sometimes a forlorn petal from a sunflower or an autumn crocus was caught up and swung aloft. Then it would break away and plane to the ground to settle on the edge of a stone, where it tiptoed precariously balanced, ready to be caught up again and whirled round with the rest into a dance that mimicked in miniature the great drama of sky and earth in the far distance.

Spellbound I watched the approach of the storm. As I listened to the distant rumble I heard also the rustling of the reeds down by the stream. The wind had swept them with a hand as it went by, and I saw them bend and quiver under that rippling touch. In the white light of the sun which struggled to break through they shimmered, not green but like olive trees and ilexes with a silvery sheen under the pewter sky. The house nestled in its nook of rusty green, its walls yellow and warm, its roaming roof cluttered up with chimneys, waiting to be woken from sleep. My eyes wandered from the storm to the house, from the house to the lichen of my stone-seat. Fascinating lichen! It looked as if the pattern had been drawn with a delicate point by the steady hand of a master, for the thin line wound in curves, springing forward and bending into sharp right angles to form a design so geometrical and subtle, so penetrating and concentrated as to outstrip the imagination even of a Klee. As for the colours, the blobs and spots, the nuances of shade and depth, the edges of light and the spaces of emptiness! Every abstract painting I could recall paled into insignificance.

The dropping of a swallow which had been swooping low hit the ground close by and drew my attention to a line of ants hurrying along, anxious to get their loads stored safely away before the deluge.

I sat and listened to the storm approaching, petrified not with fear but with awe and expectation. Acratas was still asleep. Would it ever awake? Would I be the one to awake it, or would I let myself be pulled in and feel myself sink into the softness of its embrace as into a mire? But was it asleep? Perhaps it only stood there watchful behind an apparent mask of innocence. If there was an evil force with a hold on Acratas waiting to drag me down, as I repeatedly felt there was, would I not stand up against it and drive it out? If Acratas was not yet mine, I determined to make it so, to remould it according to my will. I would open the sluices of health and life and let the clear waters sweep the mire of past influences from the ground and walls of Acratas. Why was the mud pond still there, the useless thing? Away with it! I would have my stone fountain after all and my kitchen-garden, and with lime I would whitewash the whole circuit of wall. I would have access to every room, every corner of Acratas, and I would sweep out every cobweb, every particle of dust into the air and sun. There would be light everywhere, if necessary electric light, with shining lamps on every side dispelling the shadows from the bedrooms, drawing-rooms, underground vaults and dungeons. Nobody before me had ever thought of light. I would break the inimical spell, or it would break me. There was no room for us both; which of us was stronger? Which of us would prevail?

Suddenly I saw the struggle as a matter of life and death. How I loved Acratas! What would I not do for it! And Orestes, did I not love him? No, one could not love a husband so soon, it needed time. No doubt I would in due course; surely I would, such a gentle, kind-hearted, considerate man. . . . But where did he come into the struggle, that was the point. His position seemed equivocal I thought. I would have to get to the bottom of it of course; the bottom of what though? Besides, was there not something odd in my having fallen in love with Acratas and not with my husband? But what was I to do about it? One thing, however, was clear in my mind, the struggle had to be fought to the end even though I knew not exactly what I was resolved to fight. But I felt it. And if it were to prove stronger than myself, for doesn't the intangible or unknown often prove stronger than *oneself*? I shuddered at the thought, scarcely noticing the first heavy drops on my naked shoulders. Nor had I heard the rush of the wind which preceded the downpour. It must have come sweeping from the reeds by the stream in a few split-seconds while I meditated. All at once I heard the leaves overhead swish and creak as if shaken by a blast of hurricane, and saw the branches heaving, bowing, twisting, writhing and the cypresses bending as though they wanted to show they could still touch the ground with the tips of their fingers. My scarf started blowing into my face, but so tight was I clinging to my thoughts, as one clings to a lover, that I did not stir or wake up until a blinding flash shattered the world and brought me to my feet with a start.

At first I thought the house had been struck or a tree felled. No, all seemed well, house, chapel, steeple and trees, though enveloped now in the cloudburst. I did not mind getting wet; I loved the rain that would freshen the air and heal the cracks of the earth. I stood there as if I too was thirsty for rain; but then it occurred to me that I had left my book in the open on the drawing-room steps leading to the back-garden. And, besides, I'd better make sure, I thought, that all the windows were properly shut. Spurred on by another clap of thunder, I rushed back. My dress, drenched and transparent like a veil, clung to my body in the wind. In spite of its wet weight I felt as light and determined as a Nike. When I reached the steps I found my book safe but soaked. Before opening the glass door to go in I scanned the whole back of the house lest a window had been left open by mischance.

All was well, everything seemed securely shut; but no, there was one window, I now noticed, wide open and banging wildly in the wind. It was the far window of the upper floor, the window at the south-eastern corner. I had never seen it open before. With a strange feeling down my spine I realized that it was the forbidden room. Disregarding the wind and lashing rain I stepped down into the garden to have a better view. Fascinated I kept looking at the window, as I stood by the mud pond where the frogs were now croaking their lustful delight. Was it not from that window that I had thought somebody or something was watching me earlier in the day? I pulled myself together and decided to act. Before leaving, Orestes had probably forgotten to make sure that the window was securely shut and now the storm had flung it open. Most likely the rain was pouring into the room. In such an emergency it was surely right to do something about it. There was no time to tarry and think further, for any minute now the window-panes could be smashed to pieces and the frames hurled off their hinges. So I rushed in, firmly closed the glass door behind me, picked up my bunch of keys, flung off my sandals and dripping all over ran bare-footed upstairs. Along the corridor I could hear the rain smiting the windows and, as I rushed beyond the more familiar apartments into the darker end, from one of the rooms to the right came the noise of a drip-drip on the floor which kept time with the beat of my heart. If the roof was leaking, damn it, I could not help it now. I had to hurry on. After another tearing blast of light and thunder I got to the end and stopped in front of the forbidden door, my heart throbbing faster still. Clutching the bunch of keys I listened, my ear to the panel. I heard the window banging inside. There was not a second to waste. I inserted a key, but it would not turn. I tried several, my hands were trembling, I got impatient, cursed, and the sound of my voice steadied me. At last a key turned after some encouragement. The door yielded under the pressure of my body, but not before I had heard a crash from within followed by a smash of glass splintering on the terrace below. The noise merged with another clap of thunder like a loud metallic tinkle bursting into an explosion.

As I opened the door a blast of air swept into my face from the window opposite and I noticed sheets of paper blown about in the draught. My first reaction was to rush to the window and shut it to stop the rain forgetting in my excitement that the window-panes had been smashed to pieces some seconds previously. But I had not advanced more than a few steps when I stopped short, stiffen-ing into ice.

The sight that held me aghast at that very moment keeps emerging with merciless clarity on the screen of memory from those shadows with which the years endeavour to blur it but in vain. The vision breaks through and I still see those claws out-stretched from another world, stiff and trembling in the wind, cry-ing out for my flesh, for my soul.

It was Pylades. I knew it. I knew all along, at the back of my mind, that Pylades was there, somewhere. Subconsciously I knew all along that he ruled Acratas, that I was merely a puppet. I loved

Acratas and had held on till breaking-point. This breaking-point had now come.

There he rested in state on a huge four-poster bed of heavily carved oak, under a canopy of red damask. Stretched out full length on his back and naked, on a thick black velvet pall bordered in gold, he radiated a presence beyond the limits of animality, the tail hanging right down over the end of the bed, the tip just touching the floor. His shoulders and head, crowned with a diadem of rubies, were propped up almost to sitting position by a large cushion of silvery grey satin. His eyes, glazed and yellow, stared at me with a haunting look, while his huge jaws, stiffly protruding, were set slightly apart in a grin, showing the rows of sharp yellow teeth. His scaly body of immense girth was of a muddy brown, much as it had been described to me. His belly shaded off from brown to emerald green, and from emerald green to lemon yellow. It glistened and seemed smoother, tenderer than the rest. His forelegs looked short, like the naked arms of a corpulent but muscular lady, and stretched out paws like fleshy hands which were furnished, however, with long sharp claws. Quivering and twitching in the turbulent gusts of the storm they stuck out as if longing to finger me, to clasp me. The glassless window kept banging in the wind, the rain poured in, the papers went whirling round, while I stood riveted to the floor, staring into that dark end of the room where the four-poster loomed in all its glory, where Pylades lay in state grotesquely, monstrously beautiful.

Though in shadow, the rubies glistened and the whole bed intermittently flared forward into blinding clarity under the whip of the lightning which lashed away at a mirror swaying on the wall.

I stared and stared horror-struck and yet fascinated. Then I became aware of the scream of my own voice, like a shriek tearing in from another world, and at last my feet came unstuck. I felt the whole effort of breaking loose from a hold which was repellent and yet gripping, as if bursting from a metal clasp that both hurt and enthralled with its barbaric beauty. The snap gave pain and relief at the same time. I flung myself out of the room and ran barefooted and wet down the endless corridor; I heard the keys jingle in my hands and felt my hair stream behind in the draught as the doors banged and the house shook.

Now that I think of it, what a sight I must have been! More

than enough to send Andrew into fits of laughter. But he sees things only from outside so that to him life is an eternal joke.

At last I got to my room, pushed the door open and collapsed, still screaming, I believe, on my bed, demented, convulsive. The lightning went on breaking into thunder and the intervals were so short that I knew not whether it was my voice, or God knows what, that kept on tearing my eardrums without stop until it subsided into the noise of sobs, my sobs, all that was left of my own.

However, I did not lie there on my bed for long. I sprang to my feet spurred by a single resolve, to get out of the accursed house; quick, quick, out of it and away for ever. I slipped on another pair of sandals, grabbed a small leather case, hastily packed a few necessaries, including passport and money, and opened the window, still lashed by the rain, to take a last look at my hibiscus below which, alas, I could not carry away. Its roots went too deep into the soil of Acratas. I gazed at it and saw that its petals had been torn off by the storm; it stood there dripping, a thing unhappy and unlovely. But my pot of basil was fresh, thick and bursting with green and scent. I plunged my face in and breathed deeply, holding it tight in my arms. I wanted to take it with me but it was too heavy, for I had a long way to go. As I replaced it on the window-sill the noise hurt. Then I wrenched myself away and rushed down and out of the house through the front-garden to the gates, turning round from time to time as if I were being followed, or as if, from the bed of black velvet, Pylades might still stretch out a claw to drag me back. When I opened the garage my heart stopped; there was no car. I had forgotten that Orestes had taken it to Sepheria. Orestes! A shiver went down my back at the thought of him; but I had no time to think. The three-mile track to a point on the main road where I might catch a bus to the port, had to be tackled at once. What about a horse? It seemed the obvious solution. But then I realized that in going to the stables I would be drawing the attention of the gardener or of a farm-hand: it was essential to get away unobserved as quickly as possible. Already I thought I had seen a shadow moving and disappearing at the far end of the garden near the house-door, which looked like that of the major-domo. Why on earth did I keep imagining the outlines of that man?

I made up my mind to set out on foot without further delay despite the burden of my bag. It was raining less now and the wind had dropped. I decided on a short-cut by a rough path which avoided the farm houses. So clutching my leather case I plunged ahead through the wet ferns of the wood and through the olive groves beyond, without daring to look back and catch a last sight of Acratas, my feelings being so mixed, so torn and desperate.

At first I ran, but soon my bag felt heavy and my pace slowed down to an unsteady gait over the rough path, through the puddles and runnels of murky rain water. I kept thinking I was being followed. Stumbling, out of breath, picking myself up, bruised by the stones, scratched by the thistles and bespattered with mud, I plodded on, away from Acratas at all costs; my heart thumped and felt as if it were pressing against a sharp edge of stone.

Little by little the rain thinned away and the thunder subsided into the receding blackness of the horizon. Between the gnarled olive trunks the autumn crocuses glistened at me, mauve and lilac in the after-storm light. Suddenly the warm rays of a sinking sun tore through the clouds, and lit up the white crags of Mount Kratanos. My heart ached with nostalgia and regret. But when my eyes sank to the foreground again I felt my blood curdle at the sight of a familiar shape, whether imaginary or real I knew not. In the shadow of a knotted olive tree I perceived once more the major-domo's outline, skinny and elongated like an autumn weed. He stood leaning against the trunk, looking at me with a leer of triumph across his swarthy face. I turned away and hurried on, with feelings which welled up in a turmoil of fear, hatred and vexation.

By the time I had reached the high road it was dusk and a thin rain had started again. Exhausted I sank under a great olive tree whose moss-covered roots twisted snake-like over the ground. I lay there wet and benumbed I know not how long. At length the rumbling clatter and headlights of an old bus shook me into renewed action. I leapt forward into the road to stop it and then felt myself pulled into a welter of bodies and voices. At Sepheria I was lucky to find a ship sailing that very night, and the next day a plane took me back to London.

"A crocodile! A stuffed crocodile!" My sisters with their marital complications and difficult love-lives giggled when we met again. "Not possible! Do you mean to say you let yourself be done out of everything by a stuffed crocodile? You never seem to find the right thing." As if they ever did.

Uncle Andrew's reaction was more outspokenly hilarious and healthy. He broke into an uncontrolled fit of laughter. He thought the whole story roaringly funny, but considered my reaction silly beyond bounds and that alarmed him, so he said. I was to go back immediately. He would see to everything, explain anything I liked to Orestes, if I wanted. Surely the stuffed crocodile could be removed? But didn't I like stuffed animals? Didn't I used to have a stuffed monkey or teddy-bear as a child?

Whether stuffed or embalmed, whether real or imaginary, I knew Pylades would stay. He had gained spiritual as well as corporeal permanency. For that very reason I had torn myself away from Acratas, which I loved. I kept remembering my mother-in-law's words. They had seemed cryptic to me then; now they were clear. For Acratas I had been prepared to struggle and indeed had put up a fight, but Pylades had proved stronger. I would not go back; I insisted on my divorce. Andrew roared with laughter, then he stormed because I remained adamant and because he could not see deeper. He has always remained blind to the real significance of things despite, or perhaps because of, his sense of humour, a cruel humour without subtlety. All this I realized years later. At that time I was too lame, too shaken and defenceless, but my instinct guided me, protected me. "You don't understand," I kept telling him, "you don't understand, you never do, it's not just . . . I wish I could explain, o well . . . never mind." But it is when we don't know, or don't quite know, or have not yet quite understood, that we desperately want to explain. Now I do know and feel no need to explain.

I stuck to my guns; I got my divorce. Now I am back with my horses in Yorkshire, back to my books, to my writing, and years have gone by. Uncle Andrew is getting old. I am still fond of him, he still laughs and is amusing whenever one feels like being amused. And often when I ride out over my Yorkshire hills the white crags of Mount Kratanos spring to memory and the yellow walls and tawny roofs of Acratas call out to me with a voice I love, to be smothered at once by what I then felt and saw and never can forget.

And Orestes? What about him? Well, he must be getting on by

now. I hear from Andrew that he still comes on his yearly visits to the British Isles, puts up at the Reform as usual, and then tours the country in search of a wife. Perhaps when hoary and very old he will find a woman who will either accept or succeed in ousting Pylades. I wish her good luck.

THE UNATTACHED SMILE

BY HARRY CREWS

THEY were the first mountains he had ever seen and they rose out of the sea like some dark childhood dream, and it was the same as it had been at every port. At first there was only the gentle unrest in his stomach as the land loomed gray and indefinite on the horizon; then as the shoreline rose into heavy focus, his fear hardened and lay like a weight in his heart. On the long wooden docks from the ship to land, he carried himself as delicately as though walking a tightrope, never feeling safe again until he had lain with a woman and was back aboard ship with the land slipping away into the sea. Then later, when he could no longer recall the woman's face but only the hard, bought flesh, he would be very still inside himself and say, in a small voice, that everything was all right.

He was drunk enough now. Since morning he had climbed with Tom Ash through the steep alleys of San Juan from one bar to the next, knowing that he must try himself again with a woman's flesh. Gradually he had been able to keep his eyes fastened longer and longer to the women that passed him, to the thin cloth covering their heavy, vulnerable haunches. It was only possible with those of the grinding thighs. He could not bear to look upon the others, the thin high-breasted girls with flat stomachs who carried themselves as light as pollen in the wind, because in each of them was stamped the raw image of his sister's face.

They had drunk more than he had thought they would, and their money was almost gone. He was sitting at a table wondering where in the world the money would come from, when suddenly he saw the watch on Tom's wrist.

"I tell you a watch is a useless thing," he said.

"What makes you say that?" Tom asked.

"A man always knows what time it is," he said.

Tom let his arm slide off into his lap. "My mother gave me this one."

He pushed back in his chair and gripped the edge of the table. He couldn't rush it. If he forced Tom about the watch, there'd never be the money. He would have to wait. And waiting, now that he was ready, would only bring the memory again. He was like a man about to vomit, hating it, willing against it, but all the while feeling it rise uncontrollably. There was never enough air in the world when it was upon him. He twisted in his seat, stretching his neck to breathe, and through the window the moon over the gently swelling ocean pulled at him like a great yellow magnet. And the moon had been much like that looking through the hay-loft window toward the dark house and the trees beyond the house. The green smell of hay hung in his nostrils, and in the distance a twelve o'clock rooster crowed. Beside him in the darkness he had felt her soft, almost silent breath. He was afraid she would move, and she did, her shoulder pressing against his arm, the flesh unrestrained and moving. Through the sudden summer nights and the long winter evenings with the odor of frost seeping under the door, the hay-loft had been theirs. It had been a kind of magic playhouse that neither of them ever had to explain to anyone, not even to themselves. They always had between them the memory of the place where they talked and sat, sometimes with their elbows touching. Already there was good-natured ribbing around the supper table about how soon she would be married, or should be married, or at least pick out a favorite feller.

"I want to dance," said Tom.

Suddenly, through the window, there was nothing but the heavy moon lying solid on the horizon. He turned his drink up and finished it, but it fell on his stomach like ice water.

"Dance if you want to," he said. "I'm for another drink."

Tom walked away from the table and he watched him embrace a woman on the dance floor, their bodies curved together and unmoving. When he saw them touch, he could wait no longer. Each time he had come ashore there had been this moment, the moment when he had consciously gathered himself to find a woman and let the trial begin. He opened his mouth to breathe and sucked deeply

on dry air that filled his lungs like dust. If the woman he was about
to find had only a woman's flesh and a woman's face, then he knew
he could rise from her and walk carefully back to ship and live to
the next port.

He braced himself to step away from the table and demanded
of his heart that he do it.

The bland, brown faces of the women were lined against the
wall like so much fruit. A cab driver with a golden heart embedded
in the enamel of one of his front teeth pushed a woman out toward
him. He refused her and passed on to a girl wearing a white dress.
He led her to the floor and as they danced, he felt her belly pressing below the hard brass buckle of his trousers, and under his hand
her massive hips rolled to the music. But what he felt was not important. He knew that he had set his feet in a path that was direct
and inalterable; all he had to do now was walk it.

When the dance was over, he held her hand and led her back to
the table.

"Now why did you bring her over here?" asked Tom. "You
know they always expect you to buy them drinks."

"Drink. Rum," she said.

"See," Tom said. "What the hell did I tell you?"

He caught the sleeve of a passing waiter and held up three fingers.

"Now listen," said Tom. "We got little enough money without
you buying drinks for every whore in the joint."

"You're beautiful," he said, not taking his eyes off the girl.
"She looks more like someone's sister than . . . than that."

"Being someone's sister never kept a woman from being a
whore," said Tom.

"I'm going to bed with her," he said.

"What do you intend using for money?" asked Tom. "Maybe
she'll do it for love. Go on—ask her for love."

He looked away from the girl for the first time and took Tom
by the wrist and pushed his shirt sleeve back from the watch. Tom
snatched his hand away as though he had burned it.

"My mother gave me this watch," he said evenly. "Don't think
I'm going to sell it so you can go to bed with this."

"I've got to have the money," he said, the muscles knotting
along the edge of his jaw. "You see that table of chiefs back there? I

could sell it to one of them and when we get back to the ship, I'll pay you the difference."

The girl had been following their voices with her eyes and she had picked up the argument.

"You good man," she said to Tom. "I very good for friend." She looked steadily into his eyes while he sat not speaking, and then finally added in a lower voice, "I very good."

Tom looked at the girl for a long minute and then snapped the watch off his wrist and laid it on the table. "I'll say I lost it," he said.

"Wait until I sell it," he said. "I'll split the money with you and you can drink some more or maybe go with me." He was talking too rapidly. He did not mean it about Tom going with them.

Tom said something else to him, but he didn't listen. He pushed his way through the crowd to a table where the chiefs sat drinking in a circle of smoke. The man he stopped beside was shuffling a deck of cards. A girl was outlined in blue on the back of one of his freckled hands. He was looking at the girl moving in the freckles and stiff red hair when the cards stopped and the man turned towards him. He had a ragged cigar between his teeth. He didn't speak. He just sat looking up at him.

"Say, I wanted to know if I could sell . . . that is . . ." He stumbled on, and as he talked he could see the face above the hand stretch into a smile. He said more than he meant to say. All the while the smiling eyes in the thick face kept turning to the table where Tom sat with the girl.

"Now let me get this straight," said the chief. "It's your buddy's watch but you're gonna sell it."

"Yeah, yeah," he said. "A give-away practically. I don't need but a little bit."

"A little what?" asked the chief.

"A little money," he said.

"Now how come you say you're sellin' the watch?" asked the chief.

"I told you already," he said. "The girl."

"Yes," said the chief. "And you say you don't need but a little bit."

The chief slapped the table and laughed until he started coughing and then slapped the table again.

He stood straight and still. He wanted desperately to turn and walk away, but he could not. He simply stood with the watch in his open hand while the chief wiped tears from his eyes.

"Here," said the chief, "take your money and go. Go on, you only need a little bit."

Tom had not left the table. He sat hunched forward, his shoulders curving in a bow. The girl's hand was beneath the table, the round white spot of her elbow moving slowly and surely.

"You have money now?" asked the girl.

"Yes," he answered.

"My house good," she said, rising.

Tom stood up with her as if raised by invisible threads from her body.

"How much did you get?" asked Tom. His voice sounded like he was talking with sand in his throat.

"Twenty dollars."

"Let's go then," said Tom.

"What are you going to do?" he asked.

"Go with you."

"You better get a girl," he said.

"I'm going with you," Tom said and then as an afterthought, "she has a sister."

The girl moved between them, linking her arms in theirs, and led them into the street where the taxi drivers smoked cigarettes, grouped in front of their cars. In the back seat with the girl in the middle, he was almost sick. He leaned forward with his hand over his mouth but the feeling passed. It was all wrong. He wanted to be alone with the girl, with a lamp in one corner, with the dark outside the door but not caring because the night had nothing to do with him now. He wanted to take off the girl's clothes and touch her all over and say the things he had carried with him all day, through all the days. But finally, coupled with her flesh, he must look into her eyes and find there only this woman's face.

Through the window he watched the mountainside slip past in a blur of darkness, speeding him on to the place where he would, or would not, meet her. And now, sitting still in the inevitable waiting, he thought: God, I've been down this road before.

This old familiar road that was terrifying in its familiarity. He knew when it would be straight, when a house would flash into the

headlights, and when the sides of the road would darken with the
flat wall of trees. And when it finally leveled into the dusty street of
the town, the car would stay parked all day in front of Tillit's store
baking in the sun and smelling of the groceries in the back seat and
the four new leather hame strings in the floorboard.

"Pa gave me more than you. Take a piece of mine," his sister
would say. She held the candy sack toward him, her brown eyes
turning the color of rosin over her cheeks. She smiled the slow,
deliberate smile but pretended it was not for him by staring at a
bonnet in a store window. He fell behind and watched her walk
and remembered the look of the wet curve of her back standing
knee-deep in the creek which ran behind the mule lot when the
sun was red through the trees. They went there to wash, soaping
each other's neck and back. And gradually, as they had grown
older, there had been the smile which she had pretended was not
for him.

"We can't go in there," he said. "Pa said stay out of that cotton
gin."

"They ain't ginning," she said. "Pa won't know, and we can eat
our licorice in the sacks where it's cool."

They sat in the cool, stale air of the croker sacks eating the
licorice, and her thin legs were bared to him as her dress worked
up around her hips, and once he rubbed her cheek with the flat of
his hand as she smiled the slow smile into the candy sack.

"Pay him."

The hand was hard on his shoulder. The motor of the cab idled
quietly. His head hurt behind his eyes and he wondered vaguely if
he had slept. The odor of croker sacks was still in his nostrils.

"Where are we?" he asked.

"Home." He heard the girl's voice in the darkness.

"Pay him," repeated Tom.

Tom and the girl got out of the taxi. He could hear their shoes
on the graveled road. Far below, through the window on his left,
he saw the now steady, now flickering lights of the city. He sat on
the edge of the leather cushion with one hand on the frame of the
window and the other hand on the back of the seat in front of
him.

"Like another world," he said softly, as if afraid of his own
voice.

"The money, amigo," the driver said, twisting in his seat to face him. The driver smiled and there was the golden heart, the same driver he had seen earlier in the evening. The gold embedded in the enamel of his tooth looked dull as brass, almost dark, in the reflected light from the dashboard. He felt a skip in the flutter of his heart. He had refused a girl from this man once today, and yet had he? Did it matter from whom? With whom? He pulled some money from his pocket and put it in the driver's hand, not stopping to count it, and fled through the open door. The cab motor roared once and was gone, the tail light disappearing around a bend in the mountain road.

A pair of shallow ruts slanted off to the right and he followed them, setting his feet carefully in a path that he could barely see. He rounded a bend and there, stuck in the side of the mountain like a huge fist of clay, was a house. The flat shadow of some wild growth, taller than a man's head and unmoving in the airless night, ascended the slope behind the house.

Suddenly, he heard a giggle and he strained to see them.

"Tom?" he called.

"Over here," a voice answered.

He walked closer. Tom had a jug in his hand.

"Where'd you get that?"

"Inside," said Tom. "Here, take some."

As he took the jug, he saw the light in the girl's eyes as she moved closer to the window. She looked back at him, her face flat and unsmiling.

"Why'd you come back out here?" he asked.

"They're going to bed."

"Who's going to bed?"

"Her people."

Off in the distance a mule brayed, a hoarse squealing sound that echoed hollowly against the mountain. His knees weakened and he leaned against the house for support. The mules braying when the night is down and her people are going to bed. Inside the house a chair scraped and fell and was followed by a soft Spanish word.

He turned toward the sound of metal hinges as a door opened. A girl was there in the lighted arch. She said something in Spanish and took Tom by the hand and led him into the house. He heard the soft alien voice in the door again. She had her hand stretched out, reaching for him. He refused it. She retreated and left the door open. He stood for a moment; and then as calmly and deliberately as he could, he walked into the light and through the arch.

Across the room, her face halved by shadow and light, stood a young girl. She was thin with sharp features, but as she glanced up at him momentarily before averting her face, he saw the full expressiveness of her mouth, the lips stretched in a shy, knowing smile.

He turned and walked stiffly to the low table where Tom was standing with the other girl. Just as he got to them, Tom leaned forward and said something in his ear that he did not understand and laughed. Then suddenly, without remembering how it happened, he found himself holding the jug and watching a door close behind Tom and the girl. He threw the jug to the floor and bolted for the door. He got half through it and Tom was pushing him back saying:

"I left the sister for you. She's yours."

And so the door closed and he stood facing the wall, afraid to turn around. Directly behind him, between him and the door leading to the outside, he could feel the girl standing. He moved slowly, keeping his face to the wall. He strained to hear her move. No movement came, but in the stillness he heard the sound of breathing. At first he thought it was his own. He held his breath but the sound was still there. It was close now, almost over his shoulder. He stood rigid, listening to the steady, rhythmic pull of heavy lungs.

There was no other way; he had to turn. He had to face her.

She was naked in front of the lamp, her long black hair covering her face like a mourning veil. She looked taller now without the dress to hide her adolescent thinness. And he stood transfixed, not by her body or her nakedness but by the curtain of hair and the anonymous face. He took a step toward her and she toward him. She seemed to float, to hang suspended, her body shining dully in the light from the lamp. He reached out and took her shoulders gently with all the strength of his will. The girl raised her hands and took his arms. She led him to a bed beside the window where the lamp flickered. His mind wavered like an inconstant flame; and behind her hands and hot mouth, he could see the shape of his terror. It came down from the lamp, an anonymous, unattached smile. As if in a dream, as if a part of him were aloof and detached from the scene, he saw himself sinking into that smile, through those dark lips into darkness. And before him spread a vast and airless field, vaster than the eye and without direction.

A COURTSHIP

BY WILLIAM FAULKNER

THIS is how it was in the old days, when old Issetibbeha was still the Man, and Ikkemotubbe, Issetibbeha's nephew, and David Hogganbeck, the white man who told the steamboat where to walk, courted Herman Basket's sister.

The People all lived in the Plantation now. Issetibbeha and General Jackson met and burned sticks and signed a paper, and now a line ran through the woods, although you could not see it. It ran straight as a bee's flight among the woods, with the Plantation on one side of it, where Issetibbeha was the Man, and America on the other side, where General Jackson was the Man. So now when something happened on one side of the line, it was a bad fortune for some and a good fortune for others, depending on what the white man happened to possess, as it had always been. But merely by occurring on the other side of that line which you couldn't even see, it became what the white men called a crime punishable by death if they could just have found who did it. Which seemed foolish to us. There was one uproar which lasted off and on for a week, not that the white man had disappeared, because he had been the sort of white man which even other white men did not regret, but because of a delusion that he had been eaten. As if any man, no matter how hungry, would risk eating the flesh of a coward or thief in this country where even in winter there is always something to be found to eat;—this land for which, as Issetibbeha used to say after he had become so old that nothing more was required of him except to sit in the sun and criticize the degeneration of the People and the folly and rapacity of politicians, the Great Spirit has done more and man less than for any land he ever heard of. But it was a free country, and if the white men wished to make a rule even that foolish in their half of it, it was all right with us.

Then Ikkemotubbe and David Hogganbeck saw Herman Basket's sister. As who did not, sooner or later, young men and old men too, bachelors and widowers too, and some who were not even widowers yet, who for more than one reason within the hut had no business looking anywhere else, though who is to say what age a man must reach or just how unfortunate he must have been in his youthful compliance, when he shall no longer look at the Herman Basket's sisters of this world and chew his bitter thumbs too, aihee. Because she walked in beauty. Or she sat in it, that is, because she did not walk at all unless she had to. One of the earliest sounds in the Plantation would be the voice of Herman Basket's aunt crying to know why she had not risen and gone to the spring for water with the other girls, which she did not do sometimes until Herman Basket himself rose and made her, or in the afternoon crying to know why she did not go to the river with the other girls and women to wash, which she did not do very often either. But she did not need to. Anyone who looks as Herman Basket's sister did at seventeen and eighteen and nineteen does not need to wash.

Then one day Ikkemotubbe saw her, who had known her all his life except during the first two years. He was Issetibbeha's sister's son. One night he got into the steamboat with David Hogganbeck and went away. And suns passed and then moons and then three high waters came and went and old Issetibbeha had entered the earth a year and his son Moketubbe was the Man when Ikkemotubbe returned, named Doom now, with the white friend called the Chevalier Soeur-Blonde de Vitry and the eight new slaves which we did not need either, and his gold-laced hat and cloak and the little gold box of strong salt and the wicker wine hamper containing the four other puppies which were still alive, and within two days Moketubbe's little son was dead and within three Ikkemotubbe whose name was Doom now was himself the Man. But he was not Doom yet. He was still just Ikkemotubbe, one of the young men, the best one, who rode the hardest and fastest and danced the longest and got the drunkest and was loved the best, by the young men and the girls and the older women too who should have had other things to think about. Then one day he saw Herman Basket's sister, whom he had known all his life except for the first two years.

After Ikkemotubbe looked at her, my father and Owl-at-Night and Sylvester's John and the other young men looked away. Because he was the best of them and they loved him then while he was still just Ikkemotubbe. They would hold the other horse for him as, stripped to the waist, his hair and body oiled with bear's grease as when racing (though with honey mixed into the bear's grease now) and with only a rope hackamore and no saddle as when racing, Ikkemotubbe would ride on his new racing pony past the gallery where Herman Basket's sister sat shelling corn or peas into the silver wine pitcher which her aunt had inherited from her second cousin by marriage's great-aunt who was old David Colbert's wife, while Log-in-the-Creek (one of the young men too, though nobody paid any attention to him. He raced no horses and fought no cocks and cast no dice and even when forced to, he would not even dance fast enough to keep out of the other dancers' way, and disgraced both himself and the others each time by becoming sick after only five or six horns of what was never even his whiskey) leaned against one of the gallery posts and blew into his harmonica. Then one of the young men held the racing pony, and on his gaited mare now and wearing his flower-painted weskit and pigeon-tailed coat and beaver hat in which he looked handsomer than a steamboat gambler and richer even than the whiskey-trader, Ikkemotubbe would ride past the gallery where Herman Basket's sister shelled another pod of peas into the pitcher and Log-in-the-Creek sat with his back against the post and blew into the harmonica. Then another of the young men would take the mare too and Ikkemotubbe would walk to Herman Basket's and sit on the gallery too in his fine clothes while Herman Basket's sister shelled another pod of peas perhaps into the silver pitcher and Log-in-the-Creek lay on his back on the floor, blowing into the harmonica. Then the whiskey-trader came and Ikkemotubbe and the young men invited Log-in-the-Creek into the woods until they became tired of carrying him. And although a good deal wasted outside, as usual Log-in-the-Creek became sick and then asleep after seven or eight horns, and Ikkemotubbe returned to Herman Basket's gallery, where for a day or two at least he didn't have to not listen to the harmonica.

Finally Owl-at-Night made a suggestion. "Send Herman Basket's aunt a gift." But the only thing Ikkemotubbe owned which Herman Basket's aunt didn't, was the new racing pony. So after a while Ikkemotubbe said, "So it seems I want this girl even worse than I believed," and sent Owl-at-Night to tie the racing pony's hackamore to Herman Basket's kitchen door-handle. Then he thought how Herman Basket's aunt could not even always make Herman Basket's sister just get up and go to the spring for water. Besides, she was the second cousin by marriage to the grand-niece of the wife of old David Colbert, the chief Man of all the Chicka- saws in our section, and she looked upon Issetibbeha's whole fam- ily and line as mushrooms.

"But Herman Basket has been known to make her get up and go to the spring," my father said. "And I never heard him claim that old Dave Colbert's wife or his wife's niece or anybody else's wife or niece or aunt was any better than anybody else. Give Her- man the horse."

"I can beat that," Ikkemotubbe said. Because there was no horse in the Plantation or America either between Natchez and Nashville whose tail Ikkemotubbe's new pony ever looked at. "I will run Herman a horse-race for his influence," he said. "Run," he told my father. "Catch Owl-at-Night before he reaches the house." So my father brought the pony back in time. But just in case Her- man Basket's aunt had been watching from the kitchen window or something, Ikkemotubbe sent Owl-at-Night and Sylvester's John home for his crate of gamecocks, though he expected little from this since Herman Basket's aunt already owned the best cocks in the Plantation and won all the money every Sunday morning any- way. And then Herman Basket declined to commit himself, so a horse-race would have been merely for pleasure and money. And Ikkemotubbe said how money could not help him, and with that damned girl on his mind day and night his tongue had forgotten the savor of pleasure. But the whiskey-trader always came, and so for a day or two at least he wouldn't have to not listen to the har- monica.

Then David Hogganbeck also looked at Herman Basket's sister, whom he too had been seeing once each year since the steamboat first walked to the Plantation. After a while even winter would be over and we would begin to watch the mark which David Hoggan- beck had put on the landing to show us when the water would be tall enough for the steamboat to walk in. Then the river would reach the mark, and sure enough within two suns the steamboat would cry in the Plantation. Then all the People—men and women and children and dogs, even Herman Basket's sister because Ikkemotubbe would fetch a horse for her to ride and so only Log-in-the-Creek would remain, not inside the house even though it was still cold, because Herman Basket's aunt wouldn't let him stay inside the house where she would have to step over him each time she passed, but squatting in his blanket on the gallery with an old cooking-pot of fire inside the blanket with him—would stand on the landing, to watch the upstairs and the smokestack moving among the trees and hear the puffing of the smokestack and its feet walking fast in the water too when it was not crying. Then we would begin to hear David Hogganbeck's fiddle, and then the steamboat would come walking up the last of the river like a race-horse, with the smoke rolling black and its feet flinging the water aside as a running horse flings dirt, and Captain Studenmare who owned the steamboat chewing tobacco in one window and David Hogganbeck playing his fiddle in the other, and between them the head of the boy slave who turned the wheel, who was not much more than half as big as Captain Studenmare and not even a third as big as David Hogganbeck. And all day long the trading would continue, though David Hogganbeck took little part in this. And all night long the dancing would continue, and David Hogganbeck took the biggest part in this. Because he was bigger than any two of the young men put together almost, and although you would not have called him a man built for dancing or running either, it was as if that very double size which could hold twice as much whiskey as any other, could also dance twice as long, until one by one the young men fell away and only he was left. And there was horse-racing and eating, and although David Hogganbeck had no horses and did not ride one since no horse could have carried him and run fast too, he would eat a match each year for money against any two of the young men whom the People picked, and David Hogganbeck always won. Then the water would return toward the mark he had made on the landing, and it would be time for the steamboat to leave while there was still enough water in the river for it to walk in.

And then it did not go away. The river began to grow little, yet still David Hogganbeck played his fiddle on Herman Basket's gallery while Herman Basket's sister stirred something for cooking into the silver wine pitcher and Ikkemotubbe sat against a post in his fine clothes and his beaver hat and Log-in-the-Creek lay on his back on the floor with the harmonica cupped in both hands to his mouth, though you couldn't hear now whether he was blowing into it or not. Then you could see the mark which David Hogganbeck had marked on the landing while he still played his fiddle on Herman Basket's gallery where Ikkemotubbe had brought a rocking chair from his house to sit in until David Hogganbeck would have to leave in order to show the steamboat the way back to Natchez. And all that afternoon the People stood along the landing and watched the steamboat's slaves hurling wood into its stomach for steam to make it walk; and during most of that night, while David Hogganbeck drank twice as much and danced twice as long as even David Hogganbeck, so that he drank four times as much and danced four times as long as even Ikkemotubbe, even an Ikkemotubbe who at last had looked at Herman Basket's sister or at least had looked at someone else looking at her, the older ones among the People stood along the landing and watched the slaves hurling wood into the steamboat's stomach, not to make it walk but to make its voice cry while Captain Studenmare leaned out of the upstairs with the end of the crying-rope tied to the door-handle. And the next day Captain Studenmare himself came onto the gallery and grasped the end of David Hogganbeck's fiddle.

"You're fired," he said.

"All right," David Hogganbeck said. Then Captain Studenmare grasped the end of David Hogganbeck's fiddle.

"We will have to go back to Natchez where I can get money to pay you off," he said.

"Leave the money at the saloon," David Hogganbeck said. "I'll bring the boat back out next spring."

Then it was night. Then Herman Basket's aunt came out and said that if they were going to stay there all night, at least David Hogganbeck would have to stop playing his fiddle so other people could sleep. Then she came out and said for Herman Basket's sister to come in and go to bed. Then Herman Basket came out and said, "Come on now, fellows. Be reasonable." Then Herman Basket's aunt came out and said that the next time she was going to bring Herman Basket's dead uncle's shotgun. So Ikkemotubbe and David Hogganbeck left Log-in-the-Creek lying on the floor and stepped

down from the gallery. "Goodnight," David Hogganbeck said.
"I'll walk home with you," Ikkemotubbe said. So they walked
across the Plantation to the steamboat. It was dark and there was
no fire in its stomach now because Captain Studenmare was still
asleep under Issetibbeha's back porch. Then Ikkemotubbe said,
"Goodnight."

"I'll walk home with you," David Hogganbeck said. So they
walked back across the Plantation to Ikkemotubbe's house. But
David Hogganbeck did not have time to say goodnight now because Ikkemotubbe turned as soon as they reached his house and
started back toward the steamboat. Then he began to run, because
David Hogganbeck still did not look like a man who could run
fast. But he had not looked like a man who could dance a long time
either, so when Ikkemotubbe reached the steamboat and turned
and ran again, he was only a little ahead of David Hogganbeck.
And when they reached Ikkemotubbe's house he was still only a
little ahead of David Hogganbeck when he stopped, breathing fast
but only a little fast, and held the door open for David Hogganbeck to enter.

"My house is not very much house," he said. "But it is yours."
So they both slept in Ikkemotubbe's bed in his house that night.
And the next afternoon, although Herman Basket would still do
no more than wish him success, Ikkemotubbe sent my father and
Sylvester's John with his saddle mare for Herman Basket's aunt to
ride on, and he and Herman Basket ran the horse-race. And he
rode faster than anyone had ever ridden in the Plantation. He won
by lengths and lengths and, with Herman Basket's aunt watching,
he made Herman Basket take all the money, as though Herman
Basket had won, and that evening he sent Owl-at-Night to tie the
racing pony's hackamore to the door-handle of Herman Basket's
kitchen. But that night Herman Basket's aunt did not even warn
them. She came out the first time with Herman Basket's dead uncle's gun, and hardly a moment had elapsed before Ikkemotubbe
found out that she meant him too. So he and David Hogganbeck
left Log-in-the-Creek lying on the gallery and they stopped for a
moment at my father's house on the first trip between Ikkemotubbe's house and the steamboat, though when my father and Owl-
at-Night finally found Ikkemotubbe to tell him that Herman Basket's aunt must have sent the racing pony far into the woods and

hidden it because they had not found it yet, Ikkemotubbe and David Hogganbeck were both asleep in David Hogganbeck's bed in the steamboat.

And the next morning the whiskey-trader came, and that afternoon Ikkemotubbe and the young men invited Log-in-the-Creek into the woods and my father and Sylvester's John returned for the whiskey-trader's buckboard and, with my father and Sylvester's John driving the buckboard and Log-in-the-Creek lying on his face on top of the little house on the back of the buckboard where the whiskey-kegs rode and Ikkemotubbe standing on top of the little house, wearing the used general's coat which General Jackson gave Issetibbeha, with his arms folded and one foot advanced onto Log-in-the-Creek's back, they rode slow past the gallery where David Hogganbeck played his fiddle while Herman Basket's sister stirred something for cooking into the silver wine pitcher. And when my father and Owl-at-Night found Ikkemotubbe that night to tell him they still had not found where Herman Basket's aunt had hidden the pony, Ikkemotubbe and David Hogganbeck were at Ikkemotubbe's house. And the next afternoon Ikkemotubbe and the young men invited David Hogganbeck into the woods and it was a long time this time and when they came out, David Hogganbeck was driving the buckboard while the legs of Ikkemotubbe and the other young men dangled from the open door of the little whiskey-house like so many strands of vine hay and Issetibbeha's general's coat was tied by its sleeves about the neck of one of the mules. And nobody hunted for the racing pony that night, and when Ikkemotubbe waked up, he didn't know at first even where he was. And he could already hear David Hogganbeck's fiddle before he could move aside enough of the young men to get out of the little whiskey-house, because that night neither Herman Basket's aunt nor Herman Basket and then finally Herman Basket's dead uncle's gun could persuade David Hogganbeck to leave the gallery and go away or even to stop playing the fiddle.

So the next morning Ikkemotubbe and David Hogganbeck squatted in a quiet place in the woods while the young men, except Sylvester's John and Owl-at-Night who were still hunting for the horse, stood on guard. "We could fight for her then," David Hogganbeck said.

"We could fight for her," Ikkemotubbe said. "But white men

and the People fight differently. We fight with knives, to hurt good
and to hurt quickly. That would be all right, if I were to lose.
Because I would wish to be hurt good. But if I am to win, I do not
wish you to be hurt good. If I am to truly win, it will be necessary
for you to be there to see it. On the day of the wedding, I wish you
to be present, or at least present somewhere, not lying wrapped in
a blanket on a platform in the woods, waiting to enter the earth."
Then my father said how Ikkemotubbe put his hand on David
Hogganbeck's shoulder and smiled at him. "If that could satisfy
me, we would not be squatting here discussing what to do. I think
you see that."

"I think I do," David Hogganbeck said.

Then my father said how Ikkemotubbe removed his hand from
David Hogganbeck's shoulder. "And we have tried whiskey," he
said.

"We have tried that," David Hogganbeck said.

"Even the racing pony and the general's coat failed me,"
Ikkemotubbe said. "I had been saving them, like a man with two
hole-cards."

"I wouldn't say that the coat completely failed," David Hogganbeck said. "You looked fine in it."

"Aihee," Ikkemotubbe said. "So did the mule." Then my father said how he was not smiling either as he squatted beside David
Hogganbeck, making little marks in the earth with a twig. "So
there is just one other thing," he said. "And I am already beaten at
that too before we start."

So all that day they ate nothing. And that night when they left
Log-in-the-Creek lying on Herman Basket's gallery, instead of
merely walking for a while and then running for a while back and
forth between Ikkemotubbe's house and the steamboat, they began
to run as soon as they left Herman Basket's. And when they lay
down in the woods to sleep, it was where they would not only be
free of temptation to eat but of opportunity too, and from which it
would take another hard run as an appetizer to reach the Plantation for the match. Then it was morning and they ran back to
where my father and the young men waited on horses to meet
them and tell Ikkemotubbe that they still hadn't found where under the sun Herman Basket's aunt could have hidden the pony and
to escort them back across the Plantation to the race-course, where

the People waited around the table, with Ikkemotubbe's rocking chair from Herman Basket's gallery for Issetibbeha and a bench behind it for the judges. First there was a recess while a ten-year-old boy ran once around the race-track, to let them recover breath. Then Ikkemotubbe and David Hogganbeck took their places on either side of the table, facing each other across it, and Owl-at-Night gave the word.

First, each had that quantity of stewed bird chitterlings which the other could scoop with two hands from the pot. Then each had as many wild turkey eggs as he was old, Ikkemotubbe twenty-two and David Hogganbeck twenty-three, though Ikkemotubbe refused the advantage and said he would eat twenty-three too. Then David Hogganbeck said he was entitled to one more than Ikkemotubbe so he would eat twenty-four, until Issetibbeha told them both to hush and get on, and Owl-at-Night tallied the shells. Then there was the tongue, paws and melt of a bear, though for a little while Ikkemotubbe stood and looked at his half of it while David Hogganbeck was already eating. And at the half-way he stopped and looked at it again while David Hogganbeck was finishing. But it was all right; there was a faint smile on his face such as the young men had seen on it at the end of a hard running when he was going from now on not on the fact that he was still alive but on the fact that he was Ikkemotubbe. And he went on, and Owl-at-Night tallied the bones, and the women set the roasted shote on the table and Ikkemotubbe and David Hogganbeck moved back to the tail of the shote and faced one another across it and Owl-at-Night had even given the word to start until he gave another word to stop. "Give me some water," Ikkemotubbe said. So my father handed him the gourd and he even took a swallow. But the water returned as though it had merely struck the back of his throat and bounced, and Ikkemotubbe put the gourd down and raised the tail of his shirt before his bowed face and turned and walked away as the People opened aside to let him pass.

And that afternoon they did not even go to the quiet place in the woods. They stood in Ikkemotubbe's house while my father and the others stood quietly too in the background. My father said that Ikkemotubbe was not smiling now. "I was right yesterday," he said. "If I am to lose to thee, we should have used the knives. You see," he said, and now my father said he even smiled again, as at the end of the long hard running when the young men knew that he would go on, not because he was still alive but because he was Ikkemotubbe; "—you see, although I have lost, I still cannot reconcile."

"I had you beat before we started," David Hogganbeck said. "We both knew that."

"Yes," Ikkemotubbe said. "But I suggested it."

"Then what do you suggest now?" David Hogganbeck said. And now my father said how they loved David Hogganbeck at that moment as they loved Ikkemotubbe; that they loved them both at that moment while Ikkemotubbe stood before David Hogganbeck with the smile on his face and his right hand flat on David Hogganbeck's chest, because there were men in those days.

"Once more then, and then no more," Ikkemotubbe said. "The Cave." Then he and David Hogganbeck stripped and my father and the others oiled them, body and hair too, with bear's grease mixed with mint, not just for speed this time but for lasting too, because the Cave was a hundred and thirty miles away, over in the country of old David Colbert—a black hole in the hill which the spoor of wild creatures merely approached and then turned away and which no dog could even be beaten to enter and where the boys from among all the People would go to lie on their first Night-away-from-Fire to prove if they had the courage to become men, because it had been known among the People from a long time ago that the sound of a whisper or even the disturbed air of a sudden movement would bring parts of the roof down and so all believed that not even a very big movement or sound or maybe none at all at some time would bring the whole mountain into the cave. Then Ikkemotubbe took the two pistols from the trunk and drew the loads and reloaded them. "Whoever reaches the Cave first can enter it alone and fire his pistol," he said. "If he comes back out, he has won."

"And if he does not come back out?" David Hogganbeck said.

"Then you have won," Ikkemotubbe said.

"Or you," David Hogganbeck said.

And now my father said how Ikkemotubbe smiled again at David Hogganbeck. "Or me," he said. "Though I think I told you yesterday that such as that for me will not be victory." Then Ikkemotubbe put another charge of powder, with a wadding and bullet, into each of the two small medicine bags, one for himself and one for David Hogganbeck, just in case the one who entered the Cave first should not lose quick enough, and, wearing only their shirts and shoes and each with his pistol and medicine bag looped on a cord around his neck, they emerged from Ikkemotubbe's house and began to run.

It was evening then. Then it was night, and since David Hogganbeck did not know the way, Ikkemotubbe continued to set the pace. But after a time it was daylight again and now David Hogganbeck could run by the sun and the landmarks which Ikkemotubbe described to him while they rested beside a creek, if he wished to go faster. So sometimes David Hogganbeck would run in front and sometimes Ikkemotubbe, then David Hogganbeck would pass Ikkemotubbe as he sat beside a spring or a stream with his feet in the water and Ikkemotubbe would smile at David Hogganbeck and wave his hand. Then he would overtake David Hogganbeck and the country was open now and they would run side by side in the prairies with his hand lying lightly on David Hogganbeck's shoulder, not on the top of the shoulder but lightly against the back of it until after a while he would smile at David Hogganbeck and draw ahead. But then it was sundown, and then it was dark again so Ikkemotubbe slowed and then stopped until he heard David Hogganbeck and knew that David Hogganbeck could hear him and then he ran again so that David Hogganbeck could follow the sound of his running. So when David Hogganbeck fell, Ikkemotubbe heard it and went back and found David Hogganbeck in the dark and turned him onto his back and found water in the dark and soaked his shirt in it and returned and wrung the water from the shirt into David Hogganbeck's mouth. And then it was daylight and Ikkemotubbe waked also and found a nest containing five unfledged birds and ate and brought the other three to David Hogganbeck and then he went on until he was just this side of where David Hogganbeck could no longer see him and sat down again until David Hogganbeck got up onto his feet.

And he gave David Hogganbeck the landmarks for that day too, talking back to David Hogganbeck over his shoulder as they ran, though David Hogganbeck did not need them because he never overtook Ikkemotubbe again. He never came closer than fifteen or twenty paces, although it looked at one time like he was.

Because this time it was Ikkemotubbe who fell. And the country was open again so Ikkemotubbe could lie there for a long time and watch David Hogganbeck coming. Then it was sunset again, and then it was dark again, and he lay there listening to David Hogganbeck coming for a long time until it was time for Ikkemotubbe to get up and he did and they went on slowly in the dark with David Hogganbeck at least a hundred paces behind him, until he heard David Hogganbeck fall and then he lay down too. Then it was day again and he watched David Hogganbeck get up onto his feet and come slowly toward him and at last he tried to get up too but he did not and it looked like David Hogganbeck was going to come up with him. But he got up at last while David Hogganbeck was still four or five paces away and they went on until David Hogganbeck fell, and then Ikkemotubbe thought he was just watching David Hogganbeck fall until he found that he had fallen too but he got up onto his hands and knees and crawled still another ten or fifteen paces before he too lay down. And there in the sunset before him was the hill in which the Cave was, and there through the night, and there still in the sunrise.

So Ikkemotubbe ran into the Cave first, with his pistol already cocked in his hand. He told how he stopped perhaps for a second at the entrance, perhaps to look at the sun again or perhaps just to see where David Hogganbeck had stopped. But David Hogganbeck was running too and he was still only that fifteen or twenty paces behind, and besides, because of that damned sister of Herman Basket's, there had been no light nor heat either in that sun for moons and moons. So he ran into the Cave and turned and saw David Hogganbeck also running into the Cave and he cried, "Back, fool!" But David Hogganbeck still ran into the Cave even as Ikkemotubbe pointed his pistol at the roof and fired. And there was a noise, and a rushing, and a blackness and a dust, and Ikkemotubbe told how he thought, *Aihee. It comes.* But it did not, and even before the blackness he saw David Hogganbeck cast himself forward onto his hands and knees, and there was not a complete blackness either because he could see the sunlight and air and day beyond the tunnel of David Hogganbeck's arms and legs as, still on his hands and knees, David Hogganbeck held the fallen roof upon his back. "Hurry," David Hogganbeck said. "Between my legs. I can't——"

"Nay, brother," Ikkemotubbe said. "Quickly thyself, before it crushes thee. Crawl back."

"Hurry," David Hogganbeck said behind his teeth. "Hurry, damn you." And Ikkemotubbe did, and he remembered David Hogganbeck's buttocks and legs pink in the sunrise and the slab of rock which supported the fallen roof pink in the sunrise too across David Hogganbeck's back. But he did not remember where he found the pole nor how he carried it alone into the Cave and thrust it into the hole beside David Hogganbeck and stooped his own back under it and lifted until he knew that some at least of the weight of the fallen roof was on the pole.

"Now," he said. "Quickly."

"No," David Hogganbeck said.

"Quickly, brother," Ikkemotubbe said. "The weight is off thee."

"Then I can't move," David Hogganbeck said. But Ikkemotubbe couldn't move either, because now he had to hold the fallen roof up with his back and legs. So he reached one hand and grasped David Hogganbeck by the meat and jerked him backward out of the hole until he lay face-down upon the earth. And maybe some of the weight of the fallen roof was on the pole before, but now all of the weight was on it and Ikkemotubbe said how he thought, *This time surely aihee*. But it was the pole and not his back which snapped and flung him face-down too across David Hogganbeck like two flung sticks, and a bright gout of blood jumped out of David Hogganbeck's mouth.

But by the second day David Hogganbeck had quit vomiting blood, though Ikkemotubbe had run hardly forty miles back toward the Plantation when my father met him with the horse for David Hogganbeck to ride. Presently my father said, "I have a news for thee."

"So you found the pony," Ikkemotubbe said. "All right. Come on. Let's get that damned stupid fool of a white man—"

"No, wait, my brother," my father said. "I have a news for thee."

And presently Ikkemotubbe said, "All right."

But when Captain Studenmare borrowed Issetibbeha's wagon to go back to Natchez in, he took the steamboat slaves too. So my father and the young men built the fire in the steamboat's stomach to make steam for it to walk, while David Hogganbeck sat in the upstairs and drew the crying-rope from time to time to see if the steam was strong enough yet, and at each cry still more of the People came to the landing until at last all the People in the Plantation except old Issetibbeha perhaps stood along the bank to watch the young men hurl wood into the steamboat's stomach:—a thing never before seen in our Plantation at least. Then the steam was strong and the steamboat began to walk and then the People began to walk too beside the steamboat, watching the young men for a while then Ikkemotubbe and David Hogganbeck for a while as the steamboat walked out of the Plantation where hardly seven suns ago Ikkemotubbe and David Hogganbeck would sit all day long and half the night too until Herman Basket's aunt would come out with Herman Basket's dead uncle's gun, on the gallery of Herman Basket's house while Log-in-the-Creek lay on the floor with his harmonica cupped to his mouth and Log-in-the-Creek's wife shelled corn or peas into old Dave Colbert's wife's grand-niece's second cousin by marriage's wine pitcher. Presently Ikkemotubbe was gone completely away, to be gone a long time before he came back named Doom, with his new white friend whom no man wished to love either and the eight more slaves which we had no use for either because at times someone would have to get up and walk somewhere to find something for the ones we already owned to do, and the fine gold-trimmed clothes and the little gold box of salt which caused the other four puppies to become dead too one after another, and then anything else which happened to stand between Doom and what he wanted. But he was not quite gone yet. He was just Ikkemotubbe yet, one of the young men, another of the young men who loved and was not loved in return and could hear the words and see the fact, yet who, like the young men who had been before him and the ones who would come after him, still could not understand it.

"But not for her," Ikkemotubbe said. "And not even because it was Log-in-the-Creek. Perhaps they are for myself: that such a son as Log-in-the-Creek could cause them to wish to flow."

"Don't think about her," David Hogganbeck said.

"I don't. I have already stopped. See?" Ikkemotubbe said while the sunset ran down his face as if it had already been rain instead of light when it entered the window. "There was a wise man of ours who said once how a woman's fancy is like a butterfly which, hovering from flower to flower, pauses at the last as like as not where a horse has stood."

"There was a wise man of ours named Solomon who often said something of that nature too," David Hogganbeck said. "Perhaps there is just one wisdom for all men, no matter who speaks it."

"Aihee. At least, for all men one same heart-break," Ikkemotubbe said. Then he drew the crying-rope, because the boat was now passing the house where Log-in-the-Creek and his wife lived, and now the steamboat sounded like it did the first night while Captain Studenmare still thought David Hogganbeck would come and show it the way back to Natchez, until David Hogganbeck made Ikkemotubbe stop. Because they would need the steam because the steamboat did not always walk. Sometimes it crawled, and each time its feet came up there was mud on them, and sometimes it did not even crawl until David Hogganbeck drew the crying-rope as the rider speaks to the recalcitrant horse to remind it with his voice just who is up. Then it crawled again and then it walked again, until at last the People could no longer keep up, and it cried once more beyond the last bend and then there was no longer either the black shapes of the young men leaping to hurl wood into its red stomach or even the sound of its voice in the Plantation or the night. That's how it was in the old days.

CLOUD NINE

BY CAROLINE GORDON

"These things never were, but always are."

SALLUSTIUS,
Concerning the Gods

O N A CERTAIN afternoon—one of those which cannot be measured on any calendar devised by man—Zeus, the Father of Gods and Men, ascended to the highest peak of Mount Olympos. He was accompanied by his son Phoebos Apollo, and his attendant eagle, Morinthos. The bird, whose task it was to speed the lightning and thunder bolts which Zeus every now and then loosed upon mankind, perched on a heap of stones at the foot of the crag. Apollo, who had never before visited this particular mountain peak, was glancing about him curiously. Zeus made a peremptory gesture and Apollo obediently started up the path to the summit. Zeus paused long enough to inform his attendant of his plans for the afternoon. He had invited Apollo to join him in this retreat which was unknown to the other Olympians because he had something of importance to discuss with him, something which could only be discussed in private. The eagle, as the result of his long and close association with Zeus, had acquired a certain amount of sagacity. He said that in that case the Father of Gods and Men would do well to surround his retreat with some barrier —the kind that the younger deities would hesitate to break through. Glancing over his shoulder a few minutes ago he had discerned a female figure pacing back and forth upon the battlements of Heaven. He was not certain (though he was famed for his far sight), but in his opinion (for what it was worth) the pacing female figure was that of Zeus's wife, Hera, Queen of Heaven. As

Zeus knew, she required less repose than her consort. He himself had observed that she tended to grow more restive as the afternoons wore on.

Zeus groaned and clapped his eagle on the back so hard that the bird lost his footing and went fluttering about over the rocks before he could gain his usual perch. Zeus, meanwhile, had turned and with sweeping motions, first of his right hand, then of his left, was gathering clouds to encircle his resting-place. They floated in from every quarter of the globe. Some, shaped like pillars, were darkly purple and swollen with rain. Others were of a greenish hue, with yellow streaks zigzagging down their sides. In and out, among the larger clouds, floated smaller clouds, gossamer thin sometimes, sometimes curdled as thick as the fleece on the back of a young lamb. They eddied about the headland so thickly that for a moment Zeus's countenance was hidden. He blew them aside with a mighty breath and with a few negligent motions of his right hand ranged them to form a rampart, the larger, darker clouds rearing themselves like pillars, the smaller clouds clinging to them or floating over the rocks which were scattered all about.

Zeus, who, when he was not irate, was uniformly courteous to gods and men, birds and beasts, then thanked Morinthos for his timely warning and ascended to what he sometimes referred to as his "favorite throne." It was of granite but so richly veined with marble that it scintillated when the sun shone upon it. Nature had fashioned it in the shape of a huge chair and had placed it upon the topmost peak of Mount Olympos. As Zeus approached he leaned his lotiform lightning and thunder bolts against the side of the chair, then removed from his shoulders his violet-colored *chlamys* sprinkled with gold stars and hung it over the back of his "throne." His lower limbs were swathed in a long *himation,* deep blue in color, its hem bordered with purple. He loosened the upper folds of his *himation* and leaned back with a sigh of relief.

Apollo had gone to stand on the brow of the mountain and was looking down upon the earth—as if, Zeus thought, with the touch of petulance which occasionally overcame him, he had never seen it before. One could not deny, however, that he cut a fine figure outlined there against the blue sky. The long priestly robe which he wore could not conceal the grace of his straight limbs. A wreath of laurel was set upon his golden curls. He was carrying his lyre in his hands. He realized that he was being observed and advanced towards his father, smiling. Zeus pointed to a nearby boulder. Apollo took his seat upon it and enquired how he could be of service.

Apollo was not only the handsomest of Zeus's many children. He was also the most intelligent. That was why Zeus had asked him to come here today. There was a matter he wanted to discuss with him. But now that he was face-to-face with Apollo, he found himself wishing that he had chosen to confer with some other Olympian. There was something about Apollo's level gaze that he found disconcerting. But he asked himself now whether he would have fared any better if he had asked advice of any of the other gods. Of Ares, for instance. The fellow was intent only on bloodshed. The sacking of cities was his chief delight. As for Apollo's twin sister, Artemis, she cared only for the chase—and the fortunes of women. She protected women in childbirth and other trials. If a man fell under her displeasure she sent a wild boar or some other monster to ravage his fields. Pallas Athene was wiser than all the rest, but she was, after all, a woman and hence likely to be swayed by her passions. What she loved best was to whisper into some warrior's ear the words that would inspire him to victory. But a warrior equally brave, with a cause equally just, if he happened to incur her wrath, might find himself in the midst of battle crushed by a stone fallen apparently from Heaven! Hephaestos, of course, was incapable of reasoned discussion. What intellect he had was in his fingers. As for Aphrodite . . . Zeus shook his ponderous head. The less said of *her* in this connection the better!

Zeus's concern at the moment was the woeful condition of mortals. Ever since he had ascended the throne of Olympos he had been giving much thought to it. It seemed to him that Apollo, who exerted so much influence over mortals through his Oracle at Delphi, must feel some of the concern which he himself felt; they came from all over the world to ask the Delphic Oracle's advice as to how they should conduct their affairs. He enquired of Apollo now whether the number of pilgrims to Delphi was increasing yearly. Apollo had laid his lyre across his knees when he sat down. He plucked one of its strings carelessly before he replied. His priests, he said, informed him that there were four times as many pilgrims this year as the year before. Some of them came from as far away as Lydia.

"And do you find that they generally profit from the Oracle's advice?" Zeus asked.

Apollo shook his head. "Not all mortals are willing to follow the Oracle's advice, Sire."

Zeus said that that was to be expected.

"Others are anxious to follow the Sibyl's instructions to the letter but misinterpret them as often as not."

"That too is in the nature of things," Zeus said.

Apollo went on as if Zeus had not spoken. "Take the case of King Laïos of Thebes. While a guest at the court of Pelops he fell in love with Pelops's son Chrysippos, kidnapped him, and carried him off to Thebes. The immortal gods, remarking his homoerotic tendencies, thought it as well that he live and die without issue. I myself," he added indignantly, "gave him contraceptive advice, counselling him not to untie his bulging wine-skin under certain circumstances. Laïos, being a mortal, interpreted the words 'bulging wine-skin' literally rather than figuratively. He abstained, for the most part, from wine but did not refrain from begetting a son."

"His name was Oedipous," Zeus said. "It comes to me now. But in the end, Oedipous worked your will. He murdered Laïos and thereby brought so many disasters upon the family that the stock was exterminated . . ." He stopped speaking suddenly and eyed Apollo with suspicion. "Are you sure that these events have already taken place?" he demanded. "Laïos was the son of Labdakos who was the son of Agenor who was the son of Libya who was the daughter of Epaphos . . ."

". . . who was the son of Zeus and the beautiful maiden Io, daughter of the river-god Inachos, and priestess in Hera's great temple in Argos," Apollo said, smiling. "I would not compete with you, Sire, in a recitation of generations. Some of these events have already taken place—as you, who have concerned yourself so largely with generation, well know. As for others, if they have not yet taken place, they will. Does it matter when?" He looked about him appreciatively. "I must congratulate you on your choice of a retreat, Sire. Morinthos reminds us that the Queen of Heaven is both active and articulate. But she is not, like yourself, all-seeing. I should think that you might take your repose here undisturbed— particularly if you keep the headland cloud-wrapt."

Zeus knew that the younger gods were aware of the sufferings inflicted on him as the result of Hera's jealousy. But he did not like to hear either himself or Hera referred to so lightly. He told Apollo: "I shall keep the place cloud-wrapt or not cloud-wrapt, according to my pleasure. I invited you here this afternoon because I wanted to enquire into the efficacy of your Oracle at Delphi. As you know, there have been oracles before the one at Delphi . . ."

"Ah, yes," Apollo returned carelessly. "Chief and oldest of them the Talking Oak at Dodona where, I understand, you yourself sometimes spoke through the rustling of the leaves . . ."

"And the creaking of its branches," Zeus said. "The priests slept on the earth and went with unwashed feet. At Delphi, as you doubtless recall, the first oracular utterances came from our Earth Mother, Gaea."

Apollo nodded. "She was succeeded—regrettably—by the dragon Pytho."

"Whom you slew."

"Just so. His habits and ways of divination were deplorable . . . But all that has been changed. A tripod has been placed over the oracular chasm which was the dragon's lair. The priestess seats herself upon the tripod and waits till she is overcome by the fumes which arise from the chasm. Her prophecies take the form of words. An advance over the primitive methods employed at Dodona."

Zeus was silent. He found himself thinking, with what to a mortal mind might have seemed inconsequence, of his courtship of Apollo's mother, Leto. A great goddess, the daughter of the Titan Koios and the Titaness Phoebe. The Olympians, who were not inclined to reverence the older gods, all stood up when she entered the great audience hall! He had courted her in the shape of a quail but as soon as she became pregnant he had been obliged to transform her into a she-wolf. Jealous Hera had decreed that Leto should not give birth to a son in any land the sun shone upon. Leto wandered long in the country of the Hyperboreans. He had finally had to raise an island up out of the sea for her parturition. It was called Delos because it had not been visible until that moment. Leto came to it in "wolf light"—that is, between sunset and sunrise, the time when wolves see best. But even this barren soil showed itself inhospitable to her! At the bottom of the sea the island had heard murmurings of the great god who was to be born and feared that when he saw the light of day he might spurn Delos and with one stamp of his foot send it back into the depths from which it had just risen. From his throne on high Olympos Zeus observed the commotion and was about to launch a thunder bolt upon the recalcitrant crag when Leto herself resolved the conflict. Gripping with both hands the trunks of two palm trees, the only living things on the island, she took the oath by the waters of the Styx that her son would look upon Delos as a holy place, and gave herself up to the birth pangs. They lasted nine days and nine nights, almost as severe a labor as his own mother, Rhea, had undergone at his birth, Zeus thought proudly. Artemis, Apollo's sister, who had been born the day before on another island, acted as midwife, since Hera had contrived that Eileithyia, the goddess of childbirth, should not learn of Leto's travail. When Apollo was born the whole island of Delos became fragrant. Swans circled about it seven times singing some of the songs Apollo sang now to his lyre. Hera went without anger for one whole day!

Having recently ascended to the throne of Olympos, Zeus had had much to occupy him. As soon as he was assured of Leto's safe deliverance he turned his attention to other matters and did not lay eyes upon his divine son until Apollo was three days old. He was brought to Delphi, then, a golden-haired infant, still cradled in his mother's arms. But even at that tender age he showed himself the "divine bowman." When he caught sight of the dragon Pytho, he cried, *"Hie! . . . Hie! . . . Paean!"* and shot arrow after arrow into the huge body until the serpent's coils relaxed and he sank lifeless to the earth. It was a valorous deed and one that brought Apollo great fame . . . But he talked too much!

He was talking now about the advances that had been made in divination since he had succeeded to the Delphic shrine. Less and less attention was being paid to the flight or song of birds. "As for hieromancy, the priests, instead of observing the entrails of animals, determine which days are auspicious for prophecy by drenching a goat all over with cold water and then observing the results with great care. It is not enough for the beast to turn its head this way or that, as sacrificial beasts sometimes do when they feel the knife at the throat. The goat must shiver in every limb or the day is thought inauspicious. However, most days turn out auspicious. In the old days the priestess used to ascend the tripod only once a year, on my birthday . . ."

"The tripod?" Zeus asked.

"A three-legged stool is placed over the oracular chasm. Formerly an ordinary cooking vessel made of metal, it is loftier now and made of gilded wood. As I was saying, the priestess used to ascend the tripod only once a year. But now she prophesies every day. In fact, we have recently found it necessary to have two Pythias acting alternately, with a third to assist, in case of accident. But no matter what the number of Pythias, the procedure is the same. The priestess prepares herself by washing first in the stream Cassotis and then drinking from the Castalian spring. She enters the inmost sanctuary, wearing flowing robes, with gold ornaments in her hair. She chews a leaf of the laurel before she takes her seat upon the tripod. No one is present except the priest who interprets the meaning of the words she utters in her ecstasy . . ." He paused, frowning. "Difficulties arise, of course. But they always arise when one deals with words."

"Then don't deal with them," Zeus said.

Apollo stared at him blankly. "But how, then, can the will of the gods be known, Sire?"

"By the creaking of oak boughs," Zeus said. "Or the priests might sleep on the earth or go with unwashed feet, as at Dodona."

"I hardly think that those methods would answer today."

"What about the coils of serpents?" Zeus asked. "That dragon Pytho, whom you slew, was the son of Our Mother Earth. As I recall, you had to atone for his murder. Were you not forced to flee from Delphi and spend eight years in menial service before you could become high priest of his shrine?"

"Yes, yes!" Apollo said impatiently. "A festival called the *Septeria* is held every year in commemoration of the affair. The events are all reënacted—my slaying of the dragon, my flight, my atonement, and my return as the God of Light. A boy, both of whose parents must be living, portrays my rôle. A simulacrum of the dragon is destroyed. His house is burned. The boy is taken in procession to the temple, along the same road which I myself followed. After he has been purified he is brought back along the same road, accompanied by maidens singing songs of joy."

"A pretty sight!" Zeus murmured. "I have occasionally looked down upon it. You spoke of the dragon's methods of divination as deplorable. What, exactly, were they?"

Apollo shuddered. "It was perhaps not so much his methods as his appearance," he said. "He was repulsive in the extreme. His very coils . . . To tell the truth they were—excessive!"

"That accusation has been brought against him before," Zeus said thoughtfully. "You are aware, of course, that he is your own great-uncle."

The same faint shudder convulsed Apollo's limbs. "The great goddess Gaea has a multitudinous progeny," he said. "Some of them are uncouth—by present-day standards."

"It is true that the Kyklopes have only one eye apiece and that set in the middle of their foreheads," Zeus said. "And the Hekatoncheires present an extraordinary appearance because each one has a hundred hands. It was because of their monstrous appearance that your great-grandfather Ouranos consigned his elder children to the caves beneath the earth as soon as they were born."

"One must admit that it was a wise precaution," Apollo said.

"When I contended for the throne," Zeus told him, "I had to wage war against my father, Kronos, and his brother Titans. I sought counsel of the Earth Mother, Gaea, before I entered the conflict. She advised me to enlist the aid of the Kyklopes and the Hekatoncheires. If I had not had them on my side I could not have gained the throne. In that case where would *you* be, my fine son?"

Apollo, smiling radiantly, said that in such a case he, in all probability, would never have seen the light of day. "If you had not raised up the island of Delos for my birthplace, my mother would have sunk to the bottom of the sea. I would then have been born a subject of Poseidon instead of being the son and subject of Zeus, the Father of Gods and Men. Everyone who dwells on high Olympos must feel overwhelming gratitude to you, Sire! But the war against the Titans has been won. Kronos has been dethroned. You rule the earth and the kingdom of the upper air. The Kyklopes and the Hundred-Handed Ones fought valiantly on your side, but now that the war is won it is best that they retire to the caves beneath the earth to which their father so wisely relegated them. It seems to me that we Olympians will do well to follow his example—in that respect, at least. Now that you are firmly established on the throne of Olympos, need we concern ourselves with these older gods?"

Zeus did not answer. After a short silence Apollo began speaking of a class of pilgrims which he had not mentioned before.

"They are aware of the meaning of the words the Oracle utters but instead of obeying the will of the gods they resist it. There was King Akrisios of Mykenai. The Oracle told him that he would never have a son but his daughter would have a son who would bring about the king's death. Instead of resigning himself to his fate, as revealed by the Oracle, Akrisios set himself to thwart the gods. He resolved that his daughter should never have a child and imprisoned her in a dungeon which he had his artificers fashion for him out of bronze. The maid was enclosed therein for the space of a year and looked upon no mortal face except that of the nurse whose task it was to bring her food and drink. But everything man-made has its flaws: King Akrisios sought to protect his daughter from mortal men. It had not occurred to him that she might arrest the attention of a divine lover! It was a simple matter for such a lover to gain entrance to the prison. Slipping through a chink in the roof of the dungeon, he fell, in the form of a ray of light, into the maiden's lap . . ."

Zeus interrupted him. "I am familiar with the history of King Akrisios of Mykenai. It is unedifying. We will not concern ourselves with it at the moment. You have not answered my question. As you know, the condition of most mortals is woeful. They seldom conduct their affairs in ways which result in happiness. Yet they come from all quarters of the globe to ask the advice of your Oracle. Why is it that so few of them profit from the counsel they get at your shrine?"

"Because they are mortals," Apollo said promptly. "Gods are gods and men are men. In consequence, an abyss is fixed between them."

"Did it ever occur to you that that abyss might be bridged?" Zeus asked him.

Apollo shook his golden head. He reminded his father of occasions when the gods had attempted to bridge that gulf, usually with lamentable results. "The most notable instance is that of Tantalos, King of Sipylos. He had the privilege of dining with the gods. Surely, Sire," he added, "you have not forgotten what happened when the time came for him to return their hospitality?"

"He slaughtered his son Pelops and added his dismembered limbs to the stew he was preparing," Zeus said. "But there is more than one way of looking at that affair. You might say that Tantalos was guilty of enacting a sacral rite with too much exactitude. It is evident, however, that he was not able to digest his pleasures. He is undergoing punishment, suspended between earth and sky, condemned to suffer eternally the pangs of hunger and thirst. As for his son Pelops, he came out of the affair better than one might have expected. Pallas Athene, you will remember, simmered his limbs in a cauldron with magic herbs. They reknitted until they were as good as new. Indeed, he lived to beget children. In some places he is worshiped as a hero—that is to say, a demi-god."

At that Apollo smiled. He said that he was aware that Pelops had many great deeds to his credit. He had defeated King Oenomaus in chariot racing, thereby winning the hand of the king's daughter Hippodameia. Some of his male descendants had also won fame, among them Agenor and Kadmos. Here Apollo's smile grew broader. He was inclined to think that Pelops's most distinguished relative was his sister Niobe. Had she not enjoyed the honor of being the first mortal woman whose bed was visited by the Father of Gods and Men?

Zeus answered that at the moment he could not remember whether he had ever lain with the woman. Apollo said that he could well understand that Zeus's memory grew dim when he tried to recall the names of the mortal women or, for that matter, goddesses, he had lain with. He sighed. His own amorous adventures had been few, he said, and nearly always disastrous. There was Daphne, a daughter of the Thessalian river god Peneius. She had chosen to be turned into a laurel tree rather than submit to his embraces! He had wooed another mortal maiden, Koronis, daughter of another Thessalian prince, Phlegyas. He had felt confident that she returned his love—until it became evident that even though she was pregnant by him she had taken a mortal lover. He discovered Koronis's perfidy at a time when a plague was raging in her father's kingdom. His sister, Artemis, had advised that Koronis's body be cast on one of the funeral pyres which were burning all over the land. He had not been able to endure the prospect of his son's destruction and at the last moment had snatched the infant from Koronis's womb, but her body had been wholly consumed.

He sat silent for a while, his handsome head bent in dejection. When he looked up it was to direct a respectful glance at his father, along with a word of caution. His own loves, admittedly, had been unfortunate. Might he point out that the same held true, for the most part, of his august sire's loves—particularly where mortal women were involved?

King Tantalos's daughter Niobe, for instance, seemed to have inherited no small share of her father's arrogance, displaying the kind of pride which so often overtook women who had lain with a god. Indeed, she had created a public scandal, deriding his own mother, Leto, for having only two children—"a mannish girl and a girlish boy!"—whereas she herself was the mother of six handsome sons and as many beautiful daughters. He and his sister, Artemis, had been called from the chase to defend their mother's honor. As Zeus knew, they had transfixed Niobe's children with their arrows. All except one girl, who somehow survived. At the moment Apollo could not recall the details of her escape.

"She survived," Zeus told him, "because she lifted up her hands to me and prayed for deliverance. You forget, perhaps, that I am worshiped at many shrines as Zeus the Savior."

Apollo replied that he realized that the Father of Gods and Men was worshiped at innumerable shrines and under many appellations. He began to recite, in his musical voice, some of the names by which mortals supplicated Zeus. The lyre still rested on his knee. Occasionally he plucked its strings as if he were about to set his words to music.

Zeus interrupted the litany. "You seem very fond of that instrument which, as I recall, your younger brother Hermes invented."

Apollo plucked a string resoundingly. "The rascal! But I can forgive him anything—even the theft of my divine cattle—for the invention of this instrument. There has never been any to equal it. As you know, I have long had the habit of joining the Muses when they dance on Mount Parnassos. But only as a flute player. And then infrequently. But now . . ."

"Now that you have your lyre you play for them every night," Zeus said. "Is it your intention to repair to Mount Parnassos this evening?"

Apollo admitted that such was his intention.

"In that case," Zeus said, "don't let me detain you . . . . What are the joys and sorrows of mortals compared to the rounds the Muses tread?"

Apollo thanked him for his solicitude and after a few more minutes of desultory conversation took his leave. As Apollo strode off down the mountainside, Zeus reflected, as he so often did, on the complexities of his own mind. Even Apollo, who alone among the Olympians had the gift of high soothsaying, could penetrate it only a short distance. There were times when he himself was reluctant to tread its labyrinthine ways. While he was talking with Apollo some deeply buried memories had stirred. He would know no peace until they were disinterred. Fortunately, he knew how to go about that. He sat erect and with his right hand made a gesture of invocation sharper than the ones he had directed at the clouds, then sank back in his chair and awaited the vision.

A drowsiness came over him. He realized that his summons was being answered. In the land of the sunset, beyond the ocean stream, the Gate of Horn had opened. A dream was speeding towards him. He closed his eyes, the better to welcome it.

A sun showed itself, rising out of a sea whose waves were dull and leaden-colored. On the far shore of this sea, giant figures of women loomed. All about them lay rain-washed images of stone. The women lay as still as if their limbs, too, had been wrought from stone. But about the head of one of them live serpents writhed continually. The sky suddenly grew brighter. The giant female figures disappeared from view. The sun shone so brightly that all the surface of the sea glowed, then, as suddenly, turned lead-color again. The sun had gone from the sky. Somewhere words were being intoned: *"He hath set his tabernacle in the sun . . . as a bridegroom coming out of his chamber . . . His going out is from the end of heaven . . . And his circuit even to the end thereof. . . ."*

He was awakened by a low, cautious cawing. He sat upright and gazed about him. Morinthos had not left his perch but his head was turned away from his master. Zeus followed the gaze of the bright, far-reaching eye and perceived a rift in the clouds which, a few minutes ago, had been marshalled to suit his own pleasure. The rift widened. Two clouds which had clung so closely together as to seem one suddenly drifted apart—as if impelled by some alien force! The eagle turned his head long enough to give his master a warning glance, then resumed his contemplation of the clouds.

Zeus involuntarily grasped his thunder bolt and leaned for-

ward, frowning. He had ranged his sentinel clouds in the same formation in which clouds were ranged about the battlements of
Heaven. His daughters, the Hours, patrolled those ramparts. They
were efficient guardians. Even Hera, his wife, and his daughter
Pallas Athene, returning from some of their numerous expeditions
to the earth below, had to halt their chariots long enough for the
Hours to roll back the huge, cloudy gates. But these clouds parted
as if they were obeying some will other than his own!

They were so sharply sundered now that slivers of blue sky
showed between them. There was the glint of sunlight on metal. A
cloudlet, drifting aside, revealed a brawny knee. A sandaled foot
appeared.

Zeus sank back on his couch with a sigh of relief. The god
Hermes was standing at the foot of the crag, smiling up at him. He
said that he regretted having to disturb the repose of the Father of
Gods and Men, but the Queen of Heaven desired her consort's
presence in the great audience hall.

Zeus was already tightening the upper folds of his *himation*. He
paused in the act of throwing his star-sprinkled *chlamys* over his
shoulders and stared at Hermes from under lowering brows. "So
you flew straight here!" he growled. "And now every godling on
Olympos knows of my retreat!"

Hermes, keeping a wary distance, had been snapping his fingers
at the eagle, which gazed implacably past him. He left off teasing
the bird to direct a reproachful glance at Zeus. "You do me an
injustice, Sire," he murmured. "I assured the Queen of Heaven
that I would execute her commands as speedily as possible. In
order to render her the obedience which her august state requires
it was necessary for me to approach your retreat—circuitously. For
you know," he added with a disarming smile, "you would not have
been likely to grant her request if I had come here with half
Olympos at my heels."

Zeus looked at him with approval. Hermes was one of his favorite sons. Not as slow of wit as some, not as given to making costly
mistakes. Zeus thought with a fleeting pang of Hermes's mother,
Maia, a mountain nymph who possessed extraordinary powers of
discretion along with great personal charms. Although her son was
now one of the Olympians she continued to lead a life of retirement in the same cave on Mount Kyllene in which Zeus had wooed
and won her.

He sighed, thinking of the many mortal women—and god-desses—he had known whose characters differed fundamentally from Maia's, and indicated his willingness to follow Hermes, at the same time enquiring what Hera wanted of him.

Hermes, winging his way over the rocks—it was hard for him to keep his feet on the ground—answered that the Lady Hera had not confided in him what she wanted of her Lord. A conference was in progress in the great hall, however. He suspected that she wished the Father of Gods and Men to grace it with his presence.

"A *conference!*" Zeus exclaimed. "On an afternoon in mid-summer!"

Hermes said that he had noticed that the Lady Hera and the Lady Athene were indifferent to extremes of heat and cold when they were on one of their missions to the earth.

"What are they up to now?" Zeus enquired.

"They were guiding their swift coursers around Mount Kithai-ron when they discerned the figure of a mortal man standing on the topmost peak of the mountain."

"What of it?" Zeus said. "A shepherd might have climbed up there to look for a lost sheep."

"He had no shepherd's crook and he was not searching for any sheep."

"What *was* he doing, then?"

"He was praying."

"What's wrong with that?" Zeus asked after a moment's omi-nous silence.

Hermes answered that the goddesses did not disapprove of what the mortal was doing. They had halted their chariot on the moun-taintop because they wished to consult him about a matter which was occupying their attention.

"And what profit could they hope to derive from conversation with any mortal?"

Hermes said that he himself would not entertain such an ex-pectation but that the Lady Hera and the Lady Athene seemed to feel otherwise. He added that this mortal was renowned for his wisdom. He was supposed to be wiser than other mortals because his vision had been turned inward at an early age. He was now a very old man but he had been blind since he was a youth.

Zeus demanded his name.

"Teiresias . . . He has long been known to the Lady Athene."

Zeus groaned and the mountain quivered. "She *ought* to know him! It was she who blinded him."

Hermes skipped neatly around a boulder and paused to turn on Zeus a faintly reproachful gaze. "But you will admit, Sire, that this mortal offered Lady Grey-eyes great provocation. He looked upon her divine body while she was bathing in a woodland pool."

"What about the provocation she offered *him?*" Zeus countered. "Suppose *you* had come upon her bathing in a woodland pool! Would you have turned and run the other way?"

Hermes was silent. Zeus had the power of reading the thoughts of the younger gods and goddesses, although they had no clue to what went on behind his marmoreal brow other than what his looks or gestures betokened. He knew now what Hermes would have said had he answered: *"But I am a god!"*

"Yes, yes!" he said irascibly. "Your claims to divinity are well established. As I recall, you took care of that matter yourself at an age when most godlings are content with the cradle."

Hermes said modestly that he was so well content with his own cradle that he had felt impelled to bestir himself to augment its lustre even while he was in swaddling bands.

"Yes," Zeus returned in the same irritable voice. "You have done very well, both as Messenger of the Gods and as Psychopompos. Persephone has spoken to me about you and so has Hades. They both feel that no other god could surpass you in the carrying of messages or in escorting souls to the Underworld . . . *What in the name of Styx is that?*"

They had come within sight of the great hall which Hephaestos, the divine smith, had erected as a meeting place for the gods and goddesses of Olympos. The massive doors were flung wide. Zeus's attention was fastened on an equipage which, at that moment, was gliding through them. Zeus recognized the chariot as one in which his brother Poseidon traveled when he left his palace at the bottom of the sea. It was of gold, shaped like a dolphin, but its sides gave off a lustre higher than that of gold; turquoises, emeralds, and other precious stones which were blue-green in color were inset in them to form pictures of the monsters of the deep. The horses which drew the chariot had hoofs of bronze and golden manes. Poseidon wielded a golden whip over them and commonly stood when he drove his chariot over the deep. He was reclining today, however, as if to mark the fact that he was not in his own kingdom. But the robe he wore was of gold and he held his trident —his sceptre of office—in his right hand and he was attended by several of his sons. He had, in fact, brought more retainers along with him than was necessary or even seemly. Dolphins and Nereids frisked about the chariot-boat and a Triton stood on its prow, holding his conch shell to his lips—as if ready at any moment to sound a blast of victory!

Preoccupied with the spectacle, Zeus strode forward, so rapidly that he outdistanced Hermes. But Hermes skimmed the ground easily in his winged sandals and caught up with him. "The Lord Poseidon, entering the gates of Olympos," he murmured. "You will have observed that he is attended by eight Nereids and eight dolphins. And, of course, the same number of Tritons. A splendid spectacle, is it not?"

Zeus turned and glared at him so fiercely that a boulder beside the path trembled and split in two. "What is my brother Poseidon doing on Olympos?" he demanded.

"I gather that he has been invited—by the Lady Hera and the Lady Athene—to attend the conference," Hermes answered.

"And what, may I ask, is the conference about?" the Father of Gods and Men enquired.

Hermes fluttered away on his winged sandals. When he had attained what he evidently considered a safe distance, he called out, "I think, Sire, that the Lady Athene and the Lady Hera can answer that question better than I can."

Zeus waited until Poseidon and his train had passed through the vast cloudy doors, then strode the length of the great hall and took his seat. Hera was already seated upon the adjacent throne. She wore a robe which she wore only on state occasions, of finest white wool, woven in patterned squares. On her forehead she wore a golden diadem. Her hair, closely braided and coiled low on her neck, was covered with a net of fine gold threads. She was holding a pomegranate in her left hand. Her right hand grasped her sceptre, whose end was ornamented with a simulacrum of a cuckoo, fashioned for her by Hephaestos. She sat very straight and held her sceptre upright.

The page Ganymede approached and, kneeling, held Zeus's sceptre out to him. Zeus took it and was about to lean it up against the side of his throne, where his lotiform thunder bolts already rested, but, observing Hera's regal attitude, he grasped the sceptre firmly in his right hand and looked from under massive lowering brows out upon the assembly.

The air in the great hall and all the air which surrounded the higher peaks of Olympos was of a consistency different from that breathed by mortals—finer and, some mortals maintained, more fiery. Its particles, fine as they were, had all been set in motion by the entrance of Poseidon and his train. Indeed, the air immediately surrounding the King of the Sea had a watery look as if each particle had been dipped in brine. The Nereids, who held up Poseidon's long sea-green *chlamys,* turned their heads aside every now and then to release from parted lips shining bubbles. No doubt they found it difficult to breathe, as fish do on land. Poseidon, however, like Zeus, had been born on land and seemed to feel as much at home in the *aither,* as mortals called it, as in his own palace at the bottom of the sea. He had taken up his position at the far end of the hall and reclined calmly upon his couch, leaning his head on one hand as he gazed over the heads of the younger gods. The posture was one which Zeus himself favored. He did not consider that it became Poseidon—at least while he was visiting Olympos, the kingdom of the upper air. But Poseidon was by nature turbulent and unruly, forever pushing his way in where he was not wanted. Zeus turned his face away from his brother to look out over the assembly.

Every one of the Olympians was present, as well as some of the older deities. Directly in front of him Phoebos Apollo stood conversing with his sister Artemis and the divine smith, Hephaestos. Artemis and Apollo had probably requested Hephaestos to fashion some new gear for the chase, of which they were both inordinately fond. Hephaestos showed to poor advantage beside the radiant, straight-limbed deities but he seemed unconscious of that fact. He was listening attentively and kept looking from one to the other, smiling. But his eyes, under his scraggy brows, were, as ever, bloodshot. Hephaestos's brother Ares had once said that to look into the smith's eyes was like gazing at a fire burning behind a bushy thicket. Hephaestos, for all his cleverness, was not good to look upon. When he was born he had been so ugly that his mother, Hera, had straightway dropped him over the battlements of Heaven! But he was kindly of heart and always ready to do what he could to help others. Not of the same calibre as Apollo, but superior in character to Ares.

It occurred to Zeus that of all his sons Ares was the one he least favored, always warring or stirring up wars, and when he was not inciting mortals to war, he was stirring up trouble in Heaven . . . that affair with Aphrodite! Her husband, Hephaestos, had found out about it, of course, and had announced that he was going to visit his favorite island, Lemnos. Then he spread over the lovers' couch a net made of wires so fine that they had not realized that they were entangled in it until he summoned all Olympos to view their plight. Ares had threatened Hephaestos with dire vengeance but his wrath seemed to cool more quickly than usual. He had been seen in friendly converse with Hephaestos the very day the lovers had been apprehended in their illicit delights. After all, a god who went mail-clad as often as Ares did could not afford to quarrel with his armorer!

Zeus wondered now whether Ares had any part in today's assemblage and looked about until he perceived him leaning on one of the wide embrasures that framed the windows. Apparently he took little interest in the proceedings for he was staring moodily at the floor.

They were leading the old prophet Teiresias over to stand in front of the thrones. Zeus, eyeing him closely, reflected, not for the first time, on the pitiable condition of mortals who sometimes paid with a lifetime of woe for a single encounter with divinity. The last time Zeus had looked upon Teiresias he had been a youth, seemingly more flushed with the ardor of the chase than by his sight of the great goddess. A straight-backed, curly-headed lad whose sparkling glance betokened a lively awareness of all that went on around him. One of those who, in early life, develop a passion for venery and who—if the Fates do not intervene—come to be known as mighty hunters. The Fates *had* intervened! When Teiresias had been summoned before the dread tribunal, he bore himself with due reverence but stoutly, like one who knows that if he has offended it is through no conscious fault. Only his eyes, set a little slanting in his head, as is frequently the case with those who are called upon to read the future, betrayed any inkling of his predicament. While he faced his judges those eyes had roved from one countenance to the other, as if they discerned what was as yet hidden from the young hunter!

Since that day he had outlived four generations of Thebans. His hair and sparse, long beard were white; the limbs through which the red blood had coursed so hotly were pallid, knotted, and emaciated. But the eyelids which enclosed his sightless orbs were still red and swollen! The *aigis*-cape which Athene had thrown at him had struck him full in the eyes. She had felt some compassion for him afterwards and had presented him with the staff of cornel wood upon which he was now leaning and had induced Zeus to bestow upon him the gift of long life. Teiresias had had another gift bestowed upon him in recompense for the loss of his sight. He alone among mortals was to be permitted to retain his intelligence when he arrived in the underworld. Zeus wondered now whether he had done the fellow a service when he bestowed the last-named gift upon him. One who was condemned to sojourn in Hades was perhaps as well off if he did not know everything that went on there!

Hera was making the old seer give an account of himself—as if she had never laid eyes upon him before! He was answering in a voice so low that it could hardly be heard. Zeus found that he could not endure to look upon the swollen eyelids or listen to the voice which seemed already to have gone on too long. He looked away.

He had not yet caught sight of Aphrodite in the crowd and was wondering whether she had absented herself because she was bent on some mischief when he saw her moving slowly to the left of the great doors in the far wall. She wore a rainbow-colored *peplos* and a dove was perched on each shoulder. Her *peplos* was gossamer-thin but it was belted at the waist, perhaps so that the ordinary observer could not tell whether or not she was wearing her magic girdle. His daughters, the Hours, had imprudently presented her with it when she stopped off at Cyprus on her way to Olympos. This girdle had the power of inspiring love for anybody who wore it. Aphrodite herself wore it often—often enough to stir up trouble in Heaven and on earth. She was also in the habit of lending it to other goddesses when the fancy struck her. His own consort, Hera, had not been above borrowing it on occasion. He looked over at Hera, sitting straight-backed upon her throne, her sceptre held upright in her hand, gazing severely out over the assembly, in imitation, he suspected, of his own properly magisterial bearing.

Hera was stately of figure, white-armed, golden-haired, with eyes as large and lustrous as those the ox turns upon the priest when he feels the sacrificial knife at his throat. She was also vain, capricious, overbearing, and inordinately ambitious. That cuckoo which she had had Hephaestos fashion for her out of gold to ornament the top of her sceptre represented one of her first victories over him, Zeus! He had been overwhelmed by her beauty and had made no secret of his love for her. She, on the other hand, had pretended to be indifferent to him, gazing out over the world of men all the while he was wooing her. In order to secure her attention, he, the Father of Gods and Men, had been obliged to abandon his wooing and retire into a nearby thicket, where he transformed himself into a cuckoo! He had had the presence of mind to take some of his thunder bolts along and while he was in the process of transformation had launched a medium-sized bolt. The cuckoo which presently flew out of the thicket was so bedraggled by the sudden storm that Hera allowed him to perch, for warmth, in her bosom. It had been an easy matter after that to ravish her. The proceeding, on the whole, had been undignified and he preferred not to keep it in mind. . . . .

But in the early days of their marriage she had come to him frequently, of her own will, when he was reclining upon a cloud which he kept conveniently floating about the topmost peak of Ida, the mountain upon which he had been reared. She wore no diadem in those days. Her *peplos* would be all of one color, a blue that glittered all over as if fresh-dipped in dew. When she lay down beside him the cloud, which had been golden, turned rose color. Helios, perceiving the lovers in their favorite trysting place, would obligingly turn away his head. But tell-tale blossoms—daisies, windflowers, roses, crocuses, and violets—sprang up from the earth over which the cloud floated.

All the gods had brought gifts to their wedding feast. The handsomest gift was the tree hung with golden apples which Mother Earth caused to spring up in Hera's honor. It grew in a garden sacred to Hera, on the banks of the river Oceanus, and was tended by the daughters of the Titan Atlas, and guarded by the dragon Ladon.

Their wedding night had not been spent in the Garden of the Hesperides, however, but on the Island of Samos where Hera (on occasion) claimed she had been born. It had lasted three hundred years.

He could not say that the marriage had been happy. The truth of the matter was that Hera did not understand him. She did not understand, either, the proper rôle of a wife. Very soon after they were married she had begun to show signs of insubordination. On more than one occasion she had threatened to leave him and take up her residence in her splendid dower, the Garden of the Hesperides.

She had turned her head and was making a sign which signified that he should pay more attention to what was going on. He made a sign even more peremptory which indicated that she should not disturb his cogitations. A pretty state of affairs it would be if he, the Father of Gods and Men, were not free to follow the forest windings of his own mind! . . . He had just succeeded in recalling the first occasion on which she had directly opposed his will. It was in connection with that Argive priestess of hers whom Apollo had mentioned, Io, an extraordinarily beautiful girl, with eyes almost as large and lustrous as Hera's own. He had had to change the maiden into a heifer in order to protect her from Hera's jealousy. And even then Hera would not yield, sending a gadfly to sting the poor heifer so cruelly that she leaped into the sea and swam away to Libya. There had been other occasions on which Hera had allowed her jealousy to impel her to the most indecorous conduct. Once she had been so openly rebellious that he had been forced to suspend her between Heaven and Earth with golden chains and an anvil tied to each foot. The measure had not proved successful. She was as contumacious as ever when she was freed. If she understood his true nature and trusted in his might as she should, she would abet his plans instead of continually opposing them. But what woman ever saw things as they truly are?

Hera ought not to be such a thorn in his side, however. He had known her from infancy. After all, they were both children of Kronos and Rhea. A dubious heritage, he sometimes thought! Men called the reign of his father, Kronos, "the golden age." That was because mortals had lived then without care or labor, eating only acorns and wild fruit and honey, drinking the milk of goats and sheep, never growing old, dancing and laughing a great deal. Death to mortals then was no more than sleep. But for the gods— for Kronos himself—life was harder. He was afraid that one of his children might dethrone him as he had dethroned his father, Ouranos. He fell into the habit of swallowing each child as soon as it was born. His consort, Rhea, finally outwitted him, giving a stone wrapped in swaddling clothes in place of her last-born babe. Zeus's mother had borne him at dead of night in a cave on Mount Dikte in the island of Crete. He was nursed by the ash-nymph Adrasteia and her sisters and suckled by the she-goat Amalthea, with her son, Goat-Hoof Pan, for his playmate. In his early infancy his cradle, which was of gold, was swung from the bough of a tree so that Kronos might not find him on the earth or in the sea. But Kronos got wind of his birth and came in pursuit of him. He sought the counsel of the older gods and was advised to become cup-bearer to his father. He had also been furnished with an emetic which, introduced into Kronos's drink, had forced him to disgorge his sons and daughters. Hestia had been the first to tumble out of that dark abyss and after her Poseidon and Hades. At the time they expressed gratitude for their deliverance. Nowadays they were inclined to forget that but for their younger brother Zeus, they might still be imprisoned!

They were still questioning Teiresias as to how he lost his eyesight. Athene, driving her horses too fast, as usual, became so heated in her progress through the air that she descended from her chariot and, having disrobed, was bathing in a woodland pool on Mount Kithairon when the poor fellow came blundering through the trees. Hunting all morning, he had developed a raging thirst and came into the grove seeking water to quench his thirst, not the sight of a naked goddess! Still, his mortal eyes had looked upon the uncovered flanks and bosom of the great goddess. That was profanation.

He became aware that his daughter Pallas Athene had taken her stand behind his throne. She was pressing his shoulder now as if she expected him to take some kind of action. He turned his head slightly and met her flashing eyes with a look that somewhat dimmed their brilliance. She presumed upon the fact that she was his favorite daughter. The circumstances of her birth accounted for that. At the moment he could not remember whether Metis or Themis had been his first wife. He remembered distinctly, however, that early in his marriage with Metis he had received an oracle which foretold that any son born to Metis would be greater than his father. When it became evident that Metis was pregnant he had acted with his customary decisiveness and, in accordance with an old family tradition, swallowed her in the first stages of her pregnancy. He had regretted the necessity, as doubtless his own father had regretted the necessity of swallowing his children. It was only after he had swallowed Metis that he became aware of certain capabilities in himself which he had not known he had. An increase in prophetic gifts, for one thing . . . Metis's pregnancy had culminated in his head. On a certain day he had had a headache so severe that he had roared with pain. All Olympos trembled, the waves of the sea ran backwards, the clouds all but scudded off the horizon. The divine smith, Hephaestos, had had to split Zeus's head open with an axe. It had been a tremendous relief when Pallas Athene sprang out, fully armed and flashing her eyes about exactly the way she was flashing them now. He had felt a glow of pride at his first sight of her. She was, certainly, a daughter of whom a father could feel proud. She was dutiful, too, and assumed the burden of many responsibilities which otherwise would have fallen upon his shoulders. She was actually more mighty in war than Ares—if the dolt could only recognize that fact! Mistress of all womanly arts, too. Particularly accomplished in spinning and weaving. Her mastery of those arts had stood her in good stead on one momentous occasion. Hephaestos, after wooing her unsuccessfully for some time, had attempted to take her by force. Athene had torn a skein of wool off the spindle she had laid down beside her couch and had interposed it between his member and her body so effectively that he spilled his seed on the ground. But Hephaestos, for all his ill-favoredness, was a very potent fellow. He had visited the island of Lemnos once (under circumstances which Zeus did not care to recall), and the very soil had changed its character as the result of his visit. Priests were always importing parcels of it to use in their religious rites. He himself would have been glad to see Athene married to Hephaestos, but she would have none of him. A child had resulted from that peculiar union, however. Athene, though determined to remain a virgin, had shown a proper maternal concern for its welfare. The boy, who was called Erechtheus, looked upon her as his mother, though she referred to him as a "Son of Earth." He had undergone some hardships in youth because of his peculiar appearance—he was shaped like a serpent—but he was now having quite a respectable career as king of the Athenians, the inhabitants of that rock she had such a fancy for. Now that he considered the matter, he could not accuse Athene of any misconduct. And he kept close watch upon her. Having swallowed her mother, he had had to stand in the stead of both father and mother to her. He could not see, however, that she had suffered from having come into the world in such an extraordinary manner. And she seemed to have a hearty enjoyment of the life she led on Olympos. He glanced over at his wife. He had to admit that Hera was an exemplary stepmother. She railed at him occasionally for having loved Dione or Themis or Metis or Mnemosyne or Elare or Pyrrha or Asteris or Leto or Protogeneia or Io or Danaë or Niobe or Leda or Europa or Semele . . . But she had never reproached Athene with her irregular birth and she seemed to relish Athene's company more than that of any other of the Olympians. He wondered, though, whether her influence over Athene was altogether wholesome. This matter of the relationship of the sexes, for instance. It was Hera's constant preoccupation, whereas Athene repeatedly announced her intention to remain a virgin. And yet she was always becoming embroiled in Hera's follies. She had left her place behind his throne and, standing on the edge of the dais, was following the inquisition as eagerly as Hera herself.

Hera was still firing questions at the old mortal, who was leaning more and more heavily on his staff of cornel wood. But neither Hera nor Athene seemed to notice that he was tiring under the steady rain of questions. Hera was frowning—and whenever Teiresias answered one of her questions pursed her lips as if wondering whether he was answering truly.

Zeus regarded her for a moment with disfavor, then looked away. The Fates, for whom he had due regard, referred to his union with Hera as the *hieros gamos*. He wondered why this marriage to Hera was more sacred than other marriages he had contracted. There was Dione, with whom he had lived in an oak wood at Dodona. His memory of her was dim but he was inclined to think that his union with her had preceded his union with Metis.

He *had* lived with her in an oak wood at Dodona. He was certain of that. One of the oaks had turned oracular. The priests interpreted his will by the rustlings of its leaves. Dione divined the future from the meanderings of the stream which gushed out at the foot of the tree. His other wives, Dione's priestesses, kept, for the most part, to the branches of the oak. When anyone came to consult the Oracle the branches of the tree trembled for a moment and the women's voices could be heard saying, *"Zeus declares this or that."* It had not been a bad life, by any means. . . .

There was a stirring at the rear of the hall. Aphrodite, her doves still on her shoulders, was making her way through the crowd. The youth who had been her companion when she arrived on Olympos was moving beside her. There were days when he had the appearance of a child but today his bright, curly head was on a level with her own. The sling in which he carried his arrows hung from his shoulder but—Zeus was glad to note—he carried no arrows in his right hand. He was using that hand to steady himself, no doubt grasping the hair of the person who was bearing him on high. The crowd parted. Zeus had a glimpse of a shaggy head upon which Eros's hand rested. A hoof darted forward, was followed by another hoof. Aphrodite with Eros riding beside her on the shoulders of Goat-Hoof Pan! . . . She was aware that he was eyeing her. Turning her head, she regarded him steadily out of eyes the color of cold sea-water. He bent upon her a look that was even more lowering than the one he had just bent upon the Queen of Heaven. Some people maintained that Aphrodite was his daughter. But he knew better. She was as old, if not older, than he was himself! He recalled the first sight he had had of her, floating over the waves, standing erect upon a cockleshell, naked except for her long unbound hair. He had foreseen in that instant the mischief she would inflict upon mankind and gods and had taken what steps he could to forestall her. But he had had no cooperation from her, of course, and next to none from the younger gods. They were purblind in her presence and showed little concern over certain characteristics of her son Eros, which caused *him* much concern. It was no doubt part of the mischief which his own father, Kronos, had inflicted on gods as well as mortals. Armed with the sickle-shaped knife which his mother, Gaea, had produced from her flinty bosom, Kronos had crept up on his father, Ouranos, where he was reclining upon a peak on Cape Drepanum, cut off his genitals, and thrown them into the sea. A great hubbub had ensued, naturally. Nereus's fifty daughters had rushed to the surface to gape and chatter. Dolphins, squids, whales, and other sea creatures had dashed about so madly that all the waves were fretted. Aphrodite claimed that up to that moment she had been living in the depths of the ocean, in proper retirement with her husband, a cockleshell named Nerites. He was actually the son of Nereus, who had ruled the sea before Poseidon and was sometimes referred to as "the fairest of beings," but the life of a cockleshell suited him and he appeared oftenest in that form. Nerites was too kind-hearted for his own good. When his wife expressed a wish to know what was going on in the upper world he obligingly hoisted her upon his back and traversed ocean after ocean with his fair burden. They came at last to where Ouranos's severed members were floating upon the waves. The foam that was clinging to them drifted over and began gathering itself about Aphrodite's shapely ankles. The minx, who up to that time had conducted herself with the decorum proper to her station as the mate of a cockleshell, at once saw the possibilities inherent in such a situation and with little ado stepped from her husband's back out on to the waves. It was unfortunate that one of the lighter-minded Winds came along at this juncture and wafted her to the Island of Cyprus. It was then that he, the Father of Gods and Men, had made the same mistake that Nerites had made. Watching her drift over the sea, clad only in her long, golden hair, he had felt compassion for her. But he was never one to flout due authority and before taking any action, he had asked the advice of Themis, the Goddess of Justice. She had been his wife in the early days but in these later times she preferred to reign with him not as his consort but as the representative of divine justice in all its relations with man. She was renowned for her wisdom—the Delphic Oracle had been in her charge before it came into the care of Apollo. Themis, when questioned, informed him that it would be contrary to the laws governing the relations of the sexes for Aphrodite to appear on Olympos naked. He had therefore commanded his daughters the Hours to provide her with suitable garments. They had followed his instructions too enthusiastically, it seemed to him; she left Cyprus in a swirl of veilings so gossamer and so multicolored that they aroused the envy of Iris, the female Messenger of the Gods, who usually went clothed in rainbows. Aphrodite's next step, of course, was Olympos. The unfortunate Nerites accompanied her there. The two of them appeared before him to plead their respective causes. Aphrodite wanted to be allowed to remain on Olympos. Nerites, after describing some of the sufferings he had endured at her hands, prophesied that if she became an inhabitant of Olympos she would cause much disturbance. Zeus, the Father of Gods and Men, did not need that caution. One look at her had told him that much but he could not deny her a place among the Olympians; the way she had come into being established her divinity. His own sympathies were with Nerites, however. He showed that by offering to make him an Olympian, also— a handsome offer when you took into consideration the fact that the fellow was only a cockleshell! But he was also a denizen of the deep and knew secrets unknown to mortals and, Zeus suspected, to the younger gods. After one look around the great hall where the gods and goddesses were assembled, much as they were today, Nerites replied that having been born a cockleshell, he preferred to remain a cockleshell, and sank to the bottom of the ocean, whence he had never returned. It was, perhaps, just as well. Aphrodite had behaved the way Nerites had prophesied she would behave. The younger gods had behaved the way he, Zeus, had foreseen they would behave. As soon as they saw Aphrodite they crowded around her, kissed her and embraced her, and each one sought to marry her. Apollo even offered his lyre as a wedding gift; Hermes begged her to accept his staff, which carried wealth along with it. Poor Hephaestos came hobbling forward with a necklace of precious stones fresh from his forge. It was obvious that she must be married off at once—he and Hera had been in accord about that. But he sometimes wondered whether they had chosen the right mate for her. Of all the gods Hephaestos was the cleverest with his hands. There was nothing the fellow couldn't fashion. And out of any material. Gold, ivory, wood, precious stones, metals —he could work with any substance. But he had been lame ever since that unfortunate trip to Lemnos and he had been ill-favored from birth.

The younger gods maintained that it was no wonder Aphrodite sought love outside the marriage bed. Hephaestos's ugliness and infirmity were enough to make any woman restless. He himself wondered whether close companionship with Eros—he had been called Protogonos when he first arrived on Olympos—did not account for some of her vagaries. She referred to him as her son but even she could not name his father. He arrived on Olympos in the form of a slim, winged youth but he seemed to have been growing younger ever since and now looked more like a child than a man.

His spiritual growth also seemed to have been arrested. Aphrodite had had Hephaestos fashion him a bow and a sling full of arrows and he ran about all day long, aiming his arrows at whomsoever he pleased. The younger Olympians found his antics amusing but the Father of Gods and Men was of the opinion that Eros ought to be put under some kind of restraint. He had spoken to Aphrodite about this and he meant to speak to her again. . . .

She was still sidling through the crowd. He was sure now that she had some goal in mind and looked closely at the far corner of the hall. He did not need to look again to know what was going on there. His brother Hades, Lord of the Underworld, was attending the conference. But he had seen fit to come wearing his helmet of invisibility. Zeus wondered exactly what Hades had in mind. The last time he had come here equipped with that gear he had meant mischief. On that occasion he had been determined to hurl his brother Zeus from the throne which he had recently ascended. He would have succeeded in his evil design if Hermes and Goat-Hoof Pan had not come to Zeus's rescue. Zeus recalled that a moment ago he had seen Pan slipping through the crowd in the train of Aphrodite and Eros. Perhaps Pan had realized that Hades and, in all probability, Poseidon were bent on mischief, and he had come here to warn the Father of Gods and Men. Zeus looked about for Pan now but, not catching sight of him immediately, fell to musing on days that were past.

The war which he had waged against his father, Kronos, and Kronos's brother Titans had been severe. When it was over, it was agreed that Zeus, who had led the fight, was to be acknowledged as the Father of Gods and Men—that is to say, King of Heaven and Earth. Poseidon had been given the sea as his kingdom while Hades was made ruler of the underworld. Poseidon was troublesome enough, loosing storms on headlands, sending tidal waves to destroy whole cities. But he could be held in check. Hades was more dangerous because more wily. His first act after he was acknowledged Lord of the Underworld was to demand that the Kyklopes forge for him a helmet of invisibility; he pointed out that he could not rule his kingdom properly unless he had the power of becoming invisible on occasion. Zeus had observed that he chose to become invisible when he was bent upon errands of which he, the Father of Gods and Men, was not likely to approve.

Hades had actually used his helmet of darkness in an attempt to dethrone him, Zeus, the Father of Gods and Men! Doubtless with the intention of settling himself upon the throne, he had enlisted Poseidon's aid and had persuaded Hera, Zeus's consort, and the other Olympians—Zeus's own sons and daughters!—to join him in his fell design. The pretext was that Zeus had become so overbearing—in short, so drunk with power—that it would be better for all concerned if some other god ruled in his place! Poseidon, of course, hoped to be that god but it was more likely that Hades would have succeeded to the throne if the plot had succeeded. At any rate, it was Hades who organized the rebellion and led it. Wearing the helmet which made him invisible, he stole up on Zeus while he was napping and threw over him the net which he had had Hephaestos manufacture for this purpose.

Goat-Hoof Pan guessed what Hades was about and wakened Zeus with his cry which strikes terror into the hearts of gods and men. But his warning came too late. The net was fashioned of cords which were tied in knots so firm that Zeus could not untie them. He struggled unavailingly while Hera and the other gods and goddesses stood by laughing—all except Pan and Hermes. They conferred together and decided that help must be got from one of the older deities. Briareos, one of the Hundred-Handed Ones, was released from Tartarus and escorted to Olympos by Hermes. Having his hundred hands at his disposal, he was able to untie all the knots simultaneously and with such speed that Zeus rose from his couch and routed the assembled Olympians with his thunder bolt before they realized what he was about.

Hades had tried to excuse himself by maintaining that the affair was a practical joke. He had it in mind, he said, to demonstrate to the younger gods and goddesses that the Father of Gods and Men was truly invincible. Zeus had not challenged this preposterous statement except to bend one of his grimmest looks upon his brother while remarking that there had been other gods and demigods, to say nothing of mortals, who had taken it upon themselves to test his omniscience: Prometheus, Sisyphos, Ixion, Tantalos. None of them was in a position to visit Olympos at that moment. . . .

He became aware that his consort, Hera, was directing towards him a bright, compelling gaze. She wanted him to pay closer attention to the proceedings. Athene, as Hera's deputy, was questioning

Teiresias about what they referred to as his "unusual advantages." Roaming about on Kithairon—the fellow did not seem to be able to keep away from that ill-fated mountain!—he had come upon a pair of snakes in the act of coupling and had killed one of them with his staff. Zeus remembered the occasion well. He had meted out what seemed to him a fitting punishment. It was the female snake which Teiresias had killed. He had therefore been condemned to live as a woman for seven years. When the seven years were up Teiresias again encountered a pair of serpents coupling. He had promptly killed the male serpent, perhaps with a canny (if inward-turned) eye to the metamorphosis which might ensue. The *Moirai* had wanted Zeus to change the man into a snake but he, Zeus, felt that Teiresias had already undergone enough punishment with the loss of his physical eyesight and the temporary loss of his manhood. He had therefore restored him to his original sex.

He gave Hera a glance which made her turn her eyes away from his countenance. There was no need for him to concern himself with what was going on now—Athene had stepped aside and Hera had taken upon herself the task of interrogation. She was asking Teiresias whether, when he saw the goddess reclining upon the rocks, the water purling over her naked limbs, he had turned away at once—or had he lingered in the grove? Teiresias answered in a quavering voice that he had quitted the grove—as soon as he could.

Hera then wanted to know whether he at once averted his eyes —or had he allowed them to dwell on the forbidden sight? Teiresias answered in the same quavering voice that he had looked away —"as soon as he could!"

But they kept on questioning him. Teiresias's breath was coming shorter and he was bearing down more and more heavily upon his staff. Zeus decided that he would put an end to the farce. He made a sign to Hera so imperious that she could not ignore it. Her face assumed a haughty and aloof expression. Still keeping her upright posture, she folded her arms as if to signify that she wished to wash her hands of the affair.

Zeus then addressed the blind old seer in a voice so loud that it made him start and quiver in every limb. "They maintain that you have enjoyed unusual advantages, having lived for a period of years both as a man and as a woman. Be so good as to satisfy our curiosity. Tell us whether you derived more pleasure from the act of love when you lived as a man or as a woman."

The old mortal lifted his head and directed his sightless gaze at the Father of Gods and Men. "When I was living as a woman, Sire," he quavered.

Zeus stole a glance at his consort. Her face was still impassive. She still stared out over the assembly as if she herself had not brought this poor old mortal to high Olympos!

He said, "It might prevent useless speculation if you were able to estimate the pleasure each sex derives from the act."

Teiresias pondered, nodding his head slowly back and forth. Finally he intoned:

> 'Often the man enjoyeth but one part.
> Nine parts the woman fills with joyous heart.'

Hera had abandoned her rigid posture and was turning on Zeus the full blaze of her immense, dark eyes. Throughout the hall was a murmuring. Aphrodite, instead of trying to lose herself in the crowd, suddenly stepped out from behind some sheltering figure. She too was staring at him as if he had uttered some blasphemy! Was ever a god so beset? He rose from his throne and, carrying his lightning and thunder bolts in his right hand, passed through the throng. They made way for him hastily but he knew that their ranks would close as soon as he left the hall. The huge cloudy gates were swinging back before him. Hermes was at his side. Hermes did not speak until the doors had closed behind them. Then he asked, "Any commands, Sire?" "No," Zeus said impatiently. "No commands."

He waited until Hermes had turned back into the hall before he left the trodden way and took the narrow, winding path which led to the highest peak of Mount Olympos. He ascended to this summit and, taking his seat in the chair he thought of as his favorite throne, gazed off through the *aither*. Helios perceived him and sent some of his beams dazzling towards him. Zeus acknowledged the salutation with lifted hand and resumed his contemplation of the vault of Heaven. Helios still had some distance to go before his horses could quench their thirst in the ocean stream. The Winds were quiet. Below him the clouds were ranged, side by side, in close formation, like fat-backed sheep which the shepherd leaves to doze through the noonday heat. Except for the rays which Helios emitted on his round all was still in the *aither*. Below the clouds lay the earth. Men moved about there over its broad bosom, intent on their appointed tasks, breathing the *aer* which is all that mortals have to breathe. If they looked up to Heaven, as mortals sometimes did, they caught only glimpses of it; their sluggish glances could not pierce the barrier of clouds.

The sound of voices roused him from his reverie. Two female figures had appeared at the foot of the path: Hera, accompanied by Aphrodite. They were looking up at him. Extending their hands, they chanted the names by which mortals supplicated him. *"Zeus Homognios!"* they called in tones piercingly sweet. He inclined his head slightly in recognition. He *was* Zeus Homognios, the Protector of every family, both of gods and men. Yet he sat here alone on this mountain peak, unattended even by his eagle! He felt a prickling in his shoulder blade, put his hand up, and withdrew from the flesh a small, golden arrow. That boy of Aphrodite's must be roaming the mountain with his quiver full. He realized now that he had acted imprudently when he refused Hermes's offer to accompany him. But what could Hermes do against the power of the older gods? Hermes wore a winged cap and winged sandals on his feet. But Protogonos's wings grew from his shoulders. In a moment he, Zeus, would have to enwrap himself in one of those clouds if he wanted to be protected from the golden rain. Below him the goddesses were still chanting: *"Zeus Phyxios!"* He inclined his head towards them again. He was known never to have refused sanctuary when it was asked for in a spirit of true piety. The very universe might have been unframed if he had not guided Deucalion's stumbling feet to where, after the flood, the Delphic flame still sent up its vapors between two leaning rocks! *"Zeus Xenios!"* Everywhere on the earth's surface men extended hospitality to strangers, in fear of rousing his displeasure, for he was known as their protector. . . .

"Zeus Nephelegeterae!" If they only knew, this was the appellation which of all his appellations most pleased him. He averted his countenance from the goddesses and resumed his contemplation of the clouds which floated between him and earth. He *was* the Cloud-Gatherer. He was also the Shepherd of the Universe. These clouds were his sheep. Every one of them, at one time or another, had

sped across the vault of Heaven at his bidding. A large, gold-colored cloud which lay immediately beneath his feet he recognized as one he used to keep floating about the topmost peak of Mount Ida in the early days of his marriage to Hera. . . .

"Zeus Meilichios!" they called out. He *was* kind, to both mortals and immortals, and customarily sweet of tongue. One of the tales told about his upbringing was that he had been nurtured on honey made by sacred bees in the cave on Mount Dikte. Three wicked men, Laïos, Kerberos, and Aïgolios, had dared to enter the cave to steal the honey. They had encased their bodies in bronze armor and, indifferent to the bees' stings, had drawn the honey and were about to make off with their booty when they saw, cast aside in a corner of the cave, the bands with which Rhea had swaddled him when he was born. The cave blazed with lightning. The thieves would have been consumed if the Fates had not intervened, maintaining that no creature could die in that sacred spot. The thieves had been changed into birds—a green woodpecker, a blue thrush, an owl. . . .

The voices had grown faint. He looked down. Aphrodite had vanished. Hera was ascending the path alone. She was not wearing the robe she had worn in the throne room. This one was blue and embroidered all over with flowers. Something she had borrowed from Aphrodite, no doubt. He sighed and lifted his hand in a gesture of invitation and the cloud at his feet, blushing rosy-pink, rose obediently and floated towards him.

THE FUGITIVES

BY MADISON JONES

Walt heard the train again. He slowed his steps until the clap of his shoes on the pavement was dimmed to a flesh-like padding. It reached him from far off beyond the field where cotton rows merged at a distance and wove a lush unruffled fabric that fanned out wide under the moon to a dark wall of thicket. From so far away the sound was only a wail, almost painful, like the surge of a childhood memory into the heart. It came to him that way often when on summer nights through his open window he heard the trains heading south out of the city. Then he would half rouse from his pillow and follow in spirit over the rolling farm checkered land, along the delta that bounded the broad untamed river. Then he would think again of Uncle Tad, an old man hunched in a chair gripping a stick between his knees with hands burly as haunches of meat but strangely tender with mottled old-man's flesh. Walt used to sit at his feet. By the hour he sat there and looked up at him while the old man talked, recounting over and over violent tales of the days when he had been a railroad engineer. Walt used to watch his hands gripping the stick like a lever in his engine, growing white about the knuckles when he told about the time his coaches cut loose; or again, when he ran the barricade, how he throttled up his engine as he came on and hit with a force that knocked him half senseless against the iron-studded panel and yet found strength to lean out of the window and wave goodbye to the mob with a big ruddy hand. Walt used to think what those hands had done. And once he brought him an egg to break, long-ways in one hand like Uncle Tad had said he could. But now he said, "No; no more," because the strength had gone from his grip. Walt wanted his hands to be like Uncle Tad's and he used to pull at his fingers thinking that would help them grow, and hold them out ahead of him in the sun trying to make them red. Now they were big, as long as Uncle Tad's, he guessed. But the brawn and the redness were not there. People didn't have hands like his any more. And sometimes at his drafting table he had mused upon it, looking at his hands and at Walker's next to him that were thin and fragile and capable only of wielding a compass. And then he would think of what they had told him in biology about hands and evolution and he thought about men reverting because they did nothing to develop their hands. Or again, he would look out of the window over the blue tiresome sheet into the sunlight and think of a muscular hand gripping a hot steel lever, whitening at the knuckles, or perhaps twisting a compass about a single finger.

Walt shifted the bag to his other hand and moved on down the empty highway. There had been no car for half an hour. An occasional truck went by droning south to Vicksburg or New Orleans or north Memphis. They wouldn't hail at night. But he didn't care. The air was live and fresh and the pavement stretched away like an unbroken line of soft manila paper. Perhaps he would have to walk all night. It didn't matter. He had a week and some money and a few clothes in the handbag. Maybe he would make New Orleans. It was the going he liked, the feel and privacy of night, the chance he took of catching a ride or being marooned until dawn on the highway. And back home they had no notion of it. By now, his mother was thinking, he was in Nashville at Woody's house asleep. She had kept him at the door what seemed an intolerable time, holding his hand, fondling him with her eyes. When at last he broke away he felt as though he had done her some violence. It made him angry at her. He could feel her eyes as he passed along the hedge, but he did not look back. Perhaps he should have; it did no good to be unkind. They had given him everything; whatever they knew of to do they had done. Except they seemed never to have known, or else to have forgotten, that stifling sense of tedium, of meeting yourself coming back in a tiny circle which was your birthright. And he had inherited a Lilliputian world precisely rendered in minute sketches of bridges and buildings on a sheet of dull blue drawing paper. He could nearly encircle it by extending the arm of his little silver compass. And he had drawn, he knew, a million such circles. They were everywhere in the world, an infinity of circles, only waiting to be drawn. But if you did not draw them—then they were only in the mind; they did not exist. Yet his was drawn already, a little one in which the heart grew calluses from its incessant pounding against the narrow ribs of its cage. The way out was to lower your head and break through and claim your real birthright—the right to draw your own circle, or to draw none at all. And why shouldn't he do that? He was grown now and free and the road stretched out from his feet through a hundred cities where he had never been heard of and nothing was required of him but that he should mind his business. He looked down at his free hand, at the paleness of his outstretched fingers. It was only the wan light, he knew, but somehow the hand looked bigger, broader than before, and harder. He clenched it into a fist and the knuckles, whitening, showed like bulbs of ivory under the moon.

The road curved in a gentle arc and the moon was higher and the shadows not so long as before. Through the cotton to his right an embankment like a tiny levee ran and converged with the road which straightened ahead and paralleled it. On its crest twin rails glimmered away and in the distance came together with a single splash of brightness. Now he was tiring. He sat down, folding his legs up beneath him against the warm pavement. Mosquitoes whined around. One bit his cheek. He slapped it fiercely and got up and went on. There was nothing in sight but fields of cotton. He wondered if he would have to walk all night.

It was late when he saw a town. It lay back from the highway, straggling, still, like a little fortress of impregnable sleep. He stopped at the turn-off where trees cast a ragged shadow. A sign said "Rolling Fork." Up the lane scattered streetlights made vague semicircles on the dark macadam. There was no other sign of life. To try there for a place seemed almost irreverent, as though he would be treading on graves. And besides, it was too late. He stood pondering it, conscious how his legs ached. There was not even a barn nearby. Then his eyes caught something he had not seen before—boxcars, two of them, on the track only a little distance beyond the town.

Somewhere he missed the crossing and had to push through weeds. He felt his pants wet to the hips as he stepped up on the embankment. The boxcar door was sealed. He passed on to the

other car. That one too was closed, but he saw that the seal was
broken. With his free hand he pushed solidly at the door and it did
not budge and he set the bag down and with both hands pulled.
The door slid and the rasp of grating steel echoed in the hollow
interior. Inside, a rectangle of light extended half across the floor,
but beyond, the cargo of darkness seemed piled impenetrably upon
itself. He heard no sound from within and about him only the
chirping noises of night. He took up the bag and set it inside and
tried again to peer through the blackness. His hands rested on the
steel sill and he vaulted and stood upright. Here it was still with a
silence that muted the pulsing of night beyond. Then he had the
feeling of eyes fixed on him out of the dark. Cautiously he turned
his head and tried to see into the regions where no light fell. Words
formed in his mind. But a timidity restrained him, as though his
voice would make a tumult of the silence. He reached for a match.
It struck noisily against the cover, but moonlight drowned its glow
and he held it far out ahead and inched his way into the darkness.
It burned his finger. He dropped it and took another and held it
up and struck it. In the first bright flare his eye leaped to a face that
watched him from the corner. His pulses sprang; he recoiled and
the match fell extinguished from his hand. Half in the light he
stood his ground and felt the quick beating of blood in his chest
and the scrutiny of eyes from out of the dark. He felt the need for
some word or action to break the hold of silence. His own voice
startled him.

"I couldn't see you back there. Gave me a start at first."

The empty car gave an unfamiliar resonance to his words. He
got no answer, but he felt a slack in the tension, as though his
speech had thawed a subtle bodiless ice. He waited, listening for
some response. Then he said, "Mosquitoes about took me. I
thought it'd be better in here." And now he began to wonder. Perhaps it had been his imagination and no one was there at all. He
jumped at the sudden voice.

"Air this a town?"

The voice was deep and without inflection, but something in
the speech, some uncertain quality, gave him new assurance.

"Just a little village," he said. "This is the road to Vicksburg.
We're out on the delta."

He felt a certain awkwardness in his stance and he reached for a
cigarette and lit it deliberately and knew that his countenance

showed clearly in the blaze of the match. He blew a long puff and watched the smoke vanish into blackness. Then came a sudden rustling and he started again at footsteps which resounded as from a cavern and approached him out of the dark. But he held his ground. He saw a figure, tall, coming into the light. The figure moved past him, an arm's length out, and stopped a little back from the door. Walt turned cautiously and watched him sidelong from his eye. He seemed not to notice Walt's presence. He gazed through the door and out across the delta with the look of a man who watches something far away. He was tall, exceedingly tall. And in the light that reached him he stood with a straightness that seemed unnatural. He appeared to be wrought there, like the far-gazing monuments of soldiers Walt had seen, Confederates mounted on their footings in quiet southern towns. His face looked gaunt, with pockets of shadow settled in hollows beneath the protruding bones. And now Walt was conscious of smoke from his cigarette rising toward the light and the whisper of crickets outside and now, it seemed, a change in that face, a softening. The lips moved barely and the face turned to him. Walt met his gaze and knew that he wasn't afraid any more.

"How far air we from Memphis?" The man's voice had a famil-iar twang, like the speech of mountaineers Walt had heard over at Lupton's Cove.

"Hundred and fifty miles, I guess. Where are you headed for?"

The man didn't answer for a time. Then, "A ways on down yet," he murmured.

Walt heard the thin crying of a mosquito and he struck at it with his hand. "I never saw so many of the devils. You can't rest for them out there."

The man didn't reply. He stood there pensively and gazed at the landscape and finally said, "How far's this Vicksburg?"

"I'm not sure. A long way. Seventy miles, I reckon."

"You say that's a town yonder?"

"Yeah. But it's all closed up. It's just a little place."

Again Walt glanced at the face beside him and now he noticed its gauntness, and he wondered if the man was hungry. He had a sandwich in his bag. He hesitated though, waiting for something. Finally he said, "If you're hungry I've got a sandwich you can have. I don't want it."

Walt saw his lips part and an eagerness in his face that touched it with boyishness. He was younger, much younger than he had seemed, Walt's own age perhaps. Walt took the sandwich and put it into the outstretched hand. The man tore it from the paper and ate it savagely. After he had finished he turned his eyes to Walt again and in that instant they caught the moonlight. Walt returned their gaze and he half grinned at the earnest question. There was no mistaking it. He was still a boy. Walt shook his head. "That's all I've got."

The boy smiled a little. "I'm obliged to you." Now his face seemed less grave, as though quickened by something he watched out there. "Do you reckon there's any water hereabout?"

"I don't know," Walt said. "Unless it's back in that little town."

"Ain't there no creeks?"

"Yeah. But they're not fit to drink, down here in this low country. No telling what you'd catch."

"I've got to have some," he said and stepped to the door and put his hand on the sill and dropped nimbly to the ground. Then he stood motionless outside the car. Walt looked down on his ruffled hair and in the moonlight it seemed to have an auburn tint. It looked like Woody's hair. A truck was passing on the highway a hundred yards beyond and the noisy hum of its engine seemed the only sound in all that still country. The boy was following its progress with a gradual turn of his head. Walt saw that he was waiting.

"Those mosquitoes'll carry you off out there." He thought the boy shifted as though to start and Walt moved forward and came down beside him on the embankment. "Let's go," he said. They started, walking along the embankment. The slope declined from the ends of the cross-ties and made hard walking and they stepped up onto the track.

"It'd be better down on the road."

For a while the boy didn't speak. Then, "Let's stay up here."

Walt stepped rapidly to keep beside his long striding that covered two ties at a time. He glanced sidelong at him, waiting for some apology. But there was none. Gravel crunched beneath their feet. Sometimes a steel track rang from rock they kicked against it. Walt's eyes followed the rails, how they sped away like silver wires into the distance. Now he was sure of it. This boy's was no pleasure jaunt like his own. Why else should he prefer this gravel and ties to the smooth pavement of a highway. And why all that time in a boxcar hungry and thirsty, like a fugitive there in the dark. Maybe that was it. What else would a hill boy be doing there? Walt glanced up suddenly, half expecting to see him anew. But the boy looked far out ahead as though nature steered his feet, and even in the dim light his face seemed full of a strange bright exuberance. Walt watched the ties passing beneath them. Maybe he was right; maybe not. Somehow it didn't matter. Yesterday and what had come before were things shut out by the level horizon that encircled them.

The cotton field to the right never varied and in spite of their rapid walking seemed to have no end. Walt was feeling the weariness he had forgotten. "Let's stop a minute," he said. "I've been walking all night." Walt sat on the track. It was cool and wet with the dew. The boy stood for a time, then seated himself on the opposite track. The mosquitoes were back again. Walt slapped and reached for his cigarettes and held them out and the boy took one and thanked him.

"Smoke's all that'll keep them away," Walt said. He watched the smoke rise thinly from his hand.

"They wasn't hardly this bad back home. 'Less you went down in a hollow." He spoke as though thinking aloud.

"Where do you live?" Walt said.

He hesitated; then, "Point Creek," and then, "It's in Tennessee."

Walt dragged again at his cigarette. "How far is that from Carthage?"

"A right far piece. Fifty mile, I reckon."

After a moment Walt said, "Good fishing up around Carthage. I was up there once."

The boy looked down. "I used to fish all the time in Wolf Creek. Used to grab for them—I could catch them, too. Pa said it was 'cause I was so long and gangling I could get back up under them rocks where nobody else couldn't." He paused and a smile was on his lips. "Once I pulled out a snake. Pa said I jumped clean up on the hill." He laughed deep and mellow and Walt laughed too. They were quiet again except for an occasional chuckle from deep inside the boy. Walt blew smoke up into the air. Then the boy looked at him and the moon reflected in his eyes. "Where do you live at?"

"Memphis." The boy seemed to ponder it a moment. "That's a

big place," he said. Then he threw down his cigarette. "I got to have some water."

"I could use some myself."

The rest had done Walt good. His legs felt lighter. He caught the swing of his companion's stride, a rhythm like the cadence of marching men. After a long time the boy said, "Don't look like there's no water about."

"Naw it don't. Looks like we'd run on a house or something."

In his mind Walt could picture a spring welling out from rock at the foot of a hill and them on their bellies sucking deep, wetting the ends of their noses. The thought of it made him thirstier. Perhaps the boy too was thinking of a spring where he had drunk back in some mountain hollow. Walt thought how it would look and how pleasant it would be to go with him there and drink from the spring, or grab for fish in the mountain branch. Suddenly the boy began to whistle soft and fine. It was square-dance music, Walt knew; it sounded like "Turkey in the Straw." But he did not know the tune. "What's the name of that?" Walt said.

The boy reflected a moment. Finally, "I've forgot. Pa used to fiddle it all the time."

The tune ran in Walt's head. After a little he was whistling it between his teeth.

"Naw," the boy said. "It goes like this." He whistled a few bars and Walt joined in and then the boy stopped and Walt saw him nodding and heard him say, "Now you got it."

They walked for a long time and once stopped to rest and smoke and the boy sang "Barbara Allen," all of it he could remember, and laughed when he got through. But now their gaiety had passed. The boy was suffering for water, Walt knew, because he kept talking to him about it and twice stopped and pulled blades of the wet grass and put them in his mouth and chewed them. Walt was thirsty too. It had grown upon him in the last hour, as though the boy's thirst had infected him. Then the boy said, "Look," and pointed and Walt saw a roof there at the thicket which bounded the cotton field. They hurried; then they saw that it was a shed without walls and empty.

"Shore we'll find some directly," the boy said. Walt felt his disappointment, its keenness, in the wan hope of his voice.

Still the highway and the open field were on their left, but to the right now a thicket rose and shut out the light but for patches where it broke through the heavy foliage.

"I hear a frog," the boy said. "Must be water." He was right, for now Walt too could hear it. That was the reason for a thicket—because the land was too wet for cotton. "It must be a swamp," Walt said. "We can't drink swamp water."

They went on, peering down into the thicket. Now they heard clearly the frogs, their quiet clamor that swelled and died in a strange grating rhythm, like the pulse of the swamp whose breath reached up and touched their nostrils with its dankness. Here the mosquitoes were worse. Even walking they had to flail at them with their hands. Then, at the thicket's edge where the moon broke through, they saw water, slick and shining under the light. The boy stopped. Quickly Walt said, "You can't drink that. It'll kill you."

"I got to have some water," he said.

"But that stuff's full of fever. It'd be just like drinking poison."

The boy still looked down at it.

"Come on," Walt said. "We're bound to run on a house."

The boy did not answer, only grunted when again Walt warned him against the water. Now they could see that the swamp was not large, that up ahead the thicket broke as abruptly as it had begun onto another field of cotton. Then they saw the stream that fed it, how its bright placid face abruptly vanished into the shadows that darkened the swamp. Ahead it passed under the tracks. Once more Walt set his pace with the boy's, which had quickened at sight of the water.

They stepped onto the bridge and Walt looked down through the ties at the stream. It looked deep. No ripple stirred and the gloss of its surface lay tranquil as ice. Walt tasted the humid air.

"This ain't in the swamp," the boy said.

"It's the same stuff though. Look how still it is."

The boy kept on looking at it.

"Let's go," Walt said. "It'll be day pretty soon. Then we can catch a ride." But his words made him remember.

"Naw," the boy answered. "I got to have some." He started across the bridge and when Walt came up beside him he said, "I got to. I ain't had none since yesterday noon."

Walt followed him down the bank through weeds and onto a

clearing beside the stream where someone had watered stock. The boy dropped to his knees and put his hands in the water; mud clouded upward to meet his face. He straightened up again and crawled a little down the bank and leaned out beyond the stance of his spraddled hands. But he paused a moment there above his shadow. Then he began to drink. Walt watched the ripples around his head, how they shimmered the water's face, and he heard the suck of his drinking.

"Don't get too much," Walt said.

The boy did not stop or even seem to hear, as though there was no sound in the world but the noise of water coursing down his throat. Walt went to him and put his hand on his shoulder, the hard muscle that quivered with the strain.

"Don't drink any more."

The boy stopped. Walt looked at his kneeling body, the heaving of his chest, the still head that drooped a little downward toward his shadow with the look of a man in prayer. Now Walt could not hear his breathing any more; only mosquitoes and the witless chorus of frogs. The boy rocked back on his heels and struck at his arm. Walt looked at the water.

"How is it?"

"Better than nothing."

Walt looked at the water, aware that the boy stood up. The coating of light lay like varnish on its pond-quiet face. Looking at the water he heard the boy speak. He answered, "Yeah," and stepped to where the boy had been and knelt and lowered his face. His nose touched warm water; the scent of it rose up rancid and unclean into his nostrils. Beneath his eyes the water was black and lifeless as oil sopping his lips and tongue. He swallowed once, then again. As he came upright he felt the warm languid surge of it downward in his gullet. After a moment it had passed, but he shuddered. He got up and the boy was watching him. Light was in his eyes. They were gray eyes, or seemed to be, gray for looking distances. Walt held out his cigarettes and the boy took one without speaking and Walt lit it for him and then his own.

"Let's get up on the track," Walt said.

The boy sat on the rail beside him. They watched their smoke rising on the windless air. Walt said, "They don't like smoke."

"Naw," the boy answered.

But still Walt could hear mosquitoes about his head and he

slapped at his cheek. The boy got up. Walt watched him as he searched about in the weeds and pulled some grass, sage, Walt thought, that looked drier than the rest. He came back with his hands full and arranged it quickly in a criss-cross pile near Walt's feet. He tried to light it, this stem and that, and at length a flame flickered tinily. They nursed it with their breath and bits of grass they dropped on it until a slow flame with gentle hissing consumed its way through the pile.

"That'll fetch them," the boy said.

Walt listened. But now he heard the boy's whistling again, the tune he had whistled before.

"Ain't you going back?" Walt asked.

"Naw. That's the first place they'd look."

"Where you going to?"

The boy threw the stub of his cigarette into the fire. "I don't know. It don't matter. I ain't going back to Nashville."

After a little Walt said, "How long did you have?"

The little blaze was flickering.

"Life."

Walt leaned forward and laid unburnt stems on the flame. They writhed for an instant in the heat, smoking, then caught.

The boy said, "I'd rather be dead than back there." He watched the fire, its fluctuations like bursts of a dying candle. "But I ain't sorry. I give him fair warning—I told him to stay away from there."

The last of the flames swelled to a moment's brightness and reeled and vanished into embers that pulsed still with an inner fire. The smoke still rose. Walt heard only the frogs. He looked down the silver tracks.

"You might go to New Orleans. They'd have a hard time finding you there."

The boy answered "Yeah" and yawned and in the middle of it said, "Reckon I will," and reached his hands above his head and stretched. Walt yawned too. "Catching, ain't it?" he said.

The smoke, all but a wisp, was gone. Walt saw him start to move and they stood up together and Walt reached for his handbag and stepped off. But the boy was not at his side. Walt turned back and started at the look of him, the fixed body and half-raised hand and his face rigid. The boy turned his back to him.

"What is it?" Walt said.

"Listen."

That tenseness, the set of his body, stopped Walt's own slow breathing.

"Don't you hear it?" the boy whispered.

"No."

"Listen."

Now he heard it, a distance off up the tracks. Then it sounded again, clearer.

"I hear dogs."

The boy didn't say anything. They heard again the throaty yelps coming intermittently—but not a sound like barking. Walt felt the tension, the strain of gazing through light that was too unsure. He heard the hasty whisper that spoke the thought in his mind.

"They ain't no ordinary dogs."

Then Walt pointed, "Look"; he saw it glint an instant under the moon. The boy wheeled. Walt read panic in his face. He had no words, but he seized the boy's arm and the bright eyes fixed on him a wild mute appeal.

"The water," Walt said; "they can't track in the water."

Comprehending, he cut his eyes from Walt's face and bolted into the weeds toward the clearing. Walt started to call and did not. He saw the boy drawing away from him with long bounds of his shifting body; he felt sudden loneliness. The yelp of the dogs, clearer now, was advancing on him. Walt sprang into his wake. Striking the weeds he saw the boy reach the stream; he saw something else, a glimpse screened quickly by his descent, a car crawling lightless along the highway beyond. The boy was in water hip-deep wading on toward the road.

"The swamp," Walt hissed; "they're on the highway." The boy heard and wheeled and lurched back like a man dizzy with turning and sprawled in the water. Trying to run he made his way back to Walt and grasped his arm and "Quiet," Walt said, "they'll hear," and the boy's wide eyes crossed his face and Walt struggled on by his side. Under the bridge they crossed its shadow and came into light again. The water grew deeper. It rose up onto Walt's chest. The boy was gaining on him. Walt let go his handbag. The swamp was ahead with its sudden line of shadow and they began to swim a long silent breast stroke. The boy passed into the shadow first and the light was shorn from his hair. They heard the dogs, clear-voiced, nearer now. They slid on through black slick water that swirled in hollow sucks above their hands, and the voice of a million frogs dinned in their ears like soft rhythmic thunder. They made for the bank. Mud like paste gave way under their hands, but a vine was there and they seized it, the boy first, and dragged themselves on wet bellies over the shallow bank. They came upright and the boy led blindly off.

"Keep close to the creek," Walt said. They plowed on half stumbling through sticky mud and vines that caught at their feet or slid wetly across their legs. A glooming light was all around, like a spell misguiding their steps. Walt struck another vine and fell to his knees and got up and went on. They were in water, splashing, tugging against the mud. Someone called. "Wait," Walt said and the boy stopped. Above the sounds of the swamp Walt heard the dogs and then on the bridge behind them the voices of men. They waited. The voices still sounded, but they could not distinguish the words. Suddenly mosquitoes were about them thick as from a hive, brushing against their faces, swarming so that Walt held his breath for fear they would enter his nostrils. He heard the boy say, "God," and start again. But now Walt could feel a difference, a sense of something gone, some unclear haze like departed sleep that left him aware of wretchedness, of sweat and his aching legs, and then, of wonder. It was only this morning—or yesterday—he stood on his own front walk—as though it were someone else, not him, who was fleeing here through the swamp; someone who had no memory of the names of books on his shelf, of Litton's voice, the look of his mother's face. He sank in mud to his shins. He tugged free and plunged on again. Then, "Look yonder," the boy cried. He was right. A rim of clear light was there, dissected by trunks that intervened, but deep like crystal water reaching into the distance. They hurried; then they both stopped together. The men were ahead of them; they knew every swamp and thicket, the lay of every field, the habits of men in flight. "They ain't to the creek yet," the boy hissed and started angling toward the stream. Walt fought the mucky space that grew between them, calling to him as loud as he dared. Then a voice sounded beyond the swamp dead on line of their course. The boy stopped. Another voice back behind them answered. Walt came up beside him. The boy did not look at him.

"They're all around," Walt said. He watched the line of the boy's profile, the swamp light on his face. And again he felt the mosquitoes. Abruptly the boy began to flail with heavy wasteful strokes of his hands.

Walt said, "We can't stay here. It's almost day."

He quit beating the air and stood gently fanning with his hands.

"I'm going to try it—in the cotton yonder."

"You can't," Walt said. "It's too light. And besides—those dogs. Even if they missed—"

"I'm going to try it." The words were a whisper, strained, exhausted. But they did not pass; they whispered themselves like faint echoes inside the cavern of Walt's skull. He could hear nothing, think nothing, but the sound of that whispering. The boy's movement startled him; his mind filled up again. He was following through water half to his knees, through mire that sucked at his shoes and strained hot cramps into the muscles of his thighs. He shielded his face with his arms and broke through the vines; his wrists burned like sores. He felt he was blind, compelled on his course by a kind of groping instinct. Once he came hard against a stump and fell to his hands. He felt cool water on his lips, the muck like a cushion under him. Then ahead he saw light. His eyes searched the rim of the thicket, under the roof of foliage, along black trunks that stood like portals opening onto the field. He saw the boy's head. It was framed black as the trees in a square of light. Walt got up and started. The head had vanished, but he found the boy on his hands and knees in the last edge of the shadows. The boy turned his face to him as he came up and kneeled down. But the boy did not speak. His eyes looked almost white. It was dusk over the field. The moon was in the west the feeble color of milk, hung in the interregnum between day and night. Off somewhere the throaty bark of a dog, then a voice. Nothing stirred. It seemed long.

"Hear the owl?"

Walt wasn't sure the boy had said it. His head was turned away, as stiffly fixed as though he were scenting something. Then Walt saw a man. He was standing hip-deep in cotton a distance down the edge of the thicket. He had a gun.

"The creek," the boy whispered.

"They'll be looking for that," Walt answered.

They began to crawl painfully along the shadow to where it touched on the cotton. They paused. The man had not moved. Even the frogs had stopped. On a line with his eyes the cotton spread out like a glistening turgid lake.

"It's dawning," the boy said. The words came on a faint expiration of breath, like something imagined. The boy was gazing at him. Walt strained to see his face, but only the feeble whiteness of his eyes showed through the blur. He could tell when the eyes closed, deliberately, and opened again and then turned away into the field.

They were crawling in the cotton down a narrow aisle of lumpy dirt and uprooted vegetation that rustled against their arms and legs. For long spaces he held his breath and watched his hands passing one another like pale fragile duck's feet against the dark earth. Sometimes he touched the muddy sole of a shoe and hesitated. Sometimes back behind them there were voices calling. A bird in the swamp shattered the dawn with its raucous cry. He knew that they must hurry. A space grew between him and the shoes. He moved faster. Then a sudden noise startled him to a halt; a white tuft of hair bobbed off through the cotton. The rattling of stalks beat for an agonized moment against the membranes of his ears. He could not move; he felt his heart swelled up tight like stuffing against his ribs. Suddenly behind them came another crashing. He knew that this was it, but he felt only confusion, and feebleness in his muscles. Then a voice, thunderous, challenging. He felt the boy come to his feet, the earth tremble at each quick thud of the ponderous shoes. The voice calling "Halt" and again "Halt" shocked Walt into motion. But a shot answered the upward lurch of his body; the noise like a concussion blew him staggering forward in the tracks of the racing figure. He strained at the yielding dirt. And some hard object, it seemed, probed against the small of his back. Then he could not stand it any more. He dove onto his belly and behind him the voice cracked and then the shot. He heard the boy's body strike the ground, as though the gun had discharged some enormous awkward load of pulp. He bolted forward. He half heard the warning shout and came to his knees by the long still body. The boy was lying face down. An arm was crooked clumsily under him. He had the look of having been dropped there from a great height. But now his body was shuddering. Walt felt sudden panic. He hovered over the boy, forming words with his tongue that did not come out. Then, as suddenly, he felt it was all a ridiculous act and he wanted to shout, "Stop it, stop it." But he could not stand to see him lying like that. With a calm that surprised him he was gently turning the boy onto his back, gently murmuring to him in the accents of a lover. The boy's lips were faintly writhing; there was blood on them and Walt's hand was covered with blood. But he hardly noticed it. With the tail of his shirt he wiped the lips and he wiped dirt from the nostrils and forehead. And all the time those pale lidless eyes stared at him. He tried to look deep into them, past that look of white amazement, down through the channels of his mind. But the whiteness blinded him. The boy's body began to strain; a noise like gargling issued from his throat.

"Turn his head 'fore he chokes," a voice said.

He obeyed, unshaken even by the sudden intrusion of that voice. The mouth was open. The teeth looked nearly scarlet, like dirty rubies. He laid his hand on the boy's dark jacket over the heart. It was wet, grimy; it cleaved like paste to his fingers. He took his hand away. There was a sound of rattling foliage and other voices were around him answering quietly to one another. Then he knew he was being spoken to, querulously. He was answering, not looking up, not even thinking, as though the words came by rote to his tongue. Now others were kneeling beside him. They did not speak for a long time. Then one of them stood up.

"Bring him on," the man said.

Two men seized the boy's long arms and hoisted him. His head flopped back and rolled wandering on his shoulders as he came upright. Walt sprang to him. He shouldered the man aside and took the limp wet arm and encircled his own neck with it. He heard the man curse and another coldly answer him. Then he began to think with a kind of pain at his own heart, "We cannot carry him this way, with a hole through his chest." But as they plodded off and the boy's feet dragged behind him and his head toppled aimlessly on the yielding column of his neck, Walt understood that he carried a corpse.

The east was flaming bright when they got up onto the track. The arm about his neck was sticky, suffocating; his wrist and fingers ached from the grip he held on that dead hand which slipped persistently from his own on a slime of sweat and blood. He felt that he could not get his breath. Some object like a round stone seemed lodged in his gullet, swelling up, pressing the air from his lungs. He tried to swallow it back, but it surged up hot and acid into his throat and drenched his tongue. He vomited, bent under the weight of the body. The heaves came violently, knotting his muscles, straining his entrails dry. He did not know so much of that black water was in him.

It seemed a long time he was on his knees retching. When it ceased he felt too tired to get up. It was as though he had waked up from a drugged uneasy sleep and looked out at a new-risen sun. But one of the men was speaking to him. He got to his feet. The body was stretched out, staring. There were no shadows on the face now. It looked older than it had before, the features not so clean of cut. And deep indentations, like scars, angled down from the flanges of the nose past the open mouth. But more than these, death had frozen the face in a look of dull and wanton brutality. He turned away. He could not help to carry the body any more.

They left him there with one silent man and took the corpse away. He did not look after them. The sun threw coppery spangles into a dusty sky. It promised heat. He felt shattered, as though he had run hard against a barrier of stone. And as he looked up the track which they had come down so lustily last night, he imagined he saw his own figure walking slowly north. At the end of his walk his own front door was standing open and they were watching him approach and the expression on their faces was something between placid satisfaction and mild surprise.

THE WHEEL

BY SMITH KIRKPATRICK

T HE TIRES were humming on the highway. The hot rubber sang against the asphalt and its refrain steeped his brain. He had not stopped in three hours and through the heat waves rising from the plumb-straight road, he was looking for a filling station. He had meant to stop at the end of two hours. That was his rule: every two hours, stop. But he forgot. Or maybe he only thought he forgot; maybe he hadn't seen a filling station. He couldn't remember right then; it was easier to listen to the tires than to think. He could always depend on the tires. When they were rolling there was no need for thought. They put his feelings into words. He could sit there and the tires' refrain would pull the feelings from the very nerves and make them into words.

He stared unseeing across the hooded fires blazing before his feet, and on through the heat waves. The tires hummed and the splintered sun turned its midday force on the car and the asphalt. The asphalt stored the heat and the car fled its surface, a fire-enclosed oven. He was inside, the car-top burning his skull until he felt his brain boiling, his crotch melting into dry air. The air rushed by, and along the asphalt the sand lay hot and soft. The tires sang between the sand: going again, he's going again, going again, he's going again. . . .

"What are you going to have, sir?"

For a moment he was bewildered. Then he remembered and smiled. It had happened before. That time he had pulled to the curb on hearing a police whistle. He had had a good laugh at himself when he discovered it was a murder story playing aimlessly on the radio.

"What are you going to have, sir?"

A cool dampness fell against his wrist. A hand passed back and forth before his face and there was a woman's voice, "Here, here, why don't you join us and tell the man what you want."

He raised his head. The woman's face was laughing into his, a sunbrowned face with dark eyes and soft dark hair falling forward.

"What? Oh, I'm sorry." He leaned against the back of the deep-cushioned stool and turned towards the bar. "Something big with a lot of ice."

A folded cloth lay against his wrist. The bartender was bent under the bar storing bottles. The empty bottles clanked, and he could see the bartender's white apron that did not quite meet in the back.

He turned back to the woman. There was a man sitting beside her. The man was as brown as she, and the sleeves of his navy blue shirt ended above the elbows. She leaned back on her stool and waved her hand between them, "This is Albert, my husband. I'm Clara."

His hand lifted automatically to his forehead. But before he could give his name, Albert was leaning forward on the bar ready to speak, the teeth flashing white in a brown face, "I'll bet you've just crossed the desert."

Clara's head was bobbing before her husband finished. "You can always tell when someone's crossed just by looking at his face." She raised her voice. "Tommy, come out from under there and give this man a drink. He's just crossed and needs it. Tommy should take better care of the newcomers," she confided. "They're his biggest trade."

"Now, Clara, you're exaggerating again. Just look around you," Albert said.

He looked around the room. The stool felt like the moving car seat. His legs and neck were aching and cramped, to move them was a pleasant pain. Wisps of light drifted through the latticed door and lay on the floor like yellow straw. The debating voices beside him became a part of the hum of the room. He had not realized there were others there. They were lined on the stools, their faces outlined by the dim lights back under the bar. Except for the hair and lipstick the faces all looked alike. All were burned dark. He thought that curious. The faces were variously talking, smiling, or sightless across the bar; but each variation seemed no more than a different expression of the one face. Behind them and extending into shadowy vagueness were the snowy rectangles of tables, laid out and ready for the dinner hour. The bar made a graceful, drifting curve before the figures, and both the bar and the figures faded from sight. He could hear Tommy somewhere around the curve clanking bottles. Tommy was serving a woman. She was laughing. It was shrill and expectant.

Her laughter died and he could hear only the murmuring hum of the voices. He shook his head against the sound and lifted the tall thin glass from the bar. The rim of the glass hit against a metal napkin dispenser. The thin glass twanged in his fingers, but did not break. It sent a shiver through his body, from fingers to toes and back again. Then it was gone, gone from the glass and gone from himself. He raised the glass with effort. The vibrations should not have been in the glass anyway; a nearly full glass did not vibrate. He was tired and imagining things. Holding the glass close to his face, he thumped its rim with his forefinger. The movement was back, back in the glass and back in himself. He bowed his head, but before the cold glass touched his lips, he heard the hum of its vibration. Then the hum went out of the glass. The reddish liquid burned sour and acrid down his throat. He didn't know what it was; he had never tasted such a drink before. His lips felt like he had been blowing music through a comb. He could feel the tiny lashes of the tissue paper. He set the glass on the bar and rubbed his hand damp and cold over his lips. The feeling did not diminish. Under his hand the vibration spread over his face. It smeared around his mouth; wherever his hand had touched, the flesh tingled until his skin felt as red as the liquid. He tried to see the redness in the mirror, but the bar lights were too dim. He could only see the slender outline of a face, a face that was drawn, vaguely perceived.

The sound of humming welled in him, and his whole body was vibrant. He sat perfectly still, careful not to make the smallest movement. His hands were pressed immobile, each on a knee. Yet he was moving and the seat was moving. He lifted a hand from his knee and touched his fingers to the metal dispenser. Immediately the metal took up the humming vibration. Then it spread over the room rising and falling about the figures into the shadows and snowy tables. Then it separated. He heard the engine before his feet, felt the car moving under him, and outside the latticed door he could hear the rush of the wind. The highway lay straight. Straight to the west the fluid tires sang: going again, he's going again, going again, he's going again. . . .

The tires never failed him: straight like a voice of judgment they gave the final verdict, rendered his mute feelings into words. Only this time it was different; this time he had not yet decided where. He must think of this soon. He must not wait. It was important.

The tires hummed and through the seat he could feel the dampened imperfections of the road and engine. He raised a leg and pulled at the seat of the trousers stuck wet against his body. Then he held out his hand and the hot rush of dry air pushed against his arm. The small wail of the air joined the sound of the tires. He rested his arm on the door and gasped with pain at its touch. He started to rub his elbow but the car swerved, forcing his hands back to the wheel. He should not have to steer with such care here where the road was so straight and empty, not on this road.

God damn this road, a voice said. It was a hoarse, grave voice that cracked at the end. For a moment it hung in the car, then it was sucked out and lost in the churning backwash. It was gone before he decided who had spoken.

Strange not to recognize his own voice, but everything was strange. He had not seen so much as a live cactus the whole distance, only glinting beer cans and blown-out tires. The tires were like black lesions in the sand and the sun glinting on the butts of the cans nearly blinded him. The cans and tires lined the road, scattered between the asphalt and the fences. They floated in the hot sand, and the sand flowed beneath the fences and over the edges of the asphalt. The surprising, unfathomable fences hung along the road like barriers, shining and heavy, heavier even than the hog fence he had helped his father build as a boy. The hog fence was still standing strong the last time he had driven past the place four years ago. It sagged between the posts, but was still stout enough to pen a rooting boar.

He had been in low gear by the time he passed the house. It sat in the late afternoon shade of the oaks and the hickory. The trees had thickened and the hickory had a lightning scar on the side nearest the road. The steep roof and chimneys merged into the grove of cedar tops. He wondered about the new owner; the lawyer had written only a name, which he had not recognized and which meant little. He wished now he had stopped, even if for nothing more than to ask a drink of water from the well. Not that he was thirsty, but just to watch the bucket come up creaking and dripping, and to let the cold sweet water run in his throat, then to throw the dregs on the ground like his father always did. Or he might have gone up the little hill in back, where the two graves lay, and sat with them for a while under the cedars. He had seen the jonquils blooming beside the path. The new owner might have let him pick some. She would have liked that. His father had always teased her and called them Easter flowers.

But he hadn't stopped. The car was in high gear by the time he reached the corner post at the creek. The bridge boards rattled and he was fast on the new road to town.

He had never been over this new road, but he had been over the old one, how many times: swaying with his father high on a cotton wagon, riding the school bus, going in to see Jane or taking her back of a Sunday evening after she had spent the weekend. His father had teased her about the jonquils, too.

He stopped in town. He drove through the tree-lined streets and stopped in front of the old frame building that through the dusk and shrubbery looked in worse need of paint than it actually was. His leather heels popped strangely on the walk. The tall shrubbery along the walk was the same, but cement had replaced the white gravel he had expected to crunch underfoot. His heels popped and the porch gleamed in the fading light. Then he saw the ladder and smelled the fresh paint. The steps were new boards and not yet painted. He mounted the steps, taking care to miss the top one which had always been the faulty board. There from the edge of the porch he saw her, saw Jane sitting in the swing waiting as though she were expecting him. He walked towards her, not remembering the porch as being so long—it was not a great house, but it certainly seemed a long porch. His heels drummed on the porch boards, measured and slow, duller and louder than on the sidewalk. Jane's hands half lifted from her lap. And as her hands moved towards each other, he was conscious of a devil wind coming in from the street to the porch edge and whirling into a seven-year lilac bush, the bush shaking and the wind whirring and turning in the leaves. The drumming died as the wind whirred louder, turning and turning in the bush. There was no other sound, only the wind shaking the bush until the earth was loosened around the stalk. It whirred, measured and steady, and from its rhythm he heard a new drumming. Each beat became more and more a single word. The beat shaped and molded the word in his mind. But before the word could become fully molded by his lips, the wind left the bush. And he was standing beside the swing in a stillness as silent as the rising dusk. Jane's hands clasped and dropped back into her lap. And her eyes were dropping towards her hands.

They sat together in the swing. He expected her to ask about the new places he had been. But she didn't. She sat watching the steps. He talked for awhile and found he too was watching the steps. Then she held out her hand. He shook it and went down the steps into the rising dusk.

His heels popped on the cement walk, but he didn't listen for the word which the wind had nearly shaped. He could only hear the tires' going again, going again, he's going again, going again. . . .

She had never understood there were some things a man had to do. And he had to, the way he had to breathe, thirteen years ago. It didn't seem so long, but time had a way of coming at you when your head was turned. Thirteen years ago he had flipped a coin: east or west. West had won but somehow he had been diverted. He had gone to sea that time, keeping records on a ship. But now the coin was falling true. He was on his way west. And as soon as he left the desert and found a cool place to sit and think, he must decide where. Maybe he would buy a piece of land that had thick trees on it and see if he could still build a fence, if his hands could remember building.

He studied his hands, turning them. They were soft and white, almost dainty looking. The left palm was wet and cold. The lines in the palms were shallow and barely interrupted the smooth swirls of the skin pattern. A drop of water slid down one of the fingers and into the palm, leaving a cold path on his hand. Then the drop was wiped away and his hand was held between two smaller brown ones.

"Albert, just look how white his hands are."

Her hands were hot and firm. His looked pale, like a sunless
shoot lying upturned from the earth. She lifted the hand towards
Albert, who leaned forward to see. "They are awfully white.
Everybody will know you're a newcomer."

Clara dropped her head and put his palm against her cheek.
It was warmer than her hands and her dark hair tickled his wrist.
He looked at Albert who was still leaning his bare arms on the
bar.

"The sun will fix it in a couple of weeks," Albert said. "But
everybody will know meantime."

She was moving her cheek in his palm. He kept looking at Albert. "I am new here."

"Of course you are, that's what I mean, and everybody can tell
it. One look at you and—presto—just like that they'll say, 'newcomer.' Clara and I have been here for—oh, for a long time.
Haven't we, Clara?"

She raised her head and his hand slipped away. He held his
glass with both hands.

"How can you tell how long?" she asked. "We didn't know
what living was until we came here. Anyway, we're accepted. No
one, really no one, ever suspects we weren't always here. The boy
in that new place told me yesterday how glad he and the management were to have the established residents coming there. That
pretty boy, he has to stand there all day without even a stool to sit
on. And he's so *young*."

Albert put his arm about her waist. "Now, Clara, remember
you're not supposed to let those things upset you." Albert looked
at him. "Her heart just goes out to such people. She's very sensitive. That's why we're here today; we come every Sunday to let her
get away from routine, meet new people. It's good there's so much
to do out here. Something's going on all the time: everything,
everything you can imagine. And every man's his own man.
There's no limit to what a man can do in this part of the world."
Clara leaned against Albert's shoulder, watched with excitement
his brown face, now suffused, intent. Albert's voice tightened.
"Out here you could just walk around a corner and—presto—
bump into the very thing, just the right . . ." Albert's thumb and
forefinger were minutely measuring a distance that his fingers
could not find.

The voice, like the fingers, became lost in the search.

He watched the fingers seeking the magical distance. They were trembling, and between them he could see the figures along the bar lifting their glasses, holding them between their thumbs and fingers. The glasses refracted the bar lights. They glinted like the beer cans had before he entered the valley. In fact he didn't even remember seeing any beer cans *in* the valley, but then even the valley had been a surprise. Maybe he just hadn't noticed; he certainly hadn't noticed the climbing grade that the valley lay behind. He was looking for a filling station and hadn't realized the gradual ascent until he turned to look at the strip of torn rubber. It slid towards him long and twisted in the sand, and when it flashed past, he turned to look. It had blown completely in two. He hoped it had not been on a front wheel. As he watched it slide smaller away, the tires changed their pitch. They ground harsh on the sand. He jerked about and pulled the car to straddle the center. He was always looking back. Wreck at this speed and he'd never know it; never in this world would he know it, it would happen so fast. Besides there was the rear-view mirror, built especially for such a purpose. Like a small picture the mirror showed the road dropping down and back, compressed under the heat waves and between the fences and littered sand until distance merged fences and road into fluid sand.

Then there was a new sound. It grew from the familiar humming of balanced forces like a single voice growing from a choir, but straining its power to do so. It was the engine. Its laboring rose above the sound of the tires, muted the rush of air as the grade steepened and the flat terrain became broken. Great black rocks rose ahead in the sand. The land undulated and the tires pounded up and down its waves, the car dipping and swerving. The rocks, mortared with sand, were piled high, and he was among them. The curves veered sharper.

He gripped the wheel with both hands, kept his eyes close on the road that twisted over and around the growing mounds. The bases of the mounds spread, neared one to the other, then blended. the turns and mounds now followed in continuous and rolling succession. The sun slipped about the sky: now low on the horizon, now high in the heavens, and then lower even than the hill-tops.

He lost his location from the earth's center. His sensitive balances left him: when the car was turning right, his body was turning left; when the road dropped, his body rose. He knew it was not so—he had only to look at the road—but when he leaned from side to side or back and forth, he felt weightless in any position.

He pushed against the wheel, shoving his back stiff against the seat. He would at least stay upright with the car. The car burst over the top of one of the mounds; the road dipped, then jackknifed. He wrenched the wheel. The tires screamed and ground sand. A deep valley swept like a grey shadow before him, and the rocks and valley became mixed in a careening jumble, sometimes seeming to fly overhead: the valley grey, the black rocks surrounding and filling the car. Then there was a filling station jutting out between the mounds and the valley. The car glided in and stopped beside the pumps.

He cut the ignition and fell back against the seat, his head still dipping and whirling. That had been close, closer than he ever wanted to come again. From now on he would be more careful. He was too old for such frights—thirty now, and too old to tempt death.

The building behind the pumps sat unshaded in the sand, riding the jutting point where it was exposed to the sun from horizon to horizon. A high chimney tilted rakishly above it and was held in place by guy wires. Two round windows gashed its sides, the windows barely above the reach of the wind-piled sand. The door creaked and opened. An old man stepped out squinting in the sun under a matting of white hair. His feet shuffled and slid along in the sand. He was carrying a pitcher.

He thrust the pitcher through the window. The dry skin was stretched taut over an arm thick and roped with muscles.

"Drink all you want," the man told him. "You'll need it."

His face cracked and he tried to smile. Again he was surprised at the sound of his voice. "I need it already. Thank you."

"Welcome, welcome to all you want. I'm not near as mean as folks say; only you people shouldn't come through here when a man's resting. Ain't considerate."

He realized his own weariness. "I didn't mean to bother you, but I need gas. It's been a long trip; I've a long way to go."

The old man grunted, "There's plenty time." Then shaking

his head the old man went to the front of the car and raised the hood. He raised the pitcher. The water was so cold his teeth ached to its touch. The old man thumped the pitcher with his finger.

His lips lost the rim of the pitcher and the water spilled down his shirt.

"I'll fill the tank," the man said.

He started to protest but the water was cool on his chest. His head bowed and he rubbed his hand over his shirt, pressing the wet cloth against the skin. His head dropped lower. He was too tired to protest and too tired to sit there. He should get out, stretch his legs. He reached for the door handle, but the man was leaning against the door, the muscled arms reaching for the pitcher. He looked into the man's eyes. The glowing orbs looked straight into his, but they were hidden behind lids half closed as though to shield him from their full glare.

"You don't want to get out here," the man said. Then the glowing eyes took on a crafty look. "I ain't got nothing here. You wait'll you're in the valley. There's fine modern places there."

His hand dropped from the door handle. He just wanted to stretch his legs, but he was too tired to argue. The white-headed fool; he was probably crazy from the heat anyway; must be to live here in the sun this way without a soul to talk with.

"I'll even let you use my short cut to the valley and you'll be there in no time at all. About a half mile down the road. It turns off behind the biggest rock in these parts. Can't miss it."

If the old fool didn't want him to get out, then he wouldn't.

"It's a fine road, too. But no need for me to hold you here in the heat; you'll learn it your own self."

The man stepped back, and he wearily pulled the gear shift. The car swung smoothly onto the highway. He barely heard the man yell, "Can't miss it."

And the old man was right, he couldn't miss it; no doubt which was the largest of the rocks. Only he expected no road behind it. The old man was just trying to hurry him on. Besides, he wouldn't take a stranger's shortcut. No telling where or what it would lead to. It might even be a trick of the old man's to wreck and rob him. He had heard the sailors tell tales of such things, and he didn't trust those eyes.

He rounded the rock and was surprised to find there really was a road, a good road. Before he was even aware of turning the wheel, the car was on the shortcut. The road dropped straight into the valley, a natural road of packed sand. The car descended it in a long glide, and levelled off on the flat valley floor in an even flow of speed. There were no ditches to mark the road, but almost instinctively he followed the worn outlines of its course through the sand. The sand had changed: here in the valley it was bleached and bare, except for the occasional rocks which looked like lumps of alkali. The greyness of the valley made even the air seem grey, like light smoke. The air stung his nostrils; they felt lined with tiny veins. A round sun lowered itself in the smoky haze until it filled the windshield, still high above the horizon but hanging directly ahead over the road.

Then he saw another road, or what he thought was another road. It ran parallel to his. It lay like a streak of mercury in the sand, slowly converging with his. It was only when they ran side by side that he saw the other road was an easy-running canal of silvery clear water.

Then the land began to change; the bleached sand turned a rich brown. The canal now branched off into loamy-looking earth. And everywhere there were fields green with growth, the luxuriant green of the tropics that spread from one field to the next without pause. And there were houses, patioed houses opened to the sun and air, and spaced well apart with each resting serenely in the shade of deep-foliaged trees. Across the brimming canal, two cows were down under a tree chewing their cuds. Their soft eyes watched him as he passed.

All his life he had waited for a valley like this. It had been a long search, and hard, but he had found it. The problem now would be finding someone who would sell. All these places were well tended. He crossed his legs. The aching had diminished. It wouldn't be natural for places so well kept to be for sale. But he would stay here until he found one, and he would start asking right now.

They were getting off their stools when he asked, and his question brought smiles to their faces. They smiled at him as though he were a small boy.

Albert placed an arm over his shoulders. "You certainly are a newcomer. Clara and I have had two places since we've been here, and we're swapping with a man south of here next week. His house gets more sun than ours and he's tired of the glare. Just ask Tommy there. He sort of arranges all the moves. Just leave the information with him."

Arm in arm Clara and Albert moved towards the white tables. Albert looked back over his shoulder. "Meet us here next Sunday and let us know how you make out."

He watched them walk past the figures at the bar. The woman's shrill laughter rose above the hum of the voices.

He listened to the laughter and wanted to laugh himself. These people were like babies, ready at the price of a whim to give away everything he was searching for. He would take his time, look with care, and then get the richest land and the most secluded home in the valley.

He turned towards the bar. Tommy's hand was taking his empty glass.

"What kind of place you looking for?"

He stared at the thick hand holding the glass, listened with care to the familiar voice. He could feel the movement of the car through the stool. Deliberately he uncrossed his legs to receive its most delicate vibrations. Then slowly, as though there were all the time in the world, his eyes moved towards the voice, past the muscled arm, traveling the shirt's vast white plain. At the black tie they stopped. Above that he felt his gaze could not go. But the matted white head bent now to him. Carefully, deliberately the crisp curling locks hovered before him. And below the curling white, fixing him at last, the two eyes glowed.

The tires boiled and hissed through his brain: going again, going again, going again. . . . The latticed door slapped shut, and through the rhythm there came a harsh drumming like footsteps hurrying over the sand. Each step, as it advanced, molded the single word in his mind.

"What kind of place you looking for?"

Now he knew he had all the time in the world.

"It's gone," he said.

Gone.

He gripped the curving bar but the grip would not hold. He thrust his back stiff against the seat, the word whirling in his mind, his mind boiling, his crotch melting into the seat. Upon his lap lay the cold white hands. Even as he looked, a dark shadow crossed them. There was now only the word. It steadied in his mind. *Gone.* For a brilliant moment it hung there, then softly exploding, plumes of lilac leaf and cedar, green pain, filled all the void.

A MATTER OF FAMILY

BY CLAUDE F. KOCH

Matri Norberto Sorori Sancti
Pueri Cuius Narrata Haec Sunt.

I

LEANED against the railing on the sea side of the boardwalk and slid my foot out of my pumps. Just my luck with my hair done up for my birthday that *all* my brothers treated me to, to get my heel caught in a loose board or something, and now it was flapping like a biddy's tongue. Two fresh boys with large brown "R's" on white sweaters—they must have been college men because they weren't the least embarrassed to stand and stare and grin at me, and one was smoking a cigar that smelled awfully heady —these two fresh fellows tried to strike up a conversation on that old angle of sympathy. One said he'd carry me over to *The Break-ers* for a coke. "C'mon, curly," he said, "we'll carry you all the way home if necessary." I turned my back on them, though I couldn't do it in a ladylike way—having that darn shoe in one hand as I did. And then they came over and stood on either side of me, too close, and I tried to close my eyes and shut out their voices and think of the padding of feet pushing the rolling chairs behind me, and all the voices of kids in bathing suits, and the smell of the ocean. But the thick smoke of that cigar made me cough. "Go away, you," I said and opened my eyes and a gull flew past, and then I saw dad.

He was down on the beach a ways, sketching on a pad set on an old easel, and he had his back to me, but I couldn't mistake him. He was tall and thin, just as I can remember him from the very first memory, years and years ago when I rode on his shoulder long before the war, and mom herded the other four behind us down the boardwalk. That was my first memory of him, and it was here at Atlantic City too. I can't ever think of him apart from the sun and the salt air and the salt-water-taffy and cigar smells of the boardwalk. His elbows stuck out, brown from following the sun, I guessed—because none of us had seen him for a year now; and we just took it for granted that he had been at some other place along the coast, Florida or somewheres that he could pick up enough to live on and hear the ocean—but dad always called it the sea. The last year when Johnny ran into him he was demonstrating a gadget for opening cans and paring god knows what all outside a penny arcade by Convention Hall. And Johnny'd come back to the flat we'd rented with Gordie and Paul and Philip, and said "Well, I've seen the old man," and we set out right away, the five of us, to listen to him and buy a gadget. Every year since long before mom died he'd turn up that way doing some odd summer thing, and we'd always go get him and have a reunion, and even Philip, the legal eagle we call him, never could be really mad at him—and certainly not mom, who just took it for granted that that was the way he was after the war. His pension from the war came in every month, and he'd always sent her something now and then extra from the helter-skelter jobs he had. You'd have to be told he was total disability because you'd never know it looking at him there— he looked like any old beaten down fellow who'd gotten gray too soon picking up a slim living on the beach. I saw this as I tried to pull my fingers out from being crushed between that fresh college boy's and the cool rail of the walk.

"Now, princess," the fresh kid said, "you're in distress and we're here to see that you're done right by." He had a nice smile, like Gordie's, with the same kind of big, generous mouth. Mom used to say we should exhibit Gordie—that was in the days when Hunt's Pier had a Ubangi act the first year dad wandered away.

"You oaf," I said, and dug an elbow into his ribs. That's what comes of having four brothers: I learned how to crack ribs. I must have hurt because he grunted and pulled his hand away, and I hobbled down to the slim crowd leaning over the railing watching dad. There was a brown little girl with her hair to her waist on the edge of the rubbernecks, and dad must have seen her, because he was sketching her—yet he wasn't looking that way. All from memory, one glance, I guess—he could do that. He had that kind of memory, and it wasn't only for faces, but dates and names and birthdays and god knows what all. Something always came to each of us on a birthday though we mightn't of seen him for ages. Usually things he made himself out of driftwood or shells, gadgets that fell apart in a month or had strange smells when the sun got to them. Shell bracelets for me; once a conch shell for Johnny to give him the lonely holler of the sea back home in Philly because, I suspect, Johnny was like dad and he knew it. The last thing mom got from him was shell earrings and it was on their anniversary. That was three years ago and she wasn't able to get out of bed. We couldn't reach him to tell him because there was no return address on the parcel—just the postmark "Pensacola." Mom wouldn't take the earrings off for the rest of the month, but then at last she said I was to have them when she knew it was all up.

I took the other shoe off and stood in my bare feet beside the pigtailed kid and leaned my chin on the top rail, and one of those damn fresh college monkeys patted me and I whacked him with the shoes. Then dad looked around, just a quick disinterested kind of look, and seemed to not know me, but I knew that he did. He just seemed to take the both of us in, the kid and me, with those vague, good-natured, sunken eyes as indefinite colored as driftwood, and then he swung back again and kept working. But the pigtails disappeared with his quick crayon strokes that always made me proud of him and the head on his pad was all over curls. It isn't everyone whose dad can do that. And that's what it was finally, a snub-nosed kid of seven or so, with a monstrous head of brown curls, and I knew he had done me as I was that first year he went away. That must've been nine years ago, because when Phil was trying to talk mom into a divorce it was six years ago and I remember clear as rain his saying "This is three years' desertion, Mother." Only Phil called mom Mother. And mom turned away from the dishes (trust Phil not to do any) and winked at me drying. "I'm not deserted, son." Not by a long sight with that pile of dishes. Phil was in law school then, and he'd make a case of anything, without meaning much by it. "And beside," mom said, "Catholics can't get divorces." Phil's always been prissy as all get out: "A separation, then, Mother," he said, mincing each word like he'd a bad smell suspended somewhere. But mom smiled.

Then dad signed the sketch in a big hand: "Lolly," and drew a small lollypop in the corner which was what the nickname had been shortened from over those years, and took those big steps he had over without a sign that he knew me and held it up.

"Lolly, hey?" said one of those birds, "—that's right, you're sweet enough to eat." It might have been spoken to a stranger for all the attention dad paid. One of the college kids threw a quarter over into the sand and said, "Give it here, pop." And dad looked confused, as though the cigar smoke smarted at his eyes, and let it go. Then he fumbled in the sand for the quarter.

"That's mine," I yelled, and whacked that one over the head with the shoes, too.

"All right, all right, for pete's sake," and he dropped the sketch, bobbing and waving arms as long's a gorilla's, while the one with Gordie's mouth made a big pretense of hiding behind him.

"I'll see *you* at *The Breakers*," I said to dad who stood brushing the sand off the quarter and gave no hint at all that he'd heard. I set down the shoes and patted my hair in place, more for effect and to watch those two hulks' mouths hang open. Then I rolled up the sketch and picked up the shoes and strolled over to *The Breakers* and ordered two cokes.

Dad came to the open door by the salt-water-taffy counter and stood there shifting his feet. He had sure gotten gaunt and stringy since I saw him last, so god-awful burnt you'd say he'd been basted in the sun. He came clopping those old wooden sandals across the neat tiled floor of *The Breakers*—all white tile that I used to love so to feel cool beneath my feet when he brought me here as a kid like that pigtailed one. He was carting the sketch pad, and he shifted it up on the marble table and sat down—tentatively like you'd spread a seat cover that you didn't intend to stay put. He had just about as much substance front to back.

"Well, Lolly," he said, with a smile so small that it seemed to be fading out from something he'd said a moment ago.

"Who's watching your easel, dad," I said. For a minute he looked blank, as Johnny often did, but Johnny'd be putting on, because he had a memory like a steel trap. At first I thought dad was putting on too, but his hand shifted kind of aimlessly across the pad as if he was trying to pick out a tune by ear on a keyboard without any face, and I knew he'd forgotten it. That didn't strike me at first because I was watching his hand. I loved his hands. They were perfect and long and I'd always wanted them, but I got everything sawed off and short, legs and everything. I hated "curly" but I hated "shorty" worse. Mom's hands and his were meant to be held together and that's how I always thought of them because once they were always that way. Philip took me to the museum in Philly as a fourteenth birthday present last year—the cheapskate—but I did see a pair of hands there like mom and dad's worked out of a stone block that hadn't been finished. Theirs were finished, all right.

"You wait," he said, and got up and clopped off again. I saw those two wolves hitched up on the railing across the boards and grinning in, so I shifted deliberately with a look that was suitable and arch, like Grace Kelly's, and so I had my back to him when he came in again and I pretended that I was a lady waiting for a gentleman at a fancy table. He stood the easel up in the aisle between the tables and sat down; then he got up and put the pad on the easel and sat down again—all very quiet now that he didn't have to move far.

Then he looked at me with that little smile still fading from his face as though he were waiting for an answer.

"Drink the coke before the ice melts, dad," I said.

"This is very thoughtful." He stirred the ice about.

"The boys'd like to see you; we're at the same place," I said.

By the time dad got around to preparing an answer, a sawed-off character in a white striped summer suit and too neat to live was standing beside him and clearing his throat as if he'd a mouth full of distress and saying: "I hope you don't intend to leave these here much longer, sir?" The way he said "sir" I'd of whacked him with the shoes except they were on the floor under the table.

"Come on, dad," I said.

"Of course," and before I could stop him, he'd put the quarter on the table, but when he turned away to get the easel I slipped down two dimes with a hard look at the sawed-off manager and on the way out I dropped the quarter back in dad's pants' pocket. It didn't make any noise hitting anything else when it went in.

It was warm on the boardwalk curving up to the Inlet, with the sun everywhere about—in the dark brown velvet sheen of the boards, and the soft warmth up from them, and coming in on the breeze from the ocean that I could feel move against my face almost like mom's breath because it was warm and good. I took his pad from him and tucked the shoes and pad and sketch under one arm so that I could hold his arm; and we just strolled and dad began to talk. It was wonderful to listen to him, so colorful that everything seemed to, oh, seemed to be *alive*. He always knew more about us than you'd think, though it might be months old, and I knew how he did it—he'd take it into his head every few months when he could scrape together enough money to phone Jonathan Welk (that was his old friend, our next-door-but-one neighbor in Philly). But he never called us direct since that time just after mom died. Not that anybody'd ever said anything to hurt him, except possibly Phil in one of his god-almighty moods, but I think he just was afraid now that some other terrible thing like that might come to him out of the blue.

We had to walk slow because of his wooden clodhoppers, and that was the way I wanted it now—though once it had been fun to stretch my sawed-off legs to catch up with him, fun for mom, and me, and all of us.

"You're getting tall, Lolly," and I said, "Oh, get out," because it was one of our old jokes. "And that trip to the museum, how did it turn out?" Then I almost told him about the hands but it was too hard to get into words. Besides, it wasn't like him to ask me about something that'd happened more than a year ago and that I'd already told him about. I caught his hand then so that we wouldn't get separated in that awful mob that hangs about Garden Pier.

Dad's easel kept prodding people and we were mighty unpopular but I knew that without paying any mind to it because dad talked about the boys when they were young, and how Paul was almost smart enough to dodge First Confession but got caught and dragged down from where he'd hid in St. Pete's old belfry, and that he wouldn't have if he hadn't leaned against the rope. And how mom had almost sent me to a convent school at the Square but couldn't because of the war and no money. Now Paul's going in the seminary next year, and Philip's marrying some stuck-up model with nice long legs and everything else that counts and Johnny's headed for the navy, and that'll only leave Gordie and me. It seemed that nothing was ever lost the way dad remembered it all. And dad bobbed along with the easel poking people and every once in a while I'd crane around to look up into his face and see that gentle smile, and he kept searching back as he always did bringing all the old days back as though he were reaching for something and couldn't quite (but almost) put his finger on it. I didn't want the walk to end, though something kept bothering me every time I glared at someone complaining about getting nudged by that easel. I had never known him to forget anything before, but he'd almost left the easel there on the beach. I held his hand up against my cheek and rubbed it back and forth; there were tiny brown hairs matted across the back though his head was all over gray, but the skin was hard and cracked, not smooth like the stone hands at the museum that he'd forgotten I'd told him about and I wondered what kind of a menial job he'd had that winter. We had stopped for a minute and over dad's hand against my mouth I saw two old harpies staring as though they disapproved and I couldn't figure it out, and then I saw our reflection in a store window and it hit me so hard that I hated them all and their ugly old dirty minds and I wanted to hold dad and say, "Take me back with you, any-wheres; let me take care of you and bring Gordie and let everyone know it and clean your clothes and help you shave and have a home where you are even if it means being movers all the time." Because I didn't look like him at all; that was the terrible thing I saw in that window—and I didn't look like mom, who was tall and like a princess. I didn't look like anybody. . . .

Our apartment was on a side street in the Inlet section and this was the first year I'd noticed how beat-up the whole surroundings were. But from a corner of the kitchen window you could see through a slit between buildings (that somehow just went on and on as though all the buildings that were so cramped just opened up so that it would be there)—why, you could see like at the wrong end of a telescope a few yards of boardwalk and the chairs passing back and forth and beyond that the ocean that sometimes startled because it was so blue, as if it was painted there between the sick yellow brick and weather-worn wood houses. But when I left dad sitting on the edge of the couch in the old shoddy living room as though he'd a bus to catch and went into that hole-in-the-wall kitchen to make him tea, there were whitecaps on the blue in a tiny white line like lace at mother's throat or tiny white snail shells on a string that he'd made for me once. And I'd asked Johnny I guess last year why dad sat like that and he'd looked long at me with the way he had (he always had patience to answer me) and he said: "So you've noticed that too, Lolly." And I said yes I noticed things. "It's because he loves us and he's afraid, Lolly," Johnny said. He leaned down and kissed me on the forehead. " 'Jeepers creepers,' " he sang off key—only Paul can sing, " 'where'd you get them peepers?' "

"Go along with you," I said.

But now I took down the blue willow cup and saucer that didn't come from Sears but down through mother's family and was made in England years back. When I was little it used to always sit on the window sill facing the ocean wherever we were, with ivy in it or great ear-like leaves; and I remember watching it, in the white sunlight that burned off the ocean, so long that I thought I could go through the blue gate and under the Chinese arch into the garden where the tall ladies and stiff gentlemen in flowing robes walked by the water. And when we were home it was at the kitchen window and the blue gate was ajar into a green garden with a willow pond. Oh, when I was little then and mamma sang by the window that gate was into my spring garden; and I'm sure I did once run quick to the back door to get behind the cup and the blue gate and see the great ladies standing with slim hands upraised by the tall blue-capped gentlemen in our brick back yard. But maybe I only dreamed of that, and maybe I never dared look behind the cup to see if they were there. Because there is another picture of that back yard in my mind: a house of scrap boards close to the ground in the lowest branches of the mulberry tree and Phil and Johnny hanging down from it, and Gordie tossing an apple core clear over the neighbor's yard at Mr. Welk's cat on his clapboard fence. I took it into the parlor to dad, who hadn't moved from the edge of the couch.

"Ah," he said, "it isn't broken yet." There was a wonder in his voice. "Is this yours now, Lolly?"

"It's ours, daddy," I said. He held the cup in both hands. . . .

When he put it down, without a sound on the blue willow plate, he said: "I'm tired, Lolly."

That was the first time I can remember him saying that, and he didn't actually say it to me, but more to the mandarin on the cup.

What he did say to me, looking, as he often did when I knew he was thinking of more than he would say, at my hair and not my eyes— but over and beyond me as though someone'd be behind me and above me: "Is Philip's young lady here?"

I knew what he would say next, and I didn't want him to say it because it would be too off-hand and I got up to pour the tea to distract him, but he said it anyhow:

"You know, Lolly, I guess I'd better go. There're things I want to get done. . . ."

But what could he want to get done? And where? I looked down at him there, smiling up at me without any sign that he wanted anything or expected anything.

"Don't you dare," and I had to bite on my lip. "I'm making you tea."

He didn't argue, but when I'd brought the kettle back and poured the water over the tea bag in the blue willow cup, he stirred it slowly.

"If Philip comes in with his young lady," he said as though he were addressing the mandarin on the cup again, "he will be unhappy to find me here."

I didn't say anything and he continued to stir the tea. I always kept a pack of fresh *lorna doones* on the cupboard shelf for him every summer, even the summers when we never saw him at all— because they were the only kind of cookie I ever knew him to like. And I climbed up on a chair to get them down now, because they had to be kept out of Gordie's way even if he was seventeen and almost six feet. He'd eat anything that wasn't nailed down, mom said, and he wasn't getting any better with age, so I hid them with a mouse trap in front of them on a top shelf in the kitchen. I started doing that the year before we lost mom when she was mostly too sick to keep house and it became my job. Dad didn't come up that summer, and we found out later he'd got a job with a mangy circus out traveling the Midwest. That was something Johnny'd always wanted to do, and when dad told us about it the next summer, Johnny was all for giving up college where he had a full scholarship and going off with him right then and there; but dad said no, that one in the family was enough and that it was mom's wish that he should finish school and that was enough and so there was no argument.

We didn't talk any more. He was ragged, I could tell, by the way the cup shook ever so slightly when he lifted it; and once the tea spilled down his chin and he didn't have a handkerchief and I gave him mine though it was a scented one. He looked over my head again at that and smiled; and when I took the cup away, just in time to see a big sailboat, flashing white canvas and a great red painted lobster across it, move slow between the buildings out to sea, and come back, he was asleep—just sort of sprawled like he was sitting on a curb in the sun and not on a davenport at all. His breathing was so slight it frightened me for a minute, and I lifted his legs up and took off his shoes that were only wooden sandals with canvas uppers and propped a pillow under his head and spread a sheet over him though it was still warm in the late afternoon. He was my father, but I had not seen him asleep for years and years and he was like a stranger that way.

So I sat across the room from him and waited for the boys.

But watching him there I came to know why he looked a stranger and it made me easy in my mind again. Because of the pillow. You live with people for years and years and if someone asks you to describe them, you're stymied. I'm fifteen and I guess I couldn't describe my brothers for a police blotter or anything, except by one or two minutes you remember when they seem to be all there, truly there for once and forever. Like Gordie and the cookies. It was the pillow that told me why dad looked strange—that and the memory of mom pointing to Johnny one day asleep on that same couch. I was twelve and I remember it because I had just come in from watching them dance in the Ballroom of the Million Dollar Pier. You could see them dance from the boardwalk. It was the first time I ever cared to see anyone dance, but suddenly I saw it was beautiful—the music and behind the sound of waves and how graceful the girls and their fellows moved on the polished floor. I remember how strange I felt all the way home, and how it hurt to think of them. And I came in and mom was picking up magazines from the floor, looking drained out and older than usual. "Lolly," she said, but more to herself, "get a pillow for Johnny." He was asleep in the most uncomfortable mess on the couch. Mom stood over him and sighed, and I didn't know why. "He never settles himself comfortably," she said. "He just throws himself down." It all came before me so quick—so quick that I turned toward dad again, expecting to see mom there—and though she wasn't I got up, sure if I walked over to him she'd suddenly come and shake her head and sigh. And I stood over him and I saw Johnny and dad there on the couch and they were one. "Mom," I said to her out loud, "I know why he does it. . . ." Because he didn't care for himself, that was why.

Dad was still asleep when the knock came. I heard the feet first coming up the wooden steps (because we were a second-floor back apartment and didn't have a proper entrance), and I knew by the tapping and the stomping that it was Phil and his girl. They weren't saying anything so I knew they'd had another fight and would be in an awful mood. Phil glares at me when I call Allison his girl. "Allison is my fiancée—keep that in mind, Lolly," he says as though I was some felon or something. Then there was a knock —not the secret knock that we all use (two light, two heavy, one bomp)—Phil said that was silly when he started going to law school. Perhaps it is silly but we don't have enough of the old silly things any more. Anyhow, I started not having much time for Phil when he swiped my cat almost every night that I used to close up in my drawer in my bedroom at the old house in Philly because I wanted her to sleep with me. And Phil would sneak down after I was asleep and let the cat out because he said she'd smother though I knew different—all the boys wanted her to sleep with them but only Phil'd steal her off of me if I got her first at night.

I quick ducked into the bedroom and got a cover and tucked it in over dad so that old stuck-up Allison wouldn't see the rotten old clothes he was wearing, and then I opened the door and it was her all right, and Phil standing behind her with a sour look and his nose in the air.

"Dad's here," I said right past her to him, and I didn't get out of the way in any hurry.

"Well," that old snob Allison turned around to Phil—and let me tell you she could put on airs—even on those rickety old back steps. "Well, that won't make any difference, will it?"

"Of course not," though I got to admit Philip had the grace to be concerned. "Is he all right, Lolly?"

"He's all right *now*," I said, and I think he got the point, because he settled his chin down in his collar so that his neck wrinkled up like a turtle's. Oh, he'd be a success, all right; he had the double chin for it.

"And how are you, my dear?" she said to me.

"Peaches," I said, and wondered if I could stomp on one of her lacquered toes and get away with it if I'd turn quick. The door was open, but she blocked out the salt air with some god-awful svelte perfume. When she first came with Phil two years before, after she'd been finished at some slick swank junior college, she looked like Ingrid Bergman; now she looked like Grace Kelly. She always looked like someone else. And besides, she made everything look cheap: she could do that just by standing in a door.

Then there was a whoop downstairs, and it was Gordie, and I got to stomp on her after all. He was pounding up the steps and yodeling, and he was so *huge* that the old wooden steps shook and boomed like a flat drum; so I tramped across her and dug her in the ribs and it sure did me good, and fell right in Gordie's arms.

"Dad's home, Gordie! Dad's home!"

"Well . . . !" Gordie always made me feel good, because he's dumber than I am. "Hi!" he said. "How're you doing, Al?"

Oh, did that rile Phil; and, anyhow, old Allison wasn't doing so good. She was trying to hold her toe and her stomach and look like Grace Kelly at the same time.

"Allison has been injured," Philip said. "Come in, dear; you poor thing." He gave me the nastiest look.

"I'm awful sorry, Allison," I said. "Did *I* do that? I'll get you some epsom salts. . . ."

But she didn't want to be helped; except by Phil. She leaned all over him, and he was as sticky as cotton candy. So they made up, and I guess I did my good deed for the day.

"Well, let's have a party," Gordie said. He's seventeen, but I fit in under his arm, though he's not the one to encourage it. Today, though, with Allison sitting there on the old wing chair with her back up, and Phil hovering over her like an offended waiter, I made up to Gordie—I wasn't going to cross that room in front of *them* like an outsider. It was such a small room, though I hadn't thought of it before until Allison sat in that chair with her back out from it and her arms pulled in as though she didn't want to be contaminated.

In front of dad Gordie pulled up short and teetered a bit on his toes: "Is he all right, Lolly?" He wagged his head toward the cover. Gordie'd learned to keep his hands off things; he's kind of destructive. "Has he got a chill?"

"He's all right." I pulled his arm and got him in the kitchen. "It's *her*," I said.

"Al?" he winked at me. "Pretty sharp," he said; "what's she got to do with it?"

"Oh!" It was like hinting to a post. "Look," I said, "get *them* out, will you? I want dad to have a chance to sleep."

"Oh sure." I have to say one thing: Gordie was always cheerful. I guess he was never burdened with thoughts. I put on a pan to boil water, and I could hear him talking about Hunt's Pier, and then they all went out.

I didn't want any tea, I just wanted her to go. Everyone has to get married, of course, except Paul who's going to be a monk—but why did she have to come between us the way she did, so that Phil started to live up to *her*? He was always a pain in the neck, but we knew it. I guess what griped me was that *she* didn't see it; that was the way people were, for her.

Now she'd be taking Phil's name, that was dad's name and mine. We didn't need more family; we needed to hold what we'd got. That's the way I felt.

Through the aisle between the buildings I could see the sailboat passing again, dipping and catching the sun on some metal thing on the mast so that it flashed a signal down between the buildings almost, and something turned over in me right under my heart. I almost knew what it meant. It wasn't only that so much time had passed while I was in there with dad and Gordie and Phil and old Allison, so that the old boat could have gotten out and back to the inlet and out again—and I hadn't realized that time had passed. It wasn't only that, though there it was coming right back past again, dipping again there at the end of the corridor between the buildings, just as before—only this time that flash of light hit me between the eyes, and I thought: *Could anything really come back again, just as it was, even for a moment? And if it did, would I be there to see it?* Suppose there was no signal, and it was past before I knew? Suppose I was asleep, like dad, and time was running on and on? I could hardly breathe; I never hurt like that before, and it wasn't really in my body, though I pushed hard against my heart to make it hurt where I could be sure of it. It wasn't any good. I turned my back on that window, and opened the kitchen door onto the little rickety back porch where mom liked to sit on a beach chair because she could see across the roofs of houses toward the inlet and the drawbridge over to Brigantine. I put the same old chair out there each summer; though when mom was here I never sat on it and neither did anyone else in case she wanted to—to catch her breath and the sun that always beat down there because there wasn't any roof, except the canvas top that you could pull over the chair itself.

The bridge was up to Brigantine; you couldn't see what was going on though because the roofs were in the way, but you could see the red and green lights strung up there on the ends of the girders, even in daytime, as though there was some kind of celebration and they'd hung out the lanterns.

It was quiet up there, and a little wind blew the sun across my face and I could feel a tingling where I was beginning to burn; it would hurt tomorrow, but now it was like wearing a sea-scented, downy muff across my cheeks. I ran my tongue across my lips and tasted the salt. Then the sea breeze slackened off and there was the kind of calm that sucked in sails and dropped them against the masts. I sat on the chair and waited; for the wind to pick up again, I guess—I don't know. The bridge was up for so long, I tried to guess what would be coming; but sometimes it would just be an outboard motor with a sail for spare—some wobbly old fishing boat that could hardly make knots, and it would tie up the traffic for a good half-hour putting through. On other days I liked to sit up there and imagine what was passing under that bridge, and when Gordie and I were children we'd bet how long it would be before it'd go down—that was after he'd got his Ingersoll for his eighth birthday, and neither of us could really tell time except for the five minuteses across the face. But today I didn't want anything strange, and this seemed awful strange to me—the long wait while the wind stopped.

Then I saw I wasn't the only one waiting. My eyes began to water from staring at the bridge in that bright sunlight; it was important to see the bridge go down, the way it's sometimes important to touch every lamp post on the boardwalk for whole blocks at a time; but the sun made me dizzy, and I looked across the street and there were two others very still. Across the street the roofs were lower, and some had sun porches built out on them of old unpainted wood, eaten away here and there by the weather and the salt air. On one of the porches just below a little fire escape out of a third-floor window, a woman was stretched out on pillows in a bathing suit, with a towel across her face; and on the fire escape a man was standing, watching her. None of us moved; nothing moved—not the bridge nor the air nor the clouds. And very far away it seemed there was a little sound, like an outboard motor starting up far beyond the houses out in the back bay. And the man started down the fire escape, very slowly, toward her; and out of the corner of my eye I saw the bridge going down. She didn't move, and how could she breathe with the towel across her face when I could scarcely breathe watching her? He kept coming very slowly, not saying anything. I took great gulps of air; it was like drowning, and I couldn't call out to her. I jumped up and barged through the screen door, slamming it behind me.

"Lolly?" Dad was sitting up, looking sleepy and bewildered. I ran over to him and sat down in a heap at his feet and put my head in his lap. "What is it, Lolly?"

"Why don't you stay with us?" I said, not making much sense. "Why don't you stay this time?"

"But Lolly." He ran his fingers back and forth through my hair. "You see I'm here. Of course, I'm here. What is it, Lolly?"

"Well," dad said, "just like old times." But it wasn't, because it was supper, and that godawful Allison was preening herself at the inlet end of the table by the window. I guess she wanted to be seen by the gulls.

They were all falling all over themselves playing up to her, except dad, who was waiting to put through a call to Jonathan Welk; and who wouldn't have done it anyhow, because *he* was used to having a *lady* in the house. He wouldn't tell us why he wanted to talk to Mr. Welk, but he was distressed in a quiet way when the operator kept getting a busy signal. Finally he came in to the table, and sat between Johnny and me. "I hope Jonathan isn't having any trouble," he said. He sat between us, not eating though I had cooked corn on the cob especially for him, but rubbing his terribly thin hand along the side of his jaw.

"Dad," Paul said, "whatever happened to those seascapes you did two summers ago?" I saw old Allison's ears twitch at that.

"I have them," I said. "They're put away, with the other things dad did in Florida." He hadn't done anything in Florida, and I didn't have his seascapes or anything else, but as long as Allison was poking around, I wasn't going to admit it.

"I didn't know you painted, Mr. Redding?" Allison was as sweet as treacle. I could have carved her.

"These were good work," Paul said. He spoke very quietly, and he was very sure of himself in a nice way. He'll be a bishop. "I was talking to Judd down at the pier about putting some in his shop. What do you say, dad?"

"I certainly have no objection," dad said.

"Could I see them, Mr. Redding?" That woman's painted too carefully for my taste; you can't trust people who're so darn good with makeup. She knew how to lean her chin in her hands and keep all the wrinkles down at the same time. "I love art of all kinds. Are they water color? Gouache?" I'd have gouached her if I had my way.

Phil was looking around the table as if he'd just beaten the pope on a point of canon law: "Allison minored in the history of art in college," he said.

"Oh?" dad said, smiling at her like she was one of his own kin. "You've been fortunate, Allison. All I know on that subject has been picked up haphazardly."

"You should have kept them, dad," Johnny said. "If Lolly's got them, we're out of luck. I think she still has her first teething ring." I'll take that from Johnny. He leaned across dad and patted my hand. "Come on, sport, confess they're in your hope chest."

"They're in Philly," I lied, "in the cellar—we're waiting for frames."

"I think," Phil got his two cents in, "it would be a wise idea to drop in tomorrow when I'm on my way to Cartwright and Sloan and pick them up. If Judd will show them we must not let the opportunity pass." I knew what he wanted: he wanted to improve dad. He was always trying to trap him into some steady job. Phil couldn't of left the garden of Eden alone; he'd of pruned the apple trees.

"You do that," I said. I'd worry about that in the morning.

"Have you exhibited before, Mr. Redding?" Allison was back, showing her teeth like they were her own.

"No," dad said, "and I hardly think Mr. Judd will care to hang these."

"But it's such a wonderful thing to be able to paint at all." That Allison could sound as if she meant it, all right—I give her credit for that. "Did anyone inherit your talent, Mr. Redding?" she said, beaming around the table like a tooth-paste ad. "Lolly?"

"I couldn't paint a stick." It made me mad, why she should play up to me. I didn't need her attention.

"Perhaps when you go to college, you'll find you can do that," she said, "and a number of other things. The time's not far off, you know."

"I hope she will," dad said, and I wished for once he wouldn't be so darned polite to just *anybody;* but he couldn't help it, I guess. It was his nature.

"She's got a year to go," Johnny said. "She'll be out of high school at sixteen. And you wouldn't think to look at her she had any sense at all." He didn't smile, and there they were all looking at me as though they'd just discovered something. Johnny's mouth had that peculiar twist, like dad's, so tender that it always made me want to cry. I just sat there; I didn't know what to do. Then Allison put in her two cents again:

"When you get back to the city, Lolly, you come up to my college. We'll talk to the dean. Perhaps you can get a scholarship."

I was so mad and sad at the same time I almost burst; but I saw dad looking at me, and I kept the peace.

"That's very considerate, Allison," dad said. It was awful; perhaps she could take him away from me too. Then he said: "You there, Gordon," and it was no effort to him to change the subject, "I hear you're starting on the Beach Patrol."

"Why, yes, dad," Gordie grinned around at us, "came through yesterday. How did you find out?" He wasn't really surprised; we'd long since stopped trying to figure those things out—but I knew Gordie; he was proud of it, and he wanted to keep the talk going.

"Captain Pierce is an old friend," dad said. I'd forgotten; that accounted for his sketching on the beach without a license. "I knew him when your . . ." He let the sentence hang there, rubbing his chin and looking over Gordie's head toward the kitchen door. He wasn't confused, and he hadn't forgotten; he just stopped talking, and I watched the little smile form instead of words—the kind of smile that old people sometimes get when they see a child after their own have all grown up. But he was thinking of mom—I knew, though he always stopped short of saying her name. If I could remember all the times, like that one, when he'd almost let me see what they'd been like together—if I could remember and someday ask him to finish those sentences—why, I think I would know a great and important thing; though what it would be, I can't be sure. But it was like opening a door part way on a wonderful room that'd always been right there, off the parlor—a room with a light under the door, with people in it, and laughing, and sounds of old music and rustling of silk dresses, and the scent of shrub in chests. As I thought of the room it became more familiar, and pretty soon it was their room in Philly; but that wasn't the one I meant really, and the strange and wonderful one faded, and there was dad smiling that little smile and ignoring all the talk around him about Gordie and the beach patrol and how much it would bring in, and how Captain Pierce probably recognized Gordie's name on the application and so spoke up for him. I could see that Allison didn't realize how many important people like Captain Pierce dad really knew. Perhaps when you get finished off at those snob factories nobody is really important any more, except yourself. I was sorry I had put out the good china and lighted the two candles; she might have thought it was done for her.

It was done because mama loved supper above other meals, though she had much more to do and she was much more tired at the end of the day. She spread a tablecloth, and lighted candles, and put out the medium-good china—the china with the pale rose pattern and the faded gold band; and in the spring and summer she had rambler roses or wild sweet peas on the table from the small plots along the edge of the bricked yard. But even in the autumn and the winter, the evening meal was always among roses in my mind, and even now when I smell roses I can feel the crisp tablecloth and smell also the wick of the hot snuffed candles that always dripped across the cloth. She wanted everyone around her at supper, and dad's place was always left, with the plate and silverware and napkin set out, and the chair pulled over to the table for him so that, whenever he would show up, he'd know we welcomed him. I still did that, and sometimes I'd forget and set a place for her; especially on those days when I did not dare think she was gone. . . .

"Sometimes she's moody like that," Philip was saying, and I realized that he was talking about me!

"Don't you worry about me," I said.

"Of course not," Allison said, with all her company manners. "Lolly's just dreaming. We all do that, don't we, Lolly."

"Lolly doesn't dream; she hallucinates," Johnny said, and I kicked him under the table.

"She's got a boyfriend." Gordie tried one of his deadpan idiocies on me, and I resolved then and there to fix his wagon. He's a milk-drinker, a health-addict, always flexing his biceps. I got up to get him some milk, meaning to pour enough of it down his neck to dampen his spirits, when dad caught my arm.

"I think," he said, "I'll ask you to try to get Jonathan again for me, Lolly." He cleared his throat a bit, and looked up at the ceiling. "Would it inconvenience any of you if I asked him down over this weekend?"

"Of course not, dad," Paul said, very quickly—because dad had not done anything like that since the war, and it caught us embarrassed.

"I . . . ah . . . am not feeling quite up to visiting the city at the moment," dad said, "and I have a yearning to see Jonathan. It's been four years now—in fact, Paul, it was the day you took the scholarship examination. John pitched a particularly disastrous game in the Park that day—thirteen hits, if I remember correctly?"

"That stays with *me*, as well," Johnny said.

"And Gordon made off with one of the balls, I think. You have mended your ways, somewhat, son."

"Yes, sir."

"And Philip, Allison, looking every inch the future solicitor, began his clerking at Sloan and Cartwright."

"Cartwright and Sloan, dad."

"Of course."

"And what about Lolly, Mr. Redding? She was in this too, wasn't she?" I hated her for that; she was mocking him: she didn't know enough to see that this was *his* life he was talking about, not ours.

"Lolly had the measles," dad said, just as though she'd asked a lady-like question. It was true. I remember sitting in the darkened bedroom where I was supposed to save my eyes, and hearing dad and mom and Mr. Welk talking downstairs. That afternoon seemed to last forever, perhaps it was because I had to be in the darkened room, and I wasn't allowed to read; and the big old console radio was too heavy to move upstairs. So I sat and listened to the tick of the hall clock, and the voices downstairs, and I wondered if the afternoon would never end. When I think of time standing still, I think of that afternoon; and now as I listened to dad I knew that I would give my eyeteeth for that afternoon again, and I would sit in the dark contented forever if I could hear those voices downstairs, even if I didn't know what they were saying. But in my memory of it I still strained to hear. That was an important conversation, too—it must have been, everything but the words was so clear to my mind. And once mama laughed. Her laugh was different from anyone's I know: I thought that if a slim, clear fountain should rise out of the willow pond in the formal garden on our blue china cup, it would be like her laugh. Her humor was quiet and steady, like the pond. Then Allison was laughing, affected, high and gushy, like chlorinated water pumped through a hose; and Philip—like something seeping through a broken pipe; and all the rest. Even dad was smiling.

"Now what?" I said.

It was that Gordon, with a silly napkin on his head, and a hangdog face: "Does *she* bleed," he said, "when she's sick." Chatter, chatter, chatter—it's like nursing a cage of grounded squirrels. *"I* remember that one—she threw a box of powder at me when I took up her juice. Mean! I tell you . . ."

That did it. I said: "Excuse me, I'll get dessert." And on the way back I did pour the milk down his neck.

II

"Lolly," dad said after supper, "when Philip doesn't find those watercolors in the cellar, you'll have some explaining to do."

"What did you do with them, dad?"

"Jonathan is keeping them, at the moment."

"Well, why didn't you tell Philip?"

"The whole matter caught me rather unawares. I did them for your mother, you know."

Everyone had left, and I was proud of the way dad said goodby to Allison. People talk of old-fashioned courtesy, and I guess there are fashions in that like in hair-do's; but courtesy with dad was as real as his elbow-bone—no fashion, but foundation that he could no more ignore than he could ignore his skeleton. She was subdued, for her; she had probably never met a real gentleman before.

Paul wanted to help me with the dishes, but I wanted to have dad to myself—so I told him to go to a novena, or something. Finally, he went with the rest to see Allison to the train, and we had some peace at last.

Dad poked around in his pockets for a few minutes, and he finally said: "Lolly, what happened to my pipe? I left it on the corner of that bureau."

It was true, he had left it there—but that was last summer. I had it put away with fresh tobacco in my box—hope chest, Johnny calls it—and I watched him light it on the back porch. There was still an hour of daylight, and he settled on the beach chair to smoke. I had seen him do just that so many times during so many past summers, that I felt I was being given something back, some thing that I had almost lost, that I didn't know I had been in the way of losing until he settled down there.

"Now, Lolly," he said. "We won't try to exhibit those pictures. I'll get Jonathan to bring them with him, and I want you to have them. They'll last a while, you know; and they really aren't bad at all."

It was his first gift to me as the lady of the house; and even though it had come about more or less by accident—as an afterthought, you might say, I knew how important it was. All the really big things come by accident, like Darwin reading Malthus, and that science-fellow who stumbled on his big idea on the top of a bus, and Johnny going in the navy because he went up the wrong stairs at the Customs House and missed the Marine floor, and met a petty officer he liked. It took no time to do the dishes, because I was imagining all the places in the Philly house where the paintings would go well.

Dad was asleep when I finished. I covered him. Everything was quiet. No one was lying on the roof across the way. The door to the fire escape was closed. It was like the conversations I never quite heard downstairs when I had measles. I would never know about that. But I was too content with the thought of the pictures to have it bother me.

This was the best time at the shore, this and early morning; especially when the tide is out, and you can walk along the edge of it and know that the few people on the boardwalk are walking along the edge of something too. They are quieter then, and they steer clear of the shops and loaf in a thoughtful way along the railing. During the day the boardwalk is just a street like any other, but in the morning and in the evening, just before the light changes, it's truly board sounding hollow under your feet, and lifted over the edge of the ocean there like a boundary. I like to get farther out, to take off my shoes and walk half-in and half-out of the last curling of the water. I imagine then that I can go either way; that I can make a wonderful decision if I want to. I can never really be sure what the decision is, but just being in that state is good. I find beautiful things by the way, while the sandpipers start up and run on ahead, and the ends of waves make a little sound as faint as grackles in the back yard just before sun-up.

So I walked down 5th Avenue toward the beach. There are no trees like at home; the cement and the pushed-in, jumbled wood and brick and asbestos-siding of the rooming houses and little hotels are as bare as dunes to the sky. The street is a straight line to the boardwalk. In the evening it's as soft as crayon to the eye. I was the only one on the street—it was still supper-time—and on the boards the people walked away, up and down. I went in under the Walk where the sand was damp still from the afternoon tide, and took off my loafers. Out along the water's edge the sand was salmon-tinted and the ocean a dark green, rippled like artificial stone. Far down the beach a dog was barking, and terns cried like lost children from the pilings. The breeze picked at my hair and patted against my cheek like soft gloves. A person can be alone at the edge there and not be lonely. I slapped my feet in water on one side and wet sand on the other, stomping down to hear the splash and the suck of the sand. Sand crabs burrowed in ahead of me, each one going a separate way, like the terns and gulls that circled alone and made their cries. I didn't disturb them; I was as independent as any of them.

Up farther on the beach, nearer the boardwalk, there were patches of seaweed and the shells and claws of crabs—all the waste of a day of tides—but down along the edge it was clean. I wanted to leave my dress on a piling and walk into the furry breeze to the end of the island, and beyond, perhaps, with never any company but sandpipers and sand crabs. I was thinking that, and suddenly I was under the pilings of Garden Pier without expecting it. The breeze had no leeway there, and it was very still and very dark and very cold. There were no gulls there, and water sounded different; it splashed against the bulkhead of the pier with a threatening sound.

I was alone then, and the twilight on either side of the pier supports seemed far away. A huge pipe opened just in front of me and ugly discolored water seeped from it. The pier came together with the boardwalk like the back of a frightful throat, and the broken pilings from some old construction jutted up in the dimness back there like teeth. I was so upset that I stepped into an old piling hole partially filled with water and lurched over onto my knee in the cold damp sand, and I was scared. I don't know what of. It never looked that way under here in the day when people strolled back and forth and children pushed boats in the pool. Then I heard someone call my name. I swear I heard someone say "Lolly"—very low, and far back in that throat of darkness. But no one moved there, and I began walking, fast, but casual, toward the far side of the pier. The pilings stretched like bars on both sides of me. It was awful strange, to have my name come out of nothing like that. I was too proud to look back, and so all the way to the edge of the pier I felt something following me, close enough to touch me; and I knew I would scream if it said my name again.

When I came out on the other side, the whole earth had changed; the sun was down at the level of the rooftops in back of the stores. Across the boardwalk, over the pilings, out to the ocean horizon, it was as though a golden net had been flung, and through the strands of the net the old beaten shore and sand and bulkhead glistened like treasure far under the sea. Then I stole a look backwards and saw that the gold was beyond the pier too; but in between, the darkened maze of sand and pilings where I had left my name.

Just for a moment I thought I might not get back, but that was foolish because the steps were right there up to the boardwalk and

I didn't have to go under the pier at all. So I shook off the feeling about the pier and faced down the beach again. I didn't see anyone at first, just the bare beach kindled under the net of gold; and then, down at the next jetty, a lady stood as though she were rising out of the sea.

It happened so suddenly that I knew I had imagined it, like the voice from the pier. But then when I saw she was truly there, it seemed that the voice must be there, too—and I was caught on a line between air and darkness, and the sea and light, and a lady rising as though she'd been summoned by a magician that I couldn't see there where the sand seemed to have molten gold behind it. Her back was to me, and her hair was down to her waist, and the wind blew her white dress against her. She stretched her arms out like a priestess praying to the setting sun. I couldn't move for fear I'd distract her and interrupt whatever ritual she was following. While I watched, she ran her hand under her hair and fluffed it out, and then she stepped down, holding her body straight and moving only her hips. As though she had a burden on her head, of fruit and jewels.

The sun was down behind the boardwalk stores now; I didn't look at it (I couldn't take my eyes from her), but I could see the shadow advancing up from the water, and a color like old rose was changing everything into a strange uncertainty. Her dress and her skin and her hair were all of a piece with the sand and the pilings and the sky. I looked down at my dress and hands for fear I had changed, too. I had. Then she turned toward me. When she saw me she hesitated, as though she were surprised, and then she came toward me slowly and I saw she was smiling.

"It's late, child," she said when she came up to me.

"Yes. You're not going through *there?*"

"Of course I am."

"I'd be scared."

"Then come with me." She held out her hand. A huge oval stone of a clear, whitish kind was on a finger.

She wasn't young, but there were no lines in her face, and her body was full, as though she had children of her own. Her face was tranquil, and in that light it was as though she wore a calm mask. She seemed detached from such things as the creepiness I felt with the pier behind me. Even her hand, when I touched it, didn't so much hold mine as guide it. She was kind, and austere, and there was something odd about her features, as though she were eastern like the queens of old dynasties in Junior history.

"Come along," she said. "I'll keep you company."

Where would she have taken me, I wonder, if I had gone with her?

There was too much darkness now. I couldn't see the patch of light beyond the pilings of the pier. So I loosed my hand and said as politely as I could: "No, thank you. My brothers are waiting for me down the beach." She was looking straight into my eyes all this time, and she must have known it wasn't true; but she nodded her head as though she knew more than that and understood: "Then you must go to them." She walked away from me, gracefully; and when she got to the pier, for just a moment she stood there and turned and raised her hand, and I thought how she looked like the caryatids that held the old temple roofs as easily as baskets on their heads.

I was very tired; so tired that my arm ached when I waved to her. It seemed that hours had passed since I first went in under the pier; and since I had covered dad on the porch, days might have gone by and been forgotten. It was that way this summer: whole blocks of time would drift by like the sails through our kitchen window, and then there'd be moments that lasted and lasted, everything fixed in place like the figures on the willow cup or the children playing statues under the plane tree outside our living room window at home. I couldn't play any more, of course; but I watched them from the window sill, and sometimes I thought my heart would stop when they did and everything would be the same forever.

Then it was dark—that quick. We used to play, Gordie and me, that the sun was a ship burning in the bay behind the stores and the houses and the church steeples of the city, and the one to see the last streamer of fire through the aisles between the boardwalk shops could claim her cargo. On the way home between mom and dad we'd argue about it: what the cargo was, and each of us would try to outdo the other in imagining what we had salvaged when we won. My biggest haul was a unicorn, but Gordie wouldn't believe it, and I couldn't pronounce it, and I had to show him the picture —but that was a month later when we got back to Philly and Johnny's books. We argued all month about it; I could have asked mom or dad, but it was against the rules of the game. That rankled

Gordie for three years, because the best he could come up with was a blackamoor and then we just stopped playing. That summer I read for myself that there are no unicorns. And that there are blackamoors. I was glad, for Gordie's sake. He never asked for anything, and that was a hard year all around. But he was too old.

So it was just the sun that went down.

III

That Saturday Jonathan Welk came; dad and I met him at the train. I saw him first, way up the platform, towering over the mob with kids and lunch baskets who were down just for the day. He walked like I'd imagine a tree would walk if it could, stiff but swaying from side to side. He came straight down the platform, not pushing anyone, but not diverted to either side once he'd seen us. People seemed to sense him behind them and make way.

Our neighbors thought Jonathan Welk was queer. He once told me that he leaned against trees for strength, that what was in the tree flowed into him; and once he told me he would never die. Johnny said he was an Original, and Phil said he was a nut; I know Paul prayed for him on the sly, and Gordie got him to do his homework. He lived next door to us in the house he'd been born in, and he taught in a fashionable Catholic college for girls. He'd served in the same outfit with dad in the war, and I once overheard him say to mom that he worked with women all day and he'd be damned if he'd marry one. He was Uncle Jon to all of us, and we were as close to a family as he had.

I wanted to run up to him, but dad held me back with that little smile on his face. He enjoyed watching Jonathan come through the crowd, and I wondered what he was remembering that gave him such pleasure. They didn't shake hands, but stood, a few feet from one another, just looking at each other and smiling.

"Well," Jonathan said, "home is the sailor." He shifted the green bag that anyone else would use for laundry but that he used for books, from his right hand to his left, and held out the hand to me, palm up, and I put both hands in it; and one hand closed around both of mine.

"Lolly, you've lost six inches since I saw you last. Has it been baked away?"

"Oh, stop it." I felt that I could leave all that bothered me in that hand of his.

"She'll be a midget soon at this pace." He hitched the bag across his shoulder and pulled my arm through his. I put my other arm through dad's and we crossed the waiting-room together.

"I can't offer you much choice in transportation," dad said.

"I have no objection to walking," Jonathan said, "as long as we stay away from the beach. Beach and ocean are two aspects of this life I cannot tolerate. Have you no tree-lined streets?"

They talked back and forth over my head; I didn't listen to what they said—just the murmur of their voices like a comfortable hum of bees; and their arms holding me on either side like strong fences.

The place had three bedrooms: I had mom's to myself now, the one I had shared with her for as far back as I can remember. Then there was the room that Dad and Johnny slept in, and the third for Phil and Paul and Gordie. Phil had gone home, and now Johnny moved in with the other two. So I unpacked Jonathan's bag in the room he was to share with dad. I asked if I could do it for him, and he looked startled for a moment. He had forgotten he was carrying a bag. "Oh, yes, thank you, Lolly. And your pictures are in there— rolled up, so be careful."

Bags are odd things to go into. I liked to imagine they were packed by people with orders to get out or be shot, and so they could take only what they absolutely needed to live. Jonathan's sack looked more like that kind of thing than most, I guess. The pictures were there, very carefully rolled and set in a cardboard tubular container—but that was all that made much sense. There was one black and one dark brown sock, a huge bottle of sunburn lotion, a pair of monstrous sneakers, a sweatshirt with Holy Child College for Women stitched across it, and six paperbacks. It looked as though it'd been packed *after* he'd been shot. The sweatshirt was small size, and the paperbacks were all mysteries with the wildest covers. He came in while I was unpacking, and leaned against the doorjamb, watching me. "Where's my shaving cream?" he said.

"You'll have to borrow dad's. That's not all you forgot."

"I never forget anything, young lady. I planned it this way, to test your charity. That sweatshirt's for you."

It was what I hoped. I did not want to grow so quickly to that

time when Jonathan would not be able to bring an odd thing—
and the boys mostly had.

"And the books are for Gordon—to improve his mind."

"Thank you, Uncle Jon, for both of us." I turned with the
sweatshirt in my hands, holding it up for him to see how well it
would fit. "The very latest thing," I said.

"Later than you think, young lady."

Dad came in: "When you get settled, Jon, I'd like to talk to
you. Perhaps we could stroll along the Walk."

"I've never been on a boardwalk in my life. But if you say
so . . ." He seemed to reach across the room to pull the sneakers
from my hand: "Those are mine; get your own."

I held on to them, and we tugged back and forth. He was a
strange man; I don't ever remember being uncomfortable with
him, ever feeling that he was pretending an interest in any one of
us, so that we had to pretend in turn. Most adults are on stage; I
could see that now in my own relations with the children of our
block in Philly.

"Watch his arm, Lolly; his pencil arm." Dad was standing with
his head cocked to the side when I gave up. He had changed his
shirt, and wore an old sweatshirt with the sleeves rolled up, and a
pair of summer pants that'd shrunk so that they came to only
within four or five inches of his shoe tops; but he looked like a man
who was rich—it's hard to describe an expression like that: it's
something behind the face that shows through the way spring
shows through individual trees and shrubs. I might not have noticed it, except just then I felt that way myself; imagine, and all it
was, was roughhouse over an old pair of sneakers.

"Lolly," dad said, "you don't mind waiting here, do you?
When the boys come home, you tell them Jonathan is here." He
picked up the cardboard tube and weighed it in his hands for a
moment. Then he handed it gravely to me.

"We'll see the town tonight, my girl," Jonathan said.

I took the tube into the bedroom that had been mama's and sat
on the bed. The ends were open, and I could squint an eye and
look through it. Dad and Jonathan would be walking up 5th Avenue now toward the boardwalk. I ran into the kitchen, and by
standing on tiptoe I could spy through the tube onto the street.

They were just coming out from beneath the roof of the porch below, and I followed them like a sailor in a crow's nest—the space was round like a world, and they filled it almost. They were walking very slowly, their heads bent; dad's hands were clasped behind his back, and that funny, shambling and bobbing step of his was odder than ever next to Jonathan's stiff tramping stride. They walked away, getting smaller and smaller, and there was no way to focus this spy-glass to bring them back to me. Soon they passed into the crowd among the rolling chairs, and I didn't even see the direction they took.

Back in the bedroom again I sat on the edge of the bed and looked at the tube. Try as I would I could not remember what the pictures had been like, but everything *that* year was blurred for me; all I could remember was that they had come through the mail too late, and Paul had taken them in and spread them on the dining room table. I remember sitting in the corner of the living room under the stairs where it was dark and out of the way. Perhaps I saw them when I must have moved them from the table to set it for supper that night, and that must have been when Jonathan had taken them; because he came in from next door each evening at supper for a month or so and was just *there* if we needed him.

Mom had never seen these paintings that were made for her; and all my excitement of the other day faded in the face of those second thoughts. They were some sort of communication between her and dad. Should I really look at them as I knew I wanted to— as an eavesdropper, to see in them what dad put there for her and what she would know to look for? It didn't seem right. I never thought I was alone and no one would see: I knew that she would see.

The room was quiet, and I listened far back in my memory for some answer. If I opened it and could not see what it was that he was saying to her—would it mean that I could not be what she would have wanted me to be? That I could not make the home for them all that she wanted them to have?

My hand was cold and damp when I picked up the tube again so that my fingers made a dark smudge across the cardboard. Then there was a terrible roar and the old tube went clattering to the floor and rolled under the bed, and Gordie came barging in with the old mousetrap dangling from the fingers of his right hand—

bellowing that he'd murder me and serve me up in pie, and screaming for the iodine.

Gordie always roars; it's the sure sign he's not hurt. And the ham in him won't let him miss a chance.

"This serves you right," I said to him. "Those are dad's. Keep your greedy paws off the *lorna doones.*" The trap was so weak I could pry it loose with two fingers.

He stuck the sore fingers in his mouth: "There's nothing to eat in this house. I'm starved. Can't even get anything to eat in my own house. What do you want me to do? Beg from door to door . . . ?"

"You're fading away." I pulled his fingers down to my level. There was a slight pink line across the knuckles. "We get some big rodents, I tell you."

"It couldn't happen anywhere else in the world." He jammed his hand in his pocket and hulked around the room. "Where'd you get that sweatshirt?"

"Jonathan's here. He brought you some blood-and-thunder." I took his arm and pulled him into dad's room. "How you can read this trash . . ." The book on the top had a bloody cover, and the faint outline of a woman in an evening gown with a curved knife in her back.

"H'mm." Gordie looked me up and down. "Turn around."

"Ape."

"You're not dressed for it," he said. "Later."

"I thought you started the Beach Patrol today."

"Forgot my lunch," he said, "so they let me go for a half-hour."

"You'll never last, Gordie. You have absolutely no sense of responsibility." He had barged into the kitchen, and I could hear milk bottles jarring against one another.

"Set traps for your blood kin," he was muttering. "What next."

I watched him poking in the refrigerator. I wished I could set a trap for him that would hold him 'til the end of time. Instead I fried him bacon and eggs.

IV

Then he went back to the beach, and I was all alone. It gets quiet there the way it is never quiet in Philly—so high above the street, and only, if you listen close and there's a sea breeze, that crash of the waves at high tide like cymbals far away. All the people I knew were out there and below me, and there were none of them I could reach. I went into the bedroom where all the familiar old furniture waited; and that one thing I was kind of wary of under mom's bed. I sat down on the floor a minute, and then rolled over on my stomach and looked under the bed at it. It was a big double bed, and the tube had rolled all the way back against the wall. It was odd in many ways—it could stay there forever because I didn't have to account for it to anyone—anyone who'd complain, that is. Only to myself. But it was as though she were reaching out to speak to me, and though I wanted desperately to hear, I wanted too to wait until I would not miss a word. The sweatshirt Jonathan had given me was hanging there over the edge of the bed and (I don't know why I did it—perhaps because there was dust on the underside of the springs) I put it over my hair and made a bow of the arms at my neck. Then I started to crawl under the bed. It was tight, like getting into a low box, and dark: I didn't want to go all the way. I raised up a bit on my elbow to reach out and just barely touch it, and my back hit something that jabbed into it, like teeth. I heard an odd sound as if a string had broken, and then my name again: I swear I heard someone say my name. It was hot and I couldn't breathe, and I began to back out, sobbing and scraping my back on the springs all the way. It was only a few seconds, I guess, but I thought I'd never get out. I jumped up and pressed the sweatshirt against my ears and ran for the back porch, all the way to the railing, and leaned over it, trying to breathe. The sweatshirt flopped down over my eyes, and I pushed it up, and there—across a canyon deeper than the ocean—the man and woman were standing, close together on that other roof, as still as the sky and as distant as sculptured stone. Her hands were pressed to his back, and I wondered how *she* could live so tightly held. I felt the pain of that great weight myself, and only when she turned as in the movement of a slow dance and looked from far away at me, did I realize that it was the sharp railing against my stomach and the spindles sharp against my legs.

Then from the doorway behind me I heard Allison's voice, pitched high and strange: "Lolly! For heaven's sake, Lolly . . . !"

I swung around and pulled the sweatshirt down over my eyes: "Go away, you thief! I hate you . . . go away, go away. . . ."

She was in gold, a gold sheath dress; and a gold parasol that she held by the middle, pressing the handle that was a star against her teeth as if she was forcing back another cry. I could see her teeth and the way her mouth was twisted against the umbrella handle: everything about her was enamelled and faultless as if someone had made her with great skill out of ivory and shell. Over the arm that wasn't holding the umbrella she had hooked four or five picture frames; and my head cleared then because I knew what she had come for. It was as if someone had dumped a bucket of ice water on top of me.

"I *do* hate you," I said.

"No," she said, and she held out the hand with the umbrella toward me so that the star was pointing right at me. Then I felt the ice down my spine: it was like one of those terrible dreams when I was very small and someone with a wand was reaching out to touch me—to make me into something horrible by a touch, to make me like herself perhaps.

"Go away!"

"No, Lolly. Look, I've brought you . . ."

"Go away." I backed against the railing. "Go away or I'll jump." And I climbed over the railing to the ledge over the street.

"For God's sake . . ." And she was gone. It was as though she had evaporated. So I climbed back and sat in mother's chair and covered my eyes with my hands. Then I was really scared when I thought of that drop to the street, and between anger and fright I shivered like a frozen pup. It was a job, but I got quieted at last by thinking of mom knitting and counting the stitches as she worked her beautiful hands. Then I got the frames together and hid them under Jonathan's bed (in case she came back and tried to change her mind), and started to get into my bathing suit when I heard the door open and dad and Jonathan talking on the landing.

So the strangest hours of my life began, with Jonathan and dad speaking outside my door about G. I. insurance and loans and scholarships. It was something I wasn't to hear—that was clear from the surprise they tried to cover when I came out of my room with the sweatshirt Jonathan had given me over my bathing suit, and my bathing cap in my hand.

"Sometimes," Jonathan said, "you don't make enough racket for your size. We might have been talking about you. . . ."

Dad pulled at his lower lip, and said nothing.

"I'll make some lunch," I said.

"No." Dad pulled me close to him and rubbed his chin in my hair. "You go down the walk with Jonathan. He's going to treat you today."

"What about you?" I said.

"I'm slimming." He took me by the shoulders and turned me around. "She's all yours, Jonathan. I'll expect you when you return."

"First," Uncle Jon said, "you must change to more formal attire: put on your sneakers."

"All *that* formal?"

"Indeed yes. When I join those idiots out there in the sun, it's an occasion. Take it as a sign of great affection, my girl."

Signs are fine things, though Jonathan never gave many and those he gave you could only see if you had a practiced eye. He wasn't the only one who was chary with signs. I got phrases of Catechism in my head with idiotic things like "Pepsi-cola hits the spot, twelve full ounces that's a lot." I guess I have to thank the nuns that more of the slogans in my head aren't idiotic. But what jumped to my mind when Jonathan said that was about the Sacraments: "A Sacrament is an outward sign instituted by Christ to give grace." And there're only seven of them. Perhaps there're a lot of inward signs—but how do you get to them?

"Down the boardwalk," Jonathan said, "your father and I saw a fancy place. You walk in off the beach by the Haddon-Hall."

"It's awfully expensive, Uncle Jon. We've never been able to go there."

"Then that's where we're headed. Get your feet on."

It was expensive. Jonathan screwed up his face when he got the check. "All good things come high," he said. "Do you know what I want to do now?"

"No?"

"I want to fly a kite. All my life people who are generally respectable have been telling me that the beach is the very best place to fly a kite." He counted out the change, rubbing the bills to be sure they didn't stick. "If I am to sacrifice my peace of mind by walking the beach with you, I will educate my hands at least in the philosophical craft of the kite."

"I didn't know we were going to walk the beach."

"I wouldn't do it for anyone else, but there are things I want to talk to you about, and the only place in this damn city where there's any peace is somewhere on that beach between Margate and Longport."

"That's a long walk, Uncle Jon. And there's not a tree."

"You, my dear, have it in you to annihilate all that's made to a green thought in a green shade. We'll make our own trees as we need them."

"Now what does *that* mean?"

"What, indeed. Come along."

We got his kite, all right, at a toy store on the Walk. We went into a pavilion where Jonathan got it together. Then we both took off our sneakers and he tied them so they hung around his neck. He rolled up his trouser legs while I held the kite and people watched. We climbed down to the beach and started along the water's edge, with Jonathan playing the kite so that it bobbed and dived in the breeze about ten feet out from his shoulder.

"No point in putting it up until we get past the piers," he said.

I shall never forget that I went down the beach that day with Jonathan and his kite. He was very good with it, and except for once when it came down on a lifeguard's skull because he was sitting on top of his stand instead of in it, we had absolutely no trouble. We walked it down the length of the island, out of Atlantic City, along the beach of Ventnor, through Margate, and right to Longport—with people showing all sorts of interest all along the way. Jonathan was so much *bigger* than everyone else. You know how it is when a building goes up where there's never been a building before: everything looks different in relation to it. Well, Jonathan seemed like a tower to me; and the men got respectfully out of his way, and the women tried to get in it. It was an education to watch Uncle Jon handle the kite and the people.

At Longport, we sat on a jetty out in the water and Jonathan played out the thousand feet of string.

"When it gets that high," he said, "it's not really yours any more. You have to be prepared to see it go sometime. Even that can be a beautiful thing, you know. That one strange moment when it tugs itself free." He pulled in a bit as though he were fishing in the sky, and far out over the water I could see the blue kite dip. "Here," he said; "you hold it now, Lolly."

"Gosh, there's a strong wind up there."

"Yes."

He swung his feet in the water, and I watched him out of the corner of my eye. When the tide came in, he would not be able to do that because it would submerge the entire jetty. If I were King Canute I might try to hold back the tide, so that Jonathan could sit there until doomsday, kicking his feet in the water as though it were the study of his life—so quiet. In one way he was different that day: he seemed younger; or, perhaps, I was older—I don't know.

"There's something to be said for this, you know," he said, sweeping his arm around to take in the whole horizon, "but I haven't much cared for salt water since the war."

"Dad doesn't seem to mind."

"No." He pushed his hair back from his eyes and squinted at me, and suddenly I felt as though a hand were pressing my heart. The whole sky and sea seemed to turn over, and my hands were weak as water. "Take the kite, Jonathan," I said.

"You're not much of a flyer, you know," he said. "You have to play those gusts up there. Of course, the trick is to bring it in."

"What did you want to talk to me about?"

"Later," he said. "Later."

And we didn't talk any more until it was time to go home. I lay back full length, and occasionally, as the tide rose, water sloshed up the length of the pilings. I could feel its spray on my hands dangling over the jetty's sides. Perhaps I slept; it's so easy to drift away on a dream of a watery world, with the pilings a warm raft in the sun. I do it often, but this was the first time I did not seem to take that voyage alone. Sometime along in the afternoon, I heard Jonathan say: "It's time to bring it in, Lolly."

"You do it," I said. "I'll watch."

"I want you to do it."

He had tied the end of string about a twisted piece of drift-wood, and I took it from him, and began to roll it in my hands. The first five hundred feet or so were all right, but my hands were awful tired; and then it began to jig and give and tug. He was watching me all the time.

"This is work," I said.

"It's more than work, Lolly. You have to give a little there; you have to play it."

Gulls and terns were wheeling in and out between me and the kite, and I could see they were having a hard go of it. With the rising tide, the breeze seemed to have picked up, and the spray was splashing higher all around us. It would have been exciting, except my hands began to hurt; and once when I let it out to save the kite from a perilous dive, the string cut across my palm.

"I don't think I can do this, Jonathan. Won't you pitch in?"

"Not this time, young lady. You're on your own."

"Oh!" I was getting mad. The kite was about a hundred feet out and swinging low over the water. It swept back and forth like something alive. I played the string to catch it with my right hand, and suddenly my left hand went numb and the driftwood with its wound twine tumbled into the water. "Oh, damn," I said.

"You've still got the kite," he said.

"Oh, you . . ."

"It doesn't want to come in, Lolly. That's what that dancing's about."

"I'll bring it in, and then I'll wrap it around your neck. . . ."

You have to be stubborn. You have to be, if you want to deal with brothers or men in general. But my hands hurt too much, and the kite was sawing the air as if it was alive. I couldn't help it: I began to cry.

"Oh, now," Jonathan said, "here. . . ." He reached his hand over mine, but just then a gust greater than the others got it and the twine snapped somewhere out over the water. The blue kite soared for one beautiful minute, and then it dove into the sea.

We watched until it seemed to sink. I felt exhausted, as though I had been fighting for my life. Jonathan turned my hands over. He drew his finger along the red welt the string had made. "I think that's enough," he said.

"Oh, what was the use," I said. "You knew all the time I couldn't hold on to it."

"Yes," he said.

"And it was so beautiful. . . ." Even as I tried to remember it as it had soared and danced out there where now only the gulls overcame the breeze, I could see that it would have had to go anyhow because a rain squall was low over the horizon. It had come so quickly it seemed it would be on us before we made the beach.

We picked our way back Indian file along the jetty, and Jonathan helped me up on the bulkhead because the tide was all the way up the beach. We walked along the bulkhead Indian file, too, until we came to the wider beaches, and then we climbed down to paddle up to our ankles in the water. He was ahead of me; his head was bent and he kicked occasionally at the foam that glided back from the last edge of the exhausted waves.

"What did you want to tell me?"

"That," Jonathan said.

"Wait for me. Look at me. What do you mean?"

He turned and waited until I caught up to him. My head just reached his chest, and I had to tilt it to see into his face. He could have been some ancient, distant carved image, some sculptured god from the Mayan cities we studied one term (it seemed long ago). The sun had burned the bones of his cheeks and his forehead, and his eyes were as blue as the kite that had gone down in the sea.

"Everything is like that kite, Lolly—everything. Sooner or later it enters an element from which you can't retrieve it—and then you have to let it go. It hurts more than the hands to learn it—but that's a sign, and you'll remember." He clasped his hands behind his back, and I came up to his side and walked with him. After a long while, he said: "And I think the soul must go that way when we die: not outward and outward, but inward, deeper and deeper until it sinks in that terrible element whose dimension it must discover. . . ."

I pulled at his arm: "Please, Jonathan, don't frighten me. . . ."

He found a slight golden shell and gave it to me. It was translucent, and it held the last of the sun like golden water in a shallow cup. Then it began to rain, and we ran to Atlantic Avenue and climbed onto one of the old open trolleys. We sat in the middle of one of the cross-seats while the rain pounded in, and I fell asleep against his side. Perhaps he carried me from the trolley to the flat; I don't remember walking home. But I dreamt of the kite lying broken there against the bulkhead when the tide went out, and I was crying over it when I awoke.

It was dark and very late. I got down under the bed and pulled out the tube. By the light of my bedlamp I could see how pretty the pictures were—but that was all. So I went in and sat in the dark by dad's bed, listening to the low crash of the waves, and the rain blown against the window. His breathing rose and fell, as regular as a metronome; and pretty soon I was asleep again, and sailing out to sea where the kite had gone, on the tides of his breathing.

SOMETHING JUST FOR ME

BY GEORGE LANNING

Jack met Mrs. Michigan one summer in Connecticut—at a writers' conference, as it happens, though given Jack's kind of luck the same misfortune could have hit him anywhere. He was an instructor and Mrs. Michigan, arriving straight from the breakup of her marriage, was a student. That put them at once, in her view, on a suitable footing for whatever arrangement they might come to. If she was older, he was *better.*

Knowing no one when he arrived on campus, Jack smiled anxiously, placatingly in every direction—placatingly because he was a flop as a writer and was sure the whole conference would be on to him in a matter of days: a fraud passing himself off as a success in front of trusting people who'd paid a lot of money to get the straight word. Mrs. Michigan was not alone in smiling back, but she was alone in also smiling first. Jack was trapped instantly between those two smiles, and from that moment on their intimacy increased at a fast clip.

"Call me Mildred," she said. "I'm going back to my maiden name right after the divorce, and already I don't feel like a Michigan. Just think of me as that friendly Mildred, hardly able to wait for your classes to start."

Except for registration, she scarcely left his side during the rest of the opening day. That evening, at the reception which officially launched the conference, she managed briefly to insert herself into the faculty receiving line, between Jack and "noted juvenile writer" Lily Potter Plummer. Only Lily's experienced and ample hip, smoothly closing the gap between her brown lace gown and Jack's dinner jacket, prevented Mrs. Michigan from doing her share to make the new students welcome. Even so, as she yielded to social

179

pressure, she managed to whisper, "You look gorgeous. I bleed to see you tethered to such a cow."

Mrs. Michigan was, as she herself said, in the full flower of maturity at the time they came together. "Would you guess I'm 59?" she asked. "Take a look at my chest."

They were alone when Mrs. Michigan—Mildred—got on this subject of her age and chest, and Jack was pretty sure he was expected to pooh-pooh the former and run his hands over the latter. Honesty forbade astonishment, and despite all the continental novels he'd read, in which youth (comparative) and age share a moment of exquisite fulfillment, he couldn't bring himself to gratify Mrs. Michigan's only slightly veiled invitation. (She had, soon after their first meeting—while lying on his bed, in fact—quoted Benjamin Franklin to him. Or had it been Lord Chesterfield? The advice to younger men, anyway, about seeking out older women, who are not only better but more grateful. Jack remained vague about the source of the quotation because, at the time, he was preoccupied with trying to remember how she'd managed to get into his room and onto his bed, and worrying about getting her off and out again.)

The trouble was, or so Jack told himself, that she was exactly his own mother's age. Mrs. Michigan did not seem at all motherly —although she had a son, she said, "years younger" than Jack was— but still her importunity struck him as not quite respectable.

He wondered, as he often had in the past under similar circumstances, what gave mature ladies so much strength of persistence. But he knew, tiredly, that the speculation was futile. Where he was concerned, at least, they all exhibited a wonderful energy and single-mindedness, and a tendency toward the horizontal. It had begun, at 18, with the pleasant elderly lady of 43 whom he'd visited for the purpose of reading aloud his stories for criticism. She had almost instantly got flat on his arrival, and she'd never risen again except to open a fresh bottle of wine when the first one on the floor at her side went dry. As the evening progressed and her clothing, inexplicably, achieved a state of sad disorder, he'd been much disheartened by the acidity of her criticism.

Later, when others began to come along, he got to know their bag of tricks: first they asked about his "work," next they clutched his hands, then they stroked his nearest available knee and murmured of how "we understand each other," and finally they scolded.

If the tack that Mrs. Michigan took was far from new to him, her aggression was, for she observed none of the rules which her predecessors had kept to. ("I walked by your window last night, and you looked adorable, sitting at your desk with nothing but your shorts on and that beautiful tan." Jack, occupying a ground floor room, kept his shades pulled all the way down, and to get such a comprehensive view Mrs. Michigan must have pasted herself against his screen and peered through the slit between the edge of the shade and the casing of the window.)

She was, Jack admitted conscientiously, a handsome woman. It wasn't just the chest that had held its own. The jawline had too. Her hair was a bold, metallic orange which, certainly, Jack's mother couldn't have carried off with Mrs.—Mildred's—aplomb. As the relationship became increasingly a matter of public interest, some of Jack's students urged him to do the decent thing by the old girl. There were times (when she appeared at the pool in a white bathing suit, for instance) when he wavered. But later on, spread once more across his bed and fully clothed, she didn't look the same. And he couldn't love her for her mind, that was for sure. The last books she'd read were a couple by Floyd Dell and something pretty strong, though she didn't recall the title, by Grace Lumpkin.

To be sure, she meant to catch up, and even had a list based on recommendations by various literary friends: Rupert Hughes, Viña Delmar, Ben Ames Williams, Adela Rogers St. John, and Vincent Rose Benét. Since coming to the conference, she'd naturally added Jack's name, and meant to get to him first—in fact, was on him right now. How on earth had she missed his marvelous things all this time? How could she have settled for Floyd Dell and Grace Lumpkin?

Jack had published a novel some years earlier, and, before that, a scattering of dull but respectable stories—stories that even he, in his sizable vanity, couldn't bear to look at. (Mildred could, though; from the college stacks she hauled out dusty issues of forgotten magazines, read his contributions devoutly, and pronounced them "tiny classics.") She meant to have a go at his novel any minute now.

For some time Jack had been trying to finish a second novel— for such a time, in fact, that most people had forgot about the first one. He was, as a result, discouraged, defensive, belligerent toward other and better writers, and conscious of his age and failure. Willy-nilly, his new fan chinked up his morale. In future he'd be linked, wherever she went, to Floyd Dell and Grace Lumpkin: a kind of fame, for whenever people talked of Faulkner, Proust, Dostoevsky, she'd haul out Floyd and Grace and Jack and feel that she was more than holding her own. Word of mouth publicity, Jack reminded himself. The trinity was so confounding that out of morbid curiosity a few people might look them up.

Mrs. Michigan, having been such a great reader all her life, had decided to join the ranks of those whose work had given her so much pleasure. Besides, now that she'd cut off her husband "like a cancer," as she put it—and didn't this bold use of figurative language indicate a real talent?—she wanted to make a lot of money. Someone had told her the heartwarming story of a lady named Emilie Loring, who at 87 or thereabouts had taken up the writing of fiction and had earned twenty-nine million dollars before she died some thirty-six years and seventy-four novels later. The story might be exaggerated, but nobody could say you didn't run into Emilie Loring everywhere you went. Why shouldn't she eventually move over and make room for some spicier pieces by Mildred P. Michigan?

"Not Michigan, of course," she said. "My maiden name that I'm going back to. Putzig. Mildred Putzig."

"Stick to Michigan," counseled Jack.

Mrs. Michigan said that that was just the kind of thing she'd come to the conference to find out. She liked the quick way he tackled a problem. It was what was so good about his lectures, and made him show up that poor little hack he shared the period with for the mess she was.

In the peculiar parlance of that particular summer school, Jack was junior lecturer in "long fiction." The senior lecturer was a middle-aged woman named Caroline Coulter who brought out a romantic novel every year and was well thought of by both the dollar book clubs and the bigger rental libraries. Before Mrs. Michigan's scorn Jack remained silent, but he felt a twinge of disloyalty. The poor little hack was a fixture at the school and, despite the administration's preference for minor writers who came cheap, was used to a partner of rather greater renown than she'd been landed with this time. Yet she'd shown him every possible kindness and gone out of her way to let him make an impression on their joint class. In addition, she was plump, tiny, and pretty. Although there was no attachment between them, he liked working with the kind of rosy little woman he could imagine growing old and fat with, and snuggling up against in bed: a delicious goosedown pillow of a woman. More to the point, she had a way of handling captious editors which commanded all his admiration—"I said I'd go to Doubleday if they took that scene out." Also, he was dazzled by her ability to bone up on a subject and get a book out of it within a twelve-month period. "I didn't know if the Reformation would be too much or not; luckily, it wasn't."

Still, he felt grateful to Mildred—why not call her Mildred?—for understanding that this was not quite the method by which one produced a *Bovary* or an *Antonia*. Not that he was producing a *Bovary* or *Antonia* either, just at present, but Mildred obviously meant to suggest that her money was riding on him, of the two, and that *he* was the one whose advice would make her famous.

It was moments like this which produced in Jack the softening which led him to agree to little jaunts in the country in Mildred's car, or to the shore, which was only thirty miles distant, or to a funny bar she'd found. Little jaunts led to long drinks—"Let me pay," said Mildred; "I haven't started writing yet, so I'm not as poor as you are"—and further confidences: "My husband and I didn't . . . *You* know. Not after the first week. Later, he got a job traveling, and he used to come home and tell me about the things he did. Then he'd cry and beg me to forgive him. All the women were flat-chested. My analyst says that Victor is really attracted to men, but flat-chested girls are as near as his middle-class morality lets him get. This woman he's gone off with is like the rest. And I stood it for twenty years."

"Still," Jack countered the first time, "you have a son—"

"That was by my *first* husband," said Mildred, and she smiled in a way she had, as if they were (in this case) sharing a common recollection of how efficiently husband number one had been disposed of (some broken glass in the frozen Daiquiri?). Her eyes—hard, prominent, pale blue like winter sky reflected in ice—

opened wide, wider. Jack drew as far backward as the rigid upright wall of the booth would permit. Those eyes might at any moment detach themselves from their sockets and dart at him and stare and stare until he gave in to their demands.

After this exchange, he went back, for a day or two, to addressing his disciple as Mrs. Michigan.

Husband number one had indeed gone beyond the veil, but to hear Mrs. Michigan he'd departed peacefully. Not really peacefully, of course, because he'd been shot down in a revolution; but *legitimately,* so to speak. He'd been, said his pious relict, a crack correspondent for the AP. A stray bullet had got him. Jack wanted to ask whether Mrs. Michigan—Mrs. Tischman, as she then was— had been accustomed to accompany her spouse on his reportorial jaunts, and from which camp the bullet had seemed to come: the government's or the rebels'? But as well as Mrs. Michigan assured him that they knew one another, he lacked the courage.

The subject of Mr. Tischman led, of course, to that of his sole surviving exploit: his and the present Mrs. Michigan's son. "Peter and I are very close," said Mrs. Michigan. "He tells me everything. Are you and your mother that close?"

"No," said Jack. "Yes, but no. She wouldn't be interested. Or I mean she wouldn't want to know that there was anything like that that she *might* be interested in."

"We're like brother and sister," Mrs. Michigan went on. She finished her old fashioned and he watched her chew a piece of glass. Ice, he meant. "Once he brought a little gal he'd been shacked up with home for the weekend. He'd written me about her and I was glad to have a look. He was glad, too. He wasn't sure, he said, until Mom said nix. Do you show your mother your girls, Jack?"

"Not conscientiously," said Jack; and then (for he was under the impression that Peter was in his late 'teens) he asked her: "What does your son do?"

"He teaches at M.I.T. He's been there six years—ever since he finished his doctor's."

Mrs. Michigan was not officially enrolled in "long fiction." She was doing "short fiction" and "articles." But she appeared faithfully at Jack's classes, and she addressed all her questions pointedly to him, even when it was Caroline who was carrying the particular session. "I have this thing I've got to work out of me," she explained. "This hideous barren marriage. That's why I've sold my house and bought a trailer."

"You think that travel will . . . ?"

"No. But I'm going to Arizona for the winter and live in my trailer and write the whole thing. As a novel, of course. I'll change the names. Therapy for my trauma, the analyst says."

"You ought to talk to Caroline. She can give you some really practical advice about how to do it."

"I don't want to make this a hack job. It's my life. She'd give me a list of reference books to read. Pretty soon I'd find I was writing about passion in the Punic Wars, not about *me*. I want to get the thing over with so I can go on to more commercial stuff. That's why I hang on your every word."

Jack was surprised to learn that he struck his auditors as so conversant with the market. He even had a moment in which he determined to take his own advice, before it struck him that there was none to take. Whatever Mrs. Michigan's motive for attending a course she wasn't enrolled in, it wasn't the literary horse-sense she claimed to find there.

There were only two periods in the day when Jack could be sure of being free of Mrs. Michigan's presence on his bed, at his side at the pool, before him in class, or approaching him at a rapid pace down corridor or across lawn. One period was lunch and the other was dinner, both of which he ate in the faculty dining room. At these meals his colleagues scolded him unmercifully for his tolerance of "that really appalling woman," as Mrs. Michigan had come to be known.

"People like that should be drowned in bags, like cats," said an elderly Jew, one of the lecturers in "articles" and therefore necessarily another of Mrs. Michigan's victims. "You think you're the only one she's stalking? You're just the patsy when the rest of us give her the freeze."

"But I *can't* . . ." Jack would protest miserably. And what was it he couldn't?—cut her off? put her in her place? let her know, through some unmistakable rudeness, that she was a spectacular nuisance? He wished he could at least reply that he felt sorry for her, but the fact was that he didn't. Maybe the relationship was the more difficult to break off because he felt that he *should* pity her early widowhood, her humiliating second marriage, her present loneliness and resolve to get some mileage out of the therapy recommended for her "trauma." Wasn't this sad? And quoting Thomas Jefferson—or whoever the hell it was—and peeking in at windows, and prowling around waiting to grab somebody, anybody: weren't these just brave little things she did, a way she had of flinging out a lifeline between herself and the world?

As the conference moved into its closing week, Jack's life was complicated by a second and equally unrewarding relationship. He became the confidant of a lady poet and fellow lecturer named Eunice. Ten years earlier, Eunice had won a major literary prize for a long verse narrative on an Early American theme. It had been published in two parts in either *Look* or *Life,* with Thomas Hart Benton-like "paintings," and later had been the dual selection of a book club. "In all, I made $40,000 out of it," Eunice told him, and her voice—normally that of an aging tenor reaching for a series of high notes—grew plump, sleek, silken. Since publication of *A Benevolence in Sudbury,* which was the unlikely title of her book, Eunice hadn't been able to whip out even one perfect iambic pentameter. ("I was distracted by dactyls," she liked to explain—and invariably Jack saw prehistoric monsters waving their flippers at her, hypnotizing her, drawing her from her desk into a hideous metric wilderness. *"Dump* dump dump!" Eunice would add. "The rhythm got into my blood; but I couldn't *write* anything in it. *Dump* dump dump!")

Her long literary silence—longer than Jack's by four years—may have been what first drew him to her. He thought that they shared a common agony and humiliation, and it was good to find a fellow sufferer. Also, it was bracing for him to remember that Eunice was farther along the road to failure than he was. Something would certainly happen for him in another four years, but even if it didn't he'd be no worse off than Eunice was now—whereas *she'd* be in the very devil of a fix (his sympathy was not so great that he allowed Eunice, in his imagination, any second triumph in the years ahead—not until he'd got in first with one, anyway). The clincher was that even if time went by and nothing came right for Jack, either, there was Eunice always before him, a figure ever-receding at a steady, dactylic *dump* dump dump! In short, she gave him fresh courage.

Eunice, less affected by her failure than Jack might have wished, was part of the regular faculty at the conference: another lecturer on "articles," as it happened. (Her only experience in this field, she told Jack, had been a brief piece called "Let's Explore Monument Avenue" which had appeared in one of those fancy magazines distributed by automobile manufacturers—"They paid me $450," she said, once again sounding rich and plump.) She was a woman of about 29, if you calculated on the basis of the chronology she threw out with careful casualness, with a bony white intense face, a lot of straight black hair which smelled strongly of tobacco and always got loose from the single comb she held it back with, and a body as trim as a fountain pen.

("You should see her in the shower," said Mrs. Michigan. "Remember Slim Summerville? In fact, I wish you could get a look at the whole bunch of them in there. I hold up good.")

Nevertheless, Eunice had such a deep faith in her own desirability that she actually exuded a kind of hilarious allure. Jack began by having lunch with her a couple of times; then dinner; and finally both, with cozy walks and talks in between. Eunice gave him useful advice about dealing with magazine editors and book publishers, and Jack was flattered to be treated as someone who actually had things to deal with them *about*. Sometimes, though, he had the feeling that Eunice was really Clara Kimball Young and he was really Wallace Reid, and they'd met at Hollywood and Vine to discuss all the television shows on which neither of them would ever appear.

After three or four days of what Jack considered a prolonged courtship, he invited Eunice to his room for a drink (Mildred, as she'd once again turned into, was mercifully out; no doubt scouting around for more funny bars). In public, Eunice had the endearing habit of emphasizing her remarks by swatting whatever part of whatever male anatomy was adjacent to her, and now, in private, Jack thought that she might enjoy being swatted back. But Eunice, settling down with warm bourbon and water in a paper cup, made plain at once that she had other matters on her mind.

She had a problem, she said, and it did her good to talk it out. She was in love with a worker in a nearby woolen mill whose name was Ernest. They'd met during the first summer when she'd lectured at the conference (Ernest, enrolled in "poetry," had sung some of his own work one evening to the accompaniment of a guitar, and Eunice, metaphorically, had been ravished). "He's a natural," she explained; and then, more thoughtfully, "A kind of American primitive." That first summer, Ernest had still been living with the frightful woman who was his wife. This unwholesome relationship had since been severed, but Ernest seemed no closer to a divorce than ever. He was a stubborn, dyed-in-the-wool Yankee—no pun intended—and he couldn't agree to a settlement which gave his wife most of their property and the better part of his subsequent income. Unfortunately, the youngest child (there were five) was still a minor.

"My family, as you might guess, oppose the whole thing," said Eunice.

"They don't like divorce?" asked Jack, pouring more bourbon into her extended cup.

"Not just that. Ernest is twenty years my senior." Twenty? Ernest, then, was . . . "He's 63," said Eunice. "I suppose they're right. I ought to find a younger man." She looked coyly at Jack, round the edge of her paper cup, and curled herself up on his bed. "Like you."

Jack's intentions wavered. Twenty from 63 . . . Was he to push out one Mrs. Michigan only to make room for the next?

"Have another drink," said Jack gloomily.

Eunice smiled at him. "Just like you," she giggled. "Like you, like you, like you. . . . I've got a drink."

If arithmetic only made Eunice something besides 43, Jack thought. The age revived so vividly the image of the lady who had drunk wine and commenced to snap. And now here was Eunice, too, uncurling with what might be purpose, settling her flat little bones along the mattress.

"Then you only see Ernest when you're up here—in the summer, I mean?" he asked hurriedly. (During the school year, Eunice taught at a women's college in Virginia.)

"Not quite." She closed her eyes and burrowed her head luxuriously into Jack's pillow. The paper cup, balanced on her chest, slopped its contents onto the peculiar blouse she was wearing. Really, a very peculiar blouse, now he took a good look at it: the effect was of fishnet, through which large misshapen tropical creatures—distant kin of the dactyl, possibly—peered glumly forth from their green and orange depths. They wobbled and dipped with Eunice's breathing. Her bony—fine-boned, he meant—shoulder blades stuck out of the blouse like reefs. "He comes down for a reading once every winter," she explained. "The girls love him."

Jack, afflicted by the heat of the day or simply by too much liquor, saw Ernest slowly swimming south along the green and orange Atlantic shore, his guitar clutched under a fin; saw Eunice cast out her net and haul him in as he got opposite Virginia.

"He usually stays a week," Eunice added, opening her eyes and fixing him with one of those intense stares that Mildred was so fond of. Jack didn't doubt the implication, but he found it implausible. To begin with, Ernest would be so exhausted after that long swim...

Eunice suddenly sat up and mopped at her shoulders with the side of her cup. "You and I could have fun together," she went on, once again immobilizing him with her direct gaze. "But what would it lead to?"

A few speaking engagements, Jack thought. Except I can't play a guitar.

"I need a father figure," she explained with manly frankness. "You've guessed that from *Benevolence in Sudbury*, of course." Jack hadn't, since Wallace Stevens was as far as he went with popular poets, but he nodded sympathetically. Eunice required a father figure and Mildred wanted a husband figure. As for him, he needed a girl figure—and an enthusiastic editor. Look what life had dished up. They were all the clowns of fate.

The next day Mildred proposed an expedition to one of the more distant beaches. The conference would soon be over and they might not have another chance to see something of the countryside. En route, they could look for a literary shrine to visit, thus justifying the fact that they'd be playing hookey from an afternoon lecture by a New York publisher. Except for Wallace Stevens, Jack couldn't think of a single respectable author who came—or ever had come—from Connecticut, unless you counted Mark Twain. And they'd be going nowhere near Hartford. Besides, he'd hoped to meet the publisher and make an impression on him which later might be useful. He gave in, of course—not with the best grace, but with the knowledge that Mildred was so used to refinements of attitude that she took no notice of them.

"Wear that tiny *teeny* bathing suit of yours," she said joyously. "I love your legs, and I want to get some pictures."

The trouble was, she probably *did* love his legs, and the more he thought about them being all alone in a car with her, or stretched naked and defenseless on a deserted beach, the more apprehensive he got. Also, she belonged to the generation when cars ran "out of gas" or "broke down" in convenient isolation, and with the conference ending so soon there was no telling what old-fashioned ingenuities she might dream up.

At noon that day, meeting Eunice as usual at the faculty dining room, he said, "Would you like to go to the beach today? Mildred wants to make up a party. I know what you think of her, but we haven't much longer, and it won't be bad with the two of us there. A little human kindness, you know . . ."

An hour later he said to Mildred: "Would you mind awfully if Eunice came? Like a fool I mentioned it to her and she went wild. It shouldn't be too painful since we'll have each other."

Mildred had worked out a picturesque route which led along a series of teeth-jarring gravel roads. Since she'd brought her camera, they paused regularly before abandoned farmhouses and alongside stony out-croppings, and at each of these places Jack and Eunice were photographed by Mildred; then Jack and Mildred were photographed by Eunice. At the first stop, Jack offered to take a picture of the girls, but the deafness which simultaneously afflicted both of them was too striking to be risked a second time. Jack was also photographed alone: leaning against a peeling gate (his face carefully lifted to the sun, to erase the incipient double chin), standing with one foot on a broken step, and looking myopically toward the horizon from atop a spur of rock. It was at this last place that Mildred suggested he get into his bathing suit. They would just pretend that they were somewhere along the shore. It would make a marvelous picture. But Jack, looking below into two sets of voracious, glittering eyes, two mouths thinned out by hunger and bafflement, managed again the laugh by which he usually turned Mildred's proposals into jokes, and shinnied down the rock and rejoined them.

The beach which Mildred achieved by her system of unmarked roads was so crowded that they all turned in horror from the prospect of swimming there. It was perhaps the day's single moment of rapport, if you didn't count Mildred and Eunice's common glee as they pointed out to each other the pretty young mothers chasing fat babies across the sand, the healthy young men tossing beach balls back and forth or lying beside sunflushed and diapered girls in an intimacy which perhaps was never realized in private.

Appalling, of course: that is, it was the sort of beach one never went to. And yet, before the spectacle of so much health and energy, before the imagined spectacle of happy, uncomplicated people, people free of problems, people making promises of love under a glittering August sky, Jack felt shabby; he felt old, and disappointed in other than literary matters; he felt like a fool, trailing these two cackling, malicious, scruffy hens in his wake. In a moment the whole beach would rise and turn and point a collective finger at them, and laugh. Before such scorn the three of them would dry up and blow away in the wind off the water. How was it that these women found him better than what they saw before them, along this sweep of coast? But of course they didn't; they only thought that he, unlike the beauty they laughed at, might be attainable. For he was of their kind—not as the member of a common profession but as an outcast, an incompetent, a plain damned fool who was getting old.

They had a couple of beers in a roadhouse and then started back. Somehow—maybe because of all the picture-taking—the afternoon was gone. To the west, thunderheads mounted. They stuck to the highway this time, and Eunice pointed out the drive which led to the house of one of the judges for the club which had taken *Sudbury*. She'd been to dinner there, soon after her book was published.

So after all, thought Jack, we've found our literary shrine, or one sufficient to the day. He wondered what the New York publisher had had to say—a good novel is hard to find?—and whether he might still be around tonight. He wondered how much further they had to go, and whether Mildred would insist on stopping for dinner somewhere. He thought of happy people on a beach. He decided that he never wanted to visit Connecticut again.

The last days of the conference passed swiftly. The director gave his annual party, at which the guests were served a warm wine punch with so much citric acid in it that whole groups succumbed to heartburn on the spot. Then there was a rather peculiar evening seminar featuring a man and woman who edited a writers' magazine. They were like a competent vaudeville turn, one speaker leading into the other's jokes, and each working hard to build the act. They had many valuable things to say about "the right market" and "current editorial needs." They brought along with them a woman with extraordinarily long legs who wrote plays for children. Her relevance to the general topic was never clear, but she held her own anyway: the successful author of 169 one-act plays, most of them in book form, who'd started out as nothing more than a Poughkeepsie housewife. With those legs, she should have gone farther, or at least in a different direction.

Also, there was the final dinner—lobster Newburg—in the women's gymnasium. This was enlivened by the hunt for a washroom for the men and a reading by the year's winner of the annual conference poetry-writing award. For Jack, it was also livened up by his hunt for a seat somewhere distant from both Eunice and Mildred. But Mildred was ever brisker and more alert than he, and when the assembly sat down he found that they were directly across the table from one another. The dinner was formal, and Mildred wore a taffeta dress in electric blue. It was off the shoulder, off the arm, and almost off the chest.

"I want to see you later," she said, leaning toward him. This was near the end of the meal, and the director of the conference was already on his feet, introducing the poetry winner. As a result, Jack was able to nod noncommittally.

The poetry winner began to read—from his prize poem, presumably.

"Oh, fecund earth, mother strong and fierce—"

". . . been good friends, haven't we?" whispered Mildred.

"The very best," said Jack warmly, thinking of how they'd all be dispersed come morning.

"And so revere your binding sheets of sperm!" cried the poet.

". . . last favor," said Mildred.

A favor in the sheets? No, no, that couldn't be what she meant. Still, she was giving him that hard look again. But surely not. The last night. They were all so *fed up!* And there was a room party in the students' dorm that he wanted to go to.

"Now toss your belly seaward to the wind!" the poet suggested.

You do that, thought Jack. You go back to the beach and just *do* that.

". . . time finding it, but I finally managed to get a copy," Mildred added.

"Fine," said Jack. Copy? Of his book, did she mean? "Swell," he said. She might mean anybody's book, of course: she was perfectly capable of handing him something by Grace Lumpkin—or even by Emilie Loring.

"And then with *ong dee plooey* do I rest," the poet declared in conclusion.

Ong dee plooey?

There was a quite unnecessary amount of applause.

". . . going on, is there?"

He'd lost the whole of that speech. "What?" he said.

"We could have a last chat, couldn't we? There's nothing going on tonight, is there?" Mildred had raised her voice just as the applause was dying away, and her words carried clearly to everyone in their vicinity.

"*I* know what's going on," said the elderly Jew, Jack's neighbor at the right, speaking from behind his napkin. With his elbow he struck Jack a sharp, brotherly blow in the ribs and then subsided into the napkin, coughing with laughter.

The poet, by God, was on his feet again, flushed with the pleasure of his success and ready to read something else, from the look of him. "*Ong dee plooey,*" muttered Jack, and pushing his chair back softly he stood up. He waggled his head at Mildred, smiled sheepishly, and thought that he'd probably managed to get across the idea that he was off to the men's room. But what a bore, having to make a fool of himself in order to give her the slip. And she'd be along as soon as the dinner was over; straight for his bed she'd make, and a last "chat," book in hand—somebody's book. His strategy gained him nothing but a respite, a chance to think up a way of shaking her before the party really got going. "Come up early," one of his students had said (a young twig of 50 or so). "It'll be a ball—we'll maybe go on all night, the liquor holds out. But give the old girl the brush, will you? We've had it—and she's had it. Take her for a walk and drown her in the pool."

It wasn't as simple as that. For one thing, the gate to the pool

was locked. And she'd never take a hint and exit gracefully; she
didn't know a hint from a handrail, if that was the expression. He
sighed in exasperation. Life was full of *ongst*. No wonder the poet
shouted *plooey*! He understood exactly why the late Mr. Tischman
had arranged to intercept a bullet. He congratulated Mr. Michigan
on his taste for flat-chested girls. Go bind your belly deep within
the sea, he thought. Oh, please, just for tonight, drop dead.

But Mildred had no consideration. She turned up in his room
twenty minutes after he made it there himself. "I looked all *over*
for you!" she cried happily.

"I couldn't very well go back in," he answered. "And I got
tired of hanging around outside. . . ."

"No," she agreed. "You didn't miss a thing—except three more
songs to mother and the sea. Thank heavens it's over." She tossed a
large black plastic briefcase on his bed—containing, he decided
gloomily, her nightgown and slippers, and possibly a few sand-
wiches. Freed of her encumbrance, she leaned against his door, her
hands behind her, and crossed one foot over the other. The attitude, rather that of a voluptuous inclined plane, reminded him of
the way some actress used to look—Carole Lombard, was it? or
Constance Bennett?—in overwrought movies about women who'd
got abandoned in the tropics. *Were* abandoned, so to speak. He
regarded Mildred apprehensively. She was breathing heavily, but
mercifully her eyes were closed. For the moment her attention was
withdrawn from him. Then he realized that she was out of breath.
Perhaps she'd run all the way from the women's gymnasium to her
room, where presumably she'd acquired the briefcase, and then
across the quadrangle to his building. In fact, she must have run
—and at top speed—for not a sound came from the hallway beyond his partly-open door. No one else had returned yet.

Just then Mildred leaned farther backward and the door closed.
She opened her eyes and smiled at him and he felt a spasm of un-
welcome pity; no, not pity; kindred feeling, as if they'd come to
share something that now they must talk about. She moved over to
the bed and from the briefcase withdrew his book, neat and bright
in its jacket, the orange and yellow ink only slightly faded from its
years of storage in the publisher's warehouse or on the shelf in an
out-of-the-way bookstore.

"I want you to write something specially for me," she said.
"Nothing you've put in anybody else's."

There hadn't been anybody else, not lately, certainly not on this go-round. It struck Jack suddenly, as he took the book from her, that there hadn't been anybody else for anything at all for quite a while. What was there to choose between their situations, his and Mildred's? Nothing—except that she, like Eunice, was farther along the route, had less time to make it in—make whatever it was each of them wanted. This was the thing they shared; but it was unbearable and couldn't, after all, be acknowledged, let alone talked about.

"I'll have to find my pen," he said, going over to a suitcase which stood, partly packed, beneath a window. He groped in the pockets along each side and finally came upon the pen clipped to the rolled-up manuscript of his lecture notes. Then at last he felt the evening's finality; the end of summer. For those closely-written sheets represented not only the days of the conference but the weeks he had given to preparation. He *had* to make that party tonight, round off his summer with some kind of bang, however slight.

As he got up from his knees, he saw Mildred's face and body reflected in the windowpane. She was seated on the extreme edge of the bed, and, in the light of the unshaded overhead bulb, she looked like a skull in an orange wig propped on an electric-blue bolster. Her gaze was directed away from him, straight across the narrow room; her naked shoulders drooped and, as nearly as he could tell, her mouth had gone slack. He cleared his throat sharply, said "Found it!" in a voice too loud and hearty, and turned around.

He'd given her what time she needed—or it might be that he'd seen wrong, in the dark glass. She dazzled for him, light running like water off the folds of blue taffeta. Her bold eyes sought his boldly, without pretense; but without calculation, too. Her skin, sun-brown fading to yellowish-white, was a little moist. One long wild hair, which she couldn't see, curled outward from a mole on her back.

"A really special inscription," he said; making noise. Abruptly he was overcome by a lassitude more painful than irritation or even disappointment and loneliness. He looked at the book which had cost him so much effort but had brought him none of the praise and respect he'd longed for, none of the kindred spirits he'd hoped would find him through its pages.

"Something just for me to look at," she said. When he made no response, she leaned forward slightly, and one hand rose in wavering supplication. "We've had a lot of fun together, haven't we? I don't know that I've got much out of the conference—I suppose I'm too advanced for this kind of thing—but I've certainly learned from you, Jack."

Have you? he thought grimly.

"Jack," she said a moment later, into his continuing silence, "I could— Do you want me to give you a lift down to New York? With all the stuff you've got to carry . . . I'm going up to Peter's, but he doesn't know when I'm finished here. I mean—"

He had put the book on top of the chest of drawers and opened it to its endpaper. "You're distracting genius from its work," he told her, and hoped that he'd struck a tone of jocular ferocity. "If you want something just for you . . ."

Rather curiously, she seemed to find his words reassuring. She contrived a little girl's laugh and wriggled backward onto the mattress. She leaned sideways on one elbow, with a provocation which might not have been intended, and got a cigarette from the briefcase and lighted it.

What could he say in her damned book—*his* damned book. It was a desecration, to take this thing he'd loved so much and concoct a few lines to bloat her swollen vanity with. "For Mildred, who's getting out of my life and better stay there. In memory of all our lousy trips and talks." Will that do, Mildred? Milly, dearest Milly? "For Milly, whose scholarship has brought Benjamin Franklin to the awareness of a whole new generation." "For Mildred P. Michigan, the biggest case of summer complaint I've ever had."

"I always have trouble writing these things," he said.

"Let's have a little drinkie first, and maybe that'll warm you up." She opened the briefcase again and brought out a fifth of bourbon. "I got this in town today."

True, a fresh bottle. Did she picture them sitting here together, slugging it down? Warmed up for what?

Mildred knew exactly where he kept everything, and from the bottom drawer in his desk she extracted the venerable paper cups.

"That looks like Caroline's lipstick," she said, examining a fresh smear on one of them.

"Eunice's," said Jack while his mind sought frantically for an excuse to skip the drink, cut the session short. Look, there's a party I'm going to—a sort of private party. . . . No good. Mildred would just say she loved private parties.

"Did you notice," asked Mildred gleefully, "what Eunice had on tonight?"

"I didn't see her all evening."

"I think—I'm not *sure*—it was a pair of exercise bloomers. And I'll swear that the top was a black lace bra. She looked like the cleaning woman in a harem." With a whoop of laughter, Mildred opened the door and carried the cups out to the water fountain in the hall. Glumly, Jack tore the sealer off the bourbon. Mildred returned, her face flushed pink with laughter and the good feeling that the fun had started. "And her *shoes* . . . !" she exclaimed, but could say no more. Still whooping and hiccoughing, she took the drink he made for her and went back to the bed. She dabbed at her eyes and then, peeping at him over the rim of the cup much as Eunice had done earlier, she solicited his response.

He made a few perfunctory noises which, with Mildred, were as good as the real thing—*were* the real thing for her, probably, since an authentic response was something she mustn't have encountered in years.

As silence closed in on them once more, and the animation and hope died from her face, he was seized with compassion. He said, "That's a beautiful dress"—and knew, before the words were out, that he'd said too much.

"I wore it for you," she replied. "I even bought it for you."

"For me?" he echoed in genuine astonishment.

"For the you I knew I was going to meet some day, I mean. I bought it right after Victor left me, but this is the first time I've had it on."

In a moment, he feared, she'd have it off. "My mother has—" he began, hoping the presence of his mother might regularize the situation. But what did she possess which could be brought out to meet Mildred's gown? His mother's clothes, made for her, would only be puzzled by this poor little machine-cut-and-stitched imitation of the high fashion of a season which had already gone into history.

It didn't matter, for Mildred had no intention of letting another woman get into the room. "I could see you looking at me in the mirror," she said lyrically. "Right there in the shop. And yes," —she examined him critically—"fantastic as it may seem, it really was *your* face. You nodded your head—this was the perfect one for my coloring."

Orange and blue, thought Jack dazedly. Wasn't there a college . . . ? "Well, I should say so!" he declared, nodding his head —no, no, better not nod. That got them back to the mirror again. The power of suggestion: was this what she put her faith in? He bolted his drink and stood up. "I'd better see what I can write in this book of yours. I know you're tired, and you've got a long drive in front . . . Certainly enjoyed the drink. Better than a sleeping pill, any day."

He hastened across the room to the chest of drawers and once again took up his pen. Mildred, with the monolithic calm, the careful languor, of women who do not choose to be hustled off, only smiled and, bending over for the bottle which he'd placed beside her feet, filled her cup again. Straight.

He wrenched his mind away from the awful, portentous sight, and stared at the endpaper. "From the me you was sure you'd meet some day, to the you I wish I hadn't." No, no, no. "For a darned good pal and a really snappy dresser. . . ."

"Look, Mildred," he said at last, desperately, "I draw a blank when I have to perform with somebody looking at me. And I want . . . I want to write a nice one."

"You'd better," she said. "One I can look at when I'm in my trailer this winter and remember the fun we had. When I'm trying to get that dirty dog out of my system. Twenty years, Jack! Jacky, twenty long miserable years! There are plenty of things I haven't told you yet. Things I didn't have the courage to tell my analyst, even."

"Well, that's just fine . . ." he said. "Or—"

"What's *really* fine," she declared, "is that it's just the two of us here. I'm so bored with those stupid room parties, and in the daytime Eunice follows you around like a hamster on the edge of menopause, and in class you're so polite to that fat sack with wind on her brain that she does all the talking. . . . Jack, aren't you glad we're alone, to have a real talk together? We're like two crazy kids, aren't we, Jack? We get so excited about ideas, I mean. Don't you think so? And, you know, things. I guess we understand each other —you do *me,* I know! And this is our last night!"

"When do you go to Arizona?" he asked.

"When do I . . . ?" She appeared, briefly, bewildered. "Oh. I don't know. I'll probably spend the fall with Peter. We're going to take an apartment. Maybe you could come up for a weekend. Could you?"

"Wait a minute," he said. "Wait a minute now. I think I've got it."

"No, you wait," she said, with such urgency that he couldn't pretend to ignore her. "There's one thing I want to tell you. What you've done for me. I was in pretty low spirits when I started out for here. Victor and everything. Selling the house and all our furniture. Deciding about Arizona. I've never been to Arizona. Besides, the people here aren't very chummy, are they? It would have been horrible except for you. We could . . . That is, we're really friends, aren't we? We're among the lucky few who find something precious and have the good sense to recognize it. If you want . . . If there's anything you want, you know I'm right here, Jack."

Jack didn't reply. Throughout her speech he'd kept his eyes down, his face half-turned away from hers. Now, in rage and humiliation, he gripped the pen and bent above the book and began to write. "For our wonderful 'Mom,'" he put down, "the life of the Connecticut writers' conference and the wickedest old gal who ever set the whole East Coast on its ear. Long may she reign! From one sinner to another, with kindest personal regards." Then he signed his name and the date. He blew on the ink and handed the book to her, still open. He could feel sweat running down his arms, feel his hands turning cold, feel his stomach beginning already to revolt at the cruelty he'd done to her with this inscription, and to himself as well.

"Maybe you'd rather read it later," he told her, as a poisoner might urge his victim to finish the nice hot drink in bed.

She glanced at the words he had written and he thought he saw her stiffen. She, too, blew on the ink, and then she waved the book back and forth in the air.

"You're wonderful!" she said. "I love it! I just love it!" She laughed loudly and, laying the book on the coverlet, got up and brushed cigarette ashes off her lap. "You're the only person who

ever seems to know when I'm kidding. It's what I like about you.
'Mom'!" she repeated. "Wait till Peter sees this. And it's just what
I feel about all you kids. Old, wicked Mom! You've got my num-
ber, all right."

"Well, it's been grand," said Jack, feeling his sickness rising up
behind his teeth. "Every minute of it. I wish I could have said it
better."

"No, I wanted it like this, off the cuff. It's wonderful. It shows
your wonderful humor." She looked down at the liquor which remained in her cup, started to drink it, and then changed her mind
and set the cup on Jack's desk. "I guess old Mom's had enough."
She took a deep breath and swung round to face him squarely.
"Bad for the complexion. I want to look good so I can catch me a
millionaire dude out West." She smiled. "I guess I'll see you in the
morning. To say goodbye."

"Oh, sure. Sure. We'll all see each other. Here." He stooped
and picked up the bottle and the briefcase and put them in her
hands.

She took them blindly, and blindly, it seemed, she started for
the door. "Beauty sleep!" she cried. "Beauty sleep!"

"Wait a minute. Don't forget your book." He swept it off the
bed and crossed the room to her.

"My . . . ? Oh, yes. And after I came all the way over here just
to get you to write in it." She went out into the hall.

"Goodnight, Mildred," he said, following her as far as the doorway.

She didn't answer. She had begun already to move away from
him, down the empty, silent corridor. Her dress and her hair
flamed up as she passed beneath a ceiling light. Then the vitality
died away as she went beyond into a stretch of darkness. He was too
exhausted, too near being sick, to cheer her out of sight, to call
reassuring phrases which might ease both their savaged dignities.
He did manage to say "See you at breakfast for sure!"—but she was
at the stairs now; perhaps she didn't hear him. He saw her put one
foot on a riser, teeter slightly as if she were dizzy, and then begin
slowly to ascend.

He closed his door and leaned against it in a posture which, by
accident, was a travesty of Mildred's own earlier travesty. And he
thought: it's over, over! He moved across to the window and flung

it up, although the night was cold for August, and leaned his forehead against the screen. He breathed deeply, damp earth and grass,
clean impersonal air, and closed his eyes. Then he had an uneasy
moment in which he imagined that another forehead was pressing
against his—that of Mildred leaning in to tell him how adorable he
looked leaning *out*. He closed the window and turned back into
the room. There on the desk stood the drink she'd left. He lifted
the cup in a toast. *Salud!* Mildred P. Michigan, he said silently.
And goodbye forever. He drank off the bourbon in a gulp. It was
time to get a move on. Time—oh, God! and more!—to go and
have a ball.

THE GUIDE

BY ANDREW LYTLE

THE BIG CAR rolled smoothly into the night. The sharp bright smudge of the headlights slid under the darkness with mathematical exactitude. Dressed in his hunting clothes, the boy sat beside his uncle and watched the road. He sat rather stiffly. His new boots, greased by his mother, prodded the boxes of shells piled carelessly onto the floor of the car. He was not comfortable. The shells gave him no easy rest for his feet, his clothes were strange in their bulk, and he could not make up his mind how to act with his Uncle Bomar. This was to him at the moment the most serious matter in the world. He tied himself into knots thinking about it. He rather felt that the childish deference to an elder was out of place now that they were going hunting together, and not merely hunting but to the Lake for ducks. The invitation was plainly Bomar's way of accepting him as a man. Bomar did not take boys duck shooting. Quail or dove hunting, but never duck. He had begged too often not to know. The boy felt that at last he was ready for a man's pleasures and responsibilities. This thought made him all the more anxious to behave as he should. This and the way his mother had seen them off.

But how was he to behave? Nobody had told him, just as nobody had told him what it meant to put on long pants. His mother had cried, his father had asked the cost, his grandfather had spouted Latin about the *toga virilis*. And his brother Bob, all he had said was, "Keep it buttoned up, kid." "Of course I'll keep buttoned up," he had answered with shame and petulance, thinking only of the technical handling of the clothes. He knew at once he had made a mistake, even before he saw the smirk on his brother's face. Suddenly the long months of expectation, at last realized, turned bitter under his tongue and he did not know rightly why. Vaguely and with confusion it came to him how narrow had been his understanding of what he had wanted. His wish had been little more than to masquerade in grown-up clothes. But the fact was another thing. Changing clothes had changed him. He felt the same and yet he was not the same. For days it puzzled him how this could be, then he gave it up as he grew accustomed to his new condition, but for a while longer he carried about him a feeling of unease. This made him sensitive and timid, so that he would cross over to the other side of the street rather than speak to someone he had known all his life.

The car took a curve. From the darkness a large stock barn with white doors appeared, disappeared. A board fence made a slapping noise as they passed down its narrow lane. He watched the posts go down like piles. The air sucked in, the fence was gone, and he knew they were entering poorer country.

"Tommy phoned me the big flights were coming in," Bomar said. "Had been for two days."

The boy stiffened in his seat, thinking desperately hard what reply a sportsman would make to such an important statement. The moment of his indecision dragged interminably, so that he blurted out, "You reckon they'll still be there?" His cheeks burned with shame at the over-eager, inadequate words.

"If the weather holds," Bomar replied in his slow, unexcitable voice. "It's got to be cold enough for the streams and back water to freeze over before the ducks come on to the Lake in any number. It's pretty cold. I expect they'll be there."

The boy leaned back in his seat. His uncle had answered him seriously. His question no longer seemed to him childish and ineffective. He even recovered from the humiliation of the leave-taking, his mother following them to the car, pulling his scarf about his neck, telling him not to get shot, not to take cold, and to promise her, if his feet got wet, to tell the man to row him in, a few ducks is not worth pneumonia. . . . Great God, Effie, the boy's going duck shooting, not to the North Pole. He had been grateful for Bomar's words then. He was more grateful now. They had not meant regret for asking him to come along. Maybe Bomar, too, knew what it was to be hindered by the solicitude of women.

The older man reached up and turned on the car's spot. He

played it about the countryside, objects in the rough fields, then set it to the center of the road. The headlights swelled to a new fulness and the car took up speed. "A spot is a good thing to have in the country," Bomar said, as if his gesture needed some explanation.

"It sure is," the boy replied.

His uncle had turned as he spoke, turned easily, almost lazily, and yet all his movements showed perfect coördination. The boy felt a slight shock of surprise. His uncle was not so old a man as he had always thought, or rather he had never thought about his age at all. He had been Uncle Bomar, his mother's younger brother, sometimes whispered about in the family, but one of the opposition nevertheless who stood for authority, dullness, and obstacles to freedom. Except that he had never been so dull as the others. He had threatened older boys with Bomar's name and he would always let you go along to pick up doves. And Bomar had taken time to teach him how to shoot. He looked at the older man's eyes as if for the first time. They wore a look of furious haste which seemed out of keeping with his fleshy cheeks. As the boy looked more closely, it seemed to him that the fury had grown cold and the haste had set like the film over the racer's pupils as he is being led from the track, blinded to the shouting in the stands, to winning and losing, to all but the burning strain of the race and the gorged heart.

Bomar said, "You had better take that heavy coat off. You won't feel it in the morning. It gets cold as hell out on that Lake."

Hastily the boy took off the coat, for the second time thinking bitterly of his mother, whom he had allowed in his ignorance to dress him as she had once done for parties and Sunday school, as if the whole affair were no more than a fashion parade. His uncle wore his good clothes. Hunters changed for the Lake after they got there.

"How do you think you will like it, kid?"

"Oh, fine," he said hastily. "I've always wanted to go. Old Jake used to tell me about grandfather Laus going there. He said he went in a wagon and it took him two weeks to go, and he always stayed two or three weeks hunting and fishing. Jake said he was a little boy, and they took him along to gather up fat pine and keep the fires."

"It's quite a difference these days," the older man said.

"Oh, yes, sir. When will we get there?"

"Well, we could make it tonight, but I think we'll stop off and sleep at Center. There's a good hotel there. The quarters at Hornbec are pretty rugged. And the guides keep you up drinking your whiskey."

"Oh," the boy said. He kept silent a moment, then resumed eagerly. "Jake said there were all kinds of hunting, and on one trip grandfather Laus brought back a live bear."

"The old boy must have been quite a sport."

"Oh, he was. Sometimes he would sleep under the trees, by a spring or creek. Jake said when he put up with people along the way, he would copy the design of a quilt he liked and have his wife make it when he got back home."

Bomar looked curiously at the boy at his side. "You seem to know a lot about that old guy. Which one was he?"

"He's the one that hangs to the right of the mantel in the living room."

"Let's see. That's the . . ."

"He hangs in the mahogany frame."

"Yeah. He was the one that was such a rounder."

"But he reformed. Mother says he received the mantle of grace when the Methodists held their great revival, and built a Church for his slaves."

"When the hell was that?"

"Oh, a long time ago. I don't know rightly."

"You might know it would be a long time. The United Daughters like'm dead."

The boy regarded his uncle with a puzzled expression. "You mean the United Daughters of the Confederacy, sir?"

"I mean all united daughters. The club don't make any difference. In union is strength. That's their battle cry. But hell, boy, you don't know what I'm talking about," Bomar said with impatience. "What I mean is the only man they'll have any truck with is a dead one. After a certain age, that is. The deader the better, if he's buried deep enough so he don't stink."

The boy nodded knowingly, although his head was awhirl. He had heard his father and his father's friends occasionally refer to women in disparaging terms. One spoke of women and preachers, he discovered, in the same tone of voice. It apparently was a thing one did to relieve certain difficult situations, but there was never a particular woman, or a particular preacher, named. The reference was invariably general. And his grandfather—only with him it was religion. He never spoke impolitely of ladies, but he could fling himself into a passion about the Church, especially at the dinner table when the conversation fell off. And his grandmother gave always the same reproving speech, in the same falsely affronted manner, "Don't blaspheme before these young men, Mr. Hancock." And Mr. Hancock would reply with righteous vehemence, "The truth, Madam, cannot blaspheme." None of this banter had he taken to mean anything, but with his Uncle Bomar he felt a difference. Bomar had actual women in mind and a grievance which seemed, however mysterious, real and vaguely threatening. He could not help but be disturbed the more he thought about Bomar's remark. Did he mean his own mother? She talked a great deal about her family, living and dead. The truth heretofore hidden in things familiar confronted him: most of the people she talked about were dead.

After a while, in the silence which had fallen between the man and boy, Bomar said, "Forget it, kid." And the boy knew it was hard for him to speak, that inadvertently he had allowed talk which he considered unseemly to pass between them.

But he could not forget so easily. Considerations too disturbing to be summarily dismissed had been set loose in his head. Was it true that ladies of his mother's years thought only of the dead, or thought of them to the disfavor of the living? He was sure it could not be so with his mother. The tales she told never called to mind the dead but only the very dearest of kin who perhaps lived too far away to visit. Above all was this true of grandfather Laus, whom she set him for example. "Hold your head up and step lightly," she would say and he knew who it was she had in mind. Or, "Always be able to look any man in the eye." And again, "Think what you please but never speak loosely and you'll have nothing to take back." These admonitions he was conscious of but never in the forepart of his mind. They underlay and gave firm texture to all he found delightful in his great-grandfather's life, and he somehow knew that had they been lacking the stories which won his heart would have seemed less true. But now that he thought of things in a way he never had thought before, all which touched him dearly lay bright and clear before his vision, the beginning, the middle, and the end clarified in a burst of illumination, where the parts

were the whole and the whole defined the parts. And so it came to
him that from his mother he got most of the admonitions but the
stories he had from his grandfather or from Jake.

The near duel with General Jackson he liked best of all, for the
two friends were parted over a horse race. This seemed to him
right and fitting, for only some such great occasion was proper
cause to break the bonds between two "gentlemen who held each
other in the highest esteem." The story as it was told, without directly accusing the General, was told to his discredit. Large sums
had been placed on the race. In the last half mile, the General's
horse was gaining, when his grandfather Laus's horse threw his
rider and crossed the finishing line several lengths ahead of his
rival. Proud of himself, he turned to the stand where his master sat,
and whinnied. At this point in the story his grandfather would
pause dramatically. "The spectators to a man rose and cheered the
gallant animal." But of course no riderless horse could win a race.
Words passed, just what words he was never told, a challenge was
given and taken, but the night before the morning of the duel
friends intervened and the matter was disposed of to the honor of
both parties. "Else," his grandfather would say, "Else," he would
repeat, looking significantly about him, "the history of our nation
had been played out in different fashion."

Tall, gallant, and forever young, this was the man whose image
he carried, not that of the picture in the mahogany frame. That
never made him think of grandfather Laus. It looked like the dead
or would have so looked if the straight-glancing eyes had been
closed. But they narrowed too sharply out of some great reserve,
above the stiff neck and stock and the black broadcloth coat. He
could never imagine the man in the picture lying under the trees,
wrapped in a bear skin, with the shine of the camp fire on his face
and the sound of the hobbled horses grazing in the dark. The grandfather who was hunter was the man he liked to think about. Now he
was going over the same road he had taken and to the Lake where
he had had such great sport with all kinds of game. The road was
changed, there was no more a forest, but the Lake at least would
still be wild and the guides simple, noble men.

"Wake up, kid, we're here."

He opened wide his eyes, but for a moment his senses delayed.
Startled, he thought the car was drawing up before the hotel in

Center under its large neon sign glowing evilly red in the darkness. Here the night before they had stepped out of the frosty air into the shabby newness of the lobby, had been shown to their room by a grey-haired elevator boy. It had seemed to him that he had scarcely closed his eyes before his uncle was shaking him awake. Behind the desk the proprietor greeted them. He was dressed in hunting clothes. His eyes were bright as a bird's and he jerked about like a mechanical toy as he cocked his head to one side and talked glibly of the shooting, but what he wanted to find out was whether they would be back that night. "Bastard," Bomar said as they turned away. It was still dark as they passed a second time under the neon sign. The car was white and glistened in the dark. The exhaust made a loud noise in the deserted street. In the distance he had heard an ash can clattering. . . .

"Well, here we are," Bomar said and got out of the car with a motion which was quick for a man his size. He called into the darkness, "Anybody seen Tommy?"

A voice answered, "He stepped up to his house. He'll be on down in a little."

"Are we really here?" the boy asked. He noticed that he had lowered his voice. His uncle had spoken right out.

"This is Hornbec. There's the Lake over there."

The boy glanced towards a rough pier, but it was all dark beyond and he could see nothing of the water. They walked up the narrow street which bordered the Lake. Lights from the windows and door of a plain two-story building glared from its porch and threw a milky shadow onto the steps. But the light did not penetrate, although he could see his uncle's face and the half-solid forms of men stirring busily around him. He was wide awake now, with the cold wind from the Lake blowing his face, but he felt as if he were acting in a dream, where all was topsy-turvy yet all seemed natural. It was this very naturalness of things which made him feel as he did: people going about their business, talking in a normal voice, but all in the dead of night.

"Let's go in the hotel," Bomar said.

Inside it was warm and bright. Some dozen men dressed in their hunting clothes, several of them in hip boots, sat around a pot-bellied stove. It was red-hot about its middle. He shivered and walked over to warm himself.

"How about a little breakfast, Nelly?" Bomar called out and walked into the long dining room.

The walls were plain and unfinished. Most of the tables were in disarray and he could see that the guests of the hotel had already eaten. Where he sat, there were crumbs on the cloth and somebody had spilled catsup. The woman Nelly came in with fried eggs shining white with grease, thick bacon, large thick biscuits, and coffee in heavy china cups. She flung her head and shoulders about as she walked. The boy thought he had never seen less sense in a face, but he could see the hunters liked her or at least that she thought the hunters liked her.

"Good old Nelly. She won't let us starve," Bomar called out with too loud a heartiness and grabbed playfully at her waist. She tossed her head and flung herself out of the way, but her wide bright eyes grew brighter.

"Quit, now-wah," she said.

The brazen stupidity in her dare that was not a dare chilled his spirits. The eggs were cold, but he ate the bacon and poured a lot of milk and sugar in his coffee and drank it. The coffee was steaming hot.

"Paul's wife may come up with him today," Bomar said to the girl.

"I hope she does."

"Do you now?"

"Why not. I ain't got nothing to hide."

"No. Nothing to hide. Nothing at all."

"That's right."

"Who did I see kissing you?"

"He was jest being jolly."

"Yeah. Jolly. Good old jolly Paul."

"That's right," she said. "Jolly and friendly. You all want lunches?"

"Sure. You want us to go hungry on that Lake?"

"I didn't know. I thought maybe you'd brought lunches with you."

Bomar turned to his nephew. "This hotel thinks it's got a monopoly."

"We don't care where you stay." Her head came up. A light flush at the cheekbones rushed to her eyes. For the first time the woman seemed real to the boy. His mother had told him that plain people were quick to take offense but it was her show of pride which gave her being, and he understood that it was a thing she held in common with those around her as she shared a speech which his mother called country.

"Well, will you be here tonight?" she continued.

Bomar paused. "Yeah. The kid and I'll be here."

"I jest wanted to know. I have to plan about supper."

She left the dining room, and the man and boy ate hurriedly and in silence. From the other room they heard spurts of talk. None of it flowed easily, as happens with men who are idling. It jabbed at the silence, a silence enclosing a time of waiting upon action, when the mind grows fearful lest its edge grow dull from images. The boy was trying to catch the drift of the talk. He had not heard the soft steps approaching. He heard only the words, "Now if you ain't a pretty bastard."

He stiffened and waited for the blow which Bomar in all honor must give. He waited a second. There was no stirring of the chair. He raised his eyes upon his uncle's smiling, placid features.

Bomar's lips were moving. "You ain't no handsome son-of-a-bitch yourself," they said.

"Getting in here this time of day. You drive all night?"

"Hell, no. We stopped off at Center to get a few hours' sleep."

"What you think you are, a goddam tourist?"

"You got an interest in this hotel?"

"Hell, no. It's just the company you keep. When I want to sleep in a whorehouse, I don't want no pimp to show me my bed. That mealy-mouthed bastard dressing up like a hunter to catch the suckers like you, only I didn't know you was a sucker before. And they'll steal there, too."

"Hell, Applegate."

"Hell they don't. Last week a man from Indiana lost his purse with ninety-seven dollars in it."

"You're just afraid he'll take away your business."

"Hell. None of the guides around here will go up there. And we don't let him down here."

Bomar turned to his nephew. "Kid, shake hands with Tommy Applegate."

The boy rose and gave the small heavy-set man his hand. He

was a little dazed. Bastard and son-of-a-bitch were fighting words, not friendly greetings. He didn't understand. He knew his uncle had fought for less, much less. And he well knew that no such greeting would have passed between grandfather Laus and his lean, weathered guide, when they met again at the return of the hunting season. But of course there were no professional guides in those days. The people who lived about the Lake at that time hunted or trapped for a living. They might go along with a friend out of pure courtesy, or for companionship, but he was sure they took no money for it. But it was not money either. It was the greeting which shocked and puzzled him. For a second his hand gripped the guide's hand. He felt the inert calloused flesh, and the strength within, near the bone, but there was no response to his clasp. The man was not being unfriendly, but as he drew away the boy felt he had been rebuffed. Later he remembered the eyes. They were brown, which he did not expect. And there was something else, something wrong about them. They lacked the sharpness of a hunter's eyes.

"We are about ready to shove off, kid," Bomar interrupted. "We're going to the first pocket. Tommy got you a good guide. Watch him, though, or he'll shoot up too many of your shells. And you give him this at the end of the day."

The boy looked at the money. "All of this, Uncle Bomar?"

"Yeah, I know. It's too damn much, but it's what they charge."

Outside the darkness was thinning. The Lake spread out for a way like a black floor. The boy hesitated on the edge of the porch. His clothes were slick from the cold, but the blood charged through his body. It seemed a trivial thing that he had worried at not finding the place and the people what he had expected, for the surroundings are nothing. The only thing that mattered was the shoot. Hunters passed him on the steps, all with a common purpose, the same thoughts, the same sense of excitement and expectation. He could feel it as they went by. One or two looked curiously at him. He knew he must go on or they would think him strange, but still he delayed to savor the full measure of the experience before it was played out by the act. All this stir, the time of day, the learning of the guides, the rich men who hunted, who came from places where their word was law, others who came out of some urgent need they did not rightly understand—all of them, now and in his

great-grandfather's day, were guided, were governed by the in-
stincts of a bird. Bomar half turned. "Where are you?" he called
sharply.

"Coming," the boy answered and hurried down the steps. He
noticed that Bomar's bulky clothes spreading out over his hips enlarged them. He looked from the rear like his mother.

At the water's edge two boats were drawn close into the bank.
Tommy was standing in one. Bomar was handing him his gear.

"Your gun unloaded?" Tommy asked.

"You know I wouldn't hand you any loaded gun," Bomar replied.

"Be God-damned sure. I don't want you to blow my ass off."

"Don't put it where it'll get wet."

"If it gets wet, you'll get wet. Hand me that sack of charcoal."

"Your arm's not broke. Pick it up."

"What's the matter with your back? Been riding it too much?"

"My back's all right. This is Jack Daniels' number seven. Catch
it."

"Three's my lucky number."

"Well, this will more than double your luck. Won't it, Goosetree?"

A man looked up from blowing the charcoal burner in the adjoining boat. The light from the charcoal showed a pair of flat eyes,
with sharp points at their centers. Even in the steady red glow his
features seemed pale. He said dryly, "He'll double your drinks."

"This is the kid, Goosetree, that's going with you," Bomar said.

The man nodded. "They'll make the noise, sonny," he said.
"We'll bring in the meat."

"Hell," Tommy said with heavy scorn.

"I've got the gun will do it," Goosetree added. "And this boy
looks like he can shoot."

"You may get a mud hen or two."

"I'm going to hole up at the point. We'll bring'm in."

"Bring in my ass," Tommy said.

"Now that ud be a right heavy load."

The boy no longer felt ill at ease with these people. At first he
had been repelled by their obscenities. The words had struck him
with all the force of their literal meaning. And in his disgust there
had been fear, not so much of the men and the place, as of his own

sensations. All things he had found different from his imaginings. Bomar's unintended remarks in the car had begun it. He had got in beside his uncle, never doubting that things could ever be otherwise than as they seemed. He had found that even a fact about which there could not be the slightest uncertainty, such as Bomar's eyes, was not a fact at all. Almost without attending it, so fast did it happen, one certainty after another had slipped away from him until he felt exposed in all his privacy. Now this in some way had changed. He had scarcely listened to the guides' talk. He watched them get the boats set for the shoot. What they did went quickly, but there was no haste to their movements, and their banter was spoken with as little attention to the meaning as the congregation repeating the doxology on Sunday.

Goosetree straightened up. His movement was unmistakable. There came a pause and Bomar turned hastily. "Now, kid," he said, "you got to lead these duck."

"Like doves?"

"Yeah. Maybe further. I can't tell you exactly. You'll have to judge. But when they come flying in at you, shoot at their bills." He stepped into the boat. "All ready, me lads?"

"We been ready," Goosetree replied.

The boy sat forward in the boat, astraddle the charcoal burner. There was barely room for his legs and he had to watch to see that his boots didn't burn. They pushed off and he thought surely the ice must chew up the bottom of the boat. The going got better after a while, but every now and then the guide had to strike the ice several times before he could set the oars to water. The darkness thinned and the cold began to bite into him. It had a different quality over water. He felt weight as well as chill. He wore two wool shirts, a heavy wool coat and next to his body close-knit woolen underwear, but it went through all these garments like air through a sack in a broken windowlight. He got to wondering if he could stand it all day and leaned forward to rub his hands over the open mouth of the burner.

His teeth began to chatter and he drew down his chin so it wouldn't be seen. He could hear Bomar and Tommy. Their voices had the flat clear sound of coming from a distance and yet they were not far away. And then he looked up. . . . Dawn had swamped the sky. There was no light and yet he could see. He was first conscious of a wonderful ease to his eyes. Wide open, without a thread's strain, they saw everywhere through the colorless haze. Never had he been able to see so clearly and so far. He thought it must be like this with animal eyes at night or whenever they hunt, to see and not know they are seeing, when the vision and prey are made one for the spring. A wonderfully fresh strength streamed through his body. All things seemed at a beginning. It was the world on the first day.

The boat struck a snag. He looked more closely about. Black slick tree trunks stuck up out of the water like the splintered piles of a pier which has rotted away. Occasionally they passed a stump that was still alive, but its stunted growth only made the desolate surroundings more forbidding. And the Lake, he saw, was forbidding. Miles upon miles of saw grass, more grass than water, and everywhere the illusion of solid ground. Slimy ooze, even quicksand, was its floor. His first elation drained away. He told himself the place was not meant for man. It was more foreign and distant to his experience than the most outlandish reaches of human habitation. Over him came a great and terrible loneliness.

The boats entered an open pocket of frozen water. His boat began to rock and he grasped the sides.

"Give with the boat," Goosetree commanded.

"What's the matter, Mr. Goosetree?"

"Nothing's the matter. I'm breaking the ice."

"What for?"

"To throw out the blocks." Goosetree's voice made him feel the depth of his ignorance.

The ice broke up in sheets and the boat sloshed it out of the way. Into the open water the guide began to throw his decoys. He unwound the string, glanced at the water with quick precision, and then threw out the painted block. In no time the false birds rode their anchors in front of the blind. Goosetree now drove the boat into the edge of the grass. He handed the boy a pole. "When I pull, you push on that," he said and stepped into the water. His hip boots sank down and he said, "All right." At each push the boat slid further into the blind. Empty shells and cigarette butts soiled the flattened tufts of grass. One cigarette, scarcely smoked, touched the water, its damp brown insides spilling and staining the paper. A smear of lipstick gashed its upper end. Instinctively the boy averted his gaze. A blot formed in the blue-gray haze, hung for a moment to the air, desperately, noiselessly fluttering its wings, turned and disappeared. Motionless, he watched the spot where it had been, feeling he could almost have touched the duck, if duck it was, for how could its wings beat so and not make a sound?

"I reckon it's hid," Goosetree said.

"No, it just melted away," the boy replied.

Goosetree's eyes came on guard. The boy said hastily, "Oh, the boat. Yes, sir, it looks hid."

"What'd you think I meant?"

"I didn't hear you well."

He felt that his guide was studying him, trying to make up his mind whether he was responsible enough to risk in the close quarters they must keep. At last Goosetree pulled himself out of the water and began to prepare the boat for action. He set the burner between them, changed the seats so that they faced each other, set his lunch beside him, his water bottle to the rear. He took bunches of grass from both sides and tied them together over the boat. Carefully he loaded his gun and set it down pointing into the grass. He loaded the boy's and handed it to him. "Point it that way," he said, "and always keep the safety on until you get up to shoot. And don't get up until I tell you."

"Where are Uncle Bomar and Tommy gone?" he asked.

The guide was dropping charcoal into the burner. "They went to the other side of the pocket." He leaned over to blow the coals. The boy noticed that his hands were black and his face sooty from handling the coal. When the fire suited him, he dropped a tomato can over the low tin chimney, then rose in the boat. He stood with his body half bent and with a short jerk of the head looked up. A shadow passed over his eyes as he flicked them across the arc of the sky.

"See anything?" the boy asked.

"They'll be in," he replied.

Then they sat in silence, leaning towards each other over the burner. Around the boat, out of the grass, the cold boiled up through a slimy mist. Now that they were settled and waiting the boy felt his body relax and his head grow dull. He was wondering how he could get up from his cramped quarters in time to shoot. He did not see the guide rise. He heard the shot and looked up, his heart fluttering, in time to see the red feet draw up under the white belly, see the inert body slanting to the Lake.

"When they hit the ice, they don't git up no more," Goosetree said. He added, "I seen him too late to call you."

His first feeling was chagrin and resentment. A guide should give others a chance to shoot. But in his heart he knew he had been a bad hunter. Too much excitement had worn him out. He must learn how to wait, be idle and still wound up, like a spring. That was it. Like a spring.

"There they come," Goosetree hissed.

"Where?" he breathed.

"A Susie. In front of you."

Almost overhead and to the left he saw the duck. The spring in him snapped. He heard the report of his gun, saw the bird falter, fly for a hundred yards and then go down. He shot at another passing to his front, missed, shot and missed again. He tried to aim but his eyes felt frozen and wide open. His gun and Goosetree's went off together. The bird stopped short in flight and fell straight down. For the first time Goosetree smiled.

"I missed the second shot," the boy said and his voice was trembling and his throat dry.

"You didn't lead him enough. The air from your load fanned his tail."

"We both shot at the same time. Think we both got him. I expect you got him."

"It was a teal," Goosetree said, glancing swiftly around. The sky seemed to open out of his eyes.

It seemed a long time before the next ducks flew over. At last he heard, "There!" He grabbed his gun, half rose. "Git down," the guide ordered and hastily put his hands to his mouth and called, the reedy imitation of the duck's cry rasping the air. The call seemed too urgent to the boy, faster than a bird would make. The birds dipped and turned, then flew away.

"No use aiming. Whenever they see you, it's too late."

"Did they see me?"

"Hell, yes. Never get up until you're ready to shoot."

The nasal call to death and the sound of guns travelled from different parts of the Lake, gradually drifted into silence until the whole world grew as still as the painted ducks riding their anchors in the pool of rotten ice. He and the guide were close enough to touch. The intimacy which was not intimacy began to close in on him. He felt that he ought to say something. He said, "Is your son going to follow in your footsteps, Mr. Goosetree?"

"Hell, no. There's no money in guiding. Soon's he's old enough I'm going to send him to college."

"I would think this was a wonderful life," the boy said in surprise, "being able to hunt or fish every day and get paid for it."

"It gits stale, up before day freezing your balls off sloshing around in this ice."

The guide picked up a jug of milky water and poured it into a pan and set the pan on the open mouth of the burner. "I'll make us some coffee," he said. "And we can eat. The ducks won't be back until about eleven o'clock. I've noticed that's the time they been coming in."

He measured the coffee and dumped it into the water, took a dirty rag and carefully wiped out two cups and put them beside him. Then he took a spoon and began to stir the coffee and blow the coals. "No," he said, "it's hard on you. I'm going to quit it soon. I bought me the finest summer house ever built around this Lake. Old man Simpkins built it, a rich lumber man from Mississippi. He spent eight thousand dollars on it. Built it of pine and not a knot in it, plumbing, lights, frigidaire, and good water. I heard his widow wanted to sell and I let her know by the woman who looks after it that I might, might mind you, try to buy it. So old lady Simpkins called me long distance. And I asked her what she wanted for it and she commenced telling me how much she'd put in it. I cut her off. I said I'll give you two thousand cash for it. She couldn't listen to any such figure, it was giving it away. Two thousand's my offer. Take it or leave it. She hung up on me. But a week later I got a letter from her son saying his mother couldn't bear to come up here no more since her old man had went away and that they'd close the deal." Goosetree poured a cup of coffee and handed it to the boy. "I'd of give twenty-five hundred as easy as I give two thousand." He unwrapped a sandwich. "I'm going to build two cabins, put a toilet and shower in em, they's eight rooms to the house, and rent by the week or month. A man and his wife can come up and fish. They come sometime with women they claim to be their wives. There'll be money in it."

"How many'd you get?" a voice from the Lake asked.

It was Bomar and Tommy. Goosetree rose. "Aw, we got'm, boys. How many'd you knock down?"

"None," Tommy said. His face was grave and averted, as though still turned from the incomprehensible workings of Fate.

"We shot twice, but they were too high," Bomar added apologetically.

Tommy began throwing out his decoys.

"Don't throw them blocks out here," Goosetree said.

Tommy rowed about, continuing to throw them out. He asked, "Don't we work together?"

"Hell. The quarters is too close."

Bomar said in his slow, soothing voice, "Goosetree, I believe you are afraid we'll outshoot you."

"Who's got the duck?"

"Well, how many did you get?"

"Three," Goosetree said, his voice less belligerent.

"I really got one, Uncle Bomar. On the nose."

"Fine, kid."

"Yes, sir, this boy's gonna knock'm," Goosetree said. The boy felt a glow of pleasure. He was beginning to think more of his guide.

Tommy masked his boat in the grass behind the others.

"You want some coffee?" Goosetree asked.

"We got something better'n coffee," Tommy replied.

"Here, take a drink," Bomar said.

Tommy turned up the bottle. His Adam's apple worked like a piston as the bright brown liquid flowed down his throat. He wiped the mouth of the bottle on his sleeve and returned it casually. "Warms you better than any charcoal," he said matter-of-factly.

From where he reclined in the boat Bomar took a drink. The boy noticed it was much less than Tommy took. "How about it, Goosetree?"

"I got ulcers. Drinking too much in Arkansas," Goosetree replied. "God, but that stuff lightened you as it went down. Set your tail on fire."

"Kid?"

"No, thank you, sir." The boy knew by the way the whiskey

was offered that he was supposed to refuse, but he mightily wanted to taste it. He drank his coffee instead and took a bite out of a ham sandwich. There was too much bread for the meat and he threw away the top slice.

"My daddy tole me to stay out'n Arkansas," Goosetree continued.

"Ain't nothing there," Tommy added sourly.

"I went over there to a duck-calling contest oncet. I called as purty as ever you please." Goosetree added bitterly, "They give the prize to a eleven-year-old boy."

"Ain't nothing for nobody in Arkansas," Tommy said.

The boy tried another sandwich, peanut butter and jelly spread together on the bread. It tasted good. At least it wasn't so dry. He finished his coffee and felt better for the food.

"Tommy, where are these duck you called me about?"

Tommy looked shocked at the question and glanced over the Lake towards the woods. "They're roosting on the reserve," he said.

"Government birds, eh?" Bomar said. "Well, they'll sit on their fat asses until we starve to death."

Tommy looked even more serious. "They'll come out after a while," he said.

"That was humor, Applegate. You wouldn't recognize it, though. It bore no reference to fornication."

Bomar drank again and passed the whiskey to his guide. Tommy took it and turned it up in one motion. He swallowed like a thirsty man drinking water. "That's seven times seven," he said. "What does it make?"

"You drunk," Bomar replied.

"It'll make you holler." He opened his mouth and his voice rang lustily over the Lake.

Bomar examined his companion's face for a moment. "Applegate," he said, "if you had rings in your ears, you'd look like a damn pirate."

Tommy shouted again. "Hi-yo!"

The boy thought he did look like a pirate, anyway like a foreigner, the way his eyes didn't suit his rough, swarthy features but looked both boldly and evasively at the same time. With Mr. Goosetree it was different. He looked like a guide ought to look, although he was a little small and didn't think much of guiding, which was a disappointment the boy didn't explore but which lay uneasily in the back of his head. But Tommy at least was human and it was somehow because of his eyes. Watching the sky, they absorbed it like a blotter. Maybe it was this which made him seem always on guard. When Mr. Goosetree looked at the sky, he skinned it.

"Hi-yo!" Tommy shouted again. As if suddenly spent by the shouting, he said, "My daddy was a Jew and my mother an Indian. Now ain't that a hell of a combination?"

He had half turned away. Bomar looked at him but said nothing. Tommy continued in a conversational tone. "He used to trade up and down this country. I reckon he made a pretty good living until he took to drinking. When I was a shirt-tail boy, he'd come in on Satday nights and run all of us out of the house. I sort of liked it in summer, like a kid will. My mother would bed us down in the leaves and moss. It didn't seem to worry her much. I reckon Indians are sort of used to the woods. There was generally plenty to eat. She made a good truck patch. She'd take the littlest one and go out in the corn when it was tosselling and sing to it. Homesick kind of a singing. As I got older, I didn't like it so much. Looked like he didn't do so well trading. He'd come in during the week drunk and beat her up. She never hollered, but if he tried to take his scantling to one of us young-uns, she'd scratch and bite him like a cat.

"I was about eleven, I guess. We still had plenty to eat, well not a plenty but enough. She always managed to keep us in victuals, but we was all ragged. It takes money to buy clothes. He wasn't doing no trading at all, except he'd take her corn and swap it for licker. Well, he come a night of the worst blizzard that ever you saw, mean drunk and dirty. He looked like he'd been laying out for a week. He commenced cussin' and stumbling around and hollered, 'Clear all these half-breeds outer here.' I said, 'Daddy, I don't aim to go out in no blizzard.' His red eyes kind of bulged at me. He picked a old table leg that was laying around and come toward me. I raised the gun. He still kept coming. I let him have it right in the belly." Tommy's voice ceased. He said after a while, "Sober, he wasn't no mean-natured kind of a man."

Without saying anything Bomar passed the whiskey over to Tommy. Nobody spoke again for a long while. Goosetree had covered himself up and gone to sleep. Bomar lay back, reclining in the boat. The day had advanced but there was no sun to relieve the cold. The frozen clouds stretched tight across the sky. After a while the boy became conscious of Bomar's soothing voice. It flowed too smoothly. It was getting confidential. He recognized the signs. Miserable from the cold and the long, trying wait, he felt the shoot would be a failure. Nobody would watch for the ducks, maybe there wouldn't be any more to come in. He felt the need to stand up. It was a little less cold up in the air. There was not a duck in the sky. He looked down and his blood danced. Three were playing in the water before a jutting strip of the grass. "Look, Tommy," he cried.

"Mud hens," Tommy said and sat back down.

Bomar had turned where he lay. His eyes were gay. "What," he asked, "would the old boy, what's his name, Menelaus, say if he knew his grandson had taken a mud hen for a duck? The pious Menelaus, our noble ancestor, unequalled in the arts of field and stream and Ovid's pupil. What would he say, kid?"

He was too surprised to say anything—Bomar wondering about grandfather Laus, too, for it was plain that he only pretended to recollect his name. . . .

"Never, oh, never, would that nonpareil, that prince among men, that cock of the walk, have mistaken a mud hen for a duck. Or so we're told. What I like, Applegate, about this revered ancestor of mine and the kid's, was his timing. Now I know that timing is everything, but damn if I can bring it off. But this guy Menelaus did. When he was young, he went the rounds. When it came time to settle down, he didn't settle, but nobody held it against him, least of all his large female connection. He hunted when he wanted to, he had plenty of money, he played the races and was a family man all at the same time. He was a genius, Applegate. And while he stepped high, wide and handsome, his Helen stayed at home making quilts and raising his young. That's the way to do it, Applegate. Be fruitful and multiply. And don't forget the quilts. He didn't. He made it a point to keep her in fresh patterns, just in case. . . . And then when he had dropped all the grains of corn from one jar to the other and it was time to change'm back, he saw the light. At a camp meeting at Walnut Grove the dove, not the kind you're thinking about, Applegate, but the blessed, the miraculous dove, came bearing the twig of salvation." He paused. His voice had grown harder as he spoke. "Don't take it hard, kid, you're not the first to take a wooden nickel."

He couldn't make heads or tails of what his uncle was saying. What did a wooden nickel have to do with it? It was very important. He could tell by Bomar's voice. Before he could try to figure it out, Tommy interrupted.

"There was a lady here fishing once named Helen," Tommy said. "She come here with a doctor from Chicago. They claimed they was married, but I been rowing a long time. These two didn't much care whether they caught anything or not. She wasn't having much luck and I said—I wasn't thinking anything—'diddle on this side.' I meant her hook of course, and she said, 'What? Right there?' and giggled. You know, it was the way she giggled. And the doctor, he laughed too. They did a sight of loose laughing." Tommy leaned over and stirred the charcoal in the burner. "When I first took up guiding people, didn't no women come here to hunt or fish."

Bomar raised his bottle. "Here's to Argive Helen and all her kin."

The boy felt the boat move. Goosetree was awake and staring at Bomar's large, well-wrapped body. "Look at him," he said, "laying over there like a fattening hog."

Far away, over near the island, a lone gun shot once. It made no more noise than a popgun but the men in the two boats grew very quiet. They all rose to their feet. Goosetree took out his watch. "Eleven twenty," he said.

The importunate duck calls, still at a distance, now buzzed like insects. More guns went off over by the reserve. The firing was scattered. Then somebody said, "Get down." The boy didn't see anything and he got panicky. "Coming over you." "Where, where?" he asked in a tight voice. And then all four of them were shooting furiously. He thought he hit one but he wasn't sure. Two of the ducks turned and flew over a blind across the channel. The hunters there shot up a lot of shells but the ducks went on their way. Goosetree called out, "You want my gun?" His voice was taunting and cheerful. "You can have my gun if you want it."

"How about that for shooting, Applegate?" Bomar asked. His voice was even and full.

"Boy, you stopped him."

"Didn't I stop him, though?"

"Did you? A mallard, too."

"Purty good shooting," Goosetree said. "But look over here in the water."

"Here's where to look," Tommy called back. "Them ducks jest killed theyselves, but we had to shoot to bring'm down."

"Hell."

"We're hitting them, ain't we?" Bomar said.

"Watch it, boys," Goosetree snapped.

Down in the boat Tommy was calling. The hunters across the channel called. The boy crouched and watched the bird, the bending wings, the red feet drawn in. . . . The duck dipped and dove toward the water. The world vanished. There was nothing but space, a streak in space. The moving bolt was all. His ears crashed, the thud against his shoulder, another crash, the red feet gashed the white breast. The dead body dropped and the world was.

"Not bad, kid."

"I think you got him, Uncle Bomar."

"Hard to say. We shot together."

The two of them, the boy and his uncle, were alone in the boat. They watched the guides row from place to place, gathering in the ducks. At last the long full day was over. Behind the island the darkness crouched. As if sensing the hunters could no longer shoot, the ducks now lighted everywhere around them. "God, God . . ." Bomar whispered. Then the guides turned their boat about. It sped toward the hunters. Quietly the water parted about the prow, quietly closed behind the rippling wake. No sign of passage marred its surface—waiting to receive the falling night.

"It's been a good shoot," Bomar said evenly. "But it's over."

The boy turned towards his uncle. What he saw made him raise his hand, as though for support. Bomar stood erect and waiting. His eyes were regarding the boy; they were the eyes in the mahogany frame.

LULA BORROW

BY THOMAS MABRY

LULA BORROW was fifteen years old when she came to work for the MacFarlands in 1914, but to Wade MacFarland, who was nine, she seemed to be a grown Negro woman, an adult like his mother or even his grandmother: an old person. Otherwise, looking back, how could he excuse himself—a poor excuse even so—for his behavior in the earliest incident he could remember Lula's having had a part in? The scene had always remained with him. It was summer, there had been a rain during the night, the green earth around him was steaming and above him the boughs bent down as if under the weight of so much sunlight. Rain puddles still dotted the driveway. Lula was sitting on the front porch rocking Wade's baby sister to sleep, or rather she was pushing the baby carriage back and forth where his sister lay sleeping. Wade had been playing in the sandpile that surrounded the black base of one of the stalwart white-oaks that stood in the sloping tree-filled yard. Behind him, the street along which he could hear a cart going past now and then, seemed at a great distance. In front of him, up and across the more open sweep of sunlit grass, the flower garden too seemed far away. He glanced up and saw the Negress's knees stretched apart and her skirt tight over them. Her head rested on the back of the rocking chair and she also might have been sleeping except that she held in her hand a folded newspaper with which she now and again attacked the lazy flies that circled above the baby-carriage. A sense of quietness lay on the morning air. He rose to his feet and, wiping the gritty sand from his hands by rubbing them on his knickers, walked over to the porch steps and stood gazing up at Lula, who smiled down at him. . . . Did he smile back at her? He could not remember. His mind had been too full of the ambient air, too excited by the impulse that had risen within him. What he distinctly remembered was that he had thrust his forefinger into his nose and pulled out a bit of greenish-brown mucus, walked up the steps, leaned daringly over Lula's lap and deposited the mucus on the bosom of her dress.

He had not been prepared for the effect of his action.

Lula jumped to her feet. "You, boy! What you mean, wiping your boogers on my clean dress!" Suddenly her brown hand shot out and slapped him. He heard the sound and felt simultaneously the sting on his cheek. Lula looked down at her starched, white bosom. "Miss Dora just gimme this dress this morning." She took a handkerchief out of her pocket and wiped off the slime. "Why you want to go and do a thing like that?"

Wade stood back on his heels. The sunlight, piercing the green boughs behind him, warmed his shoulders and lit up Lula's face. "I'm going to tell Mother you slapped me," he said. "I'm going to tell her as soon as she comes back from town."

Lula leaned over the baby carriage. "Shsh now," she said softly. "Shsh now." She straightened up and faced him. "What you say you going to tell her?"

"I'm going to tell her you slapped me."

Lula stared at him a moment before she laughed. She nodded towards the street. "There she comes, now," she said.

Wade turned and saw his mother stepping out of a carriage. There were other ladies in the carriage. She stood talking to them and presently stepped back and waved to them, while the horses were turned round. She waved again and turned and walked slowly across the green grass, up the hill under the trees to the porch and up the steps. She put her arm around his shoulder.

"Well, Lula," she said, "has the baby been good?"

"Good as gold, Miss Dora," Lula said. "Slept all morning."

Mrs. MacFarland pressed Wade more closely to her side. "And what about this big baby here?"

Wade's heart was beating faster. The sense of a secret intimacy that was about to be broken was almost unbearably exciting. He waited for Lula's answer, and heard her say:

"He's *growing* so, Miss Dora! He's gona be growed up into a man before y'all knows it."

"I do know it," Mrs. MacFarland said with a sigh. She opened the screen door and as she disappeared into the cool hall she added: "And I just can't stand it."

Linked with that memory was another memory, of an incident of even less consequence. But just as from the first he had learned the excitement of assault, so from the second he learned the despair that comes from the knowledge of the limitless distance that separated him from another human being. It was Lula who gave him words for it. . . . Beyond the sandpile stood a swing, an elaborate wood construction, a "two-seater" which could hold four people. The seats, facing each other, were connected at the foot by a sort of open lattice platform by means of which, working the feet and legs rigidly back and forth, the swing could be "pumped." Next to the swing grew a Japanese quince, as high as the swing and dankly sheltering it. The time was perhaps a year later. Lula was still house-girl and nurse—she had not yet moved into the kitchen— but she had become such an accustomed part of the household that he never thought of home (from the distance of town or school-house) that she was not in the image. This time it was again summer, and again his baby sister was asleep. But the hour was later because his mother was also asleep, taking her usual afternoon nap, and he and Lula were alone in the swing together.

He was pleased to have her to himself. Most of the time she was busy either cleaning the house or nursing the baby. That afternoon she had come out to rest in the swing. During the past year she had grown more plump and her beautiful tan-colored cheeks were smooth and full, and the short wiry black hair that curled about her broad forehead glistened in the sunlight. They sat facing each other in the swing. Wade felt the gentle airy balance of it that was still new and a constant pleasure to him. He raised his feet and folded them under him on the seat. "You pump a while, Lula," he said, and shut his eyes, waiting for the thrust of the stronger movement. Lula obliged him, and he relaxed to the sensation. As he felt the repeated upward thrust it seemed to him that each time the swing went higher; that he had left the earth altogether now and was up in the very midst of the green leaves whose height had before always eluded him. Up here the air smelled sweeter. Up here the quality of sunlight was different: it was thinner, dryer, yet all the more piercing. He tried to will that this delicious movement go on forever. Then the swing stopped. He opened his eyes and saw that Lula had closed hers. "All right," he said. "Now I'll pump you." He went to work and the swing sailed back and forth, as high as he could make it go. After a little, Lula opened her eyes.

"That's mighty nice," she said, "but it's time to pick the baby up."

The sensation of sailing abruptly ceased as Lula's feet pressed down against the platform.

"Not yet," Wade said. "Not yet."

"Next thing you know the baby will be waking your mamma," Lula said, and half rose from the seat.

"No," Wade said, and began a vigorous pumping. The swing swerved to the side, and Lula, caught off balance, fell back into her seat.

"Let me out of here, boy."

"You can't go yet," Wade said. He had been conscious of being in command while the swing was moving. It was too soon to relinquish that power. Besides, he believed he had been giving Lula pleasure too. Their eyes met, and Wade saw the lovely smile that would never, he knew, deny him any indulgence. "We've just begun," he added.

"It's time to pick the baby up," Lula repeated, and put a foot out on the ground to steady the swing.

He decided to use his authority. "You've got to stay," he said boldly. "I order you to stay. You've got to stay so I can swing you."

Lula rose to her feet. Her brown arms clasped both sides of the swing while she looked down at him. "I ain't *got* to do nothing but die," she said quietly, and left him there in the swing alone.

He used to wonder later if Lula could have had any idea of how successfully her remark had detached him from her, at least for a while. It seemed to separate her from him by a million miles. And though the remark wounded him he soon forgot it: he did not know, then, that it represented the bare rock she clung to, her last residuum of strength; that because of it she had been able to rally from despair the year before and seek work until she found it at the MacFarlands'. . . .

Lula had been born and raised down in Stewart County, down in the back country, thirty miles from the town of Mount Ashton where the MacFarlands lived. By the time she was ten years old she was keeping house for her widowed father, who was a sharecropper on a farm owned by a white man. That was in addition to working in the corn and tobacco patch when the weather was good. She never saw anybody to talk to except her father and an elder sister who was married and lived on another farm three miles away. Lula used to walk the distance every night after the dishes were done. One night—she was eleven then—she arrived to find the cabin door flung open. From inside there came a low guttural moaning that made her hair stand up. She ran through the door. Her sister was sitting in a pool of blood on the floor. The moaning came from her. The lamplight burned evenly on the table. Lula looked across the room and saw her sister's husband lying dead in the bed. Her sister—Alice was her name—half dead herself, was waiting for the police to come and take her away. Lula never saw Alice after that except when she visited her once a year in the penitentiary at Nashville.

Lula married when she was thirteen. She was lonesome without her sister, her father was old and cranky, and she had fallen in love with a dark-skinned young man she saw riding the mules back and forth from the stable. He passed in front of the cabin twice a day, and the way he sat on the lead-mule and managed the others (better than any other man on the place) pierced Lula's heart. He spoke to her in the field while they were setting out tobacco. She had been carrying plants to the men from the plant bed. She lowered the tow-sack from her shoulder and unfolded it at his feet, revealing the pale green spindly shoots she had dug. She could never believe in May that by July those shoots would grow into sturdy plants, high as her shoulder, with each sticky odorous leaf as broad as her waist. He asked her to fetch him the water jug. The sight of his bare feet, the luxuriant sound of his low voice, and the movement of his shiny black neck excited her more deeply than she had ever been excited before. She flew to the edge of the field where the water jug lay under a persimmon tree, and flew back. He started courting her regularly after that, and by June they were married. The ceremony took place on a fine day, full of sunshine. Lula remembered thinking as she walked to the church and looked out across the fence at the peach orchard she was passing where the fruit was already ripening that she would be able to make plenty of peach preserves for her husband that summer.

Lula was a good housekeeper. She liked to make things. Her

husband had told her he had a house for her, ready and waiting, but when he took her there after the marriage ceremony, and threw open the door, what she saw before her was a single-room cabin without a piece of furniture in it, not even a bed or a cook-stove. He pushed her down on the floor, and later fell asleep lying on top of her. She extricated herself from his drunken slumbering embrace and went home and brought back a broom and the corn-shuck ticking from her own bed, and helped him onto it. While he slept she swept out the room, and by nightfall had borrowed a coal-oil stove and enough food and cooking utensils to cook his supper. By the end of the week she had sewed together flour sacks for the window, constructed a table and wash-stand and put together some planks to form a kind of bed. In a month's time she had papered the room with newspaper, made a rag rug and found a calendar and a looking-glass somewhere.

She carried water for herself and her husband from her father's house, but in July her father married, and his new wife refused to let Lula use the cistern any more. Thereafter she made a daily trip to the pond that lay a half mile from her own house. The pond water, however, was warm and muddy from cattle standing in it, and Lula fell ill from drinking it. She managed, nevertheless, to gather the hard red clingstone peaches that grew on the peach tree near the cabin—it was the only tree in the yard, in fact—and these she cut open and spread out on the roof to dry. All during the late summer and autumn she prayed that a baby girl would be born to her. She wanted to name it after her sister Alice whom she deeply missed and with whom she had long imaginary conversations. She felt that a daughter would partly take her sister's place. When in January she gave birth to twins, a boy and a girl, she was overjoyed.

For a while she was hardly aware that her husband paid little attention to her now except to beat her when he came home drunk. Almost a child herself, she shared a child's inability to es-cape from another's cruelty and could only suffer from it, mutely. It was during this period that she developed her passion for eating sweet things. Sitting with the two babies feeding at her breast she would sometimes experience so sudden and imperious a hunger that she would have to put them down and run to the sugar sack and swallow half a cupful before she could pick them up again.

Her husband was growing more sullen. It seemed that the very presences of his wife and the two babies were an irritation to him beyond endurance. He would sit and stare at them after supper, his black narrow face like an angular bird's beak in the lamplight. At intervals he would stretch back his lips involuntarily. The grimace would show his blue-black gums and even white teeth. Seeing them, she began to tremble.

It was not for herself that she trembled. She had begun to sense that his malice had grown to include the babies too. This knowledge left her dazed and uncertain until the Saturday night when, drunk and cursing, he slapped them from her arms. Until that moment she had loved him, as a child might love its parent, because it was natural to do so, because the parent is the child's world and the child's first outward movement towards the world is a movement of love. But when he struck the babies from her she cried out and her heart seemed to turn to ice. She stooped down and gathered them into her arms and ran out of the cabin. That night she hid in the privy, wondering what she would do if he followed her, because he could have pushed the frail structure to the ground. But he did not follow her. She hid there, listening, until just before daybreak when she slipped out and walked the five miles to Bumpus Mills crossroads. She begged some crackers and cheese from the storekeeper and during the day was able to find work for herself and a place to stay. But she was not left in peace for long. She had got work as cook in the logging camp at Bumpus Mills, and she lived in a shack near the kitchen. She would feed the twins and put them to bed and go about her work, making trips to the shack in the intervals between rush hours. The babies slept quietly, waked happy, and played together in silence like two wild cubs, instinctively wise at concealing their whereabouts. One rainy night when she returned from her duties in the kitchen she found the babies gone . . . No need to ask where they were or who had taken them: she knew.

For a few minutes all her faculties left her. She threw herself on the pallet and lay there groaning. The sound was more like the sound of some agonized animal than that of a woman crying. But after a time it turned into the sound of ordinary weeping: her mind came back to her: she was again able to force her body to act. She got up and ran out of the shack. The black rain was like a multitude of stones beating against her and she could not see the road or, for that matter, any object by which she might get her bearings. Finally her feet detected the muddy track that led to the highway, and she began running towards it.

In an hour she had run the distance between Bumpus Mills and her husband's cabin. All the way she imagined her babies calling to her although they were only three months old. Yet she endowed them with speech and kept answering them in her heart. She could in fact hear them screaming when she staggered through the gate into the slick clay yard, and it took all her will power to keep from crying out herself as she flung open the cabin door. Her husband evidently expected her. He was sitting in one of the two chairs she had made, facing the entrance, with his back to the two infants who lay in a corner of the room on the floor, barricaded by the table. She started towards them but he sprang in front of her and grasped her arms and pinned them to her sides while he stared down into her face. His lips stretched back into the grin she had learned to fear. Her clothes were sodden with rain, and water dripped down her cheeks from her head. She saw that he too was still wet, and the thought came to her and so filled her mind that it obscured all else: he had carried the babies unprotected through the rain, and they were wet now. Sobs broke from her, but she controlled herself. She tried to peer around him to see her children. The light from the single lamp was obstructed by the table that stood on its edge pinning the children in the corner, but the nature of their crying told her that they were cold and wet and shivering. Before her husband had even spoken she had made up her mind.

"I'll stay here," she said calmly, leaning back and trying to fix his eyes with her own. "I'll stay here and cook for you iffen you won't hit them no more."

For a week she was certain both babies were going to die. They lay gasping from croup. She would snatch them up in their paroxysms of coughing and hold them by their feet, head downwards, trying to shake out of them whatever it was that seemed about to stop their breath. She would massage their hot bodies and in her ignorance apply to their foreheads pieces of cloth soaked in vinegar. She prayed to God to spare them. It was not her husband she blamed for exposing them to the spring rain, but herself. Forgetting that her fear for their safety had in the first place made her run away with them, she told herself that if she had not taken them to Bumpus Mills their father would not have so cruelly exposed them. The first sin was her sin; she alone was the cause of their suffering. The night that the male infant died she left the cabin and went out to the privy which had become her hiding-place in times of danger. She shut the door behind her and knelt down and relinquished his soul to God. Then in her prayer she made a covenant with God that if the boy alone would be acceptable as payment for what she had done she would henceforth dedicate every waking hour of her life to the welfare of her daughter and to praising Him.

Not long afterwards, after her husband had beaten her again and threatened to beat the baby, she left him permanently. This time she travelled thirty miles, to Mount Ashton, where she put her child to board with another Negro woman and she herself went to work for the MacFarlands. At fifteen years old she passed easily for an unmarried girl. Mrs. MacFarland was delighted to find a servant girl so docile, so good-natured, so eager to please her, and apparently without close family ties. All Lula said was that she had come from "down around Bumpus Mills" and had no acquaintances in Mount Ashton. Mrs. MacFarland was relieved to think that there would be no tote-basket after supper every night and, at least for a while, no Negro man lounging on the kitchen porch steps.

Lula had worked for Mrs. MacFarland for nearly two years before anything occurred that Mrs. MacFarland could take even the slightest exception to. (Lula's position had changed during this period gradually from nurse to house-girl to cook. As nurse her wages were two dollars a week, as house-girl two-twenty-five, but after Mrs. MacFarland decided to dispense with a nurse for Wade's baby sister, she moved Lula into the kitchen and raised her wages to three dollars a week.) The incident that annoyed Mrs. MacFarland was of no consequence—it merely ran counter to her "iron rule" that the children were not to accompany any of the servants to their homes. Yet to Wade it was of great importance: he saw her room, he saw where Lula lived. Until then where she lived had been a mystery to him. Fitfully he had wondered about what sort of place Lula inhabited, but any image evaded him. The actual journey, however, led him to see more than her room, and what he saw became a bond between them, so secret, so intimate, that he almost hid it from himself.

Lula always took home with her any old bits of furniture or

trinkets that Mrs. MacFarland wanted to get rid of. These gifts were accepted by Lula with what seemed to Wade not so much ordinary gratitude as delight. Her round full face would glow with pleasure and the smile that perpetually enchanted him would deepen, become more inward, more intense. "Aw Mrs. MacFarland, yess'm" she would say when the objects were displayed before her. There was in Mrs. MacFarland's mind another category of unwanted possessions upon which she had placed a mental label, SELL, and which included for the most part clothes: Mr. MacFarland's old suits, shoes, and shirts, her own worn-out dresses and shoes, Wade's shoes, and all the clothes his baby sister no longer wore. And although Lula paid whatever price Mrs. MacFarland asked for them—Mrs. MacFarland owned a little notebook in which she kept an unending account showing the nickels and dimes Lula contributed each week—Lula seemed to show the same quality of pleasure over these bought objects as over those that were given to her. Sometimes in the evening when the family was gathered in the sitting-room after supper Mrs. MacFarland would bring out her little black book and make entries. "But what on earth can she possibly *do* with them all?" she would remark to her husband.

One Saturday Wade was standing in the parlor looking out the window with his nose pressed against the pane. The day was near the end of March and the atmosphere of the soft grey afternoon seemed to hang between fog and rain. Close to the house a narrow walk of concrete ran from the front porch all the way round back to the kitchen porch. Concrete was considered something of a luxury in Mount Ashton in those days, and Wade's father had indulged rather ostentatiously in it the summer before. While Wade stood dreaming he caught sight of Lula out of the corner of his eye as she made her way slowly along the walk. She was loaded down with bundles and fat paper bags, and a small infant's chair was slung by a string from her shoulder. When she came directly opposite his window he tapped on the glass. She looked up, and the jerk of her head caused the chair to slip from her shoulder and fall to the walk. Wade raised the window and leaned out. His head was on the same level as Lula's. He could have touched her.

"You scared me, Wade," Lula said and leaned over and picked up the chair.

"Where're you going?" he asked.

"I'm going home. That's where I'm going," Lula said.

Her answer piqued him. He had already—many times before—been discomforted because Lula apparently did not consider where he and his family lived "home." It was home to him. Lula spent most of her waking hours there. Why wasn't it home for her, too? Lately he had begun to tease Lula. He was getting bigger, growing taller. He could not any longer run and jump into her lap. Teasing her was one of the few ways left to stay close to her.

"You're already at home," he said now. "So you can't be going there."

A paper bag slipped from her grasp. "Go 'way from me, Wade," she cried. The impact of the bag in its fall against the concrete had split the flimsy brown paper. "Now looka there," she added.

Wade turned from the window, picked up a newspaper, and ran out the front door and round to the walk where Lula had knelt down and was trying to tie a string around the broken bag.

"Here's some newspaper," he said. He pulled the bundle away from her and wrapped it up.

"How you know Miss Dora'n them done finished reading that paper?" Lula said. They were squatting together on the concrete walk.

Wade looked her in the eyes. "If they haven't, they ought to have," he said.

They stood up.

"Let me take that other bag too," Wade said, and they started down the driveway. When they reached the street it seemed natural to turn with her onto the wider concrete walk. Halfway down the block Wade grasped the packages tighter and said,

"I'm going to carry these all the way home for you."

Lula had increased the speed of her stride. She moved so smoothly that Mrs. MacFarland's old hat, set firmly forward on her wiry hair, barely quivered with her steps.

"Make hase, then," she said, "so I can git on back and git my supper started."

They turned from Elm Street (where the MacFarlands lived) into Seventh, and immediately the less prosperous-looking dwellings became noticeable. They crossed Harrison and passed the gloomy, witch-like cottage on the corner that belonged to Miss Ivie

Duke, a venerable, retired schoolteacher who had taught Wade's mother and who had given him *Hans Brinker* the Christmas before and brought him a dish of wine jelly when he had the measles. Beyond Miss Ivie's garden fence the squat Negro houses began. At the next corner the paving and concrete stopped. No trees lined the streets here. There was only an occasional telephone pole. Presently they were in the heart of nigger-town. A passerby, seeing them together, might have thought the trip but an ordinary passage. But as Wade's feet stumbled over the loose or broken brick of the pavement and as his eyes noted the solid lines of washing that filled the yards, and now and then an ancient Negro sitting on a porch, as he felt himself more and more surrounded by house after house where no single white person lived, a sense of excitement invaded him. He was on his way to Lula's room and nobody in his family had ever been there. He would know what his mother did not know. "Lula is so vague about where she lives," he had heard his mother at intervals say. And his father would reply: "Well, what difference does it make?" Ah, but then his father did not share as much of Lula's life as he did; his father never saw her except at mealtimes when she brought in the food, and when he paid her each Saturday night.

They crossed a street Wade did not know the name of. Lula indicated with a slight nod of her head (her arms were full of bundles even though Wade was carrying two bags) a one-story wooden structure that stood in a small yard of dry Bermuda grass at their left. It was merely a box-like room that might have held no more than sixty people. No steeple extended above the roof, but on each side wall a row of five ordinary windows apparently let in an abundance of light. "That's my church," she said in a tone of affection. They passed it. She nodded her head again. "And that there's where I live."

"Right next door!" Wade said and smiled.

"As close as I can git," Lula said and laughed.

Wade looked back at the structure. "Why?" he said, wondering.

"Why?" Lula exclaimed in a tone of disapproval. "Wouldn't you, if you could!"

"I hadn't thought about it," Wade said. "What church is it?"

"Sanctified," Lula said, "I thought you knowed that." She

leaned against the sagging gate to let Wade enter the yard in front of her. But he stood back and let her lead the way across the short yard towards her room, which appeared to be a lean-to attached to that side of the house next to the church. She unlocked the door.

He was to wonder why the beating of his heart had accelerated as he crossed that threshold. Perhaps unconsciously he was already aware of his commitment to Lula, and yet through all her life he was never able to give a name to that commitment. Years later when he thought of Lula it was as of someone who existed for him with an intensity of existence unlike anything else in his life, but he could hardly have called that a "commitment."

Outside it had been foggy and the trees had dripped with moisture, but as he stepped into Lula's room the air seemed to lighten, become less dense, and when she closed the door behind him the room appeared to be illuminated by some mysterious dry white light that came from every direction. The light was both pleasing and unearthly, and for an instant he had the confused thought that they had by mistake entered a room or crypt of the church next door. For indeed the room was almost bare and there were no windows. Then he realized that what had seemed strange was simply the effect of light coming through a skylight in the slanted ceiling and striking against walls which had been freshly whitewashed.

"Why, there's my old bed," he said, reassured at the sight of something so familiar as the gilded brass bed that had once stood in his room. In these austere surroundings it seemed almost gaudy. There was little else in Lula's room. A wardrobe, a single straight chair, and over against the wall two orange crates, stood on end, which together evidently formed a sort of dressing-table, for there was a small looking-glass—the kind that gives the effect of being splintered around the edges—hanging from a nail above the crates. That was all except a trunk. The trunk served as a table next to the bed and on it were a coal-oil lamp, a Bible, a Kewpie doll, and a photograph. That Kewpie doll, he had won the thing at a carnival so long ago he could not remember what year it was. . . .

"Lemme take those bags you're holding," Lula said. She had deposited her own bundles and the infant's chair in a corner on the floor. Wade went over and added his two bags to the pile. He was again struck by the powdery atmosphere in the room. Even the thin plank floor reflected the white pervasive light. Nothing seemed to cast any shadow. He shivered.

"You haven't got any heat in here, Lula," he said.

"Don't need no heat," Lula said. "I'm too busy to think about whether I got heat or not."

A question came into his mind. He hesitated to ask it, but his sudden curiosity forced the question from him.

"What're you going to do with all those things we brought from home?" he said. He was thinking that he had seen her carry off many things before, yet there was no sign of them in the room, except the Kewpie doll.

"Sell 'em," Lula said.

"*Sell* 'em!" Wade said, shocked at such an idea. He had forgotten for the moment that some of the objects had already been sold to Lula by his mother. "Why, you must be rich!"

The word seemed to focus her attention on the packages in the corner. She walked over and knelt down to examine them. Wade followed and stood above her. "I mean if you keep selling all these things you bring from home . . . ," he said, as if in explanation. Lula looked up at him and smiled, and he was ashamed of the words he had spoken.

"Rich?" she said. "Honey, I *is* rich." She leaned over and pulled a pair of his father's old shoes from one of the paper bags. "All this-here needs is some polish," she said, more to herself than to him, "and I know that nigger will buy them." Then louder: "Yes sir, I is rich. And one half goes to my church and the other half goes for my baby."

"What?" He could not believe he had heard Lula correctly. "Did you say for your baby?"

"Go yonder and look at that picture," Lula said, pointing to the trunk beside the bed.

Wade went over and picked up the photograph. He had noticed it when he came in but only as ornament to the trunk. Now he held it in both hands and tried to concentrate on the picture of the smiling Negro child, but he was thinking of Lula herself, trying to adjust his mind to this new vision of her. His old conception of her was suddenly valueless.

"That's my baby girl," Lula said proudly.

"Is she dead?" he asked.

"Course she ain't dead," Lula said, and laughed. "What makes you ask a thing like that?"

"Where is she, then?"

At this question Lula's face darkened, caught itself up, as if their conversation had already gone too far, as if she had been trapped into some misstatement. "Where's who?" she said blandly.

" 'Where's who?' " Wade repeated, confused. Then, because of his confusion and his love and his innocence, and because he saw Lula being separated from him by ghostly presences closer to her than he himself, he exclaimed in his arrogance, his ignorance:

"Then she must be dead. She'd be here if she wasn't dead."

Lula rose to her feet. She snatched off her hat, and with the gesture her black head of hair seemed to bloom more abundantly.

"Hush up your mouth! *Hush up your mouth!*" She took a step towards him and held the hat aloft like a weapon. "Don't you never say nothing like that again." Suddenly she dropped to her knees in the middle of the floor, and buried her face in her hands.

"Lula, Lula," Wade cried out at the agonizing sound of her sobbing. He stooped down beside her on the floor and stared at her plump shaking shoulders. "Lula," he said again, bewildered. He noticed that he was still holding the photograph. It was of a child about the age of his own sister, with skin darker than Lula's. He leaned over farther to catch what she was saying. She was speaking with difficulty.

"My baby ain't dead. Lord God, my baby ain't dead!"

"I didn't mean it, Lula, really I didn't."

He put out his hand and touched her shoulder tentatively. After a minute she raised her face and seeing that he was holding the photograph, she took it from him. "Ain't she cute?" she said. She had regained control over herself. "I sure do miss that pretty thing." She rose to her feet with a sigh. "Time to start back."

She went over to the door and held it open for him. Wade hesitated on the threshold. It was imperative to clear up the mystery. "But where *is* your baby?" he asked.

Lula's eyes swept the room before she answered, as if to be certain there were no spying ears to hear what she might say. She pushed him gently through the doorway and turned and locked the door behind them. "I'm boarding her 'cross town with Sister Mary Margaret," she said.

They started back across the yard.

"Why don't you bring her to our house?" Wade asked.

"You know Miss Dora don't want no nigger baby sitting in her kitchen," Lula said. She turned and faced him. "Besides," she added, "I ain't aiming to let her get too used to me."

They had crossed the yard when the main door of the house opened and a voice called out to Lula, who turned back. Wade leaned against the fence pondering what she had told him. The word "Why?" had formed on his lips but he had not spoken it. He felt himself in the presence of an emotion which he respected even if he did not understand. And yet, dimly, he did understand it. He knew that Lula wanted to protect her child from something, something that she herself had not been protected from.

Suddenly he heard Lula's voice cry out behind him. He whirled round. She was talking to a Negro woman who stood half in the doorway. He heard Lula say "Here?" incredulously. Then she was coming back across the yard towards him. She reached him, passed him, and the single word she said was "Hurry!"

He never forgot that journey back home. Lula spoke little but from what she said so meagerly he learned that her husband had discovered where she was living and that he had come there, and that she was afraid if he found her he would force her to tell him where she had hidden her child. She spoke so haltingly and in such fragments that afterwards he could never remember exactly what she said. In later years when he looked back, his own life seemed to him to have begun with that journey. Even at the time he knew at least that his childhood was ending with it, for it was a journey into the knowledge of evil, and when he arrived again at his own front porch and Lula left him to go round the back to the kitchen he was assaulted with the pain of separation from her and assaulted, too, with the realization that she had moved into regions remote from him. He sat down on the porch step, and it was as if he had been cast out alone in the middle of a desert.

After a while as he sat there, however, he began to feel a certain curiosity. He had never known before what it was to be curious about another person's actions. Now, he wondered what Lula would do. (The short walk home had changed more than the world he lived in; it had changed him.) Not only was he curious about Lula but he was aware of another emotion: the desire to help her.

That night after supper instead of going up to his room to study he slipped out of the house and went out and sat under the hawthorn tree in the corner of the yard and waited for Lula. When he saw her emerge from the rear of the house after her work was done, he stood up and went forward to meet her on the pavement.

Lula kept on walking. "Why ain't you in the house getting your lessons like you ought to be?" she asked him calmly.

He fell into step beside her. "I'm going with you," he said.

"Naw you ain't," Lula said.

"Yes I am," he said. "What are you going to do, Lula?"

She did not answer at once. They reached the corner and turned down Seventh Street before she said:

"I'm moving out of that room and moving fast."

"I'll help you move," Wade said.

"You better go on back home," she said.

But he had detected in her tone a lack of the usual vehemence with which she addressed him. He remained with her and she did not speak again until they were within a block of where she lived. Then she said, more to herself than to him:

"I got plenty of time. If I know that nigger he'll wait till he's good and drunk."

"What do you want me to do, Lula?" Wade asked.

"You just stand here," Lula said. "And if you see a tall black lanky nigger turn in the yard, you just go on back home. I can handle him."

She left him then, and he took up his guard. He could see her moving about in her room in the lamplight. Presently she came out dragging her trunk, and dragged it over to the porch of the main part of the house. A woman came out of the house and the two of them went into Lula's room and came out again carrying pieces of Lula's brass bed. They carried the bed and the trunk into the woman's house. In a few minutes Lula's room was empty.

Wade had looked up and down the street several times in the deepening twilight. Nobody had passed him except a single Negro woman, obviously a cook going home after work. It occurred to him that his own task was over. He waited a moment longer. Then he heard Lula's voice call out to him.

"I'm all moved out now. You go home and get your lessons."

"All right," he called back. "I'm going."

He hurried home feeling that he had discharged a duty honorably. He was filled too with an agreeable excitement, an excitement that must have been noticeable in his eyes, for when his mother met him in the hall on his return she gave him a sharp look and said:

"Good gracious! Where have you been?"

"I walked home with Lula, that's all," he said.

Mrs. MacFarland did not approve of her son's having walked home with her servant. She did not consider it suitable. She told him so, and took him in the sitting-room where her husband was, and asked her husband to speak to him about it. The next morning she also told Lula that she did not approve of it. Lula promised not to let him walk home with her any more. When Wade protested that it was he who had asked Lula to let him go with her, his mother said, "Nonsense."

That was the beginning of a series of things Mrs. MacFarland did not approve of. She did not approve of Lula's asking permission to store her "furniture" in a corner of the carriage house— Lula had said she was boarding in the home of her clergyman now, and had no place for her furniture—but, as Mrs. MacFarland said, what could she do? The furniture was just a few old things she had herself given to Lula, so she could hardly refuse her. Mrs. MacFarland did not approve, either, of the way Lula ate nothing but Karo corn syrup, or the way she had of hurrying through supper and going to prayer meeting, now not on Wednesday nights alone but on every week-day night. Mrs. MacFarland's disapproval was touched with good humor. She said she supposed Lula had to sweeten herself up for church, she went so often, but a half-gallon can of Karo every week—that was too much! She had a serious conversation with Lula. She said she did not mind a bit buying the Karo (it was cheaper than anything else) but that eating nothing but sweet things was not good for anybody's health.

After her conversation with Mrs. MacFarland Lula tried to stop eating so much Karo. She conceived the idea of making candy with it. She surprised Mrs. MacFarland with a gleaming white dish of divinity fudge which the whole family admired. Mr. and Mrs. MacFarland each ate a piece, and Wade ate two pieces, but the remainder grew hard and dusty and landed back in the kitchen. Nevertheless, thereafter Lula kept a dish of it on hand. Sometimes she would vary the white by coloring it green, or pink. Wade often found these pieces of candy in his school lunch box.

Wade never walked home with Lula again, not because of his mother's disapproval, but because he did not want to remind Lula of anything unpleasant. He knew that she had moved from her old room out of fear of her husband, and it seemed to him that she wanted to disappear into thin air whenever she left the MacFarland kitchen—disappear to appear only at church. In between church and the kitchen she wanted to become invisible.

He would have helped her do so had he known how. He thought of asking his mother to let her live in the room over the carriage house, but he was afraid that if he spoke to his mother she would find out how much he himself knew about Lula, she would want to know why *he* wanted Lula to live on the place, and he felt instinctively that he must not reveal Lula's secret; he felt that Lula's safety and the safety of her daughter depended on his silence.

He was right insofar as his mother was concerned: if she had found out about Lula's child she would undoubtedly have caused some sort of trouble. But the fact that Wade never referred to the visit to Lula herself made Lula feel that he was ashamed of her. So she did not tell him when she sent her daughter away. Sister Mary Margaret moved to Detroit that fall and agreed to take the little girl with her. That took a heavy burden off Lula's heart but it added another, for then she became a victim of such loneliness that she fell ill and for two weeks lay in her rented room with her eyes closed. Mrs. MacFarland sent word to ask how she was. Lula got up the third week and went back to work. Time passed. Her sister Alice died in the penitentiary during the winter. Sister Mary Margaret rarely wrote—a postcard every few months that Lula would spell out with difficulty—so all Lula had to remind her of her daughter was the aging photograph and the ache inside her heart. There was no one near at hand to love now except Wade.

Walking home in the spring rains from school Wade would often wonder what Lula had done about her daughter. He could not bring himself to speak of it to her nor ask her the question that haunted his mind. It was not exactly that he felt himself to blame in any way for the afternoon trip he had made to her room the spring before, but the memory of the sudden violence she had shown when he asked if her daughter was dead kept him from mentioning the child, and the silence he imposed on himself ended by making him uneasy in Lula's presence. More than that. In times past nothing had pleased him so much as to settle down on a stool in the kitchen in the late afternoon and, as the cracks in the old coal stove showed red in the dusk, watch Lula cook supper. Such moments of quietness had fed his spirit. But now he felt an embarrassment even to look into Lula's eyes. Those black eyes, so beautifully set behind black lashes and under the smooth brown forehead, those eyes full of candor, those eyes he had always taken for granted, now seemed to look at him in an intimacy he did not understand but which he found uncomfortable. He was embarrassed by the question in them, whatever the question was. They appeared too real, too demanding, to be the eyes of a Negro. His mother's eyes sometimes embarrassed him so.

No rift occurred between them. He was aware of a debt he owed Lula, the debt for so many of the good times of his childhood. But he was growing up fast these days and he could not spend as much time with her as formerly. Gradually he adopted to a certain degree the attitude of his family towards Lula: good-natured tolerance. She began to appear to him as "funny," and he would recount Lula's preachments—for she was closer to the church than ever before and her attitude towards the world at large was becoming somewhat severe. She was growing away from him, he felt, just as he was growing away from her, and the realization of this caused him to feel that he had somehow failed her. He made up for this by joking with her. He would question her about her church and when he heard her singing—which was often—he would ask her to repeat to him the words of the hymn. He was particularly fond of the words of one hymn. Their ominous sound amused him, and he wrote them down in a copybook:

> Tell them preachers they better stop lying:
> They lied in the mountains, they lied in the valley,
> But they gotta reap just what they sown.
>
> Tell them deacons they better stop lying:
> They lied in the mountains, they lied in the valley,
> But they gotta reap just what they sown.

He asked Lula what the difference was between the Sanctified Church and other denominations. There was a great deal of difference, Lula said. If you were a member of the Sanctified Church—if you were *sanctified,* in other words—all your sins had been washed away and you could do no evil.

"You mean no matter what you do it isn't wrong?" Wade said.

"Certainly I mean that," Lula said.

"You mean you, Lula Borrow, can't commit a sin?"

"I'm sanctified," Lula said. "Don't you understan' that? If you was sanctified you wouldn't want to commit no sin, either."

"I'd like to go to that church some time," Wade said.

"You're welcome to come," Lula replied. "You're welcome to come any time."

Wade and Lula's conversations were usually composed of fragments like that, never resolved, never finished, but all leading by a curious alchemy towards their separation and ultimately their estrangement. Possibly for most people it is by such fragments of talk that attitudes are formed, decisions hardened, a point of view unconsciously adopted to appear later as a stand taken. In July of that year Wade finally attended a meeting at Lula's Sanctified Church. Later that night, taking a bath, he remembered mostly the singing, which was lively. Not until weeks later was he to realize that for Lula his presence there must have appeared to be an indication of his first step towards sanctification.

He had found the church easily enough. Although he had never returned to that part of Mount Ashton since the night he had stood guard for Lula, his feet carried him straight to the frame structure—it must once have been a grocery—that served as her church. Even from the outside he could tell that there was considerable activity inside. Light from the windows cut into the black hot July night. An uneven row of Negro men, stragglers evidently, lined the whitewashed boards on either side of the wooden steps. In the anemic light from the street lamp, they glanced at him and lowered their gaze. Wade mounted the three plank steps fortified by the fact that Lula, a member of the congregation, had invited him. He touched the door. It moved inward, pulled by an unseen hand, and he was confronted at once by an elderly Negro with a benign countenance. Wade had the sudden unpleasant sensation of having been waited for. He rejected the effort of the Negro to escort him forward and sat down near the rear on one of the picnic-like benches that lined both sides of the modest room. Although the room was lit by only two electric bulbs hanging from two cords, one near the rear where he sat and one above the raised platform at the other end, they were so brilliant that the light dazzled him, causing him to feel unduly exposed in his white shirt and blue serge pants and fresh haircut. His eyes sought Lula but he did not see her plump shoulders among the thirty or forty backs. Then he recognized her. She was sitting immediately in front of the platform in front of a man who stood at a rough wooden lectern, reading or, it seemed to Wade, mumbling, from a large book Wade imagined was some white family's discarded family Bible. Behind the preacher, in chairs arranged in a semicircle, sat a man with a tambourine, another man with a drum, and three women holding what Wade supposed were hymn books.

At first he tried to follow what the preacher was saying, but it was so incoherent that presently he became overcome with a kind of fatigue from the effort. Also, at first, he had been exhilarated by the tension created by the reader's voice. It rose and fell in regular periods, and its effect was hypnotic. The congregation swayed and moaned in response, and now and again sharp cries would burst from various parts of the room. Cries for the most part inarticulate but now and again emerging from constricted throats in words: "Praise Jesus," "Amen," "Praise Him," "Sanctified, praise Jesus." But soon the excitement of the congregation began to make Wade feel ill at ease. It appeared to involve him, too, and the involvement made him nervous. The speaker paused and raised his arms and said:

"Praise Jesus. We have a fine young white gentleman with us tonight, praise Jesus."

"Amen." "Oh, praise Him," came from several parts of the room at once.

"This rich young white gentleman has left his fine big house and come all the way here to find Jesus!"

"Yes, Sir!" a voice cried out.

"He didn't go up yonder to one of those big marble churches . . ."

"Praise Jesus!"

"He didn't walk down the aisle on no red velvet carpet . . ."

"Praise Jesus!"

"He didn't dress up in no fine clothes . . ."

"No, Jesus."

"He walked right up them plank steps into this-here plank room!"

"Yes, Lord."

During this passage Wade's heart was pounding in his chest and his cheeks were burning hot. He sat transfixed with a horrified, sickly smile on his face, and his dry lips slightly open. Although the preacher's words and the responses had taken only a few seconds it seemed to Wade that he had lain exposed and naked under a searchlight for hours. Yet he saw that no head had once turned towards him, no eyes had glanced in his direction. Even in his extreme embarrassment he was aware of a certain decorum in the ceremony.

A chorus of exclamations had gone up at the preacher's last remark. The preacher turned and pointed at the man behind him who was holding the tambourine. Immediately the man began shaking the instrument. The drummer began beating his drum, and one of the three women began singing. After a few words the other two joined her, then the whole congregation joined in, and the hymn swelled out into the little room, flowed over Wade sitting in the rear, flowed so passionately that for a moment he didn't recognize the words. They were more words to the hymn Lula had written down for him:

> Tell them brothers they better stop lying:
> They lied in the mountains, they lied in the valley,
> But they gotta reap just what they sown.

A man in the front row jumped up and clapped his hands once over his head. His body began to shake; he clapped his hands again and his feet began to move. The rhythm, which seemed to be in syncopation with the rhythm of the hymn, suggested tap-dancing, but there was a solitary, trance-like, isolated air about the angular black figure that was far from the air of a "performance." The dancer danced for himself alone. As he turned slowly around he bent his head back on his limber neck and in the glare of the single electric bulb Wade saw that his eyes were tight shut.

But *Lula* dancing! Wade would never have expected to see such a thing.

When she rose to her feet the click of the tambourine quickened sharply. The two standing figures, Lula and the man, were on opposite sides of the aisle, and they did not move towards each other as Wade would have supposed. Each stayed in his own confined, solitary orbit, Lula relaxed and immobile. The man, whose movement had been decreasing, presently sat down. Only then did Lula prepare to dance. She stretched out her arms, and the drumbeat and hand-clapping swelled out as if to support her. Wade, whose cheeks had reddened when the preacher had so openly referred to him, felt himself even more exposed now. Lula kept her eyes shut, like the dancer before her—she did not look at Wade once. Yet there seemed to be invisible wires connecting her body with his, taut wires the pull of which was a mixture both painful and pleasurable to him. She began to tremble and then her knees started making quick bending movements, and as the high nasal hymning increased in volume her body began whirling and bending and bobbing in rhythm with the song. He kept his eyes fixed on her, hardly believing what he saw. How could she do such a thing? How could she exhibit herself so grossly, she whose modesty and good humor had always warmed him? But here she was, with sweat running down her face, her teeth bared and her lips stretched back in a kind of grin, her eyes shut and her body bobbing up and down like a cork. The relation between Lula and the congregation puzzled him; even in his embarrassment he noted its nature: although the congregation seemed intimately related to Lula's dancing, its frenzied rhythmic clapping and singing at once taking on its character from her intensity and at the same time buoying her up, the relationship was impersonal, too. The congregation and Lula, while serving each other, served their own ends. He kept his eyes fixed on her—he could hardly do otherwise—and all at once he understood why Lula appeared remote from the congregation. She was dancing in celebration of something that had nothing to do with them. She was dancing in celebration of his presence. He had come at last to her church and she was dancing for the joy it gave her. She was dancing for the thankfulness she felt.

Suddenly he could no longer bear it. He stood up abruptly and turned in one bound and pushed through the door. Outside were the same lounging fresco of figures, the same pale greenish light from the corner street-lamp. The figures did not stir. Wade walked away slowly and as he walked he felt their eyes upon him as he disappeared from their view towards the part of town where the white people lived.

That was on a Sunday night. He did not see Lula alone the next day but after supper he met her in the "butler's pantry." They had had ham for supper and Wade, thirsty from the salty meat, had gone out to get a swallow of ice water from the water-cooler that stood on a stool at one end of the dark little hallway throughout the summer months. (Sometimes his mother would dump the water out and store a watermelon on top of a piece of ice in the round cylindrical chamber. At such times Wade would turn on the spigot and hold his mouth underneath to receive the icy drops.) Lula had just carried a tray full of clean dishes into the dining room and was returning to the kitchen. She stopped and looked at him, looked up at him, for he was now a trifle taller than she was. Something of the transport of the night before still remained on her face. What happened then took only an instant but afterwards it seemed to Wade that it had dragged out for hours. Lula let go of the tray and as it clattered to the floor she threw her arms around him, and, raising her face towards the ceiling, said:

"Sanctify him, Jesus!"

Wade was so surprised he couldn't speak at first. Lula had pinned one of his arms down with her impetuous gesture, but his other arm was bent upward. Water, from the glass he held in his hand, had sloshed down his shirt-front. He jerked away from her and, as he did so, dashed the rest of the water into her face.

"Get away from me, Lula," he cried out, half laughing, much as he might have shouted while he repulsed the sudden advances of a large and friendly dog. "Get away from me!"

Lula withdrew without saying anything more.

After that Wade began to avoid Lula, not altogether of course, but sufficiently for him to imagine she noticed the difference. He did not go into the kitchen unless for some particular reason; he never went there any more just to sit and talk and watch Lula prepare the food. He denied himself the pleasure of those visits with some difficulty, and so it was a relief to him when he went off to the Boy Scout camp on the first day of August. The first week he received a box of plain divinity fudge, the second week, a box of divinity fudge with walnuts, each accompanied by a letter from his mother saying that Lula had asked her to send the candy to him. He buried both boxes in the woods, thinking the presents too girlish to be offered to his companions in camp. The week before he came home he received a letter from his mother in which she said she had had to discharge Lula—"fire" was the word his mother used.

Wade was surprised, but not excessively so. His mother's explanation that Lula had begun to take religion entirely too seriously for her own good and had got too uppity to stand any longer appeared reasonable enough to him when he considered the experience he himself had had with her. He would miss her though, he admitted that.

When Lula left the MacFarlands' kitchen she did not pass entirely out of their lives. Yet the connection was tenuous. Occasionally Mrs. MacFarland would run into her on the street and come home and announce to the family that she had seen Lula and that the two of them had had a good visit. But Wade went off to school that year and did not hear about even those infrequent encounters.

Lula hardly knew what to do with herself during the first year after she left the MacFarlands. Over the years she had grown accustomed to their ways. She missed them. And the kitchen at the Mac-Farland house remained in her memory like a home lost. She hired herself out for a while as cook to one of Mrs. MacFarland's acquaintances, which pleased her because through her employer she would now and then hear news of the MacFarland family. But after a few months that relationship ceased to content her; indeed, it grew to distress her to such an extent that one morning she could not force herself to go to work. She sent a little boy for her pay and never went back.

For a long time now she had had no communication from Sister Mary Margaret about her daughter. She wrote regularly—a sentence asking how they were—and regularly sent money to the latest Detroit address she knew. But no answers came back. Lula had never ridden on a train but one day she got on the Louisville & Nashville's "Pan American" that stopped for two minutes at Mount Ashton, and rode all the way to Detroit. She spent half a day walking from the railroad station to the address on Garfield Street. It turned out to be a rooming house and the woman who ran it said that Sister Mary Margaret had moved to St. Louis and, so far as she knew, had carried Lula's daughter with her. She said she had been forwarding Lula's letters to General Delivery there which was the only address Sister Mary Margaret had left with her. Lula asked the woman if she could sit down on her front porch a while. Later that afternoon she walked back to the railroad station and, since she did not have enough money to buy a ticket to St. Louis, returned to Mount Ashton.

By this time she had only five dollars left of the money she had saved while she was working for the MacFarlands. She wanted three things: to keep up her payments on her burial insurance, to continue sending money to Sister Mary Margaret—the envelope was addressed to St. Louis, General Delivery, now—and to get enough money to make the trip out to St. Louis. She took a job cleaning the floors down at the Kandy Kitchen, but she didn't seem able to put her mind to it. She would stand lost in a sort of day-dream or be drawn irresistibly to the glass cases in which were piled the neat pyramids of pink and white and green candies. After the three Greek gentlemen who ran the store found Lula eating candy a few times they let her go.

Sometimes Lula walked past the MacFarland place, but it seemed more shut up than it used to be. During the period that she had been away from the family Mr. MacFarland had died. When Lula heard about it she went to see Mrs. MacFarland, but that was already a week after the funeral. Mrs. MacFarland was too grief-stricken still to come downstairs to see her, and Wade had gone back to school. Lula hardly recognized Wade's baby sister in the tall girl who spoke to her.

"You remember me?" Lula asked. She was standing on the back porch. The girl had the kitchen door half open and was holding onto the doorknob.

"Yes, I think so," the girl said. "You're Lula, aren't you?"

"I certainly am," Lula said.

"I remember you as fatter," the girl said.

Lula laughed. "That was when you was a baby," she said. "You sure loved to sit in my lap, too."

"I'm sorry Mother is still taking her nap," the girl said.

"Yes'm," Lula said. She was on the point of asking the girl to let her go out and look at her furniture that was still stored in the room above the carriage house but on second thought she decided not to. She had no place to put it.

Lula got one job and lost it, got another and lost that, too. She was not only not saving enough money to get to St. Louis—she was having trouble paying her room rent at the preacher's house and sending the weekly envelope to the General Delivery office at St. Louis. She would have to let her burial insurance drop or give up her room, so she gave up her room at the preacher's and found another, a cheaper one. It was a lean-to tacked on to the end of a coal-house in some white woman's back yard. Lula was never sure of the woman's name; she just knocked at the kitchen door and asked her if she could use the room. . . .

Lula entered a new period of her life now. She was wholly engrossed in trying to think how she could get enough money for the trip to St. Louis. She went to church every night as she had done for many years but she did not dance any longer. She spent her time during the service on her knees praying to God to show her how to get to St. Louis. It was not until there was a church supper and she had begged from the white woman a one-burner oil stove and made some divinity fudge for the supper that she thought of making divinity fudge as a way to earn her living. Then she began to appear with her basket at the back doors of the houses of the white people of Mount Ashton, and though at first she was able to sell a little of the candy, after the initial sale most people smiled and shook their heads and said it was just too sweet for them. And that was in spite of the fact that Lula let her insurance premium lapse once and bought a package of rainbow confection dyes with which she dyed the divinity fudge various shades of colors. So after each trip around town she would go back to her room and eat the candy herself. She could never understand why other people did not like it as much as she did. She did not have to bother about food as long as she had all that candy to eat.

One May afternoon when she was returning from her efforts at peddling she met Mrs. MacFarland. Something had kept her from ever having tried to sell any of the candy to Mrs. MacFarland. It might have been because she remembered how she always ate more Karo corn syrup than Mrs. MacFarland wanted her to but, anyway, the sight of her former employer embarrassed her. She hung her head and tried to conceal the basket on her arm and indeed would have passed by without speaking had not Mrs. MacFarland leaned over to the side and said:

"Isn't that Lula?"

Lula stopped but her body pivoted from side to side like that of a demure yet friendly child. The old smile was on her face.

"Yes'm, it's me."

"Well, Lula. I haven't seen you for such a long time."

The smile broadened. "No'm. How you, Miss Dora?"

If Lula had been able to think in the clichés familiar to Mrs. MacFarland it would have occurred to her that the woman who stood before her had "visibly aged."

"I haven't been well, Lula," Mrs. MacFarland said. Then, as if to brush aside a subject too serious to go into, she said, "What's that you've got in that basket?"

Lula lowered her head again. "Candy," she said simply.

Mrs. MacFarland stepped back to make a little distance between them. She laughed. "That sweet tooth of yours is going to be the death of you yet, Lula," she said.

Lula lifted the piece of brown paper that covered the divinity fudge for Mrs. MacFarland to see. "I'm selling it," she said.

Mrs. MacFarland held up her hand in a gesture of distaste.

"What for?" she asked.

A cloud came over Lula's face. It was difficult to put the matter into words. "To go to St. Louis," she said.

"You wouldn't like St. Louis," Mrs. MacFarland said, and added, "small-town people just don't like big cities."

"My daughter lives there," Lula said. "I'm going to see her."

"Your daughter!" Mrs. MacFarland said in surprise. "Why you never told me you had a daughter, Lula. All the time you worked for me and you never told me that!"

Lula suddenly realized she was talking to an old woman. The last time she had stood in front of Mrs. MacFarland and had herself talked to like this was when Mrs. MacFarland looked like a young woman. That was when Lula's daughter was living across town and she could see her when she wanted to, or at least it was when her daughter was in Detroit and Lula got letters or postcards now and then from Sister Mary Margaret. It was when Wade was at home; it was when she stood in the MacFarland kitchen bending over the hot stove and thinking about getting ready to go to church as soon as she got the dishes washed. . . . The years seemed to roll up into a huge ball and almost knock Lula down. Through all those years she had not seen her daughter, not once, not once since she sent her away with Sister Mary Margaret and stored her furniture in Mrs. MacFarland's carriage house. Lula looked down at her own arm crooked under the basket handle. It was almost as scrawny as the arm of the white woman, curled round her handbag.

"No'm," she said.

"Well, I declare," Mrs. MacFarland said.

Mrs. MacFarland seemed to be thinking. After a minute she said:

"Mr. Wade asked about you not long ago, in a letter. I wrote back and told him I hadn't seen you in a month of Sundays." She took a step forward as if to continue her walk.

"I'd sure like to see Mr. Wade," Lula said. "I'll bet he's growed by now into a bigger man'n his daddy was."

"Thank goodness he'll be here the first of the month," Mrs. MacFarland said. "Thank goodness for that. This is his last year of school." She sighed audibly. "I certainly hope he won't go off and leave me again, Lula."

"Now won't that be nice," Lula said.

"If his father had lived, of course he would want to go off to college," Mrs. MacFarland went on, as if to herself.

"Sholy," Lula said.

". . . but I wrote him he would just have to come back and take charge of things, that I was simply not equal to it any longer."

"Mr. Wade always was a good boy," Lula said.

"Yes he was," Mrs. MacFarland said. She stiffened slightly. "To think you never told me you had a daughter all that time."

Lula covered up the candy. She was wondering whether or not to ask Mrs. MacFarland to buy some. She had sold none now for more than a week. Mrs. MacFarland turned round.

"Speaking of letters. That reminds me. I knew there was something in the back of my mind I wanted to see you about." She leaned over and unclasped the large black leather handbag that depended from her arm. After a few moments she extracted from the bottom of it a dog-eared letter. "I've been carrying this around with me for I don't know how long," she said and handed the letter to Lula.

"Thank you ma'am," Lula said.

"I knew I was bound to run into you some time," she said. She smiled down at Lula. "You better stay in Mount Ashton where folks *do* run into each other." She resumed her journey.

When Lula got to her room she set the basket of candy down on the floor where it was cooler and went over and stood beside the window to see better. She looked down at the letter. It was post-marked from Chicago and addressed to Lula in the care of Mrs. MacFarland. She tore open the envelope and recognized the writing of Sister Mary Margaret. She had trouble making out the faint pencil scratching and she wished she had asked Mrs. MacFarland to read it to her. The letter was a short one. Lula read it through twice. It told her that her daughter had run off with a man. Sister Mary Margaret did not know where. The letter did not contain a return address.

Lula sat down on the pallet. Although the afternoon was warm and humid, she felt cold, and her tongue was dry in her mouth. She reached out and automatically picked up a piece of divinity fudge. For the last few months she had been subjected to violent spells of dizziness—at times she would almost faint—and the candy was the only thing that seemed to relieve the spells. This time, however, not even the candy did any good. Presently she lay down. She would never be really sick, she told herself, because she was sancti-fied, and if you were sanctified you were free from all evil and from all illness. She shut her eyes and thought about that. Her lips moved and she found she was praying to God to keep her sanctified so she could go to Chicago. Then she repeated the prayer that she had prayed every day for fifteen years, the prayer in which she had asked God to sanctify her daughter and to sanctify Wade.

The afternoon waned. Lula lay on the pallet thinking about how she was going to get the money to go to Chicago. She consid-ered trying her hand at taking in washing although she knew she was not very good at ironing. There would be washtubs to buy, too, and she was not at all sure whether the white woman who owned the place would let her use the water. She thought of nurs-ing, but the thought made her stomach turn. Cooking was what she could do best but she hadn't been able to get a cooking job for so long a time that her hand was out. No, she had better go on mak-ing candy and trying to sell it. Now and again she could count on finding a cleaning job as well. Gradually the sun sank and the air grew cooler, and Lula left off thinking and began listening to the birds that had sprung up now that the end of the day had come. Before the light faded she had fallen into a deep sleep.

When she awoke it was day, and at first she thought she had had her eyes closed for only a few minutes. Then she had the sensation of having been asleep a long while, and decided she had slept around the clock, for sunlight was blazing through the window the way it did in early afternoon. She was thirsty so she got up to get a dipperful of water. As she walked across the room to where the water bucket sat on the window sill she realized that all her strength had come back to her. She dropped down on her knees beside the window and thanked God for having answered her prayer, the prayer she had prayed for herself. She knew now that she would get to Chicago some way, and that she would find her daughter once she got there. She rose to her feet and, seeing that there was a scant and lukewarm dipper of water in the bottom of the bucket, she set out across the yard toward the cistern. She drew the bucket full of fresh, cool, amber-colored cistern water and had started back to her room when the white woman at the kitchen window, startled by the clatter of the bucket against the ground, looked out to see Lula fall forward on her face.

She went out and turned her over. She slapped her face but that did not revive her. Then the woman dragged Lula out of the sun and propped her up against the wall of the coal-house and ran back into her kitchen and poured out a cup of coffee and put some sugar in it. Lula had revived by the time the woman returned. She thanked her for the coffee, drank it, and felt considerably better. The woman helped her to her room and asked her if she wanted her to call the doctor, but Lula said no, and presently she put on her hat and walked across town to ask her preacher if he and the congregation would pray for her at Church that night because, she said, she was feeling too sick to be there herself. The preacher said they would pray for her that night and if she wasn't cured they'd pray for her tomorrow night and if that didn't cure her they would fast and pray all night the next night. So Lula went back to her room content and easy in her mind. The next morning she felt so much better that she set to work cooking up all the sugar she had on hand into divinity fudge in order to have it ready when she would feel well enough in a day or so to start peddling it again.

Getting well took longer than Lula expected. She kept telling herself that she *was* well but that she did not feel like going into the sun. She lay on her pallet most of the day. Towards evening the white woman would bring her something to eat, and Lula thought she had never known a white person so generous and thoughtful but she still wasn't sure what the woman's name was.

But lying around her room was wasting time, so after a week Lula started out again with her basket of divinity fudge on her arm. Although she had to have the money if she ever hoped to get to Chicago, she was, in a way, almost sorry to part with any of the candy. It was true that she didn't sell much, but every little bit she did sell seemed to her to sap her strength somehow. The candy was so pretty, sitting in plates on the floor around the room; it tasted so good. She used what money she earned from sales in buying the ingredients to replenish her supply.

The first of June came. She remembered that Mrs. MacFarland had told her that Wade was coming the first of June, and one morning the idea came to her that she would ask him to go to Chicago for her if something should happen to keep her from going herself. It was not that she doubted in the least her own ability to get there, but sometimes on the street she felt such a faintness that she could hardly find her way back to her room. She was not certain of the propriety of asking a white person to do such a thing but she knew Wade was a good boy and she recalled the time he had stood on the street on the lookout for her husband while she moved from her room. That was years ago, now, and she had not seen him in a long time. On the other hand, she was aware of daily communication with him through her prayers. She put on her hat and set out for the MacFarland house. Halfway there it occurred to her that she still did not have sufficient money for a ticket to Chicago and she did not think she had the right to pledge Wade to such a journey unless she could give him the money for it. She turned back.

She thought she might meet him on the street. If she should run into him accidentally she believed she would have the courage to speak to him more openly than she would if she went to the MacFarland house and knocked on the kitchen door. If she could see him alone without Mrs. MacFarland or his sister crowding around him, she might be able to say what was in her heart. So as she went about she kept her gaze fixed at a distance in order to take in all the cars and the people crossing at street corners. That gave her a curious abstracted look that caught then repelled the glances of passers-by.

A lassitude had come over her and she went out now only in the afternoons. Another week had passed and she had not seen him. But on Friday afternoon of the following week she was standing on the pavement in front of Sites' Jewelry Store. It was in the heart of the business section of Mount Ashton, and she had been on the street for three hours, yet had sold no candy. She shifted the basket on her arm to get it out of the sun's rays which at that time of the year even at that late hour were still hot enough to melt her candy. She was tired and faint and had decided to go back to her room. Suddenly the pressure of a hand lay across her shoulders and the pressure of another hand ran down the center of her back. An instantaneous chill went through her, she shivered violently, and for a second longer turned her head this way and that unable to see who it was behind her who had seized her. The hold on her shoulders relaxed and she turned to look up into Wade's laughing face.

"Mister Wade!"

"Did you know who it was?" Wade said, shaking her hand.

Lula scrutinized his face. He was the same boy she remembered, the same boy she prayed for every night. For a moment she could not speak. Then she saw that he was not alone. Mrs. MacFarland and his sister were standing on the curb, opening the door of a car. She said:

"I might 'a knowed nobody but you'd do such a thing like that."

Wade laughed again. "Where you going?" he asked again.

Lula hesitated. She looked down the street. "Nowhere, specially," she said.

"Well, come on. We'll drive you home," Wade said, pushing her towards the car.

"It ain't far," Lula said.

Mrs. MacFarland and Wade's sister had already arranged themselves in the front seat.

"Hello, Lula," they said.

Wade opened the back door. "Get in," he said. He shut the door after her and went around and got into the driver's seat. After the car was moving he said:

"Well, Lula, I certainly am glad to see you. Where do you live?"

"Down here on Seventh Street behind a white lady's house. I'm glad to see you too, Mister Wade. You going to be here long?"

"I certainly hope so, Lula," Mrs. MacFarland said. "I hope he's going to be here for good."

"That's no distance at all," Wade said. "You show me which house it is."

"I know he'll be a mighty big help to you," Lula said, "if he does. I know that for a fact."

"Are you still selling divinity fudge?" Mrs. MacFarland asked presently, as if to change the subject.

"Yes, ma'am," Lula said, and removed the handkerchief that covered the top of her basket. "Would you like to have a piece? I got some right here."

"No thank you," Mrs. MacFarland and Wade's sister said.

"Would you, Mister Wade?"

"I'd like to buy a piece," Wade said. "I'd like to buy a dollar's worth."

"There ain't that much here," Lula said.

"That's all right," Wade said. "Give me what you've got and we'll call it a dollar's worth." He handed a dollar bill over his shoulder to Lula.

"Thank you, Mister Wade," Lula said.

Wade appeared to be meditating. After a few minutes he turned round and looked briefly at Lula.

"Wade!" Mrs. MacFarland exclaimed. "Watch where you're going!"

"Well, Lula, it's been a long time," Wade said and turned his head towards the front again. His tone had suggested that the remark was more general than specific, as though a great many things had been "a long time." He added after a moment, "What've you been doing all this time?"

"Nothing specially, Mister Wade," Lula said from the back seat. "Little bit of this, little bit of that."

"Lula's become quite a candy-maker," Mrs. MacFarland said. "Haven't you, Lula?"

"Yes'm, I guess so," Lula said.

Wade turned the car into Seventh Street. "She always was a wonderful candy-maker," he said.

"It's that third house over there on the right, Mister Wade," Lula said.

Wade stopped the car in front of the house.

"I never noticed that house there before," Mrs. MacFarland said. "Who lives there, Lula?"

"Widow-lady," Lula said. "She calls herself Mrs. Chara."

"Charon?" Mrs. MacFarland said. "Did you say Chara or Charon?"

"I guess so," Lula said. "I ain't for certain."

"Chara," Mrs. MacFarland said. "I never heard that name before. I thought I knew everybody in Mount Ashton. Are you sure that's right, Lula?"

"No'm," Lula said. "Sounds like Chara to me." She opened the car door. "I'll leave my basket on the seat here, Mister Wade."

"Won't you need it?" Mrs. MacFarland asked.

Lula got out of the car. "No ma'am. I got another," she said. She held onto the door for a moment, giving herself time to examine Wade's face once more. She studied the deep brown eyes, the full red lips. She noted the high color of his cheeks, the down on his upper lip. But mostly it was the expression in his eyes that told her he was the same boy she had trusted long ago. Yet she could think of no way she could tell him what she needed to tell him. All she could say was, "You take good care of your mammy." She stood on the curb while they told her good-bye and she watched Wade turn the car round and head it the other way. She watched it until it disappeared up Seventh Street towards Elm Street. Then she started back to her room. But she had never felt this way before. She had felt bad plenty of times, but never like this. She could hardly force one foot in front of the other, and her teeth were chattering so hard she tasted blood in her mouth from her bitten tongue. Her back was wet from sweat and she was shivering so violently from the pain between her shoulders that her hands made erratic movements in the air, movements over which she had no control. She started to sit down on the concrete curbing that separated the pavement from Mrs. Chara's yard but she was afraid that if she sat down she could not get up. Instead, she staggered forward and clutched the fence that ran close beside the driveway, and holding onto it step by step she finally made her way to the back and into her room.

She crawled over to her pallet and lay there, panting. She thought of the divinity fudge she had left on the back seat of the car, and she was filled with a ravenous hunger for the candy, filled with more than hunger, for it seemed to her that she had left there a vital part of herself without which she would surely die. But she remembered she still had a supply in her room and she reached out and was reassured when her hand touched a plate piled with candy. She drew the plate closer and as she ate the green and pink and white squares a measure of calm returned to her.

Someone was at the door. With an effort Lula moved her eyes and saw that the woman she called Mrs. Chara had entered the room. She came over and stood above Lula.

"I noticed you coming in the drive and I knew you was sick."

Lula shook her head but she could not speak.

The white woman bent down and put her hand on Lula's forehead. Then she straightened up.

"You need a doctor, Lula Borrow, and I'm going to get one."

Lula's eyes tried to protest. She was afraid of doctors and what they might do to her. They would send her off some place and she would never come back. She would never be able to talk to Wade.

The white woman saw the brown forehead wrinkle, and noted the pain and fear in the black eyes. "Don't you worry, Lula," she said. "I'll take care of you." And she left the room.

Lula sank back. When, after a few minutes, she looked towards the window, she thought a storm had come up—the way they do suddenly in summer—because the room had grown so dark. But she heard no sound of rain or of wind, or even any increased noise of birds that ordinarily was the prelude to a summer storm. She thought then that perhaps she had fallen to sleep unknowing and that now it was night. In that case there would be no sound of birds at all, unless it was an owl or a whippoorwill, whereas she could hear distinctly the late afternoon sound of birds and, as well, the sound of activity in the street and from neighboring yards. But she could not see!

The thought came to her suddenly that she had made a mistake to lie down, that she ought to have got to her church somehow instead of coming in here to this room. A deep longing to be in church took hold of her. Her heart seemed to overflow with the desire. She said aloud:

"I better get up from here and get myself over there."

But she made no move to rise up. Instead she closed her eyes which were dry and painful from their sightless staring, and immediately she was seized with a dizziness that seemed to snatch her body up in the air and fling it sharply this way and that so that the pallet appeared at intervals to fall away from her altogether. Then it was herself that was falling, and the pallet and her room were left far behind. Words formed on her lips. "Sweet Jesus!" she thought she had whispered. Then she tried to open her eyes again. She decided it was beyond her strength to do so. She made a final effort. This time she succeeded. But what her eyes opened to was not her room but her church. She was not surprised at this, yet some voice deep within her said as though with ultimate relief, "I made it."

At first she thought no one was in the room but herself. She was standing alone on the platform right where the preacher always stood, except there was no lectern in front of her. "I ain't supposed to be up here," she heard her voice say. But while she was hearing the voice she felt the pressure of an arm around her shoulders and she looked and saw Wade was standing on her right hand and that it was his arm around her. But he was not looking at her—he was looking straight in front of him and smiling. So Lula looked to the left and as she did so she felt another arm around her shoulders and saw that her daughter was standing on her left hand, and that it was she at whom Wade was smiling. Lula thought what a fine woman her daughter had grown up to be, and the thought filled her heart with happiness such as she had never known before. Now she began to hear a sound which at first was a kind of dry rattling. She did not know what the sound was until she realized that she and Wade and her daughter were not alone together in the room as she had supposed but that behind them sat the drummer and the tambourine player. The sound she had heard was the drum. In a minute the tambourine started too, and to that vibrant conjunction of sounds she began dancing. She looked down at her feet and saw that not only was she herself dancing but that Wade's feet and her daughter's feet were moving also. She looked up at their faces. Their eyes held nothing but joy. Their arms closed around her, and Lula, sharing the joy in their eyes, knew that neither Wade nor her daughter nor herself would ever again stop dancing.

After they had left Lula standing on the pavement and had ridden the few blocks to Elm Street and the car had turned into Elm Street, Mrs. MacFarland rearranged the handbag on her lap and said,

"I never heard of any Mrs. Chara." She turned to her daughter. "Did you?"

Her daughter looked out the car window. "No, Mother," she said. "I never did."

"Lula's obviously mistaken," Mrs. MacFarland said. "There is no such name. Unless it's some country woman recently moved to town."

They had come abreast of their own driveway and Wade was about to turn in.

"Why don't we drive on out in the country a little," his mother said. "It's such a pleasant afternoon now that the sun's gone down some."

Wade swerved the car back into the street and drove on out Elm. In a few minutes they had passed beyond the town and were headed out the Guthrie Road. They crossed the covered bridge that spanned Red River. It rattled and shook with the weight of the car.

"This bridge isn't going to last much longer," Mrs. MacFarland said. "I read in the paper the other night where the County engineer recommends tearing it down." When neither her son nor her daughter made any reply she turned to Wade. She patted his knee. "Cat got your tongue?"

Wade kept his eyes fixed on the road ahead. "I was thinking of Lula," he said.

Mrs. MacFarland let her hand remain on her son's knee. She gave his knee a slight pressure. "I knew you were," she said with a smile. Then she sighed and added after a pause, "Poor Lula. She has greatly deteriorated, I'm sorry to say."

Wade moved his knee. "Deteriorated?" he said. "She certainly looked thin, but I don't know what you mean by 'deteriorated.' "

His sister laughed.

"What's so funny?" Wade asked.

"Your sister knows what I mean," Mrs. MacFarland said.

"Well, what do you mean?" Wade said.

"I mean," said Mrs. MacFarland, "that any woman, black or white, who spends her time on the streets all day is looking for trouble. That's all."

"Mother!" Wade exclaimed.

"Well, I can't help it," his mother said. "I'm sorry, but that's the fact of the matter."

Wade drove on in silence. The road was not a smooth one. It was rarely used nowadays because of the new highway that had replaced it.

"I want to get in the back," his sister said suddenly. "Will you stop or do you want me to climb over?"

"I'll turn round," Wade said. "There's not much point in going on any farther anyway. You can get in the back when I turn around." He drove on, looking for a suitable place to stop.

"Well please hurry up," his sister said.

"Don't be so impatient," Mrs. MacFarland said.

Wade found a lane and turned into it and stopped the car. His sister got out and got into the back seat. Wade turned the car round and started back towards town. Presently from the rear seat his sister made a sound of disgust. She thrust an arm between Wade's and Mrs. MacFarland's shoulders and exhibited between her thumb and forefinger a piece of Lula's divinity fudge.

"Imagine," she said. "Imagine anybody's eating a piece of this stuff!"

Mrs. MacFarland looked at it. "Don't!" she said and turned her head away.

"Put that back," Wade said sharply. "She has to make her living some way."

His sister moved the candy nearer Wade's mouth. "Take a bite," she said. "You paid for it."

"Put it back, I said."

"Since you don't want it and Mother and I don't want it I'll throw it away," his sister said and tossed the white square across in front of Wade's face and out the window. It disappeared in the dry roadside grass.

Wade jammed on the brakes. "You little bitch!" he muttered, and stopped the car with a lurch. He jumped out and threw open the back door and dragged his sister out into the dusty road. She made no protest but her face had gone white. "You're not too big to whip," he cried out at her. He caught her by the waist and gave her a hard slap with his right hand on the buttocks.

"Children!" Mrs. MacFarland cried out from the car. "This is disgraceful!"

Wade stepped away from his sister. She was looking at him with a smile on her lips and with her eyes glazed in hatred. "And now," she said, still smiling, "may I get back into the car?"

Wade turned away without speaking. He climbed in behind the wheel and waited while his sister got in the back. No one spoke. But as they rode back into town Wade was aware that his mother was silently weeping.

He turned the car in the driveway and stopped at the side entrance of the house, and after his mother and sister got out he drove on back and parked the car in the old carriage house that was now used for a garage. He cut off the engine but sat a while longer behind the wheel. A melancholy had settled over him. He tried to confront it, to define its limits, but he felt himself eluded as if by some ghostly substance that yet had power enough to overcome him. He thought of his mother. Why did she have to cry like that, he asked himself, just because his sister had acted in such a beastly way. Both of them, his mother and his sister, had said things about Lula that were not true. They had acted as though they wanted to destroy Lula. But whether the things they said were true or not, their putting them into words had left him dispirited, forsaken. The thought came to him suddenly that in striking at Lula they were striking at him. But why should his mother want to strike at him? He was here in Mount Ashton because she had begged him to come back. . . . His fingers tightened on the wheel. It had been a mistake to come home. He had known it would be a mistake, all along. He told himself that he should not have succumbed to his mother's numerous entreaties, but should have stayed away, as he had originally planned. Yet her daily letters had been so importunate. "You will simply have to come home to take charge of things," she had written, over and over, "because I am simply not equal to it. And I am just too unwell to try to discipline your sister any longer." So now he had come home; had promised to stay; had taken charge of things. And behold, what a mess he made even trying to discipline his sister! His heart sickened at the thought of the scene on the highway. Her body had felt so soft and limp, so fragile, in his arms. And she had stood there smiling and smiling: daring him, in her triumph.

He started up abruptly and got out of the car, but paused beside it, his hand on the door. He reflected that his melancholy did not actually arise because he had not wanted to come home. In all honesty he had wanted to come. The melancholy was the result of what happened after he got there. It was what they did to him, what they said. A pall seemed to hang over everything they said or did at home, and the pall crushed them down until their voices died. Or rather, he thought, whenever they spoke at home their words seemed always to issue from some deep resentment, some contempt, but at what the contempt and resentment were directed he was not sure. He recalled that his sense of their disenchantment had existed even before his father's death, and he had secretly, guiltily, exulted for a little while after his father died, believing that then he would be able to breathe more easily, move about more freely there, feel less the chains upon his limbs. But actually the gloom had deepened. The black circle in which he found himself had shrunk even more.

He leaned against the car. For the last few minutes he had been staring into the dark corner of the carriage house, beyond the car. He noticed now that what his eyes had been fixed upon was the flight of wooden steps that ascended to the room above. Years had passed since he had climbed that stair. His mind filled with the blurred images of all the dusty afternoons he had played in the room above. He walked over to the staircase and set his foot upon the stair.

The first thing he thought of when he emerged from the stairwell was how small the room had become. Its slanting roof was so low that he could stand upright only in the center of the floor. But the room was still full of light, just as he remembered it. The two windows in each end, although they were covered with dust and cobwebs, let in the late afternoon sunshine. Dust was thick on the rough planks under his feet, and plaster had fallen in places from the walls. Yet the dry powdery smell was immediately so familiar that he smiled in recollection. Two ancient children's sleds had been thrown in one corner near a stack of faded green shutters. He had forgotten that once the house had had shutters at every window! A disorderly pile of harness lay in the center of the room, and on top of the harness lay a single carriage-wheel. Beyond that, in another corner, was some furniture. He stepped closer. He could not imagine who it was who had stored furniture in this dust-filled place. Not until he went over and laid his hand on the rounded foot-piece of the brass bed did he know. His hand closed more firmly round the ornate metal rod. The bed had once been his own bed. His earliest memories of sleep, of waking, were connected with that bed. Later, it had been discarded and given to Lula. He remembered the pleasure he had felt upon again finding it in her room. But why had it been here so long, gathering dust? Didn't Lula need it? To whom did it belong now? He stood there, holding on to it, feeling its voluptuous curves, and suddenly there rose in his mind another question. What am I? he asked himself. What am I here for? What am I trying to find out?

They were at breakfast the next morning at their accustomed hour. During the night it had rained sharply, and now the air was cool and the sunlight, falling through the kitchen window shone with an unusual clarity. Wade sat between his mother and his sister, but until he glanced up from the table and looked out the window into the green boughs of the maple tree he had not known how bright the morning was. He realized at the same moment how well he had slept the night before, how refreshed he felt. It was as if he had been transported to a former day when sleeping and waking were equal parts of a calm and benevolent infinitude of time. And yet, he thought, there is a difference. He tried to think what the difference was.

His mother lifted a folded newspaper from her lap and pushed it gently towards him across the table. "You might like to see the morning paper," she said.

"Thank you," he said, but did not pick the paper up.

She took a sip of coffee and added, "Although I must confess there's nothing in it." Her hand paused, holding the cup above her saucer. She turned her head sideways. "Don't I hear someone at the front door?"

"I don't think so," Wade said.

She set her cup down. "I thought I heard someone knocking," she said and looked questioningly at her daughter. Her daughter kept her eyes fixed on her plate.

"There!" Mrs. MacFarland said. "I was sure I did."

Wade glanced at his sister. She shrugged her shoulders.

Mrs. MacFarland turned to her daughter. "Aren't you going to answer it?" she said.

"I didn't hear anything," her daughter said.

Mrs. MacFarland half rose from her chair.

Wade got up hurriedly. "I'll go," he said.

He left the bright kitchen and crossed the vacant dining room and walked through the dark hall towards the front door. As he approached it he could see, through the translucent curtain that covered the upper glassed half of the door, the head and shoulders of a woman. He unlocked the door and pulled it open and faced the stranger. For a second he stared out at the figure, startled by her disheveled hair and by the excited lustre in her eyes. Then he said politely,

"Good morning."

"Good morning," the woman said. "Is this where Mrs. MacFarland lives?"

"Yes," Wade said.

"Are you her son?"

"Yes," Wade said. "I am."

"You-all the folks Lula Borrow used to work for?"

"Yes, we are," Wade said, opening the door wide. "Won't you come in?"

The woman shook her head. She clasped her hands against her bosom and stared at him with her bright eyes.

"I came to tell you Lula's dead," she said.

"Dead!" Wade said. "Did you say 'dead'?"

"Yes sir," the woman replied emphatically. "She died yesterday afternoon."

"We just saw her yesterday afternoon," Wade said. "We . . ."

"I know it," the woman said. "When she came in the drive I said to myself, 'Lula's sick.' I saw you-all leave."

Mrs. MacFarland had come up behind them. She slipped her hand through Wade's arm. "What is it, Wade?" she said. "Someone wants to speak to me?"

He turned quickly, brushing her hand away. "Lula's dead," he said.

"Why, that's impossible," his mother said, and took a step forward as if to challenge the stranger. "She was perfectly well yesterday afternoon."

"She warn't well," the woman said. "She was sick."

Mrs. MacFarland inclined her head slightly. "I don't believe we're acquainted," she said. "I'm Mrs. MacFarland."

The woman looked at her speculatively. "Lula lived on my

place," she said, evidently supplying what she considered sufficient identification. "I got her a doctor. I held her when she died."

Mrs. MacFarland withdrew a step, apparently convinced. "How perfectly shocking! What was the matter with her?"

"Diabetes, for one thing," the woman answered. "Must of had it a long time, the doctor said."

"How sad," Mrs. MacFarland said. "How terribly sad."

"Had a carbuncle, too," the woman said. "Right between the shoulder blades. Big as a grapefruit. Doctor said she couldn't of died of that, though."

"Oh *dear!*" Mrs. MacFarland said, pained by these details. "If we'd only known, we might have been able to do something. . . ."

The woman had turned and faced Wade. She put out her hand and grasped his arm. "Lula talked about you," she said. "Right up till she died. That's why I'm here. I thought you'd want to know she was dead."

Wade did not answer but he nodded his head in acknowledgement. He had been standing perfectly quiet, listening. And while he listened, the woman's words had come to him strangely, like an echo, a corroboration. She released his arm and moved down the steps. It was not until she had started towards the street that he bounded forward and caught up with her.

"Where's Lula now?"

The woman paused in her progress. "At the undertaker's, I guess," she replied. "Doctor called him last night and he come got the body." She glanced back once more at the figure of Wade's mother who still stood in the doorway, then started again towards the street.

Wade did not immediately rejoin Mrs. MacFarland, but stooped down on the concrete walk and, taking his knife out of his pocket, opened it and began picking at the thin line of moss that grew in the narrow crack between the concrete slabs. He was trying to accustom himself to the sensation in his chest before he again faced his mother. It was grief he felt, but it was not grief only. What else he was aware of he recognized almost as a feeling of excitement.

His mother came down the steps and bent over and placed her hand on his shoulder. He stood up. She drew him to her. "Poor Lula," she said. "It's terribly sad . . . But I don't know what we can do about it, do you?"

"I'm going to see her," Wade said.

"But Wade . . . ," his mother said.

He started up the steps. "I'm going now."

"But Wade," his mother said again, following him into the house. "I can't let you do such a thing alone. If you're going, I will go with you."

Wade paused. "I'd rather go alone," he said.

"It's out of the question," his mother said. "I'll come just like I am."

He started to speak again, but changed his mind, and walked on ahead of her out through the kitchen and into the yard towards the garage. As he got in the car he noticed on the back seat the basket of candy Lula had left there the day before. The only piece that had been removed from it was the piece his sister had thrown away. He waited for his mother at the side entrance, the engine of the car running. Already he felt calmer. His mother kept him waiting only a moment, and as he turned the car out of the driveway into the street he looked at her and smiled and heard himself say:

"I'm glad you're coming."

She returned his smile but made no answer.

There was only one Negro undertaking establishment in Mount Ashton, and Wade made the trip in a few minutes. Neither of them spoke on the way. When they drew up beside the neat cottage with the white-painted picket fence his mother turned to him and said,

"I'll wait in the car."

Wade opened the gate and walked the few feet to the porch. He paused for a moment under the blue neon sign that even in daylight set forth the words brilliantly: Roberts' Funeral Home. He was met at the door by a tall black Negro.

"I've come to see Lula Borrow," Wade said.

"Why, the body ain't here," the Negro said, and his teeth shone whitely in the black face. He bent his head a little to come through the door and stand beside Wade on the porch. "It's already at the church."

"Thank you," Wade said.

"Do you know where the church is?" the Negro asked.

"Yes," Wade said and turned to leave.

"I know y'all'll be pleased to see how nice I fixed her up," the Negro said. "She looks mighty pretty."

Wade got in the car again. They were silent as before while they traversed the several blocks between the undertaker's house and Lula's church, but when Wade drew up at the curb and cut off the engine he said,

"I want to know something, Mother."

Mrs. MacFarland folded her hands in her lap. "What is it you want to know, Son?"

"This morning," Wade said and turned in his seat so that he faced her, "I was going to ask you to ask Lula to come cook for us again. I woke up this morning thinking we needed Lula to cook for us again . . ." He paused. "What I want to know is, would you have asked her?"

"Why, Wade," his mother said and looked down at her hands. "I hadn't thought of such a thing. The extra expense of keeping a regular servant . . ."

Wade broke in. "Would you have asked her if I'd asked you to?"

His mother seemed to hesitate. Wade opened the car door. His mother raised her eyes and looked at him. "Yes, Son," she said. "I would have asked her."

He left his mother in the car and walked across the treeless church yard to the church. He had not seen it since his trip to it years ago. It was the same fragile, box-like structure with the same warped frame door except that now the whitewash had washed away and had not been renewed, so that the raw pine boards showed more plainly. He opened the door and walked in. He thought at first the room was empty, but a Negro woman rose from a chair in the corner at his right and came forward. She wore a black shawl over her head, and he could not tell whether she was old or young until she spoke to him, and then he knew that she was old because nowadays no young Negro ever used that form of address:

"The funeral's not till ten o'clock, white folks."

"I came to see Lula," he said.

Her eyes seemed to give him permission for they turned then in the direction of the raised platform that filled the other end of the room. A table had been placed in the center of the platform, and on the table a coffin. He moved towards it.

Until that moment Wade had not asked himself why he had

made this journey. He had come because it had seemed natural to him to come. Now, for some reason, perhaps because of the presence of the Negro woman, he felt a certain embarrassment; he felt the need of an excuse to explain his own presence in this empty Negro church. I've simply come to tell Lula goodbye, he thought, and at the thought blushed deeply. The inadequacy of such a thought, the banality of it, pained him as if from a pain that he had inflicted upon himself physically. He strode up the few steps at the end of the platform, walked over, and looked down into the open coffin.

His first impression was that he was looking at a pigmy. The figure that lay before him was so shrunk, so much of it had been drained away, exhumed, that he could not believe he was looking at the human being that he had known. But if it was a pigmy, how much care had been spent, and by an expert hand, what a lavishment of skill, to enliven the pigmy features! Wade clenched his hand. He had not expected to see such a thing as this. The abundant hair he remembered as rising so richly from the smooth forehead was slicked down as though by wax and parted in the middle. The glowing brown forehead itself had become only stretched skin over bone, and below the shut eyes the sunken cheeks were bright with rouge. The tight prim line of carmine was Lula's lips. He bent over the face.

"Lula, Lula," he whispered and felt suddenly the tears stinging his eyes. It was clear now how little his reason for coming was to tell such a monstrosity "goodbye." No, the reason he had come— he asked himself how he could ever not have known it—the reason he had come was for a far different purpose. He had come to ask himself a question, the same question that he had asked in the attic of the carriage-house the day before, the question he knew was the most compelling question he would ever ask. He had come to ask it here and to find the answer, here. Already, that morning, when he had looked out and had seen the brilliant sunlight, he thought he had an intimation of the answer. He had felt a tremor of the answer when the woman had come to tell him Lula was dead. Now, he was sure of the answer. He looked down into the coffin again. This pitiful thing before him was not Lula. Surely Lula was not *here*. Then where was she, what was she? He recalled the time he had accompanied her to her room and had marked the powdery

light with which the room was infused. Something of the same
white ineffable lightness seemed also to surround him here. Lula,
the Lula he remembered, was not in that room years ago. She was
not here in this coffin. Yet she had always been close beside him,
ever since he could remember her. She was still beside him. Only
now, she was not locked away from him in the body she once wore;
now she was closer . . . dispersed into the air—he lifted his eyes
to the windows that lined the bare walls of the room—into the thin
air of the world. He would find her wherever he went, wherever he
breathed. He breathed in deeply now, and as he breathed in, it
seemed to him that he was breathing in love.

THE LAME SHALL ENTER FIRST

BY FLANNERY O'CONNOR

I

SHEPPARD sat on a stool at the bar that divided the kitchen in half, eating his cereal out of the individual pasteboard box it came in. He ate mechanically, his eyes on the child, who was wandering from cabinet to cabinet in the panelled kitchen, collecting the ingredients for his breakfast. He was a stocky blond boy of ten. Sheppard kept his intense blue eyes fixed on him. The boy's future was written in his face. He would be a banker. No, worse. He would operate a small loan company. All he wanted for the child was that he be good and unselfish and neither seemed likely. Sheppard was a young man whose hair was already white. It stood up like a narrow brush halo over his pink sensitive face.

The boy approached the bar with the jar of peanut butter under his arm, a plate with a quarter of a small chocolate cake on it in one hand and the ketchup bottle in the other. He did not appear to notice his father. He climbed up on the stool and began to spread peanut butter on the cake. He had very large round ears that leaned away from his head and seemed to pull his eyes slightly too far apart. His shirt was green but so faded that the cowboy charging across the front of it was only a shadow.

"Norton," Sheppard said, "I saw Rufus Johnson yesterday. Do you know what he was doing?"

The child looked at him with a kind of half attention, his eyes forward but not yet engaged. They were a paler blue than his father's as if they might have faded like the shirt; one of them listed, almost imperceptibly, toward the outer rim.

"He was in an alley," Sheppard said, "and he had his hand in a

273

garbage can. He was trying to get something to eat out of it." He paused to let this soak in. "He was hungry," he finished, and tried to pierce the child's conscience with his gaze.

The boy picked up the piece of chocolate cake and began to gnaw it from one corner.

"Norton," Sheppard said, "do you have any idea what it means to share?"

A flicker of attention. "Some of it's yours," Norton said.

"Some of it's *his*," Sheppard said heavily. It was hopeless. Almost any fault would have been preferable to selfishness—a violent temper, even a tendency to lie.

The child turned the bottle of ketchup upside-down and began thumping ketchup onto the cake.

Sheppard's look of pain increased. "You are ten and Rufus Johnson is fourteen," he said. "Yet I'm sure your shirts would fit Rufus." Rufus Johnson was a boy he had been trying to help at the reformatory for the past year. He had been released two months ago. "When he was in the reformatory, he looked pretty good, but when I saw him yesterday, he was skin and bones. He hasn't been eating cake with peanut butter on it for breakfast."

The child paused. "It's stale," he said. "That's why I have to put stuff on it."

Sheppard turned his face to the window at the end of the bar. The side lawn, green and even, sloped fifty feet or so down to a small suburban wood. When his wife was living, they had often eaten outside, even breakfast, on the grass. He had never noticed then that the child was selfish. "Listen to me," he said, turning back to him, "look at me and listen."

The boy looked at him. At least his eyes were forward.

"I gave Rufus a key to this house when he left the reformatory —to show my confidence in him and so he would have a place he could come to and feel welcome any time. He didn't use it, but I think he'll use it now because he's seen me and he's hungry. And if he doesn't use it, I'm going out and find him and bring him here. I can't see a child eating out of garbage cans."

The boy frowned. It was dawning upon him that something of his was threatened.

Sheppard's mouth stretched in disgust. "Rufus's father died before he was born," he said. "His mother is in the state penitentiary.

He was raised by his grandfather in a shack without water or electricity and the old man beat him every day. How would you like to belong to a family like that?"

"I don't know," the child said lamely.

"Well, you might think about it sometime," Sheppard said.

Sheppard was City Recreational Director. On Saturdays he worked at the reformatory as a counselor, receiving nothing for it but the satisfaction of knowing he was helping boys no one else cared about. Johnson was the most intelligent boy he had worked with and the most deprived.

Norton turned what was left of the cake over as if he no longer wanted it.

"You started that, now finish it," Sheppard said.

"Maybe he won't come," the child said and his eyes brightened slightly.

"Think of everything you have that he doesn't!" Sheppard said. "Suppose you had to root in garbage cans for food? Suppose you had a huge swollen foot and one side of you dropped lower than the other when you walked?"

The boy looked blank, obviously unable to imagine such a thing.

"You have a healthy body," Sheppard said, "a good home. You've never been taught anything but the truth. Your daddy gives you everything you need and want. You don't have a grandfather who beats you. And your mother is not in the state penitentiary."

The child pushed his plate away. Sheppard groaned aloud.

A knot of flesh appeared below the boy's suddenly distorted mouth. His face became a mass of lumps with slits for eyes. "If she was in the penitentiary," he began in a kind of racking bellow, "I could go to seeeeee her." Tears rolled down his face and the ketchup dribbled on his chin. He looked as if he had been hit in the mouth. He abandoned himself and howled.

Sheppard sat helpless and miserable, like a man lashed by some elemental force of nature. This was not a normal grief. It was all part of his selfishness. She had been dead for over a year and a child's grief should not last so long. "You're going on eleven years old," he said reproachfully.

The child began an agonizing high-pitched heaving noise.

"If you stop thinking about yourself and think what you can do for somebody else," Sheppard said, "then you'll stop missing your mother."

The boy was silent but his shoulders continued to shake. Then his face collapsed and he began to howl again.

"Don't you think I'm lonely without her too?" Sheppard said. "Don't you think I miss her at all? I do, but I'm not sitting around moping. I'm busy helping other people. When do you see me just sitting around thinking about my troubles?"

The boy slumped as if he were exhausted but fresh tears streaked his face.

"What are you going to do today?" Sheppard asked, to get his mind on something else.

The child ran his arm across his eyes. "Sell seeds," he mumbled.

Always selling something. He had four quart jars full of nickels and dimes he had saved and he took them out of his closet every few days and counted them. "What are you selling seeds for?"

"To win a prize."

"What's the prize?"

"A thousand dollars."

"And what would you do if you had a thousand dollars?"

"Keep it," the child said and wiped his nose on his shoulder.

"I feel sure you would," Sheppard said. "Listen," he said and lowered his voice to an almost pleading tone, "suppose by some chance you did win a thousand dollars. Wouldn't you like to spend it on children less fortunate than yourself? Wouldn't you like to give some swings and trapezes to the orphanage? Wouldn't you like to buy poor Rufus Johnson a new shoe?"

The boy began to back away from the bar. Then suddenly he leaned forward and hung with his mouth open over his plate. Sheppard groaned again. Everything came up, the cake, the peanut butter, the ketchup—a limp sweet batter. He hung over it gagging, more came, and he waited with his mouth open over the plate as if he expected his heart to come up next.

"It's all right," Sheppard said, "it's all right. You couldn't help it. Wipe your mouth and go lie down."

The child hung there a moment longer. Then he raised his face and looked blindly at his father.

"Go on," Sheppard said. "Go on and lie down."

The boy pulled up the end of his t-shirt and smeared his mouth with it. Then he climbed down off the stool and wandered out of the kitchen.

Sheppard sat there staring at the puddle of half-digested food. The sour odor reached him and he drew back. His gorge rose. He got up and carried the plate to the sink and turned the water on it and watched grimly as the mess ran down the drain. Johnson's sad thin hand rooted in garbage cans for food while his own child, selfish, unresponsive, greedy, had so much that he threw it up. He cut off the faucet with a thrust of his fist. Johnson had a capacity for real response and had been deprived of everything from birth; Norton was average or below and had had every advantage.

He went back to the bar to finish his breakfast. The cereal was soggy in the cardboard box but he paid no attention to what he was eating. Johnson was worth any amount of effort because he had the potential. He had seen it from the time the boy had limped in for his first interview.

Sheppard's office at the reformatory was a narrow closet with one window and a small table and two chairs in it. He had never been inside a confessional but he thought it must be the same kind of operation he had here, except that he explained, he did not absolve. His credentials were less dubious than a priest's: he had been trained for what he was doing.

When Johnson came in for his first interview, he had been reading over the boy's record—senseless destruction, windows smashed, city trash boxes set afire, tires slashed—the kind of thing he found where boys had been transplanted abruptly from the country to the city as this one had. He came to Johnson's I.Q. score. It was 140. He raised his eyes eagerly.

The boy sat slumped on the edge of his chair, his arms hanging between his thighs. The light from the window fell on his face. His eyes, steel-colored and very still, were trained narrowly forward. His thin dark hair hung in a flat forelock across the side of his forehead, not carelessly like a boy's, but fiercely like an old man's. A kind of fanatic intelligence was palpable in his face.

Sheppard smiled to diminish the distance between them.

The boy's expression did not soften. He leaned back in his chair and lifted a monstrous club foot to his knee. The foot was in a heavy black battered shoe with a sole four or five inches thick.

The leather parted from it in one place and the end of an empty sock protruded like a grey tongue from a severed head. The case was clear to Sheppard instantly. His mischief was compensation for the foot.

"Well Rufus," he said, "I see by the record here that you don't have but a year to serve. What do you plan to do when you get out?"

"I don't make no plans," the boy said. His eyes shifted indifferently to something outside the window behind Sheppard in the far distance.

"Maybe you ought to," Sheppard said and smiled.

Johnson continued to gaze beyond him.

"I want to see you make the most of your intelligence," Sheppard said. "What's important to you? Let's talk about what's important to *you*." His eyes dropped involuntarily to the foot.

"Study it and git your fill," the boy drawled.

Sheppard reddened. The black deformed mass swelled before his eyes. He ignored the remark and the leer the boy was giving him. "Rufus," he said, "you've got into a lot of senseless trouble but I think when you understand why you do these things, you'll be less inclined to do them." He smiled. They had so few friends, saw so few pleasant faces, that half his effectiveness came from nothing more than smiling at them. "There are a lot of things about yourself that I think I can explain to you," he said.

Johnson looked at him stonily. "I ain't asked for no explanation," he said. "I already know why I do what I do."

"Well good!" Sheppard said. "Suppose you tell me what's made you do the things you've done?"

A black sheen appeared in the boy's eyes. "Satan," he said. "He has me in his power."

Sheppard looked at him steadily. There was no indication on the boy's face that he had said this to be funny. The line of his thin mouth was set with pride. Sheppard's eyes hardened. He felt a momentary dull despair as if he were faced with some elemental warping of nature that had happened too long ago to be corrected now. This boy's questions about life had been answered by signs nailed on pine trees: DOES SATAN HAVE YOU IN HIS POWER? REPENT OR BURN IN HELL. JESUS SAVES. He would know the Bible with or without reading it. His despair gave way to outrage. "Rubbish!" he snorted. "We're living in the space age! You're too smart to give me an answer like that."

Johnson's mouth twisted slightly. His look was contemptuous but amused. There was a glint of challenge in his eyes.

Sheppard scrutinized his face. Where there was intelligence anything was possible. He smiled again, a smile that was like an invitation to the boy to come into a school room with all its windows thrown open to the light. "Rufus," he said, "I'm going to arrange for you to have a conference with me once a week. Maybe there's an explanation for your explanation. Maybe I can explain your devil to you."

After that he had talked to Johnson every Saturday for the rest of the year. He talked at random, the kind of talk the boy would never have heard before. He talked a little above him to give him something to reach for. He roamed from simple psychology and the dodges of the human mind to astronomy and the space capsules that were whirling around the earth faster than the speed of sound and would soon encircle the stars. Instinctively he concentrated on the stars. He wanted to give the boy something to reach for besides his neighbor's goods. He wanted to stretch his horizons. He wanted him to *see* the universe, to see that the darkest parts of it could be penetrated. He would have given anything to be able to put a telescope in Johnson's hands.

Johnson said little and what he did say, for the sake of his pride, was in dissent or senseless contradiction, with the club foot raised always to his knee like a weapon ready for use, but Sheppard was not deceived. He watched his eyes and every week he saw something in them crumble. From the boy's face, hard but shocked, braced against the light that was ravaging him, he could see that he was hitting dead center.

Johnson was free now to live out of garbage cans and rediscover his old ignorance. The injustice of it was infuriating. He had been sent back to the grandfather; the old man's imbecility could only be imagined. Perhaps the boy had by now run away from him. The idea of getting custody of Johnson had occurred to Sheppard before, but the fact of the grandfather had stood in the way. Nothing excited him so much as thinking what he could do for such a boy. First he would have him fitted for a new orthopedic shoe. His back was thrown out of line every time he took a step. Then he would encourage him in some particular intellectual interest. He thought of the telescope. He could buy a second-hand one and they could set it up in the attic window. He sat for almost ten minutes thinking what he could do if he had Johnson here with him. What was wasted on Norton would cause Johnson to flourish. Yesterday when he had seen him with his hand in the garbage can, he had waved and started forward. Johnson had seen him, paused a split-second, then vanished with the swiftness of a rat, but not before Sheppard had seen his expression change. Something had kindled in the boy's eyes, he was sure of it, some memory of the lost light.

He got up and threw the cereal box in the garbage. Before he left the house, he looked into Norton's room to be sure he was not still sick. The child was sitting cross-legged on his bed. He had emptied the quart jars of change into one large pile in front of him, and was sorting it out by nickels and dimes and quarters.

That afternoon Norton was alone in the house, squatting on the floor of his room arranging packages of flower seeds in rows around himself. Rain slashed against the window panes and rattled in the gutters. The room had grown dark but every few minutes it was lit by silent lightning and the seed packages showed up gaily on the floor. He squatted motionless like a large pale frog in the midst of this potential garden. All at once his eyes became alert. Without warning the rain had stopped. The silence was heavy as if the downpour had been hushed by violence. He remained motionless, only his eyes turning.

Into the silence came the distinct click of a key turning in the front door lock. The sound was a very deliberate one. It drew attention to itself and held it as if it were controlled more by a mind than by a hand. The child leapt up and got into the closet.

The footsteps began to move in the hall. They were deliberate and irregular, a light and then a heavy one, then a silence as if the visitor had paused to listen himself or to examine something. In a minute the kitchen door screeked. The footsteps crossed the kitchen to the refrigerator. The closet wall and the kitchen wall were the same. Norton stood with his ear pressed against it. The refrigerator door opened. There was a prolonged silence.

He took off his shoes and then tiptoed out of the closet and stepped over the seed packages. In the middle of the room, he stopped and remained where he was, rigid. A thin bony-faced boy in a wet black suit stood in his door, blocking his escape. His hair was flattened to his skull by the rain. He stood there like an irate drenched crow. His look went through the child like a pin and paralyzed him. Then his eyes began to move over everything in the room—the unmade bed, the dirty curtains on the one large window, a photograph of a wide-faced young woman that stood up in the clutter on top of the dresser.

The child's tongue suddenly went wild. "He's been expecting you, he's going to give you a new shoe because you have to eat out of garbage cans!" he said in a kind of mouse-like shriek.

"I eat out of garbage cans," the boy said slowly with a beady stare, "because I like to eat out of garbage cans. See?"

The child nodded.

"And I got ways of getting my own shoe. See?"

The child nodded, mesmerized.

The boy limped in and sat down on the bed. He arranged a pillow behind him and stretched his short leg out so that the big black shoe rested conspicuously on a fold of the sheet.

Norton's gaze settled on it and remained immobile. The sole was as thick as a brick.

Johnson wiggled it slightly and smiled. "If I kick somebody *once* with this," he said, "it learns them not to mess with me."

The child nodded.

"Go in the kitchen," Johnson said, "and make me a sandwich with some of that rye bread and ham and bring me a glass of milk."

Norton went off like a mechanical toy, pushed in the right direction. He made a large greasy sandwich with ham hanging out the sides of it and poured out a glass of milk. Then he returned to the room with the glass of milk in one hand and the sandwich in the other.

Johnson was leaning back regally against the pillow. "Thanks, waiter," he said and took the sandwich.

Norton stood by the side of the bed, holding the glass.

The boy tore into the sandwich and ate steadily until he finished it. Then he took the glass of milk. He held it with both hands like a child and when he lowered it for breath, there was a rim of milk around his mouth. He handed Norton the empty glass. "Go get me one of them oranges in there, waiter," he said hoarsely.

Norton went to the kitchen and returned with the orange. Johnson peeled it with his fingers and let the peeling drop in the bed. He ate it slowly, spitting the seeds out in front of him. When he finished, he wiped his hands on the sheet and gave Norton a long appraising stare. He appeared to have been softened by the service. "You're his kid all right," he said. "You got the same stupid face."

The child stood there stolidly as if he had not heard.

"He don't know his left hand from his right," Johnson said with a hoarse pleasure in his voice.

The child cast his eyes a little to the side of the boy's face and looked fixedly at the wall.

"Yaketty yaketty yak," Johnson said, "and never says a thing."

The child's upper lip lifted slightly but he didn't say anything.

"Gas," Johnson said. "Gas."

The child's face began to have a wary look of belligerence. He backed away slightly as if he were prepared to retreat instantly. "He's good," he mumbled. "He helps people."

"Good!" Johnson said savagely. He thrust his head forward. "Listen here," he hissed, "I don't care if he's good or not. He ain't *right!*"

Norton looked stunned.

The screen door in the kitchen banged and someone entered. Johnson sat forward instantly. "Is that him?" he said.

"It's the cook," Norton said. "She comes in the afternoon."

Johnson got up and limped into the hall and stood in the kitchen door and Norton followed him.

The colored girl was at the closet taking off a bright red raincoat. She was a tall light-yellow girl with a mouth like a large rose that had darkened and wilted. Her hair was dressed in tiers on top of her head and leaned to the side like the Tower of Pisa.

Johnson made a noise through his teeth. "Well look at Aunt Jemima," he said.

The girl paused and trained an insolent gaze on them. They might have been dust on the floor.

"Come on," Johnson said, "let's see what all you got besides a nigger." He opened the first door to his right in the hall and looked into a pink-tiled bathroom. "A pink can!" he murmured.

He turned a comical face to the child. "Does he sit on that?"

"It's for company," Norton said, "but he sits on it sometimes."

"He ought to empty his head in it," Johnson said.

The door was open to the next room. It was the room Sheppard had slept in since his wife died. An ascetic-looking iron bed stood on the bare floor. A heap of Little League baseball uniforms was piled in one corner. Papers were scattered over a large roll-top desk and held down in various places by his pipes. Johnson stood looking into the room silently. He wrinkled his nose. "Guess who?" he said.

The door to the next room was closed but Johnson opened it and thrust his head into the semi-darkness within. The shades were down and the air was close with a faint scent of perfume in it. There was a wide antique bed and a mammoth dresser whose mirror glinted in the half light. Johnson snapped the light switch by the door and crossed the room to the mirror and peered into it. A silver comb and brush lay on the linen runner. He picked up the comb and began to run it through his hair. He combed it straight down on his forehead. Then he swept it to the side, Hitler fashion.

"Leave her comb alone!" the child said. He stood in the door, pale and breathing heavily as if he were watching sacrilege in a holy place.

Johnson put the comb down and picked up the brush and gave his hair a swipe with it.

"She's dead," the child said.

"I ain't afraid of dead people's things," Johnson said. He opened the top drawer and slid his hand in.

"Take your big fat dirty hands off my mother's clothes!" the child said in a high suffocated voice.

"Keep your shirt on, sweetheart," Johnson murmured. He pulled up a wrinkled red polka dot blouse and dropped it back. Then he pulled out a green silk kerchief and whirled it over his head and let it float to the floor. His hand continued to plow deep into the drawer. After a moment it came up gripping a faded corset with four dangling metal supporters. "Thisyer must be her saddle," he observed.

He lifted it gingerly and shook it. Then he fastened it around his waist and jumped up and down, making the metal supporters dance. He began to snap his fingers and turn his hips from side to side. "Gonter rock, rattle and roll," he sang. "Gonter rock, rattle

and roll. Can't please that woman, to save my doggone soul." He
began to move around, stamping the good foot down and slinging
the heavy one to the side. He danced out the door, past the stricken
child and down the hall toward the kitchen.

A half hour later Sheppard came home. He dropped his raincoat on a chair in the hall and came as far as the parlor door and
stopped. His face was suddenly transformed. It shone with pleasure.
Johnson sat, a dark figure, in a high-backed pink upholstered chair.
The wall behind him was lined with books from floor to ceiling.
He was reading one. Sheppard's eyes narrowed. It was a volume of
the Encyclopedia Britannica. He was so engrossed in it that he did
not look up. Sheppard held his breath. This was the perfect setting
for the boy. He had to keep him here. He had to manage it somehow.

"Rufus!" he said, "it's good to see you boy!" and he bounded
forward with his arm outstretched.

Johnson looked up, his face blank. "Oh hello," he said. He ignored the hand as long as he was able but when Sheppard did not
withdraw it, he grudgingly shook it.

Sheppard was prepared for this kind of reaction. It was part of
Johnson's make-up never to show enthusiasm.

"How are things?" he said. "How's your grandfather treating
you?" He sat down on the edge of the sofa.

"He dropped dead," the boy said indifferently.

"You don't mean it!" Sheppard cried. He got up and sat down
on the coffee table nearer the boy.

"Naw," Johnson said, "he ain't dropped dead. I wisht he had."

"Well where is he?" Sheppard muttered.

"He's gone with a remnant to the hills," Johnson said. "Him
and some others. They're going to bury some Bibles in a cave and
take two of different kinds of animals and all like that. Like Noah.
Only this time it's going to be fire, not flood."

Sheppard's mouth stretched wryly. "I see," he said. Then he
said, "In other words the old fool has abandoned you?"

"He ain't no fool," the boy said in an indignant tone.

"Has he abandoned you or not?" Sheppard asked impatiently.

The boy shrugged.

"Where's your probation officer?"

"I ain't supposed to keep up with him," Johnson said. "He's supposed to keep up with me."

Sheppard laughed. "Wait a minute," he said. He got up and went into the hall and got his raincoat off the chair and took it to the hall closet to hang it up. He had to give himself time to think, to decide how he could ask the boy so that he would stay. He couldn't force him to stay. It would have to be voluntary. Johnson pretended not to like him. That was only to uphold his pride, but he would have to ask him in such a way that his pride could still be upheld. He opened the closet door and took out a hanger. An old grey winter coat of his wife's still hung there. He pushed it aside but it didn't move. He pulled it open roughly and winced as if he had seen the larva inside a cocoon. Norton stood in it, his face swollen and pale, with a drugged look of misery on it. Sheppard stared at him. Suddenly he was confronted with a possibility. "Get out of there," he said. He caught him by the shoulder and propelled him firmly into the parlor and over to the pink chair where Johnson was sitting with the encyclopedia in his lap. He was going to risk everything in one blow.

"Rufus," he said, "I've got a problem. I need your help."

Johnson looked up suspiciously.

"Listen," Sheppard said, "we need another boy in the house." There was a genuine desperation in his voice. "Norton here has never had to divide anything in his life. He doesn't know what it means to share. And I need somebody to teach him. How about helping me out? Stay here for a while with us, Rufus. I need your help." The excitement in his voice made it thin.

The child suddenly came to life. His face swelled with fury. "He went in her room and used her comb!" he screamed, yanking Sheppard's arm. "He put on her corset and danced with Leola, he . . ."

"Stop this!" Sheppard said sharply. "Is tattling all you're capable of? I'm not asking you for a report on Rufus's conduct. I'm asking you to make him welcome here. Do you understand?

"You see how it is?" he asked, turning to Johnson.

Norton kicked the leg of the pink chair viciously, just missing Johnson's swollen foot. Sheppard yanked him back.

"He said you weren't nothing but gas!" the child shrieked.

A sly look of pleasure crossed Johnson's face.

Sheppard was not put back. These insults were part of the boy's defensive mechanism. "What about it, Rufus?" he said. "Will you stay with us for a while?"

Johnson looked straight in front of him and said nothing. He smiled slightly and appeared to gaze upon some vision of the future that pleased him.

"I don't care," he said and turned a page of the encyclopedia. "I can stand anywhere."

"Wonderful," Sheppard said. "Wonderful."

"He said," the child said in a throaty whisper, "you didn't know your left hand from your right."

There was a silence.

Johnson wet his finger and turned another page of the encyclopedia.

"I have something to say to both of you," Sheppard said in a voice without inflection. His eyes moved from one to the other of them and he spoke slowly as if what he was saying he would say only once and it behooved them to listen. "If it made any difference to me what Rufus thinks of me," he said, "then I wouldn't be asking him here. Rufus is going to help me out and I'm going to help him out and we're both going to help you out. I'd simply be selfish if I let what Rufus thinks of me interfere with what I can do for Rufus. If I can help a person, all I want is to do it. I'm above and beyond simple pettiness."

Neither of them made a sound. Norton stared at the chair cushion. Johnson peered closer at some fine print in the encyclopedia. Sheppard was looking at the tops of their heads. He smiled. After all, he had won. The boy was staying. He reached out and ruffled Norton's hair and slapped Johnson on the shoulder. "Now you fellows sit here and get acquainted," he said gaily and started toward the door. "I'm going to see what Leola left us for supper."

When he was gone, Johnson raised his head and looked at Norton. The child looked back at him bleakly. "God, kid," Johnson said in a cracked voice, "how do you stand it?" His face was stiff with outrage. "He thinks he's Jesus Christ!"

II

Sheppard's attic was a large unfinished room with exposed beams and no electric light. They had set the telescope up on a tripod in one of the dormer windows. It pointed now toward the dark sky where a sliver of moon, as fragile as an egg shell, had just emerged from behind a cloud with a brilliant silver edge. Inside, a kerosene lantern set on a trunk cast their shadows upward and tangled them, wavering slightly, in the joists overhead. Sheppard was sitting on a packing box, looking through the telescope, and Johnson was at his elbow, waiting to get at it. Sheppard had bought it for fifteen dollars two days before at a pawn shop.

"Quit hoggin it," Johnson said.

Sheppard got up and Johnson slid onto the box and put his eye to the instrument.

Sheppard sat down on a straight chair a few feet away. His face was flushed with pleasure. This much of his dream was a reality. Within a week he had made it possible for this boy's vision to pass through a slender channel to the stars. He looked at Johnson's bent back with complete satisfaction. The boy had on one of Norton's plaid shirts and some new khaki trousers he had bought him. The shoe would be ready next week. He had taken him to the bracc shop the day after he came and had him fitted for a new shoe. Johnson was as touchy about the foot as if it were a sacred object. His face had been glum while the clerk, a young man with a bright pink bald head, measured the foot with his profane hands. The shoe was going to make the greatest difference in the boy's attitude. Even a child with normal feet was in love with the world after he had got a new pair of shoes. When Norton got a new pair, he walked around for days with his eyes on his feet.

Sheppard glanced across the room at the child. He was sitting on the floor against a trunk, trussed up in a rope he had found and wound around his legs from his ankles to his knees. He appeared so far away that Sheppard might have been looking at him through the wrong end of the telescope. He had had to whip him only once since Johnson had been with them—the first night when Norton had realized that Johnson was going to sleep in his mother's bed. He did not believe in whipping children, particularly in anger. In this case, he had done both and with good results. He had had no more trouble with Norton.

The child hadn't shown any positive generosity toward Johnson but what he couldn't help, he appeared to be resigned to. In the mornings Sheppard sent the two of them to the Y swimming pool, gave them money to get their lunch at the cafeteria and instructed them to meet him in the park in the afternoon to watch his Little League baseball practice. Every afternoon they had arrived at the park, shambling, silent, their faces closed each on his own thoughts as if neither were aware of the other's existence. At least he could be thankful there were no fights.

Norton showed no interest in the telescope. "Don't you want to get up and look through the telescope, Norton?" he said. It irritated him that the child showed no intellectual curiosity whatsoever. "Rufus is going to be way ahead of you."

Norton leaned forward absently and looked at Johnson's back. Johnson turned around from the instrument. His face had begun to fill out again. The look of outrage had retreated from his hollow cheeks and was shored up now in the caves of his eyes, like a fugitive from Sheppard's kindness. "Don't waste your valuable time, kid," he said. "You seen the moon once, you seen it."

Sheppard was amused by these sudden turns of perversity. The boy resisted whatever he suspected was meant for his improvement and contrived when he was vitally interested in something to leave the impression he was bored. Sheppard was not deceived. Secretly Johnson was learning what he wanted him to learn—that his benefactor was impervious to insult and that there were no cracks in his armor of kindness and patience where a successful shaft could be driven. "Some day you may go to the moon," he said. "In ten years men will probably be making round trips there on schedule. Why you boys may be spacemen. Astronauts!"

"Astro-nuts," Johnson said.

"Nuts or nauts," Sheppard said, "it's perfectly possible that you, Rufus Johnson, will go to the moon."

Something in the depths of Johnson's eyes stirred. All day his humor had been glum. "I ain't going to the moon and get there alive," he said, "and when I die I'm going to hell."

"It's at least possible to get to the moon," Sheppard said dryly. The best way to handle this kind of thing was with gentle ridicule.

"We can see it. We know it's there. Nobody has given any reliable evidence there's a hell."

"The Bible has give the evidence," Johnson said darkly, "and if you die and go there you burn forever."

The child leaned forward.

"Whoever says it ain't a hell," Johnson said, "is contradicting Jesus. The dead are judged and the wicked are damned. They weep and gnash their teeth while they burn," he continued, "and it's everlasting darkness."

The child's mouth opened. His eyes appeared to grow hollow.

"Satan runs it," Johnson said.

Norton lurched up and took a hobbled step toward Sheppard. "Is she there?" he said in a loud voice. "Is she there burning up?" He kicked the rope off his feet. "Is she on fire?"

"Oh my God," Sheppard muttered. "No no," he said, "of course she isn't. Rufus is mistaken. Your mother isn't anywhere. She's not unhappy. She just isn't." His lot would have been easier if when his wife died he had told Norton she had gone to heaven and that some day he would see her again, but he could not allow himself to bring him up on a lie.

Norton's face began to twist. A knot formed in his chin.

"Listen," Sheppard said quickly and pulled the child to him, "your mother's spirit lives on in other people and it'll live on in you if you're good and generous like she was."

The child's pale eyes hardened in disbelief.

Sheppard's pity turned to revulsion. The boy would rather she be in hell than nowhere. "Do you understand?" he said. "She doesn't exist." He put his hand on the child's shoulder. "That's all I have to give you," he said in a softer, exasperated tone, "the truth."

Instead of howling, the boy wrenched himself away and caught Johnson by the sleeve. "Is she there, Rufus?" he said. "Is she there, burning up?"

Johnson's eyes glittered. "Well," he said, "she is if she was evil. Was she a whore?"

"Your mother was not a whore," Sheppard said sharply. He had the sensation of driving a car without brakes. "Now let's have no more of this foolishness. We were talking about the moon."

"Did she believe in Jesus?" Johnson asked.

Norton looked blank. After a second he said, "Yes," as if he saw that this was necessary. "She did," he said. "All the time."

"She did not," Sheppard muttered.

"She did all the time," Norton said. "I heard her say she did all the time."

"She's saved," Johnson said.

The child still looked puzzled. "Where?" he said. "Where is she at?"

"On high," Johnson said.

"Where's that?" Norton gasped.

"It's in the sky somewhere," Johnson said, "but you got to be dead to get there. You can't go in no space ship." There was a narrow gleam in his eyes now like a beam holding steady on its target.

"Man's going to the moon," Sheppard said grimly, "is very much like the first fish crawling out of the water onto land billions and billions of years ago. He didn't have an earth suit. He had to grow his adjustments inside. He developed lungs."

"When I'm dead will I go to hell or where she is?" Norton asked.

"Right now you'd go where she is," Johnson said, "but if you live long enough, you'll go to hell."

Sheppard rose abruptly and picked up the lantern. "Close the window, Rufus," he said. "It's time we went to bed."

On the way down the attic stairs he heard Johnson say in a loud whisper behind him, "I'll tell you all about it tomorrow, kid, when Himself has cleared out."

The next day when the boys came to the ball park, he watched them as they came from behind the bleachers and around the edge of the field. Johnson's hand was on Norton's shoulder, his head bent toward the younger boy's ear, and on the child's face there was a look of complete confidence, of dawning light. Sheppard's grimace hardened. This would be Johnson's way of trying to annoy him. But he would not be annoyed. Norton was not bright enough to be damaged much. He gazed at the child's dull absorbed little face. Why try to make him superior? Heaven and hell were for the mediocre, and he was that if he was anything.

The two boys came into the bleachers and sat down about ten

feet away, facing him, but neither gave him any sign of recognition. He cast a glance behind him where the Little Leaguers were spread out in the field. Then he started for the bleachers. The hiss of Johnson's voice stopped as he approached.

"What have you fellows been doing today?" he asked genially.

"He's been telling me . . ." Norton started.

Johnson pushed the child in the ribs with his elbow. "We ain't been doing nothing," he said. His face appeared to be covered with a blank glaze but through it a look of complicity was blazoned forth insolently.

Sheppard felt his face grow warm, but he said nothing. A child in a Little League uniform had followed him and was nudging him in the back of the leg with a bat. He turned and put his arm around the boy's neck and went with him back to the game.

That night when he went to the attic to join the boys at the telescope, he found Norton there alone. He was sitting on the packing box, hunched over, looking intently through the instrument. Johnson was not there.

"Where's Rufus?" Sheppard asked.

"I said where's Rufus?" he said louder.

"Gone somewhere," the child said without turning around.

"Gone where?" Sheppard asked.

"He just said he was going somewhere. He said he was fed up looking at stars."

"I see," Sheppard said glumly. He turned and went back down the stairs. He searched the house without finding Johnson. Then he went to the living room and sat down. Yesterday he had been convinced of his success with the boy. Today he faced the possibility that he was failing with him. He had been over-lenient, too concerned to have Johnson like him. He felt a twinge of guilt. What difference did it make if Johnson liked him or not? What was that to him? When the boy came in, they would have a few things understood. As long as you stay here there'll be no going out at night by yourself, do you understand?

I don't have to stay here. It ain't nothing to me staying here.

Oh my God, he thought. He could not bring it to that. He would have to be firm but not make an issue of it. He picked up the evening paper. Kindness and patience were always called for but he had not been firm enough. He sat holding the paper but not

reading it. The boy would not respect him unless he showed firm-
ness. The doorbell rang and he went to answer it. He opened it
and stepped back, with a pained disappointed face.

A large dour policeman stood on the stoop, holding Johnson by
the elbow. At the curb a patrol car waited. Johnson looked very
white. His jaw was thrust forward as if to keep it from trembling.

"We brought him here first because he raised such a fit," the
policeman said, "but now that you've seen him, we're going to take
him to the station and ask him a few questions."

"What happened?" Sheppard muttered.

"A house around the corner from here," the policeman said.
"A real smash job, dishes broken all over the floor, furniture
turned upside-down . . ."

"I didn't have a thing to do with it!" Johnson said. "I was walking along minding my own bidnis when this cop came up and
grabbed me."

Sheppard looked at the boy grimly. He made no effort to soften
his expression.

Johnson flushed. "I was just walking along," he muttered, but
with no conviction in his voice.

"Come on, bud," the policeman said.

"You ain't going to let him take me, are you?" Johnson said.
"You believe me, don't you?" There was an appeal in his voice that
Sheppard had not heard there before.

This was crucial. The boy would have to learn that he could
not be protected when he was guilty. "You'll have to go with him,
Rufus," he said.

"You're going to let him take me and I tell you I ain't done a
thing?" Johnson said shrilly.

Sheppard's face became harder as his sense of injury grew. The
boy had failed him even before he had had a chance to give him
the shoe. They were to have got it tomorrow. All his regret turned
suddenly on the shoe; his irritation at the sight of Johnson
doubled.

"You made out like you had all this confidence in me," the boy
mumbled.

"I did have," Sheppard said. His face was wooden.

Johnson turned away with the policeman but before he moved,
a gleam of pure hatred flashed toward Sheppard from the pits of his
eyes.

Sheppard stood in the door and watched them get into the patrol car and drive away. He summoned his compassion. He would go to the station tomorrow and see what he could do about getting him out of trouble. The night in jail would not hurt him and the experience would teach him that he could not treat with impunity someone who had shown him nothing but kindness. Then they would go get the shoe and perhaps after a night in jail it would mean even more to the boy.

The next morning at eight o'clock the police sergeant called and told him he could come pick Johnson up. "We booked a nigger on that charge," he said. "Your boy didn't have nothing to do with it."

Sheppard was at the station in ten minutes, his face hot with shame. Johnson sat slouched on a bench in a drab outer office, reading a police magazine. There was no one else in the room. Sheppard sat down beside him and put his hand tentatively on his shoulder.

The boy glanced up—his lip curled—and back to the magazine.

Sheppard felt physically sick. The ugliness of what he had done bore in upon him with a sudden dull intensity. He had failed him at just the point where he might have turned him once and for all in the right direction. "Rufus," he said, "I apologize. I was wrong and you were right. I misjudged you."

The boy continued to read.

"I'm sorry."

The boy wet his finger and turned a page.

Sheppard braced himself. "I was a fool, Rufus," he said.

Johnson's mouth slid slightly to the side. He shrugged without raising his head from the magazine.

"Will you forget it, this time?" Sheppard said. "It won't happen again."

The boy looked up. His eyes were bright and unfriendly. "I'll forget it," he said, "but you better remember it." He got up and stalked toward the door. In the middle of the room, he turned and jerked his arm at Sheppard and Sheppard jumped up and followed him as if the boy had yanked an invisible leash.

"Your shoe," he said eagerly, "today is the day to get your shoe!" Thank God for the shoe!

But when they went to the brace shop, they found that the shoe had been made two sizes too small and a new one would not be ready for another ten days. Johnson's temper improved at once. The clerk had obviously made a mistake in the measurements but the boy insisted the foot had grown. He left the shop with a pleased expression, as if, in expanding, the foot had acted on some inspiration of its own. Sheppard's face was haggard.

After this he redoubled his efforts. Since Johnson had lost interest in the telescope, he bought a microscope and a box of prepared slides. If he couldn't impress the boy with immensity, he would try the infinitesimal. For two nights Johnson appeared absorbed in the new instrument, then he abruptly lost interest in it, but he seemed content to sit in the living room in the evening and read the encyclopedia. He devoured the encyclopedia as he devoured his dinner, steadily and without dint to his appetite. Each subject appeared to enter his head, be ravaged, and thrown out. Nothing pleased Sheppard more than to see the boy slouched on the sofa, his mouth shut, reading. After they had spent two or three evenings like this, he began to recover his vision. His confidence returned. He knew that some day he would be proud of Johnson.

On Thursday night Sheppard attended a city council meeting. He dropped the boys off at a movie on his way and picked them up on his way back. When they reached home, an automobile with a single red eye above its windshield was waiting in front of the house. Sheppard's lights as he turned into the driveway illuminated two dour faces in the car.

"The cops!" Johnson said. "Some nigger has broke in somewhere and they've come for me again."

"We'll see about that," Sheppard muttered. He stopped the car in the driveway and switched off the lights. "You boys go in the house and go to bed," he said. "I'll handle this."

He got out and strode toward the squad car. He thrust his head in the window. The two policemen were looking at him with silent knowledgeable faces. "A house on the corner of Shelton and Mills," the one in the driver's seat said. "It looks like a train run through it."

"He was in the picture show down town," Sheppard said. "My boy was with him. He had nothing to do with the other one and he had nothing to do with this one. I'll be responsible."

"If I was you," the one nearest him said, "I wouldn't be responsible for any little bastard like him."

"I said I'd be responsible," Sheppard repeated coldly. "You people made a mistake the last time. Don't make another."

The policemen looked at each other. "It ain't our funeral," the one in the driver's seat said, and turned the key in the ignition.

Sheppard went in the house and sat down in the living room in the dark. He did not suspect Johnson and he did not want the boy to think he did. If Johnson thought he suspected him again, he would lose everything. But he wanted to know if his alibi was airtight. He thought of going to Norton's room and asking him if Johnson had left the movie. But that would be worse. Johnson would know what he was doing and would be incensed. He decided to ask Johnson himself. He would be direct. He went over in his mind what he was going to say and then he got up and went to the boy's door.

It was open as if he had been expected but Johnson was in bed. Just enough light came in from the hall for Sheppard to see his shape under the sheet. He came in and stood at the foot of the bed. "They've gone," he said. "I told them you had nothing to do with it and that I'd be responsible."

There was a muttered "Yeah," from the pillow.

Sheppard hesitated. "Rufus," he said, "you didn't leave the movie for anything at all, did you?"

"You make out like you got all this confidence in me!" a sudden outraged voice cried, "and you ain't got any! You don't trust me no more now than you did then!" The voice, disembodied, seemed to come more surely from the depths of Johnson than when his face was visible. It was a cry of reproach, edged slightly with contempt.

"I do have confidence in you," Sheppard said intensely. "I have every confidence in you. I believe in you and I trust you completely."

"You got your eye on me all the time," the voice said sullenly. "When you get through asking me a bunch of questions, you're going across the hall and ask Norton a bunch of them."

"I have no intention of asking Norton anything and never did," Sheppard said gently. "And I don't suspect you at all. You could hardly have got from the picture show down town and out here to break in a house and back to the picture show in the time you had."

"That's why you believe me!" the boy cried, "—because you think I couldn't have done it."

"No, no!" Sheppard said. "I believe you because I believe you've got the brains and the guts not to get in trouble again. I believe you know yourself well enough now to know that you don't have to do such things. I believe that you can make anything of yourself that you set your mind to."

Johnson sat up. A faint light shone on his forehead but the rest of his face was invisible. "And I could have broke in there if I'd wanted to in the time I had," he said.

"But I know you didn't," Sheppard said. "There's not the least trace of doubt in my mind."

There was a silence. Johnson lay back down. Then the voice, low and hoarse, as if it were being forced out with difficulty, said, "You don't want to steal and smash up things when you've got everything you want already."

Sheppard caught his breath. The boy was thanking him! He was thanking him! There was gratitude in his voice. There was appreciation. He stood there, smiling foolishly in the dark, trying to hold the moment in suspension. Involuntarily he took a step toward the pillow and stretched out his hand and touched Johnson's forehead. It was cold and dry like rusty iron.

"I understand. Good night, son," he said and turned quickly and left the room. He closed the door behind him and stood there, overcome with emotion.

Across the hall Norton's door was open. The child lay on the bed on his side, looking into the light from the hall.

After this, the road with Johnson would be smooth.

Norton sat up and beckoned to him.

He saw the child but after the first instant, he did not let his eyes focus directly on him. He could not go in and talk to Norton without breaking Johnson's trust. He hesitated, but remained where he was a moment as if he saw nothing. Tomorrow was the day they were to go back for the shoe. It would be a climax to the good feeling between them. He turned quickly and went back into his own room.

The child sat for some time looking at the spot where his father had stood. Finally his gaze became aimless and he lay back down.

The next day Johnson was glum and silent as if he were ashamed that he had revealed himself. His eyes had a hooded look. He seemed to have retired within himself and there to be going through some crisis of determination. Sheppard could not get to the brace shop quickly enough. He left Norton at home because he did not want his attention divided. He wanted to be free to observe Johnson's reaction minutely. The boy did not seem pleased or even interested in the prospect of the shoe, but when it became an actuality, certainly then he would be moved.

The brace shop was a small concrete warehouse lined and stacked with the equipment of affliction. Wheelchairs and walkers covered most of the floor. The walls were hung with every kind of crutch and brace. Artificial limbs were stacked on the shelves, legs and arms and hands, claws and hooks, straps and human harnesses and unidentifiable instruments for unnamed deformities. In a small clearing in the middle of the room there was a row of yellow plastic-cushioned chairs and a shoe-fitting stool. Johnson slouched down in one of the chairs and set his foot up on the stool and sat with his eyes on it moodily. What was roughly the toe had broken open again and he had patched it with a piece of canvas; another place he had patched with what appeared to be the tongue of the original shoe. The two sides were laced with twine.

There was a excited flush on Sheppard's face; his heart was beating unnaturally fast.

The clerk appeared from the back of the shop with the new shoe under his arm. "Got her right this time!" he said. He straddled the shoe-fitting stool and held the shoe up, smiling as if he had produced it by magic.

It was a black slick shapeless object, shining hideously. It looked like a blunt weapon, highly polished.

Johnson gazed at it darkly.

"With this shoe," the clerk said, "you won't know you're walking. You'll think you're riding!" He bent his bright pink bald head and began gingerly to unlace the twine. He removed the old shoe as if he were skinning an animal still half alive. His expression was strained. The unsheathed mass of foot in the dirty sock made Sheppard feel queasy. He turned his eyes away until the new shoe was on. The clerk laced it up rapidly. "Now stand up and walk around," he said, "and see if that ain't power glide." He winked at Sheppard. "In that shoe," he said, "he won't know he don't have a normal foot."

Sheppard's face was bright with pleasure.

Johnson stood up and walked a few yards away. He walked stiffly with almost no dip in his short side. He stood for a moment, rigid, with his back to them.

"Wonderful!" Sheppard said. "Wonderful." It was as if he had given the boy a new spine.

Johnson turned around. His mouth was set in a thin icy line. He came back to the seat and removed the shoe. He put his foot in the old one and began lacing it up.

"You want to take it home and see if it suits you first?" the clerk murmured.

"No," Johnson said. "I ain't going to wear it at all."

"What's wrong with it?" Sheppard said, his voice rising.

"I don't need no new shoe," Johnson said. "And when I do, I got ways of getting my own." His face was stony but there was a glint of triumph in his eyes.

"Boy," the clerk said, "is your trouble in your foot or in your head?"

"Go soak your skull," Johnson said. "Your brains are on fire."

The clerk rose glumly but with dignity and asked Sheppard what he wanted done with the shoe, which he dangled dispiritedly by the lace.

Sheppard's face was a dark angry red. He was staring straight in front of him at a leather corset with an artificial arm attached.

The clerk asked him again.

"Wrap it up," Sheppard muttered. He turned his eyes to Johnson. "He's not mature enough for it yet," he said. "I had thought he was less of a child."

The boy leered. "You been wrong before," he said.

That night they sat in the living room and read as usual. Sheppard kept himself glumly entrenched behind the Sunday New York *Times*. He wanted to recover his good humor, but every time he thought of the rejected shoe, he felt a new charge of irritation. He did not trust himself even to look at Johnson. He realized that the boy had refused the shoe because he was insecure. Johnson had been frightened by his own gratitude. He didn't know what to make of the new self he was becoming conscious of. He understood that something he had been was threatened and he was facing himself and his possibilities for the first time. He was questioning his identity. Grudgingly, Sheppard felt a slight return of sympathy for the boy. In a few minutes, he lowered his paper and looked at him.

Johnson was sitting on the sofa, gazing over the top of the encyclopedia. His expression was trancelike. He might have been listening to something far away. Sheppard watched him intently but the boy continued to listen, and did not turn his head. The poor kid is lost, Sheppard thought. Here he had sat all evening, sullenly reading the paper, and had not said a word to break the tension. "Rufus," he said.

Johnson continued to sit, stock-still, listening.

"Rufus," Sheppard said in a slow hypnotic voice, "you can be anything in the world you want to be. You can be a scientist or an architect or an engineer or whatever you set your mind to, and whatever you set your mind to be, you can be the best of its kind." He imagined his voice penetrating to the boy in the black caverns of his psyche. Johnson leaned forward but his eyes did not turn. On the street a car door closed. There was a silence. Then a sudden blast from the doorbell.

Sheppard jumped up and went to the door and opened it. The same policeman who had come before stood there. The patrol car waited at the curb.

"Lemme see that boy," he said.

Sheppard scowled and stood aside. "He's been here all evening," he said. "I can vouch for it."

The policeman walked into the living room. Johnson appeared engrossed in his book. After a second he looked up with an annoyed expression, like a great man interrupted at his work.

"What was that you were looking at in that kitchen window over on Winter Avenue about a half hour ago, bud?" the policeman asked.

"Stop persecuting this boy!" Sheppard said. "I'll vouch for the fact he was here. I was here with him."

"You heard him," Johnson said. "I been here all the time."

"It ain't everybody makes tracks like you," the policeman said and eyed the club foot.

"They couldn't be his tracks," Sheppard growled, infuriated. "He's been here all the time. You're wasting your own time and you're wasting ours." He felt the *ours* seal his solidarity with the boy. "I'm sick of this," he said. "You people are too damn lazy to go out and find whoever is doing these things. You come here automatically."

The policeman ignored this and continued looking through Johnson. His eyes were small and alert in his fleshy face. Finally he turned toward the door. "We'll get him sooner or later," he said, "with his head in a window and his tail out."

Sheppard followed him to the door and slammed it behind him. His spirits were soaring. This was exactly what he had needed. He returned with an expectant face.

Johnson had put the book down and was sitting there, looking at him slyly. "Thanks," he said.

Sheppard stopped. The boy's expression was predatory. He was openly leering.

"You ain't such a bad liar yourself," he said.

"Liar?" Sheppard murmured. Could the boy have left and come back? He felt himself sicken. Then a rush of anger sent him forward. "Did you leave?" he said furiously. "I didn't see you leave."

The boy only smiled.

"You went up in the attic to see Norton," Sheppard said.

"Naw," Johnson said, "that kid is crazy. He don't want to do nothing but look through that stinking telescope."

"I don't want to hear about Norton," Sheppard said harshly. "Where were you?"

"I was sitting on that pink can by my ownself," Johnson said. "There wasn't no witnesses."

Sheppard took out his handkerchief and wiped his forehead. He managed to smile.

Johnson rolled his eyes. "You don't believe in me," he said. His voice was cracked the way it had been in the dark room two nights before. "You make out like you got all this confidence in me but you ain't got any. When things get hot, you'll fade like the rest of them." The crack became exaggerated, comic. The mockery in it was blatant. "You don't believe in me. You ain't got no confidence," he wailed. "And you ain't any smarter than that cop. All that about tracks—that was a trap. There wasn't any tracks. That whole place is concreted in the back and my feet were dry."

Sheppard slowly put the handkerchief back in his pocket. He dropped down on the sofa and gazed at the rug beneath his feet. The boy's club foot was set within the circle of his vision. The pieced-together shoe appeared to grin at him with Johnson's own face. He caught hold of the edge of the sofa cushion and his knuckles turned white. A chill of hatred shook him. He hated the shoe, hated the foot, hated the boy. His face paled. Hatred choked him. He was aghast at himself.

He caught the boy's shoulder and gripped it fiercely as if to keep himself from falling. "Listen," he said, "you looked in that window to embarrass me. That was all you wanted—to shake my resolve to help you, but my resolve isn't shaken. I'm stronger than you are. I'm stronger than you are and I'm going to save you. The good will triumph."

"Not when it ain't true," the boy said. "Not when it ain't right."

"My resolve isn't shaken," Sheppard repeated. "I'm going to save you."

Johnson's look became sly again. "You ain't going to save me," he said. "You're going to tell me to leave this house. I did those other two jobs too—the first one as well as the one I done when I was supposed to be in the picture show."

"I'm not going to tell you to leave," Sheppard said. His voice was toneless, mechanical. "I'm going to save you."

Johnson thrust his head forward. "Save yourself," he hissed. "Nobody can save me but Jesus."

Sheppard laughed curtly. "You don't deceive me," he said. "I flushed that out of your head in the reformatory. I saved you from that, at least."

The muscles in Johnson's face stiffened. A look of such repulsion hardened on his face that Sheppard drew back. The boy's eyes were like distorting mirrors in which he saw himself made hideous and grotesque. "I'll show you," Johnson whispered. He rose abruptly and started headlong for the door as if he could not get out of Sheppard's sight quick enough, but it was the door to the back hall he went through, not the front door. Sheppard turned on the sofa and looked behind him where the boy had disappeared.

He heard the door to his room slam. He was not leaving. The intensity had gone out of Sheppard's eyes. They looked flat and lifeless as if the shock of the boy's revelation were only now reaching the center of his consciousness. "If he would only leave," he murmured. "If he would only leave now of his own accord."

The next morning Johnson appeared at the breakfast table in the grandfather's suit he had come in. Sheppard pretended not to notice but one look told him what he already knew, that he was trapped, that there could be nothing now but a battle of nerves and that Johnson would win it. He wished he had never laid eyes on the boy. The failure of his compassion numbed him. He got out of the house as soon as he could and all day he dreaded to go home in the evening. He had a faint hope that the boy might be gone when he returned. The grandfather's suit might have meant he was leaving. The hope grew in the afternoon. When he came home and opened the front door, his heart was pounding.

He stopped in the hall and looked silently into the living room. His expectant expression faded. His face seemed suddenly as old as his white hair. The two boys were sitting close together on the sofa, reading the same book. Norton's cheek rested against the sleeve of Johnson's black suit. Johnson's finger moved under the lines they were reading. The elder brother and the younger. Sheppard looked woodenly at this scene for almost a minute. Then he walked into the room and took off his coat and dropped it on a chair. Neither boy noticed him. He went on to the kitchen.

Leola left the supper on the stove every afternoon before she left and he put it on the table. His head ached and his nerves were taut. He sat down on the kitchen stool and remained there, sunk in his depression. He wondered if he could infuriate Johnson enough to make him leave of his own accord. Last night what had enraged him was the Jesus business. It might enrage Johnson, but it depressed him. Why not simply tell the boy to go? Admit defeat. The thought of facing Johnson again sickened him. The boy looked at him as if he were the guilty one, as if he were a moral leper. He knew without conceit that he was a good man, that he had nothing to reproach himself with. His feelings about Johnson now were involuntary. He would like to feel compassion for him. He would like to be able to help him. He longed for the time when there would be no one but himself and Norton in the house, when the child's simple selfishness would be all he had to contend with, and his own loneliness.

He got up and took three serving dishes off the shelf and took them to the stove. Absently he began pouring the butterbeans and the hash into the dishes. When the food was on the table, he called them in.

They brought the book with them. Norton pushed his place setting around to the same side of the table as Johnson's and moved his chair next to Johnson's chair. They sat down and put the book between them. It was a black book with red edges.

"What's that you're reading?" Sheppard asked, sitting down.

"The Holy Bible," Johnson said.

God give me strength, Sheppard said under his breath.

"We lifted it from a ten cent store," Johnson said.

"We?" Sheppard muttered. He turned and glared at Norton. The child's face was bright and there was an excited sheen to his eyes. The change that had come over the boy struck him for the first time. He looked alert. He had on a blue plaid shirt and his eyes were a brighter blue than he had ever seen them before. There was a strange new life in him, the sign of new and more rugged vices. "So now you steal?" he said, glowering. "You haven't learned to be generous but you have learned to steal."

"No he ain't," Johnson said. "I was the one lifted it. He only watched. He can't sully himself. It don't make any difference about me. I'm going to hell anyway."

Sheppard held his tongue.

"Unless," Johnson said, "I repent."

"Repent, Rufus," Norton said in a pleading voice. "Repent, hear? You don't want to go to hell."

"Stop talking this nonsense," Sheppard said, looking sharply at the child.

"If I do repent, I'll be a preacher," Johnson said. "If you're going to do it, it's no sense in doing it halfway."

"What are you going to be, Norton," Sheppard asked in a brittle voice, "a preacher too?"

There was a glitter of wild pleasure in the child's eyes. "A space man!" he shouted.

"Wonderful," Sheppard said bitterly.

"Those space ships ain't going to do you any good unless you believe in Jesus," Johnson said. He wet his finger and began to leaf through the pages of the Bible. "I'll read you where it says so," he said.

Sheppard leaned forward and said in a low furious voice, "Put that Bible up, Rufus, and eat your dinner."

Johnson continued searching for the passage.

"Put that Bible up!" Sheppard shouted.

The boy stopped and looked up. His expression was startled but pleased.

"That book is something for you to hide behind," Sheppard said. "It's for cowards, people who are afraid to stand on their own feet and figure things out for themselves."

Johnson's eyes snapped. He backed his chair a little way from the table. "Satan has you in his power," he said. "Not only me. You too."

Sheppard reached across the table to grab the book but Johnson snatched it and put it in his lap.

Sheppard laughed. "You don't believe in that book and you know you don't believe in it!"

"I believe it!" Johnson said. "You don't know what I believe and what I don't."

Sheppard shook his head. "You don't believe it. You're too intelligent."

"I ain't too intelligent," the boy muttered. "You don't know nothing about me. Even if I didn't believe it, it would still be true."

"You don't believe it!" Sheppard said. His face was a taunt.

"I believe it!" Johnson said breathlessly. "I'll show you I believe it!" He opened the book in his lap and tore out a page of it and thrust it into his mouth. He fixed his eyes on Sheppard. His jaws worked furiously and the paper crackled as he chewed it.

"Stop this," Sheppard said in a dry, burnt-out voice. "Stop it."

The boy raised the Bible and tore out a page with his teeth and began grinding it in his mouth, his eyes burning.

Sheppard reached across the table and knocked the book out of his hand. "Leave the table," he said coldly.

Johnson swallowed what was in his mouth. His eyes widened as if a vision of splendor were opening up before him. "I've eaten it!"

he breathed. "I've eaten it like Ezekiel and it was honey to my mouth!"

"Leave this table," Sheppard said. His hands were clenched beside his plate.

"I've eaten it!" the boy cried. Wonder transformed his face. "I've eaten it like Ezekiel and I don't want none of your food after it nor no more ever."

"Go then," Sheppard said softly. "Go. Go."

The boy rose and picked up the Bible and started toward the hall with it. At the door he paused, a small black figure on the threshold of some dark apocalypse. "The devil has you in his power," he said in a jubilant voice and disappeared.

After supper Sheppard sat in the living room alone. Johnson had left the house but he could not believe that the boy had simply gone. The first feeling of release had passed. He felt dull and cold as at the onset of an illness and dread had settled in him like a fog. Just to leave would be too anticlimactic an end for Johnson's taste; he would return and try to prove something. He might come back a week later and set fire to the place. Nothing seemed too outrageous now.

He picked up the paper and tried to read. In a moment he threw it down and got up and went into the hall and listened. He might be hiding in the attic. He went to the attic door and opened it.

The lantern was lit, casting a dim light on the stairs. He didn't hear anything. "Norton," he called, "are you up there?" There was no answer. He mounted the narrow stairs to see.

Amid the strange vine-like shadows cast by the lantern, Norton sat with his eye to the telescope. "Norton," Sheppard said, "do you know where Rufus went?"

The child's back was to him. He was sitting hunched, intent, his large ears directly above his shoulders. Suddenly he waved his hand and crouched closer to the telescope as if he could not get near enough to what he saw.

"Norton!" Sheppard said in a loud voice.

The child didn't move.

"Norton!" Sheppard shouted.

Norton started. He turned around. There was an unnatural

brightness about his eyes. After a moment he seemed to see that it was Sheppard. "I've found her!" he said breathlessly.

"Found who?" Sheppard said.

"Mamma!"

Sheppard steadied himself in the doorway. The jungle of shadows around the child thickened.

"Come and look!" he cried. He wiped his sweaty face on the tail of his plaid shirt and then put his eye back to the telescope. His back became fixed in a rigid intensity. All at once he waved again.

"Norton," Sheppard said, "you don't see anything in the telescope but star clusters. Now you've had enough of that for one night. You'd better go to bed. Do you know where Rufus is?"

"She's there!" he cried, not turning around from the telescope. "She waved at me!"

"I want you in bed in fifteen minutes," Sheppard said. After a moment he said, "Do you hear me, Norton?"

The child began to wave frantically.

"I mean what I say," Sheppard said. "I'm going to call in fifteen minutes and see if you're in bed."

He went down the steps again and returned to the parlor. He went to the front door and cast a cursory glance out. The sky was crowded with the stars he had been fool enough to think Johnson could reach. Somewhere in the small wood behind the house, a bullfrog sounded a low hollow note. He went back to his chair and sat a few minutes. He decided to go to bed. He put his hands on the arms of the chair and leaned forward and heard, like the first shrill note of a disaster warning, the siren of a police car, moving slowly into the neighborhood and nearer until it subsided with a moan outside the house.

He felt a cold weight on his shoulders as if an icy cloak had been thrown about him. He went to the door and opened it.

Two policemen were coming up the walk with a dark snarling Johnson between them, handcuffed to each. A reporter jogged alongside and another policeman waited in the patrol car.

"Here's your boy," the dourest of the policemen said. "Didn't I tell you we'd get him?"

Johnson jerked his arm down savagely. "I was waitin for you!" he said. "You wouldn't have got me if I hadn't of wanted to get caught. It was my idea." He was addressing the policemen but leering at Sheppard.

Sheppard looked at him coldly.

"Why did you want to get caught?" the reporter asked, running around to get beside Johnson. "Why did you deliberately want to get caught?"

The question and the sight of Sheppard seemed to throw the boy into a fury. "To show up that big tin Jesus!" he hissed and kicked his leg out at Sheppard. "He thinks he's God. I'd rather be in the reformatory than in his house, I'd rather be in the pen! The Devil has him in his power. He don't know his left hand from his right, he don't have as much sense as his crazy kid!" He paused and then swept on to his fantastic conclusion. "He made suggestions to me!"

Sheppard's face blanched. He caught hold of the door facing.

"Suggestions?" the reporter said eagerly, "what kind of suggestions?"

"Immor'l suggestions!" Johnson said. "What kind of suggestions do you think? But I ain't having none of it, I'm a Christian, I'm . . ."

Sheppard's face was tight with pain. "He knows that's not true," he said in a shaken voice. "He knows he's lying. I did everything I knew how for him. I did more for him than I did for my own child. I hoped to save him and I failed, but it was an honorable failure. I have nothing to reproach myself with. I made no suggestions to him."

"Do you remember the suggestions?" the reporter asked. "Can you tell us exactly what he said?"

"He's a dirty atheist," Johnson said. "He said there wasn't no hell."

"Well, they seen each other now," one of the policemen said with a knowing sigh. "Let's us go."

"Wait," Sheppard said. He came down one step and fixed his eyes on Johnson's eyes in a last desperate effort to save himself. "Tell the truth, Rufus," he said. "You don't want to perpetrate this lie. You're not evil, you're mortally confused. You don't have to make up for that foot, you don't have to . . ."

Johnson hurled himself forward. "Listen at him!" he screamed. "I lie and steal because I'm good at it! My foot don't have a thing to do with it! The lame shall enter first! The halt'll be gathered together. When I get ready to be saved, Jesus'll save me, not that lying stinking atheist, not that . . ."

"That'll be enough out of you," the policeman said and yanked him back. "We just wanted you to see we got him," he said to Sheppard, and the two of them turned around and dragged Johnson away, half turned and screaming back at Sheppard.

"The lame'll carry off the prey!" he screeched, but his voice was muffled inside the car. The reporter scrambled into the front seat with the driver and slammed the door and the siren wailed into the darkness.

Sheppard remained there, bent slightly like a man who has been shot but continues to stand. After a minute he turned and went back in the house and sat down in the chair he had left. He closed his eyes on a picture of Johnson in a circle of reporters at the police station, elaborating his lies. "I have nothing to reproach myself with," he murmured. His every action had been selfless, his one aim had been to save Johnson for some decent kind of service, he had not spared himself, he had sacrificed his reputation, he had done more for Johnson than he had done for his own child. Foulness hung about him like an odor in the air, so close that it seemed to come from his own breath. "I have nothing to reproach myself with," he repeated. His voice sounded dry and harsh. "I did more for him than I did for my own child." He was swept with a sudden panic. He heard the boy's jubilant voice. Satan has you in his power.

"I have nothing to reproach myself with," he began again. "I did more for him than I did for my own child." He heard his voice as if it were the voice of his accuser. He repeated the sentence silently.

Slowly his face drained of color. It became almost grey beneath the white halo of his hair. The sentence echoed in his mind, each syllable like a dull blow. His mouth twisted and he closed his eyes against the revelation. Norton's face rose before him, empty, forlorn, his left eye listing almost imperceptibly toward the outer rim as if it could not bear a full view of grief. His heart constricted with a repulsion for himself so clear and intense that he gasped for breath. He had stuffed his own emptiness with good works like a glutton. He had ignored his own child to feed his vision of himself. He saw the clear-eyed Devil, the sounder of hearts, leering at him from the eyes of Johnson. His image of himself shrivelled until everything was black before him. He sat there paralyzed, aghast.

He saw Norton at the telescope, all back and ears, saw his arm shoot up and wave frantically. A rush of agonizing love for the child rushed over him like a transfusion of life. The little boy's face appeared to him transformed; the image of his salvation; all light. He groaned with joy. He would make everything up to him. He would never let him suffer again. He would be mother and father. He jumped up and ran to his room, to kiss him, to tell him that he loved him, that he would never fail him again.

The light was on in Norton's room but the bed was empty. He turned and dashed up the attic stairs and at the top reeled back like a man on the edge of a pit. The tripod had fallen and the telescope lay on the floor. A few feet over it, the child hung in the jungle of shadows, just below the beam from which he had launched his flight into space.

BY THE WATERS

BY CHARLES ROSE

IT WOULD take Stanley an hour to sober her up. He would stand beside her, hearing her sing as she swayed and splashed in the bathtub.

"Marie," he said, again and again.

When she began to weep, he knew that the worst was over. She sat with her knees drawn up in the water and her face in her hands. After he lifted her out of the tub and dried her off, he led her shuffling in her floppy houseslippers to their bedroom. She fell asleep almost immediately.

He emptied the ashtrays, heaped with her cigarettes, and turned off the T.V. set. After he straightened up, he looked in on the twins. They were awake, naturally. Morrie asked if Mother were sick again, and Joannie insisted that Daddy take Mother to the hospital.

"Nobody at the hospital can help her," Stanley said. He told them the story of Frank Fearnot and of how he'd chased the bank robbers on his bicycle. Then he kissed them on their chilly lips, and turning out the bedlamp he tiptoed out of the room.

Her drinking lasted through July, reminding Stanley, in its prolonged intensity, of the long hot spells they used to have on the lake, when in the shallows the lily pads spread shimmering and the brown weeds chafed the water. It turned cool, early in August. Quite suddenly, she had stopped drinking, except for a little beer with supper. She usually quit when there was someone else in her life, but since she stayed at home every night, as she had done when she was drinking, he knew that there were only the children and himself.

One day, early in August, the twins came out of the water with blue lips and prickly skin. They were huddled together in a thick, snowy bathtowel. He saw just the white of the towel, so white, even with the sun under, caping their heads and shoulders. As they came up the pier, Morrie grabbed the towel and began lashing at the pilings. Morrie hung back a little from Joannie, who would stop every few seconds for him to catch up. Then she would move on, with a very slight exaggeration in the motion of her hips, and Morrie would fall back again. Suddenly, the towel snapped, and Joannie yelled, and then they were fighting for it. Stanley ran to separate them.

"Morrie, say you're sorry!"

"I'm not sorry!" Morrie set his lips while Joannie writhed and twisted. "Let me at him," she yelped. "Let go, Daddy!"

"You sorry, son?" That was a last warning. He'd have to whip them before Marie heard. She'd tar the living daylights out of them.

"Daddy!"

Joannie shut up fast when Marie stomped out with the hairbrush. "I'll teach you two to mind!" Marie grabbed Joannie and laid it to her. Stanley wanted to tell Morrie to run for it, feeling the white arm stiffen. When Morrie's turn came, he didn't make a sound.

"That's enough," Stanley said. Marie stopped then, with the hairbrush raised. Then Joannie quit yelling, and for a minute there was just Marie's labored breath and the water slapping the pilings.

"You think it's enough!"

Her face was white as the sky. Presently, she began to breathe easier and the color came back into her face. She told the twins to run on; Joannie bolted immediately. Marie laid one hand on Morrie's hair.

"Now try to be a good boy. And mind your father."

"I apologize, Daddy," Morrie said quietly. Stanley squeezed the chilly hand set in his.

"Son, you should have more respect for your mother. She's not feeling well."

"Mother, why don't you feel well?"

Marie didn't answer right away, fixing her eyes on the wedge of a sail toward the other end of the lake. With the smothered laugh from Joannie she whirled, crying, "You want some more!" Joannie sat on the front steps, her chin in her hand, for just a moment longer. When she scampered off, Marie picked up the towel. "Don't you feel well now?"

She bent to kiss Morrie on the forehead. "I'm fine, honey. Now run along and play with your sister."

They stood awhile on the pier, watching the wind ruffle the waters. At last, Marie said, "I ought to tell you something, Stanley." She stood a moment longer, watching the lake, her feet spread wide, her thighs bulging, the wind snapping strands of her blond hair. Abruptly, she turned and went inside.

He sat down beside her in the windowseat, flanked by the potted ferns, the gray afternoon slitting the venetian blinds. He was surprised that she asked for a drink, even relieved, for it was worse to see her deny herself, day after day. She took half of it down in one swallow, wedging the glass between her knees.

"Why have you stuck with me, Stanley?" she asked, her face averted.

"I was needed. That's why you married me, because you knew I'd feel that way."

"You know that's not the reason."

"Maybe not. But you have needed me." He noticed the lines in her face, remembering its softness once, the soft full lips, nearly eight years ago, remembering that he'd said *you're mine darling*, and her sigh, *yes yours*. And now the seamed face and the brittle eyes. "What is it you want to tell me?"

He started to take her glass, rising from his seat, but she arrested his hand, with just the tips of her fingers. "I don't think it matters now. You'll find out."

She got up and walked to the bathroom, a little unsteadily, although she had just had one drink. He heard the sound of running water, while he sat before the T.V. set, without turning it on. He sat there for some time before he realized that he heard something else. By the time he reached her, she was trying to clean up the mess with a washrag.

"It's the first time I've been sick," she gasped. "I wanted to tell you before it happened."

"I want you to know who it is," Marie insisted. She lay on their bed with a washcloth across her forehead. Stanley held one of her hands, the fingers damp like the washcloth. The twins were playing fish on the living room carpet.

"I don't want to know, Marie. We can manage."

She sat up on one elbow. "We're the ones who are responsible, Stanley, not you. He should do something."

"He could sell his goddam convertible." Surprised at his own virulence, he let her hand flop on the counterpane.

"So you know who he is."

"Not his name. He was parked up the road once."

She removed the washrag and dropped it on the floor. "I haven't told him yet."

"Then let's forget about him."

"No, I won't forget him."

"All right. Now try to get some sleep."

She lay back on the pillow, staring at the ceiling. "I'll call him first."

"You don't have to." He told her that he didn't care, yet he wondered who had come that night, waiting in his convertible down the road. He had played his radio, even after she went to him, still playing it after they drove off in the convertible. The others he had never seen, but they did not count. Shadows soiling her need, they left her drained, left her to the bottle and the long nights at home. From the living room, he heard the twins, their voices raised in shrill imprecations over the card game.

"I'll call him. I have to." Marie sat up, glancing at the bedroom door. "I'd better put them to bed first."

"You're sure."

She caught his hand and shoved it against her belly, low, where the flesh was drum tight. "I have to do something." The rigid flesh, hers. Higher up it was loose, almost puffy. At last she released him.

"You'll put them to bed first."

She gave him a wan smile. "I said I would, Stanley. Then I'll call him."

Morrie went right to bed, but Joannie made some trouble. From the kitchen he heard Marie threaten Joannie with the hairbrush. He poured himself a shot, drinking it off fast and pouring another, which he carried with a glass of water to the front porch. Marie was at the telephone, asking for Missiniwa long distance. She hung up and came out on the porch. "He's out. I left word for him to call."

"You mean he drove all the way up here from Missiniwa. It's over sixty miles."

"He liked me a lot," Marie said. "I decided to end it."

"And then this happened."

"I guess I should have stuck with him."

He offered her a drink, but she refused, adding that she needed to get some sleep. Before she left, she said, "Stanley, what I do is up to you." Then he heard her houseslippers flopping on the carpet.

He sipped his drink, watching the lake. The wind was getting stronger, frothing the waves as they came into shore. The sky was egg white, with gray clouds banking the horizon, and across the lake, way up at the northern rim, the cottages were strung nestling into the trees, like pearls in velvet. Nearly eight years they had lived there, and many a gray Saturday he had sat here. The cottage —it was a house really—was his gift to her; how he'd sweated to pay for it. Now he could wait at the threshold, the wind jostling his hair.

After awhile he turned to gaze at the mulberry tree in the side yard. A robin darted in and out of the branches, reminding him of the time he'd discovered the truth about Marie. She was sitting right where he was sitting now, with a bottle on the floor and the newspaper spread out on her lap. Robins were swarming in the leaves of the mulberry tree, flicking in and out, rising in a sudden flurried wingbeat at the sound of a car on the road. He could hear the berries pattering on the roof and the steady rustle of leaves, like rain, and the sharp throaty cries. He had hurried home as soon as he'd heard the news, that Ed Kray had been killed by a sniper in Korea. When he saw the bottle, his first thoughts were for the child, for she was nearly eight months gone. It was terrible to see her that way, tilting the bottle into the glass propped against her belly, whisky slopping over the rim to stain her blouse. She raised her glass, in what seemed a ludicrous toast, and gazing off at the robins, she said, "Why couldn't it have been you?" So he knew then, though she did not tell him right away—the child would not be his. The twins, they were not his.

And now another, a third to care for. And not love this time, though she said he was fond of her, the man in the convertible whom he had seen one night, parked about thirty yards from the house, idling his motor, even playing his goddam radio, the music blaring raucously while he slapped one hand on the dashboard in time to the music. And she said he was fond of her. Playing his goddam radio, not thirty yards from the cottage.

She had loved Ed Kray, and in his own way Ed must have loved her. He should have known that, despite the smile, so swift, that ripped open the lips, a smile you turned from as from an obscenity. For he had seen them together, coming out of the movie or the drugstore, her head dropping a little to his shoulder, not quite touching, his arm around her, up close to her breasts, but not quite touching. Ed had never said a word, keeping it all to himself, probably for the first time in his life, not telling, not even in the pool hall. He could still see Ed Kray chalking the cue, bending with casual deliberation, the whipcord arm and shoulder muscles rippling the shirt, the splayed fingers. Ed Kray lining up the shot, with one piston thrust, and then the gentle contact and the ball caressed into the pocket. And then the smile as Ed racked up. It all seemed one motion now, compressed into that smile containing the brilliantined hair and the gridiron swagger and just about everything that made Ed Kray the son of a bitch that he was. But when Ed talked about Marie, he did not smile that way, and there was a reserve, a constraint that wrenched the face, that made him seem almost girlish whenever anyone mentioned her. But he had not seen, not runt Stanley, who would watch Marie dance with Ed at the Y.M.C.A. dance after the basketball game, watch her press her body to his. For even as he watched, nursing the dream of just touching her some day, while the jukebox purled its maudlin consummation, he knew that he had something that Ed could never have, what he kept at the edge of the crowd, clean in the sweat and clamp of flesh, the callow laughter.

What he had was the way she'd looked at him, the first time he'd seen her. She had known only that he was runt Stanley, who had never made any team, who couldn't even dance. That moment —yes, it was winter. She was a sophomore in high school, spilling out of class, swaying arms linked with her girl friends down the icy sidewalk. She passed Nicopoulos's candy store, her cries coming toward him. He stepped aside just before she slipped, her legs splitting, and he turned his face away, then back, drawn by her gaze. Her eyes widened as she pulled at her skirt, covert, surprised, even a little curious. With that look, prefiguring everything, he felt that he knew who he was, telling himself that he didn't want it to be true, before her voice was lost in the cold.

But it had come true, his silly dream. After Ed busted out of college, he sold insurance for awhile, and then he joined the Marines. They were already engaged when he saw Ed for the last time, home on leave after basic. He ran into Ed at George and Cecil's, where he used to stop after work for a draft, usually just one draft, which he would drink very slowly, watching the gray smoke in the back room. He seldom played pool now that he was engaged to Marie, but it was still pleasant to sit there, knowing that he would leave it all soon, that in an hour or so he would be with her, yet enjoying the delay, the protracted anticipation of delight. Every now and then he would go to the back room and play a game of snooker, but only one.

When Ed came in, he tried to stare at the baseball scores. He remembered the creak of Ed's shoes as he approached.

"One for me and one for the bridegroom."

Ed sat down beside him, smoothing out his overseas cap on the bar. The smile was slower now, frayed at the edges, and there was a tightness of the face, as though the flesh were stretched over bone, that he had not seen before, and deep circles under the eyes. He wondered just what he was supposed to say. "I'm enjoying myself while I can, Ed."

"Me too. Live it up, I say."

Ed finished his beer and ordered another round, while he told runt Stanley he was shipping out to Korea. He told Stanley that he wished to hell he hadn't joined the Marines, and congratulated him on being 4-F. Ed wouldn't let him go, and with each beer it seemed harder for Ed to keep his shoulders back. Suddenly, Ed looked like he was fifteen again, like his picture in the high-school yearbook, the first year he had played football, a green wide-eyed kid trying to look tough. Ed had tried to look tough then but it hadn't worked. "You know, Marie needs a guy like you." Ed's voice faltered, and again there came the sudden reserve that made you wonder if it had been Ed at all who had spoken. "For God's sake, look after her." The voice was husky, and the eyes flitted aimlessly. And then the smile twisted across the face as Ed threw back his shoulders. "Hell, you know what I mean. I'm not her kind of guy."

In that moment before Ed walked out of the bar, he caught the smell of sweat, shot with tobacco and stale beer. He shrank from the familiarity as Ed laid a moist hand on his shoulder. "Take care of her, buddy boy," Ed said coarsely. He kept the rude touch after Ed left, staring at the smoke from the poolroom. The rough clash of voices came with the virulence of endearments, a waste of passion sucked up in smoke. He told himself that he had seen her slowly meet his gaze, surrendering more than he felt she ever would again. But her image was lost in the curling smoke.

Lost, at that moment. Because the son of a bitch had been doing it even then, drunk, desperate, after a game of pool or late at night, in a blind clutch, calling it love, even weeping once. Marie had told him that, everything really. She told him on the same day, splashing whisky into the bottle, her sobs coming in short regular spasms.

"We didn't mean to, Stanley. Can you understand?"

The tree outside shook and the berries hit the roof like hailstones. The robins swirling, tumbling in a feverish chaos, their sharp cries deriding her loss. Yes, he could understand. He gently took the bottle from her, knowing that it was no more than a gesture, like comforting one bereaved. She was staring at the robins, swarming in a final fury, then suddenly drifting off in a cloud of wingbeats. The tree was very still now, denuded, spreading limply, without catching the breeze that wrinkled the lake. She wiped her eyes.

"It won't help, will it."

"No, Marie. He's gone."

"I'll go too, if you want me to."

"It wouldn't help."

"No, I suppose not. I thought you could help, Stanley." She spoke simply, with a clarity augmented by the stillness. "I thought you could make me forget him."

"I should have done something."

"It wasn't your fault. There was nothing you could have done."

"He came back, didn't he."

"It wouldn't have mattered. You see, I had him inside me. That's a joke, isn't it. A goddam dirty joke." She looked again where the robins had been, with a hint of surprise that they had gone.

"It's the truth."

"Yes," she said. "Now we both know that."

They hadn't forgotten it. Lying awake that night, he heard the twelve o'clock train from Chicago, the whistle dwindling from the far side of the lake, then squeezed up in his own heartbeat. He said *goddam* then, in that constriction of silence, not that anyone was to blame, not Marie, not even the poor bastard who used to be Ed Kray. But he said it, breathlessly, as though hugging his dearest possession. He said *goddam you oh goddam*, feeling life seep out of him, while the wind shook the curtains into gnarled grimaces. Just as he thought he couldn't stand it any more, he saw the kid in the football uniform, and he heard Ed's voice. *Look after her.* The plea, rotting now with Ed, in Ed, that too was true. In his own odd way, Ed had meant it for him. And there was Marie, sleeping quietly beside him, on her back. He saw the rise and fall of her belly under the sheet. With a detachment that he could already accept, he touched her lightly, feeling the kick of life against his fingertips. He knew, then, that it was possible to go on.

No one was responsible, but the son of a bitch played his radio, not thirty yards from her home. After Marie had the baby, there would be another bartender, another hot hand, and then the drinking before it all started again. He had only wanted to touch her.

The phone rang as he finished the last drop of whisky.

Joannie answered the phone before he could get to it. "A man wants to speak to you, Mother." He was sure he heard her say this before he saw what she had done. Her mouth was slashed with Marie's lipstick. Then he saw Morrie, his eyes foggy from sleep, peering out of the bedroom door. Grabbing the receiver, he held it until Marie got up.

"Morrie told me to," Joannie whined.

"I didn't," Morrie cried. "It was her idea." He shut the bedroom door when Marie came out.

"Can't you learn to behave!" Marie grabbed Joannie by the shoulders and shook her.

"He told me to."

"I don't care who told you to." He thought for a minute that Marie would slap Joannie, conscious of the sound beneath his hand. That was one thing he didn't want heard. He started to protest, but Marie stood with her hands light on the girl's shoulders, as though about to hug her. But Marie's eyes, narrowing furtively, were fixed on the receiver.

"It's a man," Joannie repeated, with a slight smile, garish, faintly malicious because of the lipstick. "For you, Mother."

"For me?" Her voice was almost inaudible, like a whisper in sleep. She slowly lowered her hands. "Oh yes, Garvin. I'd better talk to him." As she took the receiver, her fingers were chilly, vibrating like the sound. As though nearly forgetting something, she turned to Joannie, ordering her to wash up. "Then go to your room." He heard the bedroom door shut and Joannie complaining to Morrie. Marie reached to clasp his arm. As she spoke to Garvin, he felt the cold tensile strength of her fingers, and the weight behind them, it seemed her whole body.

The muted sounds from the bedroom stopped when Marie said she was going to have a baby. She said it slowly, breathing deeply. Only when she finished saying it did she release Stanley's arm.

"I have to talk to you tonight." Her breath came more surely, yet when he moved away she caught his arm again. "No, tonight. My husband will be here. No, you must come here."

And then wearily, "I'm glad you said that. All right, nine."

After she hung up, she seemed about to give out all over. He put his hand over hers, limp on his arm. When her eyes steadied and life came back into her hand, he saw that she knew he could not comfort her. "I need a drink," she said mechanically. "I'll get it."

"Maybe it'll help," he said, but she didn't answer, shuffling off to the kitchen. He went to the window, looking out at the lake. The wind had died down and the water spread in a listless opacity, flecked with a sluggish spittle of light. A few fishermen were out, and a speedboat churned up a pale foam, slightly rocking the fishing boats. Evening would come unobtrusively, and then night, thickening to merge with the torpid water. He was still looking out the window when she came out of the kitchen, coming up beside him. She had a glass in one hand and the bottle hugged to her breast.

"He'll be here at nine," she said. "I told him you'd be here."

"Yes, I heard."

"He said he wanted to have it out with you. It surprised me to hear him say that."

"You said he was fond of you."

"He is." She poured some more whisky, without drinking it.

"He's like Ed in some ways." Light stained the water, rising slick on the horizon. Evening, so neatly on them. She gulped the whisky. "But he's not a part of me."

"And the child."

"The child. It's not the same thing."

Light, flowing out of the sun, suddenly unmasked in a blank effulgence. No, the child wasn't the same. But all she had really. That and the whisky, which ran smoothly down her gullet. You wouldn't think she was afraid, not now.

"I'm going to wash my hair. Will you start dinner?"

He said that he would, and she went off still hugging the bottle. He knew that she would manage to stay sober for a few hours, which might be long enough. He slashed the blinds shut and drew the curtains, standing in the half-darkness. From the bedroom he heard muffled laughter, and he remembered how Joannie looked, the harlequin's face, and Morrie watching.

As he fixed supper, the light waxed in the kitchen, gleaming fitfully on the cabinets. It seemed that he was alone in the house, her house, in an evening that moved on tiptoe, gently solacing while his fingers went through their hapless ministrations. Morrie and Joannie must be asleep, or be feigning sleep, perhaps waiting themselves for what this evening would bring. For awhile he did hear water running in the bathroom, and then the whir of an electric hair dryer. She would look her best tonight, for the man whose name he knew now. He understood, and knew its futility. Could she cloak her heart, its raw dread?

He had dinner on and was setting the table when the light went, very quickly after such a long evening. It seemed to shrink to a hard point, the way a television screen does when you turn the set off, with dusk spreading out from the point. As easy as turning a switch, he thought, and easy too to call them, Marie and the children. Yet he paused a moment, starting for the cabinet for a drink before he remembered that Marie had the bottle. He thought he heard a car on the road. It couldn't be Garvin, not this early. He heard the car pass with relief, waiting a moment longer for the sound to thin. Then he placed another sound. The crickets had started up without him realizing.

Through supper he still found himself listening for the convertible. He could scarcely eat, nor could he respond to Marie, who seemed unnaturally exhilarated. She was in her housecoat, her face slightly flushed, her hair twisted in curlers, it seemed cruelly. And there was a cruel twist to her voice, lurking in the banter she made with the children. It showed when she chided Joannie for eating with her fingers. "You're worse than a monkey," she said, with that hard gaiety. She seized Joannie's hands, lightly slapping each palm. "Now keep them in your lap where they belong."

"But how can I eat?" Joannie stuck out her chin, clicking her teeth without parting her lips. "You tell me, Daddy."

He forced himself to look at her as she very primly put her hands in her lap. "Use your fork, like Morrie does." With a slight smile of embarrassment, Morrie laid down his fork.

"Oh Morrie's so nice. He does everything right."

"Morrie's a little gentleman," Marie said. "And you're a monkey."

"I'm a turkey," Joannie insisted, making sharp gobbling noises. Morrie stared at his plate.

After dinner, Marie told them to go outside and play. Joannie hung on the screen door, letting it sway with her weight. "Mother, who's coming to see you tonight?"

Marie stopped scraping off a plate, glancing quickly at Morrie, who was outside waiting, his back turned. "Your Uncle Garvin. He wants to meet your father."

"I thought I saw him once," Joannie continued, "in his car."

The knife rasped on the plate. "That's none of your business. Now run on and play."

He could hear Joannie protest that nobody ever told her anything. She moved even with Morrie, past him without touching. Morrie turned around and took one step to the door. The blue eyes, dilated, were like a reproach. "I saw him, Daddy. He had a new convertible."

"You'll see him again if you behave," Marie said. She put the plate on the kitchen table and then laid the knife beside it. Joannie approached her brother, timorously slipping her hand in his. "Will he bring us a present, Daddy?" She squeezed Morrie's hand.

"I don't want a present."

Peering out the bedroom door, only that afternoon. Now the shadows ringing his eyes gave the illusion of sleeplessness, and in the kitchen light the face took on a yellowish cast. So Morrie had also seen Garvin. It was hard to meet the blue eyes, hard to answer. He could only tell them to ask their mother.

"Yes, ask me!" Light glinted in the metallic curlers and the voice came harshly. "Ask me and I'll tell you it's none of your business what I do. Go on, ask me."

Morrie stepped back, his eyes fixed now on the curlers, tugging to free his hand. But Joannie drew it to her chest, squeezing it.

"I'm sorry, Mother."

"We're both sorry," Joannie said.

Marie bit her lip. "It's all right," she said weakly. "Will you run along now. I'm sure he'll bring you a present."

"Come on, Morrie."

He saw Morrie's eyes film, with the hurt. Marie, too, was about to weep. "Go on, son," he said. "Go with your sister."

Joannie turned and ran a few steps, releasing Morrie's hand. Then she stopped, hopping on one foot as she waited for Morrie. "Hurry up, Morrie." When Morrie reached her, he turned to look back. He waved, once, and then squared his shoulders, moving off into darkness.

"You see." Marie took a cigarette from the pack on the drainboard, without moving the pack, and tapping it roughly she put it to her lips. He hurried to scratch a match. When he brought the flame to her mouth, the fingers she laid on his hand were trembling. "You see what I'm like with them."

"It's not your fault."

"Yes it is." She turned to gaze out the kitchen window, drawing in on the cigarette. The smoke came out easily, puffing against the window, dissolving. "You'll do what's best for me, won't you."

"For them too. And the baby, his," he said.

"He's like the others. Like Ed, really. You know I used to think that Garvin was Ed sometimes. I'd say to myself, 'You're Ed, honey.' Then I could let myself go for awhile. But I'd finally realize what I was doing."

"It might be different."

"Yes, he might help. He's fond of me. Anyway, I've got to dress now. I'm going to look my best for him." Before she left, she touched his cheek, her fingers fluttering like moth wings. "You'll be happy when I go, Stanley." Then he was alone with the imprint of her touch, soon lost.

It would not be long now, fifteen minutes perhaps. She would go off again, as she had so many times. He had seen her once, with Garvin. The convertible had been parked down the road, and standing at the back door he had seen the man's shape and Marie, not actually running, walking with short quick steps. The door to the convertible swung open and Marie got in. She threw her head back, one hand ruffling Garvin's hair. She must have done it deliberately, for it happened close before the end, before she was back drinking. He could still hear the radio, in the moment before the convertible opened up, and through it, like a shriek, the thin cry of endearment, and then the sound of the car and dust settling on the road. Not thirty yards from the house, in the evening, so anybody could see, even the children. Yes, they too had seen, but he had forgiven her that, he had to. *You're Ed, honey.* She had tried so hard.

He heard her singing in the bedroom. Her voice smoothed into an old favorite of hers, a song she used to sing when they were courting, sliding through the pulsing crickets, then riding tipsily, with a gay buoyancy. It had meant so much on that spring night, the night he'd proposed. They were walking home from the movie, holding hands, imprisoned in the cool tingle of flesh. They didn't talk much, listening to their footsteps ring on the pavement. There was a wind in the trees, brushing their faces, stirring the leaves that spread above them, and then no leaves, the bowling sky, the full moon nimbused in a mellow beneficence. Imprisoned, then released as she began to sing, a tawdry song he'd heard a thousand times. She kept the light pressure on his fingers, and he moved with her, almost afraid to breathe. The moon and stars rolled quietly. He did not dare tell himself that he was happy, for the moon might stop, and her voice. But he had to finally. His fingers ached, with the bitter surge in his loins. He had to seize her, crushing her to him, forcing his lips on hers. *You're mine, darling.* Her lips were dry, and her shoulders taut with fear, but he could not stop. And then her lips were too warm, her body too yielding, as she sighed, "Yours." Now the song lurched repetitively, her voice swaying, tightening, breaking the keen edge of hysteria. Oh he must go to her now . . .

He heard the screen door shut. He turned, and Morrie stood quietly before him, dead still, one hand on the doorknob, until

Marie's voice stopped. Behind Morrie, outside the screen door, Joannie's thin form wavered in darkness. Morrie's hand slid off the doorknob as the glass smashed, and Joannie ran a few steps. Again, the tinkle of glass, this time the bottle. Morrie bent his head.

"Why do you let her, Daddy?"

He could not raise those bright blue eyes. And behind, a blur in the darkness, Joannie. They had seen her hand in Garvin's hair. Eight years, and the boy would not look at him.

"Why does he let you?" Morrie raised his eyes before he spoke, with the first light footstep. In the glare of the kitchen, Marie's face was a chalky white, the full lips slightly parted, the eyes filmed in a dreamy impassivity. She was watching Morrie. "It's no use, honey. We can't stay here any longer."

"But he's my father."

"Yes, but we don't need him any more. We don't need you, Stanley. You've done enough for us."

"I won't go!" How Morrie stripped his withered need. The boy craved only the husk, already crumbling. *Why couldn't it have been you,* Marie had said, years ago. Did you hear her song again, gliding with a leisurely mockery? With a tremor of horror, he knew he heard it. It came from the pale form grazing the edge of darkness, spreading like an effluvium, hanging like oil on water even after Joannie stopped. Ed's sweat, the stink of their bodies, it was all in the song, slopping over the rim. Sweat, tears, semen clotting the bone, a cloven runnel choked in excrement. Yet all so dry. So goddam dry.

"Is that what you want?" Now Marie was looking at him. A breeze caught her hair, shaking it in brazen tendrils while her fingers rose and fell on her belly. Then they opened, rising, spreading as though she were holding the throbbing life within her, warm in her hands. *For God's sake look after her.* The son of a bitch had left him that, just a word, rattling in an empty vessel.

"I can't," he cried. "You'll be better off, both of you. Can't you see?" Even as the words broke from his lips he moved to clasp the child he'd lost. But the razored eyes cut deeper.

"He's coming." Morrie's voice came with a distant clarity, like ice dropping from a limb. Yes, that must be Garvin at last, his true father. Now the boy cocked his head, listening, dead still, bending every faculty to the thin filament of sound, waiting in that prescient trance that held them all, his eyes looped in shadow. They glowed like coals as the car drew closer. The wraith of Ed's smile racked the face, wrenched the voice in the hopeless shriek. "I'll stop him, Mother! I won't let you go!"

"Stanley!" Marie cried.

But his hands closed on nothingness.

Morrie was now in darkness. Like a ghost he met his sister, merged, then slipped away, swallowed. Marie stumbled after him, lurching into Joannie, mother and daughter struggling in a senseless pantomime. Then like a sudden flame the headlights caught Morrie running. They glimmered in his yellow hair, floating like a leaf through the squeal of brakes, through Marie's scream.

When he opened his eyes, he still saw the headlights, making a cold prismatic pool in front of the car. He had not stopped moving, yet it seemed to take him a long time to reach them. Garvin stood beside the convertible, holding Joannie, who had buried her face in his arms. Garvin's face was blurred in a thin penumbra, neither light nor shadow, like Joannie's hair. He fastened his eyes on Garvin, guiding his steps by the small, almost womanish hands. Now he was close enough to see them tremble. Garvin's chest brushed Joannie's hair.

"I didn't see him, honey," Garvin said, over and over. He seemed to be talking to Joannie. How small Garvin was, shaking with Joannie's sobs. He felt himself concentrating with a dull detachment on the little man, a bystander now, gone really, like Ed. The poor son of a bitch was gone.

"My little boy."

He heard her first. Then he made himself look at what was in the headlights. She was bent over the body, in a cloud of mosquitoes that swarmed in the light, streamed from her face, her hair. He heard them whine in his ears, and heard the insane drizzle of the crickets, the burr of a locust, flooding the thick night. Now the headlights licked at his feet, yellow like a jaundice, like the lake that evening, which lay open to the stars now, unruffled, fulfilled. He had built her a house by the water and there he had heard her sing. Now there was no blood on the yellow hair, where her hand lay protectively, heedless of the mosquitoes lighting on the white face, on the waxen lips. White hand on his hair.

"I asked to go once. Remember, honey! Oh do you remember?"

The robins, that other loss. Her voice scored the crater of light, the bright orifice spread at his feet. Now he too must enter, pierce the center, dry, gaping like the little boy's mouth. His feet sank softly in the simmering dust, as Marie, shedding light, slowly lifted the body. He had only to reach out and touch her now, for Garvin was still at the edge, holding the little girl whose sobs merged with the night. *Marie.* Did her eyes open again, to the raw instant, opening? They were so small in such an immensity, but he must look at them if he were ever to atone for the life he'd smothered. *All* and Morrie's face, so still. Light reamed the hollow of his hand, the blood beating *all*. Now her blood, through flesh hollowed in his hand, beating, a cry, a joy, a searing pain. Her eyes, scorched by the terrible stars.

"He's ours now, Stanley."

"Our own. Our dead son."

Then his tears came, stronger than life, deeper than love, like the lip of a wave, breaking.

JUJITSU

BY ELEANOR ROSS TAYLOR

IT WAS the best of June days. They drove up early, he in white shirt and tie, his speech in his brief case, she in jeans and scarf, for she planned to stop off at the cabin and spend the day in idle solitude.

"I wish you were going with me."

Fifi, asleep on her lap, stirred irritably.

The cabin appeared in a hole in the valley, a well of morning sun. (Turn up refrig. Fill kettles. Open windows. Check garden.)

The lettuce was up, the squash sprouted. Up on the hill shone glossy laurel clumps with clusters of pale buds. Fifi snorted among the bushes by the creek. Rabbits, groundhogs, skunks. Perhaps a deer. Or a bear.

He kissed her goodbye; then, his hand on the car door, turned back.

"Sure you won't just change and come with me?"

"Not on your life!"

Now it was all hers. Jubilate. Spirit, dominate.

She made for the rock. But when she left the meadow and began the hill, she turned, her eyes narrowed in a sort of ecstasy, to look at the unfortified cabin on its marshy nest, to take in the sheltering rhododendron along the creek. Up on the rock she would watch for the green heron. And perhaps it would be her day to see a deer.

A cardinal, thinner, wilder, and less brilliant than those that came to her feeder at home, fidgeted in the alders. She willed him hers for his wildness, his fugitive nature.

Halfway up the hill she stopped to behold a Michaux's lily, a

327

gemini. It was exceedingly rich, black-peppered blood-orange. The petals were voluptuously extended, overlapping behind the blossom face. She did not touch it, but knelt and partook paganly, her face to its divided face, its pendant bosom. Only in a nunnery, such purity.

On the rock, big as a porch, she stood a moment scanning the world, valley from north to south, mountain facing her, loving its stature, its bones, its pine whiskers. Then she sat down on the moss-scabbed rock and put the binoculars to her eyes.

She found the heron. He was stationed stiffly, below the bushes at the edge of the pond. He was hunting. And he was on the lookout for other hunters. She was too late to see him circling and hear his cries over the meadow. But when they were there overnight Richard was always clipping things, driving places, calling her, as if they were still on Globe Street, so that even then the heron, the hedgehog, all the wild things abandoned them early. Small wonder Richard marvelled at her observations.

Why had she never seen a deer? They were known to be in the valley. Mr. Otterbein had seen a doe with two fawns in front of their cabin last week. She settled, knees up, searching with the field glasses. What size would it be? Small, she reminded herself. Smaller than a horse, larger than a dog. Of course, this was the day she really should go to see Mrs. Otterbein . . . downright un-Christian not to make yourself known to any of your neighbors.

Something unbending in the list of the rhododendrons before the wind attracted her. A groundhog was standing up, his nose to the wind, his Oriental eye on the meadow. He dropped fluidly to the ground and disappeared. She found his hole and his bare doorstep among the rhododendron roots. She was alone, human-being-among-the-creatures. My spiritual refill, she said wryly to herself.

She returned to the groundhog during the morning and closing her eyes in the sunlight imagined his underground quarters, the dirt corridors where there was still enough light for casting small shadows. Once she thought she made out dirt on the end of his nose. He listened long before any move, smelling out mysteries. Had he had a brush with violence? The final expectation of a wild thing was ambush, murder, fatal error—to be by natural weakness annihilated. And of every civilized thing? It lived by inner strength—if one had the solitude, the time to draw on it.

She tramped her paths. She greeted with passionate eyes the ferns, the brambles, the ground lichens. She crouched in the under-pines dens covered with needles. She left the garden for last, to ease the transition. Perhaps, sometime—in the future—one could stay up here. *From this dark world I would draw thee apart.*

Solitude is strength. Spirit, dominate. There was no joy in giv-ing birth; it was painful and degrading. Though she loved her children, there was no joy in nursing one's babies; it was an animal dependence. Defecating, urinating, menstruating, eating—why had these ignominies been inflicted on human beings? She hated her heartbeat when she sat still, her pulse when she lay quietly at night; when she was aware of her breathing it annoyed her, some-times almost maddened her. Coupling was the only acceptable hu-man office, the one inseparable from spirit. And of the senses, hear-ing was a doubtful blessing, touch useful. Smell was so of the mind and so untranscribable as to be almost spiritual—the hair-splitting spectrum of smell—is it a lilac or a narcissus? The pepper of one rose and the musk of another. Peach, cantaloupe, or apple? . . . But seeing was life, was light, was truly understanding.

The sun had warmed the rock like the top of a cake-baking oven. There suddenly came, like the pain in her side, the thought of Richard, of where he was. Richard was on the platform. Alone, he was alone. Strange, she had always thought of his audience as being part of him. But there he was, in need of support. It was not one of the old days or nights when she had sat waiting for the car that would bring him from the party. The same party, the same friends, the same struggle between them. . . . But she had been strong enough to bear it, to bear it all alone.

She squatted, pulling up carefully with two fingers the tiny weed plants among the lettuce seedlings.

The wind creaked a locust branch. She looked up. For a mo-ment in a vision there were, around her, playground swings, chains creaking, and slides, her grandchildren laughing the already artifi-cial laughter of the social group. Yet her neck held inclined, wait-ing for their soft, sweatered arms.

Fifi came wet from the cold creek and ran wildly around the grass and naughtily through the garden. She ran with Fifi around the cabin.

When she had raked the spot where the tomatoes would go and put the rake back into the shed, it was five.

She began expecting Richard. The grosbeaks were making a last food round-up. The light was going. She locked the windows, covered the tables, turned down the refrigerator.

At five-thirty she went to the window. Bridge and road were empty. A car tore by on the highway. It was an isolated spot. Sometimes when they came there were hunters' footprints, horses' hoofmarks, by the pond.

She settled in the rattan chaise by the window and watched the bridge. The sun was set. The green heron flapped across high over the meadow. Her intent ears caught that dull ringing of absolute silence like the grinding of the universe. Was it really only the blood pulsing in the ears? How *like it,* to be just that. Nothing still, on the bridge, nothing coming down their own little road. Everything was graying out.

But beyond the bridge there was something, or somebody, under the apple tree. She leaned forward and searched into the dusk. A large animal was surveying the cabin.

She took the binoculars to the window. A dog, a German Shepherd lightly colored like the twilight, sat on the threshold of the bridge watching the cabin intently. He was bigger than a dog; he looked big as a man. Why should he be watching from so far? He knew she was here. Did he come with some trespasser when the cabin was empty? She did not like the look of him. She called Fifi, who had been ranging near the foot of the big rock, and latched the screen door. Perhaps it had been a mistake not to have a telephone. What would she do if something had kept Richard overnight? Not spend the night here alone.

She had forgotten to put foil over the kettle spouts.

When she looked back the dog had stationed himself closer. Through the glasses his eyes, in spite of the dusk, were bright. The contradiction of his immobility and his advance was eerie. Fifi put her forepaws on the window sill and looked toward him, but did not bark or growl. In comparison to him Fifi was hardly a dog.

It was suddenly night. An inexplicable uneasiness filled her. After all, it was only a dog. He would go away. She checked the supplies. There were some cans of soup. After nine the place on the highway closed. Could that unnatural dog ambush Richard? No, again some chill in her extremities insisted—it was after her.

Had it got cold with dark? Silly. She went again to the window. Was he gone? Where was he?

She was too late. He had moved around the cabin to the garden. Now he could be seen without the binoculars, just presenting himself in the edge of the porch light. It was uncanny how he moved behind her back. As if an image in the eye shifted with the eye's glance from place to place. His posture was unchanged, his eager eyes had the same glitter, but now his tongue panted out. Did dogs really crash through windows? This dog had the look of a killer. Fifi was growling now, and staring as if hypnotized. She called her into the cabin—the porch was an unsubstantial structure—and thought to lock the door. But as she did so, Fifi, still growling to herself, lunged with a ghastly force through the rotting screen door and streaked into the dark toward the enemy.

She slammed the door, trembling, and snapped off the light. Slipping close along the wall to the window, she saw the dog still sitting in the yard gazing soulfully toward her. There was no sign of Fifi, no sound. All was silence. All was gray and dreamlike. She pushed the table against the door, slid the chairs next to it.

The rifle. Then she stopped, her foot on the loft ladder, for her impulse had been to point it not at that decoy, but at herself for the *coup de grâce.*

She felt tears. What was this beast? What did it stand for? She only knew Richard and Fifi were gone. Except for this strange adversary she was alone.

She expected it through the back door, and stood with her hand on the front doorknob, ready to play a last desperate game for salvation. When the moment came, and that horror stormed her barricade, at that moment she threw herself out the front door, slamming it to behind her. But she slipped, on the great stone step, on Fifi's blood, and her head cracked, with a sound like target practice, on the rock.

She lay dazed, arms flung outward. The rock's paralyzing magnetism seeped through her slowly. She did not try to move. She was sure she could never move again.

The headlights wheeled their twin rays over the valley as the car turned at the bridge. The doe, munching an alder sprout, looked up and, taking no chances, stepped down the bank and splashed delicately downstream; and the heron, his eyes blinded, spread his wings angrily in his secret nest.

THE DEATH OF A KINSMAN
A Play

BY PETER TAYLOR

Cast of Characters

ROBERT WADE
MARGIE, his wife
AUNT LIDA WADE
MISS BLUEMEYER, their housekeeper
MYRA WILLIS, family servant
LENNIE, upstairs maid, Myra's niece
PARIS, houseboy, Myra's nephew
The Wade children
 JAMES
 NANCY
 ALFRED
 CHARLES WILLIAM
 LIDA SUE

SCENE I

It is long before daybreak, but in the Wade house lights have been put on in the halls and in the pantry and in the upstairs sitting room and in nearly every room in the whole house and on the side porch as well. Nobody has been left sleeping. The curtain rises on the scene in the upstairs hall. It is a rectangular room running the entire width of the stage. A large stairwell is in the center and back of the stage. On the wall beyond the balustrade which guards the descending stairs is an enormous mirror. Doors to the bedrooms are at either end of the hall. A door at the extreme right in the back wall opens into the service hall where there is presumably another

332

*stairway. The door at the head of the stairs (left, back) leads to the
bedroom of Mr. and Mrs. Wade. The general effect is that all of the
wall space, except that beyond the stairwell, is taken up by the
doorways. The elaborate doorfacings and the oak balustrade and
the pilasters at the four corners of the stairwell indicate that the
house is one of those mansions put up in Midwestern cities during
the early part of the present century. The floor is not carpeted, but
it is partly covered by two large rugs. The one on the left is a handsome, though rather worn and faded, oriental rug. On the right is
an obviously new imitation of the same thing, with extremely
bright colors and a general effect of silkiness. The end of the hall to
the left (and front) is furnished as an upstairs sitting room. There
are several upholstered chairs, a footstool, a small table and lamp.
The only other furnishings are a table and chair at the right (front)
corner of the balustrade. The table is an old-fashioned card table,
the typical Southern antique, and the chair a ladder-back imitation
antique with a cushion on the seat. On the table are an electric
clock, a modern French-style telephone, and an ultra-modern desk
lamp which, except for the dimly lit table lamp, is the only light
burning as the curtain rises.*

*Simultaneously two negro maids enter from doors at opposite
ends of the hall. One is a tall, thin, stooped woman with a good deal
of grey in her hair. The other is a somewhat more than plump
young woman. Both are black. They advance hurriedly toward the
middle of the room until simultaneously children's voices call from
the rooms they have just quitted.* "Myra, where are my good
socks? What did you do with . . ." "Lennie, where's the brush I
put . . ." *The two women halt, exchange first exasperated grimaces and then indulgent smiles, and return to the children. Aunt
Lida Wade appears from one of the doors at the left. Her thin
white hair is in rollers and she is attired in a cinnamon-colored
kimono. As she enters she is addressing her great-niece Nancy over
her shoulder:* "No, I don't know which dress you mean, Nancy, but
it must be one of those in the back hall closet." *Nancy's eleven-
year-old whine can be heard from within:* "You know the one,
Aunt Lida; the one with the long sash." *Aunt Lida answers in an
impatient but conciliating voice:* "I'll see. I'll see." *She closes the
door behind her and moves across the stage taking the small, practiced lady-like steps of a long-legged woman who would naturally
move with great strides. She goes into the service hall, closing the*

*door behind her. Now quick footsteps are heard on the dark stair-
way, and presently a negro houseboy, wearing an unbuttoned white
jacket, dashes up into the hall. He places a pair of highly polished
brown shoes by the door at the head of the stairs and turns at once
to descend the stairs. Seeing the dark stairwell before him, he inadvertently reaches out and flicks the light switch on the wall beside him. The light does not come on, and grinning at himself he
says, "Ah, shoot!" Meanwhile, the older negro woman has entered
from a door at the right; she addresses him contemptuously: "Ain't
fix 'at even yit, have you, Paris?" His grin broadens into a big, silly
smile, showing a mouth full of gleaming white teeth: "I cain't fix
it, Aunt Myra." He puts his hand on the rail and disappears down
the stairway. Now Aunt Lida enters from the service hall with
three of Nancy's dresses over her arm. She passes Myra, who is moving slowly toward the head of the stairs.*

AUNT LIDA: What an hour of the day to be gotten up, eh, Myra?

MYRA: Ain't it the truth, Miss Lida? An' him not on this place
more'n three times in ten year.

AUNT LIDA: But he was the only relative any of us have in Detroit, Myra.

MYRA: Not much kin. An' gettin' all them chillun up.

AUNT LIDA: I don't see why the children should be gotten up,
but you know Mr. Robert.

MYRA: I know white folks.

AUNT LIDA: Listen here, don't you talk about white folks to me,
Myra Willis. If it were *your* Cousin Harry, you'd be off work for a
week. (*She has now opened the door to Nancy's room.*)

MYRA: (*At the head of the stairs, looking down into the darkness. Still addressing Aunt Lida.*) Nobody ain't fix 'at light yit.

AUNT LIDA: Mr. Robert said he would do it today.

MYRA: He say.

AUNT LIDA: I know, I know. (*Closing the door behind her*)

*Mr. Wade opens the door of his room to fetch his shoes. Myra
looks over her shoulder at him.*

MR. WADE: Morning, Myra.

MYRA: It's still night to me. An' this here light ain't fix yit.

MR. WADE: By George, it's not. You tell Paris to bring the ladder up, and we'll fix it right now.

MYRA: Now? This now? At five o'clock in the mornin'? (*He picks up his shoes and closes the door.*)

MYRA: Lord God.

Miss Bluemeyer, the housekeeper, enters from the service hall. She is a large woman dressed in navy-blue with tiny white ruffles at the collar. Her hair, cut like a man's, has obviously not been combed this morning, and she is still wearing her flat-heeled bedroom slippers. She is carrying a small tray with one cup of coffee and a silver sugar and cream set.

MISS BLUEMEYER: Are you in a great rush, Myra?

MYRA: Not me.

MISS BLUEMEYER: Then I would like to see you a minute, please. About something.

MYRA: Yassum.

Meanwhile, the housekeeper strides across the hall and knocks at the door at the head of the stairs.

MRS. WADE: (*from within*) Just a minute! Who is it?

MISS BLUEMEYER: It is I . . . Miss Bluemeyer.

Mrs. Wade opens the door. She is an extremely small woman of about forty. Her long brown hair falls about the shoulders of her negligee. She is pregnant.

MRS. WADE: Oh, I'm *so* much obliged to you, Miss Bluemeyer. You know that I'm not a bit of good till I've had my coffee. I'll just bet you had to make it yourself.

MISS BLUEMEYER: I did, Misses Wade. But that's all right; I made a cup for myself too.

MRS. WADE: Isn't it a hideous hour? (*Beginning to close the door*)

MISS BLUEMEYER: Yes, it is, but I am awfully sorry about your cousin.

MRS. WADE: Yes, it is sad of course. He was very old, you know, and we knew him very little, really.

MISS BLUEMEYER: I see.

Mrs. Wade closes the door, and Miss Bluemeyer turns to Myra. With a movement of her head she indicates that Myra should follow her. Then she crosses the stage and seats herself at the telephone table. Myra follows and stands before Miss Bluemeyer, with her hands folded and resting against her white apron.

MISS BLUEMEYER: (*smiling intimately and a little sadly*) Myra, tell me, did you ever know their Cousin Harry?—Mr. Wilson, that is.

MYRA: Yassum, oh, yassum. (*casually*) My sister Cora used to work for his own sister, Miss Jamie, in Nashville, way back yonder. Most of them Wilsons is dead though. He muss be the lass of 'em, I reckon.

MISS BLUEMEYER: That is not what I mean, Myra. I know that all of you knew one another back in Tennessee, but that is ten years or more—

MYRA: Yassum, we been in Deetroit ten year. Now, the two oldest chillun was born'd in Tennessee, but—

MISS BLUEMEYER: That is not what I mean, Myra. I mean—that is, I have been keeping house for Misses Wade nearly a year now and had never heard Cousin Harry's name—Mr. Wilson, that is to say—mentioned until his stroke a few weeks ago.

MYRA: No'm. He never come aroun' here much. He warn't congenial with 'em; that's all.

MISS BLUEMEYER: I . . . I did not mean to imply that there was more to it, Myra. I only mean that they are such wonderful people to feel so responsible for a person they hardly know.

MYRA: (*quickly*) Yes'm, but he *war* kin to 'em.

MISS BLUEMEYER: Yet he never came to see them.

MYRA: It warn't because he warn't invited. (*resentfully*) He didn't care nothin' bout kinfolks. Stuck off to hisself and worked down in the depot up here. He was jess—(*Breaks off suddenly, and begins again with an entirely different tone*) Well, anyhow, he 'uz kin to 'em, and the only one here kin to 'em. That's all.

MISS BLUEMEYER: I did not mean to be prying, you understand, Myra. It is only that it seems odd that they should make such to-do over a man they knew so slight.

MYRA: He didn't have no money, sho God.

MISS BLUEMEYER: That, Myra, is not what I meant.

MYRA: I don't know what you been meanin', Miss Bloomer, but he's daid an he war kin to 'em.

From the left the voice of Charles William, aged five-and-a-half, is heard calling, "Myra! Myra!" A door is thrown open and a tow-headed little boy rushes into the hall with his shoestrings flopping about.

CHARLES WILLIAM: Myra, Alfred won't tie my bows!

MYRA: *(who has turned around and advanced several steps in his direction)* I'll buss his back wide op'n.

CHARLES WILLIAM: You tie 'em, Myra.

MYRA: *(Already on her knees before him)* Come here, chile.

CHARLES WILLIAM: Is Cousin-Harry-Wilson dead, Myra?

MYRA: Sho.

CHARLES WILLIAM: Was he eighty-three years old?

MYRA: 'Course he was, C. W.

CHARLES WILLIAM: Still?

MYRA: He'll be eighty-three from hereout, C. W.

CHARLES WILLIAM: *(Obviously comforted, he places his hand on the head bent over before him.)* I love you, Myra.

Myra lifts her dark oval face and grins broadly at him. He whispers to her, "You haven't got your teeth in, Myra." She bends with laughter as Charles William runs back to his room. During their conversation Miss Bluemeyer examines her wristwatch and the electric clock very closely. She dials a number on the telephone and says after a moment, "Will you repeat that? Will you repeat that?" She dials the number again and then sets her watch and moves the hand of the clock a fraction of an inch. When Charles William is gone, she says:

MISS BLUEMEYER: Myra—

MYRA: *(Rising and moving toward the dark stairs)* I got go fetch Paris an the ladder for Mista Robert. This here light!

MISS BLUEMEYER: You *could* use the back stair, Myra.

MYRA: Not me. Not them straight-up-and-down steps. *(She goes down the steps)*

Miss Bluemeyer rises and strides toward one of the doors at right. Aunt Lida Wade opens the door from Nancy's room, left, and the two women face each other in silence a moment. "Oh," says Aunt Lida, "I thought you were my nephew, Mr. Wade." Miss Bluemeyer makes her exit, and Aunt Lida remains a moment to giggle girlishly. Then she withdraws into Nancy's room again and closes the door. Lennie enters from door at right and moves sluggishly across the hall to head of stairs. Aunt Lida opens her door again and says, "Oh, I thought you were my nephew, Mr. Robert." Lennie answers, "No'm, it's jess me." Aunt Lida closes her door again, but before Lennie has begun to descend the stairs Mr. Robert Wade, master of the house, opens the door to his room and steps into the hall. Mr. Wade is six feet, three inches in height. His hair and his small moustache are dark. The belt to his silk dressing robe is tied, but the robe is not brought together in front; and so his dark trousers and white shirt and his bow tie may be seen. He wears usually a pouty expression on his face and has little to say except when giving directions or explaining some matter to his family.

MR. WADE: Lennie, a full half hour ago I sent word for Paris to bring me the ladder.

Lennie makes no answer but fairly dives down the dark stairwell. Her feet on the steps make a frightful racket. Aunt Lida opens her door again.

AUNT LIDA: Well, now, did you ever? No wonder the women in the house have been insulted when I mistook their steps for yours. How do you do it?

MR. WADE: That was Myra's little niece descending the stair. *(He walks around to the front balustrade and leans out over the stairs to peer up at the fixture.)*

AUNT LIDA: Ah! the dungeon stair. This is the moment I've been waiting for. Rumor has got around that my nephew has roused his family at five A.M. to watch him change light bulbs over the stairway.

MR. WADE: True . . . true. *(Still looking up at the fixture.)* And, incidentally, my wife's cousin is dead.

AUNT LIDA: *(Matter-of-factly)* Poor Harry. You ought, in all conscience, to have made him come live with us years ago, Robert.

MR. WADE: He wouldn't live with his own sister, much less us. He had an allergy to the very idea of blood-relations. *(Turning to Aunt Lida)* You know, one of the few times I saw him he asked me how I could stand living under the same roof with you.

AUNT LIDA: I'm sure he did. And he told me that he left Tennessee to get away from his own flesh and blood, and that you and Margie and your younguns had to pursue him up here. *(They laugh merrily.)*

While they talk, the top of a ladder rises from the stairwell.

AUNT LIDA: But we ought to have gotten him to come here and live, somehow.

MR. WADE: He'd have been miserable here, Aunt Lida. And he'd have made us more than miserable. He wouldn't have fitted in.

AUNT LIDA: Pooh! That's why it would have been all right. (*She whispers.*) When I selected Miss Bluemeyer for Margie's housekeeper I was careful to choose someone who wouldn't fit in. If she were congenial with us, her presence here would be an intrusion. That's why my presence is an intrusion, don't you see?

MR. WADE: Tut-tut, Auntie. (*pronounced "ontee"*)

The head and shoulders of Paris have now appeared from the top landing where he is setting up the ladder. The ladder leans backward and forward, backward and forward, and Paris can be heard panting and grunting.

AUNT LIDA: Oh, but what I say about Miss Bluemeyer is really pretty true, Robert. She's always happy when we're sad, and sad when we're happy; and that's right convenient. This morning, for instance—. Well, notice for yourself.

MR. WADE: Aunt Lida, you're just awful! The poor woman.

AUNT LIDA: Why, I'm crazy about her. She's perfect. And have you seen her this morning? She's mourning your Cousin Harry, as none of us would think of doing—Poor old codger's got his blessed relief at last—and, Robert, (*rolling her eyes thoughtfully*) she never even saw him once, did she? Once even? No! . . . But if she were showing the kind of relief that we feel for him, it *would* be kind of bad, now. You see!

MR. WADE: Oh, what difference does it make that she's—(*breaking off*) What *in* the devil?

He whirls about. Paris, having steadied the ladder and having climbed uneasily to the top of it, has been sitting there tapping first his lip and then his forehead with his finger, trying hard to think of something, then with a stupid but still speculative expression on his face he has reached down and brought up a long broom with the handle of which he has now bent forward and poked (between the balusters) the back of Mr. Wade's knee. Mr. Wade's knee bends slightly. He whirls about, saying, "What in the devil." Paris jerks back the broom, gives a short, hysterical laugh, and splutters out:

PARIS: Mista Robert!

MR. WADE: What in the name of sin do you mean by that, boy!

PARIS: (*Solemnly*) Somehow, I couldn't call yo name, Mista Robert, why you reckon? couldn't think of it till you whull aroun an say, "Whut *in* de debil?" (*catching Mr. Wade's exact intonation*)

MR. WADE: (*Leaving Aunt Lida, who stands in open-mouthed wonder and amazement at Paris's behavior, and going round the balustrade to the head of the stair*.) Come down off that ladder! Did you bring the screwdriver and the bulb?

PARIS: I brung the screwdriber, Mista Robert.

MR. WADE: Well, go brung me a big bulb and a dust rag from the pantry.

Paris disappears from the ladder and down the stairs. Mr. Wade has now come down the stairs to the landing and climbed to the top of the ladder. The ladder shakes violently, and Aunt Lida cries out in a voice unlike her rather deep speaking voice:

AUNT LIDA: Robert, mind; do be careful, honey!

MR. WADE: Careful, hell! (*He clambers down the ladder.*) Paris! Paris, you come hold this ladder for me!

At the sound of Aunt Lida's voice doors from both right and left and from the back are opened. Now the children come one by one to the head of the stairs and watch their father who is climbing the ladder again. The two older children come first and watch their father in silence; they are Nancy, from left, and James, from right —aged eleven and twelve respectively. Quick on James's heels come Charles William, who is five-and-a-half, and behind him Alfred, aged nine, still wearing the "niggery" stocking cap he sleeps in. Then the fifth child, Lida Sue, the youngest of all, comes chattering. No one can understand what she says, for she has been slow learning to talk and now at four she stammers and lisps alternately. When the doors to the children's rooms opened, the door to their parents' room, at the head of the stairs, opened also; and Mrs. Wade, having glanced at her husband and smiled at Aunt Lida, has turned back into her room, leaving the door open. Her hair is now pinned up, and she wears a maternity dress. She can be seen moving about the room, making up the bed etc. During the conversation that follows, Lida Sue, instead of watching her father, as she has sat down to do, allows her attention to be distracted by the glimpse she has had of her mother, and lying back on the floor and rolling on her left side she watches her mother's movements in the room. Aunt Lida, still wearing her cinnamon-colored kimono, has moved away from the balustrade on which the children are now leaning. She stands, arms akimbo, in the center of the hall, with the back of her head of sparse, uncombed, grey hair to the audience.

AUNT LIDA: (*to Mrs. Wade in a loud voice*) Margie, he's taking the whole business apart, screw by screw.

MRS. WADE: *(from the bedroom)* It's the only way to do it, Aunt Lida.

AUNT LIDA: He has poor Paris holding the ladder, who ought to be down setting the table.

MRS. WADE: *(still from the bedroom)* There's plenty of time.

AUNT LIDA: I should say plenty of time. The greatest plenty. There was no earthly reason in his getting the whole house up at this hour.

MRS. WADE: No sense, I admit. *(only slight interest)*

AUNT LIDA: And did you ever in your life hear of a man's choosing such a time for such a job?

MRS. WADE: Never in my life. *(complete indifference)*

AUNT LIDA: I've been after him for weeks to do it, myself, and I know you have. There's really no earthly reason why Paris shouldn't learn to take down a chandelier. Otherwise, let's take him back to Tennessee and bring Mamie's brother up here. Or let Paris learn to drive, and bring Sellars in the house. Sellars's too old to drive, anyway. *(She pauses. All of this is being delivered in a shaky but resonant voice that Mrs. Wade and possibly even the servants in the kitchen can hear.)* Sellars can do anything if you show him once. But the main thing, though, is the time for such a job, the unheard-of hour of the morn . . .

MR. WADE: *(interrupting with a booming voice, his early morning hoarseness adding to the onomatopoeic effect)* Thunderation, Aunt Lida!

Aunt Lida seems only to have been waiting for this; immediately she dismisses from her mind the problem of the light fixture and all of this business in the hall. She raises her little right forefinger to her chin and frowns meditatively, trying to recollect for what she has originally come into the hall. Then of a sudden she turns and goes out the door leading to the service hall.

MR. WADE: Now, you see, children, this is not a very simple undertaking. Each of the glass sections must be removed separately, and for each there are three screws. Observe: one at the top and one on each side. Now, this protector must be broken down into its five component parts, and to do this you must understand the real structure of the fixture. Mind, now. *All* of the five pieces must be removed before the bulb—because of its large size—can be inserted. Once the bulb is in, each piece must be dusted and cleared of all dead bugs, lint, dust, trash etcetera before being replaced.

Mr. Wade works in silence for several moments. Then suddenly the light shines brightly above the stairwell. Mr. Wade, atop the ladder in a white shirt and a polka-dot bow tie with a sprinkling of dust on his black moustache, is a bright figure of enchantment for the five children who all fix a charmed gaze upon him, like five little green-eyed kittens. The spell is so absolute that they are momentarily blind and deaf to the sudden hilarious commotion on the part of Paris. This lantern-jawed houseboy, whose complexion is a dull copper color, who is supposed to be giving support to the unsteady ladder, has become so convulsed by laughter that he has thrown his whole weight against the ladder. One stern word of rebuke from Mr. Wade, however, makes Paris jump back from the quivering ladder.

MR. WADE: Get away from this ladder, you idiot!

Paris runs up the steps until he is in plain view of the audience. He continues to cavort about, twisting and bending his body, completely unable to restrain himself, giggling and pointing to the mirror on the wall beyond the stairs. All the while he is sputtering, "Look-a-there! Look-a-there!" and pointing to the mirror. Mr. Wade sits uneasily atop the ladder, staring at Paris in exasperation. As Paris runs up the steps, the children by the balustrade all turn their faces toward him but move not a muscle in their bodies.

PARIS: Do y' see what I see, Mista Robert? Look-a-there, Mista Robert.

Slowly the five children move their eyes from the houseboy to the mirror opposite them. Then Mr. Wade, steadying himself on the ladder, looks in the mirror too. What he sees there are the eight brown-stockinged legs of the four older children and the row of brown balusters interspersed with the legs.

PARIS: I thought them posts was movin'! They's jest alike—all of them legs and all them little stair posts, Mista Robert. In the mirror they all seem alike—posts and legs. Same size an same color. *(His words are interrupted now and again by his own giggling.)*

Mr. Wade's moustache twitches involuntarily, and his eyes narrow into little slits. Recognizing the ridiculous likeness of the legs to the balusters, he tosses back his head and laughs aloud. And the children one by one, even down to Lida Sue who has picked herself up from the floor, join in the laughter. Their mirth has just reached its peak when Miss Bluemeyer, the housekeeper, appears from left. Her short hair is now combed, and she has exchanged her slippers for a pair of oxfords. She advances toward the head of the stairs without showing any interest in the cause of their mirth. She passes the children with a tolerant smile, affecting to be absorbed in her own thoughts. When she reaches the head of the stairs, Lida Sue and Paris step to one side; and Lida Sue reaches for the negro man's hand which she holds to until the housekeeper has passed. Miss Bluemeyer descends the first three or four steps and then stops as she addresses Mr. Wade.

MISS BLUEMEYER: If you will pardon me, Mr. Wade, I would like to try and get by. I am going to run down and see how breakfast is going.

MR. WADE: Goodmorning, Miss. Isn't that a sight up there in the mirror?

MISS BLUEMEYER: *(glancing briefly in the general direction of the glass)* Oh, yes, isn't it? *(She takes another step as she speaks.)* I was going to say—*(She begins, but finding Mr. Wade's eyes fastened on her she hesitates.)* If you will pardon me, Mr. Wade, I must ask you to let me pass. *(fearlessly, courageously)*

MR. WADE: *(sternly)* I suggest that you use the back stairs since we haven't quite finished operations here, Miss Bluemeyer.

Miss Bluemeyer gazes defiantly at Mr. Wade for a moment, then at Paris and Lida Sue, then at the four children who are lined up along the balustrade and who, like sheep, have drawn closer together, their slight movement having been almost imperceptible to the audience.

MISS BLUEMEYER: *(utterly without expression, as though answering a question about the day of the week or the title of a book)* Goodmorning, kiddies. *(Presently she retreats to the head of the stairs, at which point she stops to address Mr. Wade again.)* I was going to say that when Paris has put away the ladder, it will be time to set the table for breakfast. That is, if you have an early breakfast in mind, Mr. Wade.

MR. WADE: I had an early breakfast in mind, Miss Bluemeyer, for there is a busy day ahead for us all.

MISS BLUEMEYER: *(in a sympathetic stage-whisper)* The funeral won't be until tomorrow, I presume, Mr. Wade?

MR. WADE: Well . . . there'll be a little service in the undertaker's chapel today. I'm taking the body back to Tennessee on the train tonight.

MISS BLUEMEYER: I see . . . I see. *(in a gentle voice, full of sentimentality*) He must have been a fine old man—Mr. Wilson. The few times I saw him he seemed very, very polite. I imagine to ladies especially, being Southern.

MR. WADE: I suppose so . . . Yes, I suppose he was. (*He turns his attention back to the light fixture for a moment, and then as though only now realizing what she has said he turns again to her with a little jerk of his head.*) Did I understand you to say you had seen him? But I didn't know you had ever seen our cousin, Miss Bluemeyer.

MISS BLUEMEYER: Oh, really? (*significantly, as though perceiving that there had been some conversation about her not having seen Mr. Wilson*)

MR. WADE: Yes, indeed . . . really. (*With parts of the fixture in his hands he goes down several rungs of the ladder, then jumping nimbly off onto the stairs and coming up into the hall he hands these pieces to Paris. Miss Bluemeyer has meanwhile moved past the children and as far as the telephone table in the direction of the door to the service hall.*) I don't recall Mr. Wilson's having been to see us since you came, Miss Bluemeyer.

MISS BLUEMEYER: That is quite right.

MR. WADE: (*his usually direct manner exaggerated somewhat*) Miss Bluemeyer, I think you are behaving and speaking in a mighty strange manner.

MISS BLUEMEYER: I am sorry if that is your opinion, Mr. Wade.

MR. WADE: Well, I think . . .

MISS BLUEMEYER: Remember, I am not one of the servants, Mr. Wade, not one of your servants.

When Mr. Wade came up into the hall, all of the children turned about and faced him and Miss Bluemeyer; and now he turns and gives them a "look" which sends them off quietly but quickly to their rooms, the older ones leading the younger. Paris, who has until this time been standing on the stairs with the parts of the light fixture in his hands, now moves down toward the ladder, ascends it, and begins hurriedly and skillfully to reassemble the fixture.

MR. WADE: I am aware that you are not one of the servants, and I am not speaking to you as such. In fact, I don't mean to provoke any unpleasantness this morning.

MISS BLUEMEYER: (*repentantly, mournfully*) And *I* am truly sorry to have been any bother this morning, Mr. Wade—this morning of all mornings. The truth is I used to see Mr. Wilson elsewhere. I never met him, you understand.

MR. WADE: I see. But you never mentioned having seen him to my wife or my aunt?

MISS BLUEMEYER: I didn't know the family would be interested that I had seen him. You understand, he lived a door from a lady with whom I am great friends.

MR. WADE: I see, I see.

MISS BLUEMEYER: He was a solitary figure, Mr. Wade, and this friend of mine had noticed him. She was an invalid, you understand, and when I was staying with her she would sometimes look out the window and say, "There goes that old Mr. Wilson. He seems to be an independent sort like us, Madge." That is all there was to it, Mr. Wade, and I used to notice him quite of-ten.

MR. WADE: But this happened when you were staying with your invalid friend?

MISS BLUEMEYER: Yes. You will think it is odd, I know, but that was before I even came here, Mr. Wade.

MR. WADE: I was thinking just that. And when was it you first made the connection between your Mr. Wilson and our Cousin Harry Wilson? That is, when did you discover that the old man you watched from your friend's window was my wife's cousin?

MISS BLUEMEYER: Only the shortest time ago, Mr. Wade, only a few weeks. Only when I happened to mention to this friend of mine that Misses Wade's only relative in Detroit had had a stroke. "What is his name, Madge?" she asked me. I told her his name and she said, "Why, Madge, that must be the same old Mr. Wilson I have pointed out to you. They tell me *he's* had a stroke," she said. It quite struck me at the time, Mr. Wade, that it was quite a coincidence, but I didn't want to bother the family at the time in their grief with idle, outside talk.

MR. WADE: Of course not. I'm sure you didn't. And it was very considerate of you.

A pause, during which Mr. Wade straightens his tie and casts his eyes about the room as though trying to decide how this conversation should be concluded.

MISS BLUEMEYER: If you would not think it was too odd, Mr.

Wade, would you mind telling me to what Funeral Home the remains will go?

MR. WADE: Why! *(taken aback)* Of course I wouldn't mind. To Lewis Brothers, I believe.

MISS BLUEMEYER: Lewis Brothers, you say? I don't believe I have heard of . . . ?

MR. WADE: No, it's a small, uh, shop, uh, concern on the other side of town. But the Lewises were from Tennessee, from my mother's county, and my aunt thought it would be—uh—nice.

MISS BLUEMEYER: I see . . . yes . . . Well I *do* thank you, Mr. Wade. *(Turning quickly to Paris, as though to change the subject)* Paris, you can set the table now!

She walks rapidly toward the door to the service hall. As she reaches for the door knob, the door opens and Aunt Lida enters with still another dress for Nancy, a black one. Paris has meanwhile reassembled the light fixture. Mr. Wade turns toward him and exclaims in genuine surprise at Paris's achievement, "Say!" Simultaneously Mrs. Wade enters from the door to her room.

MR. WADE: Boy, how did you know how to put that thing together?

PARIS: *(giving one glance at Mr. Wade, and then descending the ladder)* I had to do somepn to make myself scass. I thought you gwine eat 'at woman alive, way you come down off 'at ladder.

AUNT LIDA: What in the world do you make of it, Margie?

MRS. WADE: What do you think, Aunt Lida?

The two women have met in the center of the stage, in front of Mr. Wade, and by first addressing each other, instead of Mr. Wade whose conversation has roused their interest, they reveal their mutual sympathy and understanding and their slight regard for any interpretation which Mr. Wade might put upon his own conversation.

MR. WADE: *(having completely forgotten the episode with Miss Bluemeyer)* Margie! Aunt Lida! Look what Paris has learned! *(Paris sits beaming atop the ladder.)*

AUNT LIDA: *(paying no attention to him)* Did you hear every word of what she said?

MRS. WADE: I think so.

AUNT LIDA: I could hear every word. She said she had watched him from her friend's window even before she came here. All through his sickness she has known he was the man she and her cripple friend watched. She *is* a weird one, now, I'll tell you.

MRS. WADE: It's a curious picture, isn't it—those two lonely women watching that lonely old man. Why hasn't she spoken of it, do you suppose?

MR. WADE: Margie! Aunt Lida! This is a great day. This is important. This is a turning point in Paris's life, in the life of us all. He has learned to put that fixture together. Now he can have a try at the chandelier downstairs. (*When the women continue to take no notice of him, Paris begins to descend the ladder.*)

AUNT LIDA: It's from sheer perversity that she hasn't mentioned it, poor creature. She seems to delight in the dreariness of her own life and in finding other dreary "solitary figures." And I suppose we mustn't begrudge her her greatest pleasure.

Paris has now disappeared down the ladder, and as the ladder is seen being slowly lowered from view, Mr. Wade begins to show interest in what the women are saying.

MR. WADE: Now, Auntie, a while ago it was her sheer perversity that made Miss Blue so suitable for our household. You know, I think you are downright vicious about that "poor creature."

AUNT LIDA: Why, I'm not at all, Robert Wade!

MR. WADE: Indeed, you are. You seem to have developed a special voice, a special expression, a special vocabulary for talking about her.

MRS. WADE: That's nonsense, Robert. How could you accuse Aunt Lida of being vicious about *any*body, *ever?*

AUNT LIDA: There, you see.

MRS. WADE: A fine way your house would be in if it weren't for Aunt Lida. And your children, and your wife, and yourself!

MR. WADE: (*waving his hands before his face*) I didn't mean to start such a furor. I wasn't serious. That is, it's not a very serious crime of Aunt Lida's. That Bluemeyer is a strange duck. Anybody can see that.

AUNT LIDA: Now who's being cruel? I am interested in all people, Robert, and am not without sympathy for . . .

MR. WADE: But this seems a very special—. You have a wonderful interest in the ways and doings of all your friends and especially in your family, in us particularly (*indicating this household, by a gesture*). A kindly, gentle, womanly interest. You have a real knowl-

edge of people, too. You know us all better than we know each
other. You are a wonderful, wonderful woman, Aunt Lida, and we
couldn't live without you. But (*holding up one finger*) I still maintain that regarding Miss Blue—

AUNT LIDA: Her name is not . . .

MRS. WADE: Robert! What nonsense!

AUNT LIDA: And at such an hour. (*unruffled*)

*When interrupted, Mr. Wade turned and began walking
toward the door to his room. Now he hesitates at the doorway.*

MR. WADE: Has my blue serge come back from the cleaners,
Aunt Lida?

AUNT LIDA: It'll be back today, Robert.

*Mr. Wade goes into his room and closes the door. Mrs. Wade
moves to the front of the stage and sits down in one of the upholstered chairs, at left.*

MRS. WADE: Where are the children, Aunt Lida?

AUNT LIDA: (*calling, in a voice almost as deep as Mr. Wade's*)
Chill-drun!

*Doors on both sides of the stage open. The children peer out at
their Aunt Lida.*

AUNT LIDA: Come say goodmorning to your Mama-dear.

*The children run across the stage to Mrs. Wade, all hugging
and kissing her at once, saying, "Goodmorning, Mama-dear. Goodmorning, Mama-dear. How pretty you are, Mama." Mrs. Wade
kisses each of them, pushing the older ones slightly aside in order
to lean over and kiss little Lida Sue who says, "P-p-puhty muh-
muh." Aunt Lida watches approvingly. Presently she says:*

AUNT LIDA: Not one of you has noticed how charmingly your
Mama-dear has done up her beautiful hair this morning.

MRS. WADE: Aunt Lida, I declare! (*smiling and shaking her
head*)

*All of the children go behind her chair and admire her coiffure,
Nancy lifting Lida Sue up to where she can see.*

JAMES: It's all plaited and fixed.

NANCY: It's fixed in a bun. It's charming, Mama-dear.

ALBERT: How long is it now, Mama-dear?

MRS. WADE: Too long, too long. I'm going to cut it again before . . .

CHILDREN: No, no, no.

AUNT LIDA: (*coming forward*) We won't let her cut that beautiful hair, will we, children? . . . Nancy, let me fix your sash. It's all twisted.

MRS. WADE: It's impractical. Especially now. It will be too much trouble.

AUNT LIDA: Nonsense. We'll take turns arranging it for you. We'll never let her cut this beautiful hair, will we children?

CHILDREN: Never, never.

MRS. WADE: I'll do as I like about my hair, thank you, all. You'll some day all be sorry for spoiling me so. I'll be the spoiledest of spoiled women. I'll cut off all my hair and wear a ring in my nose, just to show you I can if I want to.

The children are delighted and they scream with laughter. "No, no, we won't let you, we won't let you."

MRS. WADE: I will. And I'll wear tow-sacks for dresses and old tennis shoes with the toes cut out. I'll wear a stocking cap like Albert's.

The children laugh again and chant, "No, never. No, never. No, never."

AUNT LIDA: Turn around, Charles William. I do believe you've managed to get your bottom rompers on backwards again.

CHARLES WILLIAM: I like 'em.

AUNT LIDA: Stand still, child. (*She has got down on one knee and begun unbuttoning his little pants. Without more words about it, she makes him step out of his pants; she turns them around and puts them on him properly. Meanwhile, Charles William continues to gaze at his mother.*) (*Addressing the children as she buttons-up Charles William*) We're going to keep Mama-dear the ornament of this household, aren't we? She ought to let us get her a personal maid, instead of a housekeeper.

MRS. WADE: One day you'll all be sorry. And I can hear you mumbling behind my back about *she.*

AUNT LIDA: Take off that stocking cap, Albert. You'll be bald before you're in long pants. (*Albert hesitates, turns his face away and gazes at the wall, pouting.*) Take it off, Albert, I said. (*He snatches off the cap, revealing a flat pompadour with every hair in place, and continues to stare at the wall, right.*) Look at him pouting, children. Stick a pin in his cheeks and they'd pop like a balloon. (*The children laugh; even Albert gives up pouting and laughs with them.*) Margie, every one of your children has a different way of pouting while being reprimanded. Only a slightly different way, however, for they are all gazers. Albert here gazes at a blank wall. James likes to gaze up at the ceiling. (*She mimics each as she describes his form of gazing. The children and Mrs. Wade laugh appreciatively after each piece of mimicry.*) Nancy is a window gazer. Charles William is a hand gazer, or a plate gazer, if we're at the table.

JAMES: What about Lida Sue, Aunt Lida?

AUNT LIDA: (*Still on one knee after buttoning Charles William's pants, she turns to Lida Sue, who is nearby.*) Why, she's the fearless type who stares a hole right through you and makes you feel that you couldn't possibly be right. (*She places her hands on Lida Sue's shoulders and stares, with a ridiculous frown. Lida Sue and the other children laugh hysterically. But Mrs. Wade has become aware of the presence of Miss Bluemeyer, who has entered several moments before from the service hall with Mrs. Wade's breakfast on a tray. Mrs. Wade watches the housekeeper, whose eyes are fixed on Aunt Lida. During that moment Mr. Wade, now wearing his suit coat, enters from the bedroom.*)

MR. WADE: (*Observing all that is taking place*) Is there breakfast for the rest of us downstairs, Miss Bluemeyer?

MISS BLUEMEYER: Yes, there is, Mr. Wade.

MR. WADE: Then let's break up this dog and pony show, what say? Breakfast, children! James! Nancy!

The children go frolicking to the head of the stairs and disappear down the steps. Aunt Lida has got to her feet and turned about so quickly that she catches Miss Bluemeyer's gaze still upon her.

AUNT LIDA: Is my petticoat showing, Miss Bluemeyer?

MISS BLUEMEYER: No, Miss Wade, not that I can see.

AUNT LIDA: Then, what is it, please? You were staring so, I thought something must be wrong. (*She pretends to examine her dress.*)

MISS BLUEMEYER: I beg your pardon.

MR. WADE: (*coming forward*) (*Cordially*) Ah, that's a mighty fine-looking breakfast a certain person's going to get this morning. (*Taking the tray from Miss Bluemeyer*) Ah, look-a-here. I believe they've got you on double rations, Margie.

MRS. WADE: (*Clearing the coffee table that Aunt Lida has pushed before her*) Well, I should think so.

Miss Bluemeyer, continuing to scrutinize the group until the very last, has finally retreated down the front stairs. Aunt Lida goes and looks over the balustrade into the stairwell. Mr. and Mrs. Wade observe her action and exchange glances.

MR. WADE: Now, Aunt Lida! What is it? What's the matter? If that woman bothers you so, why don't you give her her walking papers?

MRS. WADE: Don't talk so, Robert. Don't make a mountain out of a molehill.

AUNT LIDA: No, dear. He's right. This is more than a molehill. When I looked over the bannister just now I could see Miss Bluemeyer. She was running her hand through her hair, like this, and clenching her other fist with all her might. (*She comes to the front of the stage and speaks, as to herself, while Mr. and Mrs. Wade look on in wide-eyed amazement.*) That poor, embittered creature! My God, my God, when I looked down that stairwell I felt that I had been given a quick glimpse of a soul suffering the tortures of Hell. (*Turning to Mrs. Wade*) And it's our happiness that is her Hell, mind you, Margie. She can't abide the sight of our family happiness. Particularly not this morning when one of her sort—a man who reveled in his own bitterness and despised all those who tried to make his life a less lonesome, a less dreary business—lies dead in an undertaker's parlor. She cannot endure the presence of our happiness. Particularly not mine. (*Now angrily*) Can you tell me how the good Lord can endure the existence of such a mean and jealous being in His world? She watched me there on my knees fondling those children, and it filled her with nothing but resentment and hatred. (*Quietly again*) No, you are right, Robert. She shall have her proverbial walking-papers the moment you and the corpse of our Cousin Harry are safely on the night train to Tennessee.

MR. WADE: Aunt Lida, what a tirade! What a fit of temper! And at such an hour of the morning! Who ever heard of making such an important decision before breakfast?

Aunt Lida stares blankly at Mr. Wade for a moment; then she turns her face slowly from him to the audience. She is not smiling and she makes no answer. She doesn't seem to have heard what he said.

CURTAIN

SCENE II

The curtain rises on a second scene in the upstairs hall. It is the evening of the same day. One table-lamp is lit, front and left, and as the curtain rises Miss Bluemeyer switches on the desk lamp, seats herself, and begins dialing a number on the telephone. She is alone in the hall. The Wade family is still at dinner. During the late afternoon a funeral service has been held in the undertaker's chapel.

MISS BLUEMEYER: (*Speaking into the telephone*) Merton? It's Bluemeyer speaking. Quite well, thank you. And you? Oh, that's too bad. (*Pause*) Well, let me tell you . . . (*Pause*) Ah, that's too bad, Merton. (*Pause*) I want to tell you . . . (*Pause*) Well, have you taken something? (*Pause*) Merton, I want to tell you . . . (*Impatiently*) Of course I am interested in how you feel, but you said yourself for me to call you when they got back. Yes, they have been back a couple of hours, Merton. . . . No. . . . Why, I mean exactly this: When I talked to you a few hours ago, when they had just left for the funeral home—all but Misses Wade. She didn't go; she took her nap.—I said to you then, you remember, they were sure to guess whose flowers they were. Yes, I know you thought so too, Merton, and that is not what I am calling to tell you. We both knew they would, and I have already heard all about it, but not the last of it, I am afraid. This is what I mean: I dreaded, as you said you dreaded for me, that they would come home all sentimentalized and would gush over me with their thanks. The thing I was afraid of, Merton, was that they would think I was playing up to them. . . . Don't rush me, Merton. I will tell you the whole story right now if there is time. They are all at dinner now, you see, and if I am interrupted I will call you back from the kitchen phone when the Negroes have gone to bed. . . . I *am* going to get on with it, Merton. Don't be rude to your best friend. On the card I sent with the flowers, you remember, I had the young man write, "From Two Friends." Well, when *she* came back with the rest of the family, from the funeral, she had our card tucked in her little grey glove. I was downstairs in the side-hall, you understand, when they came in, and she just stopped beside me for a minute as though she were thinking of something. Then she slips the card out, like she was a magician—she had that air, Merton, that I should be surprised where she got it—and says in a deep, business-like voice, "Many thanks, Miss Bluemeyer, and thank the other friend for the family of the bereaved." Bereaved, indeed! They spent breakfast poking their sly fun at the child Nancy for wanting to wear a black dress. . . . No, that is all there was to it, Merton. No, not a question about who the other friend was. No, not another word, not from any of them. . . . No, I didn't want their thanks any more than you. What I mean is they have hardly spoke another word to me since, except about the usual things. Dinner was just awful, and I left just now without dessert. I couldn't have eat (*pronounced eet*) it, and the children carrying on so as if nobody had ever passed away, much less a poor lonesome old man. But the grown-ups are all hopping mad, I can tell you. *Mad,* you understand, because we had the presumption to send flowers to somebody who was their relation. Wouldn't you think *she* would understand, though, Merton, how it is. . . . Of course, she does, and she is ashamed. If *he* had been one of those who care to fawn over their relations, as *she* has! anybody who has so little pride and independence, indeed! Of course, I know you know, but . . . (*Hearing someone on the stairs*) Well, that will be all. Thank you. Goodbye, Merton. (*sotto voce*) Of course, I am not angry. Somebody's . . . Yes. Goodbye, Merton.

Mr. and Mrs. Wade are ascending the stairs, arm in arm. Miss Bluemeyer moves toward her room, at right. Lennie enters from door to service hall, right and back.

MISS BLUEMEYER: (*Just before entering her room*) Lennie, you need not turn down my bed tonight. I have some patterns spread out.

LENNIE: Yehsm.

Miss Bluemeyer closes the door behind her. Lennie enters the boys' room through the other door, right. Mr. and Mrs. Wade come forward and take seats in the sitting-room end of the hall, extreme left. They have been talking quietly as they came up the stairs and crossed the hall. Now their words become audible.

MR. WADE: The children couldn't have behaved better. I think even Lida Sue would have behaved all right if I had taken her.

MRS. WADE: I still feel a little as though I should have been there. Mama always felt so sorry for Cousin Harry. She used to say he was offish and surly even as a child. He never *was* happy.

MR. WADE: God! Eighty-three years of it! . . . Well, did you wire Cousin Lula what time I arrive with the body?

MRS. WADE: Oh, I wired her this morning. They'll want to have a little service in Nashville, I'm sure.

MR. WADE: Oh, I'm *sure* they will. And I suppose I'll have to attend that too?

MRS. WADE: Darling, I hope you will. It'll mean so much to them.

MR. WADE: I know. I know. And it won't be nearly so bad without Aunt Lida there.

MRS. WADE: Did she really behave badly?

MR. WADE: Well, I don't suppose the undertakers noticed, and there was nobody else to notice it. But as soon as they brought in that big wreath—it was a tremendous thing (*He holds his hands out to indicate the size.*)—she took herself up to where they set it by the coffin and looked at the card.

MRS. WADE: And just what did the card say?

MR. WADE: "From Two Friends."

MRS. WADE: (*smiling*) Isn't that incredible?

MR. WADE: And a strange expression came over Aunt Lida's face that didn't leave it until after we were home. She sat through the whole service as stiff as a broom and didn't sing a word of either hymn.

MRS. WADE: She was obviously making her plans. I doubt if Miss Bluemeyer will still be on the place as late as noon tomorrow.

MR. WADE: Do you think she'll let her stay the night?

MRS. WADE: Aunt Lida ought to restrain herself. The woman is merely peculiar. I wish you would talk to Aunt Lida about it before you go, Robert.

MR. WADE: *You* will have to talk to her, Margie. She has never been known to take a man's advice on anything but money matters.

MRS. WADE: Aunt Lida's a mighty clever woman.

MR. WADE: Be serious, dear. There's more in this than meets the eye.

MRS. WADE: Speak for your own eye, Robert.

MR. WADE: Then, what is it? I know I am a mere unimaginative man, but . . .

MRS. WADE: (*casually, as she settles herself in her chair*) You make us out awfully ugly, honey—Aunt Lida and me.

MR. WADE: And how do you two make me out?

MRS. WADE: I really think you are coming to believe literally in our womanly contempt for mankind. I think you're good for lots more than breadwinning, my love. Our contempt is only skin-deep. It's only a tiresome old joke that makes life easier for two women under the same roof.

MR. WADE: I wish it made it easier for three. . . . Tell me, then, what is it you see in this business that I don't see? What is it about Miss Bluemeyer's queerness that disturbs Aunt Lida so? Are we only detecting the first signs of old age in her?

MRS. WADE: It has nothing to do with old age. It is simply that someone has entered the field who won't play the game according to Aunt Lida's rules.

MR. WADE: What sort of nonsense is that? You and Aunt Lida are forever . . .

MRS. WADE: Robert Wade, stop linking me with your Aunt as though there were no difference between us.

MR. WADE: Then her age . . .

MRS. WADE: I'm not speaking of the difference in our ages. Don't you really know that your wife and your maiden aunt are two quite different people? (*Hotly*) If you haven't perceived *that* in thirteen years, how can you hope to comprehend the niceties of a problem between your maiden aunt and an old-maid housekeeper?

MR. WADE: What in the devil are you getting so worked up about?

MRS. WADE: Worked up! I say!

MR. WADE: Have you and Aunt Lida been quarreling, too?

MRS. WADE: Have we . . . ? (*Quietly*) God in Heaven, give me strength. For the ten years we have been in Detroit, Robert Wade, your Aunt Lida and I haven't had a cross word; and now you ask me calmly, have we been quarreling!

MR. WADE: And why is that such an outlandish question?

MRS. WADE: Don't you really know why it is? And don't you really know why Aunt Lida and I have such smooth sailing? It's because we have arranged our lives as we have. It's because Aunt Lida and I have played our roles so perfectly, as we've always seen them played in Tennessee: She, the maiden aunt, responsible and capable! I, the beautiful young wife, the bearer of children, the reigning queen! (*She laughs, and Mr. Wade jumps to his feet, obviously alarmed.*) Why, suh, sometimes ah can almos' heah the darkies a-croonin in the quawtuhs! (*Her laughter is now definitely hysterical.*)

MR. WADE: Margie, I won't have you flying off like this!

MRS. WADE: (*Coming to her feet*) I may fly off further than you think. (*Then she bursts into tears and throws her arms about his neck, weeping on his shirt front.*) Robert, forgive me. You know I adore Aunt Lida. (*But she continues to weep.*)

MR. WADE: (*Putting his arms around her*) There, darling. Of course you do.

As he eases her into her chair again, Miss Bluemeyer throws open her door and hurries across the stage.

MISS BLUEMEYER: Oh, the dear thing! She has been such a brave lady up until now. It has been a very sad day for her, and I feel . . .

MR. WADE: (*seated on Mrs. Wade's chair-arm with his arms still around her*) (*To Miss Bluemeyer*) Hold on, Ma'am. You're mistaken.

MISS BLUEMEYER: Indeed, I have been very much mistaken. Grief has strange ways, Mr. Wade. Let me get her a cup of coffee.

She turns and strides toward the door to the service hall. Suddenly she faces Lennie, who has been observing events from the door to the boys' room.

MISS BLUEMEYER: Lennie, bring Misses Wade a cup of coffee.

LENNIE: Yehsm, but she's jess havin a nachal spell.

MISS BLUEMEYER: A natural spell?

LENNIE: (*impatiently*) She's six months gone, Miss Bloomer. (*She goes to fetch the coffee.*)

MISS BLUEMEYER: She's . . . ? Oh, of course.

The housekeeper glances quickly in the direction of Mr. and Mrs. Wade, and her glance is met by Mr. Wade's glare. She turns and makes a hurried exit into her own room. Aunt Lida's voice is heard on the stairs, and the three children come romping up the steps ahead of her.

MRS. WADE: (*completely recovered*) How silly of me.

MR. WADE: That Bluemeyer woman *is* morbid, Margie.

MRS. WADE: You mustn't worry yourself about her, Robert. What time does your train leave?

AUNT LIDA: (*Crossing from head of stairs to sitting room*) Robert, I told Paris to bring up your Gladstone. Isn't that what he should take, Margie?

MRS. WADE: I think so, Aunt Lida.

AUNT LIDA: (*Standing, hands clasped loosely before her*) You feel like packing for him, don't you, Margie?

MRS. WADE: There, you see, Robert!

AUNT LIDA: See what, Margie?

MR. WADE: Yes, what?

MRS. WADE: *He* knows very well what.

Charles William has now climbed on his mother's knees. Alfred is tugging at his father's hand. Lida Sue is walking round and round Aunt Lida.

AUNT LIDA: You children run and play.

ALFRED: Can we play in your room, Aunt Lida?

AUNT LIDA: (*Severely*) Yes, but don't touch one thing on my dresser. (*They scamper away to Aunt Lida's room, left.*)

MRS. WADE: I've made a little scene since we came upstairs, Aunt Lida. I've had a good cry and everything.

AUNT LIDA: Are you feeling right tired, honey?

MRS. WADE: I guess I am. I must be awfully tired, for I was protesting Robert's linking our names so eternally.

MR. WADE: Jealous of you, Aunt Lida!

AUNT LIDA: Pshaw! It *is* tiresome of you, Robert.

MRS. WADE: And what I was just now pointing out to him was an example of how well we know our roles and how clearly defined are our spheres of authority. (*Turning to Mr. Wade*) Aunt Lida saw to it that your bag should be brought up, but she would leave the packing of it to me.

AUNT LIDA: (*In good nature*) Now, if I am to be embarrassed by your referring to your private conversations about me, be good enough to explain what set you off on the subject.

There is a moment's silence.

MR. WADE: We were trying to fathom the reasons for your sudden strong feelings against the housekeeper.

There is another moment of silence. Aunt Lida puts her hand self-consciously to her string of pearls. Lennie enters from service hall with coffee.

AUNT LIDA: Oh, I see.

MRS. WADE: (*Uncertain of what she is going to say*) Robert . . .

AUNT LIDA: Put the tray on the table here, Lennie. Are you right sure you want to drink coffee at this hour of the night, Margie?

MRS. WADE: Come to think of it, I guess I won't.

AUNT LIDA: Leave it there, Lennie, and I'll drink it.

LENNIE: Yehsm. (*She goes into the girls' room, left.*)

AUNT LIDA: What time is your train, Robert?

MR. WADE: I've got just about an hour. (*Looking at watch*)

AUNT LIDA: Then you'd better set about packing. Margie's plainly not up to it.

MR. WADE: (*Rising from chair*) You're dead right.

MRS. WADE: Do you mind?

MR. WADE: Not a bit, honey. (*He goes into his bedroom.*)

Aunt Lida sits down in the chair that Mr. Wade was occupying a few minutes before. With her foot she draws a footstool in front of her and rests her feet on it. She rests her head on the chairback and with her elbows raised she interlocks her fingers and places her hands over her eyes.

AUNT LIDA: Margie, I'm right tired, myself.

MRS. WADE: Poor dear, I know you are. It's been an awful strain on you, Aunt Lida.

AUNT LIDA: What has, Margie?

MRS. WADE: Oh, all of Cousin Harry's illness, with me in this condition, and the funeral today especially.

AUNT LIDA: Margie, I hope you don't ever think I underestimate you.

MRS. WADE: How so?

AUNT LIDA: I mean your powers of perception and understanding.

MRS. WADE: I'm a simple, artless little mother-woman from upper Middle-Tennessee.

AUNT LIDA: And I, I am a pore relation, a maiden aunt from the Cumberland Plateau. (*They laugh, and Aunt Lida removes her hands from before her eyes.*)

AUNT LIDA: That's how your Cousin Harry saw us to the very end, you know.

MRS. WADE: That's how we *are* to the very end, isn't it, Aunt Lida?

AUNT LIDA: I don't know, Margie. It's sometimes hard, isn't it?

MRS. WADE: Aunt Lida, it's great fun mostly. And what else is there better, with the given circumstances? When I was a girl I used to think . . .

AUNT LIDA: Yes, and so did I, even I, even then. But what chance has a person? It's like throwing away money, the horrid stuff. Yet it's the coin of the realm, and you'd best use what you have of it.

MRS. WADE: But I also thought . . .

AUNT LIDA: Ah, and so did I. But that part was harder for me, not being the pretty little thing.

MRS. WADE: Now, Aunt Lida, I was always told at home that you were a mighty attractive young girl.

AUNT LIDA: Well, as your husband's great-aunt Rhody Baird from East Tennessee used to say of herself, (*In the voice of a crone*) "Like any other, I had my little lovyer. Hee-he—he—hee." And let me tell you I made them step and fetch for me; but I used to hate myself. Sometimes I hate myself now and think that your Cousin Harry was right about it all. People like him, and like her (*Pointing with her thumb in the direction of Miss Bluemeyer's room*), make it hard. They point an accusing finger.

MRS. WADE: I know what you mean.

AUNT LIDA: Yes, I thought you did. And that's how we began this conversation.

Mr. Wade appears at the door of his room.

MR. WADE: Aunt Lida, does Paris think I'm not leaving till midnight?

AUNT LIDA: (*Rising from chair*) I told that boy . . .

MR. WADE: (*Seeing Lennie as she comes out of the girls' room*) Never mind, Aunt Lida. Lennie, you tell Paris to get up here with my Gladstone!

LENNIE: (*Stepping into the hall*) Yehsuh, he's on the back stair, wipin' it. You wouldn't-a tetched it the way it wuz.

AUNT LIDA: (*To Mrs. Wade*) Lennie *always* has to add her nickel's worth.

LENNIE: Aw, Miss Lida, I got beds to tunn back.

AUNT LIDA: Girl, that sounded to me just this side of uppity. I'll have to speak to *your* Aunt Myra.

LENNIE: Wull, there's uppitier niggers than I be in this house.

MR. WADE: (*Coming forward*) By George, this isn't getting me my Gladstone.

At this moment Paris enters from the service hall, and Lennie turns toward Aunt Lida's room. Simultaneously Myra appears on the stairway with a stack of clean, highly starched rompers and dresses for the smaller children piled high in her arms. She is mouthing over her shoulder at James and Nancy who are behind her: "Wull, make hase! Come ohn by me if y'aim to come, and mine these-here close." *Nancy and James brush past her and gallop up the few remaining steps before her. Each carries a large walking cane with a crook handle. Meanwhile, Mr. Wade addresses Paris the length of the hall.* "Paris, is that the bag Miss Lida told you to bring me?" *Paris replies,* "Yessuh, it the Glodstone." *And Aunt Lida is saying to Lennie whom she has called back from her room,* "You can leave my bed; the children are playing in there. And if you're going to change Miss Margie's sheets tonight, get Nancy to help you. I want her to learn to look after things."

MR. WADE: (*Still to Paris, who has stopped in his tracks at the far end of the hall*) It's a Glodstone, I'll grant you. It's the one Miss Margie's papa took to the Tennessee Centennial in 1896.

AUNT LIDA: (*Turning toward Paris*) What's this about the Gladstone?

MR. WADE: (*To Aunt Lida*) Do you think I'm going to travel with that old carpet bag? Did you tell Paris . . . ?

AUNT LIDA: I *did* not!

MRS. WADE: (*Whose attention has been attracted by the noise of the children, James and Nancy, behind her—looking over her shoulder to Myra*) Myra, the clothes look lovely. Come let me see them.

MYRA: Yassum. 'At James come mighty nigh spillin' 'um "lovely close."

JAMES: I did not, Myra. It was Nancy.

AUNT LIDA: Don't contradict Myra, James.

LENNIE: Come ohn, Nancy.

AUNT LIDA: Paris, you march right back down there and get the new Gladstone.

MRS. WADE: (*Holding up one of Lida Sue's dresses*) They're positively lovely, Myra. Look, Aunt Lida! Of course, these ruffles here ought to be pressed over this way.

NANCY: Aunt Lida, I know how to turn back an old bed! Don't make me do it tonight, Aunt Lida. James and I want to roll back the big rug yonder and play slide-on-the-rag-rug.

MR. WADE: You *are not* going to play that game while I'm in this house. Do as your Aunt Lida says; and James, put that walking cane down and come help me pack.

PARIS: I don't know which-a-one you mean, Miss Lida.

AUNT LIDA: *(Stepping nearer to Mrs. Wade and examining the dress she holds up)* Of course, it should be over that way. I told you so, explicitly, Myra; and you knew how I wanted it. *(Suddenly laughing)* Myra Willis, admit it! You just liked it better this way.

MYRA: *(Bending forward and laughing)* Aw, Miss Lida, ain't you a sight.

PARIS: I don't know which-a-one you mean, Miss Lida.

NANCY: Aunt Lida, don't make me . . .

MR. WADE: For God's sake, tell him the right one, Auntie.

LENNIE: She ain't comin', Miss Lida.

MRS. WADE: Aunt Lida . . .

AUNT LIDA: *(Raising her voice)* Now, see here, all of you . . .

At this moment Aunt Lida realizes that Miss Bluemeyer is standing in the open doorway to her room, right. Since Mr. Wade came from his room saying, "Does Paris think I'm not leaving till midnight?" she has been standing there, watching.

MISS BLUEMEYER: Mr. Wade.

MR. WADE: *(Furiously)* Yes—Ma'am!

MISS BLUEMEYER: I will see that you get the right luggage. *(Taking a step in the direction of door to service hall)* Come with me, Paris.

AUNT LIDA: That won't be necessary, Miss Bluemeyer. Paris knows the suitcase we mean now.

PARIS: *(Quickly)* Yessum, I suhtnly do.

He hurries through the service hall doorway, closing the door after him. At the same moment Lennie takes Nancy's hand and pulls her into her parents' room. "Come ohn, Nancy!" As they are closing the door, James rushes after them, pushing his way through the half-closed door and then closing it after him. Miss Bluemeyer begins walking slowly across the hall toward Aunt Lida who watches her intently.

MRS. WADE: *(Pushing the child's dress at Myra and nodding her head significantly toward the girls' room)* Here, Myra. *(Half whispering)* Robert, you will miss that train if you don't hurry.

MR. WADE: By George, yes! *(Looking at his watch)*

Paris now runs up the stairs with a yellow-brown Gladstone bag. Myra goes into the girls' room.

PARIS: Here, Mista Robert. (*He sets the bag down at the head of the stairs.*)

MR. WADE: (*Striding in the direction of Paris*) Tell Sellars to bring the car round.

PARIS: Sellars waitin' in the potecoshay.

Paris glances at Miss Bluemeyer, who has now reached the center of the hall, and runs down the stairs. Mr. Wade goes into his room and closes the door. Miss Bluemeyer suddenly turns about-face and hastens to her room, leaving the door ajar.

MRS. WADE: (*In alarm*) Aunt Lida!

AUNT LIDA: (*Reassuringly, in her deepest voice*) She's only going to fetch her hat and coat. She's quitting. She's not going to stay the night.

MISS BLUEMEYER: (*Enters with a light coat thrown over her left arm, a handbag in her left hand, and a soft felt hat in her right hand. With the latter she gesticulates rather wildly as she speaks in a loud, masculine voice.*) No, not another hour in the house with such as you. (*Striding the length of the hall to face Aunt Lida*) My conscience would burn me out before morning.

AUNT LIDA: (*Sternly, calmly*) Just leave us your address, Miss Bluemeyer. We'll send your things tomorrow.

MISS BLUEMEYER: Send 'em or not, Miss Wade, as you like. Do I care if I never see them again? Not one thing that will remind me . . .

MRS. WADE: (*Rising from chair*) Good night, Miss Bluemeyer! (*Miss Bluemeyer turns submissively and goes to the head of the stairs.*)

AUNT LIDA: Wait a moment.

MRS. WADE: No, Aunt Lida!

AUNT LIDA: Miss Bluemeyer, can't you calm yourself sufficiently to tell me what you have to say in a civilized manner? You and I will never see each other again, and you might be glad some day that you told me. (*Miss Bluemeyer laughs ironically.*)

MRS. WADE: Good *night*, Miss Bluemeyer.

MISS BLUEMEYER: No, Misses Wade, I will stay a bit. (*She returns to the group of chairs.*) I want to talk to you about your husband's aunt.

MRS. WADE: (*Turning her back and taking several steps in the direction of her room*) I have no interest in what you may say. Good night.

MISS BLUEMEYER: Ah, shame, Misses Wade. You who are so kind to your husband's aunt ought to be kind to other lonesome beings in this world. (*Mrs. Wade stops and turns halfway round.*) Doesn't it seem maybe that's what is wrong with all the family falderal your sort go in for?

AUNT LIDA: It was not to hear your criticism of my niece that I called you back, Miss Bluemeyer.

MISS BLUEMEYER: It was not to criticize her I am staying. . . . (*Mr. Wade enters with his Gladstone. He pulls the door to behind him and stands listening.*) Misses Wade, I have a thing or two to say. . . .

MRS. WADE: If those things concern my aunt. . .

AUNT LIDA: Miss Bluemeyer, I asked you to stop a moment because I thought you had something to say about our late cousin, Mr. Wilson.

MISS BLUEMEYER: (*Suddenly, with emotion*) Mr. Wilson! Mr. Wilson! Your *cousin*, Mr. Wilson! (*Then speaking in a hoarse monotone, obviously making a conscious effort at self-restraint*) Can you not hear yourselves? Aunt! niece! nephew! father! son! daughter! cousin! *Cousin!* I can see the poor old fellow now tramping past Merton's window to the lunch room or going up to the corner with a little package of laundry under his arm.

AUNT LIDA: Are you accusing us of unkindness to Cousin Harry?

MISS BLUEMEYER: Not to Cousin Harry, but to Mr. Wilson.

MR. WADE: I thought it had been definitely established that Cousin Harry *was*. . .

AUNT LIDA: Your distinction isn't quite clear, Miss Bluemeyer.

MISS BLUEMEYER: Oh, it is clear enough!

AUNT LIDA: (*Calmly*) If only you could calm yourself. I do think you may have a point to make.

MRS. WADE: Aunt Lida, this whole interview is uncalled-for. . . . Even if you have no respect for our family, Miss Bluemeyer, remember that one near to us has died this day. We simply do not understand each other. Please say no more and go.

MISS BLUEMEYER: Do we not understand each other, Misses

Wade? I understand a good deal of how this family business works. It makes a woman safe and sure being related this way and that way to everybody around her. And it keeps you from having to bother about anybody else, since they are not "kin folks." I understand how it works, for I was one of nine, and I saw the women in my family making the most of it too. And I might have done the same, but I was a queer sort who couldn't make herself do it.

AUNT LIDA: Is that all, Miss Bluemeyer?

MISS BLUEMEYER: Not quite all. For a solid year I have watched you here giving directions and making this house your own. And I have seen it right along that you are really the same as I in lots of your feelings, Miss Wade, that you were really lost and alone in the world, but you would not have it so, you just wouldn't. All along I have seen you were really a brainy woman and yet to see you here saying the things you say and play-acting all the time! And then when the old man Wilson was dying, you, like the rest of 'em, talked of nothing but that he was kin, kin, kin. You have mocked and joked all this day and gave him a funeral only because he was a kinsman.

MR. WADE: Miss Bluemeyer.

MISS BLUEMEYER: I am going now, Mr. Wade. (*She goes to the head of the stairs where he is standing by the door.*) Goodbye, Mr. Wade.

MR. WADE: Goodbye, Ma'am. And believe me, to us all our Cousin Harry was just a poor, lonely old man that we would have befriended if he had let us.

MISS BLUEMEYER: I know your feelings are good, Mr. Wade. But you are a man. For a man it is easier. (*She goes down the stairs. There is a moment's silence when each of the three persons present seems to be concerned with his own thoughts.*)

MRS. WADE: What could have so embittered a person?

MR. WADE: Why, the woman's crazy, and naturally Aunt Lida was the first to make it out. How long have you known she was insane, Aunt Lida?

AUNT LIDA: I don't know.

MR. WADE: (*Taking several steps forward, slowly*) What do you mean?

MRS. WADE: She means that she doesn't know when she realized it.

MR. WADE: By the way she said it, I thought she meant she wasn't sure she was crazy.

MRS. WADE: (*Taking his arm*) Oh, could a sane person possibly have been so critical and questioning of a happy family life?

AUNT LIDA: Robert, aren't you going to miss your train?

MR. WADE: By George! Well, aren't the children going to tell me goodbye?

AUNT LIDA: (*Calling*) Chill-drun!

Mr. Wade kisses Mrs. Wade.

MR. WADE: So long, Auntie.

AUNT LIDA: (*Casually*) Toodle-loo. Hurry back, Robert.

The children have now appeared in the doorways from Aunt Lida's room and their parents' room. "Yes, ma'am!" "What, Aunt Lida?"

AUNT LIDA: Tell your Daddy goodbye. (*Slowly letting herself down into chair*)

NANCY: Oh, of course!

JAMES: Sure!

All of the children rush toward their father to be kissed. As he bends and stoops to kiss each of them, he is saying, "Goodbye, Alfred. Goodbye, Nancy. Goodbye, Lida Sue. Goodbye, James. Goodbye, Charles William." But Mrs. Wade is watching Aunt Lida, who, as the curtain falls, sits with her hands over her face, as before.

CURTAIN

STATEMENT OF ASHBY WYNDHAM

BY ROBERT PENN WARREN

I

SHERIFF'S OFFICE,
THE JAIL,
MULCASTER COUNTY.

THE PORE human man, he ain't nuthin but a handful of dust, but the light of God's face on him and he shines like a dia-mint, and blinds the eye of the un-uprighteous congregation. Dust, hit lays on the floor, under the goin-forth and the comin-in, and ain't nuthin, and gits stirred up under the trompin, but a sun-beam come in the dark room and in that light hit will dance and shine for heart-joy. I laid on the floor, and hit was dark. I wasn't nuthin. I was under the trompin, which was cruel-hard. But a man don't know, fer he is ignorant. There ain't nuthin in him but meaness and a hog-holler and emptiness for the world's slop. A man don't think of nuthin but sloppin, and dodgin, when the kick comes. I laid on the floor, and didn't know, and the trompin. But the light come in the dark room, like a finger a pointin at me through the hole, and it was the hard trompin had stirred me. I shined in the light.

It was so, and truth sober. Then, that time, and for a long time, me goin or stayin, on dry land or the river. Oh, Lord, make me to be shinin agin, and do not turn away yore face. For I have spelled how hit is writ, and water come sweet from the smote stone, and light in the dark place.

But a man don't know, nor was made to. Salvation has laid hid behind a dark bush, like a enemy man up to meaness and waitin for him was comin, when the moon had got down under the ridge.

Hit holds out hits hand, and there ain't no sayin what is in hit. A stickin-knife or a five-dollar bill. But the Lord, he made the world and what walks on hit, and hit out of pure love. The copperhead, and him layin for sun in the path where the women-folks and the children goes down to the spring for water. And the wicked man in his power of meaness, he puts out his hand, and he don't know, but the Lord's love is in hit, in a far country, and hit only retches out to lay holt and come home. He figgers he's grabbin for the toys and garnishments and the vain things which is his heart's desire, but hit ain't so. The Lord's love in him is retchen out for the light of the Lord's face, and is pore and peaked like a potato-sprout in a dark cellar, where the sun don't come. But the Lord's love in him, hit knows what hit hones for. Hit's him what is ignorant, and deceit laid on his eyes like a blind-folt at a play-party, and him retchen out to lay holt.

Take Pearl. She et and lay down in the house of the abominations, and hit was the roof of that house kept the rain offen her. But the time come, and hit never kept out the light of His face. They ain't no ridge-pole hewed nor shingle split, red oak nor white, will do hit, when the time comes. Her hand retched out to lay holt. It was my blessedness to be standin there. The Lord led me, and he laid the words on my tongue. I named them, and hit was ample. She come down the river with me and mine, frost or the hot sun, freshit or drout and the mud stinken when we tied up. We all broke bread and taken our sop in rejoicin.

I done what was moved in me. What I knowed to do. And what I wouldn't know, hit may be, to do different and hit to do agin. I figured on telling her of salvation, and us movin and rejoicin, which we done. And now she lays there, and the dungeon-key turned in the lock, and her heart is full of hate. She won't unsquinch her eyes, they say, nor take sup nor morsel. How does a man know, not made to? She retched out her hand to lay holt on salvation, and done hit, back in Hulltown. Her hand retched out that night, and hit has retched nigh three years, and laid holt on that old squirril rifle.

If I hadn't never come, and named the words on my tongue, she would been there yet, and hit the house of abominations, but her face smilin. Salvation, what good has hit done her? She taken off one sin, lak a man his shirt sweat-dirty, and flung hit down, but she has done swapped one Bible-sin for another, and hate in her heart, and the cold stone wall round and about where she lays down. And my wife and them what follered and trusted me, movin on the river, they is come amongst strangers, and the bitterness. God's will, hit runs lak a fox with the dogs on him, and doubles, and knows places secret and hard for a man's foot. But a man wants to know, but hit is his weakness. He lays in the night, when the Lord has done turned away His face, and he worries his head and shakes his mind lak a tree, but what fruit falls, hit is tart-lak and wries up the tongue. He looks back on what is done. He tries to see hit lak hit was, and recollect. But hit don't do no good. Remembrance is lak the smoke what still hangs over the rifle-barril, but the squirril fallin, bumpin the limbs. Oh Lord, I have laid down in the night.

They treat me good. I ain't got nuthin agin them here. They is doin accordin to their lights. If they turn the key in the lock, hit ain't in man-meaness. Hit is laid on them so. They told me to tell them all what happened, and hit would be more easy. They said tell them and they'd put hit down, and hit would help Pearl when the time come. And help me. But me, what help I need, hit ain't in feeble man to give. But I said, I would give testifyin for the Lord. I would write hit down myself, I said, for a man can't say hit all at once, how hit was. Sometimes hit comes when a man ain't thinkin. Hit comes before you lak you was there, and hit daylight but gone in a blink. So they give me paper and ink and a pen staff. I will put hit down, spare not, fear nor favor, and I will write hit as fair as I can . . .

II

. . . I was born and had my raisin in the County of Custiss, which is a good country yit if a man can git him a patch of bottom or on the hill before the washin and rain-scourin commences. But hit ain't what hit was before the change of time, lak in the days of my grandpappy, who was a old one but spry and his hand never shook and him nigh ninety, when I was a sprout. He told me how hit was, ground idle for the takin and clearin, or slashin and burnin, and the timber there for a man's axe to square and lay for his four walls, when he left his pappy's and taken him a wife. And the woods full of varmints yit, and squirrils fat in the trees, lak apples when the limb bends, and turkeys gabblin whar the sun broke through to a open place where they taken forage. And the skillet never groaned empty, he said, save once in a spell when the Lord laid down His hand on man's neglectful pride, and a woman's never had to grabble in the lard-barril nor a man's gut rumble dry and the young uns standin round about, big-eyed for the famish. Which I seen, and not me only.

But come the change of time and newfangleness, with the ground wore out and the washin, hit ain't what hit was, lak my grandpappy named hit. My grandpappy was a godly man when I knowed him and had been a long time, he said, but there was a time he stood amongst the scoffers and scorners or lay down in the bushes to lewdness and carnal carryins-on. There was always sin and human meaness in Custiss, and he never said no contrary, but now they is churches in Custiss with the door done sagged off the hinges and the weather beats in where the roof leaks and sassafrass and elder quick-growin where folks used to stand and talk before the bell rung, and in the walkin-out season, not even waitin for dark and hit more decent, they is abominations under the ridge-pole of the Lord's house. I know hit because I misbehaved and put my immortal soul in danger, but for the mercy, and I sweat in the night for it yit. And what churches they is in Custiss ain't full lak I seen when I was a young un, women and old folks now and the children too little for devilmint, and the men folks too few so you don't much hear a good bass-burden to the song worship. Folks has got one eye cocked hot after lewdness and the other on the almighty dollar, and the Lord, He has seen and has laid down his hand, for He is the Lord God and is a jealous God, lak hit is writ. Times hard in Custiss and misery, and folks lays the blame on one thing and another, how the ground's done washed and the rich folks done bought up or took the country for the timber or the coal down under the mountains, but they forgit the Lord God and how He don't have to be huntin for a stick to lay on the bare back of wickedness. What comes to His hand is His, and His hand clever past runnin or hidin.

They is good folks in Custiss yit, I ain't denyin, but for the blindness. My mammy was good and feared God. My pappy was a good man and stout for work and providin, and he never did my mammy no meaness, but for likker and fightin. He couldn't take nuthin off no man hit looked lak. He was good, but he was not God-fearin and never taken his sins to Jesus, not for all mammy prayin and pleadin. He died sudden and hit nigh dinner time, and the vittles what had been put in the pot for him scorchin on the stove. He went out in the mornin and put his axe to the tree, and the tree what looked true, hit slipped and back-bucked of a sudden. The butt hit pappy on the side of the head. The men brung him to the house and laid him on the bed, him breathin but his eyes closed. Mammy prayed by the bed, and the folks washed the blood off. He opened his eyes one time, and hit looked lak they would pop out of his head, and they went wild around the room like birds what bat-ters to git out when they done flew in the house. Then he was dead, and gore blood on the piller. Him buried, Mammy set in a cheer for three days, nor said nuthin. Then at night time and the third day she stood on the floor, and us young uns looked at her. He died a saved man, she said. Jesus give me salvation, and I'll never see him agin. Oh, what to pray for, and me a woman ignerant and weak. Then the tears come, and for the first time, quick as a freshit. And we put her in the bed. The next mornin she et a little somethin.

My mammy was a Porsum, and they was good folks and clever. What they laid hand to, good or bad howsobeit, they taken hit hard. They was wicked men amongst them, but they never had no name for corner meaness, and folks give them a name for drivin a true furrow, once they set to hit. My mammy was a cousin to Private Porsum, what was in the big war over the other side of the ocean and made a name for himself and for Custiss that folks can read in the books. He was quiet talkin, they said, for I never seen him but one time, and he testified in the churches for salvation, but he was a man with a rifle you never seen the lak of, nor nobody in Custiss. He come back from the war, and there was big carryins-on over him in New York and in Washington, and in the city, and folks standin in the streets half a day, not workin nor nuthin, to see him come ridin past in a automobile, setting with ginrals and sena-tors and sich. And him Private Porsum from Custiss. They wanted to make him a officer and put trimmins on his coat, but he said, naw, he was Private Porsum, and he had not done nuthin but what come to his hand, and what air man would, with God's help to uphold him. And they named him Private Porsum. He was book clever, and when he come back from the war he went to the Legislature. He done good there, and after a while he never come back to Custiss much except to be makin speeches. He has got him a little place up in Custiss yit, where he goes to be huntin and fishin, but he has got him a big house down nigh the city, here. My mammy was his cousin and blood-kin, and me. But the Wyndhams, my pappy's folks, was good folks, too.

The Porsums laid hand to the plow and held on, and my mammy never was one to be turnin and laggin. She done what she could, and reared us in sweat and God's name. I seen her barefoot in the field and the plow lines hung over her neck like a man, and her humped to hit, afore us young uns was big enuff. And her not no big woman, and slight-made. I seen her, nights after she done put us to bed and me the biggest layin wakeful, I seen her settin weavin or patchin and the fire so low she squinched to see, or plaitin them hickory baskits, to sell in the settlemint. I shet my eyes for sleep, her settin there the last thing in them. We growed up and done what we could, and taken over the plowin. She did not work in the field no more, but to chop corn when we got in a tight and the grass taken a strangle holt after the wet. But she never was no sluggart, and taken no ease, with times hard till the day the women folks come in to wash her and I heard the hammer in the shed where they put the nails in and made her box staunch-tight.

Jacob my brother, he laid holt on Jesus afore mammy shet her eyes on day, and hit was a joy for her. But me, I never and I groan to deny hit to her. Hit was not in me, for blindness. I worked and done, but Saturday toward sun, hit was me down the big road, and many is the time I come back the dew done dried on a Sunday. Lak yore pappy, Ashby, she said to me, a hand for gallivantin and revellin, and him dead in the dark past Jesus' sight. He would not take nuthin offen no man, and the strong man is done brought low. Her heart grieved. And what she said last, and her lips blue lak a vilet, was to name my salvation. Ashby, she said, and tried to lift up her hand what was feeble on the cover, lay holt while hit is yit day. I stood there. My heart in my bosom, hit was lak flint rock for hardness and sharp edges cuttin, but I could not git out a word nor a tear to the eye socket. I tried to retch out and tetch the foot-board of the bed where she was layin, lak that was sumethin to do. But my arms was lak frozen. Hit was the last she said, and then the black vomit.

I seen three die mortal on that bed, and me standin there. My pappy, lost and his eyes poppin, and my mammy, safe in Jesus, and that pore old man, the Frencher, wayfarin and far from home, comin off the big road and died amongst strangers. Hit was a time after my mammy was done gone, and Jacob and me lived there and made out, him livin by Jesus' word and me hittin off ever Saturday with my hat cocked on the side of my head and lookin for what mought be. Hit was gittin along in August, and the sun not down yit and the day was a scorcher. I come round the corner of the house from the wood-pile, my arm full of stove wood, and I seen a wagin comin up, and Jacob a walkin afore hit. I went on in and throwed down them stove lengths, and heard Jacob callin. I went out there, and Jacob was pickin up a old man out of the wagin. He handled him lak he was nuthin for lightness, him wropped up in a old quilt and his arms ploppin out to drag down. His eyes was open, but he never looked at nobody nor noticed, but he looked up at the sky and never blinked. Then him was drivin the wagin jumped down and come runnin round to the old man, and leaned over to grab holt of the old man's hand, and the big old straw hat fell off, and I seen hit was a woman, not more than a gal, and long black hair come undone and tumblin down. Then Jacob yelled fretful at me standin there gapin, Hit's a pore old man sick to die, and you standin there. Git the bed ready. And I done hit.

Jacob had done met them down the road, and the gal ast him where to git some drinkin water for the old man sick. So Jacob brung them in, lak air man would, and him Christian. We put him in the bed, where had laid the saved and the unsaved to taste the bitterness. We unwrapped that old quilt offen him, and hit dirty from the journeyin, and taken off his pants and shirt. There was not no meat to him, for the wastin and fever, and the skin hung off him lak a tow sack hung on a barb wire fence. The gal washed off his face and hands, and give him water to sup, but he never said nuthin. He laid there. He had a white beard, and his head was bald like a punkin on top, and yeller, with white hair bristlin off the sides. His eyes was blue lak a baby's, and he looked up to the ceiling, and hit the house of the stranger, where he had done come all that way and all that time, from Canady, whar they is the deep snow.

The gal never said a word. She set there and leaned towards him and had holt of his hand. She did not cry, but they was dust from the journeyin on her cheeks, and you could see how the tears had done come down from her eyes and made streakin down her face. Her comin down the road in the wagin, and the old man layin there, and the sun bearin down, and the tears come down from her eyes. She set there till he was dead, after Jacob had got the doctor from Cashville. He was a gone goslin, the doctor said, and taken his leave. Hit was nigh midnight when Jacob come with the doctor, and he did not stay no time to speak of after he looked at the old man. Hit was toward day the old man crossed over. That gal did not cry none. She looked at his face for a minute real hard. She still had holt of his hand, lak all that time. Then she put her head down on his chist and let hit lay. She shet her eyes, and for all you could say, she mought been asleep, and her hair loose over his chist. I taken a look at her, and I went outside and stood there lookin off towards Massey Mountain. The first day was comin over the mountain, the sky there the color of blue-johnny spilt, and the mountain black under hit.

They is good folks in Custiss and they taken holt. They buried that pore old man and was Christian kind to Marie, which was that gal's name. Old Mrs. Marmaduke, who had the place next ouren, she taken her in for four days, till she got ready to leave. She was goin on, she said, to some place where she could git some work. She had been headin south, she said, to git the old man where hit would be warm in the winter time, lak she had heard tell. They had been comin down a long time, she said, nigh four years, stoppin and workin to git a little somethin to eat, and movin on. She mought as well keep on goin that way, she said, not havin nobody of kin nor kind. She would make out, she said.

The mornin she was leavin, I got up and started out the door and towards the gate. Whar you goin? Jacob said. I didn't say nuthin, but kept on goin. I went down the road toward Marmaduke's. I got to a place whar you can see the house, then I squatted down lak a man will to take his ease. I seen smoke comin out the chimney, and knowed they was stirrin, if haven a name for late risin. A time, and Old Man Marmaduke brung the wagin out, and I seen that gal Marie come out, and Mrs. Marmaduke. That gal was wearin a dress now, lak she done after her pappy died. Then I seen her put her valise up in the wagin, and git up, and the wagin start rollin, and the folks wavin after her. Then Old Mrs. Marmaduke went in and Old Man Marmaduke went off toward the shed. I moved down the road a piece, round the bend, and squatted down, where the cedars was.

She come down the road. She was settin there straight, and lookin down the road, not this way nor that, till I riz up by the cedars when she had done got nigh, and said good mornin. And she said good mornin, in that way she talked, not lak ouren. I kept on walkin alongside the wagin, not sayin nuthin for a spell, nor she. Then she not sayin nuthin, I said, I am goin a way down toward Cashville, I wonder can I ride with you. She said I could, and I laid hand to the side board, and lept up.

How far you aimin to get today? I ast her.

They say I kin git to what they call Tomtown, she said.

Hit is a way past Cashville.

Not too far, they say.

Hit is a heap too far, I said, for today.

Then I will rest where I can, she said. Lak we done, afore. I got a little somethin left yit, and I kin pay. She did not say nuthin for a minute, then she said right sharp, I tried to pay Mrs. Marmaduke, and not be beholdin for bread.

Hit is too far, I said, for tonight.

I'll git there tomorrow.

Hit is too far, I said, for tomorrow.

I'll git there when I git there, she said sober, lookin down the road.

No, mam, I said, you won't.

How far is hit?

Hit is too far, I said, for mortal time.

And she looked at me right sudden, and her eyes was big and blue like her pappy's.

And mortal time, hit is, we live in, I said.

Then I told her how I had done gone to Cashville yestiddy, and she could git work to do there, and not leave so far from where folks knowed her name and had put forth their hand to her in sorrow, and where her pappy was laid in the ground. One of them boardin houses up nigh the Massey Mountain Company sawmills could use a woman could cook and was willin.

She did not say nuthin for a time. She looked down at her hands layin togither in her lap. Them wagin wheels screaked lak they do, and the dust puffed up where the mule put his hoofs down. The road, hit was deep dust up over the rim, hit a drout from way back. Hit did not look lak she was goin to say nuthin, settin there, her head bowed down. Then she said, I will do what I can, Meester Ween-ham. Which was what she called me, her comin from way up in Canady, where they do not talk so good.

III

They hired her up at the boardin house on Massey Mountain to be cookin and helpin to give their vituls to the men what was workin. I takin her up thar, and I seen what hit would be lak, them two big cook stoves, big as a saw-mill boiler, and her havin to be firin up one of them stoves and cookin fer hit looked lak a army, them tables was so long whar the men set down. And dishes to wash and the floor to sweep and mop. And her not no big woman, no way. I seen how hit would be, and I said, naw, you ain't a stayin here, not and you no bigger than a rabbit.

You brought me here, Meester Ween-ham, she said in that-air way she talked.

Yeah, I said, and I kin take you away agin.

You brought me here, she said right quiet and looked at me with them big eyes, and I'm stayin, Meester Ween-ham.

Her mind was set, nor cant-hook ner crowbar could budge hit. She taken her valise and put hit in that-air little room they give her, you could see daylight through the roof hit was so shack-built, and she taken my hand. Goodbye, Meester Ween-ham, she said.

So I got in the wagin and went home, for she told me to take hit and keep hit for her.

I stopped down at the foot of Massey whar a man could git him a bottle of moonshine whiskey from Buck Barkus what made it and sold it and stirred up abomination and taken silver for it, for hit looks lak ain't nuthin pore man won't do for money, and what he won't do for money he up and does for lust of his flesh and sinful pride, and hit for pride the angels fell out of heaven and God's sight. So Buck Barkus he taken my four bits and hit was his sin, and me, I taken that air bottle, and hit was my sin, for a man takes a pull on the bottle and it is lak he taken a fire in his bowels and lust hit's name and his fingers itch. I done drunk up that air bottle and bust hit on a lime rock, and I come toward the house standin up in the wagin bed whuppin that pore old mule and the wagin jouncin and me standin up and whoopin and yellin in my lust and sinful pride.

My brother Jacob was standin thar and lookin at me when I come.

Ain't that that Canady-girl's mule? he done ast me, and I said hit was, and she said for me to keep hit.

You nigh kilt it, he said.

Hell, I said, I ain't kilt nuthin but me a bottle of Barkus pan-ther-piss.

You nigh kilt this here mule, he said, and I looked at him how his face was, and I spat over the wagin wheel on the ground.

Jesus Christ, I said, I ain't kilt no mule.

Git down, Ashby, he said, quiet, and I'll unhitch.

Jesus Christ, I said, for hit was not nuthin them days for me to take the name of our sweet Jesus and hit in vain. You ain't un-hitchin nuthin. I'm unhitchin. Hit's my wagin and hit's my mule and hit's my woman, I said.

Ashby, he said, quiet again, you git lak this and you ain't fit to unhitch no mule. You ain't fit for nuthin.

I looked down and I seen him standin there nigh the mule's head. I just looked down at him a half minute. Then I spat a spew over the wagin wheel, gittin ready slow to let fly lak a man will settin on his porch takin his ease nigh sun. Then all of a sudden I let out a whoop and I whupped that air old mule with that rope and fit to draw blood, and that old mule jumped lak hit was a race horse, and Jacob jumped back just in time, and I whooped and whupped.

We come round the corner of the house, me whoopin and whuppin and headed for the lot gate, what was open. I never seen how hit happened. But hit looked lak a wheel got hung on the gate post, what was locust and deep-set, and I seen that air old mule go down and me flyin. Hit seemed lak I flew slow, lak when a man dreams he can fly. Hit seemed lak I whooped once and me in the air. Hit seemed lak I was in the air flyin nigh a half hour. That was all I knowed.

I must have hit my head on a rock or somethin. Or maybe the ground what was tromped hard, hit being drout and the ground dry-hard. I didn't know nuthin till next mornin. I woke up, and I was layin in bed and a knot on my head the size of a simlin.

Then Jacob come in. How you feelin, Ashby? he ast, and I said I was feelin all right. I said there wasn't nuthin could faze me.

He didn't say nuthin. He just give me a cup of coffee. When I done drunk hit, he taken the cup and set hit on the table. Ashby, he said, that mule is dead.

I got out of the bed, not payin him no mind.

Ashby, he said, agin, that Canady-girl's mule is dead.

Well, I said, drag hit off. Drag hit off and give hit to the buzzards. That old mule, hit was not nuthin no-way but buzzard bait.

Hit was the Canady-girl's mule, Jacob said.

Shore, I said, and I'll pay for hit, buzzard bait or no.

We can't pay for no mule, he said. Not right off. We got to grabble to pay.

You can't pay, I told him, but me, I can pay.

You can pay? he ast me.

By God, I said, I can and will. I ain't stayin here to grabble. They ain't nuthin here. I'm sick of it here and primed to puke. I'm goin to Massey.

He shook his head, slow, and said, They ain't nuthin at Massey.

They's money at Massey, I said. I was puttin on my pants and bucklin my belt. They's payin hard money at Massey.

Yeah, he said, and chargin you for board and bed, if you ain't got a house over there you can stay in. And hit's too far a piece to stay here and work at Massey. And ain't many's got a house over there now, the Company done throwed folks off the Mountain.

I'm goin, I said.

Leavin me? he ast. Leavin me and this here place?

I'm goin, I said.

Hit was your Pappy and Mammy's place, he said.

And I ain't Pappy and Mammy, I said. I'm Ashby Wyndham, and I ain't stayin here to rot and grabble.

Hit was lak that, and I made me a bundle of my stuff, and I walked out the door.

IV

Marie said that old mule was not no matter. She said hit was not no use to her. She said hit was God's will and she taken hit for a sign. Hit was a sign for her not to be movin down the big road, and her amongst strangers.

That was what she said when I kept sayin I was goin to pay.

I tried to pay. I tried and strove. They was money at Massey, but hit looked lak what they give you with one hand on Saturday night they taken back with the other hand afore Monday morning. But I kept on tryin, if air man did. I taken what I could ever week and helt hit out. Hit was not much, and me there two months. Hit was nineteen dollars, or nigh hit. I could helt out a little more if I had not bought Marie them pretties. I bought them pretties down at Cashtown where they got stores full of them things, and they is vanity and no denyin. But a man, and a young man he full of vanity and flesh-forwardness, and hit ain't nuthin but his lust and flesh-hotness if you scan clost and name hit. He sees a woman and he gits her on his mind and he wants to put pretties on her so he can see her with them things, but hit ain't nuthin but Bible lust comin out of his eyes.

I bought Marie them things. I bought her a necklace and hit was all gold or nigh, like the man said. Hit had a sparklet in it and hit had a shine lak a diamint, you let the sun git it clear. Hit looked to me lak I had to git hit for Marie. I seen hit layin there, and I knowed I had to git it. So I ast him how much and he named hit and I taken four dollars and give it to him. I didn't say yea nor nay. I did not hem nor haw. I just give him that money, for I knowed Marie had to have hit. Marie was one of them little women, and not too much meat on them. She was spry lak them little women, and quick when she aimed to. But she was a quiet one. She was quiet and still. She would be settin or standin there, and you never knowed hit. You look at her and you did not think nobody could be that quiet, and hit natchel. You looked and you never knowed hit was breath comin and goin in her bosom, hit moved so gentle for a marvel. She was lak water layin in the sun, and hit deep and nary a riffle. But a little wind what a man can not feel blowin on his cheek, and a sparkle runs all over that water all of a sudden. She moved her hand just easy or hit was her eyes got bright of a sudden, and hit was lak that wind blowed on the water and hit was all sparkle. I bought that necklace to wear on her bosom for that sparkle what was in her.

She would be done work and I would be waitin. Axe or layin to a cross-cut all day, and I would see her comin out of that there kitchen and me waitin in the dark and the weariness was not nuthin. Hit was lak I was wakin up fresh and a sunbeam done smote you on the eyeball and roused you. We would go to them frolics at Massey on Saturday night. She would stand quiet and watch them folks dance and stomp and the caller called the figgers and them fiddles goin. She stood right quiet, but you could see the sparkle in her. If you looked clost. Then maybe we would dance a set or twain. But I did not git no more of Barkus moonshine, nor offen nobody else. At least not when I was with Marie. She did not lak for me to. And when I was with Marie I never felt no call.

I never taken likker lak I use to, and likker is a sin. But a man can not be good out of plain humankindness. He can not be good for it ain't in a pore man. He can not be good unlest it is good in the light of God's eye. God's eye ain't on him and he just swaps one sin for another one, and hit worse maybe. I laid off likker, but I swapped for another sin. I laid off likker for Marie but hit was because of pore human love and not for God's love. Then hit was for pore human love I taken that there worse sin, and I shame to say hit.

Week nights when there wasn't no frolic at Massey, we walked on the mountain. Hit was moonlight on them clearins, or stars, and on them roads where the wagins went in the daytime, and dark under the bushes and them trees. You look off west at night offen Massey, and you know they is the big valley and the hills off there, but you ain't seein it. Hit is lak the world is way down there and the black dark to yore sight, and the folks down there and the folks doins ain't nuthin. The sky is way up, and the stars. I was up on the mountain and hit was Marie with me. Hit was right brisk to cold on the mountain with the fall comin on, but we never taken no mind. We set down on a log or on a lime rock chunk, and hit was lak we done built a warm fire for a camp and put our hands to the brightness. We never taken thought on the cold. A man don't take no thought on what he was or is or what will come.

I taken no thought and hit was my sin. I ain't never said hit was Marie's sin. When a man ever does a sin he ain't done hit secret and him private. He has done taken his own sin on his shoulders, but another man's sin too to bear him down. You throw a rock in a pond and hit don't make but one splash but they is ripples runs out from hit. I sinned and I taken Marie's sin on my shoulders for Judgmint. Hit was my fault she taken spot and had blemish laid on to her. Hit was for pore human man's love, but love ain't nuthin if hit ain't in God's eye.

Hit was after Christmas she told me she was heavy. She did not say nuthin or complain. She just named hit and looked at me quiet. I just bust out laughin. Lord God, I said, hit ain't nuthin, yore Mammy and mine come to hit. Lord God, I said, hit ain't a thing in the world. I bet he will be a buster, I said. I bet he will be a ring-tail. We will just go down to Cashtown and git married. I got me half of Pappy's place and me and Jacob we will sell hit and me take my half.

She said would Jacob mind to. She said maybe Jacob wanted to stay on where his Pappy and Mammy was afore him.

Hell, I said, half is mine and I by God aim to have hit.

I said we would take my half and git us a place to stay in on Massey so I could git to my work. I said she would not be standin over them cook stoves to git vittles for other folks. I said she could stay home and git my vittles and the young uns for a change. I said I aimed to git my half.

I knowed Jacob would squeal lak a suckin pig caught under the bottom rail, but I never cared. I aimed to git my half. I come down the road on a Sunday evenin, and I seen Jacob settin under a cedar tree with his chair cocked back for hit was onseasonable warm and January. I seen him settin there but I knowed he never taken his ease. I knowed hit was the Bible layin on his lap.

I ast him how he was makin out. He said he did not have no complaint, and he made to git me a chair from the house. Naw, I said, I did not have no time for settin. I said how hit was business I come for. I said I was gittin married.

That Canady girl, he ast me.

I said hit was.

He said she was a good girl, and he knowed hit the way she was to that pore old man the Frencher.

I said, yeah, she was a good girl but I never put my foot in the big road and come twelve miles to git him to tell me. I said I come on business, lak I done said.

He said, what was hit.

The place, I said.

Hit is yores to come to, yores and that Canady girl's, he said.

And mine to sell and git my half, I said. That was what I said, right out. Good or bad, winter or summer, cold or hot, I never was one to let no word git spit-soft on my tongue. I never beat around no bush.

He just stood there shakin his head and never said nuthin.

I come to git my half, I said.

Ashby, he said, and shaken his head, hit ain't in me. Not to sell this here place and be leavin. Ashby, you ain't meanin hit. Not and yore Pappy and Mammy dyin here, and the bed they was in.

They is dead, I said, and ain't no talk makin hit different. They is dead and ain't this place or no other nuthin to them now.

I ain't sellin this place, he said, quiet.

This place, this place, I said. Lord God, you talk lak this here place was gold and diamints. This place is lak air other place. A place is dirt. And I spat on the bare ground where hit was tromped hard in front with the comin and goin.

Hit is dirt, Jacob said. But man, he is dirt, he said. He ain't nuthin but dirt, he said, but the God All Mighty breathed his breath in him and he ain't common dirt no more.

I told him this place was common dirt to me, by God.

Hit is not common to me, Jacob said.

I told him I was not breakin no wind if hit was common or not common dirt to him, but I was havin my half.

Ashby, Ashby, he said, ain't I yore brother.

I nigh wish to God you was not, I said.

Ashby, he commenst, and put out his hand lak to lay holt on me, but I never knowed what he aimed to say. I have laid awake in the dark and seen how hit was, and ain't never knowed.

By God, I said, and I looked in his face, and I knowed he would not sell never for no man's price. But that was not hit. Hit was some other thing come on me lookin at him.

By God, I said, and I give hit to him. I give hit to him on the side of the head.

I stunned him flat.

He laid on his back I ain't sayin how long, not lookin at me, just up at the sky and blinked lak a baby you put him in the light. Then he rolled on one side and got up, and stood there and looked at me.

You sellin, I yelled at him, but hit did not matter what I yelled for I knowed he was not sellin and I never waited for him to say. Hit was on me, and I was blood-guilty in my heart. I give hit to him again.

I give hit to him in the mouth, and he lay there and I seen the blood come out of his mouth.

By God, I yelled, by God. I looked where he laid. Then I turned my back and left him layin and started down the big road.

I walked down the road fast. I reckin I done gone a mile and I looked down and seen my hand was bloody. I done cut my knucks and they was bloody. I reckin I cut them on his teeth.

I wish I had kilt him, I said out loud, but they was not nobody there. By God, I said, I wish I had kilt the bastard.

I walked down the road and sucked the blood out of my knucks where they was cut, and spat the blood and spit out in the middle of the road where folks goes.

V

The woods boss for the Company he give me the letter that lawyer writ me from Cashtown. He said he had some money to give me what was left fer me and fer me to come to see him. I bust out laughin. I knowed no lawyer was not givin me nor nobody no money. I tore up that air letter. Then the next week the boss said for me to go to Cashtown to see that lawyer what had writ me the letter. So come Saturday I went to Cashtown. I seen that lawyer. He laid the money on the table. Hit was thirteen twenty dollar bills and them new and green lak sallet, and one ten dollar bill and three one dollar bills and handful of chicken feed nickels and dimes and pennies and such, nigh a dollar. He counted hit out, ever bit. Hit was two hundred and seventy-three dollars and eighty-five cents, that air chicken feed. Hit is yoren, he said to me, and you sign yore name here.

How come, I ast him.

To sell yore place, he said, and I ast him about Jacob, and he said Jacob done hit.

Well I am God durned, I said. And I said, Mister, gimme that pen staff.

I signed my name. I put my John Henry where he said and I taken care and pains fer I never wanted no mistake. Hit was not plain writin, hit was fair a pitcher of my name Ashby Porsum Wyndham for full. I always was a hand to write good give me time and a pen not no old stub.

I ast him who bought the place and he said it was the Massey Mountain Company. They goin out yore way, he said, out Fiddler's Fortune Creek section. Yore timber was not nuthin to speak on but they kin use the house for cook house and all. They give a fair price, he said.

I ast him how much.

Three thirty, he said.

Hell, I said, Jacob never taken much. He will be wantin to git more offen me.

He never taken any, the lawyer feller said, he told me to give hit all to you.

Hell, I said, you ain't give hit all to me, you ain't give me nigh sixty dollars.

Hit was for fees and titles and such, he said, lak them lawyers talk.

Who gits hit, I ast him plain.

He said he did, him and the court house.

How come, I ast him.

He said the Company had to be shore me and Jacob owned hit true and right.

Lord God, I said, my pappy owned hit. My grandpappy owned hit, and nobody said him nay. And I heard say my great-grand-pappy afore him.

Hearsay, he said, hearsay ain't the law.

I knowed hit was not no use to argify for he done had the money.

Mister Wyndham, he said to me, you done thought how you investin yore money. I advise you to buy some stock lak they call hit in the Company. You buy a piece of the Company. Then you will be workin for yoreself. You will git yore pay and you will git some more too. If you put yore money in the Company.

The Company ain't nuthin to me, I said.

The Company will make money for you, he said.

Lord God, I said, that fool Jacob give you my money and you taken sixty dollars and I shore God ain't givin the Company none of my money.

You better put hit in the bank, he said, and not tote hit.

You taken sixty dollars, I said, and the bank, I bet they take a hundred if I give them the chanst.

He said they would keep hit safe for me.

Keep hit safe, I said, and looked at him square. Mister, I said, I am six foot and two inches and I weigh a hundred and ninety pounds and I can handle me a axe ten hours and never be blowed. Ain't no man I ever seen can take what is true mine offen me.

I taken that air money up. I put hit in my pants.

And let air man try, I said. I said that and I went out the door. I left him standin there blowin his breath on his eye glasses and wipin them with his handkichief.

I come back to Massey and I told Marie how hit was. You can quit cookin and scourin, I told her. You can cook my vittles, I said. We was married aready, but she was still cookin for the Company.

Ashby, Ashby, she said soft, and hit looked lak she was gittin ready to cry.

Hell, I said, ain't you glad.

She said yes. She said she was glad not to be doin that cookin and scourin. But hit looked lak she was gittin ready to cry.

Hell, I said, what you look that way for.

Jacob, she said, hit was for Jacob.

Hit made me mad for fair. I told her. I said, I do not want to hear you namin his name. Not no more. What is betwixt me and him is betwixt me and him, and not nobody else. Not nobody. That was what I said. Hit looks lak a man can not bear and endure to look in the lookin glass when somebody has helt hit up to him. He can not endure to see his pore sinful face. She named Jacob's name and hit was lak she helt up a lookin glass for me to see my sinful face.

Then somebody ast me where Jacob had done gone.

No where as I knowed, I said.

But they said, yeah, he had done gone.

Hit stuck in my mind. I never wanted hit to, but hit stuck. I was workin or was eatin or I was layin in bed and Marie there sleepin alongside of me, and hit would come in my head. How had he done gone. Hit was lak when you git a little bitsy fish bone stuck in yore throat, little nigh to nuthin, and you think hit is done gone for you ain't feelin nuthin and all of a sudden you swaller or you turn yore neck, and hit is not gone. Hit is there. Hit is lak you swallered a pin.

Saturday evenin I taken out for Fiddler's Fortune Creek. I come there nigh four o'clock. I seen the house. The door was open and I walked in. They was not nobody there. They was not nuthin there. Everthing was gone. The chairs and cook stove and the bedstid. I seen a chunk layin in the fireplace not all burnt up on one end and the ashes layin there, white ashes lak when good hard wood is done burnt. I squatted down and tetched that chunk, lak a man will to see if may be the fire ain't long been out. But I knowed hit had been a long time. But I squatted and tetched hit lak I never knowed.

I stood up and looked round. I seen the place where everything had been set. Where the chist had been set and the bedstid. Hit looked lak I could nigh see them settin there. I stood there hit ain't no sayin how long. A man stands in a house and there ain't nobody there but him and he listens and hearkens and hit is plum quiet but he listens lak he is tryin to hear somethin. Hit is lak somebody was tryin to tell him somethin. Hit was plum quiet.

I went up to Old Man Marmadukes place. I seen Mrs. Marmaduke and I ast her. She said Jacob was done gone. She said he come and taken his leave. He give her Mammys bedstid, she said. He told her he did not want strangers to lay in hit and tetch head to piller. She showed me the bedstid.

I ast her where Jacob had done gone.

He never said, she said. He said he was goin to walk in the world. Hit was all he said, and she seen him walkin down the big road.

VI

I taken Marie out of that kitchen where she was cookin and fixin for strangers and put her in my house. I give a man a hundred and fifty dollars for that air house and give him two dollars ever month till hit was goin to come two hundred and twenty dollars. I could give hit all cash money but I helt out for Marie. She was not gittin on so good and I helt that money for medicine and such if need come. She said she was goin to be all right when the young un come. She said she was not nuthin but a little puny.

The young un come. He was a buster. He was nigh as big as his Mammy. He come some afore his time and all of a sudden but he was a buster. He never said by yore leave. She was washin dishes we et offen for supper and she yelled, Ashby, Ashby, all of a sudden. Hit was comin. There was not nobody there but me for we never knowed hit was time. Ain't nobody ever knowin hit is time for nuthin. Man figgers and calkilates but he ain't knowin. He looks at the sun and he knows what time of day hit is but there ain't no sayin the time of what is comin. The Bible says there is a time for everything, but pore man never knows the time. Hit ain't got no foot he can hear treadin. Hit comes lak an Injun. Hit lays lak a copperhead amongst the dead leaves. Hit lays on the bare ground, but a man never takes no notice for hit has got the color the ground has got.

I done what I could. What I seen them women do for Old Man Marmadukes wife one time when she come to bed. Marie laid there, and hit looked lak she was gittin ready to die. She yelled, and there was not nuthin I could do but name her name. Then I could not do that no more. Hit looked lak hit was not Marie layin there. Maybe hit was not me standin there, hit looked lak. Lak that time my Mammy was dyin and named my salvation and I stood there and my heart was lak flint rock in my bosom. His was hard and hit cut me, but I never even lifted up my hand. A hardness comes on a man. He is done froze up, and there ain't thaw nor freshit. Pore human love, hit is lak that unless hit is in Gods eye. In Gods eye and in his blessed name.

I seen Marie layin there and moanin and yellin when the pain taken holt. I said, she is goin to die. I said that but hit looked lak I taken no count of hit. Hit was lak hit was not nuthin to me. I seen her lay and twist. I heard her yell. And hit come on me to just turn my back and walk out the door and leave her lay. I seen myself walk off down the mountain where hit was dark and no stars to speak of, and hit was quiet and no yellin. I never done hit, but hit come on me. Hit don't matter I never done hit. Hit come on me, and I say hit is my shame.

The young un come and she did not die. She laid there quiet. I taken hit and washed hit and done lak them women done at Old Man Marmadukes. I laid hit down on the bed alongside of Marie, and I covered hit and her up good. Then I chunked up the fire, what was gittin low to ash, and put on some more wood. Then I set down in a chair. I set there till day.

VII

We named him Frank for the old Frencher her father who had a name like Frank in French talk. He had blue eyes lak the old Frencher had. He was a buster and he thrived good. But Marie was puny. Hit looks lak you can't tell about women. A man gits him one of them big stout-looking women whats got good teeth and is full of laughin and bouncin, but she has her a young un and it ain't no time till she is draggin and ain't no good for nuthin. And I seen lots of them little spry women quick lak Marie when she had a mind what has a half a dozen kids and hit ain't nuthin to them. My Mammy was little and spry and nuthin never fazed her. Marie, hit got so she was not no account for nuthin. She taken yerbs and such what the women give her and boughten medicine. And hit got so bad I got a doctor from Cashtown. But he could do nuthin but retch out his hand and say gimme when payin time come.

She done her work, but hit was trial and strain. She done her best, but many a time I come in from work and she was settin there white in the face and hit was me put the skillet on the stove. She always was a hand to set still and quiet, but now she was still and there was not no sparkle come. There was not no sparkle in her no more. Except maybe and hit rare when she taken up little Frank and helt him.

I spent money for her, but hit did not do no good. She seen me when I taken money out of that tin can where I kept hit, and she said for me not to. She said she didn't want Jacob's money spent on her. Hell, I said, hit is my money. She said to keep hit that a time might be comin when we would need hit worse. Hell, I said, we couldn't need hit no worse.

But the time come. The Company boss said they wasn't goin to pay us like afore. They was goin to cut our pay ten cents for ever hour. Hit come to a lot ever week. They said the Company wasn't makin nuthin and they couldn't pay hit lak afore.

A man was there workin in the sawmill by the name of Sweetwater. Nobody knowed where he come from but he come there short after me. He was a chunky built man and stout and he was a good hand at the mill everybody said. He never got in no trouble or nuthin. He was good-dispositioned and laughed. But he said the Company had plenty of money. He said he knowed hit had plenty. He said he knowed who got the money and hit was them rich fellers what taken the money from the Company. He said they was rich fellers what taken the money what by rights ought to come to them as had bought a piece of the Company and to us what worked for the Company. He said he knowed. He said if everybody quit workin for the Company all of a sudden and didn't nobody work for them, then they would have to pay us good. They would have to pay us more than afore. He said hit was ourn, and that was the way folks done to git paid better. He got folks to listen to him, and them as listened to him talked to other folks. Three weeks and everybody quit. Hit was a strike, what they called hit.

They was fellers from the city come to talk. They made speeches and talked and said how the Company couldn't pay no more and how folks ought to know hit and git back to work. Unless they wanted to starve and not git nuthin. But they wasn't but a few and them not many what wanted to git back to work. Then they brung in strangers to the Mountain to work. They was all sorts of folks. They wasn't no tellin where they come from. They was goin to do our work, and them strangers, and us git nuthin. That was what Sweetwater said. He said was we goin to let them sons of bitches do hit and us git nuthin. He said wan't true man would do hit. He said he wouldn't. He taken his stand and ast them as would be true men to git by his side. He talked good. They come to him. I wasn't the fust, but I never tarried. I was amongst them as stood by his side.

He said not let them fellers work. He said not let them git in the sawmill nor touch a axe or crosscut in the tool sheds nor lay hand to harness to hitch air mule nor put yoke on ox. He said to git somethin be it axe handle or canthook or lug hook or roll hook, and stand up there and keep them fellers off. But he said not to use no gun or cuttin knife. He said not to use no canthook nor nuthin but yore bare knucks if them fellers did not use nuthin else. He said just have them things layin there.

We kept them fellers off. They tried three times. Two times hit was bare knucks and then they come with one thing and another they had laid holt to. Sweetwater picked him up a canthook and yelled, come on boys hit is goin to be a play party. Hit was not no play party for some of them fellers. Hit was busted heads and busted arms and legs. They was layin on the ground and they drugged them off. Them fellers didn't stay on the Mountain. Then the Company brung more fellers and constables and depities with guns. Them constables come up with guns, and told us to git off, and Sweetwater looked at them and said, hell, they ain't goin to shoot nobody, they shoot somebody and they ain't got enuf bullets to go round if the boys git mad. He told them to shoot him if they wanted to start. They never shot him. Them other fellers stayed there on the Mountain but they never bothered us for two days more. Then they said they was another big strike nigh Cashtown, and another one in the coal.

Then Private Porsum come on the Mountain. He made another speech at Tomtown, and told how the Company could not pay no more and how we was breakin the law. Folks from Cashtown and Tomtown come and told us. They said the folks hearkened good to the Private. Sweetwater said the Private was with the rich fellers and was lyin, and a feller said Private Porsum never lied, he was not no man to lie. That feller said he believed the Private because he come off the Mountain.

He has done come a long way off the Mountain, Sweetwater said.

He ain't forgot, the feller said.

Maybe he ain't forgot, Sweetwater said, but he ain't forgot neither how hit feels to have money in the bank and he ain't forgot where he gits his money. He gits it from them rich fellers for talkin lak they tells him. And he gits hit off yore back and gits hit off yore table.

Hit is a lie, the feller said.

Then everybody looked for Sweetwater to do somethin, to hit him or somethin for callin him a liar. We seen how he told that constable to shoot him and give him the dare, and then Sweetwater didn't do nuthin but let that feller call him a liar.

I ain't sayin how Sweetwater didn't do right. Maybe he done Bible right. I swear and believe he done right. But then it made me plum disgusted. I was not no Bible man in them days. I was in the dark and the wicked world. I was sunk down in the world's ways. I was plum disgusted for Sweetwater.

Then Sweetwater ast him, you got kids ain't you?

The feller said, yes.

They got shoes on the feet, Sweetwater ast him.

Naw, the feller said.

They got plenty cover on the bed, he ast him.

Shet up, the feller said.

They got meat and bread on the table, Sweetwater ast him.

The feller never said nuthin, he just looked at Sweetwater.

They don't stand round, Sweetwater ast him, and say Pappy gimme somethin to eat.

The feller never said nuthin but I seen him squinch up round the eyes lak he was sightin down a gun barrel, and aimin at Sweetwater.

They don't wake up in the night, Sweetwater ast him, and say Pappy I'm hongry.

Then that feller just yelled God damn yore soul. And he jumped at Sweetwater swingin his arms.

But he never hit him. They grabbed him fust.

Folks was standin there and seen hit. But they seen too how Sweetwater taken a lie offen him.

Then Private Porsum come on the Mountain. He stood on a wagin and made a speech. I knowed he was my cousin but I never seen him afore. I knowed how he was in the war and what he done to them Germins. I knowed how he never taken nuthin for killin no human man, and how he would not be nuthin but a Private soljer. I heard him talk. He was a big fine lookin man, standin up there on that wagin, and he talked good.

A feller standin alongside of me, he said, Ashby ain't he yore cousin.

I said he was my cousin. He was my second blood cousin.

The Private said the Company was doin good as hit could. He said they couldn't pay no more. He said if they paid more there wouldn't be no Company in no time, and everybody would be ruint. He said to git back to work lak the folks done nigh Cashtown and at Tomtown and down at the coal mine. He said he come to say hit because he had not never forgot how the folks on the Mountain was his own folks. He said he come to ease his mind because he did not want to know of no trouble amongst his own folks.

Then somebody yelled, Private how you git yore money.

I knowed hit was Sweetwater. He was standin nigh me and I knowed his voice.

The Lord has prospered me, Private Porsum said, and he said he give thanks.

The Lord and the Massey Mountain Lumber Company, Sweetwater yelled.

Folks stepped back from round Sweetwater. There was just me and him standin nigh.

The Lord and the Atlas Iron Company, Sweetwater yelled agin.

Then somebody yelled for him to shet up.

But he never stopped. He yelled, Private who sent you up here.

I come to ease my mind, the Private said, and do right.

Private Porsum, Sweetwater yelled, do you stand there and say before God and man nobody sent you up here.

I say hit, the Private said.

And I, Sweetwater yelled, and he stopped and everybody looked at him, say hit's a God damn lie. And he laughed.

I was standin nigh, and I seen him when he called the Private a lie. He had done taken the lie hisself offen a feller and everybody standin by and no shame hit looked lak. And now give the Private a lie. Hit made me disgusted and sick to puke when Sweetwater taken that lie hisself and just laughed, and now he give the Private a lie and a man as takes a lie and don't do nuthin but laugh, he ain't got no right, hit looked lak to me, to be puttin the lie on nobody. I didn't say hit so to myself all of a sudden, but hit come to me later thataway. I just seen him put a lie on the Private and him my cousin, and lak I got disgusted afore I got mad. I got mad all of a sudden. I give hit to Sweetwater.

I give him a jolt on the side of the head. He come down on his knee, and I give hit to him agin. But he was tough. Afore I knowed hit he done butted me in the stomach and grabbed me. He wasn't no big man, but stout in the arms. He nigh throwed me and me beatin on him. But I snaked him with my leg and we come down. He got my arm twisted and nigh broke hit and me beatin on him. He would broke hit if I hadn't laid holt of a chunk of rock. I never knowed I grabbed hit. I give hit to him right in the face. He slipped his holt and I seen the blood on his face and him layin there. I seen the chunk in my hand lak I never knowed I had helt hit. Then I seen him and hit looked lak I didn't care if I had hit him with a chunk.

I done a lot of fightin in my time of sin and revelin. But I always fit fair. If hit was bare knucks hit was bare knucks, if hit was stomp and gouge hit was stomp and gouge. I always let the other feller call the tune and hist the burden. I never used no chunk on nobody. But hit was a chunk I give Sweetwater, and hit looked lak I didn't care. Hit was on me so. He started to git up and I kicked him. Right in the side.

Then some fellow come at me. They was fightin all round of a sudden. Some fellers was aimin to help Sweetwater, but not no plenty, and fellers was fightin them. Sweetwater tried to git up but some feller was beatin on him.

They was not many fellers with Sweetwater. Them others beat them good. Constables taken Sweetwater and some of the others with him and put them in jail down at Cashtown. I never seen him agin. They said he was bad beat up.

I am sorry and grieve I used a chunk on Sweetwater. I ought never kicked him. I ought never lifted up my hand agin him in no way. If I had helt my hand, maybe nuthin would happened. Maybe they would not been no fightin. Maybe the Company would paid us good and decint. Maybe they would not come no bad times on the Mountain lak come, and not long. Hit has come to me Sweetwater was a good man.

But I ain't never said the Private was not no good man. A big man lak what never taken nuthin for doin what he done to them Germins, he ain't goin to take money offen pore folks, and them his own folks and with young uns. I ain't never said he did not aim to do good lak he said when he come on the Mountain. Hit ain't for me to judge. Not him or no man. Not and me what I been and what I am. Oh Lord, I was dirt and you taken me up from the dark ground and blowed yore breath in me, but I am sinful and weak.

VIII

Next day they was work. Folks started cuttin and haulin and workin in the mill again. Nigh everybody went to work agin, but them what was in jail down to Cashtown or too bad beat up. But they was some said they be God damn if they would work for the Company no more, and left. If they had anywheres to go. But not many, for a man has to git bread and meat. The pay wasn't good as afore, but the Company did say they wouldn't cut hit no ten cents ever hour. They cut hit eight cents, what helped some. But hit was tight, and I seen folks hongry.

I went to work agin. I worked five weeks lak afore. Then one Saturday the woods boss said to me, Wyndham, they ain't no use comin back Monday mornin, they ain't no work for you. And I ast him, why, ain't I done good. He said, good as the next un. I said, why, and he said, hit looks lak they's cuttin down, and they said to git shed of these fellers. He helt a piece of paper in his hand and hit had five names on hit. They was five of us got told not to come back.

I tried to git somethin to do. I went down to Cashtown and tried to git hit. But they wasn't nuthin. I tried the Atlas Iron Company and they wasn't nuthin. I went plum down to the coal mine, and they said they didn't have no use for me. Hit taken me a day to git down there and a day to git back and after night. I left Marie with Frank home and nobody there, but I had to git down and see. I went to Tomtown. Hit was the same. Hit was winter and I couldn't make no gardin patch nor nuthin. I couldn't help nobody farmin. I tried cuttin stovewood with a feller had a wagin and sellin hit in Tomtown and we got a few dollars. But then we cut some more and couldn't git shed of hit. I taken nigh all what money was left in the tin can where I kept hit hid to git somethin to eat for Marie and Frank. They et somethin, and Marie made no complaint. I paid on the house one month, then I didn't pay. I wasn't goin to take money for somethin to eat and pay on the house. I told the man I would make hit up. I ast him to let me work hit out, but he said he didn't have no work.

I was comin down the road and I met a feller named Bud Jeffers. I knowed him workin for the Company. He ast me how I was makin out. I said I wasn't makin out. He said he wasn't makin out neither. Ain't you workin, I ast him. Naw, he said, they told him to git out. He said they told some more to git out. Eleven hit was. He ast me didn't I hear tell, and I said naw. Everybody, he said, what taken sides with Sweetwater at fust, ever one. Everybody what talked for Sweetwater about not workin, ever one.

They told me they was just cuttin down, I said.

Cuttin down on them as was with Sweetwater at fust, he said, and taken his side. You taken his side. I taken his side. All them fellers taken his side.

Hit can't be so, I said, for hit was me knocked Sweetwater down. For callin the Private a lie. Hit was me knocked him down.

You was a durn fool to do hit, he said.

That was what he named me. A durn fool.

I seen a time I busted a man for callin me a durn fool. I come nigh bustin Bud Jeffers standin there in the road. Hit looked lak I was goin to. Then all of a sudden they wasn't no mad-meaness in me. They wasn't nuthin in me, meaness or nuthin else. Hit was lak the bottom drops out of a bucket of a sudden and the water is spilt. I just stood there and they wasn't nuthin in me lak a old man done used up. I seen Bud Jeffers walk on down the road.

I looked up in the sky. Hit was gray, lak to snow. Not gray clouds seperit lak, but all gray and low hangin. I looked acrost the valley over them black trees what didn't have no leaves, and over them few houses I seen but they was little hit was so far, and lak they wasn't nobody in them. Lak folks had done gone and left them. I looked acrost the valley where the sky come down to the hills, but hit was mist-smoky hit was so far, and a man couldn't say for sure where the hills left off and the sky begun. The sky was layin on the hills.

Hit was lak a man knowed how hit was to be by hisself. To be by hisself and not nuthin. Hit was lak I was myself in the world, and not nobody else. Not Marie. And not Frank. Lak there hadn't never been no Marie and no Frank and no Pappy and Mammy and no Jacob. Not nobody but me, and me nuthin.

Hit was lak the time Frank died. Hit was lak I was standin there in the road by myself and the time was comin and everwhere was so quiet I could nigh hear hit steppin stealthy. Lak a man out at night hears somethin and stops of a sudden and hearkens. Then

he says, naw, hit ain't nuthin but the wind maybe. And he goes
on.

A man listens quiet and he can hear the Lord's foot mashin
down the hills. Lak they wasn't nuthin but old ruts in the road
with the mud done dried where the wagin wheel squeshed hit up
soft. He hears hit but he don't know to name hit.

Frank died in February. Hit was in his throat and hit looked
lak he couldn't git no breath. He died all of a sudden, lak he come
of a sudden and his Mammy not ready. It was lak he come of a
sudden and was in a hurry for he knowed he didn't have no time
much to stay.

They put him in the ground, and we seen hit.

We come home and we was in the house, but we never knowed
one another. Marie laid on the bed and shet her eyes, and I wasn't
nuthin to her. I kept tryin to git her to listen to me, but she
wouldn't unshet her eyes for nuthin. Hit come dark, and I set
there. Now and agin I put some wood on the fire. Marie laid there,
but I wasn't nuthin to her. I looked at her, and I knowed she
wasn't nuthin to me. She was lak a old coat somebody done flung
down, and I didn't know who. I couldn't look at her of a sudden
and know she wasn't nuthin to me. I knowed why she wouldn't
unshet her eyes. She couldn't bear and endure to see my face. I
knowed hit. Ain't nobody nuthin of his own strength when the rub
comes, and a man knows hit of a sudden and hit is lak he was
crossin a river on the ice at night and the ice breaks. Hit is lak he
goes down of a sudden. The cold water is on him, and the blackness, and ain't nobody to hear him yell.

I knowed Marie wasn't nuthin to me, and hit was lak I went
through the ice. I couldn't bear and endure to see her layin there
and know hit.

I stood up and I went out the door. That night when Frank
come into this here world of sin and pain, I stood and seen his
Mammy layin there and heard her yell, and it come on me to walk
out of that air house, and hit night time, and walk and keep on
walkin where hit was dark and there wasn't no yellin or nuthin.
Hit come on me but I never done hit. But this time when I seen
her layin there with her eyes shet and I knowed of a sudden she
wasn't nuthin to me and my heart was like a orange squoze dry and
thowed down, I up and went out the door. I never made up my

mind to git out. I didn't even know I had done left. One minute I was standin lookin at her lay and the next I was out in dark and I was runnin up the road with my feet hittin on the froze-hard ground and my head throwed back lookin up in the sky where the stars was showin, lak they do in winter time. I never knowed how I got there.

I run on the Mountain. I wasn't carin where. Just so I was runnin. I wasn't on no road. I was going acrost rock and dead bresh. I run into hit and hit snatched and tore me. I kept on runnin. I never felt hit. I fell down on them rocks, and I got up and run agin.

I fell down and I didn't git up. I laid and I didn't know nuthin. Then I knowed the breathin was lak fire in my chist when I drawed hit, but hit didn't matter none to me for hit was lak hit was somebody else's chist. I laid and hit was quiet and I seen how them stars was in the sky and steady.

I was hearin my name. Maybe I was hearin hit for a long spell layin there and didn't know, lak when you ain't waked up and somebody keeps callin yore name. You hears yore name named and knows hit, but you ain't hearin either. Then hit was clear. Hit said, Ashby, Ashby, Ashby Wyndham.

Hit was Frank callin me. He was callin his Pappy. He hadn't never said mortal word in this world. He never got big enuff to say no word true and proper. But I knowed hit was him. I knowed hit lak he was a growed boy and I had knowed his voice.

Frank, I said, Frank.

And he said, Yes sir, Pappy, lak he was a mannered boy.

Frank, I said, where are you.

I am right here, Pappy, he said.

Frank, I said, I can't see you for the dark.

Hit is dark to mortal eye, he said.

Oh, Frank, I said, and hit looked lak my heart would bust, why did you up and leave, why did you git up and go, didn't we treat you good.

Oh, Pappy, he said, Oh, Pappy, I grieve to tell.

Why did you have to up and go, I said.

Oh, Pappy, he said, I couldn't thrive none and hit the vittles of wickedness. I couldn't thrive and hit vittles and sop taken in blood wrath and wickedness. And from Jacob. Hit was from yore brother

Jacob you taken hit. Them vittles come in my throat and my throat swelled for wickedness and I had to up and go.

Oh, Frank, I commenst, but wouldn't no words come.

I come lak the Lord sent me little and pure, he said, and the Lord he taken me so.

Oh, Frank, I said, and the big tears bust like a freshet.

Pappy, Pappy, he said.

Oh, Frank, I said, what can I do.

Don't cry, Pappy, he said.

What can I do, I said.

You can git up and find Jacob, he said, and take him by the hand.

I can't never find him, I said.

You can walk in the world, he said, till you find him. He is walkin in the world amongst strangers, and you can walk in the world. You can ast folks. You can tell folks how it was with you, and how you lifted up yore hand agin him and them others, and how no man ought never to. You can ast have they seed him. And the Lord will lead you and put yore hand in Jacob's hand.

Frank, I commenst.

Give my Mammy a kiss for me, he said.

Frank, Frank, I said, but he was done gone. He had said his say, and he was done gone.

I got up offen the cold ground. I went down the Mountain. Light was just showin blue and weak over Massey when I come to my house and entered in hit.

I seen Marie layin there. She was sleepin. I went to her and I lent over and I kissed her lak Frank said. She opened her eyes slow and looked at me. Hit was a kiss from little Frank, I said.

And I knelt down beside the bed and let my head lay and she put her hand on my head.

IX

We give what little truck and plunder we had to them as needed hit more than we did. We taken some clothes to keep clean and decent in a bundle, and a skillet to cook in, and nigh four dollars I had, and we walked down off the Mountain. We come to a settlemint, and then they was more settlemints and towns, and I ast folks had they met with Jacob, and told them how I come to be huntin him. I done forgot the names of haf them places. We stopped in them places and I done what I could git to do. We was hungry and hit no lie more than one night when the sun went down. We laid down and the belly was drawed, and the sun come and hit was the same. But the Lord taken mind on the sparrow, and the Lord taken mind on us. He give me work to do, and he put bread and meat in our mouth. Folks taken us in and they give us bite and sup and we give thanks. I never ast for nuthin. I done somethin ever time to pay.

I stood in the street and I told folks how hit was. How the Lord had laid hit on me to tell folks. I told them my wickedness and how the wicked man will come down low. I met folks in the big road and I told them. I told them how peace come in my heart and hit was lak sunshine when the clouds are done gone. And I met folks as taken heed. You meet a man in the road as has got a coat on his back and his belly full and folks give him a good name and got a tight roof over his head and money in his pants. Hit looks lak he ain't thinkin on nuthin but gittin and thrivin and takin his ease, and you tells him how peace come in yore heart. But you name peace in yore heart and you look in his face and hit is drawed of a sudden. Hit is lak they was a old stitch or a old pain in him and he ain't thought nuthin on hit and all of a sudden he knows somethin is in him growin and he gits cold all over and knows he is goin to die and wrys up his face. Maybe he will make his heart hard and he will tell you to git out of his way. But you know they ain't no peace in his heart. And he knows hit and wrys up his face. But I met a man in the road nigh a settlemint by the name of Sumatry and I told him how hit was. You got peace in yore heart, he ast me.

I told him I did, and give praise. He looked at me nigh half a minute. The Lord bless you, he said of a sudden. Then he said, and the Lord have mercy on my soul.

He was a big man with a black beard all curly, and he had on a black coat and a gold watch and chain and he was ridin in a buggy. He said that to me and then he went off down the road in the buggy.

I come to towns and I stood in the street where the folks was and I read to them folks out of the Bible. I give them the Lords word lak hit come to me and I told them how hit was with me.

Hit was eight months when we come to Mitchell Landin. Hit is a settlemint on the river, and they was buildin a bridge there. I got me work on the bridge, and Murry got him work. Murry was a big boy, and he could do work lak a man. He taken up with us from a town up the valley. He did not have no folks. He was a orfin in the world, and he come with us. He could not read none but he would set and listen and hearken when I read what the Bible said. I read hit and he never moved.

They was a feller workin on the bridge by the name of Jasper Littlefoot. Me and him, we was workin alongside, swingin a pick and shevil where the road was goin to the bridge. I ast him did he live in Mitchell Landin, and he said, naw he did not. I ast him where he come from, lak a man will and him civil. He did not say nuthin and I reckined he did not ketch me good. So I ast him agin. He histed up his shevil lak he was gittin ready to blast me over the head, and he said you son of a bitch. He said hit agin. I did not do nuthin. I looked at him and I said, you named me a son of a bitch, I am a pore sinful man in Gods sight but I ain't no son of a bitch. He did not say no more, and he put down his shevil.

They was a feller seen hit and hit was afterwards he said to me, that feller Littlefoot nigh killed you.

Why, I ast him.

He done kilt one man, he said.

Why was he fixin to kill me, I ast him.

Because you ast him where he come from, he said. And he laughed and he spat out on the ground and he said, he is right touchous if you ast him where he come from, he is touchous because he come from the pen.

He told me that feller was in the pen ten years for killin a man. He had not been out no time, and he was touchous. He did not have nuthin to do with folks. He lived in a old shanty boat on the river by hisself.

The next day when we quit workin about sun, I seen Littlefoot start walkin off. I walked aside of him. I said to him, I was in a dark prisen and I laid in the dark.

He did not say nuthin. He just kept walkin and lookin down the road lak they was not nobody but hisself.

I laid in the dark, I said, and I was a lost man and somebody put a key in the lock and throwed the door wide open and the light come in so strong I blinked blind for the brightness.

Yeah, he said, yeah, they put a key in my lock and they throwed the door open but hit taken them ten years.

He said hit but he never looked at me when he done hit.

I laid longer, I said.

How long, he said.

Not ten years, I said, hit was more than a score.

He looked at me right clost, and he seen I was not no old man, and he said, they must have put you in for bitin yore Mammy on the tit.

Naw, I said, naw, but I laid in the dark nigh all my life, I laid in the prisen cell but hit was the dark of sin and wickedness where I laid.

He looked at me agin. He stopped in the road and looked at me and scan me clost, and he did not say but one word. Hit was a word I ain't goin to put on no paper. Hit was a word of filthiness and abominations. But he give me a look and hit was all he said. Then he started walkin down the road.

But when the job out at the bridge was done finished he taken up with us. I had done told him how hit was with me. I had done read the Lords blessed word to him. We had done been down on our knee bones together afore God and him most High.

I done said he lived by hisself on a shanty boat. He taken us on the shanty boat with him. We was goin down the river and we was goin to tell the Gospel to them as had ears.

We come to towns and places on the river. We worked to git money to buy a little somethin to eat. We fished in the river. Jasper had him a old squirril rifle and we kilt squirrils and rabbits and et them. We was a long time on the river, comin down. We stayed at places a long time and worked and told folks about Gods blessed word and how peace come in our hearts. Then when hit come on us to be goin we went down the river. A old man and his wife taken up with us at a town they named Cherryville. The house they had had done burnt plum down to the ground and the grandbaby they was raisin. That baby was all the folks they had. Our baby has done gone to the Lord, the old man said, and we done turned our eyes to the Lord. They had the name of Lumpkin. He was a old man, but he washed a lot and kept hisself clean. He had been a hand to chaw and smoke, he said, but when the Gospel taken holt he give hit up. Hit was a filthiness, he said.

We seen days hungry and we seen days cold on the river. But we taken what the Lord sent and knowed hit was good. We give praise and rejoicin.

I always ast if folks had seen Jacob. At one place they was a man as thought he had seen him. But he was not positive of a certain.

Hit was nigh a year on the river and we come to Hulltown. Hit was a big town. Hit was the biggest town I ever seen afore we come to the city here where the Lord has done led us. At Hulltown they was a furnace where they melted the iron out of the rock they taken out of the ground. I got me a job workin at the furnace. And Jasper got him a job. Hit was the Lords blessin for we needed money bad. Old Sister Lumpkin was down and porely. Marie watched her and tended on her but we needed money to git her somethin to eat as would stay on her stummick and to git her medicine.

In Hulltown we taken Pearl from the house of abominations.

Hit was summer and I was comin down the street in a part of town where I had not never been. Hit was Sunday evenin at sun, and I was just walkin for hit had come on me so. Hit was not dark yit but them lights in the street come on just a minute after I seen the house. Them lights in town come on long afore a man had good need. I seen the house and I seen the two of them settin on the porch laughin and talkin. Hit was a yeller house set by a alley. The other houses nigh hit was not houses for folks to dwell in, and they was closed up for a Sunday. Hit had a fence around hit and a gate. I seen the woman and the man settin there, and I stopped at the gate. I give them a good evenin as best I knowed. The woman said good evenin but the man did not say nuthin.

She was a medium size woman and her hair was yeller. The man was a big man. They both had on fine clothes, I seen. They was settin in a swing and the man had his arm around the woman. The woman had on a yeller dress.

I ast could I come in. I had not aimed to but the Lord laid hit on my tongue lak he done them days. I seen somebody and the Lord laid hit on my tongue may be. If he did not I never said nuthin. But I ast them could I come in a minute.

They ain't nuthin stoppin you, the woman said. The man did not say nuthin. He just looked at me lak I was a mule he might buy but did not reckin he would.

I said thank you kindly, and I went in that air gate. I come on the porch.

The lady said the other girls would not be back till nigh eight o'clock. She ast did I want to see one of the girls.

I said, no mam.

Well you better git on and peddle yore apples, the man said to me. You ain't got no business here, he said.

I know I ain't, I said, but the Lord has.

For Christ sake, the man said, and he knocked the ashes off his cigar.

What do you want, the lady ast me.

Hell, the man said, he dont want nuthin he can pay for. Then he said to me, buddy, this is a high class place and you better git.

I was gittin ready to say excuse me please and git on, but the lady ast me what did I want.

Hell, says the man, he wants a dime to git him a cup of coffee. He retched in his pants and he taken a dime. He throwed the dime on the floor in front of me. I let hit lay.

I dont want no dime, I told him. I was gittin ready to go, I said, but yore wife ast me what I come for.

Wife, the man said, and he bust out laughin.

The lady did not laugh. He shaken her with his arm lak he was tryin to make her laugh. She said, I dont see nuthin so God dam funny.

He stopped laughin of a sudden and he said to me, you git on.

But the lady said to him, Claude you act too dam big, you act lak you own the place. She told him to shut up and take his God dam hands offen her.

He got mad. You could see he was gittin mad. You talk that way to me, he said, and you let that God dam trash come in here, and he ain't got a dime.

I am a pore man, I said, but I ain't trash. I am a pore man but I got Jesus in my heart.

This is a hell of a place to bring Jesus, the man said and he laughed agin. I seen his heart was hardened.

She did not pay no mind. She ast me what did I want.

I did not want nuthin, mam, I said, the Lord just laid hit on me to come in and ast did you have the peace of Jesus in yore heart.

Well you done ast it, the lady said, and now you can git out.

You can just take yore bleedin Jesus and git out, the man said to me, afore I knock the bleedin Jesus out of you.

Mister, I said to him, I am goin to go. I come not meanin no harm. The Lord laid hit on me to come and the Lord lays hit on me to go, and not no human man.

Git out, he said.

I am, I said, but I am goin in the Lord and not for you.

I ought never said hit. A man can be proud and high in the Lord lak he can in pore human pride and hit is a sin. Hit is a worse sin.

The hell you say, the man said.

I turned round and started down the steps. I never looked back. I did not see him git up from that air swing. I did not know nuthin till I felt him kick me where a man sets down. I was on them steps and hit knocked me plum down on the ground and me not expectin hit.

The man was standing there laughin. I got up and I seen the lady was laughin too. I was surprised the lady was laughin.

I went to the gate and the lady kept on laughin. Mam, I said, hit ain't fitten for you to laugh.

All right, the man said, and I will bust you agin.

He come down off the porch. I walked on slow. I knowed he was comin but I never looked back. I heard him comin on the walk behind me. I got to the end of the fence where the alley was and he hit me on the side of the head. He knocked me down.

I will learn you to talk that way to a lady, he said.

I was layin there. Hit was night now but he was standin under the light hangin in the street and I seen him good.

I got up and he give hit to me agin. I nigh give hit back to him, but I never. I knowed hit was not the Lords will for me to. I knowed hit all come on me because I taken sinful pride in the Lord, and hit is a sin. He give hit to me three times afore he knocked me down.

The lady come out the gate and was standin there.

I got up and he knocked me down agin. I was layin in the alley.

The lady was laughin. If he won't fight lak a man, she said, kick him lak he was a dog.

I will learn him to fight, the man said.

I come up and he give hit to me three times. He knocked me down.

Kick him, the lady said. Kick him lak he was a dog.

She was laughin and goin on but hit was not lak folks laughs of a common. Hit was lak she did not know she was laughin and she could not stop hit.

I got up agin when I could. I got up slow because he had shore messed me up. He was a big man. He was nigh as big as they come. He was gittin fat but he had his strength.

I got up and he give hit to me. But just then I seen a man come round the corner of the alley. I seen hit was a police man. But just then that man give hit to me on the jaw just that time the lady stopped laughin and looked at that police man. That police man said somethin but I never understood what hit was. I did not understand for hit was right then I done hit. I did not aim to and I did not rightly know I done hit till I seen that man layin there and his head on the brickwalk. Somethin must have went pop inside me for I never knowed what I done. That man must have turned round to see who that police man was. He must have got offen his balance. He must have not been careful or somethin to let a man what was fixed lak I was knock him down.

I seen him layin there and I seen the police man. I knowed he was goin to take me.

He said, Miss Pearl what is goin on here.

Miss Pearl was that ladys name.

She stopped laughin and she pointed at him was layin with his head on the brick walk and she said, hit is him.

She said somethin else but I never knowed what hit was. I did not know nuthin. I just sunk down on the ground.

I come to and I was layin on a bed. Hit was a good bed and sweet smellin. Then I seen that lady standin there. She ast how did I feel.

I tetched my face with my hand. Hit was swole up lak a punkin.

You done stopped bleedin, she said, but you ain't no pretty pitcher.

I ast was the police man goin to take me to jail.

Why that was Mr. Duffy, she said, why Mr. Duffy has done taken him.

Ain't they goin to take me, I said.

Naw, she said, Mr. Duffy is a friend of mine and he takes what ones I say take. I said for Mr. Duffy to take him and he taken him. They had to take him in a ambulance and I bet he ain't come round yit with his head bust lak hit was.

I ought never done hit, I said.

Hit was not yore fault, she said, I reckin hit was Jesus fault. Jesus just taken his eyes offen you a secont lak he had not ought to. He must have winked, maybe.

I said I had to git on home.

You ain't fitten to go no wheres, she said.

I said I had to git on home.

She ast me where did I stay at.

I told her on the shanty boat. And I got offen that bed.

Hit is a long way, she said, and you ain't in no shape.

I said I was goin.

She said she was goin to git me there. I am goin to see you git there, she said.

She done hit for all of me.

X

We was movin on the river. They was me and Marie and Old Man Lumpkin and Mrs. Lumpkin and Murry what was gittin to be nigh a man and Jasper and Pearl. They was sevin of us countin Pearl. She come to the shanty boat that night with me. Hit was the Lords will she come for I lak not to got there. Just afore we got there she nigh had to tote me. We got right to hit and I sunk down and did not know nuthin. I come to and I seen I was on the boat. I seen Marie standin there, and she ast me how did I feel. I said I felt better than I did last night.

Last night, she said, last night, this ain't tomorrer, this is the day after tomorrer and hit is gittin nigh to sun.

I had laid there the enduren time and not known.

And we is on the river, she said. We is a long way on the river from Hulltown.

How come, I ast her.

She pointed and I seen where she pointed and there was that lady standin. She said for us to git on, Marie said.

She had ast Marie to git on. She said she aimed to pray God and worship and rejoice if he would stretch out his hand and learn her. But she said she did not reckin she would learn good in Hulltown, and her weak and frail.

I seen her standin there and I lak not to knowed her. She was not wearin that yeller dress lak she had been. She was wearin a old dress belonged to Mrs. Lumpkin. Just a old common dress down to her feet and decent.

Marie said how that night she brung me she set there all night or helped her and Mrs. Lumpkin fix for me. When light come she ast them to git on. She taken Marie by the hand and ast her. And when they got started good she ast Mrs. Lumpkin who was nigh of a size did she have air old dress, and she taken off that yeller dress and put on Mrs. Lumpkins dress and she throwed that yeller dress in the river. She said she would not give hit to nobody. Said no decent woman would not want to wear a dress of hern.

I seen her standin there in that old dress and barefoot. She had throwed her pointed shoes in the river.

Her hair was still yeller but hit was not all curly lak afore. She looked lak she was oldern I knowed. She was oldern me and Marie.

She done her part. When we stopped at them towns she worked when she could git work to do. If she could not git no work she taken care of the boat and cooked the vittles for us. She had laid soft one time and now she laid hard. She had been in a bed was soft and sweet smellin and now hit was a pallet on the hard floor. But she did not never complain and she praised God how he taken her from the house of abominations. She prayed the Lord to take her by the hand and learn her to rejoice. She ast us to pray for her and named how she wallered in sin and grunted lak a hog after the worlds slop and taken no thought. She named hit and they was tears come in her eyes.

Marie said how of a night when the women was layin on the side of the curtin where they taken there rest and was sleepin she would wake up for Pearl grabbin holt of her hand. Pearl would grab holt of her hand in the dark.

Hit looked lak Marie was a sister to her.

When Marie come sick hit was Pearl set beside her and fanned them flies and give water for the burnin fever and taken no rest or ease.

Marie was sick eight days and she died.

Hit was sevin days and Marie said to me, Ashby I am goin to go.

She was nigh too weak to talk.

No, I said, hit can not be.

Yes, she said, hit is, I am flowin and movin away from here lak water down hill.

No, I said, and I did not know I had yelled hit out till the sound come lak I was yellin to somebody acrost the river.

Don't you fret and grieve Ashby, she said. Don't you take on.

No, I yelled.

Yes, she said, and I do not grieve for me. I grieve because I never brought you no good lak hit is for women, Ashby.

Oh Marie, I said, you give me what was to give. I laid in the dark till you come and they was a sparkle in you give light to my eyes. I seen the sparkle and I put out my hand towards hit lak a child baby not knowin what hit is. I sinned and I made you take on my sin and hit was flesh lust. A man dont love no woman true but in Gods eye but if he loves her in his pore man way maybe hit can learn him to love the Lord. Hit is lak a school and the young un goes to school and they learns him to spell and if he studies on hit he gits so he can read the Lords blessed word. Oh, Marie, I said to her, you learned me to spell, and I see hit clear.

She did not say nuthin, but she looked at me and I seen the sparkle in her. Hit come of a sudden lak long afore, and her layin sick now.

Marie, I said, I see hit clear now and not never afore.

She looked at me and she said, I will give little Frank a big kiss and a hug for his Pappy. She said not air other word.

The next evenin her sperit taken hits flight and left me to mourn.

Hit was Pearl washed her and fanned them flies after she was layin dead. We was not near no town or settlemint. We did not see no houses or nuthin but woods and cane thickits all that next day. I did not want to put her in the ground in no woods or cane thickit lak a varmint. Hit was August and the river was low with drout. The water did not hardly move. I set and looked at a old black stub of a dead tree and hit taken nigh all that mornen to git where hit was. Then hit taken all evenin to git where I could not see hit. We taken two days to git to a settlemint. Pearl set there and fanned them flies and tears come down her cheeks.

At the settlemint we bought them boards to make a coffin for Marie. We paid two dollars and twenty cents and Jasper and me made hit. We put her in the ground where they was a church and Christian folks was standin there.

I mourned for Marie. When my Pappy died I did not mourn for him. When my Mammy lay cold and dead, hit was not in me to mourn. My heart was lak flint rock in me and cuttin, but hit was not mournin. When little Frank died hit was not mournin I done. I run mad lak a dog on the mountain. But now I mourned for Marie and for all them I seen taste the bitterness and take there flight. When a man ain't in God he can not mourn. He can not truly mourn. I seen them not in God as fell down on the ground and tore there hair, but hit is a way of puttin a curse on God. Hit ain't mournin of a truth. After Marie died I set on the boat and looked at the river and smelled the mud stinkin where the water had done gone down low, and I seen how Marie was goin to lay in the stinkin ground, and I nigh put a curse on God. But hit was not mournin. Hit was a wildness and hit tears a man in two pieces. But to mourn in God and of his will is a kind of sweetness. Hit is gittin closter to them as is dead than ever you was and them livin and drawin breath. Hit is a gift God give, and I give praise.

They put Marie in the ground and I knowed how hit is to mourn. I mourned for her and for my Pappy and my Mammy and for Frank, and knowed Gods will.

We stayed in the settlemint three weeks and we worked and was amongst Christian folks and we give testifyin for the Lord.

Then we come agin on the river.

We come where they was fields and the corn was standin tall and yeller and ready for folks to come with wagins. I never seen no corn lak hit in Custiss. And I seen big fields for pasture and horses and cows standin. I seen them houses. They was big and white with paint on them and I seen folks settin in front or standin. Hit was lak a country I never heard tell.

Then we come nigh the city. They was smoke on the sky. Murry seen the smoke was fer off, and Pearl said hit was the city.

We come in the city under them bridges and seen all the folks walkin and ridin. We come in to the bank and Murry jumped off and taken the rope. They was folks ever where. More than a man could name. They was thick lak the corn we seen.

They is folks here as walks in sin, I said, and folks as walks in God. Hit is a field to the harvest. We are here and we are goin to testify to the saved and to the unsaved.

Old Man Lumpkin said amen.

We stood in the street and we testified. Folks was comin and goin. They was them as scoffed and scorned and them as heark-ened. We went in the city where the folks was thickest and we stood on the street and sang a song and rejoiced. Pearl sang good and Murry, and me and Mr. Lumpkin we taken the bass burden. We sang about Mary and her only son.

> Mary had a only son
> The Jews and Romans had him hung
> Keep yore hand on the plow hold on.
>
> They taken him to Cavalree
> And there they hung him on a tree
> Keep yore hand on the plow hold on.

We sung how they done hit and how he died to save. We told how he had done saved our souls and hit was peace in our hearts.

A police man come and said how we could not sing and testify. I told him how the Lord said his blessed word was for ever man. I showed him the place in the book. He said he could not help what hit said for us to git on.

We went to another place where they was folks movin and standin. We sung and testified. Hit was another police man come and said to git on.

We taken another stand and hit was the same. Ever where hit was the same. I tried to tell them how hit was and showed hit to them in the book but they said for us to git on. I was sore in my heart.

A saved man has got joy and rejoicin in his heart and he is bustin to tell. He has got Gods word in him and he has got peace and he has got to pour hit out to them as has ears. Hit is a joy to pour hit out and the joy is withouten end. But you dont let him tell and pour hit out of his heart and his heart is sore. He is lak a woman got a baby and her breast has got milk for that air baby and hit is a joy when hit takes hits suck and is helt to the tit. But you take that woman away from that air baby and her breast is swole and sore for the fulness. My heart was sore.

I told them was with me how hit was.

Pearl said for us to git to the boat and git on hit and leave.

I said why.

She said she was afeard of them police.

Jasper said he knowed them. He said they could not do nuthin but put you in jail. He said they would not beat no woman.

Pearl said she was not afeard of bein beat.

I am afeard of bein beat, Jasper said. They shore beat me one time when they taken me. I am afeard of bein beat but I will do what Ashby says. I aim to do Gods will.

I ain't afeard of bein beat, Pearl said. But they put you in jail and you lay there and they ain't nuthin for you. You are alone. And they let you out and they ain't nuthin for you or nobody. Hit does you harm.

They is God for you, I said.

Oh, God, she said, I am a pore woman and I am afeard to be alone. I need what help they is. I need them with me as has God in there heart to lift me up. Oh, God, she said, I am weak and frail.

I did not say nuthin. We went on down to the boat. I did not know nuthin to say. I was waitin for hit to come on me what to say.

We et and I read to them out of the book what is a ever present help. We prayed to God.

What we goin to do, Pearl ast.

I dont rightly know, I said. Hit will come on me, I said.

We taken our rest for hit was dark.

I nigh never slept that enduren night. I laid and called to God.

When light come I rose up and taken the book. I opened hit and looked and lo, I seen. Hit said, and Jesus said unto him no man havin put his hand to the plow and lookin back, is fittin for the Kingdom of God.

I knowed hit for a sign and come of God.

What we goin to do, Pearl ast me.

I read her what hit said.

Oh God, she said.

I laid in jail, Jasper said, when I was a sinful man, and taken hit. I reckin I can take hit now I aim to walk in God.

Oh God, Pearl said, I am weak and frail.

The Lord will keep holt on you with his hand, I said.

We went in the city lak afore. We sung and we give testifyin. Ever time a police man come and said for us to git on. But hit was all. They did not take nobody to jail. And ever time we come to another place and taken our stand.

Hit was after dinner time Mrs. Lumpkin come sick. She set on the pavemint and puked. After a spell she said she did not feel so bad. But I said for Old Man Lumpkin and Pearl to git her to the boat. And they done hit. Me and Jasper and Murry, we stayd and give testifyin some more. Then we come to the boat.

Mrs. Lumpkin was some better but porely.

She was porely the next mornin. I said for Pearl to stay with her while me and Jasper and Old Man Lumpkin went in the city. We come to a big market where folks brung vegitibles and chickins and such to sell and folks in the city comes and buys hit. We stood where they come in and went out and I read to them out of the book.

A police man come and said, for Christ sake you all git on somewheres else so I won't have to run you in.

I said to him we done come in Gods name.

Well for Christ sake, he said, you go somewheres else in Gods name and quit worryin folks.

I read to him what the book said.

Save hit for Sunday, he said, and git on.

We went round to another door where folks was.

Old Man Lumpkin said how he was worrit how Mrs. Lumpkin was makin out. I said I would go down to the boat and see how she was makin out. He was a old man and hit was hard for him to climb back up the hill. I said I would git a docter if she was not makin out so good and come tell him. I told him and Jasper to wait and not do no readin or testifyin or nuthin. I did not want them to git in no trouble and me not there.

I come to the boat and Mrs. Lumpkin was still porely. I said I was aimin to git a docter and she said naw, for the money. I said the money was not nuthin and her layin there and not makin out no better. She said naw, and I was argyin with her and of a sudden Pearl yelled somethin. Pearl was out front of the house part. She yelled agin, and I come out.

Hit is Murry, she yelled.

I seen Murry runnin down the hill. Then I seen a man behind him. Hit was a police man. The police man was yellin for him to stop but he never paid him no mind. They was another police man back up the hill was comin too. The first police man had a pistil in his hand I seen. I yelled for Murry to stop but he never.

The police man shot off his pistil but I seen he did not mean to shoot Murry.

Murry run up the board we had laid to the boat. He yelled they done taken Jasper and Old Man Lumpkin. He kicked that board in the water and he tried right quick to cut that rope as helt the boat. He taken out his knife to cut hit. They says how Murry taken out his knife to cut the police man but he never. He is a good boy and has got true peace in his heart. He did not mean nuthin when he broke loose from the police man up to the markit and tripped him up and run. He was afeard lak a young un, and taken no thought.

The first police man got there and he grabbed that big board out of the water. He was tryin to lay hit to the boat. Murry tried to kick hit loose but he slip and fell.

The other police man got there and he was yellin.

Then Pearl yelled right behind me. I looked round and seen her. She had that there old squirril rifle of Jasper in her hand.

Hit looked lak I could not say nuthin. Hit all come of a sudden.

Them police men throwed the board on and was yellin. One of them put his foot on the board.

Oh God, Pearl said loud.

Pearl, I yelled, Pearl. And I aimed to grab holt of that rifle.

She shot off that old squirril rifle.

I seen that police man put his hands on his stummick afore he fell in the water.

Murry had got up and was cuttin on the big rope. He cut hit.

I felt the river take holt of the boat. Hit was not much for the water was low with the drout but we had done slipped out good from the bank. The police man was gittin the other one out of the water.

I seen Pearl standin there. She still had holt of that rifle lak she never knowed she helt hit. She was watchin that police man and them folks what come runnin.

Pearl, I said.

She turned right slow, and looked at me.

I said, Pearl, give me that rifle.

Then she looked down at hit. Then she said, Oh God.

Give hit to me Pearl, I said.

All of a sudden she throwed hit in the river.

Pearl, I said then and knowed what she was goin to do. Hit was lak somebody told me. I made to ketch her by the barest. She nigh lak to got in the river. But I had my holt good.

We laid there where we fell. She was tryin and strivin to git loose but I helt my holt. She was beatin on me with her hands to git loose. Then she started to cry and she said God damn me. She said God damn you Ashby Wyndham, God damn you to hell you Ashby Wyndham you son of a bitch. She said them things and more what she never meant or knowed. She scratched my face with her finger nails till the blood come out. She bit me on my arm to make me let go my holt, but I never.

I yelled for Murry to help me and he done hit. We got holt of her good and helt her hands. Then I said to Murry I could keep holt of her and for him to git the oar and put the boat to the bank. Then he taken the oar lak I said and was tryin when I heard that motor boat comin. Hit was them police men as taken us.

They come to us and got on and I said I was tryin to put the boat to the bank and wait for them lak hit was Gods will.

I bet, one of them said but hit was the truth I spoke.

They taken us to the jail.

I am in the jail now and I lay here. I lay here and I pray to God to show me his face. Oh God make me to rejoice agin and in my salvation. I ast to know and hit is my weakness. Pearl laid holt on salvation and come out from the house of abominations. She put off her sin and she was rejoicin. Her heart was full of joy and all she aimed to do was testify to folks and name her joy and salvation. But if salvation had not taken holt on her she would be in Hull-town and smilin yit. She would not be layin and holdin her eyes squinched up and not sayin nuthin nor not takin bite or sup. Oh God she laid off one sin for salvation and salvation taken her to another sin. She kilt a man and hit is a bigger sin.

Oh Lord yore salvation hit moves lak the wind. Hit blows the pore mans heart lak a dead leaf. Hit is lak the wind and no man ain't seen hit come or go. Oh Lord yore foot has been set in the dark place and hit is not seen. Oh Lord yore will has run lak the fox and sly. The pore mans mind sniffs after hit lak a hound dog. But the scent is done lost and the ways of hits goin.

Oh Lord have mercy on Pearl where she lays.

Have mercy on me and not turn yore face away.

I have writ down the truth lak hit was.

I am rispectfully

ASHBY PORSUM WYNDHAM.

MOON LAKE

BY EUDORA WELTY

I

FROM the beginning his martyred presence seriously affected
them. They had a disquieting familiarity with it, hearing the
spit of his despising that went into his bugle. At times they
could hardly recognize what he thought he was playing. Loch
Howard, Boy Scout and Life Saver, was under the ordeal of a
week's camp on Moon Lake with girls.

Half the girls were county orphans, wished on them by Mr.
Nesbitt and the Men's Bible Class after Billy Sunday's visit to
town; but all girls, orphans and Battle Hill girls alike, were the
same thing to Loch; maybe he threw in the two counselors too. He
was hating every day of the seven. He hardly spoke; he never spoke
first. Sometimes he swung in the trees; Nina Forrest in particular
would hear him crashing in the foliage somewhere when she was
lying rigid in siesta.

While they were in the lake, for the dip or the five-o'clock
swimming period in the afternoon, he stood against a tree with his
arms folded, jacked up one-legged, sitting on his heel, as absolutely
tolerant as an old fellow waiting for Kress to open, being held up
by the wall. Waiting for the girls to get out, he gazed upon some
undisturbed part of the water. He despised their predicaments,
most of all their not being able to swim. Sometimes he would take
aim and from his right cheek shoot an imaginary gun at something
far out, where they never were. Then he resumed his pose. He had
been roped into this by his mother.

At the hours too hot for girls he used Moon Lake. He dived
high off the crosspiece nailed up in the big oak, where the Ameri-

415

can Legion dived. He went through the air rocking and jerking like an engine, splashed in, climbed out, spat, climbed up again, dived off. He wore a long bathing suit which stretched longer from Monday to Tuesday and from Tuesday to Wednesday and so on, yawning at the armholes toward infinity, and it looked black and formal as a minstrel suit as he stood skinny against the clouds as on the stage.

He came and got his food and turned his back and ate it all alone like a dog and lived in a tent by himself, apart like a nigger, and dived alone when the lake was clear of girls. That way, he seemed able to bear it; that would be his life. In early evening, in moonlight sings, the Boy Scout and Life Saver kept far away. They would sing "When all the little ships come sailing home," and he would be roaming off; they could tell about where he was. He played taps for them, invisibly then, and so beautifully they wept together, whole tent-fulls some nights. Off with the whip-poor-wills and the coons and the owls and the little bob-whites—down where it all sloped away, he had pitched his tent, and slept there. Then at reveille, how he would spit into that cornet.

Reveille was his. He harangued the woods when the little minnows were trembling and running wizardlike in the water's edge. And how lovely and altered the trees were then, weighted with dew, leaning on one another's shoulders and smelling like big wet flowers. He blew his horn into their presence—trees' and girls'—and then watched the Dip.

"Good morning, Mr. Dip, Dip, Dip, with your water just as cold as ice!" sang Mrs. Gruenwald hoarsely. She took them for the dip, for Miss Moody said she couldn't, simply couldn't.

The orphans usually hung to the rear, and every other moment stood swayback with knees locked, the shoulders of their wash dresses ironed flat and stuck in peaks, and stared. For swimming they owned no bathing suits and went in in their underbodies. Even in the water they would stand swayback, each with a fist in front of her over the rope, looking over the flat surface as over the top of a tall mountain none of them could ever get over. Even at this hour of the day, they seemed to be expecting little tasks, something more immediate—little tasks that were never given out.

Mrs. Gruenwald was from the north and said "dup." "Good morning, Mr. Dup, Dup, Dup, with your water just as cold as ice!"

sang Mrs. Gruenwald, fatly capering and leading them all in a singing, petering-out string down to the lake. She did a sort of little rocking dance in her exhortation, broad in her bathrobe. From the tail end of the line she looked like a Shredded Wheat Biscuit box rocking on its corners.

Nina Forrest thought, There is nobody and nothing named Mr. Dip, it is not a good morning until you have had coffee, and the water is the temperature of a just-cooling biscuit, thank Goodness. I hate this little parade of us girls, Nina thought, trotting fiercely in the center of it. It ruins the woods, all right. "Gee, we think you're mighty nice," they sang to Mr. Dip, while the Boy Scout, waiting at the lake, watched them go in.

"Watch out for mosquitoes," they called to one another, lyrically because warning wasn't any use anyway, as they walked out of their kimonos and dropped them like the petals of one big scattered flower on the bank behind them, and exposing themselves felt in a hundred places at once the little pangs. The orphans ripped their dresses off over their heads and stood in their underbodies. Busily they hung and piled their dresses on a cedar branch, obeying one of their own number, like a whole flock of ferocious little birds with pale topknots building themselves a nest. The orphan named Easter appeared in charge. She handed her dress wrong-side-out to a friend, who turned it and hung it up for her, and waited standing very still, her little fingers locked.

"Let's let the orphans go in the water first and get the snakes stirred up, Mrs. Gruenwald," Jinny Love Stark suggested first off, in the cheerful voice she adopted toward grown people. "Then they'll be chased away by the time *we* go in."

That made the orphans scatter in their pantie-waists, outwards from Easter; the little gauzes of gnats they ran through made them beat their hands at the air. They ran back together again, to Easter, and stood excitedly, almost hopping.

"I think we'll all go in in one big bunch," Mrs. Gruenwald said. Jinny Love lamented and beat against Mrs. Gruenwald, Mrs. Gruenwald's solid, rope-draped stomach all but returning her blows. "All take hands—march! Into the water! *Don't* let the stobs and cypress roots break your legs! *Do* your best! Kick! Stay on top if you can and hold the rope if necessary!"

Mrs. Gruenwald abruptly walked away from Jinny Love, out of

the bathrobe, and entered the lake with a vast displacing. She left them on the bank with her Yankee advice.

The Battle Hill girls might never have gone in if the orphans hadn't balked. Easter came to a dead stop at Moon Lake and looked at it squinting as though it floated really on the Moon. And mightn't it be on the Moon?—it was a strange place, Nina thought, unlikely—and three miles from Battle Hill, Mississippi, all the time. The Battle Hill girls pulled the orphans' hands and dragged them in, or pushed suddenly from behind, and finally the orphans took hold of one another and waded forward in a body, singing "Good Morning" with their stiff, chip-like lips. None of them could or would swim, ever, and they just stood waist-deep and waited for the dip to be over. A few of them reached out and caught the struggling Battle Hill girls by the legs as they splashed from one barky post to another, to see how hard it really was to stay up.

"Mrs. Gruenwald, look, they want to drown us."

But Mrs. Gruenwald all this time was rising and sinking like a whale, she was in a sea of her own waves and perhaps of self-generated cold, out in the middle of the lake. She cared little that Battle Hill girls who learned to swim were getting a dollar from home. She had deserted them, no, she had never really been with them. Not only orphans had she deserted. In the water she kept so much to the profile that her single pushing-out eyeball looked like a little bottle of something. It was said she believed in evolution.

While the Boy Scout in the rosy light under the green trees twirled his horn so that it glittered and ran a puzzle in the sun, and emptied the spit out of it, he yawned, snappingly—as if he would bite the day, as quickly as Easter had bitten Deacon Nesbitt's hand on Opening Day.

"Gee, we think you're mighty nice," they sang to Mr. Dip, gasping, pounding their legs in him. If they let their feet go down, the invisible bottom of the lake felt like soft, knee-deep fur. The sharp hard knobs came up where least expected. The Battle Hill girls of course wore bathing slippers, and the mud loved to suck them off. The alligators had been beaten out of this lake, but it was said that water snakes—pilots—were swimming here and there; they would bite you but not kill you; and one cottonmouth mocca-sin was still getting away from the niggers—if the niggers were still

going after him; he would kill you. These were the chances of getting sucked under, of being bitten, and of dying three miles away
from home.

The brown water cutting her off at the chest, Easter looked
directly before her, wide awake, unsmiling. Before she could hold a
stare like that, she would have had to swallow something big—so
Nina felt. It would have been something so big that it didn't matter to her what the inside of a snake's mouth was lined with. At the
other end of her gaze the life saver grew almost insignificant. Her
gaze moved like a little switch or wand, and the life saver scratched
himself with his bugle, raked himself, as if that eased him. Yet the
flick of a blue-bottle fly made Easter jump.

They swam and held to the rope, hungry and waiting. But they
had to keep waiting till Loch Howard blew his horn before they
could come out of Moon Lake. Mrs. Gruenwald, who capered before breakfast, believed in evolution, and put her face in the water,
was a quarter of a mile out. If she said anything, they couldn't hear
her for the frogs.

II

Nina and Jinny Love, with the soles of their feet shocked from
the walk, found Easter ahead of them down at the spring.

For the orphans, from the first, sniffed out the way to the spring
by themselves, and they could get there without stops to hold up
their feet and pull out thorns and stickers, and could run through
the sandy bottoms and never look down where they were going,
and could grab hold with their toes on the sharp rutted path up the
pine ridge and down. They clearly could never get enough of
skimming over the silk-slick needles and setting prints of their feet
in the bed of the spring to see them dissolve away under their eyes.
What was it to them if the spring was muddied by the time Jinny
Love Stark got there?

The one named Easter could fall flat as a boy, elbows cocked,
and drink from the cup of her hand with her face in the spring.
Jinny Love prodded Nina, and while they looked on Easter's
drawers, Nina was opening the drinking cup she had brought with
her, then collapsing it, feeling like a lady with a fan. That way, she
was going over a thought, a fact: Half the people out here with me

are orphans. Orphans. Orphans. She yearned for her heart to twist. But it didn't, not in time. Easter was through drinking—wiping her mouth and flinging her hand as if to break the bones, to get rid of the drops, and it was Nina's turn with her drinking cup.

Nina stood and bent over from the waist. Calmly, she held her cup in the spring and watched it fill. They could all see how it spangled like a cold star in the curling water. The water tasted the silver cool of the rim it went over running to her lips, and at moments the cup gave her teeth a pang. Nina heard her own throat swallowing. She paused and threw a smile about her. After she had drunk she wiped the cup on her tie and collapsed it, and put the little top on, and its ring over her finger. With that, Easter, one arm tilted, charged against the green bank and mounted it. Nina felt her surveying the spring and all from above. Jinny Love was down drinking like a chicken, kissing the water only.

Easter was dominant among the orphans. It was not that she was so bad. The one called Geneva stole, for example, but Easter was dominant for what she was in herself—for the way she held still, sometimes. All orphans were at once wondering and stoic—at one moment loving everything too much, the next folding back from it, tightly as hard green buds growing in the wrong direction, closing as they go. But it was as if Easter signalled them. Now she just stood up there, watching the spring, with the name Easter— tacky name, as Jinny Love Stark was the first to say. She was medium size, but her hair seemed to fly up at the temples, being cropped and wiry, and this crest made her nearly as tall as Jinny Love Stark. The rest of the orphans had hair paler than their tanned foreheads—straight and tow, the greenish yellow of corn-silk that dimmed black at the roots and shadows, with burnt-out-looking bangs like young boys' and old men's hair; that was from picking in the fields. Easter's hair was a withstanding gold. Around the back of her neck beneath the hair was a dark band on her skin like the mark a gold bracelet leaves on the arm. It came to the Battle Hill girls with a feeling of elation: the ring was pure dirt. They liked to look at it, or to remember, too late, what it was—as now, when Easter had already lain down for a drink and left the spring. They liked to walk behind her and see her back, which seemed spectacular from crested gold head to hard, tough heel. Mr. Nesbitt, from the Bible Class, took Easter by the wrist and turned her around to him and looked just as hard at her front. She had started her breasts. What Easter did was to bite his right hand, his collection hand. It was wonderful to have with them someone dangerous but not, so far, or provenly, bad. When Nina's little lead-mould umbrella, the size of a clover, a Crackerjack prize, was stolen the first night of camp, that was Geneva, Easter's friend.

Jinny Love, after wiping her face with a hand-made handker-chief, pulled out a deck of cards she had secretly brought in her middy pocket. She dropped them down, bright blue, on a sandy place by the spring. "Let's play cassino. Do they call you *Easter?*"

Down Easter jumped, from the height of the bank. She came back to them. "Cassino, what's that?"

"All right, what do *you* want to play?"

"All right, I'll play you mumblety-peg."

"I don't know how you play that!" cried Nina.

"Who would ever want to know?" asked Jinny Love, closing the circle.

Easter flipped out a jack-knife and with her sawed fingernail shot out three blades.

"Do you carry that in the orphan asylum?" Jinny Love asked with some respect.

Easter dropped to her scarred and coral-colored knees. They saw the dirt. "Get down if you want to play me mumblety-peg," was all she said, "and watch out for your hands and faces."

They huddled down on the piney sand. The vivid, hurrying ants were everywhere. To the squinted eye they looked like angry, orange ponies as they rode the pine needles. There was Geneva, skirting behind a tree, but she never came close or tried to get in the game. She pretended to be catching doodle-bugs. The knife leaped and quivered in the sandy arena smoothed by Easter's hand.

"I may not know how to play, but I bet I win," Jinny Love said.

Easter's eyes, lifting up, were neither brown nor green nor cat; they had something of metal, flat ancient metal, so that you could not see into them. In Battle Hill there had been a queer old music teacher with a box of coins from Greece and Rome. Easter's eyes could have come from Greece or Rome that day. Jinny Love stopped short of apprehending this, and only took care to watch herself when Easter pitched the knife. The color in Easter's eyes

could have been found somewhere, away—away, under lost leaves
—strange as the painted color of the ants. Instead of round black
holes in the center of her eyes, there might have been women's
heads, ancient.

Easter, who had played so often, won. She nodded and accepted
Jinny Love's barrette and from Nina a bluejay feather which she
transferred to her own ear.

"I wouldn't be surprised if you cheated, and don't know what
you had to lose if you lost," said Jinny Love thoughtfully but with
an admiration almost fantastic in her.

Victory with a remark attached did not crush Easter at all, or
she scarcely listened. Her indifference made Nina fall back and listen to the spring running with an endless sound and see how the
July light like purple and yellow birds kept flickering under the
trees when the wind blew. Easter turned her head and the new
feather on her head shone changeably. A black funnel of bees
passed through the air, throwing a funnelled shadow, like a visitor
from nowhere, another planet.

"We have to play again to see whose the drinking cup will be,"
Easter said, swaying forward on her knees.

Nina jumped to her feet and did a cartwheel. Against the spinning green and blue her heart pounded as heavily as she touched
lightly.

"You ruined the game," Jinny Love informed Easter. "You
don't know Nina." She gathered up her cards. "You'd think it was
made of fourteen-carat gold, and didn't come out of the pocket of
an old suitcase, that cup."

"I'm sorry," said Nina sincerely.

As the three were winding around the lake, a bird flying above
the opposite shore kept uttering a cry and then diving deep plung-
ing into the trees there, and soaring to cry again.

"Hear him?" one of the niggers said, fishing on the bank; it was
Elberta's sister Twosie who spoke as if a long, long conversation
had been going on, into which she would intrude only the mildest
words. "Know why? Know why, in de sky, he say 'Spirit? Spirit?'
And den he dive *boom* and say 'GHOST'?"

"Why does he?" said Jinny Love, in a voice of objection.

"Yawl knows. *I* don't know," said Twosie, in her little high, helpless voice, and she shut her eyes. They couldn't seem to get on by her. On fine days there is danger of some sad meeting, the positive danger of it. *"I* don't know what he say dat for," Twosie spoke pitifully, as though accused. She sighed. "Yawl sho ain't got yo eyes open good, yawl. Yawl don't know what's out here in woods wid you."

"Well, what?"

"Yawl walk right by mans wid great big gun, could jump out at yawl. Yawl don't eem smellim."

"You mean Mr. Hi Watkins? That's a flashlight he's got." Nina looked at Jinny Love for confirmation. Mr. Hi Watkins was their handy man, or rather simply "the man to be sure and have around the camp." He could be found by beating for a long time on the porch of the American Legion boat house—he slept heavily. "He hasn't got a gun to jump out with."

"I know who you mean. I hear those boys. Just some big boys, like the MacLain twins or somebody, and who cares about them?" Jinny Love, with her switch, indented the thick mat of hair on Twosie's head and prodded and stirred it gently. She pretended to fish in Twosie's woolly head. "Why ain't *you* scared, then?"

"I is."

Twosie's eyelids fluttered. Already she seemed to be fishing in her night's sleep. While they gazed at her crouched, devoted figure, from which the long pole hung, so steady and beggarlike and ordained an appendage, all their passions flew home again and went huddled and soft to roost.

Back at the camp, Jinny Love told Miss Moody about the great big jack-knife. Easter gave it up.

"I didn't mean you couldn't *drink* out of my cup," Nina said, waiting for her. "Only you have to hold it carefully, it leaks. It's engraved."

Easter wouldn't even try it, though Nina dangled it on its ring right under her eyes. She didn't say anything, not even "It's pretty." Was she even thinking of it? Or if not, what did she think about?

"Sometimes orphans act like deaf-and-dumbs," said Jinny Love.

III

"Nina!" Jinny Love whispered across the tent, during siesta. "What do you think you're reading?"

Nina closed *The Re-creation of Brian Kent*. Jinny Love was already coming directly across the almost-touching cots to Nina's, walking on her knees and bearing down over Gertrude, Etoile, and now Geneva.

With Jinny Love upon her, Gertrude sighed. Her sleeping face looked as if she didn't want to. She slept as she swam, in her pantie-waist, she was in running position and her ribs went up and down frantically—a little box in her chest that expanded and shut without a second's rest between. Her cheek was pearly with afternoon moisture and her kitten-like teeth pearlier still. As Jinny Love hid her and went over, Nina seemed to see her still; even her vaccination mark looked too big for her.

Nobody woke up from being walked over, but after Jinny Love had fallen in bed with Nina, Easter gave a belated, dreaming sound. She had not even been in the line of march; she slept on the cot by the door, curved shell-like, both arms forward over her head. It was an inward sound she gave—now it came again—of such wholehearted and fateful concurrence with the thing dreamed, that Nina and Jinny Love took hands and made wry faces at each other.

Beyond Easter's cot the corona of afternoon flared and lifted in an intensity that came through the eyelids. There was nothing but light out there. True, the black Negroes inhabited it. Elberta moved slowly through it, as if she rocked a baby with her hips, carrying a bucket of scraps to throw in the lake—to get hail Columbia for it later. Her straw hat spiralled rings of orange and violet, like a top. Far, far down a vista of intolerable light, a tiny daub of black cotton, Twosie had stationed herself at the edge of things, and slept and fished.

Eventually there was Exum wandering with his fish pole—he could dance on a dime, Elberta said, he used to work for a blind man. Exum was smart for twelve years old; too smart. He found that hat he wore—not a sign of the owner. He had a hat like new, filled out a little with peanut shells inside the band to correct the size, and he like a little black peanut in it. It stood up and away from his head all around, and seemed only following him—on runners, perhaps, like those cartridges for change in Spights' store.

Easter's sighs and her prolonged or half-uttered words now filled the tent, just as the heat filled it. Her words fell in threes, Nina observed, like the mourning-dove's call in the woods.

Nina and Jinny Love lay speechless, doubling for themselves the already strong odor of "Sweet Dreams" mosquito oil, in a trance of endurance through the hour's siesta. Entwined, they stared—orphan-like themselves—past Easter's cot and through the tent opening as down a long telescope turned on an incandescent star, and saw the spiral of Elberta's hat return, and saw Exum jump over a stick and on the other side do a little dance in a puff of dust. They could hear the intermittent crash, splash of Loch Howard using their lake, and Easter's voice calling again in her sleep, her unintelligible words.

But however Nina and Jinny Love made faces at they knew not what, Easter concurred; she thoroughly agreed.

The bugle blew for swimming. Geneva jumped so hard she fell off her cot. Nina and Jinny Love were indented with each other, like pressed leaves, and jumped free. When Easter, who had to be shaken, sat up drugged and stupid on her cot, Nina ran over to her.

"Listen. Wake up. Look, you can go in in my bathing shoes today."

She felt her eyes glaze with this plan of kindness as she stretched out her limp red shoes that hung down like bananas under Easter's gaze. But Easter dropped back on the cot and stretched her legs.

"Never mind your shoes. I don't have to go in the lake if I don't want to."

"You do. I never heard of that. Who picked you out? You do," they said, all gathering.

"You make me."

Easter yawned. She fluttered her eyes and rolled them back—she loved doing that. Miss Moody passed by and beamed in at them hovered around Easter's passive and mutinous form. All along she'd been afraid of some challenge to her counselorship, from the way she hurried by now, almost too daintily.

"Well, *I* know," Jinny Love said, sidling up. "I know as much as you know, Easter." She made a chant, which drove her hopping around the tent pole in an Indian step. "You don't have to go, if you don't want to go. And if it ain't so, you still don't have to go, if you don't want to go." She kissed her hand to them.

Easter was silent—but if she groaned when she waked, she'd only be imitating herself.

Jinny Love pulled on her bathing cap, which gave way and came down over her eyes. Even in blindness, she cried, "So you needn't think you're the only one, Easter, not always. What do you say to that?"

"I should worry, I should cry," said Easter, lying still, spread-eagled.

"Let's run away from basket weaving," Jinny Love said in Nina's ear, a little later in the week.

"Just as soon."

"Grand. They'll think we're drowned."

They went out the back end of the tent, barefooted; their feet were as tough as anybody's by this time. Down in the hammock, Miss Moody was reading *The Re-creation of Brian Kent* now. (Nobody knew whose book that was, it had been found here, the covers curled up like side combs. Perhaps anybody at Moon Lake who tried to read it felt cheated by the title, as applying to camp life, as Nina did, and laid it down for the next person.) Cat, the niggers' cat, was sunning on a post and when they approached jumped to the ground like something poured out of a bottle, and went with them, in front.

They trudged down the slope past Loch Howard's tent and took the track into the swamp. There they moved single file between two walls; by lifting their arms they could have touched one or the other pressing side of the swamp. Their toes exploded the dust that felt like the powder clerks pump into new kid gloves, as Jinny Love said twice. They were eye to eye with the finger-shaped leaves of the castor-bean plants, put out like those gypsy hands that part the curtains at the back of rolling wagons, and wrinkled and coated over like the fortune-teller's face.

Mosquitoes struck at them; "Sweet Dreams" didn't last. The whining lifted like a voice, saying "I don't want. . . ." At the girls' shoulders Queen Anne's lace and elderberry and blackberry thickets, loaded heavily with flower and fruit and smelling with the melony smell of snake, overhung the ditch to touch them. The ditches had dried green or blue bottoms, cracked and glazed—like a dropped vase. "I hope we don't meet any nigger men," Jinny Love said cheerfully.

Sweet bay and cypress and sweet gum and live oak and swamp maple closing tight made the wall dense, and yet there was somewhere still for the other wall of vine; it gathered itself on the ground and stacked and tilted itself in the trees; and like a table in the tree the mistletoe hung up there black in the zenith. Buzzards floated from one side of the swamp to the other, as if choice existed for them—raggedly crossing the sky and shadowing the track, and shouldering one another on the solitary limb of a moon-white sycamore. Closer to the ear than lips could begin words came the swamp sounds—closer to the ear and nearer to the dreaming mind. They were a song of hilarity to Jinny Love, who began to skip. Periods of silence seemed hoarse, or the suffering from hoarseness, otherwise inexplicable, as though the world could stop. Cat was stalking something at the black edge of the ditch. The briars didn't trouble Cat at all, it was they that seemed to give way beneath that long, boatlike belly.

The track serpentined again, and walking ahead was Easter. Geneva and Etoile were playing at her side, edging each other out of her shadow, but when they saw who was coming up behind them, they turned and ran tearing back toward camp, running at angles, like pullets, leaving a cloud of dust as they passed by.

"Wouldn't you know!" said Jinny Love.

Easter was going unconcernedly on, her dress stained green behind; she ate something out of her hand as she went.

"We'll soon catch up—don't hurry."

The reason orphans were the way they were lay first in nobody's watching them, Nina thought, for she felt obscurely like a trespasser. They, they were not answerable. Even on being watched, Easter remained not answerable to a soul on earth. Nobody cared! And so, in this beatific state, something came out of *her*.

"Where are you going?"

"Can we go with you, Easter?"

Easter, her lips stained with blackberries, replied, "It ain't my road."

They walked along one on each side of her. Though they automatically stuck their tongues out at her, they ran their arms around her waist. She tolerated the closeness for a little while; she smelled of orphan-starch, but she had a strange pure smell of sweat, like a sleeping baby, and in her temple, so close then to their eyes, the skin was transparent enough for a little vein to be seen pounding under it. She seemed very tender and very small in the waist to be trudging along so doggedly, when they had her like that.

Vines, a magnificent and steamy green, covered more and more of the trees, played over them like fountains. There were stretches of water below them, blue black, netted over with half-closed waterlilies. The horizontal limbs of cypresses grew a short, pale green scruff like bird feathers.

They came to a tiny farm down here, the last one possible before the muck sucked it in—a patch of cotton in flower, a house whitewashed in front, a cleanswept yard with a little iron pump standing in the middle of it like a black rooster. These were white people, an old woman in a sunbonnet came out of the house with a galvanized bucket, and pumped it full in the dooryard. That was an excuse to see people go by.

Easter, easing out of the others' clasp, lifted her arm halfway and, turning for an instant, gave two waves of the hand. But the old woman was prouder than she.

Jinny Love said, "How would you all like to live there?"

Cat edged the woods onward, and at moments vanished into a tunnel in the briars. Emerging from other tunnels, he—or she— glanced up at them with a face more mask-like than ever.

"There's a short-cut to the lake." Easter, breaking and darting ahead, suddenly went down on her knees and slid under a certain place in the barbed wire fence. Rising, she took a step inward, sinking down as she went. Nina untwined her arm from Jinny Love's and went after her.

"I might have known you'd want us to go through a barbed wire fence." Jinny Love sat down where she was, on the side of the ditch, just as she would take her seat on a needlepoint stool. She jumped up once, and sat back. "Fools, fools!" she called. "Now I think you've made me turn my ankle. Even if I wanted to track through the mud, I couldn't!"

Nina and Easter, dipping under a second, unexpected fence,

went on, swaying and feeling their feet pulled down, reaching to the trees. Jinny Love was left behind in the heartless way people and incidents alike are thrown off in the course of a dream, like the gratuitous flowers scattered from a float—rather in celebration. The swamp was now all-enveloping, dark and at the same time vivid, alarming—it was like being inside the chest of something that breathed and might turn over.

Then there was Moon Lake, a different aspect altogether. Easter climbed the slight rise ahead and reached the pink, grassy rim and the innocent open. Here it was quiet, until, fatefully, there was one soft splash.

"You see the snake drop off in the water?" asked Easter.

"Snake?"

"Out of that tree."

"You can have him."

"There he is: coming up!" Easter pointed.

"That's probably a different one," Nina objected in the voice of Jinny Love.

Easter looked both ways, chose, and walked on the pink sandy rim with its purpled lip, her blue shadow lolling over it. She went around a bend, and straight to an old gray boat. Did she know it would be there? It was in some reeds, looking mysterious to come upon and yet in place, as an old boat will. Easter stepped into it and hopped to the far seat that was over the water, and dropping to it lay back with her toes hooked up. She looked falling over backwards. One arm lifted, curved over her head, and hung till her finger touched the water.

The shadows of the willow leaves moved gently on the sand, deep blue and narrow, long crescents. The water was quiet, the color of pewter, marked with purple stobs, although where the sun shone right on it the lake seemed to be in violent agitation, almost boiling. Surely a little chip would turn around and around in it. Nina dropped down on the flecked sandbar. She fluttered her eyelids, half closed them, and the world looked struck by moonlight.

"Here I come," came Jinny Love's voice. It hadn't been long. She came twitching over their tracks along the sandbar, her long soft hair blowing up like a skirt in a play of the breeze in the open. "But I don't choose to sit myself in a leaky boat," she was calling ahead. "I choose the land."

She took her seat on the very place where Nina was writing her name. Nina moved her finger away, drawing a long arrow to a new place. The sand was coarse like beads and full of minute shells, some shaped exactly like bugles.

"Want to hear about my ankle?" Jinny Love asked. "It wasn't as bad as I thought. I must say you picked a queer place, I saw an *owl*. It smells like the school basement to me—peepee and old erasers." Then she stopped with her mouth a little open, and was quiet, as though something had been turned off inside her. Her eyes were soft, her gaze stretched to Easter, to the boat, the lake— her long oval face went vacant.

Easter was lying rocked in the gentle motion of the boat, her head turned on its cheek. She had not said hello to Jinny Love anew. Did she see the drop of water clinging to her lifted finger? Did it make a rainbow? Not to Easter: her eyes were rolled back, Nina felt. Her own hand was writing in the sand. Nina, Nina, Nina. Writing, she could dream that her self might get away from her—that here in this faraway place she could tell her self, by name, to go or to stay. Jinny Love had begun building a sand castle over her foot. In the sky clouds moved no more perceptibly than grazing animals. Yet with a passing breeze, the boat gave a knock, lifted and fell. Easter sat up.

"Why aren't we out in the boat?" Nina, taking a strange and heady initiative, rose to her feet. "Out there!" A picture in her mind, as if already furnished from an eventual and appreciative distance, showed the boat floating where she pointed, far out in Moon Lake with three girls sitting in the three spaces. "We're coming, Easter!"

"Just as I make a castle. *I'm* not coming," said Jinny Love. "Anyway, there's stobs in the lake. We'd be upset, ha ha."

"What do I care, I can swim!" Nina cried at the water's edge.

"You can just swim from the first post to the second post. And that's in front of camp, not here."

Firming her feet in the sucking, minnowy mud, Nina put her weight against the boat. Soon her legs were half hidden, the mud like some awful kiss pulled at her toes, and all over she tautened and felt the sweat start out of her body. Roots laced her feet, knotty and streaming. Under water, the boat was caught too, but Nina was determined to free it. She saw that there was muddy water in the boat too, which Easter's legs, now bright pink, were straddling. Suddenly all seemed easy.

"It's coming loose!"

At the last minute, Jinny Love, who had extracted her foot from the castle with success, hurried over and climbed to the middle seat of the boat screaming. Easter sat up swaying with the dip òf the boat; the energy seemed all to have gone out of her. Her lolling head looked pale and featureless as a pear beyond the laughing face of Jinny Love. She had not said whether she wanted to go or not—yet surely she did; she had been in the boat all along, she had discovered the boat.

For a moment, with her powerful hands, Nina held the boat back. Again she thought of a pear—not the everyday gritty kind that hung on the tree in the backyard, but the fine kind sold on trains and at high prices, each pear with a paper cone wrapping it alone—beautiful, symmetrical, clean pears with thin skins, with snow-white flesh so juicy and tender that to eat one baptized the whole face, and so delicate that while you urgently ate the first half, the second half was already beginning to turn brown. To all fruits, and especially to those fine pears, something happened—the process was so swift, you were never in time for them. It's not the flowers that are fleeting, Nina thought, it's the fruits—it's the time when things are ready that they don't stay. She even went through the rhyme, "Pear tree by the garden gate, How much longer must I wait?"—thinking it was the pears that asked it, not the picker.

Then she climbed in herself, and they were rocking out sideways on the water.

"Now what?" said Jinny Love.

"This is all right for me," said Nina.

"Without oars?—Ha ha."

"Why didn't you tell me, then!—But I don't care now."

"You never are as smart as you think."

"Wait till you find out where we get to."

"I guess you know Easter can't swim. She won't even touch water with her foot."

"What do you think a *boat's* for?"

But a soft tug had already stopped their drifting. Nina with a dark frown turned and looked down.

"A chain! An old mean chain!"

"That's how smart you are."

Nina pulled the boat in again—of course nobody helped her!—burning her hands on the chain, and kneeling outward tried to free the other end. She could see now through the reeds that it was wound around and around an old stump, which had almost grown over it in places. The boat had been chained to the bank since maybe last summer.

"No use hitting it," said Jinny Love.

A dragonfly flew about their heads. Easter only waited in her end of the boat, not seeming to care about the disappointment either. If this was their ship, she was their figurehead, turned on its back, sky-facing. She wouldn't be their passenger.

"You thought we'd all be out in the middle of Moon Lake by now, didn't you?" Jinny Love said, from her lady's seat. "Well, look where we are."

"Oh, Easter! Easter! I wish you still had your knife!"

"—But let's don't go back yet," Jinny Love said on shore. "I don't think they've missed us." She started a sand castle over her other foot.

"You make me sick," said Easter suddenly.

"Nina, let's pretend Easter's not with us."

"But that's what *she* was pretending."

Nina dug into the sand with a little stick, printing "Nina" and then "Easter."

Jinny Love seemed stunned, she let sand run out of both fists. "But how could you ever know what Easter was pretending?"

Easter's hand came down and wiped her name clean; she also wiped out "Nina." She took the stick out of Nina's hand and with a formal gesture, as if she would otherwise seem to reveal too much, wrote for herself. In clear, high-waisted letters the word "Esther" cut into the sand. Then she jumped up.

"Who's that?" Nina asked.

Easter laid her thumb between her breasts, and walked about.

"Why, I call that 'Esther'."

"Call it 'Esther' if you want to, I call it 'Easter'."

"Well, sit down . . ."

"And I named myself."

"How could you? Who let you?"

"I let myself name myself."

"Easter, I believe you," said Nina. "But I just want you to spell it right. Look—E-A-S——"

"I should worry, I should cry."

Jinny Love leaned her chin on the roof of her castle to say, "I was named for my maternal grandmother, so my name's Jinny Love. It couldn't be anything else. Or anything better. You see? Easter's just not a real name. It doesn't matter how she spells it, Nina, nobody ever had it. Not around here." She rested on her chin.

"I have it."

"Just see how it looks spelled right." Nina lifted the stick from Easter's fingers and began to print, but had to throw herself bodily over the name to keep Easter from it. "Spell it right and it's real!" she cried.

"But right or wrong, it's tacky," said Jinny Love. "You can't get me mad over it. All I can concentrate on out here is missing the figs at home."

" 'Easter' is real beautiful!" Nina said distractedly. She suddenly threw the stick into the lake before Easter could grab it, and it trotted up and down in a crucible of sunfilled water. "I thought it was the day you were found on a doorstep," she said sullenly—even distrustfully.

Easter sat down at last and with slow, careful movements of her palms rubbed down the old bites on her legs. Her crest of hair dipped downward and she rocked a little, up and down, side to side, in a rhythm. Easter never did intend to explain anything unless she had to—or to force your explanations. She just had hopes. She hoped never to be sorry. Or did she?

"I haven't got no father. I never had, he ran away. I've got a mother. When I could walk, then my mother took me by the hand and turned me in, and I remember it. I'm going to be a singer."

It was Jinny Love, starting to clear her throat, who released Nina. It was Jinny Love, escaping, burrowing her finger into her castle, who was now kind, pretending Easter had never spoken. Nina banged Jinny Love on the head with her fist. How good and hot her hair was! Like hot glass. She broke the castle from her tender foot. She wondered if Jinny Love's head would break. Not at all. You couldn't learn anything through the head.

"Ha, ha, ha!" yelled Jinny Love, hitting back.

They were fighting and hitting for a moment. Then they lay quiet, tilted together against the crumbled hill of sand, stretched out and looking at the sky where now a white tower of cloud was climbing.

Someone moved; Easter lifted to her lips a piece of crossvine cut back in the days of her good knife. She brought up a kitchen match from her pocket, lighted up, and smoked.

They sat up and gazed at her.

"If you count much on being a singer, that's not a very good way to start," said Jinny Love. "Even boys, it stunts their growth."

Easter once more looked the same as asleep in the dancing shadows, except for what came out of her mouth, more mysterious, almost, than words.

"Have some?" she asked, and they accepted. But theirs went out.

Jinny Love's gaze was fastened on Easter, and she dreamed and dreamed of telling on her for smoking, while the sun, even through leaves, was burning her pale skin pink, and she looked the most beautiful of all: she felt temptation. But what she said was, "Even after all this is over, Easter, I'll always remember you."

Off in the thick of the woods came a fairy sound, followed by a tremulous silence, a holding apart of the air.

"What's that?" cried Easter, sharply. Her throat quivered, the little vein in her temple jumped.

"That's Mister Loch Howard. Didn't you know he had a horn?"

There was another fairy sound, and the pried-apart, gentle silence. The woods seemed to be moving after it, running—the world pellmell. Nina could see the boy in the distance, too, and the golden horn tilted up. A few minutes back her gaze had fled the present and this scene; now she put the horn blower into his visionary place.

"Don't blow that!" Jinny Love cried out this time, jumping to her feet and stopping up her ears, stamping on the shore of Moon Lake. "You shut up! We can hear!—Come on," she added prosaically to the other two. "It's time to go. I reckon they've worried enough." She smiled. "Here comes Cat."

Cat always caught something; something was in his—or her—mouth, a couple of little feet or claws bouncing under the lifted whiskers. Cat didn't look especially triumphant; just through with it.

They marched on away from their little boat.

IV

One clear night the campers built a fire up above the spring, cooked supper on sticks around it, and after stunts, a recitation of "How They Brought the Good News from Ghent to Aix" by Gertrude Bowles, and the ghost story about the bone, they stood up on the ridge and poured a last song into the woods—"Little Sir Echo."

The fire was put out and there was no bright point to look into, no circle. The presence of night was beside them—a beast in gossamer, with no shine of outline, only of ornament—rings, earrings. . . .

"March!" cried Mrs. Gruenwald, and stamped down the trail for them to follow. They went single file on the still-warm pine needles, soundlessly now. Not far away there were crackings of twigs, small, regretted crashes; Loch Howard, supperless for all they knew, was wandering around by himself, sulking, alone.

Nobody needed light. The night sky was pale as a green grape, transparent like grape flesh over each tree. Every girl saw moths—the beautiful ones like ladies, with long legs that were wings—and the little ones, mere bits of bark. And once against the night, just before Little Sister Spights' eyes, making her cry out, hung suspended a spider—a body no less mysterious than the grape of the air, different only a little.

All around swam the fireflies. Clouds of them, trees of them, islands of them floating, a lower order of brightness—one could even get into a tent by mistake. The stars barely showed their places in the pale sky—small and far from this bright world. And the world would be bright as long as these girls held awake, and could keep their eyes from closing. And the moon itself shone—taken for granted.

Moon Lake came in like a flood below the ridge; they trailed downward. Out there Miss Moody would sometimes go in a boat;

sometimes she had a late date from town, "Rudy" Spights or "Rudy" Loomis, and then they could be seen drifting there after the moon was up, far out on the smooth bright surface. ("And she lets him hug her out there," Jinny Love had instructed them. "Like this." She had seized, of all people, Etoile, whose name rhymed with tinfoil; "Hands off," said Etoile.) Twice Nina had herself seen the silhouette of the canoe on the bright water, with the figures at each end, like a dark butterfly with wings spread open and still. Not tonight!

Tonight, it was only the niggers, fishing. But their boat must be full of silver fish! Nina wondered if it was the slowness and near-fixity of boats out on the water that made them so magical. Their little boat in the reeds that day had not been far from this one's wonder, after all. The turning of water and sky, of the moon, or the sun, always proceeded, and there was this magical hesitation in their midst, of a boat. And in the boat, it was not so much that they drifted, as that in the presence of a boat the world drifted, forgot. The dreamed-about changed places with the dreamer.

Home from the wild moonlit woods, the file of little girls wormed into the tents, which were hot as cloth pockets. The candles were lighted by Miss Moody, dateless tonight, on whose shelf in the flare of nightly revelation stood her toothbrush in the glass, her hand-painted celluloid powder box, her Honey and Almond cream, her rouge and eyebrow tweezers, and at the end of the line the bottle of Compound, containing true and false unicorn and the life root plant.

Miss Moody, with a fervent frown which precluded interruption, sang in soft tremolo as she rubbed the lined-up children with "Sweet Dreams."

> "Forgive me
> O please forgive me
> I'm sorry that I made
> You cry!
> I need you and I want you—"

They crooked and bent themselves and lifted nightgowns to her silently while she sang. Then when she faced them to her they could look into the deep tangled rats of her puffed hair and at her eyebrows which seemed fixed for ever in that elevated line of adult pleading.

"Do anything but don't say goodbye!"

And automatically they almost said, "Goodbye." Her hands rubbed and cuffed them while she sang, pulling to her girls all just alike, as if girlhood itself were an infinity, but a commodity. ("I'm ticklish," Jinny Love informed her every night.) Her look of pleading seemed infinitely perilous to them. Her voice had the sway of an aerialist crossing the high wire, even while she sang out of the nightgown coming down over her head.

There were kisses, prayers. Easter, as though she could be cold tonight, got into bed with Geneva. Geneva like a little June bug hooked onto her back. The candles were blown. Miss Moody ostentatiously went right to sleep. Jinny Love cried into her pillow for her mother, or perhaps for the figs. Just outside their tent, Citronella burned in a saucer in the weeds—Citronella, like a girl's name.

Luminous of course but hidden from them, Moon Lake streamed out in the night. By moonlight sometimes it seemed to run like a river. Beyond the cry of the frogs there were the sounds of a boat moored somewhere, of its vague, clumsy reaching at the shore, those sounds that are recognized as being made by something sightless. When did boats have eyes—once? Nothing watched that their little part of the lake stayed roped off and protected; was it there now, the rope stretched frail-like between posts that swayed in mud? That rope was to mark how far the girls could swim. Beyond lay the deep part, some bottomless parts, said Moody. Here and there was the quicksand that stirred your footprint and kissed your heel. All snakes, harmless and harmful, were freely playing now; they put a trailing, moony division between weed and weed—bright, turning, bright and turning.

Nina still lay dreamily, or she had waked in the night. She heard Gertrude Bowles gasp in a dream, beginning to get her stomach ache, and Etoile begin, slowly, her snore. She thought: Now I can think, in between them. She could not even feel Miss Moody fretting.

The orphan! she thought exultantly. The other way to live. There were secret ways. She thought, Time's really short, I've been only thinking like the others. It's only interesting, only worthy, to try for the fiercest secrets. To slip into them all—to change. To change for a moment into Gertrude, into Mrs. Gruenwald, into Twosie—into a boy. To *have been* an orphan.

Nina sat up on the cot and stared passionately before her at the night—the pale dark roaring night with its secret step, the Indian night. She felt the forehead, the beaded stars, look in thoughtfully at her.

The pondering night stood rude at the tent door, the opening fold would let it stoop in—it, him—he had risen up inside. Long-armed, or long-winged, he stood in the center there where the pole went up. Nina lay back, drawn quietly from him. But the night knew about Easter. All about her. Geneva had pushed her to the very edge of the cot. Easter's hand hung down, opened outward. Come here, night, Easter might say, tender to a giant, to such a dark thing. And the night, obedient and graceful, would kneel to her. Easter's calloused hand hung open there to the night that had got wholly into the tent.

Nina let her own arm stretch forward opposite Easter's. Her hand too opened, of itself. She lay there a long time motionless, under the night's gaze, its black cheek, looking immovably at her hand, the only part of her now which was not asleep. Its gesture was like Easter's, but Easter's hand slept and her own knew—shrank and knew, yet offered still.

"Instead . . . me instead . . ."

In the cup of her hand, in her filling skin, in the fingers' bursting weight and stillness, Nina felt it: compassion and a kind of competing that were all one, a single ecstasy, a single longing. For the night was not impartial. No, the night loved some more than others, served some more than others. Nina's hand lay open there for a long time, as if its fingers would be its eyes. Then it too slept. She dreamed her hand was helpless to the tearing teeth of wild beasts. At reveille she woke up lying on it. She could not move it. She hit it and bit it until like a cluster of bees it stung back and came to life.

V

They had seen, without any idea of what he would do—and yet it was just like him—little old Exum toiling up the rough barky ladder and dreaming it up, clinging there monkeylike among the leaves, all eyes and wrinkled forehead.

Exum was apart too, boy and nigger to boot; he constantly moved along an even further fringe of the landscape than Loch, wearing the man's stiff straw hat brilliant as a snowflake. They would see Exum in the hat bobbing along the rim of the swamp like a fisherman's cork, elevated just a bit by the miasma and illusion of the landscape he moved in. It was Exum persistent as a little bug, inching along the foot of the swamp wall, carrying around a fishing cane and minnow can, fishing around the bend from their side of the lake, catching all kinds of things. Things, things. He claimed all he caught, gloating—dangled it and loved it, clasped it with suspicious glee—wouldn't a soul dispute him that? The Boy Scout asked him if he could catch an electric eel and Exum promised it readily—a gift; the challenge was a siesta-long back-and-forth across the water.

Now all rolling eyes, he hung on the ladder, too little to count as looking—too everything-he-was to count as anything.

Beyond him on the diving-board, Easter was standing—high above the others at their swimming lesson. She was motionless, barefooted, and tall with her outgrown, printed dress on her and the sky under her. She had not answered when they called things up to her. They splashed noisily under her calloused, coral-colored foot that hung over.

"How are you going to get down, Easter!" shouted Gertrude Bowles.

Miss Moody smiled understandingly up at Easter. How far, in the water, could Miss Parnell Moody be transformed from a schoolteacher? They had wondered. She wore a canary yellow bathing cap lumpy over her hair, with a rubber butterfly on the front. She wore a brassiere and bloomers under her bathing suit because, said Jinny Love, that was exactly how good she was. She scarcely looked for trouble, immediate trouble—though this was the last day at Moon Lake.

Exum's little wilted black fingers struck at his lips as if playing a tune on them. He put out a foolishly long arm. He held a green willow switch. Later they every one said they saw him—but too late. He gave Easter's heel the tenderest, obscurest little brush, with something of nigger persuasion about it.

She dropped like one hit in the head by a stone from a sling. In their retrospect, her body, never turning, seemed to languish upright for a moment, then descend. It went to meet and was received by blue air. It dropped as if handed down all the way and was let out of sight at once. There was something so positive about its disappearance that only the instinct of caution made them give it a moment to come up again; it didn't come up. Then Exum let loose a girlish howl and clung to the ladder as though a fire had been lighted under it.

Nobody called for Loch Howard. On shore, he studiously hung his bugle on the tree. He was enormously barefooted. He took a frog dive and when he went through the air they noticed that the powdered-on dirt gave him lavender soles. Now he swam destructively into the water, cut through the girls, and began to hunt Easter where all the fingers began to point.

They cried while he hunted, their chins dropping into the brown buggy stuff and their mouths sometimes swallowing it. He didn't give a glance their way. He stayed under as though the lake came down a lid on him, at each dive. Sometimes, open-mouthed, he appeared with something awful in his hands, showing not them, but the world, or himself—long ribbons of green and terrible stuff, shapeless black matter, nobody's shoe. Then he would up-end and go down, hunting her again. Each dive was a call on Exum to scream again.

"Shut up! Get out of the way! You stir up the lake!" Loch Howard yelled once—blaming them. They looked at one another and after one loud cry all stopped crying. Standing in the brown that cut them off where they waited, ankle-deep, waist-deep, knee-deep, chin-deep, they made a little V, with Miss Moody in front and partly obscuring their vision with her jerky butterfly cap. They felt his insult. They stood so still as to be almost carried away, in the pictureless warm body of lake around them, until they felt the weight of the currentless water pulling anyhow. Their shadows only, like the curled back edges of a split drum, showed where they each protruded out of Moon Lake.

Up above, Exum howled, and further up, some fulsome, vague clouds with uneasy hearts blew peony-like. Exum howled up, down, and all around. He brought Elberta, mad, from the cook tent, and surely Mrs. Gruenwald was dead to the world—asleep or reading—or she would be coming too, by now, capering down her favorite trail. It was Jinny Love, they realized, who had capered down, and now stood strangely signalling from shore. The painstaking work of Miss Moody, white bandages covered her arms and legs; poison ivy had appeared that morning. Like Easter, Jinny Love had no intention of going in the lake.

"Ahhhhh!" everybody said, long and drawn out, just as he found her.

Of course he found her, there was her arm sliding through his hand. They saw him snatch the hair of Easter's head, the way a boy will snatch anything he wants, as if he won't have invisible opponents snatching first. Under the water he joined himself to her. He spouted, and with engine-like jerks brought her in.

There came Mrs. Gruenwald! With something like a skip, she came to a stop on the bank and waved her hands. Her middy blouse flew up, showing her loosened corset. It was red. They treasured that up. But her voice was pre-emptory.

"This minute! Out of the lake! Out of the lake, out-out! Parnell! Discipline! March them out."

"One's drowned!" shrieked poor Miss Moody.

Loch stood over Easter. He sat her up, folding, on the shore, wheeled her arm over, and by that dragged her clear of the water before he dropped her, a wrapped bundle in the glare. He shook himself in the sun like a dog, blew his nose, spat, and shook his ears, all in a kind of leisurely trance that kept Mrs. Gruenwald off as though he had no notion that he was interrupting things at all. Exum could now be heard shrieking for Miss Marybelle Flanagan, the lady who had had the camp last year and was now married and living in the Delta.

Miss Moody and all her girls now came out of the lake. Tardy, drooping, their hair heavy-wet and their rubber shoes making wincing sounds, they edged the shore.

Loch returned to Easter, spread her out, and then they could all get at her, but they watched the water lake in her lap. The sun like a weight fell on them. Miss Moody wildly ran and caught up Easter's ankle and pushed on her, like a lady with a wheelbarrow. The Boy Scout looped Easter's arms like sashes on top of her and took up his end, the shoulders. They carried her, looking for shade. One arm fell, touching ground. Jinny Love, in the dazzling bandages, ran up and scooped Easter's arm in both of hers. They proceeded, zigzag, Jinny Love turning her head toward the rest of them, running low, bearing the arm.

They put her down in the only shade on earth, after all, the table under the tree. It was where they ate. The table was itself still mostly tree, as the ladder and diving board were half tree too; a camp table had to be round and barky on the underside, and odorous of having been chopped down. They knew that splintery surface, and the ants that crawled on it. Mrs. Gruenwald, with her strong cheeks, blew on the table, but she might have put a cloth down. She stood between table and girls; her tennis shoes, like lesser corsets, tied her feet solid there; and they did not go any closer, but only to where they could see.

"I got her, please ma'am."

In the water, the life saver's face had held his whole impatience; now it was washed pure, blank. He pulled Easter his way, away from Miss Moody—who, however, had got Easter's sash ends wrung out—and then, with a turn, hid her from Mrs. Gruenwald. Holding her folded up to him, he got her clear, and the next moment, with a spread of his hand, had her lying there before him on the table top.

They were silent. Easter lay in a mold of wetness from Moon Lake, on her side; sharp as a flatiron her hipbone pointed up. She was arm to arm and leg to leg in a long fold, wrong-colored and pressed together as unopen leaves are. Her breasts, too, faced together. Out of the water Easter's hair was darkened, and lay over her face in long fern shapes. Miss Moody laid it back.

"You can tell she's not breathing," said Jinny Love.

Easter's nostrils were pinched-looking like an old country woman's. Her side fell slack as a dead rabbit's in the woods, with the flowers of her orphan dress all running together in some antic of their own, some belated mix-up of the event. The Boy Scout had only let her go to leap onto the table with her. He stood over her, put his hands on her, and rolled her over; they heard the distant-like knock of her forehead on the solid table, and the knocking of her hip and knee.

Exum was heard being whipped in the willow clump; then they remembered Elberta was his mother. "You little black son-a-bitch!" they heard her yelling, and he howled through the woods.

Astride Easter the Boy Scout lifted her up between his legs and dropped her. He did it again, and she fell on one arm. He nodded —not to them.

There was a sigh, a Battle Hill sigh, not an orphans'. The orphans did not press forward, or claim to own or protect Easter any more. They did nothing except mill a little, and yet their group was delicately changed. In Nina's head, where the world was still partly leisurely, came a recollected scene: birds on a roof under a cherry tree; they were drunk.

The Boy Scout, nodding, took Easter's hair and turned her head. He left her face looking at them. Her eyes were neither open nor altogether shut but as if her ears heard a great noise, back from the time she fell; the whites showed under the lids pale and slick as watermelon seeds. Her lips were parted to the same degree; her teeth could be seen smeared with black mud.

The Boy Scout reached in and gouged out her mouth with his hand, an unbelievable act. She did not alter. He lifted up, screwed his toes, and with a groan of his own fell upon her and drove up and down upon her, into her, gouging the heels of his hands into her ribs again and again. She did not alter except that she let a thin stream of water out of her mouth, a dark stain down the fixed cheek. The children drew together. Life-saving was much worse than they had dreamed. Worse still was the carelessness of Easter's body.

Jinny Love volunteered once more. She would wave a towel over things to drive the mosquitoes, at least, away. She chose a white towel. Her unspotted arms lifted and criss-crossed. She faced them now; her expression quietened and became ceremonious.

Easter's body lay up on the table to receive anything that was done to it. If *he* was brutal, her self, her body, the withheld life, was brutal too. While the Boy Scout as if he rode a runaway horse clung momently to her and arched himself off her back, dug his knees and fists into her and was flung back careening by his own tactics, she lay there.

Let him try and try!

The next thing Nina knew was a scent of home, an adult's thumb in her shoulder, and a cry, "Now what?" Miss Lizzie Stark pushed in front of her, where her hips and black purse swung to a full stop, blotting out everything. She was Jinny Love's mother and had arrived on her daily visit to see how the camp was running.

They never heard the electric car coming, but usually they saw it, watched for it in the landscape, as out of place as a piano rocking over the holes and taking the bumps, making a high wall of dust.

Nobody dared tell Miss Lizzie; only Loch Howard's grunts could be heard.

"Some orphan get too much of it?" Then she said more loudly, "But what's *he* doing to her? Stop that."

The Battle Hill girls all ran to her and clung to her skirt.

"Get off me," she said. "Now look here, everybody. I've got a weak heart. You all know that.—Is that *Jinny Love?*"

"Leave me alone, Mama," said Jinny Love, waving the towel.

Miss Lizzie, whose hands were on Nina's shoulders, shook Nina. "Jinny Love Stark, come here to me, Loch Howard, get off that table and shame on you."

Miss Moody was the one brought to tears. She walked up to Miss Lizzie holding a towel in front of her breast and weeping. "He's our life saver, Miss Lizzie. Remember? Our Boy Scout. Oh mercy, I'm thankful you've come, he's been doing that a long time. Stand in the shade, Miss Lizzie."

"Boy Scout? Why, he ought to be—he ought to be—I can't stand it, Parnell Moody."

"Can't any of us help it, Miss Lizzie. Can't any of us. It's what he came for." She wept.

"That's Easter," Geneva said. "That is."

"He ought to be put out of business," Miss Lizzie Stark said. She stood in the center of them all, squeezing Nina uncomfortably for Jinny Love, who flouted her up in front, and Nina could look up at her. The white rice powder which she used on the very front of her face twinkled on her faint mustache. She smelled of red pepper and lemon juice—she had been making them some mayonnaise. She was valiantly trying to make up for all the Boy Scout was doing by what she was thinking of him: that he was odious. Miss Lizzie's carelessly flung word to him on sight—the first day—had been, "You little rascal, I bet you run down and pollute the spring, don't you?" "Nome," the Boy Scout had said, showing the first evidence of his gloom.

"Tears won't help, Parnell," Miss Lizzie said. "Though some don't know what tears are." She glanced at Mrs. Gruenwald, who glanced back from another level; she had brought herself out a chair. "And our last afternoon. I'd thought we'd have a treat."

They looked around as here came Marvin, Miss Lizzie's yard boy, holding two watermelons like a mother with twins. He came toward the table and just stood there.

"Marvin. You can put those melons down, don't you see the table's got somebody on it?" Miss Lizzie said. "Put 'em down and wait."

Her presence made this whole happening seem more in the nature of things. They were glad Miss Lizzie had come! It was somehow for this that they had given those yells for Miss Lizzie as Camp Mother. Under her gaze the Boy Scout's actions seemed to lose a good deal of significance. He was reduced almost to a nuisance—a mosquito, with a mosquito's proboscis. "Get him off her," Miss Lizzie repeated, in her rich and yet careless, almost humorous voice, knowing it was no good. "Ah, get him off her." She stood hugging the other little girls, several of them, warmly. Her gaze only hardened on Jinny Love; they hugged her all the more.

She loved them. It seemed the harder it was to get out here and the harder a time she found them having, the better she appreciated them. They remembered now—while the Boy Scout still drove up and down on Easter's muddy back—how they were always getting ready for Miss Lizzie; the tents even now were straight and the ground picked up and raked for her, and the tea for supper was already made and sitting in a tub in the lake; and sure enough, the niggers' dog had barked at the car just as always, and now here she was. She could have stopped everything; and she hadn't stopped it. Even her opening protests seemed now like part of things—what she was supposed to say. Several of the little girls looked up at Miss Lizzie instead of at what was on the table. Her powdered lips flickered, her eyelids hooded her gaze, but she was there.

On the table, the Boy Scout spat, and took a fresh appraisal of Easter. He reached for a hold on her hair and pulled her head back. No longer were her lips faintly parted—her mouth was open. It gaped. So did his. He dropped her, the head with its suddenness bowed again on its cheek, and he started again.

"Easter's dead! Easter's d——" cried Gertrude Bowles in a rowdy voice, and she was slapped rowdily across the mouth to cut off the word, by Miss Lizzie's hand.

Jinny Love, with a persistence they had not dreamed of, deployed the towel. Could it be owing to Jinny Love's always being on the right side that Easter mustn't dare die and bring all this to a stop? Nina thought, It's I that's thinking. Easter's not thinking at all. And while not thinking, she is not dead, but unconscious, which is even harder to be. Easter had come among them and had held herself untouchable and intact. Of course, for one little touch could smirch her, make her fall so far, so deep.—Except that by that time they were all saying the nigger deliberately poked her off in the water, meant her to drown.

"Don't touch her," they said tenderly to one another.

"Give up! Give up! Give up!" screamed Miss Moody—she who had rubbed them all the same, as if she rubbed chickens for the frying pan. Miss Lizzie without hesitation slapped her too.

"Don't touch her."

For they were crowding closer to the table all the time.

"If Easter's dead, I get her coat for winter, all right," said Geneva.

"Hush, orphan."

"Is she then?"

"You shut up." The Boy Scout looked around and panted at Geneva. "You can ast *me* when I ast you to ast me."

The niggers' dog was barking again, had been barking.

"Now who?"

"A big boy. It's old Ran MacLain and he's coming."

"He would."

He came right up, wearing a cap.

"Get away from me, Ran MacLain," Miss Lizzie called toward him. "You and dogs and guns, keep away. We've already got all we can put up with out here."

She put her foot down on his asking any questions, getting up on the table, or leaving, now that he'd come. Under his cap bill, Ran MacLain set his gaze—he was twenty-three, his seasoned gaze—on Loch and Easter on the table. He could not be prevented from considering them all. He moved under the tree. He held his gun under his arm. He let two dogs run loose, and almost imperceptibly, he chewed gum. Only Miss Moody did not move away from him.

And pressing closer to the table, Nina almost walked into Easter's arm flung out over the edge. The arm was turned at the elbow so that the hand opened upward. It held there the same as it had held when the night came in and stood in the tent, when it had come to Easter and not to Nina. It was the one hand, and it seemed the one moment.

"Don't touch her."

Nina fainted. She woke up to the cut-onion odor of Elberta's under-arm. She was up on the table with Easter, foot to head. There was so much she loved at home, but there was only time to remember the front yard. The silver, sweet-smelling paths strewed themselves behind the lawn mower, the four-o'clocks blazed. Then Elberta raised her up, she got down from the table, and was back with the others.

"Keep away. Keep away, I told you you better keep away. Leave me alone," Loch Howard was saying with short breaths. "I dove for her, didn't I?"

They hated him, Nina most of all. Almost, they hated Easter.

They looked at Easter's mouth and at the eyes where they were contemplating without sense the back side of the light. Though she had bullied and repulsed them earlier, they began to speculate in another kind of allurement: was there danger that Easter, turned in on herself, might call out to them after all, from the other, worse, side of it? Her secret voice, if soundless then possibly visible, might work out of her terrible mouth like a vine, preening and sprung with flowers. Or a snake would come out.

The Boy Scout crushed in her body and blood came out of her mouth. For them all, it was like being spoken to.

"Nina, you! Come stand right here in my skirt," Miss Lizzie called. Nina went and stood under the big bosom that started down, at the neck of her dress, like a big cloven white hide.

Jinny Love was catching her mother's eye. Of course she had stolen brief rests, but now her white arms lifted the white towel and whipped it bravely. She looked at them until she caught their eye—as if in the end the party was for *her*.

Marvin had gone back to the car and brought two more melons, which he stood holding.

"Marvin. We aren't ready for our watermelon. I told you."

"Oh, Ran. How could you? Oh, Ran."

That was Miss Moody in still a third manifestation.

By now the Boy Scout seemed for ever part of Easter and she part of him, he in motion on the up-and-down and she stretched across. He was dripping, while her skirt dried on the table; so in a manner they had changed places too. Was time moving? Endlessly, Ran MacLain's dogs frisked and played, with the niggers' dog between.

Time was moving because in the beginning Easter's face—the curve of her brow, the soft upper lip and the milky eyes—partook of the swoon of her fall—the almost forgotten fall that bathed her so purely in blue for that long moment. The face was set now, and ugly with that rainy color of seedling petunias, the kind nobody wants. Her mouth surely by now had been open long enough, as long as any gape, bite, cry, hunger, satisfaction lasts, any one person's grief, or even protest.

Not all the children watched, and their heads all were beginning to hang, to nod. Everybody had forgotten about crying. Nina had spotted three little shells in the sand she wanted to pick up when she could. And suddenly this seemed to her one of those moments out of the future, just as she had found one small brief one out of the past; this was far, far ahead of her—picking up the shells, one, another, another; without time moving any more, and Easter abandoned on a little edifice, beyond dying and beyond being remembered about.

"I'm so tired!" Gertrude Bowles said. "And hot. Ain't you tired of Easter, laying up there on that table?"

"My arms are about to break, you all," and Jinny Love stood and hugged them to her.

"I'm so tired of Easter," Gertrude said.

"Wish she'd go ahead and die and get it over with," said Little Sister Spights, who had been thumb-sucking all afternoon without a reprimand.

"I give up," said Jinny Love.

Miss Lizzie beckoned, and she came. "I and Nina and Easter all went out in the woods, and I was the only one that came back with poison ivy," she said, kissing her mother.

Miss Lizzie sank her fingers critically into the arms of the girls at her skirt. They all rose on tiptoe. Was Easter dead then?

Looking out for an instant from precarious holds, they took in sharply for memory's sake that berated figure, the mask formed and set on the face, one hand displayed, one jealously clawed under the waist, as if a secret handful had been groveled for, the spread and spotted legs. It was a betrayed figure, the betrayal was over, it was a memory. And then as the blows, automatic now, swung down again, the figure itself gasped.

"Get back. Get back." Loch Howard spoke between cruel, gritted teeth to them, and crouched over.

And when they got back, her toes webbed outward. Her belly arched and drew up from the board under her. She fell, but she kicked the Boy Scout.

Ridiculously, he tumbled backwards off the table. He fell almost into Miss Lizzie's skirt; she halved herself on the instant, and sat on the ground with her lap spread out before her like some magnificent hat that has just got crushed. Ran MacLain hurried politely over to pick her up, but she fought him off.

"Why don't you go home—now!" she said.

Before their eyes, Easter got to her knees, sat up, and drew her legs up to her. She rested her head on her knees and looked out at them, while she slowly pulled her ruined dress downward.

The sun was setting. They felt it directly behind them, the warmth flat as a hand. Easter leaned slightly over the table's edge, as if to gaze down at what might move, and blew her nose; she accomplished that with the aid of her finger, like people from away in the country. Then she sat looking out again; in another moment her legs dropped and hung down. The girls looked back at her, through the yellow and violet streams of dust—just now reaching them from Ran MacLain's flivver—the air coarse as sacking let down from the tree branches. Easter lifted one arm and shaded her eyes, but the arm fell in her lap like a clod.

There was a sighing sound from them. For the first time they noticed there was an old basket on the table. It held their knives, forks, tin cups and plates.

"Carry me." Easter's words had no inflection. Again, "Carry me."

She held out her arms to them, stupidly.

Then Ran MacLain whistled to his dogs.

The girls ran forward all together. Mrs. Gruenwald's fists rose in the air as if she lifted—no, rather had lowered—a curtain and she began with a bleating sound, "Pa-a-ack—"

"—up your troubles in your old kit bag
And smile, smile, smile!"

The niggers were making a glorious commotion, all of them came up now, and then Exum escaped them all and ran waving away to the woods, dainty as a loosened rabbit.

"Who was he, that big boy?" Etoile was asking Jinny Love.

"Ran MacLain, slow-poke."

"What did he want?"

"He's just waiting on the camp. *They're* coming out tomorrow, hunting. I heard all he said to Miss Moody."

"Did Miss Moody *know* him?"

"Anybody knows him, and his twin brother too."

Nina, running up in the front line with the others, sighed—the sigh she gave when she turned in her examination papers at school. Then with each step she felt a defiance of her own. She screamed, "Easter!"

In that passionate instant, when they reached Easter and took her up, many feelings returned to Nina, some joining and some conflicting. At least what had happened to Easter was out in the world, like the table itself. There it remained—mystery if only for being hard and cruel and, by something Nina felt inside her body, murderous.

Now they had Easter and carried her up to the tent, Mrs. Gruenwald still capering backwards and leading on,

"—in your old kit bag!
Smile, girls-instead-of-boys, that's the style!"

Miss Lizzie towered along darkly, groaning. She grabbed hold of Little Sister Spights, and said, "Can *you* brush me off!" She would be taking charge soon, but for now she asked for a place to sit down and a glass of cold water. She did not speak to Marvin yet; he was shoving the watermelons up onto the table.

Their minds could hardly capture it again, the way Easter was standing free in space, then handled and turned over by the blue air itself. Some of them looked back and saw the lake, rimmed around with its wall-within-walls of woods, into which the dark had already come. There were the water wings of Little Sister Spights, floating yet, white as a bird. "I know another Moon

Lake," one girl had said yesterday. "Oh, my child, Moon Lakes are all over the world," Mrs. Gruenwald had interrupted. "I know of one in Austria . . ." And into each fell a girl, they dared, now, to think.

The lake grew darker, then gleamed, like the water of a rimmed well. Easter was put to bed, they sat quietly on the ground outside the tent, and Miss Lizzie sipped water from Nina's cup. The sky's rising clouds lighted all over, like one spread-out blooming mimosa tree that could be seen from where the trunk itself should rise.

VI

Nina and Jinny Love, wandering down the lower path with arms entwined, saw the Boy Scout's tent. It was after the watermelon feast, and Miss Lizzie's departure. Miss Moody, in voile and tennis shoes, had a date with old "Rudy" Loomis, and Mrs. Gruenwald was trying to hold the girls with a sing before bedtime. Easter slept; Twosie watched her.

Nina and Jinny Love could hear the floating songs, farewell-like, the cheers and yells between. An owl hooted in a tree, closer by. The wind stirred,

On the other side of the tent wall the slats of the Boy Scout's legs shuttered open and shut like a fan when he moved back and forth. He had a lantern in there, or perhaps only a candle. He finished off his own shadow by opening the flap of his tent. Jinny Love and Nina halted on the path, quiet as old campers.

The Boy Scout, little old Loch Howard, was undressing in his tent for the whole world to see. He took his time wrenching off each garment; then he threw it to the floor as hard as he would throw a ball; yet that seemed, in him, meditative.

His candle—for that was all it was—jumping a little now, he stood there studying and touching his case of sunburn in a Kress mirror like theirs. He was naked and there was his little tickling thing hung on him like the last drop on the pitcher's lip. He ceased or exhausted study and came to the tent opening again and stood leaning on one raised arm, with his weight on one foot—just looking out into the night, which was clamorous.

It seemed to them he had little to do!

Hadn't he surely, just before they caught him, been pounding his chest with his fists? Bragging on himself? It seemed to them they could still hear in the beating air of night the wild tattoo of pride he must have struck off. His silly, brief, overriding little show they could well imagine there in his tent of separation in the middle of the woods, in the night. Minnowy thing that matched his candle flame, naked as he was with that, he thought he shone forth too. Didn't he?

Nevertheless, standing there with the tent slanting over him and his arm knobby as it reached up and his head bent a little, he looked rather at loose ends.

"We can call like an owl," Nina suggested. But Jinny Love thought in terms of the future. "I'll tell on him, in Battle Hill tomorrow. He's the most conceited Boy Scout in the whole troop; and's bowlegged."

"You and I will always be old maids," she added.

Then they went up and joined the singing.

BIOGRAPHICAL NOTES

Thomas E. Adams (1937–   ) graduated from La Salle College in Philadelphia in 1958 and took his M.A. at the University of Florida in writing. "Sled" is his first published fiction; it appeared in *The Sewanee Review* in 1961 and was included in the O. Henry *Prize Stories 1962*. It has been republished many times and was once turned into a play for broadcast by The Voice of America. Mr. Adams now lives in Trenton, New Jersey, and is working on a long story.

Harry Brewster (1909–   ), after a nextensive career in the British foreign service, began to write both fiction and verse. "The Marquis and the Crocodile" is his first published story. Together with three other stories, which also appeared first in *The Sewanee Review*, it is included in *Into Deeper Waters* (1968), his collection of short fiction relating to Greece. Mr. Brewster still travels widely in Europe and Asia, living alternately in Greece, Bavaria, Italy, and England, and is an enthusiastic amateur archaeologist.

Harry Crews (1935–   ) was born in Bacon County, Georgia, and raised there on a farm. "The Unattached Smile," his first story, was published in *The Sewanee Review* in 1963, and he has published in other journals. He teaches in the writing division of the University of Florida. His novels are: *The Gospel Singer* (1968); *Naked in Garden Hills* (1969); *This Thing Don't Lead to Heaven* (1970). *Jefferson Davis Is Alive and Training in Atlanta* is scheduled for publication in 1971.

William Faulkner (1897–1962) was born, bred, and died in Mississippi. *As I Lay Dying* (1930), *The Unvanquished* (1938), *The Sound and the Fury* (1929), *Absalom, Absalom!* (1936), *Light in August* (1932), and *Go Down, Moses* (1942) are probably his best fiction. The story "A Courtship" appeared first in *The Sewanee Review* in the fall of 1948.

Caroline Gordon (1895–   ) was born and brought up on a tobacco farm in Kentucky. Her story "Cloud Nine" appeared in *The Sewanee Review* in 1969. It is a section of *The Glory of Hera*, a novel she has been working on for twelve years, which will be published in the fall of 1971. She describes the novel as "experimental—in that the action takes place on the frontiers of the archetypal conscious mind, if there is such a place." She is the author of seven other novels, including *The Malefactors* (1956); of two volumes of criticism: *How to Read a Novel* (1957) and, with Allen Tate, *The House of Fiction* (1950); and of two collections of short stories: *The Forest of the South* (1946) and *Old Red and Other Stories* (1963).

Madison Jones (1925–   ) was born in Nashville, Tennessee, and graduated from Vanderbilt University. After farming in Cheatham County, Tennessee, he took his doctorate at the University of Florida. Since 1956 he has taught at Auburn University. "The Fugitives" was published in *The Sewanee Review* in 1954. His novels are: *The Innocent* (1957), *Forest of the Night* (1960), *A Buried Land* (1965), *An Exile* (1967); this last was first printed in *The Sewanee Review*. His new novel, *A Cry of Absence*, was published this year.

Smith Kirkpatrick (1922–   ) is head of the writing program at the University of Florida, where he has done graduate work. "The Wheel" was his first published story (*The Sewanee Review*, 1955). A native of Arkansas, he has been a merchant seaman, radio news editor, newspaper editor, and naval aviator. He is working on a novel laid at sea, to be called *Ship*.

Claude F. Koch (1918–   ) studied writing at the University of Florida and is professor of English at La Salle College in Philadelphia. "A Matter of Family" appeared in *The Sewanee Review* in 1962, being a chapter from his later novel *A Kite in the Sea* (1964). Other novels: *Island Interlude* (1951), *Light in Silence* (1958), *A Casual Company* (1965). He is working on a new novel and writing verse seriously.

George Lanning (1925–   ) is a former editor of *The Kenyon Review*. He now lives and writes in Cleveland, Ohio. His published novels are: *This Happy Rural Seat* (1953), *The Pedestal* (1966), and *Green Corn Moon* (1968). His *Technique in Fiction*, written with Robie Macauley, was published in 1964. "Something Just for Me" appeared in *The Sewanee Review* in 1963.

Andrew Lytle (1902–   ) has since 1961 been editor of *The Sewanee Review* and professor of English at The University of the South. Born in Murfreesboro, Tennessee, he graduated from Vanderbilt University. Two years at the Yale School of Drama were followed by a brief experience as an actor in New York City, during which time he began his first book, *Bedford Forrest and His Critter Company* (1931). "The Guide" appeared in *The Sewanee Review* in 1945 After two years of teaching in the Writers' Workshop of the University of Iowa, he lectured in creative writing at the University of Florida from 1948 to 1961. Published novels are: *The Long Night* (1936); *At the Moon's Inn* (1941); *A Name for Evil* (1947); *The Velvet Horn* (1957). A collection of stories, *A Novel, A Novella and Four Stories,* was published in 1958, and essays in literary criticism, *The Hero with the Private Parts,* in 1966. Mr. Lytle is now at work on his "memoir of a society," which is entitled *A Wake for the Living.*

Thomas Mabry (1903–1968), a native Tennessean, was a graduate of Harvard and had his M.A. from Vanderbilt. He taught creative writing and Negro American Literature at Fisk University and was for five years executive director of the Museum of Modern Art in New York City. He did writing and research for Time, Inc., and established and directed photographic exhibitions and filmstrips for *Life.* Two of his stories were included in *The Best American Short Stories 1949* and *Prize Stories 1954: The O. Henry Awards.*

He retired to his farm in Kentucky several years before his death. "Lula Borrow" was published in *The Sewanee Review* in 1956.

Flannery O'Connor (1925–1964) began and ended her short life in Georgia. Entering the writing program at the University of Iowa, she studied under Andrew Lytle, was granted the degree of Master of Fine Arts, and received the Rinehart-Iowa fiction prize for the novel she was then writing, *Wise Blood* (published 1952). The first chapter was printed in *The Sewanee Review,* as were four of her later stories—"The Lame Shall Enter First" in the summer, 1962, issue. Her two collections of stories are: *A Good Man Is Hard to Find* (1955) and the posthumous *Everything That Rises Must Converge* (1965). Her second novel, *The Violent Bear It Away,* was published in 1960.

Charles Rose (1930–   ) did his graduate work at the University of Florida, in the writing program. He now teaches creative writing at Auburn University. He has published short stories in *The Sewanee Review* ("By the Waters" in 1962) and in several other journals. He was a Bread Loaf Scholar in 1963. He has a book of stories ready for publication.

Eleanor Ross Taylor (1920–   ) lives and writes in Charlottesville, Virginia. Her first book of poems, *Wilderness of Ladies,* was published in 1960. In 1968 she received an award in poetry from the National Institute of Arts and Letters. She has a second volume of poems ready for publication. Her story "Jujitsu" came out in *The Sewanee Review* in 1969. It was selected for *Prize Stories 1971: The O. Henry Awards.*

Peter Taylor (1917–   ) is a native of Tennessee, where he and his family still spend their summers. During the winter he teaches imaginative writing at the University of Virginia. He has published five volumes of stories. The most recent, *The Collected Stories,* appeared in the fall of 1969. A book of one-act plays will be out in the fall of 1971. *The Death of a Kinsman* was printed in *The Sewanee Review* in 1949.

Robert Penn Warren (1905–   ), poet, novelist, critic, editor, historian, is professor of English at Yale University. A native of

Kentucky, he attended Vanderbilt University and was a member of the Fugitive and the Agrarian groups which flourished there in the 1920s and 1930s. He held the Library of Congress Chair of Poetry 1944–45. Twice a Guggenheim Fellow and twice winner of a Pulitzer prize, and repeatedly honored with other literary awards, he was granted the National Medal for Literature by the National Book Committee in 1970. *Audubon, A Vision* (1969) is his most recently published poetry, his latest prose being editions of the selected poetry of Melville and of Whittier, as well as a critical study, "Homage to Dreiser," in honor of the centenary of the birth of Theodore Dreiser. Mr. Warren's "Statement of Ashby Wyndham" was printed in *The Sewanee Review* in 1943; it is a monologue which is woven through his novel *At Heaven's Gate* (1943).

Eudora Welty (1909–   ) was born in Jackson, Mississippi, and still lives there. Her first collection of stories is *A Curtain of Green* (1941). "Moon Lake" appeared in *The Sewanee Review* in 1949 and was later included in the volume *The Golden Apples*. Miss Welty has been honorary consultant in American letters for the Library of Congress since 1958, and her fiction has been honored by the American Academy of Arts and Letters, by the Howells medal for a "distinguished work of American fiction" (*The Ponder Heart*, 1954), and by inclusion in "O. Henry" and "Best American" anthologies. Her most recent novel, published in 1970, is *Losing Battles*.

*The text of this book was set in eleven point
Linotype Baskerville, leaded two points. Story
titles and authors' names are also in Baskerville;
title page and half-title display are in Caslon types.
The book has been composed, printed and bound by
American Book—Stratford Press, Inc., New York.*

Typography by Ben Birnbaum.